The Collected Supernatural and Weird Fiction of Arthur Quiller-Couch

Forty-Two Short Stories
of the Strange and Unusual

Arthur Quiller-Couch

*The Collected
Supernatural and Weird
Fiction of
Arthur Quiller-Couch
Forty-Two Short Stories of the Strange and Unusual*
by Arthur Quiller-Couch

FIRST EDITION

Leonaur is an imprint
of Oakpast Ltd

Copyright in this form © 2013 Oakpast Ltd

ISBN: 978-1-78282-142-7 (hardcover)
ISBN: 978-1-78282-143-4 (softcover)

http://www.leonaur.com

Publisher's Notes

The views expressed in this book are not necessarily those of the publisher.

Contents

A Blue Pantomime	7
A Dark Mirror	24
A Pair of Hands	27
Beside The Beehives	41
Captain Knot	45
"Doubles and Quits"	61
Frozen Margit	66
The Stranger Dances in Zeb's Shoes	97
John and the Ghosts	106
Legends of St. Piran	115
Lieutenant Lapenotiere	126
Mutual Exchange, Limited	139
Grandfather, Hendry Watty	154
Not Here, O Apollo	160
Oceanus	172
Old Aeson	184
Our Lady of Gwithian	189
Phoebus on Halzaphron	195
Psyche	212

Sindbad on Burrator	217
Step o' One Side	243
The Affair of Bleakirk-on-Sands	259
The Bend of the Road	271
The Haunted Dragoon	295
The Haunted Yacht	308
The Horror on the Stair	326
The Lady of the Ship	344
The Laird's Luck	373
The Legend of Sir Dinar	412
The Magic Shadow	418
The Miracle of the White Wolf	423
The Mystery of Joseph Laquedem	439
The Paradise of Choice	460
The Penance of John Emmet	466
The Roll-Call of the Reef	489
The Room of Mirrors	506
The Seventh Man	523
The Small People	537
The Talking Ships	542
The Two Householders	552
Widdershins	565
Daphnis	572

The Collected Supernatural and Weird Fiction of Arthur Quiller-Couch

A Blue Pantomime

1.

HOW I DINED AT THE "INDIAN QUEENS."

The sensation was odd; for I could have made affidavit I had never visited the place in my life, nor come within fifty miles of it. Yet every furlong of the drive was earmarked for me, as it were, by some detail perfectly familiar. The high-road ran straight ahead to a notch in the long chine of Huel Tor; and this notch was filled with the yellow ball of the westering sun. Whenever I turned my head and blinked, red simulacra of this ball hopped up and down over the brown moors. Miles of wasteland, dotted with peat-ricks and cropping ponies, stretched to the northern horizon: on our left three long coombes radiated seaward, and in the gorge of the midmost was a building stuck like a fish-bone, its twisted Jacobean chimneys overtopping a plantation of ash-trees that now, in November, allowed a glimpse, and no more, of the grey facade. I had looked down that coombe as we drove by; and catching sight of these chimneys felt something like reassurance, as if I had been counting, all the way, to find them there.

But here let me explain who I am and what brought me to these parts. My name is Samuel Wraxall—the Reverend Samuel Wraxall, to be precise: I was born a Cockney and educated at Rugby and Oxford. On leaving the University I had taken orders; but, for reasons impertinent to this narrative, was led, after five years of parochial work in Surrey, to accept an Inspectorship of Schools. Just now I was bound for Pitt's Scawens, a desolate village among the Cornish clay-moors, there to examine and report upon the Board School. Pitt's Scawens lies some nine miles off the railway, and six from the nearest market-town; consequently, on hearing there was a comfortable inn near the village, I had determined to make that my resting-place for the night and do my business early on the morrow.

"Who lives down yonder?" I asked my driver.

"Squire Parkyn," he answered, not troubling to follow my gaze.

"Old family?"

"May be. Belonged to these parts before I can mind."

"What's the place called?"

"Tremenhuel."

I had certainly never heard the name before, nevertheless my lips were forming the syllables almost before he spoke. As he flicked up his grey horse and the gig began to oscillate in more business-like fashion, I put him a fourth question—a question at once involuntary and absurd.

"Are you sure the people who live there are called Parkyn?"

He turned his head at this, and treated me quite excusably to a stare of amazement.

"Well—considerin' I've lived in these parts five-an'-forty year, man and boy, I reckon I *ought* to be sure."

The reproof was just, and I apologised. Nevertheless Parkyn was not the name I wanted. What was the name? And why did I want it? I had not the least idea. For the next mile I continued to hunt my brain for the right combination of syllables. I only knew that somewhere, now at the back of my head, now on my tongue-tip, there hung a word I desired to utter, but could not. I was still searching for it when the gig climbed over the summit of a gentle rise, and the "Indian Queens" hove in sight.

It is not usual for a village to lie a full mile beyond its inn: yet I never doubted this must be the case with Pitt's Scawens. Nor was I in the least surprised by the appearance of this lonely tavern, with the black peat-pool behind it and the high-road in front, along which its end windows stare for miles, as if on the look-out for the ghosts of departed coaches full of disembodied travellers for the Land's End. I knew the sign-board over the porch: I knew—though now in the twilight it was impossible to distinguish colours—that upon either side of it was painted an Indian Queen in a scarlet turban and blue robe, taking two black children with scarlet parasols to see a blue palm-tree. I recognised the hepping-stock and granite drinking-trough beside the porch; as well as the eight front windows, four on either side of the door, and the dummy window immediately over it. Only the landlord was unfamiliar. He appeared as the gig drew up—a loose-fleshed, heavy man, something over six feet in height—and welcomed me with an air of anxious hospitality, as if I were the first guest he had entertained for many years.

"You received my letter, then?" I asked.

"Yes, surely. The Rev. S. Wraxall, I suppose. Your bed's aired, sir, and a fire in the Blue Room, and the cloth laid. My wife didn't like to risk cooking the fowl till you were really come. 'Railways be that uncertain,' she said. 'Something may happen to the train and he'll be done to death and all in pieces.'"

It took me a couple of seconds to discover that these gloomy anticipations referred not to me but to the fowl.

"But if you can wait half an hour—" he went on.

"Certainly," said I. "In the meanwhile, if you'll show me up to my bedroom, I'll have a wash and change my clothes, for I've been travelling since ten this morning."

I was standing in the passage by this time, and examined it in the dusk while the landlord was fetching a candle. Yes, again: I had felt sure the staircase lay to the right. I knew by heart the Ionic pattern of its broad balusters; the tick of the tall clock, standing at the first turn of the stairs; the *vista* down the glazed door opening on the stable-yard. When the landlord returned with my portmanteau and a candle and I followed him upstairs, I was asking myself for the twentieth time—'When—in what stage of my soul's history—had I been doing all this before? And what on earth was that tune that kept humming in my head?'

I dismissed these speculations as I entered the bedroom and began to fling off my dusty clothes. I had almost forgotten about them by the time I began to wash away my travel-stains, and rinse the coal-dust out of my hair. My spirits revived, and I began mentally to arrange my plans for the next day. The prospect of dinner, too, after my cold drive was wonderfully comforting. Perhaps (thought I), there is good wine in this inn; it is just the house wherein travellers find, or boast that they find, forgotten bins of Burgundy or Teneriffe. When my landlord returned to conduct me to the Blue Room, I followed him down to the first landing in the lightest of spirits.

Therefore, I was startled when, as the landlord threw open the door and stood aside to let me pass, *it* came upon me again—and this time not as a merely vague sensation, but as a sharp and sudden fear taking me like a cold hand by the throat. I shivered as I crossed the threshold and began to look about me. The landlord observed it, and said—

"It's chilly weather for travelling, to be sure. Maybe you'd be better down-stairs in the coffee-room, after all."

I felt that this was probable enough. But it seemed a pity to have put him to the pains of lighting this fire for nothing. So I promised him I should be comfortable enough.

He appeared to be relieved, and asked me what I would drink with my dinner. "There's beer—I brew it myself; and sherry—"

I said I would try his beer.

"And a bottle of sound port to follow?"

Port upon home-brewed beer! But I had dared it often enough in my Oxford days, and a long evening lay before me, with a snug armchair, and a fire fit to roast a sheep. I assented.

He withdrew to fetch up the meal, and I looked about me with curiosity. The room was a long one—perhaps fifty feet from end to end, and not less than ten paces broad. It was wainscotted to the height of four feet from the ground, probably with oak, but the wood had been so larded with dark blue paint that its texture could not be discovered. Above this wainscot the walls were covered with a fascinating paper. The background of this was a greenish-blue, and upon it a party of red-coated riders in three-cornered hats blew large horns while they hunted a stag.

This pattern, striking enough in itself, became immeasurably more so when repeated a dozen times; for the stag of one hunt chased the riders of the next, and the riders chased the hounds, and so on in an unbroken procession right round the room. The window at the bottom of the room stood high in the wall, with short blue curtains and a blue-cushioned seat beneath. In the corner to the right of it stood a tall clock, and by the clock an old spinet, decorated with two plated cruets, a toy cottage constructed of shells and gum, and an ormolu clock under glass— the sort of ornament that an Agricultural Society presents to the tenant of the best-cultivated farm within thirty miles of somewhere or other. The floor was un-carpeted save for one small oasis opposite the fire. Here stood my table, cleanly spread, with two plated candlesticks, each holding three candles. Along the wainscot extended a regiment of dark, leather-cushioned chairs, so straight in the back that they seemed to be standing at attention. There was but one easy-chair in the room, and this was drawn close to the fire. I turned towards it.

As I sat down I caught sight of my reflection in the mirror above the fireplace. It was an unflattering glass, with a wave across the surface that divided my face into two ill-fitting halves, and a film upon it, due, I suppose, to the smoke of the wood-fire below. But the setting of this mirror and the fireplace itself were by far the most noteworthy objects in the whole room. I set myself idly to examine them.

It was an open hearth, and the blazing faggot lay on the stone itself. The andirons were of indifferently polished steel, and on either side of the fireplace two Ionic pilasters of dark oak supported a narrow mantel-ledge. Above this rested the mirror, flanked by a couple of naked, flat-cheeked boys, who appeared to be lowering it over the fire by a complicated system of pulleys, festoons, and flowers. These flowers and festoons, as well as the frame of the mirror, were of some light wood—lime, I fancy—and reminded me of Grinling Gibbons' work; and the glass tilted forward at a surprising angle, as if about to tumble on the hearth-rug. The carving was exceedingly delicate. I rose to examine it more narrowly. As I did so, my eyes fell on three letters, cut in flowing italic capitals upon a plain boss of wood immediately over the frame, and I spelt out the word *FUI*.

Fui—the word was simple enough; but what of its associations? Why should it begin to stir up again those memories which were memories of nothing? *Fui*—"I have been;" but what the dickens have I been?

The landlord came in with my dinner.

"Ah!" said he, "you're looking at our masterpiece, I see."

"Tell me," I asked; "do you know why this word is written here, over the mirror?"

"I've heard my wife say, sir, it was the motto of the Cardinnocks that used to own this house. Ralph Cardinnock, father to the last squire, built it. You'll see his initials up there, in the top corners of the frame—R. C.—one letter in each corner."

As he spoke it, I knew this name—Cardinnock—for that which had been haunting me. I seated myself at table, saying—

"They lived at Tremenhuel, I suppose. Is the family gone?—died out?"

"Why yes; and the way of it was a bit curious, too."

"You might sit down and tell me about it," I said, "while I begin my dinner."

"There's not much to tell," he answered, taking a chair; "and I'm not the man to tell it properly. My wife is a better hand at it, but"—here he looked at me doubtfully—"it always makes her cry."

"Then I'd rather hear it from you. How did Tremenhuel come into the hands of the Parkyns?—that's the present owner's name, is it not?"

The landlord nodded. "The answer to that is part of the story. Old Parkyn, great-great-grandfather to the one that lives there now, took Tremenhuel on lease from the last Cardinnock—Squire Philip Cardinnock, as he was called. Squire Philip came into the property when he was twenty-three: and before he reached twenty-seven, he was forced to let the old place. He was wild, they say—thundering wild; a drinking, dicing, cock-fighting, horse-racing young man; poured out his money like water through a sieve. That was bad enough: but when it came to carrying off a young lady and putting a sword through her father and running the country, I put it to you it's worse."

"Did he disappear?"

"That's part of the story, too. When matters got desperate and he was forced to let Tremenhuel, he took what money he could raise and cleared out of the neighbourhood for a time; went off to Tregarrick when the militia was embodied, he being an officer; and there he cast his affections upon old Sir Felix Williams's daughter, Miss Cicely—"

I was expecting it: nevertheless I dropped my fork clumsily as I heard the name, and for a few seconds the landlord's voice sounded like that of a distant river as it ran on—

"And as Sir Felix wouldn't consent—for which nobody blamed him—Squire Philip and Miss Cicely agreed to go off together one dark night. But the old man found them out and stopped them in the nick of time and got six inches of cold steel for his pains. However, he kept his girl, and Squire Philip had to fly the country. He went off that same night, they say: and wherever he went, he never came back."

"What became of him?"

"Ne'er a soul knows; for ne'er a soul saw his face again. Year after year, old Parkyn, his tenant, took the rent of Tremenhuel out of his right pocket and paid it into his left: and in time, there being no heir, he just took over the property and stepped into Cardinnock's shoes with a 'by your leave' to nobody, and there his grandson is to this day."

"What became of the young lady—of Miss Cicely Williams?" I asked.

"Died an old maid. There was something curious between her and her only brother who had helped to stop the runaway match. Nobody knows what it was: but when Sir Felix died—as he did about ten years after—she packed up and went somewhere to the North of England and settled. They say she and her brother never spoke: which was carrying her anger at his interference rather far, 'specially as she remained good friends with her father."

He broke off here to fetch up the second course. We talked no more, for I was pondering his tale and disinclined to be diverted to other topics. Nor can I tell whether the rest of the meal was good or ill. I suppose I ate: but it was only when the landlord swept the cloth, and produced a bottle of port, with a plate of biscuits and another of dried raisins, that I woke out of my musing. While I drew the armchair nearer the fire, he pushed forward the table with the wine to my elbow. After this, he poured me out a glass and fell to dusting a high-backed chair with vigour, as though he had caught it standing at ease and were giving it a round dozen for insubordination in the ranks.

"Was there anything more?"

"Nothing, thank you."

He withdrew.

I drank a couple of glasses and began meditatively to light my pipe.

I was trying to piece together these words "Philip Cardinnock—Cicely Williams—*fui*," and to fit them into the tune that kept running in my head.

My pipe went out. I pulled out my pouch and was filling it afresh when a puff of wind came down the chimney and blew a cloud of blue smoke out into the room.

The smoke curled up and spread itself over the face of the mirror confronting me. I followed it lazily with my eyes. Then suddenly I bent forward, staring up. Something very curious was happening to the glass.

2

What I Saw in the Mirror.

The smoke that had dimmed the mirror's face for a moment was rolling off its surface and upwards to the ceiling. But some of it still lingered in filmy, slowly revolving eddies. The glass itself, too, was stirring beneath this film and running across its breadth in horizontal waves which broke themselves silently, one after another, against the dark frame, while the circles of smoke kept widening, as the ripples widen when a stone is tossed into still water.

I rubbed my eyes. The motion on the mirror's surface was quickening perceptibly, while the glass itself was steadily becoming more opaque, the film deepening to a milky colour and lying over the surface in heavy folds. I was about to start up and touch the glass with my hand, when beneath this milky colour and from the heart of the whirling film, there began to gleam an underlying brilliance after the fashion of the light in an opal, but with this difference, that the light here was blue—a steel blue so vivid that the pain of it forced me to shut my eyes. When I opened them again, this light had increased in intensity. The disturbance in the glass began to abate; the eddies revolved more slowly; the smoke-wreaths faded: and as they died wholly out, the blue light went out on a sudden and the mirror looked down upon me as before.

That is to say, I thought so for a moment. But the next, I found that though its face reflected the room in which I sat, there was one omission.

I was that omission. My armchair was there, but no one sat in it.

I was surprised; but, as well as I can recollect, not in the least frightened. I continued, at any rate, to gaze steadily into the glass, and now took note of two particulars that had escaped me. The table I saw was laid for two. Forks, knives and glasses gleamed at either end, and a couple of decanters caught the sparkle of the candles in the centre. This was my first observation. The second was that the colours of the hearth-rug had gained in freshness, and that a dark spot just beyond it—a spot which in my first exploration I had half-amusedly taken for a blood-stain—was not reflected in the glass.

As I leant back and gazed, with my hands in my lap, I remember there was some difficulty in determining whether the tune by which I was still haunted ran in my head or was tinkling from within the old spinet by the window. But after a while the music, whencesoever it came, faded away and ceased. A dead silence held everything for about thirty seconds.

And then, still looking in the mirror, I saw the door behind me open slowly.

The next moment, two persons noiselessly entered the room—a young man and a girl. They wore the dress of the early Georgian days, as well as I could see; for the girl was wrapped in a cloak with a hood that almost concealed her face, while the man wore a heavy riding-coat. He was booted and spurred, and the backs of his top-boots were splashed with mud. I say the backs of his boots, for he stood with his back to me while he held open the door for the girl to pass, and at first I could not see his face.

The lady advanced into the light of the candles and threw back her hood. Her eyes were dark and frightened: her cheeks damp with rain and slightly reddened by the wind. A curl of brown hair had broken loose from its knot and hung, heavy with wet, across her brow. It was a beautiful face; and I recognised its owner. She was Cicely Williams.

With that, I knew well enough what I was to see next. I knew it even while the man at the door was turning, and I dug the nails of my right hand into the palm of my left, to repress the fear that swelled up as a wave as I looked straight into his face and saw—*my own self.*

But I had expected it, as I say: and when the wave of fear had passed over me and gone, I could observe these two figures steadfastly enough. The girl dropped into a chair beside the table, and stretching her arms along the white cloth, bowed her head over them and wept. I saw her shoulders heave and her twined fingers work as she struggled with her grief. The young squire advanced and, with a hand on her shoulder, endeavoured by many endearments to comfort her. His lips moved vehemently, and gradually her shoulders ceased to rise and fall. By-and-by she raised her head and looked up into his face with wet, gleaming eyes. It was very pitiful to see. The young man took her face between his hands, kissed it, and pouring out a glass of wine, held it to her lips. She put it aside with her hand and glanced up towards the tall clock in the corner. My eyes, following hers, saw that the hands pointed to a quarter to twelve.

The young squire set down the glass hastily, stepped to the window and, drawing aside the blue curtain, gazed out upon the night. Twice he looked back at Cicely, over his shoulder, and after a minute returned to the table. He drained the glass which the girl had declined, poured out another, still keeping his eyes on her, and began to walk impatiently up and down the room. And all the time Cicely's soft eyes never ceased to follow him. Clearly there was need for hurry, for they had not laid aside their travelling-cloaks, and once or twice the young man paused in his walk to listen. At length he pulled out his watch, glanced from it to the clock in the corner, put it away with a frown and, striding up to the hearth, flung himself down in the arm-chair—the very arm-chair in which I was seated.

As he sat there, tapping the hearth-rug with the toe of his thick riding-boot and moving his lips now and then in answer to some question from the young girl, I had time to examine his every feature. Line by line they reproduced my own—nay, looking straight into his eyes I could see through them into the soul of him and recognised that soul for my own. Of all the passions there I knew that myself contained the germs. Vices repressed in youth, tendencies to sin starved in my own nature by lack of opportunity—these flourished in a rank growth. I saw virtues, too, that I had once possessed but had lost by degrees in my respectable journey through life—courage, generosity, tenderness of heart. I was discovering these with envy, one by one, when he raised his head higher and listened for a moment, with a hand on either arm of the chair.

The next instant he sprang up and faced the door. Glancing at Cicely, I saw her cowering down in her chair.

The young squire had hardly gained his feet when the door flew open and the figures of two men appeared on the threshold—Sir Felix Williams and his only son, the father and brother of Cicely.

There, in the doorway, the intruders halted; but for an instant only. Almost before the squire could draw, his sweetheart's brother had sprung forward. Like two serpents their rapiers engaged in the candle-light. The soundless blades crossed and glittered. Then one of them flickered in a narrow circle, and the brother's rapier went spinning from his hand across the room.

Young Cardinnock lowered his point at once, and his adversary stepped back a couple of paces. While a man might count twenty the pair looked each other in the face, and then the old man, Sir Felix, stepped slowly forward.

But before he could thrust—for the young squire still kept his point lowered—Cicely sprang forward and threw herself across her lover's breast. There, for all the gentle efforts his left hand made to disengage her, she clung. She had made her choice. There was no sign of faltering in her soft eyes, and her father had perforce to hold his hand.

The old man began to speak. I saw his face distorted with passion and his lips working. I saw the deep red gather on Cicely's cheeks and the anger in her lover's eyes. There was a pause as Sir Felix ceased to speak, and then the young squire replied. But his sentence stopped midway: for once more the old man rushed upon him.

This time young Cardinnock's rapier was raised. Girdling Cicely with his left arm he parried her father's lunge and smote his blade aside. But such was the old man's passion that he followed the lunge with all his body, and before his opponent could prevent it, was wounded high in the chest, beneath the collar-bone.

He reeled back and fell against the table. Cicely ran forward and caught his hand; but he pushed her away savagely and, with another clutch at the table's edge, dropped upon the hearthrug. The young man, meanwhile, white and aghast, rushed to the table, filled a glass with wine, and held it to the lips of the wounded man. So the two lovers knelt.

It was at this point that I who sat and witnessed the tragedy was assailed by a horror entirely new. Hitherto I had, indeed, seen myself in Squire Philip Cardinnock; but now I began also to possess his soul and feel with his feelings, while at the same time I continued to sit before the glass, a helpless onlooker. I was two men at once; the man who knelt all unaware of what was coming and the man who waited in the arm-chair, incapable of word or movement, yet gifted with a torturing prescience. And as I sat this was what I saw:—

The brother, as I knelt there oblivious of all but the wounded man, stepped across the room to the corner where his rapier lay, picked it up softly and as softly stole up behind me. I tried to shout, to warn myself; but my tongue was tied. The brother's arm was lifted. The candlelight ran along the blade. Still the kneeling figure never turned.

And as my heart stiffened and awaited it, there came a flash of pain—one red-hot stroke of anguish.

3.
What I Saw in the Tarn.

As the steel entered my back, cutting all the cords that bound me to life, I suffered anguish too exquisite for words to reach, too deep for memory to dive after. My eyes closed and teeth shut on the taste of death; and as they shut a merciful oblivion wrapped me round.

When I awoke, the room was dark, and I was standing on my feet. A cold wind was blowing on my face, as from an open door. I staggered to meet this wind and found myself groping along a passage and down a staircase filled with Egyptian darkness. Then the wind increased suddenly and shook the black curtain around my senses. A murky light broke in on me. I had a body. That I felt; but where it was I knew not. And so I felt my way forward in the direction where the twilight showed least dimly.

Slowly the curtain shook and its folds dissolved as I moved against the wind. The clouds lifted; and by degrees I grew aware that I was standing on the barren moor. Night was stretched around to the horizon, where straight ahead a grey bar shone across the gloom. I pressed on towards it. The heath was uneven under my feet, and now and then I stumbled heavily; but still I held on. For it seemed that I must get to this grey bar or die a second time. All my muscles, all my will, were strained upon this purpose.

Drawing nearer, I observed that a wave-like motion kept passing over this brighter space, as it had passed over the mirror. The glimmer would be obscured for a moment, and then reappear. At length a gentle acclivity of the moor hid it for a while. My legs positively raced up this slope, and upon the summit I hardly dared to look for a moment, knowing that if the light were an illusion all my hope must die with it.

But it was no illusion. There was the light, and there, before my feet, lay a sable sheet of water, over the surface of which the light was playing. There was no moon, no star in heaven; yet over this desolate tarn hovered a pale radiance that ceased again where the edge of its waves lapped the further bank of peat. Their monotonous wash hardly broke the stillness of the place.

The formless longing was now pulling at me with an attraction I could not deny, though within me there rose and fought against it a horror only less strong. Here, as in the Blue Room, two souls were struggling for me. It was the soul of Philip Cardinnock that drew me towards the tarn and the soul of Samuel Wraxall that resisted. Only, what was the thing towards which I was being pulled?

I must have stood at least a minute on the brink before I descried a black object floating at the far end of the tarn. What this object was I could not make out; but I knew it on the instant to be that for which I longed, and all my will grew suddenly intent on drawing it nearer. Even as my volition centred upon it, the black spot began to move slowly out into the pale radiance towards me. Silently, surely, as though my wish drew it by a rope, it floated nearer and nearer over the bosom of the tarn; and while it was still some twenty yards from me I saw it to be a long black box, shaped somewhat like a coffin.

There was no doubt about it. I could hear the water now sucking at its dark sides. I stepped down the bank, and waded up to my knees in the icy water to meet it. It was a plain box, with no writing upon the lid, nor any speck of metal to relieve the dead black: and it moved with the same even speed straight up to where I stood.

As it came, I laid my hand upon it and touched wood. But with the touch came a further sensation that made me fling both arms around the box and begin frantically to haul it towards the shore.

It was a feeling of suffocation; of a weight that pressed in upon my ribs and choked the lungs' action. I felt that I must open that box or die horribly; that until I had it upon the bank and had forced the lid up I should know no pause from the labour and torture of dying.

This put a wild strength into me. As the box grated upon the few pebbles by the shore, I bent over it, caught it once more by the sides, and with infinite effort dragged it up out of the water. It was heavy, and the weight upon my chest was heavier yet: but straining, panting, gasping, I hauled it up the bank, dropped it on the turf, and knelt over it, tugging furiously at the lid.

I was frenzied—no less. My nails were torn until the blood gushed. Lights danced before me; bells rang in my ears; the pressure on my lungs grew more intolerable with each moment; but still I fought with that lid. Seven devils were within me and helped me; and all the while I knew that I was dying, that unless the box were opened in a moment or two it would be too late.

The sweat ran off my eyebrows and dripped on the box. My breath came and went in sobs. I could not die. I could not, must not die. And so I tugged and strained and tugged again.

Then, as I felt the black anguish of the Blue Room descending a second time upon me, I seemed to put all my strength into my hands. From the lid or from my own throat—I could not distinguish—there came a creak and a long groan. I tore back the board and fell on the heath with one shuddering breath of relief.

And drawing it, I raised my head and looked over the coffin's edge.

Still drawing it, I tumbled back.

White, cold, with the last struggle fixed on its features and open eyes, it was my own dead face that stared up at me!

4.
What I Have Since Learnt.

They found me, next morning, lying on the brink of the tarn, and carried me back to the inn. There I lay for weeks in a brain fever and talked—as they assure me—the wildest nonsense. The landlord had first guessed that something was amiss on finding the front door open when he came down at five o'clock. I must have turned to the left on leaving the house, travelled up the road for a hundred yards, and then struck almost at right angles across the moor. One of my shoes was found a furlong from the highway, and this had guided them. Of course they found no coffin beside me, and I was prudent enough to hold my tongue when I became convalescent. But the effect of that night was to shatter my health for a year and more, and force me to throw up my post of school inspector. To this day I have never examined the school at Pitt's Scawens. But somebody else has; and last winter I received a letter, which I will give in full:—

21, Chesterham Road, Kensington, W.
December 3rd, 1891.

Dear Wraxall,—

It is a long time since we have corresponded, but I have just returned from Cornwall, and while visiting Pitt's Scawens professionally, was reminded of you. I put up at the inn where you had your long illness. The people there were delighted to find that I knew you, and desired me to send "their duty" when next I wrote. By the way, I suppose you were introduced to their state apartment—the Blue Room—and its wonderful chimney carving. I made a bid to the landlord for it, panels, mirror, and all, but he referred me to Squire Parkyn, the landlord. I think I may get it, as the squire loves hard coin. When I have it up over my mantel-piece here you must run over and give me your opinion on it. By the way, clay has been discovered on the Tremenhuel Estate, just at the back of the "Indian Queens": at least, I hear that Squire Parkyn is running a Company, and is sanguine. You remember the tarn behind the inn? They made an odd discovery there when draining it for the new works. In the mud at the bottom was imbedded the perfect skeleton of a man. The bones were quite clean and white. Close beside the body they afterwards turned up a silver snuff-box, with the word "*Fui*" on the lid. "*Fui*" was the motto of the Cardinnocks, who held Tremenhuel before it passed to the Parkyns. There seems to be no doubt that these are the bones of the last squire, who disappeared mysteriously more than a hundred years ago, in consequence of a love affair, I'm told. It looks like foul play; but, if so, the account has long since passed out of the hands of man.

 Yours ever,   David E. Mainwaring.
P.S.—I reopen this to say that Squire Parkyn has accepted my offer for the chimney-piece. Let me hear soon that you'll come and look at it and give me your opinion.

A Dark Mirror

In the room of one of my friends hangs a mirror. It is an oblong sheet of glass, set in a frame of dark, highly varnished wood, carved in the worst taste of the Regency period, and relieved with faded gilt. Glancing at it from a distance, you would guess the thing a relic from some "genteel" drawing-room of Miss Austen's time. But go nearer and look into the glass itself. By some malformation or mere freak of make, all the images it throws back are livid. Flood the room with sunshine; stand before this glass with youth and hot blood tingling on your cheeks; and the glass will give back neither sun nor colour; but your own face, blue and dead, and behind it a horror of inscrutable shadow.

Since I heard this mirror's history, I have stood more than once and twice before it, and peered into this shadow. And these are the simulacra I seem to have seen there darkly.

I have seen a bleak stone parsonage, hemmed in on two sides by a grave-yard; and behind for many miles nothing but sombre moors climbing and stretching away. I have heard the winds moaning and wuthering night and morning, among the gravestones, and around the angles of the house; and crossing the threshold, I know by instinct that this mirror will stand over the mantelpiece in the bare room to the left. I know also to whom those four suppressed voices will belong that greet me while yet my hand is on the latch. Four children are within—three girls and a boy—and they are disputing over a box of wooden soldiers.

The eldest girl, a plain child with reddish-brown eyes, and the most wonderfully small hands, snatches up one of the wooden soldiers, crying, "This is the Duke of Wellington! This shall be the Duke!" and her soldier is the gayest of all, and the tallest, and the most perfect in every part. The second girl makes her choice, and they call him "Gravey" because of the solemnity of his painted features. And then all laugh at the youngest girl, for she has chosen a queer little warrior, much like herself; but she smiles at their laughter, and smiles again when they christen him "Waiting Boy." Lastly the boy chooses. He is handsomer than his sisters, and is their hope and pride; and has a massive brow and a mouth well formed though a trifle loose. His soldier shall be called Bonaparte.

Though the door is closed between us, I can see these motherless children under this same blue mirror—the glass that had helped to pale the blood on their mother's face after she left the warm Cornish sea that was her home, and came to settle and die in this bleak exile. Some of her books are in the little bookcase here. They were sent round from the West by sea, and met with shipwreck. For the most part they are Methodist Magazines—for, like most Cornish folk, her parents were followers of Wesley—and the stains of the salt water are still on their pages.

I know also that the father will be sitting in the room to my right—sitting at his solitary meal, for his digestion is queer, and he prefers to dine alone: a strange, small, purblind man, full of sorrow and strong will. He is a clergyman, but carries a revolver always in his pocket by day, and by night sleeps with it under his pillow. He has done so ever since someone told him that the moors above were unsafe for a person with his opinions.

All this the glass shows me, and more. I see the children growing up. I see the girls droop and pine in this dreary parsonage, where the winds nip, and the miasma from the churchyard chokes them. I see the handsome promising boy going to the devil—slowly at first, then by strides. As their hope fades from his sisters' faces, he drinks and takes to opium-eating—and worse. He comes home from a short absence, wrecked in body and soul. After this there is no rest in the house. He sleeps in the room with that small, persistent father of his, and often there are sounds of horrible strugglings within it. And the girls lie awake, sick with fear, listening, till their ears grow heavy and dull, for the report of their father's pistol. At morning, the drunkard will stagger out, and look perhaps into this glass, that gives him back more than all his despair. "The poor old man and I have had a terrible night of it," he stammers; "he does his best—the poor old man! but it's all over with me."

I see him go headlong at last and meet his end in the room above after twenty minutes' struggle, with a curious desire at the last to play the man and face his death standing. I see the second sister fight with a swiftly wasting disease; and, because she is a solitary Titanic spirit, refuse all help and solace. She gets up one morning, insists on dressing herself, and dies; and the youngest sister follows her but more slowly and tranquilly, as beseems her gentler nature.

Two only are left now—the queer father and the eldest of the four children, the reddish-eyed girl with the small hands, the girl who "never talked hopefully." Fame has come to her and to her dead sisters. For looking from childhood into this livid glass that reflected their world, they have peopled it with strange spirits. Men and women in the real world recognise the awful power of these spirits, without understanding them, not having been brought up themselves in front of this mirror. But the survivor knows the mirror too well.

"*Mademoiselle, vous etes triste.*"
"*Monsieur, j'en ai bien le droit.*"

With a last look I see into the small, commonplace church that lies just below the parsonage: and on a tablet by the altar I read a list of many names...

And the last is that of Charlotte Bronte.

A Pair of Hands

An Old Maid's Ghost-Story

"Yes," said Miss Le Petyt, gazing into the deep fireplace and letting her hands and her knitting lie for the moment idle in her lap. "Oh, yes, I have seen a ghost. In fact I have lived in a house with one for quite a long time."

"How you *could*—" began one of my host's daughters; and "*You*, Aunt Emily?" cried the other at the same moment.

Miss Le Petyt, gentle soul, withdrew her eyes from the fireplace and protested with a gay little smile. "Well, my dears, I am not quite the coward you take me for. And, as it happens, mine was the most harmless ghost in the world. In fact"—and here she looked at the fire again—"I was quite sorry to lose her."

"It was a woman, then? Now *I* think," said Miss Blanche, "that female ghosts are the horridest of all. They wear little shoes with high red heels, and go about *tap, tap*, wringing their hands."

"This one wrung her hands, certainly. But I don't know about the high red heels, for I never saw her feet. Perhaps she was like the Queen of Spain, and hadn't any. And as for the hands, it all depends *how* you wring them. There's an elderly shop-walker at Knightsbridge, for instance—"

"Don't be prosy, dear, when you know that we're just dying to hear the story."

Miss Le Petyt turned to me with a small deprecating laugh. "It's such a little one."

"The story, or the ghost?"

"Both."

And this was Miss Le Petyt's story:—

"It happened when I lived down in Cornwall, at Tresillack on the south coast. Tresillack was the name of the house, which stood quite alone at the head of a coombe, within sound of the sea but without sight of it; for though the coombe led down to a wide open beach, it wound and twisted half a dozen times on its way, and its overlapping sides closed the view from the house, which was advertised as 'secluded.' I was very poor in those days. Your father and all of us were poor then, as I trust, my dears, you will never be; but I was young enough to be romantic and wise enough to like independence, and this word 'secluded' took my fancy.

"The misfortune was that it had taken the fancy, or just suited the requirements, of several previous tenants. You know, I dare say, the kind of person who rents a secluded house in the country? Well, yes, there are several kinds; but they seem to agree in being odious. No one knows where they come from, though they soon remove all doubt about where they're 'going to,' as the children say. 'Shady' is the word, is it not? Well, the previous tenants of Tresillack (from first to last a bewildering series) had been shady with a vengeance.

"I knew nothing of this when I first made application to the landlord, a solid yeoman inhabiting a farm at the foot of the coombe, on a cliff overlooking the beach. To him I presented myself fearlessly as a spinster of decent family and small but assured income, intending a rural life of combined seemliness and economy. He met my advances politely enough, but with an air of suspicion which offended me. I began by disliking him for it: afterwards I set it down as an unpleasant feature in the local character. I was doubly mistaken. Farmer Hosking was slow-witted, but as honest a man as ever stood up against hard times; and a more open and hospitable race than the people on that coast I never wish to meet. It was the caution of a child who had burnt his fingers, not once but many times. Had I known what I afterwards learned of Farmer Hosking's tribulations as landlord of a 'secluded country residence,' I should have approached him with the bashfulness proper to my suit and faltered as I undertook to prove the bright exception in a long line of painful experiences. He had bought the Tresillack estate twenty years before—on mortgage, I fancy—because the land adjoined his own and would pay him for tillage. But the house was a nuisance, an incubus; and had been so from the beginning.

"'Well, miss,' he said, 'you're welcome to look over it; a pretty enough place, inside and out. There's no trouble about keys, because I've put in a housekeeper, a widow-woman, and she'll show you round. With your leave I'll step up the coombe so far with you, and put you in your way.' As I thanked him he paused and rubbed his chin. 'There's one thing I must tell you, though. Whoever takes the house must take Mrs. Carkeek along with it.'

"'Mrs. Carkeek?' I echoed dolefully. 'Is that the housekeeper?'

"'Yes: she was wife to my late hind. I'm sorry, miss,' he added, my face telling him no doubt what sort of woman I expected Mrs. Carkeek to be; 'but I had to make it a rule after—after some things that happened. And I dare say you won't find her so bad. Mary Carkeek's a sensible comfortable woman, and knows the place. She was in service there to Squire Kendall when he sold up and went: her first place it was.'

"'I may as well see the house, anyhow,' said I dejectedly. So we started to walk up the coombe. The path, which ran beside a little chattering stream, was narrow for the most part, and Farmer Hosking, with an apology, strode on ahead to beat aside the brambles. But whenever its width allowed us to walk side by side I caught him from time to time stealing a shy inquisitive glance under his rough eyebrows. Courteously though he bore himself, it was clear that he could not sum me up to his satisfaction or bring me square with his notion of a tenant for his 'secluded country residence.'

"I don't know what foolish fancy prompted it, but about halfway up the coombe I stopped short and asked:

"'There are no ghosts, I suppose?'

"It struck me, a moment after I had uttered it, as a supremely silly question; but he took it quite seriously. 'No; I never heard tell of any *ghosts*.' He laid a queer sort of stress on the word. 'There's always been trouble with servants, and maids' tongues will be runnin'. But Mary Carkeek lives up there alone, and she seems comfortable enough.'

"We walked on. By-and-by he pointed with his stick. 'It don't look like a place for ghosts, now, do it?'

"Certainly it did not. Above an untrimmed orchard rose a terrace of turf scattered with thorn-bushes, and above this a terrace of stone, upon which stood the prettiest cottage I had ever seen. It was long and low and thatched; a deep verandah ran from end to end. Clematis, Banksia roses and honeysuckle climbed the posts of this verandah, and big blooms of the Marechal Niel were clustered along its roof, beneath the lattices of the bedroom windows. The house was small enough to be called a cottage, and rare enough in features and in situation to confer distinction on any tenant. It suggested what in those days we should have called 'elegant' living. And I could have clapped my hands for joy.

"My spirits mounted still higher when Mrs. Carkeek opened the door to us. I had looked for a Mrs. Gummidge, and I found a healthy middle-aged woman with a thoughtful but contented face, and a smile which, without a trace of obsequiousness, quite bore out the farmer's description of her. She was a comfortable woman; and while we walked through the rooms together (for Mr. Hosking waited outside) I 'took to' Mrs. Carkeek. Her speech was direct and practical; the rooms, in spite of their faded furniture, were bright and exquisitely clean; and somehow the very atmosphere of the house gave me a sense of well-being, of feeling at home and cared for; yes, *of being loved*. Don't laugh, my dears; for when I've done you may not think this fancy altogether foolish.

"I stepped out into the verandah, and Farmer Hosking pocketed the pruning-knife which he had been using on a bush of jasmine.

"'This is better than anything I had dreamed of,' said I.

"'Well, miss, that's not a wise way of beginning a bargain, if you'll excuse me.'

"He took no advantage, however, of my admission; and we struck the bargain as we returned down the coombe to his farm, where the hired chaise waited to convey me back to the market town. I had meant to engage a maid of my own, but now it occurred to me that I might do very well with Mrs. Carkeek. This, too, was settled in the course of the next day or two, and within the week I had moved into my new home.

"I can hardly describe to you the happiness of my first month at Tresillack; because (as I now believe) if I take the reasons which I had for being happy, one by one, there remains over something which I cannot account for. I was moderately young, entirely healthy; I felt myself independent and adventurous; the season was high summer, the weather glorious, the garden in all the pomp of June, yet sufficiently unkempt to keep me busy, give me a sharp appetite for meals, and send me to bed in that drowsy stupor which comes of the odours of earth. I spent the most of my time out of doors, winding up the day's work as a rule with a walk down the cool valley, along the beach and back.

"I soon found that all housework could be safely left to Mrs. Carkeek. She did not talk much; indeed her only fault (a rare one in house-keepers) was that she talked too little, and even when I addressed her seemed at times unable to give me her attention. It was as though her mind strayed off to some small job she had forgotten, and her eyes wore a listening look, as though she waited for the neglected task to speak and remind her. But as a matter of fact she forgot nothing. Indeed, my dears, I was never so well attended to in my life.

"Well, that is what I'm coming to. That, so to say, is just *it*. The woman not only had the rooms swept and dusted, and my meals prepared to the moment. In a hundred odd little ways this orderliness, these preparations, seemed to read my desires. Did I wish the roses renewed in a bowl upon the dining-table, sure enough at the next meal they would be replaced by fresh ones.

Mrs. Carkeek (I told myself) must have surprised and interpreted a glance of mine. And yet I could not remember having glanced at the bowl in her presence. And how on earth had she guessed the very roses, the very shapes and colours I had lightly wished for? This is only an instance, you understand. Every day, and from morning to night, I happened on others, each slight enough, but all together bearing witness to a ministering intelligence as subtle as it was untiring.

"I am a light sleeper, as you know, with an uncomfortable knack of waking with the sun and roaming early. No matter how early I rose at Tresillack, Mrs. Carkeek seemed to have prevented me. Finally I had to conclude that she arose and dusted and tidied as soon as she judged me safely a-bed. For once, finding the drawing-room (where I had been sitting late) 'redded up' at four in the morning, and no trace of a plate of raspberries which I had carried thither after dinner and left overnight, I determined to test her, and walked through to the kitchen, calling her by name. I found the kitchen as clean as a pin, and the fire laid, but no trace of Mrs. Carkeek. I walked upstairs and knocked at her door. At the second knock a sleepy voice cried out, and presently the good woman stood before me in her nightgown, looking (I thought) very badly scared.

"'No,' I said, 'it's not a burglar. But I've found out what I wanted, that you do your morning's work over night. But you mustn't wait for me when I choose to sit up. And now go back to your bed like a good soul, whilst I take a run down to the beach.'

"She stood blinking in the dawn. Her face was still white.

"'Oh, miss,' she gasped, 'I made sure you must have seen something!'

"'And so I have,' I answered, 'but it was neither burglars nor ghosts.'

"'Thank God!' I heard her say as she turned her back to me in her grey bedroom—which faced the north. And I took this for a carelessly pious expression and ran downstairs, thinking no more of it.

"A few days later I began to understand.

"The plan of Tresillack house (I must explain) was simplicity itself. To the left of the hall as you entered was the dining-room; to the right the drawing-room, with a *boudoir* beyond. The foot of the stairs faced the front door, and beside it, passing a glazed inner door, you found two others right and left, the left opening on the kitchen, the right on a passage which ran by a store-cupboard under the bend of the stairs to a neat pantry with the usual shelves and linen-press, and under the window (which faced north) a porcelain basin and brass tap. On the first morning of my tenancy I had visited this pantry and turned the tap; but no water ran. I supposed this to be accidental. Mrs. Carkeek had to wash up glass ware and crockery, and no doubt Mrs. Carkeek would complain of any failure in the water supply.

"But the day after my surprise visit (as I called it) I had picked a basketful of roses, and carried them into the pantry as a handy place to arrange them in. I chose a china bowl and went to fill it at the tap. Again the water would not run.

"I called Mrs. Carkeek. 'What is wrong with this tap?' I asked. 'The rest of the house is well enough supplied.'

"'I don't know, miss. I never use it.'

"'But there must be a reason; and you must find it a great nuisance washing up the plate and glasses in the kitchen. Come around to the back with me, and we'll have a look at the cisterns.'

"'The cisterns'll be all right, miss. I assure you I don't find it a trouble.'

"But I was not to be put off. The back of the house stood but ten feet from a wall which was really but a stone face built against the cliff cut away by the architect. Above the cliff rose the kitchen garden, and from its lower path we looked over the wall's parapet upon the cisterns. There were two—a very large one, supplying the kitchen and the bathroom above the kitchen; and a small one, obviously fed by the other, and as obviously leading, by a pipe which I could trace, to the pantry. Now the big cistern stood almost full, and yet the small one, though on a lower level, was empty.

"'It's as plain as daylight,' said I. 'The pipe between the two is choked.' And I clambered on to the parapet.

"'I wouldn't, miss. The pantry tap is only cold water, and no use to me. From the kitchen boiler I gets it hot, you see.'

"'But I want the pantry water for my flowers.' I bent over and groped. 'I thought as much!' said I, as I wrenched out a thick plug of cork and immediately the water began to flow. I turned triumphantly on Mrs. Carkeek, who had grown suddenly red in the face. Her eyes were fixed on the cork in my hand. To keep it more firmly wedged in its place somebody had wrapped it round with a rag of calico print; and, discoloured though the rag was, I seemed to recall the pattern (a lilac sprig). Then, as our eyes met, it occurred to me that only two mornings before Mrs. Carkeek had worn a print gown of that same sprigged pattern.

"I had the presence of mind to hide this very small discovery, sliding over it some quite trivial remark; and presently Mrs. Carkeek regained her composure. But I own I felt disappointed in her. It seemed such a paltry thing to be disingenuous over. She had deliberately acted a fib before me; and why? Merely because she preferred the kitchen to the pantry tap. It was childish. 'But servants are all the same,' I told myself. 'I must take Mrs. Carkeek as she is; and, after all, she is a treasure.'

"On the second night after this, and between eleven and twelve o'clock, I was lying in bed and reading myself sleepy over a novel of Lord Lytton's, when a small sound disturbed me. I listened. The sound was clearly that of water trickling; and I set it down to rain. A shower (I told myself) had filled the water-pipes which drained the roof. Somehow I could not fix the sound. There was a water pipe against the wall just outside my window. I rose and drew up the blind.

"To my astonishment no rain was falling; no rain had fallen. I felt the slate window-sill; some dew had gathered there—no more. There was no wind, no cloud: only a still moon high over the eastern slope of the coombe, the distant plash of waves, and the fragrance of many roses. I went back to bed and listened again. Yes, the trickling sound continued, quite distinct in the silence of the house, not to be confused for a moment with the dull murmur of the beach. After a while it began to grate on my nerves. I caught up my candle, flung my dressing-gown about me, and stole softly downstairs.

"Then it was simple. I traced the sound to the pantry. 'Mrs. Carkeek has left the tap running,' said I: and, sure enough, I found it so—a thin trickle steadily running to waste in the porcelain basin. I turned off the tap, went contentedly back to my bed, and slept.

"—for some hours. I opened my eyes in darkness, and at once knew what had awakened me. The tap was running again. Now it had shut easily in my hand, but not so easily that I could believe it had slipped open again of its own accord. 'This is Mrs. Carkeek's doing,' said I; and am afraid I added 'Bother Mrs. Carkeek!'

"Well, there was no help for it: so I struck a light, looked at my watch, saw that the hour was just three o'clock, and descended the stairs again. At the pantry door I paused. I was not afraid—not one little bit. In fact the notion that anything might be wrong had never crossed my mind. But I remember thinking, with my hand on the door, that if Mrs. Carkeek were in the pantry I might happen to give her a severe fright.

"I pushed the door open briskly. Mrs. Carkeek was not there. But something *was* there, by the porcelain basin—something which might have sent me scurrying upstairs two steps at a time, but which as a matter of fact held me to the spot. My heart seemed to stand still—so still! And in the stillness I remember setting down the brass candlestick on a tall nest of drawers beside me.

"Over the porcelain basin and beneath the water trickling from the tap I saw two hands.

"That was all—two small hands, a child's hands. I cannot tell you how they ended.

"No: they were not cut off. I saw them quite distinctly: just a pair of small hands and the wrists, and after that—nothing.

They were moving briskly—washing themselves clean. I saw the water trickle and splash over them—not *through* them—but just as it would on real hands. They were the hands of a little girl, too. Oh, yes, I was sure of that at once. Boys and girls wash their hands differently. I can't just tell you what the difference is, but it's unmistakable.

"I saw all this before my candle slipped and fell with a crash. I had set it down without looking—for my eyes were fixed on the basin—and had balanced it on the edge of the nest of drawers. After the crash, in the darkness there, with the water running, I suffered some bad moments. Oddly enough, the thought uppermost with me was that I *must* shut off that tap before escaping. I *had* to. And after a while I picked up all my courage, so to say, between my teeth, and with a little sob thrust out my hand and did it. Then I fled.

"The dawn was close upon me: and as soon as the sky reddened I took my bath, dressed and went downstairs. And there at the pantry door I found Mrs. Carkeek, also dressed, with my candlestick in her hand.

"'Ah!' said I, 'you picked it up.'

"Our eyes met. Clearly Mrs. Carkeek wished me to begin, and I determined at once to have it out with her.

"'And you knew all about it. That's what accounts for your plugging up the cistern.'

"'You saw? . . .' she began.

"'Yes, yes. And you must tell me all about it—never mind how bad. Is—is it—murder?'

"'Law bless you, miss, whatever put such horrors in your head?'

"'She was washing her hands.'

"'Ah, so she does, poor dear! But—murder! And dear little Miss Margaret, that wouldn't go to hurt a fly!'

"'Miss Margaret?'

"'Eh, she died at seven year. Squire Kendall's only daughter; and that's over twenty year ago. I was her nurse, miss, and I know—diphtheria it was; she took it down in the village.'

"'But how do you know it is Margaret?'

"'Those hands—why, how could I mistake, that used to be her nurse?'

"'But why does she wash them?'

"'Well, miss, being always a dainty child—and the housework, you see—'

"I took a long breath. 'Do you mean to tell me that all this tidying and dusting—' I broke off. 'Is it *she* who has been taking this care of me?'

"Mrs. Carkeek met my look steadily.

"'Who else, miss?'

"'Poor little soul!'

"'Well now'—Mrs. Carkeek rubbed my candlestick with the edge of her apron—'I'm so glad you take it like this. For there isn't really nothing to be afraid of—is there?' She eyed me wistfully. 'It's my belief she loves you, miss. But only to think what a time she must have had with the others!'

"'The others?' I echoed.

"'The other tenants, miss: the ones afore you.'

"'Were they bad?'

"'They was awful. Didn't Farmer Hosking tell you? They carried on fearful—one after another, and each one worse than the last.'

"'What was the matter with them? Drink?'

"'Drink, miss, with some of 'em. There was the major—he used to go mad with it, and run about the coombe in his nightshirt. Oh, scandalous! And his wife drank too—that is, if she ever *was* his wife. Just think of that tender child washing Up after their nasty doings!'

"I shivered.

"'But that wasn't the worst, miss—not by a long way. There was a pair here—from the colonies, or so they gave out—with two children, a boy and gel, the eldest scarce six. Poor mites!'

"'Why, what happened?'

"'They beat those children, miss—your blood would boil!— *and* starved,*and* tortured 'em, it's my belief. You could hear their screams, I've been told, away back in the high-road, and that's the best part of half a mile. Sometimes they was locked up without food for days together. But it's my belief that little Miss Margaret managed to feed them somehow. Oh, I can see her, creeping to the door and comforting!'

"'But perhaps she never showed herself when these awful people were here, but took to flight until they left.'

"'You didn't never know her, miss. The brave she was! She'd have stood up to lions. She've been here all the while: and only to think what her innocent eyes and ears must have took in! There was another couple—' Mrs. Carkeek sunk her voice.

"'Oh, hush!' said I, 'if I'm to have any peace of mind in this house!'

"'But you won't go, miss? She loves you, I know she do. And think what you might be leaving her to—what sort of tenant might come next. For she can't go. She've been here ever since her father sold the place. He died soon after. You musn't go!'

"Now I had resolved to go, but all of a sudden I felt how mean this resolution was.

"'After all,' said I, 'there's nothing to be afraid of.'

"'That's it, miss; nothing at all. I don't even believe it's so very uncommon. Why, I've heard my mother tell of farmhouses where the rooms were swept every night as regular as clock-work, and the floors sanded, and the pots and pans scoured, and all while the maids slept. They put it down to the piskies; but we know better, miss, and now we've got the secret between us we can lie easy in our beds, and if we hear anything, say "God bless the child!" and go to sleep.'

"'Mrs. Carkeek,' said I, 'there's only one condition I have to make.'

"'What's that?'

"'Why, that you let me kiss you.'

"'Oh, you dear!' said Mrs. Carkeek as we embraced: and this was as close to familiarity as she allowed herself to go in the whole course of my acquaintance with her.

"I spent three years at Tresillack, and all that while Mrs. Carkeek lived with me and shared the secret. Few women, I dare to say, were ever so completely wrapped around with love as we were during those three years. It ran through my waking life like a song: it smoothed my pillow, touched and made my table comely, in summer lifted the heads of the flowers as I passed, and in winter watched the fire with me and kept it bright.

"'Why did I ever leave Tresillack?' Because one day, at the end of five years, Farmer Hosking brought me word that he had sold the house—or was about to sell it; I forget which. There was no avoiding it, at any rate; the purchaser being a Colonel Kendall, a brother of the old squire.'

"'A married man?' I asked.

"'Yes, miss; with a family of eight. As pretty children as ever you see, and the mother a good lady. It's the old home to Colonel Kendall.'

"'I see. And that is why you feel bound to sell.'

"'It's a good price, too, that he offers. You mustn't think but I'm sorry enough—'

"'To turn me out? I thank you, Mr. Hosking; but you are doing the right thing.'

"Since Mrs. Carkeek was to stay, the arrangement lacked nothing of absolute perfection—except, perhaps, that it found no room for me.

"'*She*—Margaret—will be happy,' I said; 'with her cousins, you know.'

"'Oh yes, miss, she will be happy, sure enough,' Mrs. Carkeek agreed.

"So when the time came I packed up my boxes, and tried to be cheerful. But on the last morning, when they stood corded in the hall, I sent Mrs. Carkeek upstairs upon some poor excuse, and stepped alone into the pantry.

"'Margaret!' I whispered.

"There was no answer at all. I had scarcely dared to hope for one. Yet I tried again, and, shutting my eyes this time, stretched out both hands and whispered:

"'Margaret!'

"And I will swear to my dying day that two little hands stole and rested—for a moment only—in mine."

Beside The Beehives

On the outskirts of the village of Gantick stand two small semi-detached cottages, coloured with the same pale yellow wash, their front gardens descending to the high-road in parallel lines, their back gardens (which are somewhat longer) climbing to a little wood of secular elms, traditionally asserted to be the remnant of a mighty forest. The party hedge is heightened by a thick screen of white-thorn on which the buds were just showing pink when I took up my lodging in the left-hand cottage (the 10th of May by my diary); and at the end of it are two small arbours, set back to back, their dilapidated sides and roofs bound together by clematis.

The night of my arrival, my landlady asked me to make the least possible noise in unpacking my portmanteau, because there was trouble next door, and the partitions were thin. Our neighbour's wife was down with inflammation, she explained—inflammation of the lungs, as I learnt by a question or two. It was a bad case. She was a wisht, ailing soul to begin with. Also the owls in the wood above had been hooting loudly, for nights past: and yesterday a hedge-sparrow lit on the sill of the sick-room window, two sure tokens of approaching death. The sick woman was being nursed by her elder sister, who had lived in the house for two years, and practically taken charge of it. "Better the man had married *she*" my landlady added, somewhat unfeelingly.

I saw the man in his garden early next morning: a tall fellow, hardly yet on the wrong side of thirty, dressed in loose-fitting tweed coat and corduroys. A row of bee-hives stood along his side of the party wall, and he had taken the farthest one, which was empty, off its stand, and was rubbing it on the inside with a handful of elder-flower buds, by way of preparation for a new swarm. Even from my bedroom window I remarked, as he turned his head occasionally, that he was singularly handsome. His movements were those of a lazy man in a hurry, though there seemed no reason for hurry in his task. But when it was done, and the hive replaced, his behaviour began to be so eccentric that I paused in the midst of my shaving, to watch.

He passed slowly down the line of bee-hives, halting beside each in turn, and bending his head down close to the orifice with the exact action of a man whispering a secret into another's ear. I believe he kept this attitude for a couple of minutes beside each hive—there were eight, besides the empty one. At the end of the row he lifted his head, straightened his shoulders, and cast a glance up at my window, where I kept well out of sight. A minute after, he entered his house by the back door, and did not reappear.

At breakfast I asked my landlady if our neighbour were wrong in his head at all. She looked astonished, and answered, "No: he was a do-nothing fellow—unless you counted it hard work to drive a carrier's van thrice a week into Tregarrick, and home the same night. But he kept very steady, and had a name for good nature."

Next day the man was in his garden at the same hour, and repeated the performance. Throughout the following night I was kept awake by a series of monotonous groans that reached me through the partition, and the murmur of voices speaking at intervals. It was horrible to lie within a few inches of the sick woman's head, to listen to her agony and be unable to help, unable even to see. Towards six in the morning, in bright daylight, I dropped off to sleep at last.

Two hours later the sound of voices came in at the open window and awoke me. I looked out into my neighbour's garden. He was standing, half-way up the path, in the sunshine, and engaged in a suppressed but furious altercation with a thin woman, somewhat above middle height. Both wore thick green veils over their faces and thick gloves on their hands. The woman carried a rusty tea-tray.

The man stood against her, motioning her back towards the house. I caught a sentence—"It'll be the death of her;" and the woman glanced back over her shoulder towards the window of the sick-room. She seemed about to reply, but shrugged her shoulders instead and went back into the house, carrying her tray. The man turned on his heel, walked hurriedly up the garden, and scrambled over its hedge into the wood. His veil and thick gloves were explained a couple of hours later, when I looked into the garden again and saw him hiving a swarm of bees that he had captured, the first of the season.

That same afternoon, about four o'clock, I observed that every window in the next house stood wide open. My landlady was out in the garden, "picking in" her week's washing from the thorn hedge where it had been suspended to dry; and I called her attention to this new freak of our neighbours.

"Ah, then, the poor soul must be nigh to her end," said she. "That's done to give her an easy death."

The woman died at half-past seven. And next morning her husband hung a scrap of black crape to each of the bee-hives.

She was buried on Sunday afternoon. From behind the drawn blinds of my sitting-room window I saw the funeral leave the house and move down the front garden to the high-road—the heads of the mourners, each with a white handkerchief pressed to its nose, appearing above the wall like the top of a procession in some Assyrian sculpture. The husband wore a ridiculously tall hat, and a hat-band with long tails. The whole affair had the appearance of an hysterical outrage on the afternoon sunshine. At the foot of the garden they struck up a "burying tune," and passed down the road, shouting it with all their lungs.

I caught up a book and rushed out into the back garden for fresh air. Even out of doors it was insufferably hot, and soon I flung myself down on the bench within the arbour and set myself to read. A plank behind me had started, and after a while the edge of it began to gall my shoulders as I leant back. I tried once or twice to push it into its place, without success, and then, in a moment of irritation, gave it a tug. It came away in my hand, and something rolled out on the bench before me, and broke in two.

I picked it up. It was a lump of dough, rudely moulded to the shape of a woman, with a rusty brass-headed nail stuck through the breast. Around the body was tied a lock of fine light-brown hair—a woman's, by its length.

After a careful examination, I untied the lock of hair, put the doll back in its place behind the plank, and returned to the house: for I had a question or two to put to my landlady.

"Was the dead woman at all like her elder sister?" I asked. "Was she black-haired, for instance?"

"No," answered my landlady; "she was shorter and much fairer. You might almost call her a light-haired woman."

I hoped she would pardon me for changing the subject abruptly and asking an apparently ridiculous question, but would she call a man mad if she found him whispering secrets into a bee-hive?

My landlady promptly replied that, on the contrary, she would think him extremely sensible; for that, unless bees were told of all that was happening in the household to which they belonged, they might consider themselves neglected, and leave the place in wrath. She asserted this to be a notorious fact.

"I have one more question," I said. "Suppose that you found in your garden a lock of hair—a lock such as this, for instance—what would you do with it?"

She looked at it, and caught her breath sharply.

"I'm no meddler," she said at last; "I should burn it."

"Why?"

"Because if 'twas left about, the birds might use it for their nests, and weave it in so tight that the owner couldn't rise on Judgment day."

So I burnt the lock of hair in her presence; because I wanted its owner to rise on Judgment day and state a case which, after all, was no affair of mine.

Captain Knot

Aaron Knot, master of the Virginia ship *Jehoiada*, though a member of the Society of Friends and a religious man by nature, had a tolerant and catholic mind, a quiet but insatiable curiosity in the ways of his fellowmen (seafarers and sinners especially), with a temperate zest for talking with strangers and listening to them. He liked his company to be honest, yet could stretch a point or two in charity. He knew, and liked to think, that it takes all sorts to make a world. At sea—and he had passed forty-five of his sixty years at sea—he would spend long hours, night after night, in his cabin, peaceably thinking about God, and God's wonders, and the purpose of it all.

Ashore, his heart warmed to the red light behind the blinds of a decent tavern. He was old enough, and wise enough, to know that for him the adventure would be sober. He knew at first taste good ale and good company from bad, and no stranger to whom he offered a pipeful could deny the quality of his tobacco, the best grown on the Rappahannock. He wore the strict Quaker dress, from broad hat down to square shoes with buckles. His features had a large Roman gravity. His hair, of an iron-grey, still strong in growth and combed over temples noticeably massive, was tied at the back with a wisp of black ribbon. His stature was six feet or a little over, and his build proportionate. In a man of sixty years one looks less to the waistband than to the depth of chest.

This Captain Knot, having brought the *Jehoiada* up Avon on a full spring tide, moored her off Wyatt's Wharf, settled with his crew, declared his cargo (mainly tobacco), and done all necessary business with his consignee, bent his steps towards the Welcome Home Tavern at the head of Quay Street. The date was Saturday, August 11th, 1742: the time about seven o'clock in the evening.

Of all the taverns in all the ports known to him the Welcome Home was Captain Knot's favourite house of call, and tonight it looked as cosy and well-to-do as ever; the sign newly painted and varnished, the doorstep white with holystone, the brick floor clean as a pin, fresh sawdust in the spittoons; the brass candlesticks on the chimney-piece, the brass chains of the clock-weights, the copper warming-pan on the wall, the ware on the dresser all a-twinkle in so much of evening light as drifted in by the open doorway or over the red window-blinds.

Yes, the place still prospered. "But why, then, is it so empty?" wondered Captain Knot—"and on a Saturday night?"

There were, in fact, but two customers in the room, two seafaring men seated and talking together on the settle beyond the fireplace; or rather, the one talking low and earnestly, the other listening. The listener—who was clearly the elder—held a long pipe and had a mug of beer beside him. The other had neither pipe nor mug. He leaned forward with his wrists on his knees and his hands clasped, nor did he shift his position when answering Captain Knot's "Good evening" with a "Good evening, sir." Lowering his voice, he went on with his argument, the murmur of which could not hide a Scottish accent.

Captain Knot threw the pair a look before rapping on the table. "House!" he called, threw the younger man a second, slightly longer look as if searching his face in the dusk, and walking to the window, stared out upon the street.

The landlady entered, and he whipped about.

"Mrs. Walters?"

"At your service, sir . . . Why, if it isn't Captain Knot! For a moment—and you standing there with your back to the light—"

"Husband well?"

"Quite well, sir, the Lord be praised!—and what's more, sir, he warned me the *Jehoiada* had come in . . . but with so much housework on one's mind! And I hope it's been a good passage. Captain? Haler I never saw you looking."

"Pretty fair, ma'am: nothing to grumble at," the captain answered, but absent-mindedly. His brows had drawn together in a slight frown as one of the men on the settle made a sudden shuffling movement with his feet. "Much, on the contrary, to be thankful for," he went on briskly, pulling himself together. "And pretty hale yet, as you say, for a man of sixty. But where's thy husband, that he neglects his old customers? Thou gave me a start, ma'am—a scare, till I took notice thy cap was no widow-woman's."

"Walters?" said the wife. "Oh, Walters is like every other fool in Bristol, crazy after the new preacher. You wouldn't think it in a man of his solid habits. He started at four o'clock to walk all the way to Kingswood—on a Saturday, too!"

"But who is this new preacher, ma'am?"

"Why, haven't you heard? Oh, but I forgot—you have only arrived today, and all the way from—from—"

"From the Potomac, ma'am."

"But even in America, sir, you must have heard tell of him—the great John Wesley, that is setting half England by the ears."

"Well, as a fact, ma'am," said Captain Knot coolly, "I *have* heard tell of him once or twice, and the first time was over in Georgia, where I'm sorry to say they did not think much of him."

"'Not think much of him!'" The younger of the two seamen rose abruptly from the settle and thrust himself into the conversation. "Show me the man as dares to say he doesn't think much of John Wesley, and I'll say to his face, 'John Wesley was sent straight from Heaven, as sure as John the Baptist.'" The man's hands and muscles of his still youthful face twitched with excitement.

"You mustn't mind Peter Williamson, sir," interposed Mrs, Walters. "He's young yet, and was converted almost a week ago—"

"Glory!" put in Williamson. "Hallelujah!—and I don't care who knows it."

"Though I wonder, Pete," Mrs. Walters went on, "that with all your fervour you're not out at Kingswood, too, this fine evening, but sitting here and all the time ordering nothing. One way or the other you're losing your privileges, and that you can't gainsay."

"I'm here, ma'am, on my Father's business," stammered Williamson. "If I've forgot the due of your house in this zeal o' mine—"

"Fetch Master Williamson a mug of your strong home-brewed, and another for me," ordered Captain Knot briskly. He ignored the younger seaman, who had twice made as if to rise and go, and twice faltered and sat down again.

"My young friend," said Captain Knot to Williamson, when the landlady had gone out, "so thou art on thy Father's business? And what might that be?"

"The saving of souls, sir," answered Williamson promptly. "This man's, for instance." He jerked a thumb at his companion.

"Ah? What's his name?"

"Haynes, sir—Jim Haynes. I know his need, and it's a bitter hard one."

"'Haynes'?" Captain Knot pondered. "No, I don't recall the name. Well, friend, I'll take thy word about knowing his need. As to knowing his soul, and dealing with it, on a seven-days'-old conversion, I am not so sure. Souls are kittle, friend, as they say up in thy country of North Britain. Take mine, for example—and I dare say a passable example, as souls go. It has its needs, God knows; yet I have a notion that the cure of 'em would give thee much trouble and yield me much amusement."

"I take ye for a releegious man, sir; though it beats me how you guessed I was out of Scotland. At first sight I said, 'Yon elderly gentleman has had convictions of sin at least, or I'm mistaken.'"

"Plenty." Captain Knot walked over to the empty fireplace, turned his back to it, and parted his broad coat-tails so that one hung over each arm. "Plenty, my friend, at one time and another. But I never crowd sail on my conscience, nor will I allow another man to do it. I'm master of that ship; and so it is, or should be to my notion, with every man. 'The Kingdom of God is within you.' Ah, here comes Mrs. Walters with the beer! Thy good health, my friend. As I was saying, or about to say, every man has a soul of his own, and is responsible for it. That's a tidy number, and all different. On top of that, there's animals, as some hold. Why there's Indians, over on my side of the world, make gods of the very vermin on their bodies. And what shall we say about ships now?"

"You're talking too deep for me, sir," said Williamson, rubbing his jaw. "A ship with a soul, you say?"

"Why not? I put it to thee as a seaman. Well, I won't press the word 'soul:' but there's a something belonging to her, and to her only, whats'ever ship she may be."

"I'm not denying as a ship may have a character," owned Williamson, who was young enough, and enough of a Scotsman, to rub shoulders fondly against anything hard and metaphysical.

"'Character'?" echoed Captain Knot with a faint accent of scorn, and still nursing his coat-tails. "Thou art old enough, by thy looks, to have seen a ship—ay, and felt her—running down the trades, with t' gallant sails set and stuns'ls out like the wings on a butterfly, floating and striving after heaven. Hast never had that feeling?"

"I know what you mean, sir," confessed Williamson,

"Then," advised Captain Knot, sharply, "don't pretend to me she was sailing to heaven on her character, like a servant maid after a situation. I don't know at what point in building or rigging the Lord puts the spirit in; but a spirit there is, and a soul, even in my old *Jehoiada*. For all that, she'll nag and sulk like a man's old wife. Ships? There be ships afloat comely as Mary Magdalen, and, like her, torn with devils; beautiful, born to be damned. I've known and pitied 'em, as I'd pity a girl with her pretty face set t'ards hell. Why, I could tell of the "

Here Captain Knot with a start disengaged both hands from under his coat-tails, smote the palm of his left with the knuckles of his right, and cried: "I have it! I never forget a face! That man"—he pointed a finger at the older seaman, who shrank back sideways on the settle before it—"I never heard his name till five minutes ago, but the *Rover* was his ship. I remember his face on the deck of her as we parted. Ay, the *Rover*, Captain Kennedy—Mrs. Walters!"

The older seaman staggered up from the settle. He would have made for the door; but Captain Knot had stepped to the exit and stood barring it.

"You can't harm me," stammered the seaman. "I got the King's Pardon for it these four years."

"Who wants to harm thee? "asked Captain Knot gently. "I only want to see thy face. Mrs. Walters, ma'am, the nights are closing in, and I'll ask the favour of a candle."

Mrs. Walters brought a candle and handed it to Captain Knot. "We will have a third mug of ale, ma'am, if thou please, and this one mulled hot, with a clove or two."

He took the candle, placed it on the high chimneypiece, and under it studied the seaman's features, keeping silence until the landlady had left the room. The wick burned dimly in the tallow, and at first the light showed him but a pair of eyes staring out from a frame or fringe of black hair. They were at once defiant in the surface and timid in their depths, eyes of a man at bay, hunted, and even haunted. Captain Knot took up the candle again, and held it close. The lower part of the face was weak, but neither sensual nor unrefined.

"When you've quite finished," growled the man.

"So Jim Haynes is his name?" Captain Knot set back the candle, and addressed the younger seaman, "Jim Haynes, formerly of Kennedy's gang in the *rover*. If either of ye wants to convert this man I would advise thee and thy Master Wesley against starting him to confess his sins in public."

"I got the King's Pardon," repeated Haynes. "Can't you let a man alone as has turned a new leaf?"

"I never saw the *Rover*, sir," put in Williamson. "But, as it happens, I came across a good part of her crew one time, and this Jim Haynes amongst 'em. What's more, I know how most of 'em ended."

"On the gallows, I make no doubt," said Captain Knot. "Let me hear thy tale presently. But 'tis the *Rover*—the ship herself—that I'm concerned about; the ship and the soul of her. A beautiful ship, hey?" He swung round on Haynes.

"Pretty enough," Haynes admitted in a hoarse voice.

"'Beautiful' was my word. Dutch built, as I've heard, and Dutch manned when that blackguard Howell Davies took her. But the man who designed her must have despised to call his craft by the name of any nation, for he had been up to heaven and fetched away the Lord's own pattern of a ship. The sheer of her! and the entry! It isn't enough to say that the wave off her cut-water never had time to catch so much as her heel, the dainty! For she cut no water, or none that showed. She touched it, and it made room. The first time I crossed her 'twas in a gale of wind, and she'd come up for a look at us. It couldn't have been but for that, and for wantonness, the seas being too steep and the weather too heavy for so much as hailing us, let alone boarding. I was young in those days—young and proud as a cock, it being my first command.

"My ship? Oh, the same old *Jehoiada*. I've commanded her and never another these thirty-five years. By rights I should have laid her to, hours and hours before. Nowadays I should lay-to as a matter of course. But I was proud, as I say, and venturesome, and anxious to cut a dash with my owners. So I held her on under close-reefed maintop sail and a napkin of a fo'c'sle, which answered well enough until the gale moderated, and the seas growing as it lessened began to knock the wind out of our sails, so that she fell slow to her helm in the troughs, why then I began to see my vainglory in a new light. And just then, out of the dirt astern, this *Rover* came overhauling us, leaping almost atop of us. She had sighted us, no doubt, and made sure we were running in fear of her.

"So just to give us a shake she passed us to windward and close. At one moment she was high up over our heads—high as our mainyard almost; the next I'd be holding hard by the rigging and looking over as she went down and down, craning my neck over her deck and half wondering if she'd spike our very hull as she lifted again. There were two men at her wheel, and a third man just aft of them; and right aft, on her very taffrail, a monkey, cracking nuts and grinning."

"Roberts's ape," blurted Jim Haynes.

"I reckoned the third man would be Roberts. He was grinning almost as comfortable as his ape, and once he looked up and shook his fist for a joke. A light-featured man, with a wig, as I remember; but his ship! Dancing past like a fairy on cork heels, the very deck of her dry, and three times the *Jehoiada* had taken it green. She passed us, downed helm, put breast to wave, went over it like a lark over a wall, right across our bows, and left us.

★★★★★★

"That was the first time. The second, 'twas about thirty leagues off Barbadoes, and the *Jehoiada* standing for home with a hold full of negroes from the Guinea Coast. This time she came up on us out of a summer sea, every stitch set, to her butterflies." Captain Knot turned on Haynes. "She carried a genius of a sailmaker?"

Haynes nodded. "Corson—Zepth Corson. He went with the rest."

"Ay! I can guess how. Well, then, they hanged an artist. The old Greeks or the Romans—I forget which—used to figure the soul in the shape of a butterfly. Master Haynes, what like was the soul of that ship? The beautiful !—I tell thee 'beautiful' was my word—and the hands she had passed through! Howell first, then Roberts, and now with that hulking Kennedy for master.

"Kennedy had given Roberts the slip—left him (as I've heard) to rot in a waterless boat—and now was in his shoes, full sail for Execution Dock. There's a silly proverb tells ye to speak of a man as you find him. I found Kennedy well enough. Partly in fun, belike, and it happening to be his humour, he let me off easy. But I sensed him for one of the worst rogues I had ever run across. A hollow man, filled up with dirt—that's what I made of Kennedy."

"I can tell you his end, sir," put in Williamson. "He got back to London and kept a bad house on Deptford Road. One of his women, in a tiff, laid information against him for robbery. While he was in Bridewell on this charge she sought out the ex-mate of a ship that he'd plundered. Grant was his name. Grant pays a visit to Bridewell, spots Kennedy as his man, swears to a warrant for piracy, and gets him shipped to Marshalsea. The rogue, to save his neck, offered King's Evidence against eight or ten old comrades then in hiding."

"I was one," said Jim Haynes. "He was a dirty rogue, was Walter Kennedy—as you say, sir. But the judge wouldn't listen. So they took him from the Marshalsea and turned him off at Execution Dock. That would be 'in the summer of '21, as I make out."

"There or thereabouts," agreed Captain Knot. "That would be about the length of rope I gave him. I haven't exactly what they call second sight, and yet I saw the hemp about his neck as plain as plain . . . notwithstanding that he used me very civilly.

"I have told you that I was proud in those days. On one point I've continued proud as I was then. I belong to the Society of Friends. Not a gun have I ever carried on the *Jehoiada*; not a pistol nor sword nor cutlass would I ever permit to be brought aboard of her, much less to be worn. My owners called me a fool, and, what was more, they proved it. To which I made no answer but that they must take me or leave me. They took me.

"I had a sprinkling of friends among my crew; but the rest, who would have fought the ship if we'd carried arms, treated me to some pretty black looks when the *Rover* bore down upon us. I kept my face as stiff as I could, making believe not to notice; and indeed I saw very little to fear. These gentry would have little use for my ship, which is, and ever was, a good plain sailer in sea-room, but no consort for theirs—not within six points of the wind.

"'Why,' said I to my mate, Mr. Greenaway, that stood grumbling,' the *Jehoiada*'s as good-looking as any man's wife has a right to be; but this here dancing beauty, angel or devil, is not coming to enlist the likes of the *Jehoiada*. And as for her cargo, Friend Greenaway,' I said, 'didst thou ever hear of a pirate that was hungry for a cargo of blacks? However much treasure he may carry, or however little, he takes only what stows close for its worth, and nine times out of ten he's in trouble to feed his own mouths. He'll take victual from us, and victual we have in plenty'—for I always feed my slaves fat as pigs; it's Christian, and it brings its earthly reward in the market. 'But for the rest,' said I, 'thou mark my words, he'll leave us alone.'

"Well, so it turned out, and to my astonishment even a little better. For what should prove to be this Kennedy's real reason for bringing us to? Victual he took from us, indeed, and enough to last him for three weeks. But his main purpose, he explained to me, coming aboard to my cabin. It seemed that he and his men, having taken much wealth, were weighted by it, and not only oppressed but frightened. 'Of what use is wealth. Master Quaker,' he asked, 'if it don't bring a man peace and comfort?' 'Of none at all, friend,' said I, 'and I am glad that repentance sits so heavy on thee.' 'Devil a bit it does,' said he. 'But I want to enjoy my earnings, and it's the same with my men. Now wealth made at sea will only bring enjoyment ashore, and the enjoyment we seek is not to be found in the islands, or, to my mind, anywhere on this Main. The most of us are dying to drop this trade, get back to England, bury the past, and live respectable, more or less. But that's the curse of it,' said he. 'You took note of my ship, maybe, as she came up on you?'

"'As one seaman to another. Captain Kennedy,' I said, 'she's the loveliest thing I ever saw on the face of the waters.' 'She's a devil,' says he. 'And I'm chained to her. Worse than a devil she is, being damned herself. Face of the waters—ay, there's her prison. Homeless, houseless, fleet as a bird, with all the law and the gospels in chase and giving her no rest. For all my pride in her she might sink under my shoes to-night, so I could win home to a tidy little parlour in Deptford.' 'It's there, friend,' said I, 'that I cannot help thee, being bound for the Capes.' 'No,' said he; 'but you can take off eight, or maybe nine, men of my company that have a mind to settle in Virginia. They will bring their share of the money, and I don't doubt they'll pay you well. I'm overmanned,' said he, 'for anything but fighting; and I'm sick of fighting and plundering; I only ask to get away home and live clean.'

"The upshot was that I took over eight pirates with their chests and a light cutter boat, in which four of them had a mind to make, as soon as we neared the coast, for Maryland. Eight they were, and, as I remember, Jim Haynes, thou watched 'em pull from ship to ship, yourself in two minds to make the ninth. I had my glass on thee, and I never forget a face."

"What became of them?" asked Haynes.

Captain Knot made a purring noise in his throat.

"I carried them safe," said he," and delivered them. They made me a present of ten chests of sugar, ten rolls of Brazil tobacco, thirty *moidures* and some gold dust, in all to the value of two hundred and fifty pounds. They also made presents to the sailors. But they gave me a great deal of trouble with their jovial ways, and it was difficult for me to keep any discipline because they wore arms day and night. So I was glad enough when we reached coast water, and half the party left us in the boat to make across the bay for Maryland. For the other four, I may tell thee that, coming to Hampton and anchoring, I made haste ashore to Mr. Spottswood, the governor, who sent off a guard, had them all bound, and hanged them out of hand. Nay, he did more, being a man to great energy. He sent patrols up the coast after the four that were making for Maryland, but (as it happened) had been forced by weather to land where they could, and were having good entertainment with the planters in those parts. These also he hanged. So all the eight were accounted for."

"And a d—n dirty trick!" swore Haynes, "when they had paid their passage."

"Ah, to be sure," said Captain Knot. "I forgot to tell that I handed the governor all their property taken on board, and all the presents they had made me, and forced my men to do the like. I've no taste—never had—for pirates or pirates' money."

"Well, I'm glad I made up my mind as I did,—that's all," Haynes growled.

Captain Knot fairly beamed on him. "I thought I had made it clear, friend," said he, "'twas the ship, and only the ship, that moved my bowels of pity. The beauty she was!" He sighed. "I never saw her again, nor heard what became of her."

Peter Williamson took up the story.

"I canna tell you, sir, what became of the ship. But I ken very well how the crew came to land, and it was not in this same *Rover*.

"Jamie Haynes, here, did once tell me a part of your tale, sir— how that they fell in with a Virginiaman, the master of which was a Quaker (saving your presence), and would carry no arms. He named me the eight men that went along with you, but the names, you'll understand, don't stick in my head."

"Nor in mine," Captain Knot assured him heartily.

"I dare say Jamie could put names to them now." Williamson glanced at Haynes, who had thrust his shoulders back into the settle-corner and was brooding inattentive, with his chin sunk on his chest. "But there! they're hanged long syne and don't signify. He said he'd often wished he had gone along with them."

"Ha?" was Captain Knot's comment, short and grim.

"But he said, sir, that some days after parting company with you, cruising off Jamaica, they took a sloop thither-bound from Boston, loaded with bread and flour. Aboard of this sloop went all hands that was in compact for breaking the gang and living honest—or all but Kennedy himself. They mistrusted Kennedy for his dirty ways, forbye that he had no skill in navigation, nor even in the reading and writing, but was only useful in a fight. He pleaded so bitterly, however, when they were about to throw him overboard—he having got ahead of them and sneaked into the sloop—that in the end they took him along, having first made him swear to be faithful, putting his hand upon the Bible, and taking the most dreadfullest oaths.

"So the *Rover* was left on the high seas, with the few that had a mind to hold on in her; and the sloop, with Kennedy's party (as we'll call them) and their shares of plunder aboard, shaped right away for Ireland, where they had agreed to land and scatter. By bad navigation, however, they ran away to the north-west of Scotland, and into one gale upon another; whereby, with all bearings lost, they came near to perishing.

"Upon this coast, sir, in those days, my father kept what you might call a shebeen, a mile from Clashnessie, to the south of Eddruchillis Bay. Alec Williamson his name was, a widower, and myself a lad of sixteen, very industrious to learn penmanship and the casting of accounts—my father doing some business off and on in the Free Trade, and, as he maintained, losing half his just profits by reason of his ignorance in these branches.

"Late one night, then—and the wind still blowing hard— there came a knocking at the door, and I opened it upon this very James Haynes as you see on this settle. He was wet through, and scared; and his first word was, 'Shut the door, for God's sake, and for God's sake close that chink of light between your shutters!' 'Is it a run?' asked my father, awake and coming downstairs at the noise of the latch. 'If so,' says my father, 'no warning has been put on me; and, what's more, my man, I never saw your face in my life.' 'By the smell of this house,' says Haynes, 'the usquebah is not very far away. Fetch me a drink, and in the morning, if ye're early risers, I'll make ye rich for life.'

"I went with the jug, and, that side of the house being dead to leeward, I heard a roaring of tipsy voices away beyond the cross roads. When I brought it to him the man took the liquor down like milk. 'I gave 'em the slip at the turning,' says he, and laughs. 'They're for Edinburgh, poor devils.' He would answer no questions. After another drink and a bite he laid himself down in his sodden clothes before what was left of the fire, and was asleep as soon as his head touched the hearthstone.

"But before day he was up and led us—a little unsurely, having come in the dark—down to a cove we called the Sow's

Shelter; a hole well-kenned as serviceable by the free-traders, running in narrow and steep-to, with a shelf of sand for the landing. What should we see there in the light of morning, but a good-sized sloop almost filling the hole, stern-on to the beach, and there grounded, hard and fast! . . . 'Take your run through her,' says this Haynes, pointing, 'and take your pickings before the whole country's on top of 'ee—as it will be within these two hours. For the fools who ran her here,' says he, 'are rolling south down the road and passing themselves for shipwrecked men; and the money is in their pockets and the drink in their heads. So help yourselves, honest men, while you may,' says he.

"'There's silks aboard, and chinaware, and plenty good tobacco; but to look for the dollars and the precious stones and the gold dust will only waste your time.' ''Tis hard we three must work then before his lordship's factor come and claims wreckage,' said my father. 'Begging your pardon,' says Haynes, 'but it will not be healthy for me to be taken here. You two must do without me, and that not until your lad here has taken me to safe hiding.' There was reason in this, and I led the man around a point of the foreshore to a snug cave. His clothing was stuffed with money so that he clinked as he climbed across the rocks. Well, in this cave by day, and by night in our cottage, we kept him hid for more than a month, it being sure capture for him within that time to try south after the rest of the crew. For I must tell you, sir

"I am not curious to hear about this man," put in Captain Knot, with a pretty grim look at Haynes, "seeing that I missed the pleasure to hang him. He's alive, as I see, so we will say no more about it. As for the rest, it will content me to hear that they came to the gallows—never mind how."

"Very well, sir," said Williamson; "then I'll be as short as you please. Kennedy cut loose from them at Cromarty, and by some means got himself shipped across to Ireland; which delayed his sail into Execution Dock for a season. Six or seven others had sense after a while to break away singly or in couples, and reached London without being disturbed or suspicioned. But the main gang flamed it down through Scotland, drinking and roaring at such a rate that in places folk shut themselves within doors. In others they treated the whole township to drink; which procured two of their stragglers to be knocked on the head, their bodies being found murdered on the road and their money taken from them. The residue, to the number of seventeen, won almost to the gates of Edinburgh. But, a post having ridden ahead, they were arrested and put into gaol on suspicion of they kent not what. The magistrates were not long at a loss over warrants; for two of the pact, offering themselves for evidence, were accepted; which put the others on trial: whereby nine were convicted and executed. To get back to Jamie Haynes here—"

"I tell thee," Captain Knot interrupted, "I am fair sick hearing of Haynes."

Haynes stood up, wiping his mouth weakly with the back of his hand. His knees shook as he straightened himself. He seemed like a man in a twitter after long drinking.

"Is it the *Rover*? . . . I can tell you, sir, about the *Rover*. She was a fine ship, sir. There was no mistaking her—"

"Look here, my man," put in Captain Knot. "There's no need to stand up and tell what I have been telling thee these twenty minutes."

"There was no mistaking her," Haynes went on, as though not hearing. His eyes were as if they withdrew their look deep in his head, and anon they stared out past the captain as though they saw a picture out in the twilight beyond the window-pane. He paused and gulped.

—"No mistaking her," he went on. "In the end I got away, first to Wick, then to Leith. There I shipped honest on the *Anna* brig for Jamaica. We called at St. Vincent in the Wind'ard Islands. Two days out from St. Vincent—and me forward, it being my watch—at daybreak there stood the *Rover* right ahead, and not two miles from us. There was no mistaking her, *as* you say, sir. She came on me out of the night like, as if she had been searching, with all her sins aboard—her sins and mine, sir. Instead of calling out I ran aft to the captain, and threw myself down, there by the wheel, at his feet, crying out her name, and how that was once a lost ship.

Haynes passed a hand over his eyes.

"There she was, sir—heeling to it—the main t'gallant sail blown away, and all the rest of her canvas crowded. The captain put up his glass. 'They must be mad aboard then,' says he; 'or else blazing drunk—or she 's behaving,'—For she fetched up in the wind, staggered dead, and after a bit the breeze fetched her a clap that laid her rail under. She righted, paid off again, and again she fetched up shivering. 'We'll hail her,' says our captain. 'I'm not afraid of any seaman that handles his ship so.' He hailed, and none answered.

"Our captain, manning up close, saw that her decks were empty. There was no one at the wheel, which wasn't even lashed. He ordered me and five others to board her along with him."

Haynes covered his eyes again, and henceforth to the end kept them covered.

"There was no crew aboard, sir: no trace of a crew. The hold was empty, but for nine niggers—live niggers, starved to the bone—sitting there with the whites of their eyes shining. Oh, my God! Nine niggers, and not a word to be got from them!

"What is it you say, sir? There was no trace, I swear! Not a spot of blood on her decks or anywhere. Cleaned down from fo'c'sle to cabin. Food enough on board, too. No, the men were not chained. But there they sat, the flesh shrunk on their bones and the whites of their eyes shining. . . ."

Haynes dropped back on the settle, and covered his face with both hands.

"Well?" asked Captain Knot. "What did your skipper do with her?"

"Put half a dozen hands aboard of her, sir: with orders to keep company and bear up with us for Kingston."

"And—"

"And that night she skipped ahead. . . . We never saw her again. She never came to port."

"Amen," said Captain Knot after a pause. "She never was for port."

"Doubles and Quits"

Here is a story from Troy, containing two ghosts and a moral. I found it, only last week, in front of a hump-backed cottage that the masons are pulling down to make room for the new Bank. Simon Hancock, the outgoing tenant, had fetched an empty cider-cask, and set it down on the opposite side of the road; and from this Spartan seat watched the work of demolition for three days, without exhaustion and without emotion. In the interval between two avalanches of dusty masonry, he spoke to this effect:—

Once upon a time the cottage was inhabited by a man and his wife. The man was noticeable for the extreme length of his upper lip and gloom of his religious opinions. He had been a mate in the coasting trade, but settled down, soon after his marriage, and earned his living as one of the four pilots in the port. The woman was unlovely, with a hard eye and a temper as stubborn as one of St. Nicholas's horns. How she had picked up with a man was a mystery, until you looked at *him*.

After six years of wedlock they quarrelled one day, about nothing at all: at least, Simon Hancock, though unable to state the exact cause of strife, felt himself ready to swear it was nothing more serious than the cooking of the day's dinner. From that date, however, the pair lived in the house together and never spoke. The man happened to be of the home-keeping sort— possessed no friends and never put foot inside a public-house. Through the long evenings he would sit beside his own fender, with his wife facing him, and never a word flung across the space between them, only now and then a look of cold hate. The few that saw them thus said it was like looking on a pair of ugly statues. And this lasted for four years.

Of course the matter came to their minister's ears—he was a "Bryanite"—and the minister spoke to them after prayer-meeting, one Wednesday night, and called at the cottage early next morning, to reconcile them. He stayed fifteen minutes and came away, down the street, with a look on his face such as Moses might have worn on his way down from Mount Sinai, if only Moses had seen the devil there, instead of God.

At the end of four years, the neighbours remarked that for two days no smoke had issued from the chimney of this cottage, nor had anyone seen the front door opened. There grew a surmise that the quarrel had flared out at last, and the wedded pair were lying within, in their blood. The anticipated excitement of finding the bodies was qualified, however, by a very present sense of the manner in which the bodies had resented intrusion during life. It was not until sunset on the second day that the constable took heart to break in the door.

There were no corpses. The kitchen was tidy, the hearth swept, and the house empty. On the table lay a folded note, addressed, in the man's handwriting, to the minister. It began:

> Dear Friend in Grace, we have been married ten years, and neither has broken the other; until which happens, it must be hell between us. We see no way out but to part for ten years more, going our paths without news of each other. When that time's up, we promise to meet here, by our door, on the morning of the first Monday in October month, and try again. And to this we set our names.—
> (here the two names followed.)

They must have set out by night; for an extinguished candle stood by the letter, with ink-pot and pen. Probably they had parted just outside the house, the one going inland up the hill, the other down the street towards the harbour. Nothing more was heard of them. Their furniture went to pay the quarter's rent due to the squire, and the cottage, six months later, passed into the occupation of Simon Hancock, waterman.

At this point Simon shall take up the narrative:—

"I'd been tenant over there"—with a nod towards the ruin—"nine year an' goin' on for the tenth, when, on a Monday mornin', about this time o' year, I gets out o' bed at five o'clock an' down to the quay to have a look at my boat; for 'twas the fag-end of the Equinox, and ther'd been a 'nation gale blowin' all Sunday and all Sunday night, an' I thought she might have broke loose from her moorin's.

"The street was dark as your hat and the wind comin' up it like gas in a pipe, with a brave deal o' rain. But down 'pon the quay day was breakin'—a sort of blind man's holiday, but enough to see the boat by; and there she held all right. You know there's two posts 'pon the town-quay, and another slap opposite the door o' the 'Fifteen Balls'? Well, just as I turned back home-long, I see a man leanin' against thicky post like as if he was thinkin', wi' his back to me and his front to the 'Fifteen Balls' (that was shut, o' course, at that hour). I must ha' passed within a yard of en, an' couldn' figure it up how I'd a-missed seein' en. Hows'ever, 'Good-mornin'!' I calls out, in my well-known hearty manner. But he didn' speak nor turn. 'Mornin'!' I says again. 'Can 'ee tell me what time 'tis? for my watch is stopped'—which was a lie; but you must lie now and then, to be properly sociable.

"Well, he didn' answer; so I went on to say that the 'Fifteen Balls' wudn' be open for another dree hour; and then I walked slap up to en, and says what the Wicked Man said to the black pig. 'You'm a queer Christian,' I says, 'not to speak. What's your name at all? And let's see your ugly face.'

"With that he turned his face; an' by the man! I wished mysel' further. 'Twas a great white face, all parboiled, like a woman's hands on washin' day. An' there was bits o' sticks an' chips o' seaweed stuck in his whiskers, and a crust o' salt i' the chinks of his mouth; an' his eyes, too, glarin' abroad from great rims o' salt.

"Off I sheered, not azackly runnin', but walkin' pretty much like a Torpointer; an' sure 'nough the fellow stood up straight and began to follow close behind me. I heard the water go squish-squash in his shoon, every step he took. By this, I was fairly leakin' wi' sweat. After a bit, hows'ever, at the corner o' Higman's store, he dropped off; an' lookin' back after twenty yards more, I saw him standin' there in the dismal grey light like a dog that can't make up his mind whether to follow or no. For 'twas near day now, an' his face plain at that distance. Fearin' he'd come on again, I pulled hot foot the few steps between me an' home. But when I came to the door, I went cold as a flounder.

"The fellow had got there afore me. There he was, standin' 'pon my door-step—wi' the same gashly stare on his face, and his lips a lead-colour in the light.

"The sweat boiled out o' me now. I quavered like a leaf, and my hat rose 'pon my head. 'For the Lord's sake, stand o' one side,' I prayed en; 'do'ee now, that's a dear!' But he wudn' budge; no, not though I said several holy words out of the Mornin' Service.

"'Drabbet it!' says I, 'let's try the back door. Why didn' I think 'pon that afore?' And around I runs.

"There 'pon the back door-step was a woman!—an' pretty well as gashly as the man. She was just a 'natomy of a woman, wi' the lines of her ribs showin' under the gown, an' a hot red spot 'pon either cheek-bone, where the skin was stretched tight as a drum. She looked not to ha' fed for a year; an', if you please, she'd a needle and strip o' calico in her hands, sewin' away all the while her eyes were glarin' down into mine.

"But there was a trick I minded in the way she worked her mouth, an' says I, 'Missus Polwarne, your husband's a-waitin' for 'ee, round by the front door.'

"'Aw, is he indeed?' she answers, holdin' her needle for a moment—an' her voice was all hollow, like as if she pumped it up from a fathom or two. 'Then, if he knows what's due to his wife, I'll trouble en to come round,' she says; 'for this here's the door *I* mean to go in by.'"

But at this point Simon asserts very plausibly that he swooned off; so it is not known how they settled it.

(This story is true, as anyone who cares may assure himself by referring to Robert Hunt's *Drolls of the West of England*.)

Frozen Margit

A Narrative of the sufferings of Mr. Obed Lanyon, of Vellingey-Saint Agnes, Cornwall; Margit Lanyon, his wife; and seventeen persons (mostly Americans) shipwrecked among the Quinaiult Tribes of the N.W. Coast of America, in the winter of 1807-8. With some remarkable Experiences of the said Margit Lanyon, formerly Pedersen. Written by the Survivor, Edom Lanyon, sometime a Commander in the service of the Honourable East India Company.

My twin brother Obed and I were born on the 21st of March, 1759 (he being the elder by a few minutes), at Vellingey-St. Agnes, or St. Ann's, a farm on the north coast of Cornwall, owned and cultivated by our father Renatus Lanyon. Our mother was a Falmouth woman, daughter of a ship's captain of that port: and I suppose it was this inclined us to a sea-faring life. At any rate, soon after our fifteenth birthday we sailed (rather against our father's wish) on a short coasting voyage with our grandfather—whose name was William Dustow.

A second voyage in the early summer of 1776 took us as far as the Thames. It happened that the famous Captain Cook was just then recruiting for his third and (as it proved) his last voyage of discovery. This set us talking and planning, and the end was that we stole ashore and offered ourselves. Obed had the luck to be picked. Though very like in face, I was already the taller by two inches; and no doubt the captain judged I had outgrown my strength. But it surprised me to be rejected when Obed was taken; and disappointed me more: for, letting alone the prospect of the voyage, we two (as twins, and our parents' only children) were fond of each other out of the common degree, and had never thought to be separated.

To speak first of Obed:—Captain Cook put some questions, and finding that we were under our grandfather's care, would do nothing without his consent. We returned to the ship and confessed to the old man, who pretended to be much annoyed. But next day he put on his best clothes and went in search of the great seaman, to Whitehall; and so the matter was arranged. Obed sailed in July on board the *Discovery*; shared the dangers of that voyage, in which the ships followed up the N.W. Coast of America and pushed into Behring's Strait beyond the 70th parallel; was a witness, on February 4th, 1779, of his commander's tragical end; and returned to England in October, 1780. Eleven years later he made another voyage to the same N.W. American Coast; this time as master's mate under Vancouver, who had kept an interest in him since they sailed together under Cook, and thought highly of him as a practical navigator and draughtsman.

It was my brother who, under Vancouver, drew up the first chart of the Straits of Fuca, which Cook had missed: and I have been told (by a Mr. G——, a clerk to the Admiralty) that on his return he stood well for a lieutenant's commission—the rule of the Service being stretched now and then to favour these circumnavigating seamen, many of whom worked their way aft from the hawse-hole to the quarter deck. But my father and mother dying just then, and the former having slipped a particular request into his will, Obed threw up the sea and settled down in Vellingey as a quiet yeoman farmer.

Meanwhile, in 1779, I had entered the sea service of the Honourable East India Company; and with passable good fortune had risen in it pretty fast. Enough to say, that by the spring of 1796 I was looking forward to the command of a ship. Just then my fortune deserted me. In a sudden fear of French invasion, our government bought the four new ships which the Company had building (and a bad bargain they proved). This put a stop for the time to all chance of promotion; and a sharp attack of jaundice falling on top of my disappointments, I took the usual decrease of pay and the Board's promise to remember my services on a proper occasion, and hauled ashore to Vellingey for a holiday and a thorough refit of health.

I believe that the eight or nine following months which Obed and I spent together were the happiest in our two lives. He was glad enough to shoulder off the small business of the farm and turn—as I have seen so many men play, in a manner, at the professions they have given over—to his favourite amusement of sounding the coast of Vellingey and correcting the printed charts. He kept a small lugger mainly for this purpose, and plied her so briskly that he promised to know the seabottom between Kelsey Head and Godrevy Rock better than his own fields. As for me, after years of salt water and stumping decks, I asked nothing better than to steer a plough and smell broken soil, and drowse after supper in an armchair, with good tobacco and Obed for company.

In this way we passed the winter of 1796-7; until the lambing season, which fell midway in February. The year opened wet, with fresh south westerly winds, which in the second week chopped suddenly; and for four days a continuous freezing gale blew on us from the N.W. It was then that the lambs began to drop; and for three nights I exchanged pipe and fireside for a lantern and the lower corner of Friar's Parc at the back of the towans, where the ewes were gathered in the lew.[1] They kept us so busy that for forty-eight hours we neither changed our clothes (at least, I did not) nor sat down to a meal. The sand about Vellingey is always driving, more or less; and the gale so mixed it up with fine snow that we made our journeys to and from the house, so to speak, blindfold, and took our chance of the drifts.

But the evening of the 11th promised better. The wind dropped, and in an hour fell to a flat calm: then, after another hour, began to draw easily off shore—the draught itself being

---

1. Shelter from the wind.

less noticeable than the way in which it smoothed down the heavy sea running. Though the cold did not lift, the weather grew tolerable once more: and each time I crossed the town-place[2] with a lamb in my arms, I heard the surf running lower and lower in the porth below Vellingey.

By daybreak (the 12th) it was fallen to nothing: the sky still holding snow, but sky and sea the same colour; a heavy bluish grey, like steel. I was coming over the towans, just then, with a lamb under either arm (making twelve, that night) when I happened to look seaward, and there saw a boat tossing, about a gunshot from the shore.

She was a long boat, painted white; very low in the sheer, and curved at stem and stern like a Norwegian; her stem rounded off without a transom, and scarcely bluffer than her bows. She carried a mast, stepped right forward; but no sail. She was full of people. I counted five sitting, all white with snow—one by the mast, three amidships, and one in the stern sheets, steering. At least, he had a hand on the tiller: but the people had given over pulling, and the boat without steerage-way was drifting broadside-on towards the shore with the set of the tide.

While I stood conning her, up at the house the back-door opened, and my brother stepped out and across the yard to milk the cows. His milk-pails struck against the door-post, and sounded as clear as bells. I shouted to him and pointed towards the boat: and after looking a moment, he set down his pails and started off at a run, down towards the porth. I then hurried towards the house, where I found Selina, our old housekeeper, in the kitchen, tending the lambs with warm milk. Handing the newcomers over to her, I caught up a line and made off hot-foot after Obed.

At low-water (and the tide had now scarcely an hour to ebb) the sands in Vellingey Porth measure a good half-mile from the footbridge at its head to the sea at its base. My legs were longer than Obed's; but I dare say he had arrived five minutes ahead of me. He was standing and calling to the boat's crew to get out an

---

2. Farmyard.

oar and pull her head-to-sea: for although the smoothing wind had taken most of the danger out of the breakers, they were quite able to capsize and roll over any boat that beached herself in that lubberly fashion.

I ran up panting, and shouted with him—"Pull her round head-to-sea, and back her in!"

Not a man moved or lifted a hand. The next moment, a wave tilted and ran a dozen yards with her, but mercifully passed before it broke. A smaller one curved on the back-draught and splashed in over her gunwale as she took ground. But what knocked the wind out of our sails was this—As the first wave canted her up, two men had rolled out of her like logs; and the others, sitting like logs, had never so much as stirred to help!

"Good Lord!" I called out, and fumbled with my line. "What's the meaning of it?"

"The meaning is," said Obed, "they're dead men, every mother's son. They're frozen," said he: "I've seen frozen seamen before now."

"I'll have in the boat, anyway," I said. "Here, catch hold and pay out!" Running in, I reached her just as she lifted again; and managed to slew her nose in-shore, but not in time to prevent half-a-hogshead pouring over her quarter. This wave knocked her broadside-on again, and the water shipped made her heavier to handle. But by whipping my end of the line round the thwart in which her mast was stepped, for Obed to haul upon, and myself heaving at her bows, we fetched her partly round as she lifted again, and ran her into the second line of breakers, which were pretty well harmless.

"How many on board?" Obed sang out.

"Five!" called I, having counted them. Up to this I had had enough to do with the boat; besides looking after myself. For twice the heave had tilled me up to the armpits, and once lifted me clean off my feet; and I had no wish to try swimming in my sea-boots. "Five," said I; "and two overboard—that makes seven. Come and look here!"

"Tend to the boat first," he said. "I've seen frozen seamen."

"You never saw the likes of this," I answered. So he ran in beside me.

The boat had her name (or that of the ship she belonged to) painted in yellow and black on the gunwale strake by her port quarter—*Margit Pedersen, Bergen*: but by their faces we could not miss knowing to what country the poor creatures belonged. They were—

1. A tall man, under middle age; seated by the mast and leaning against it (his right arm frozen to it, in fact, from the elbow up) with his back towards the bows. The snow was heaped on his head and shoulders like a double cape. This one had no hair on his face; and his complexion being very fresh and pink, and his eyes wide open, it was hard to believe him dead. Indeed, while getting in the boat, I had to speak to him twice, to make sure.

2. A much older man, and shorter, with a rough grey beard. He sat in the stern sheets, with his right hand frozen on the tiller. Our folk had afterwards to unship the tiller when they came to lift him out: and carried him up to the house still holding it. Later on we buried it beside him. This man wore a good blue coat and black breeches; and at first we took him to be the captain. He turned out to be the mate, Knud Lote, who had put on his best clothes when it came to leaving the ship. His eyes were screwed up, and the brine had frozen over them, like a glaze, or a big pair of spectacles.

3. Against his knee rested the head of a third man—one of the three I had first seen sitting amidships. When the other two toppled overboard this one had slid off the thwart and fallen against the steersman. He was an oldish man, yellow and thin and marked with the small-pox; the only one in the boat who might have come from some other country than Norway. His eyes were cast down in a quiet way, and he seemed to be smiling. He wore a seaman's loose frock, ragged breeches, and sea-boots.

4 and 5. Stretched along the bottom-boards lay a tall young man with straw-coloured hair and beard: and in his arms, tightly clasped, and wrapped in a shawl and seaman's jacket, a young woman. Her arms were about the young man and her face pressed close and hidden against his side. He must have taken off his jacket to warm her; for the upper part of his body had no covering but a flannel shirt and cinglet.

While we stood there the tide drained back, leaving the bows of the boat high and dry. As I remember, Obed was the first to speak; and he said "She has beautiful hair." This was the bare truth: a great lock of it lay along the bottom-board like a stream of guineas poured out of a sack. He climbed into the boat and lifted the shawl from her face.

Those neighbours of ours, friends and acquaintances, who afterwards saw Margit Pedersen at Vellingey, and for whom this account is mainly written, will not need a description of her. Many disliked her: but nobody denied that she was a lovely woman; and I am certain that nobody could see her face and afterwards forget it. It was, then and always, very pale: but this had nothing to do with ill health. In fact I am not sure it would have been noticeable but for the warm colour of her hair and her red lips and (especially) her eyebrows and lashes, of a deep brown that seemed almost black. Her lips were blue with the cold, just now: but the contrast between her eyebrows and her pale face and yellow hair struck me at once and kept me wondering: until Obed startled me by dropping the shawl and falling on his knees beside her. "Good God, Dom!" he sang out: "the girl's alive!"

The next moment, of course, I was as wild as he. "Get her out, then," I cried, "and up to the house at once!"

"I can't loosen the man's arms!" Though less than a yard apart, we both shouted at the top of our voices.

"Nonsense!" I answered: but it was true all the same—as I found out when I stepped in to Obed's help. "We must carry up the pair as they are," I said. "There's no time to lose."

We lifted them out, and making a chair of our hands and

wrists, carried them up to Vellingey; leaving the others in the boat, now for an hour well above reach of the tide. And here I must tell of something that happened on the way: the first sign of Obed's madness, as I may call it. All of a sudden he stopped and panted, from the weight of our load, I supposed. "Dom," he said, "I believe that nine men out of ten would kiss her!"

I told him not to be a fool, and we walked on. In the town-place we happened on the shepherd, Reuben Santo, and sent him off for help, and to look after the frozen people in the boat. The sight of us at the door nearly scared Selina into her grave: but we allowed her no time for hysterics. We laid the pair on a blanket before the open fire, and very soon Obed was trying to force some warm milk and brandy between the girl's lips. I think she swallowed a little: but the first time she opened her eyes was when one of the lambs (which everyone had neglected for twenty minutes or so) tottered across the kitchen on his foolish legs and began to nuzzle at her face. Obed at the moment was trying to disengage the dead man's arms. A thought struck Selina at once. "Put the lamb close against her heart," she said. "That'll warm her more than any fire."

So we did, making the lamb lie down close beside her; and it had a wonderful effect. In less than half-an-hour her pulse grew moderately firm and she had even contrived to speak a word or two, but in Norwegian, which none of us understood. Obed by this time had loosened the dead man's arms; and we thought it best to get her upstairs to bed before the full sense of her misfortune should afflict her. Obed carried her up to the spare-room and there left her to Selina; while I saddled horse and rode in to Truro, for Doctor Mitchell.

Much of what followed is matter of public knowledge. Our folks carried the dead Norwegians up to Church-town, including one of the two that had fallen overboard (the next tide washed him in; the other never came to land); and there buried them, two days later, in separate graves, but all close together. The boat being worthless, we sawed it in two just abaft the mast and set the fore-part over the centre grave, which was that of

Captain Pedersen, the young man we had carried up with Margit. The mast rotted and fell, some years ago, although carefully stayed: but the boat, with the names painted on it, remains to this day. Also we set up a small wooden cross by each man's grave, with his name upon it. Margit was able, from our description, to plan out the right name for each.

On the third day an interpreter came over from Penzance. Margit could not yet leave her bed: and before he stepped up to question her, I took him aside and showed a small Norwegian Bible we had found in the pocket of the seaman's jacket to which she owed her life. On the first page was some foreign writing which I could not make out. The interpreter translated it: first the names "Margit Hansen to Nils Pedersen": and after them, this strange verse from the *Song of Solomon*—strange, I mean, to find written in such a place—"Let him kiss me with the kisses of his mouth: for thy love is better than wine."

The interpreter, Mr. Scammel, went upstairs, and she told him her story. "Our vessel," she said (I give it in brief) "was the *Margit Pedersen*, brig. She belonged to me and was called after me. We were bound for the Tagus with a cargo of salted fish which I had bought at Bergen from the Lofoden smacks—fish for the Roman Catholics to eat in Lent. Nils Pedersen, the captain, was my husband: Knud Lote was mate."

Mr. Scammell having expressed some surprise that so young a man should have been captain, she explained, "He was twenty-two. I made him captain. My father and mother died: they had not wished me to marry him. They were proud. But they left very little money, considering; and with it I bought the brig and cargo. She was an old craft, half rotten. We had fair weather, mostly, down the English Channel and almost to Ushant. There we met a strong southerly gale, and in the middle of it a pintle of our rudder gave way and the loose rudder damaged our sternpost. We tried to bear up for Falmouth, but she would not steer; and we drove up towards the Irish Coast, just missing Scilly.

"On the 8th the wind changed to N.W. and increased. That night, as Nils tried to lay to, she carried away her fore-mast, which had been shaky for days. She was now leaking fast. At noon on the 9th we managed to launch a boat, and abandoned her. She sank at four o'clock: we saw her go down. The weather grew colder, that night. I think it snowed all the time: and the seas were too heavy to let the boat run. The men pulled to keep her nose to them and the wind, and so she drifted. I forget when they gave over pulling. For a night and a day I baled steadily. After that I lay most of the time in the bottom of the boat. Our food was almost done. It was very cold. That is all I can remember."

And this, I think, was all we ever heard from her. On his return to Penzance, Mr. Scammell sent me a Norwegian dictionary; and with the help of it Obed and I soon managed to talk a little with her, in a mixture of Norwegian and English. But she never wanted to speak of the past, and fell silent whenever we spoke of it. What astonished me more was that, though she told us the names of the dead men, she showed no further interest in them. At first, knowing how weak she was, and fearing to distress her, I fought shy of the subject; but one day, towards the end of the third week—she being strong enough to walk a moderate distance—I plucked up courage and asked if she cared to come with me to the churchyard. She agreed, and that afternoon, after a heavy shower, we walked thither together. I feared what effect the first sight of her husband's grave might work on her feelings; and all the way kept wishing that we had omitted to set up the boat and mast. But she looked at them calmly, and at the graves. "That is good," she said: "you have done great kindness to them. I will not come any more." And so she prepared to walk away.

I own that this seemed to me unfeeling. Outside the churchyard I pulled from my pocket the small Bible. "This belongs to you," I said: "I have kept it to help me with your language"—but I held it open at the fly-leaf. She glanced at it, "Oh yes, I gave it to Nils, my husband. You wish to keep it?"

"You were very fond of him, to judge from this," I said; and halted, expecting her to be angry.

But she halted too, and said quite coolly—looking at me

straight—"Yes? Oh yes; very much."

That same evening I spoke to Obed as we sat alone with our pipes. "I suppose," said I as carelessly as I could, "Margit Pedersen will be leaving us before long." He looked up sharply, and began to shift the logs on the hearth.

"What makes you say so?" he asked.

"Well, she will have friends in Bergen, and business—"

"Has she written to her friends?" he interrupted.

"Not to my knowledge: but she won't be staying here forever, I suppose."

"When she chooses to go, she can. Are you proposing to turn her out? If so, I'd have you to mind that Vellingey is my house, and I am master here."

This was an unworthy thing to say, and he said it with a fury that surprised me. Obed and I had not quarrelled since we were boys. I put a stopper on my tongue, and went on smoking: and after a while he began to talk again in his natural way on ordinary matters.

Margit stayed on; and to all appearance our life at Vellingey fell back into its old groove. As a matter of fact there was all the difference in the world—a difference felt before it was seen, and not to be summed up by saying that a woman sat at our table. I believe I may quite fairly lay the blame on Obed. For the first time in our lives he kept a part of his mind hidden from me; he made show enough of frankness in his talk, but I knew him far too well to miss the suspicion behind it. And his suspicion bred suspicion in me. Yet though I searched, I could find nothing amiss in his outward bearing. If he were indeed in love with the girl—her age, she told us, was twenty-one—he gave no sign upon which one could lay hold.

And certainly Margit's bearing towards us was cool and friendly and impartial as the strictest could desire. Of the two, I had, perhaps, more of her company, simply because Obed spent most of his time in the lugger, while I worked in the fields and within easy reach of an afternoon's stroll. Margit would be busy with housework most of the morning, or in the kitchen, helping

Selina—"domineering," Selina preferred to call it.

For, whatever our feelings, Selina had set her face against the new-comer from the first. She started, no doubt, with the old woman's whiddle that no good ever comes of a person saved from the sea. But as time went on she picked up plenty of other reasons for dislike. Margit took charge from the day she came downstairs, and had a cold way of seeing that her orders were attended to. With about twenty words of English she at once gave battle to Selina, who had bullied us two men from childhood; and routed her. The old woman kept up a running fight for a week before appealing to Obed, and this delay cost her everything. Obed flew in a rage that more than equalled her own, and had the advantage to be unusual and quite unexpected by her. She ran from him to the kitchen, in tears; and thenceforth was a beaten woman, however much she might grumble at the "foreigner" and "interloper."

For me, I will confess, and have done with it, that before a month was out my interest in this pale foreign woman, who moved about the house so quietly and surely, had grown to a degree that troubled me. That Obed had suspected me before he had any cause made it no easier now to play a concealed game at cross-purposes; and no pleasanter. In the two months that followed I hated myself pretty often, and at times came near to despise myself for the thought that before long I might be hating Obed. This would never have done: and luckily I saw it in time. Towards the end of June I made application to the Board: and left Vellingey in July, to sail for Bombay on board the *Warren Hastings*, in my old capacity of first mate. My abandoning the field to Obed would deserve some credit, had Margit ever by word or look given me the slightest reason to hope. But she had not; indeed I hoped that she had never guessed the state of my feelings.

Eighteen months passed before I returned to Vellingey—this time on a short leave. Obed had written constantly and with all the old familiarity; a good deal concerning Margit—her health, her walks, her household business—everything, in short, but what I expected and dreaded to hear. "Come," I said to myself, "five minutes' start in life and eighteen months in courtship is no such bad allowance for Obed. Perhaps he will allow me now to have *my* turn."

I had this thought in my head as I drew near Vellingey in a light gig hired from the Truro post-master. It was a rainy afternoon in January, and a boisterous north-wester blew the Atlantic weather in our teeth as we mounted the rise over Vellingey churchtown. My head being bent down, I did not observe the figure of a woman coming up the village street, but looked up on hearing the sound of her clogs close beside the gig. It was Selina, tearful, carrying a bundle.

"Whatever is the matter?" I asked, on pulling up.

"They've turned me to door!" she moaned. "My dear, they've turned me to door!"

She was tramping home to her cousins in St. Day parish. Not another night would she sleep at Vellingey—to be trampled on. Of course she accused the "foreign woman:" but I, it seemed, had started the quarrel this time; or, rather, it started over the preparations for my home-coming—some trifling matter of cookery. Selina knew my tastes. Margit professed to know them better. Such are women.

I own that as I sent the poor soul on her way, with a promise that the gig should carry back her boxes from Vellingey and a secret resolve that she should return to us within a week, I could not avoid a foolish pleasure in the thought that Margit deemed my coming of such importance. Then it occurred to me that her position now as a single woman alone at Vellingey lay open to scandal. The sooner I tested my growing hopes, the better.

I did so, the second evening, after supper. Obed had stepped out to make the round of the farm buildings and lock up. Margit had removed the white cloth, and was setting the brass candlesticks and tobacco jar on the uncovered table.

"What is going to happen about Selina?" I asked, from my chair.

Margit set down a candlestick. "Selina has gone," she said

quietly.

"But people will talk, if you stay here alone with us, or with Obed. You mustn't mind my saying this."

"Oh, no. I suppose they will talk."

I stood up. "I take it," said I, "you cannot be quite blind to my feelings, Margit. I came home on purpose to speak to you: but perhaps, if it had not been for this, I might have put off speaking for some days. If you care for me at all, though, I think you can answer. My dear, if you will marry me it will make me a happy man."

She was fingering the candle-base, just touching the brass with her finger-tips and withdrawing them gently. She looked up. "I rather thought," she said, "you would have spoken last night. Obed asked me this morning—he gave you that chance: and I have promised to marry him."

"Good Lord! but this is a question of loving a man!"

"I have never said that I like you better. I shall make Obed a very good wife."

Less than a minute later, Obed came into the room, after slamming the back-door loudly. He did not look at our faces: but I am sure that he knew exactly what had happened.

They were married in April, a fortnight after my leaving England on another voyage. We parted the best of friends; and in the course of the next seven years I spent most of my holidays with them. No married life could well be smoother than was Obed's and Margit's in all this time. He worshipped her to fondness; and she, without the least parade of affection, seemed to make his comfort and well-being the business of her life. It hardly needs to be said that my unfortunate proposal was ignored by all of us as a thing that had never happened.

In October, 1802, I reached the height of my ambition, being appointed to the command of the Company's ship *Macartney*, engaged in the China traffic. I call her the *Macartney*: but the reader will presently see that I have reasons for not wishing to make public the actual name of this vessel, which, however, will be sufficiently familiar to all who knew me at that time and who have therefore what I may call a private interest in this narrative. For the same reason I shall say no more of her than that she was a new ship, Thames-built, and more than commonly fast; and that I commanded her from October 1802 to June 1806.

She carried passengers, of course: and in the autumn of 1805 it surprised and delighted me to hear from Obed that he and Margit had determined on a sea voyage, and wished to book their passages to the Canton River and back in the *Macartney*. I had often given this invitation in jest: but such voyages merely for health and pleasure were then far from common. Yet there was no single impediment to their going. They had no children: they were well-to-do: they had now a hind, or steward (one Stephens), to whose care they might comfortably leave the farm. To be short, they sailed with me.

On the 2nd of May 1806, the *Macartney* dropped anchor in the Canton River after a fast and prosperous voyage. The events I have now to relate will appear least extraordinary to the reader who best understands under what conditions the English carry on their trade with China. Let me say, then, that in its jealousy of us foreign barbarians the Chinese government confines our ships to the one port of Canton and reserves the right of nominating such persons as shall be permitted to trade with us. These Hong merchants (in number less than a dozen) are each and all responsible to the emperor for any disturbance that may be committed by a person belonging to a foreign ship: and they in turn look for compensation to the European factors. So that, a Chinese mob being the most insolent in the world, and the spirit of British seamen proverbial, these factors often find themselves in situations of great delicacy, and sometimes of more than a little danger.

It happened that on the next day after our arrival a small party of us—Margit and Obed, the second officer, Mr. Tomlinson, and I—had taken a short stroll ashore and were returning to the boat, which lay ready by the landing, manned by six seamen. The coxswain brought the boat alongside: and I, on the lowest step of the landing-stage, stooped to hold her steady while

Margit embarked. She and Obed waited on the step next above, with Mr. Tomlinson close behind. A small crowd had followed us: and just then one dirty Chinaman reached forward and with a word or two (no doubt indecent) laid his open palm on the back of Margit's neck. Quick as thought, she lifted a hand and dealt him a rousing box in the ear. I sprang up and pushed him back as he recovered. He slipped on the green ooze of the steps and fell: this was all I saw, for the crowd made a rush and closed. Obed and Mr. Tomlinson had hurried Margit into the boat: I leapt after them: and we pushed off under a brisk shower of dirt and stones. We were soon out of range, and reached the ship without mishap.

Knowing the nature of a Chinese rabble, I felt glad enough that the affair had proved no worse; and thought little more of it until early next morning, when Mr. Findlater, the first officer, came with a puzzled face and reported that during the night someone had attached a boat, with a dead Chinaman in it, to the chain of our small bower anchor.

I went on deck at once. A good look at the corpse relieved me: for as far as my recollection served, it bore no resemblance to the man I had pushed on the landing. I told off two of the rowers of the previous day—the two whose position in the bows had given them the best view of the scuffle—to cut the thing adrift. They did so and came back with the report that they had never seen the dead man before in their lives. So I tried to feel easy.

But soon after breakfast, and almost in the full heat of the day, there came off a galley with two of the Hong merchants and no less a person than Mr. '——', the Chief of the H.E.I.C.'s factory. He brought serious news. The boat had drifted up the river and had been recovered by a crowd of Chinese, who took out the dead man and laid him on the doorstep of the factory, clamouring that he had been killed, the day before, by an Englishwoman; and threatening, unless she were given up, to seize the first supercargo that came out and carry him off to be strangled.

I answered, describing the scuffle and declaring my readiness to swear that the body bore no resemblance to the fellow whose ear Margit had boxed. But I knew how little this testimony would avail in a Chinese court. The two Hong merchants assured me that their brother, the *Macartney's* guarantor, was already in the hands of the magistrates, who had handcuffed him and were threatening him with the bamboo: that an interdiction lay on the *Macartney's* cargo, and Mr. '——' himself ran no small risk of imprisonment.

Our position was at once absurd and extremely serious. To do him justice, Mr. '——' at once agreed that there could be no question of delivering up Margit: the penalty of her offence, if proved to the satisfaction of the Chinese magistrates, being—I can hardly bring myself to write it—nothing short of strangulation. He could only promise to accept for the while the risks of delay and do his utmost to bribe the magistrates into compromising the matter for a small fine.

He proved as good as his word. For five weeks the *Macartney* lay at anchor without discharging a pennyweight of her cargo; and every day brought a new threat, edict, or proclamation. At the end of the first week the security merchant was allowed to send his agents to offer a reward of 10,000 dollars to any man of our crew who would swear to having seen the Englishwoman strike the deceased. The agents conducted their parley from a boat, and only made off on being threatened with a bucket of slops. I kept the ship's guns loaded, and set on a double watch, night and day. His wife's peril threw Obed into a state of apprehension so pitiable that I began to fear for his mind. Margit, on the other hand, behaved with the coolest composure: and I had some trouble in persuading her to remain below decks and out of sight. She relied cheerfully on us and on the crew, every man of whom she had bound to her (I suppose by her remarkable beauty) in the completest loyalty.

In five weeks Mr. '——' had spent at least as many thousands of pounds; and still matters were at a stand when, one day, Mr. Tomlinson reported a boat under our quarter demanding speech with us. I went to the side and saw a tall lank-haired man, in a suit of white duck, standing in the stern-sheets with the tiller-lines in his hands.

"No pigtail on me, Cap!" he bawled. "I'm Oliphant Q. Wills, of the American barque *Independence*: and I want to come aboard." He pointed to his vessel, which had entered the river soon after us, and now lay, ready for sea, two cables distant from us.

I saw no reason for refusing; and in less than a minute he came running up the ladder, and introduced himself again. "Business," said he; so I led him to my cabin.

"Hullo!" said he, looking over the floor. "I observe you don't chew." He glanced at the stern-window. I opened it. Our talk then ran as follows:

Capt. W. "I've come to trade."

Self. "Then you have come, sir, to a very bad ship."

Capt. W. "I allowed you would say that. I know all about it, and came in consequence. I never miss a chance."

Self. "You wish to buy, of course."

Capt. W. "Not at all. I'm here to sell."

Self. "What, pray?"

Capt. W. "A half-hogshead cask of pretty ordinary Geneva: *with* a Dutchwoman inside."

Self. "Now, where on earth could you have picked that up?"

Capt. W. (spitting out of window). "In latitude 28 degrees; in a flat calm; off a Dutch East Indiaman. The name I have at home on a bit of paper: you shall have it as warranty with the cask. The captain was drunk, and I traded with the mate. I never miss a chance. The mate said nothing of the woman inside. I believe her to be his captain's wife, preserved for burial ashore. This is painful for me to speak about; for I had the worst of the deal, and such is not my reputation. But I allowed I would sell that cask at a profit if I carried it around for a hundred years."

Self. "What do you ask?"

Capt. W. "Well, I have been enquiring of Mr. '———', your Chief Factor here; and he tells me that your brother, Mr. Obed Lanyon, was with Cook and Vancouver, and knows the coast from Cape Flattery northwards and round by the Aleutians like the palm of his hand. Now it happens I have business up there among the Russian settlements—part trade, part exploring— I needn't say more, for the United States' Government didn't send me to tell secrets. A man like your brother would be money in my pocket all the way: and at the end of the job I would undertake to deliver him and his wife safely at any American port within reason, with money to take them home like princes, and a trifle over. I'm a square man: and if I weren't, you couldn't be in a worse fix than you are."

"I think," said I, "if you do not mind waiting a few minutes, we will trade, Mr. Wills." With this I went on deck and hoisted my private signal for Mr. '——', who came alongside in less than half-an-hour. He was a practical man, and at once saw the prospect of escape held out by the American's offer, ridiculous as it may seem to those who know little of Chinese law and custom. Indeed one of the magistrates had frankly appealed to Mr. '——' to hire a substitute for Margit among the negro women at Macao: and our friend engaged that by spending a few hundred additional dollars he would get the Dutchwoman's corpse accepted as full discharge for the offence, provided that Mrs. Lanyon could be smuggled out of the Canton River.

"This Captain Wills readily undertook to do. Mr. '——' then suggested that his negotiations would be made easier by the disappearance of all implicated in the scuffle—*i.e.* Mr. Tomlinson and myself, as well as Obed and Mrs. Lanyon. Mr. Findlater, my first officer, could take command and work the *Macartney* home; and Mr. '——' engaged to make our case right with the Company, though at the cost to me of the indirect profits which a commander looks to make from a homeward voyage. We discussed this for some while, and in the end agreed to it. Captain Wills, being short-handed, was even generous enough to offer me a small sum for my services in assisting him with the navigation.

To be short, all was arranged. That same night a boat from the *Independence* brought the famous cask of Geneva alongside, and took us four English people in exchange, and by 4 a.m. we were under weigh and heading for the open sea.

The *Independence* steered through the Formosa Strait, across the Eastern Sea, and on the 25th of July entered the bay of Nangasaki under Russian colours, which she thenceforth continued to fly. Like most European captains, our American kept his straightforward dealing for certain races only. He produced his trading articles: but the Japanese wanted nothing, and demanded to know what brought him there? He answered that he wanted water and fresh provisions (we had a plenty of both), and to prove it, ordered several butts to be started, and brought empty on deck. This was enough for the hospitable Japanese; who next day brought supplies of hogs, fish, and vegetables, for which they asked no payment; besides four dozen large tubs of water, which Captain Wills emptied on deck, stopping the scuppers, and removing the plugs at night so that the water might not be perceived. On the fourth day we got under weigh again; our deluded friends even going so far in kindness as to tow us out of the bay, and parting from us with cheers and much waving of hats and hands.

From Nangasaki we made for Kamschatka and thence for the Aleutian Islands and the American coast. On his way Captain Wills sedulously prosecuted the business for which his vessel had been chartered by the Russian American Company, and distributed his cargo of nankeens, silks, tea, sugar, etc., among the Russian settlements dotted among the islands. So far, Obed's services had been in little request: and I, too, had leisure to observe and wonder at a certain remarkable change that had come over Margit—as it seemed to me, from the time of our entering the parallels above 50 degrees. Her usual calm bearing had given way to succeeding fits of restlessness and apathy.

At times she would sit dejected for hours together; at others, she would walk the deck without pause, her cloak thrown open to the cold wind, which she seemed to drink like a thirsty creature. One day, the vessel being awkwardly becalmed within a mile of an ugly-looking iceberg, her excitement rose to something like a frenzy. The weather being hazy, Obed—who was busy with the captain taking soundings—asked me to run below for his glass; and there I almost fell Over Margit, who lay on the cabin floor, her whole body writhing, her hands tightly clenched upon a handkerchief which she had torn to rags. Of course I asked what ailed her, and offered to bring help, medicines, anything. She rose in confusion. 'It was a pain at the heart,' she said; 'nothing more: it would quickly pass: the cold brought it on, she thought. I would oblige her by going away; and, above all, by saying nothing to Obed.'

To what extent Obed remarked the change, I cannot tell. He now began to be pretty busy with his soundings and sketches of the coast. We had left Kadjak on the 9th of October, and on the last day of the month were cruising off Queen Charlotte's Island. So far, considering the lateness of the season, we had enjoyed remarkable weather. The natives, too, were friendly beyond expectation. The sight of our vessel brought them off in great numbers and at times we had as many as a hundred canoes about us, the largest holding perhaps a dozen, some armed with muskets, but the most with lances and forks pointed with stags' antlers and a kind of scimitar made of whale-rib. We suffered but two or three persons to board us at a time, and traded with them for dried fish, sea-otters, beaver and reindeer skins. A string of glass beads (blue was the favourite colour) would buy a salmon of 20 pounds weight: but for beaver they would take nothing less valuable than China stuffs.

Obed had warned us against the natives of Queen Charlotte's Island, as likely to prove stronger and less friendly than any we had encountered. We felt a reasonable anxiety, therefore, when, almost as soon as we sighted the island, a thick fog came up with some wind and a heavy swell from the south and hid the coast completely. This lasted until November 2nd at daybreak, when the weather lifted and we saw land at about eight miles' distance. Unhappily the wind dropped at once, while the motion of the waves continued, and our sails being useless, we found ourselves drifting rapidly shoreward with the set of the current. In the height of our dismay, however, a breeze sprang up from the north-west, and we worked off.

But we were over-hasty in blessing this breeze, which before midnight grew to a violent gale: and for two days we drove before it in much distress—Obed and I taking turns at conning the ship, since Captain Wills had received an awkward blow between the shoulders from the swinging of a loose block, and lay below in considerable pain and occasionally spitting blood, which made us fear some inward hurt. During the night of the 4th, the wind moderated; but the weather turning thick again, we were hardly reassured.

Early on the 6th Captain Wills appeared once more on deck and sent me below to get some sleep. I believe indeed that, had fate allowed, I could have slept round the clock. But at ten that morning a violent shock pitched me clean out of my berth. The *Independence* was aground.

The place of our shipwreck you will find in 47 degrees 66 minutes N. lat., between Vancouver's Cape Flattery and the mouth of the Columbia River, but nearer to the former. Luckily the *Independence* had run in upon soft ground and at high water: so that when the tide dropped she still held together, though badly shaken and gaping in all her lower seams. To save her was out of the question. We therefore made the best of our way ashore in the dense fog, taking with us all our guns and the best part of our ammunition, as well as provisions and a quantity of sails and spars for rigging up tents.

On no side of us could we see further than twenty paces. Of the inhabitants of this dreary spot—if indeed it had inhabitants—we knew nothing. So we first of all cleaned and loaded our firearms, and then set to work to light a fire and erect a shelter. We had done better, as it turned out, to have divided our company, and told off a fairly strong party to protect the ship. As it was, Captain Wills remained on board with three men to cut away and take down some of the heavier tackling.

We had set up one tent and were at work on the second, when I heard an exclamation from Margit, who stood by the big cauldron, a few paces off, cooking our dinner of salt pork.

Looking up I saw a ring of savages all about us on the edge of the fog.

They were brown undersized men, clothed for the most part in dirty blankets and armed with short lances shod with iron, though one or two carried muskets. These last I soon discovered to be *toens*, or elders, of the tribe. They stood and observed us with great gravity (indeed in all my acquaintance with them I never knew one to smile) and in absolute silence. I could not tell how many the fog concealed. They made no aggressive movement.

I called to Margit, bidding her leave the cauldron and walk quietly towards us; and she did so. Almost at once a savage thrust his lance into the pot, drew out our dinner on the end of it, and laid it on the sand. One of the *toens* then cut up the pork with his knife and handed the portions round, retaining a large lump for himself.

Seeing this, some of our men were for hostilities: but I restrained them and we made our meal from a barrel of biscuit, eating in silence while the natives chewed away at the pork. The meal over, we fell to work and finished the second tent without opposition, though curiosity drew some of our visitors so near as to hamper the workmen. When thrust aside they showed no resentment, but after a minute drew near again and impeded us as badly as ever.

Towards nightfall the main body drew off—whither, the fog did not reveal: but one or two entered the tents with us, hung around while we supped, and without the least invitation stretched themselves down to sleep. I own that this impudence tried my temper sorely, and Obed—the only one of us who knew some scraps of the language of these Indians—went so far as to remonstrate with them. But if they understood, they gave no sign of understanding: and we resolved to forbear from violence, at least so long as Captain Wills and his three comrades remained away from our main body and exposed to any vengeance these savages might wreak.

And our fears for the captain were justified about 4 a.m. by a report of firearms in the direction of the ship. I sprang to the door and waved a torch, and in a minute or so our comrades came running in through a shower of stones and lances, several of which struck the tents. The natives, it appeared, had attempted to plunder the ship. At great risk Obed ran out to seek one of the *toens* and reason with him: but the mischief happened too quickly.

Some of our men caught up their muskets and fired. Our assailants at once broke up and fled; and half-a-dozen of us charged down to the water's edge, where we saw a score and more with torches, busily setting fire to the ship. They too dispersed before us, leaving two of their number dead on the field and carrying off several wounded. But we came too late to save the *Independence*, which was already ablaze in a dozen different places; nor could we make any effort against the flames, for we knew not how sorely we might be wanted at the tents.

So we returned and spent the rest of the night in great discomfort, the blaze of the ship colouring the fog all around, but showing us nothing. Soon after daybreak the weather lifted a little, and what we saw discouraged us yet further. For, except the beach on which we were encamped, we found the whole coast covered with thick forest to the water's edge; while our boats, in which we might have made shift to escape, had been either fired or taken off by the savages. At 10 a.m., therefore, Captain Wills called a council of war, and informed us that he could think of no better plan than to push on for a harbour (its name, if I mistake not, was Gray's Harbour) lying about seventy miles to the southward, where a ship of the Company was due to call early in the spring.

Obed remembered it, and added that the journey might be quickly made, since his map showed no creek or river that promised to impede us, and the Indians were not likely to annoy us while the camp and the remains of the barque afforded any plunder. Accordingly we packed up, and having destroyed what muskets and weapons we did not want and thrown our spare gunpowder into the sea, shortly after noon began our march through the forest.

We were nineteen persons in all: and each of us carried two muskets, a pistol and some pounds of ammunition, besides his share of the provisions. The only ones more lightly laden were Margit and Captain Wills. The latter, indeed, could with pain manage to walk at all, and so clogged the pace of the party that we made but eight miles before nightfall, when we halted in an open space, set watches, and passed the night with no more discomfort than came from the severe cold.

In the morning we started early and made a good ten miles before noon. The captain now seemed at the end of his powers and we allowed him an hour's rest while we cleaned our firearms. Margit gave no sign of fatigue: but I observed that she walked alone and in silence. Indeed she had scarcely spoken since our shipwreck.

The ground chosen for our halt lay about mid-way down a stiff slope by which the forest descended to the sea, visible here and there between the stems of the trees below us. Shortly before two o'clock, when we were preparing to start again, a big stone came crashing down among our stores; and, as we scattered in alarm, two or three others followed. Looking up, I caught sight of a couple of Indians on the crest of the slope, and fired off my rifle to frighten them. They desisted at once: but to prevent further annoyance we made for the crest, where the rocky ground made walking difficult, so that we added but another five miles or so before nightfall.

During this night the wind rose, and at length it blew and snowed so hard as to drive us off the ridge. Luckily, however, one of the men discovered a shallow cave in the hillside, and here we huddled and continued all the next day and night, waiting for the storm to abate; which no sooner happened than we were assailed again by a perfect bombardment of big stones. These, however, flew harmlessly over our shelter.

I was dozing at daybreak on the 10th when a seaman named Hogue woke me and called my attention to the captain. He was stiff and cold, and had died in the night without complaint and, as far as could be learnt, without sound. The rain of stones not being resumed with daylight, we left his body in the cave, and pushed on over the snow in sad and sorry condition: for our provisions now began to run short.

Obed assumed the lead, with the consent of all. Once or twice in the course of the morning I observed him to pause, as if listening. The cause of this became apparent at about one in the afternoon, when I, too, heard the sound of running water: and an hour later we halted on the edge of a broad valley, with a swift stream running through it, black between banks of snow, and on the near bank a few huts and a crowd of three hundred Indians at least.

They had already caught sight of us: so we judged it better to advance, after looking to our arms. We were met by a *toen* (the same that had cut up the pork) and a chief of taller stature and pleasanter features than we had hitherto happened on in the country. It now appeared that the previous silence of these people had been deliberate: for the *toen* at once began to talk in a language fairly intelligible to Obed. He proposed to supply us with boats to cross the river, if we would give up our muskets in payment. This, of course, we refused: but offered him the whole collection of beads and trinkets that we had brought with us in the hope of trafficking for food.

After some haggling—to which the handsome chief, Yootra-maki, listened with seeming disdain—the *toen* undertook to let us have the boats; and presently one appeared, paddled by three naked savages. As this would barely hold a dozen passengers, we begged for another, that we might all cross together. The *toen* complied, and sent a second, but much smaller boat. In these we allowed ourselves to be distributed—Obed and I with ten others in the larger, and Margit with five seamen in the smaller.

The boats pushed out into the stream, the larger leading. The current ran deep and swift: and when, about half-way across, the nearest savage ceased paddling, I supposed he did so that the others on the starboard side might more easily bring the bows round to it. Before one could guess his true intention he had stooped and whipped out a plug from the boat's bottom, at the same time calling to his comrades, who leapt up and flung themselves overboard.

The next moment he was after them, and the whole party swimming to shore. The current swept us down and carried us so near to a spit of the shore we had left, that the savages, who now pelted us with arrows, succeeded in killing one seaman, and wounding four others: but here most fortunately it set right across for the opposite bank, where we contrived to land just as our boat sank beneath us. Those in the smaller boat, however, fell into our enemy's hands, who clubbed the five seamen on the head, sparing only Margit; and then, supposing our muskets to be wet and useless, crossed over in a canoe to attack us.

But as Providence would have it, we had four muskets left dry—they being slung round us in bandoliers—and the greater part of our powder unspoiled. We met the foe with a volley which disposed of three and sank the canoe. The survivors swam for it, and I dare say reached shore. A second canoe put off, and from the bows of it the rascally toen (cause of all this misfortune, as we deemed) hailed Obed and offered to let us go in peace and even restore Margit if we would surrender our firearms.

I think the coldest heart must have pitied my poor brother then. He paced the bank like a mad creature, silent, directing the most agonised looks at his comrades and at me in particular. We turned our faces aside; for his wishes were madness, yet we were asking him to sacrifice what was dearest to him in the world. In his distraction then he tore off most of his clothes, and piling them in a heap besought the toen to take them for the ransom; and we too stripped and stood all but naked, adding our prayers to his. But the scoundrel, without regard of our offering, spoke to his men, and was paddled away.

I will pass over the hour that followed. We quieted Obed's ravings at length; or rather, they ceased out of pure exhaustion. We were all starving in fact, and the food left in our wallets would not keep a cat alive for another forty-eight hours. Retiring to a clump of firs about 100 yards back from the river's bank, we scooped a hole in the snow and entrenched ourselves as well as we could for the night. Some of us managed to sleep a little; the others tried to allay the pangs of hunger by chewing their musket-covers, the sponges on their ramrods, even their boot-soles.

At midnight came my turn for watching. In my weakness I may have dozed, or perhaps was light-headed. At any rate, turning after some time to glance at the sleepers, I missed Obed. An ugly suspicion seized me; I counted the muskets. Two of these were missing. After shaking one of the sleepers by the elbow and bidding him watch, I leaped over our low breastwork and ran towards the river in the track of my brother's footsteps. Almost as I started, a flash and a report of a musket right ahead changed the current of my fears. By the light of the young moon I saw two figures struggling and rolling together on the river's brink. They were Obed and our peculiar enemy, the *toen*. The body of a dead Indian lad was stretched some ten paces off beside a small canoe which lay moored by the bank.

Our comrades came running up as I flung myself into the struggle, and we quickly secured the *toen*. I believe Obed would have killed him. "Don't be a fool!" said I; "cannot you see that we now have a hostage for Margit?" I ought at the same time to have begged his pardon for my suspicions. As the reader already knows, Obed had a far keener ear than I, and it had warned him of the canoe's approach. It turned out afterwards that the *toen* had planned this little reconnoitring expedition on his own account, and on the chance perhaps of filching a musket or two.

We quickly laid our plans; and at daybreak flung my gentleman, bound hand and foot, into his own canoe, which Obed and I paddled into mid-stream, while our party stood on the bank and watched. The village opposite seemed deserted: but at Obed's hail an Indian woman ran out of the largest hut, and returning, must have summoned the good-looking chief Yootramaki; who emerged in a minute or so, and came slowly down the bank. By this time several groups of Indians had gathered and stood looking on, in all perhaps eighty or a hundred people.

Obed pointed to our prisoner and made his demand. I understood him to ask for the immediate ransom of Margit, and a supply of salmon and other provisions to take us on our journey. The chief stood considering for a while; then spoke to a native boy, who ran to the house; and in a minute or so Margit herself appeared, with the native woman who had first taken word of us. She came down the bank, and Yootramaki signed to Obed to address her; which he did.

"Margit," said he, pointing to the *toen*, "I believe that in this scoundrel here God has provided a way out of all our troubles. We caught him last night, and have brought him along as ransom for you. But stand close to the water and be ready to jump for the boat if they mean treachery. Edom and I will see that you come to no harm."

"My dear husband," she answered, very quiet and slow, "I think you are wasting your time. I am sorry, but I shall not go with you."

Obed turned a dazed look on me, and then, supposing he had not heard aright, began again—

"Stand close by the water, and jump when I give the word. All may depend on your quickness—only be bold, my dear. I will explain after."

"But it is I that must explain. I am not going with you: really I am not."

Obed turned again to me, this time with wide eyes. "God of mercy!" he cried hoarsely; "her troubles have driven her mad!"

Margit heard. "Oh no," she said; "I am not mad. The chief here has taken me: he seems to be the most powerful man in this tribe, and at least he is kind. I should be mad, rather, to wander with you through the forests, and in the end fall into worse hands, or perhaps die of starvation or cold. I do not want to be frozen—again. Go away now, when you have bartered the man there for food. You have been very good to me, but this cannot be helped."

Obed lifted his gun: then lowered it. "Dom," he muttered, "can you shoot her? I cannot!"

I was using all my strength, just then, to keep paddling the canoe against the current. I caught a glimpse of our comrades on the further bank: and then exactly what happened I know not. Perhaps Margit, having given her answer, turned back towards the house. At any rate, shrilly crying her name, Obed sprang up and discharged his musket. The shot went wide. With a second furious cry he stooped, caught up the helpless *toen*, and held him high in air. The canoe lurched heavily, and the next instant I was in the water.

I never saw Obed again: and the *toen* must have gone down like a stone. For me, I struck out for the far shore, but the current swept me down on the sandy spit where we had nearly come to shipwreck, the day before. Several Indians had gathered there. One ran into the water, waist-high, lifting a club. I turned and made a last effort to swim from him, but he flung himself on my back and bore me under.

I recovered to find myself in an Indian hut. Margit had persuaded them to spare me, and I was now, in name at least, a slave in Yootramaki's possession. As a matter of fact, however, I was allowed to do pretty much as I liked; and my employment (absurd as it may sound) for the most part consisted in designing kites and other toys for the natives, who in mind and disposition resemble children rather than grown people—sullen and rather vicious children, I should say.

I believe that Obed's body never came to land. Panic-stricken by his death (I was told), our surviving comrades turned and fled into the woods: and from that hour no more was heard of them. Probably they perished of weariness and hunger; it is at least unlikely in the extreme that they found their way back among civilised men.

Though I accompanied my master and his household northward to the village near Cape Flattery, where his chief residence lay, and remained more than three months in his service, I could never obtain speech with Margit. But I have reason to believe she accepted her new life with absolute contentment. No doubt, though, she found the sight of me an irksome reminder: and one day early in April Yootramaki took me aside and promised me my liberty if I would travel with him as far as the Strait, where an American brig had lately arrived. Of course I accepted his offer with gratitude; and we set forth next day. The captain of this brig (the *Cordelia*) was a Mr. Best, and his business in those parts seemed to consist in trading old American muskets in exchange for furs and dried fish. The Indians have no notion of repairing a gun which has got out of order, and Captain Best actually carried a gunsmith on board, whose knowledge enabled him to buy up at one place all the guns that wanted repairing, and sell them as new pieces at another.

It only remains to add that the *Cordelia* conveyed me to Valparaiso, whence I shipped for England, reaching the Downs in safety on the 4th of April, 1809.

The Stranger Dances in Zeb's Shoes
(Chapter 5 of *I Saw Three Ships*)

It was close upon midnight, and in the big parlour at Sheba the courant, having run through its normal stages of high punctilio, artificial ease, zest, profuse perspiration, and supper, had reached the exact point when Modesty Prowse could be surprised under the kissing-bush, and Old Zeb wiped his spectacles, thrust his chair back, and pushed out his elbows to make sure of room for the rendering of "Scarlet's my Colour." These were tokens to be trusted by an observer who might go astray in taking any chance guest as a standard of the average conviviality. Mr. and Mrs. Jim Lewarne, for example, were accustomed on such occasions to represent the van and rear-guard respectively in the march of gaiety; and in this instance Jim had already imbibed too much hot "*shenachrum*," while his wife, still in the stage of artificial ease, and wearing a lace cap, which was none the less dignified for having been smuggled, was perpending what to say when she should get him home. The dancers, pale and dusty, leant back in rows against the wall, and with their handkerchiefs went through the motions of fanning or polishing, according to sex. In their midst circulated Farmer Tresidder, with a three-handled mug of *shenachrum*, hot from the embers, and furred with wood-ash.

"Take an' drink, thirsty souls. Niver do I mind the *Letterpooch* so footed i' my born days."

"'Twas conspirator—very conspirator," assented Old Zeb, screwing up his A string a trifle, and turning *con spirito* into a dark saying.

"What's that?"

"Greek for elbow-grease. Phew!" He rubbed his fore-finger round between neck and shirt-collar. "I be vady as the inside of a winder."

"Such a man as you be to sweat, crowder!" exclaimed Calvin Oke. "Set you to play six-eight time an' 'tis beads right away."

"A slice o' saffern-cake, crowder, to stay ye. Don't say no. Hi, Mary Jane!"

"Thank 'ee, Farmer. A man might say you was in sperrits tonight, makin' so bold."

"I be; I be."

"Might a man ax wherefore, beyond the nat'ral hail-fellow-well-met of the season?"

"You may, an' yet you mayn't," answered the host, passing on with the mug.

"Uncle Issy," asked Jim Lewarne, lurching up, "I durstn' g-glint over my shoulder—but wud 'ee mind tellin' me if th' old woman's lookin' this way—afore I squench my thirst?"

"Iss, she be."

Jim groaned. "Then wud 'ee mind a-hofferin' me a taste out o' your pannikin? an' I'll make b'lieve to say 'Norronany' count.' Amazin' 'ot t' night," he added, tilting back on his heels, and then dipping forward with a vague smile.

Uncle Issy did as he was required, and the henpecked one played his part of the comedy with elaborate slyness. "I don't like that strange chap," he announced, irrelevantly.

"Nor I nuther," agreed Elias Sweetland, "tho' to be sure, I've a-kept my eye 'pon en, an' the wonders he accomplishes in an old pair o' Tresidder's high-lows must be seen to be believed. But that's no call for Ruby's dancin' wi' he a'most so much as wi' her proper man."

"The gel's takin' her fling afore wedlock. I heard Sarah Ann Nanjulian, just now, sayin' she ought to be clawed."

"A jealous woman is a scourge shaken to an' fro," said Old Zeb; "but I've a mind, friends, to strike up 'Randy my dandy,' for that son o' mine is lookin' blacker than the horned man, an' may be 'twill comfort 'en to dance afore the public eye; for there's none can take his wind in a hornpipe."

In fact, it was high time that somebody comforted Young Zeb, for his heart was hot. He had brought home the chest of drawers in his cart, and spent an hour fixing on the best position for it in the bedroom, before dressing for the dance. Also he had purchased, in Mr. Pennyway's shop, an armchair, in the worst taste, to be a pleasant surprise for Ruby when the happy day came for installing her. Finding he had still twenty minutes to spare after giving the last twitch to his neckerchief, and the last brush to his anointed locks, he had sat down facing this chair, and had striven to imagine her in it, darning his stockings. Zeb was not, as a rule, imaginative, but love drew this delicious picture for him. He picked up his hat, and set out for Sheba in the best of tempers.

But at Sheba all had gone badly. Ruby's frock of white muslin and Ruby's small sandal shoes were bewitching, but Ruby's mood passed his intelligence. It was true she gave him half the dances, but then she gave the other half to that accursed stranger, and the stranger had all her smiles, which was carrying hospitality too far. Not a word had she uttered to Zeb beyond the merest commonplaces; on the purchase of the chest of drawers she had breathed no question; she hung listlessly on his arm, and spoke only of the music, the other girls' frocks, the arrangement of the supper-table. And at supper the stranger had not only sat on the other side of her, but had talked all the time, and on books, a subject entirely uninteresting to Zeb. Worst of all, Ruby had listened. No; the worst of all was a remark of Modesty Prowse's that he chanced to overhear afterwards.

So when the fiddles struck up the air of "Randy my dandy," Zeb, knowing that the company would call upon him, at first felt his heart turn sick with loathing. He glanced across the room at Ruby, who, with heightened colour, was listening to the stranger, and looking up at his handsome face. Already one or two voices were calling "Zeb!" "Young Zeb for a hornpipe!"

"Now then, Young Zeb!"

He had a mind to refuse. For years after he remembered every small detail of the room as he looked down it and then across to Ruby again: the motion of the fiddle-bows; the variegated dresses of the women; the kissing-bush that some tall dancer's head had set swaying from the low rafter; the light of a sconce gleaming on Tresidder's bald scalp. Years after, he could recall the exact poise of Ruby's head as she answered some question of her companion. The stranger left her, and strolled slowly down the room to the fireplace, when he faced round, throwing an arm negligently along the mantel-shelf, and leant with legs crossed, waiting.

Then Young Zeb made up his mind, and stepped out into the middle of the floor. The musicians were sawing with might and main at high speed. He crossed his arms, and, fixing his eyes on the stranger's, began the hornpipe.

When it ceased, he had danced his best. It was only when the applause broke out that he knew he had fastened, from start to finish, on the man by the fireplace a pair of eyes blazing with hate. The other had stared back quietly, as if he noted only the performance. As the music ended sharply with the click of Young Zeb's two heels, the stranger bent, took up a pair of tongs, and rearranged the fire before lifting his head.

"Yes," he said, slowly, but in tones that were extremely distinct as the clapping died away, "that was wonderfully danced. In some ways I should almost say you were inspired. A slight want of airiness in the double-shuffle, perhaps—"

"Could you do't better?" asked Zeb, sulkily.

"That isn't the fair way to treat criticism, my friend; but yes—oh, yes, certainly I could do it better—in your shoes."

"Then try, i' my shoes." And Zeb kicked them off.

"I've a notion they'll fit me," was all the stranger answered, dropping on one knee and beginning to unfasten the cumbrous boots he had borrowed of Farmer Tresidder.

Indeed, the curious likeness in build of these two men—a likeness accentuated, rather than slurred, by their contrast in colour and face, was now seen to extend even to their feet. When the stranger stood up at length in Zeb's shoes, they fitted him to a nicety, the broad steel buckles lying comfortably over the instep, the back of the uppers closing round the hollow of his ankle like a skin.

Young Zeb, by this, had crossed shoeless to the fireplace, and now stood in the position lately occupied by his rival: only, whereas the stranger had lolled easily, Zeb stood squarely, with his legs wide apart and his hands deep in his pockets. He had no eyes for the intent faces around, no ears for their whispering, nor for the preliminary scrape of the instruments; but stood like an image, with the firelight flickering out between his calves, and watched the other man grimly.

"Ready?" asked his father's voice. "Then one—two—three, an' let fly!"

The fiddle-bows hung for an instant on the first note, and in a twinkling scampered along into "Randy my dandy." As the quick air caught at the listeners' pulses, the stranger crossed his arms, drew his right heel up along the inner side of his left ankle, and with a light nod towards the chimney-place began.

To the casual eye there was for awhile little to choose between the two dancers, the stranger's style being accurate, restrained, even a trifle dull. But of all the onlookers, Zeb knew best what hornpipe-dancing really was; and knew surely, after the first dozen steps, that he was going to be mastered. So far, the performance was academic only. Zeb, unacquainted with the word, recognised the fact, and was quite aware of the inspiration—the personal gift—held in reserve to transfigure this precise art in a minute or so, and give it life. He saw the force gathering in the steady rhythmical twinkle of the steel buckles, and heard it speak in the light recurrent tap with which the stranger's heels kissed the floor. It was doubly bitter that he and his enemy alone should know what was coming; trebly bitter that his enemy should be aware that he knew.

The crowder slackened speed for a second, to give warning, and dashed into the heel-and-toe. Zeb caught the light in the dancer's eyes, and still frowning, drew a long breath.

"Faster," nodded the stranger to the musicians' corner.

Then came the moment for which, by this time, Zeb was longing. The stranger rested with heels together while a man might count eight rapidly, and suddenly began a step the like of which none present had ever witnessed, Above the hips his body swayed steadily, softly, to the measure; his eyes never took their pleasant smile off Zeb's face, but his feet—

The steel buckles had become two sparkling moths, spinning, poising, darting. They no longer belonged to the man, but had taken separate life: and merely the absolute symmetry of their loops and circles, and the *click-click-click* on boards, regular as ever, told of the art that informed them.

"Faster!"

They crossed and re-crossed now like small flashes of lightning, or as if the boards were flints giving out a score of sparks at every touch of the man's heel.

"Faster!"

They seemed suddenly to catch the light out of every sconce, and knead it into a ball of fire, that spun and yet was motionless, in the very middle of the floor, while all the rest of the room grew suddenly dimmed.

Zeb with a gasp drew his eyes away for a second and glanced around. Fiddlers and guests seemed ghostly after the fierce light he had been gazing on. He looked along the pale faces to the place where Ruby stood. She, too, glanced up, and their eyes met.

What he saw fetched a sob from his throat. Then something on the floor caught his attention: something bright, close by his feet.

Between his out-spread legs, as it seemed, a thin streak of silver was creeping along the flooring. He rubbed his eyes, and looked again.

He was straddling across a stream of molten metal.

As Zeb caught sight of this, the stranger twirled, leapt a foot in the air, and came down smartly on the final note, with a click of his heels. The music ceased abruptly.

A storm of clapping broke out, but stopped almost on the instant: for the stranger had flung an arm out towards the hearthstone.

"A mine—a mine!"

The white streak ran hissing from the heart of the fire, where a clod of earth rested among the ashen sticks.

"Witchcraft!" muttered one or two of the guests, peering forward with round eyes.

"Fiddlestick-end! I put the clod there myself. 'Tis *lead!*"

"Lead?"

"Ay, naybours all," broke in Farmer Tresidder, his bald head bedewed with sweat, "I don't want to abash 'ee, Lord knows; but 'tis trew as doom that I be a passing well-to-do chap. I shudn' wonder now"—and here he embraced the company with a smile, half pompous and half timid—"I shudn' wonder if ye was to see me trottin' to Parlyment House in a gilded coach afore Michaelmas—I be so tremenjous rich, by all accounts."

"You'll excoose my sayin' it, Farmer," spoke up Old Zeb out of the awed silence that followed, "for doubtless I may be thick o' hearin', but did I, or did I not, catch 'ee alludin' to a windfall o' wealth?"

"You did."

"You'll excoose me sayin' it, Farmer; but was it soberly or pleasantly, honest creed or light lips, down-right or random, 'out o' the heart the mouth speaketh' or wantonly and in round figgers, as it might happen to a man filled with meat and wine?"

"'Twas the cold trewth."

"By what slice o' fortune?"

"By a mine, as you might put it: or, as between man an' man, by a mine o' lead."

"Farmer, you're either a born liar or the darlin' o' luck."

"Aye: I feel it. I feel that overpowerin'ly."

"For my part," put in Mrs. Jim Lewarne, "I've given over follerin' the freaks o' Fortune. They be so very undiscernin'."

And this sentence probably summed up the opinion of the

majority.

In the midst of the excitement Young Zeb strode up to the stranger, who stood a little behind the throng.

"Give me back my shoes," he said.

The other kicked them off and looked at him oddly.

"With pleasure. You'll find them a bit worn, I'm afraid."

"I'll chance that. Man, I'm not all sorry, either."

"Hey, why?"

"'Cause they'll not be worn agen, arter this night. Gentleman or devil, whichever you may be, I bain't fit to dance i' the same parish with 'ee—no, nor to tread the shoeleather you've worn."

"By the powers!" cried the stranger suddenly, "two minutes ago I'd have agreed with you. But, looking in your eyes, I'm not so sure of it."

"Of what?"

"That you won't wear the shoes again."

Then Zeb went after Ruby.

"I want to speak a word with 'ee," he said quietly, stepping up to her.

"Where?"

"I' the hall."

"But I can't come, just now."

"But you must."

She followed him out.

"Zeb, what's the matter with you?"

"Look here"—and he faced round sharply—"I loved you passing well."

"Well?" she asked, like a faint echo.

"I saw your eyes, just now. Don't lie."

"I won't."

"That's right. And now listen: if you marry me, I'll treat 'ee like a span'el dog. Fetch you shall, an' carry, for my pleasure. You shall be slave, an' I your taskmaster; an' the sweetness o' your love shall come by crushin', like trodden thyme. Shall I suit you?"

"I don't think you will."

"Then goodnight to you."

"Goodnight, Zeb. I don't fancy you'll suit me; but I'm not so sure as before you began to speak."

There was no answer to this but the slamming of the front door.

At half-past seven that morning, Parson Babbage, who had risen early, after his wont, was standing on the vicarage doorstep to respire the first breath of the pale day, when he heard the garden gate unlatched and saw Young Zeb coming up the path.

The young man still wore his festival dress; but his best stockings and buckled shoes were stained and splashed, as from much walking in miry ways. Also he came unsteadily, and his face was white as ashes. The parson stared and asked—

"Young Zeb, have you been drinking?"

"No."

"Then 'tis trouble, my son, an' I ask your pardon."

"A man might call it so. I'm come to forbid my banns."

The elder man cocked his head on one side, much as a thrush contemplates a worm.

"I smell a wise wit, somewhere. Young man, who taught you so capital a notion?"

"Ruby did."

"Pack o' stuff! Ruby hadn't the—stop a minute! 'twas that clever fellow you fetched ashore, on Monday. Of course—of course! How came it to slip my mind?"

Young Zeb turned away; but the old man was after him, quick as thought, and had laid a hand on his shoulder.

"Is it bitter, my son?"

"It is bitter as death, Pa'son."

"My poor lad. Step in an' break your fast with me—poor lad, poor lad! Nay, but you shall. There's a bitch pup i' the stables that I want your judgment on. Bitter, eh? I dessay. I dessay. I'm thinking of walking her—lemon spot on the left ear—Rattler strain, of course. Dear me, this makes six generations I can count back that spot—an' game every one. Step in, poor lad, step in: she's a picture."

John and the Ghosts

In the kingdom of Illyria there lived, not long ago, a poor wood-cutter with three sons, who in time went forth to seek their fortunes. At the end of three years they returned by agreement, to compare their progress in the world. The eldest had become a lawyer, and the second a merchant, and each of these had won riches and friends; but John, the youngest, who had enlisted in the army, could only show a cork leg and a medal.

"You have made a bad business of it," said his brothers. "Your medal is worthless except to a collector of such things, and your leg a positive disadvantage. Fortunately we have influence, and since you are our brother we must see what we can do for you."

Now the King of Illyria lived at that time in his capital, in a brick palace at the end of the great park. He kept this park open to all, and allowed no one to build in it. But the richest citizens, who were so fond of their ruler that they could not live out of his sight, had their houses just beyond the park, in the rear of the palace, on a piece of ground which they called Palace Gardens. The name was a little misleading, for the true gardens lay in front of the palace, where children of all classes played among the trees and flower-beds and artificial ponds, and the king sat and watched them, because he took delight in children, and because the sight of them cheered his only daughter, who had fallen into a deep melancholy. But the rich citizens clung to it, for it gave a pleasant neighbourly air to their roadway, and showed what friendliness there was between the monarch of Illyria and his people.

At either end you entered the roadway (if you were allowed) by an iron gate, and each gate had a sentry-box beside it, and a tall beadle, and a notice-board to save him the trouble of explanation. The notice ran—

PRIVATE.—

THE BEADLE HAS ORDERS TO REFUSE
ADMITTANCE TO ALL WAGGONS, TRADESMEN'S
CARTS, HACKNEY COACHES, DONKEYS, BEGGARS,
DISORDERLY CHARACTERS, OR PERSONS CARRYING BURDENS.

A sedentary life had told so severely upon one of the two beadles that he could no longer enter his box with dignity or read his newspaper there with any comfort. He resigned, and John obtained the post by his brothers' interest, in spite of his cork leg.

He had now a bright green suit with scarlet pipings, a gold-laced hat, a fashionable address, and very little to do. But the army had taught him to be active, and for lack of anything better he fell into deep thinking. This came near to bringing him into trouble. One evening he looked out of his sentry-box and saw a mild and somewhat sad-featured old gentleman approaching the gate.

"No admittance," said John.

"Tut, tut!" said the old gentleman. "I'm the king."

John looked at the face on his medal, and sure enough there was a resemblance. "But, all the same, your Majesty carries a burden,"—here he pointed to the noticeboard,—"and the folks along this road are mighty particular."

The king smiled and then sighed heavily.

"It's about the princess, my daughter," said he; "she has not smiled for a whole year."

"I'll warrant I'd make her," said John.

"I'll warrant you could not," said the king. "She will never smile again until she is married."

"Then," answered John, "speaking in a humble way, as becomes me, why the dickens alive don't you marry her up and get done with it?"

The king shook his head.

"There's a condition attached," said he. "Maybe you have heard of the famous haunted house in Puns'nby Square?"

"I've always gone by the spelling, and pronounced it Ponsonby," said John.

"Well, the condition is that every suitor for my daughter's hand must spend a night alone in that house; and if he survives and is ready to persevere with his wooing, he must return a year later with his bride and spend the night of his marriage there."

"And very handy," said John, "for there's a wedding-cake shop at the corner."

The king sighed again.

"Unhappily, none survive. One hundred and fifty-five have undertaken the adventure, and not a man of them but has either lost his wits or run for it."

"Well," said John, "I've been afraid of a great many men—"

"That's a poor confession for a soldier," put in the king.

"—when they all happened to come at me together. But I've never yet met the ghost that could frighten me; and if your Majesty will give me the latch-key I'll try my luck this very night."

It could not be done in this free-and-easy way; but at eight o'clock, after John had visited the palace and taken an oath in the princess's presence (which was his first sight of her), he was driven down to the house beside the Lord Chamberlain, who admitted him to the black front hall, and, slamming the door upon him, scuttled out of the porch as quickly as possible and into his brougham.

John struck a match, and as he did so heard the carriage roll away. The walls were bare, and the floor and great staircase ahead of him carpetless. As the match flickered out he caught a glimpse of a pair of feet moving up the stairs; that was all—only feet.

"I'll catch up with the calves on the landing, maybe," said he; and, striking another match, he followed them up.

The feet turned aside on the landing and led him into a room on the right. He paused on the threshold, drew a candle from his pocket, lit it, and stared about him. The room was of great size, bare and dusty, with crimson hangings, gilt panels, and one huge gilt chandelier, from which and from the ceiling and cornice long cobwebs trailed down like creeping plants. Beneath the chandelier a dark smear ran along the boards. The feet crossed it towards the fireplace; and as they did so, John saw them stained with blood. They reached the fire-place and vanished.

Scarcely had this happened, before the end of the room opposite the window began to glow with an unearthly light. John, whose poverty had taught him to be economical, promptly blew out his candle. A moment later two men entered, bearing a coffin between them. They rested it upon the floor and, seating themselves upon it, began to cast dice. "Your soul!" "My soul!" they kept saying in hollow tones, according as they won or lost. At length one of them—a tall man in a powdered wig, with a face extraordinarily pale—flung a hand to his brow, rose and staggered from the room. The other sat waiting and twirling his black moustache, with an evil smile. John, who by this time had found a seat in a far corner, thought him the most poisonous-looking villain he had ever seen; but as the minutes passed and nothing happened, he turned his back to the light and pulled out a penny-dreadful. His literary taste was shocking, and when it came to romance he liked the incidents to follow one another with great rapidity.

He was interrupted by a blood-curdling groan, and the first ruffian broke into the room, dragging by its grey locks the body of an old man. A young girl followed, weeping and protesting, with dishevelled hair, and behind her entered a priest with a brazier full of glowing charcoal. The girl cast herself forward on the old man's body, but the two scoundrels dragged her from it by force. "The money!" demanded the dark one; and she drew from her bosom a small key and cast it at his feet. "My promise!" demanded the other, and seized her by the wrist as the priest stepped forward. "Quick! over this coffin—man and wife!" She wrenched her hand away and thrust him backward. The priest retreated to the brazier and drew out a red-hot iron.

John thought it about time to interfere.

"I beg your pardon," said he, stepping forward; "but I suppose you really *are* ghosts?"

"We are unhallowed souls," answered the dark man impressively, "who return to blight the living with the spectacle of our awful crimes."

"Meaning me?" asked John.

"Ay, sir; and to destroy you tonight if you contract not, upon your soul, to return with your bride and meet us here a twelvemonth hence."

"H'm!" said John to himself, "they are three to one; and, after all, it's what I came for. I suppose," he added aloud, "some form of document is usual in these cases?"

The dark man drew out pen and parchment.

"Hold forth your hand," he commanded; and as John held it out, thinking he meant to shake it over the bargain, the fellow drove the pen into his wrist until the blood spurted. "Now sign!"

"Sign!" said the other villain.

"Sign!" said the lady.

"Oh, very well, miss. If you're in the swindle too, my mind is easier," said John, and signed his name with a flourish. "But a bargain is a bargain, and what security have I for your part in it?"

"Our signature!" said the priest terribly, at the same moment pressing his branding-iron into John's ankle. A smell of burnt cork arose as John stooped and clapped his hand over the scorched stocking. When he looked up again his visitors had vanished; and a moment later the strange light, too, died away.

But the coffin remained for evidence that he had not been dreaming. John lit a candle and examined it.

"Just the thing for me," he exclaimed, finding it to be a mere shell of pine-boards, loosely nailed together and painted black. "I was beginning to shiver." He knocked the coffin to pieces, crammed them into the fireplace, and very soon had a grand fire blazing, before which he sat and finished his penny-dreadful, and so dropped off into a sound sleep.

The Lord Chamberlain arrived early in the morning, and, finding him stretched there, at first broke into lamentations over the fate of yet another personable young man; but soon changed his tune when John sat up, and, rubbing his eyes, demanded to be told the time.

"But are you really alive? We must drive back and tell His Majesty at once!"

"Stay a moment," said John. "There's a brother of mine, a lawyer, in the city. He will be arriving at his office about this time, and you must drive me there; for I have a document here of a sort, and must have it stamped, to be on the safe side."

So into the city he was driven beside the Lord Chamberlain, and there had his leg stamped and filed for reference; and, having purchased another, was conveyed to the palace, where the king received him with open arms.

He was now a favoured guest at court, and had frequent opportunities of seeing and conversing with the princess, with whom he soon fell deeply in love. But as the months passed and the time drew near for their marriage, he grew silent and thoughtful, for he feared to expose her, even in his company, to the sights he had witnessed in the haunted house.

He thought and thought, until one fine afternoon he snapped his fingers suddenly, and after that went about whistling. A fortnight before the day fixed for the wedding he drove into the city again—but this time to the office of his other brother, the merchant.

"I want," he said, "a loan of a thousand pounds."

"Nothing easier," said his brother. "Here are eight hundred and fifty. Of the remainder I shall keep fifty as interest for the first year at five *per cent.*, and the odd hundred should purchase a premium of insurance for two thousand pounds, which I will retain as security against accidents."

This seemed not only fair but brotherly. John pocketed his

eight hundred and fifty pounds, shook his creditor affectionately by the hand, and hurried westward.

The marriage was celebrated with great pomp; and in the evening the king, who had been shedding tears at intervals throughout the ceremonies, accompanied his daughter to the haunted house. The princess was pale. John, on the contrary, who sat facing her father in the state-coach, smiled with a cheerfulness which, under the circumstances, seemed a trifle ill-bred. The wedding-guests followed in twenty-four chariots. Their cards of invitation had said "Two to five-thirty p.m.," and it was now eight o'clock; but they could not resist the temptation to see the last of "the poor dear thing," as they agreed to call the bride.

The king sat silent during the drive; he was preparing his farewell speech, which he meant to deliver in the porch. But arriving and perceiving a crowd about it, and also, to his vast astonishment, a red baize carpet on the perron, and a butler bowing in the doorway with two footmen behind him, he coughed down his exordium, and led his daughter into the hall amid showers of rice and confetti. The bridegroom followed; and so did the wedding-guests, since no one opposed them.

The hall and staircase were decorated with palms and pot-plants, flags and emblems of Illyria; and in the great drawing-room—which they entered while John persuaded the King to a seat—they found many rows of morocco-covered chairs, a miniature stage with a drop representing the play-scene in *Hamlet*, a row of footlights, a *boudoir*-grand piano, and a man seated at the keyboard whom they recognised as a performer in much demand at suburban dances.

The company had scarcely seated itself, before a strange light began to illuminate that end of the room at which the stage stood, and immediately the curtain rose to the overture of M. Offenbach's *Orphée aux Enfers*, the pianist continuing with great spirit until a round of applause greeted the entrance of the two spectral performers.

Its effect upon them was in the highest degree disconcerting.

They set down the coffin, and, after a brief and hurried conference in an undertone, the black-*moustachioed* ghost advanced to the footlights, singled out John from the audience, and with a terrific scowl demanded to know the reason of this extraordinary gathering.

"Come, come, my dear sir," answered John, "our contract, if you will study it, allows me to invite whom I choose; it merely insists that my bride and I must be present, as you see we are. Pray go on with your part, and assure yourself it is no use to try the high horse with me."

The dark ghost looked at his partner, who shuffled uneasily.

"I told you," said he, "we should have trouble with this fellow. I had a presentiment of it when he came to spend the night here without bringing a bull-dog. That frightening of the bull-dog out of his wits has always been our most effective bit of business."

Hereupon the dark ghost took another tone.

"Our fair but unfortunate victim has a sore throat to-night," he announced. "The performance is consequently postponed;" and he seated himself sulkily upon the coffin, when the limelight-man from the wings promptly bathed him in a flood of the most beautiful rose-colour. "Oh, this is intolerable!" he exclaimed, starting to his feet.

"It is not first-rate, I agree," said John, "but, such as it is, we had better go through with it. Should the company doubt its genuineness, I can go around afterwards and show the brand on the cork." Here he tapped the leg, which he had been careful to bring with him.

Before this evidence of contract the ghosts' resistance collapsed. They seated themselves on the coffin and began the casting of dice; the performance proceeded, but in a half-hearted and perfunctory manner, notwithstanding the vivacious efforts of the limelight-man.

The tall ghost struck his brow and fled from the stage. There were cries of "Call him back!" But John explained that this was part of the drama, and no encores would be allowed; whereupon the audience fell to hissing the villain, who now sat alone with the most lifelike expression of malignity.

"Oh, hang it!" he expostulated after a while, "I am doing this under protest, and you need not make it worse for a fellow. I draw the line at hissing."

"It's the usual thing," explained John affably.

But when the ghostly lady walked on, and in the act of falling on her father's body was interrupted by the pianist, who handed up an immense bouquet, the performers held another hurried colloquy.

"Look here," said the dark-browed villain, stepping forward and addressing John; "what will you take to call it quits?"

"I'll take," said John, "the key which the lady has just handed you. And if the treasure is at all commensurate with the fuss you have been making about it, we'll let bygones be bygones."

Well, it did; and John, having counted it out behind the curtain, came forward and asked the pianist to play "God save the King"; and so, having bowed his guests to the door, took possession of the haunted house and lived in it many years with his bride, in high renown and prosperity.

Legends of St. Piran

1.—Saint Piran and the Millstone

Should you visit the Blackmore tin-streamers on their feast-day, which falls on Friday-in-Lide (that is to say, the first Friday in March), you may note a truly Celtic ceremony. On that day the tinners pick out the sleepiest boy in the neighbourhood and send him up to the highest *bound* in the works, with instructions to sleep there as long as he can. And by immemorial usage the length of his nap will be the measure of the tinners' afternoon siesta for twelve months to come.

Now, this first week in March is St. Piran's week: and St. Piran is the miners' saint. To him the Cornishmen owe not only their tin, which he discovered on the spot, but also their divine laziness, which he brought across from Ireland and naturalised here. And I learned his story one day from an old miner, as we ate our bread and cheese together on the floor of Wheal Tregobbin, while the Davy lamp between us made wavering giants of our shadows on the walls of the adit, and the sea moaned as it tossed on its bed, two hundred feet above.

★★★★★

St. Piran was a little round man; and in the beginning he dwelt on the north coast of Ireland, in a leafy mill, past which a stream came tumbling down to the sea. After turning the saint's mill-wheel, the stream dived over a fall into the Lough below, and the *lul-ul-ur-r-r* of the water-wheel and fall was a sleepy music in the saint's ear noon and night.

It must not be imagined that the mill-wheel ground anything.

No; it went round merely for the sake of its music. For all St. Piran's business was the study of objects that presented themselves to his notice, or, as he called it, the "Rapture av Contemplation"; and as for his livelihood, he earned it in the simplest way. The waters of the Lough below possessed a peculiar virtue. You had only to sink a log or stick therein, and in fifty years' time that log or stick would be turned to stone. St. Piran was as quick as you are to divine the possibilities of easy competence offered by this spot. He took time by the forelock, and in half a century was fairly started in business. Henceforward he passed all his days among the rocks above the fall, whistling to himself while he whittled bits of cork and wood into quaint shapes, attached them to string, weighted them with pebbles, and lowered them over the fall into the Lough—whence, after fifty years he would draw them forth, and sell them to the simple surrounding peasantry at two hundred and fifty *per centum per annum* on the initial cost.

It was a tranquil, lucrative employment, and had he stuck to the Rapture of Contemplation, he might have ended his days by the fall. But in an unlucky hour he undertook to feed ten Irish kings and their armies for three weeks on end on three cows. Even so he might have escaped, had he only failed. Alas! As it was, the ten kings had no sooner signed peace and drunk together than they marched up to St. Piran's door, and began to hold an Indignation Meeting.

"What's ailing wid ye, then?" asked the saint, poking his head out at the door; "out wid ut! Did I not stuff ye wid cow-mate galore when the land was as nakud as me tonshure? But 'twas three cows an' a miracle wasted, I'm thinkin'."

"Faith, an' ye've said ut!" answered one of the kings. "Three cows between tin Oirish kings! 'Tis insultin'! Arrah, now, make it foive, St. Piran darlint!"

"Now may they make your stummucks ache for that word, ye marautherin' thieves av the world!"

And St. Piran slammed the door in their faces.

But these kings were Ulstermen, and took things seriously. So they went off and stirred up the people: and the end was that one sunshiny morning a dirty rabble marched up to the mill and laid hands on the saint. On what charge, do you think? Why, for *Being without Visible Means of Support!*

"There's me pethrifyin' spicimins!" cried the saint: and he tugged at one of the ropes that stretched down into the Lough.

"Indade!" answered one of the ten kings: "Bad luck to your spicimins!" says he.

"Fwhat's that ye're tuggin.' at?" asks a bystander.

"Now the Holy Mother presarve your eyesight, Tim Coolin," answers St. Piran, pulling it in, "if ye can't tell a plain millstone at foive paces! I never asked ye to see *through* ut," he added, with a twinkle, for Tim had a plentiful lack of brains, and that the company knew.

Sure enough it was a millstone, and a very neat one; and the saint, having raised a bit of a laugh, went on like a cheap-jack:

"Av there's any gintleman prisunt wid an eye for millstones, I'll throuble him to turn ut here. Me own make," says he, "jooled in wan hole, an' dog-chape at fifteen shillin'—"

He was rattling away in this style when somebody called out, "To think av a millstone bein' a visible means av support!" And this time the laugh turned against the saint.

"St. Piran dear, ye've got to die," says the spokesman.

"Musha, musha!"—and the saint set up a wail and wrung his hands. "An' how's it goin' to be?" he asked, breaking off; "an' if 'tis by Shamus O'Neil's blunderbust that he's fumblin' yondther, will I stand afore or ahint ut? for 'tis fatal both ends, I'm thinkin', like Barney Sullivan's mule. Wirra, wirra! May our souls find mercy, Shamus O'Neil, for we'll both, be wantin' ut this day. Better for you, Shamus, that this millstone was hung round your black neck, an' you drownin' in the dept's av the Lough!"

The words were not spoken before they all set up a shout. "The millstone! the millstone!" "Sthrap him to ut!" "He's named his death!"—and inside of three minutes there was the saint, strapped down on his own *specimen*.

"Wirra, wirra!" he cried, and begged for mercy; but they raised a devastating shindy, and gave the stone a trundle. Down the turf it rolled and rolled, and then *whoo!* leaped over the edge of the fall into space and down—down—till it smote the waters far below, and knocked a mighty hole in them, and went under—

For three seconds only. The next thing that the rabble saw as they craned over the cliff was St. Piran floating quietly out to sea on the millstone, for all the world as if on a life-belt, and untying his bonds to use for a fishing-line! You see, this millstone had been made of cork originally, and was only half petrified; and the old boy had just beguiled them. When he had finished undoing the cords, he stood up and bowed to them all very politely.

"Visible Manes av Support, me childher—merely Visible Manes av Support!" he called back.

'Twas a sunshiny day, and while St. Piran chuckled the sea twinkled all over with the jest. As for the crowd on the cliff, it looked for five minutes as if the saint had petrified them harder than the millstone. Then, as Tim Coolin told his wife, Mary Dogherty, that same evening, they dispersed promiscuously in groups of one each.

Meanwhile, the tides were bearing St. Piran and his millstone out into the Atlantic, and he whiffed for mackerel all the way. And on the morrow a stiff breeze sprang up and blew him sou'-sou-west until he spied land; and so he stepped ashore on the Cornish coast.

In Cornwall he lived many years till he died: and to this day there are three places named after him—Perranaworthal, Perranuthno and Perranzabuloe. But it was in the last named that he took most delight, because at Perranzabuloe (Perochia Sti. Pirani in Sabulo) there was nothing but sand to distract him from the Study of Objects that Presented Themselves to his Notice: for he had given up miracles. So he sat on the sands and taught the Cornish people how to be idle. Also he discovered tin for them; but that was an accident.

2.—Saint Piran and the Visitation.

A full fifty years had St. Piran dwelt among the sandhills between Perranzabuloe and the sea before any big rush of saints began to pour into Cornwall: for 'twas not till the old man had discovered tin for us that they sprang up thick as blackberries all over the county; so that in a way St. Piran had only himself to blame when his idle ways grew to be a scandal by comparison with the push and bustle of the newcomers.

Never a notion had he that, from Rome to Land's End, all his holy brethren were holding up their hands over his case. He sat in his cottage above the sands at Perranzabuloe and dozed to the hum of the breakers, in charity with all his parishioners, to whom his money was large as the salt wind; for his sleeping partnership in the tin-streaming business brought him a tidy income. And the folk knew that if ever they wanted religion, they had only to knock and ask for it.

But one fine morning, an hour before noon, the whole parish sprang to its feet at the sound of a horn. The blast was twice repeated, and came from the little cottage across the sands.

"'Tis the blessed saint's cow-horn!" they told each other. "Sure the dear man must be in the article of death!" And they hurried off to the cottage, man, woman, and child: for 'twas thirty years at least since the horn had last been sounded.

They pushed open the door, and there sat St. Piran in his armchair, looking good for another twenty years, but considerably flustered. His cheeks were red, and his fingers clutched the cow-horn nervously.

"Andrew Penhaligon," said he to the first man that entered, "go you out and ring the church bell."

Off ran Andrew Penhaligon. "But, blessed father of us," said one or two, "we're all *here*! There's no call to ring the church bell, seem' you're neither dead nor afire, blessamercy!"

"Oh, if you're all here, that alters the case; for 'tis only a proclamation I have to give out at present. Tomorrow mornin'—Glory be to God!—I give warnin' that Divine service will take place in the parish church."

"You're sartin you bain't feelin' poorly, St. Piran dear?" asked one of the women.

"Thank you, Tidy Mennear, I'm enjoyin' health. But, as I was sayin', the parish church 'll be needed tomorrow, an' so you'd best set to and clean out the edifice: for I'm thinkin'," he added, "it'll be needin' that."

"To be sure, St. Piran dear, we'll humour ye."

"'Tisn' that at all," the saint answered; "but I've had a vision."

"Don't you often?"

"H'm! but this was a peculiar vision; or maybe a bit of a birdeen whispered it into my ear. Anyway, 'twas revealed to me just now in a dream that I stood on the lawn at Bodmin Priory, and peeped in at the priory window. An' there in the long hall sat all the saints together at a big table covered with red baize and plotted against us. There was St. Petroc in the chair, with St. Guron by his side, an' St. Neot, St. Udy, St. Teath, St. Keverne, St. Wen, St. Probus, St. Enodar, St. Just, St. Fimbarrus, St. Clether, St. Germoe, St. Veryan, St. Winnock, St. Minver, St. Anthony, with the virgins Grace, and Sinara, and Iva—the whole passel of 'em.

"An' they were agreein' there was no holiness left in this parish of mine; an' speakin' shame of me, my childer—of me, that have banked your consciences these fifty years, and always been able to pay on demand: the more by token that I kept a big reserve, an' you knew it. Answer me: when was there ever a panic in Perranzabuloe? 'Twas all very well,' said St. Neot, when his turn came to speak, 'but this state o' things ought to be exposed.' He's as big as bull's beef, is St. Neot, ever since he worked that miracle over the fishes, an' reckons he can disparage an old man who was makin' millstones to float when he was suckin' a coral. But the upshot is, they're goin' to pay us a Visitation to-morrow, by surprise. And, if only for the parish credit, we'll be even wid um, by dad!"

St. Piran still lapsed into his native brogue when strongly excited.

But he had hardly done when Andrew Penhaligon came running in—

"St. Piran, honey, I've searched everywhere; an' be hanged to me if I can find the church at all!"

"Fwhat's become av ut?" cried the saint, sitting up sharply.

"How should I know? But devil a trace can I see!"

"Now, look here," St. Piran said; "the church was there, right enough."

"That's a true word," spoke up an old man, "for I mind it well. An elegant tower it had, an' a shingle roof."

"Spake up, now," said the saint, glaring around; "fwich av ye's gone an' misbestowed me parush church? For I won't believe," he said, "that it's any worse than carelussness—at laste, not yet-a-bit."

Some remembered the church, and some did not: but the faces of all were clear of guilt. They trooped out on the sands to search.

Now, the sands by Perranzabuloe are forever shifting and driving before the northerly and nor'-westerly gales; and in time had heaped themselves up and covered the building out of sight. To guess this took the saint less time than you can wink your eye in; but the bother was that no one remembered exactly where the church, had stood, and as there were two score at least of tall mounds along the shore, and all of pretty equal height, there was no knowing where to dig. To uncover them all was a job to last till doomsday.

"Blur-an'-agurs, but it's ruined I am!" cried St. Piran. "An' the Visitashun no further away than tomorra at tin a.m.!" He wrung his hands, then caught up a spade, and began digging like a madman.

They searched all day, and with lanterns all the night through: they searched from Ligger Point to Porth Towan: but came on never a sign of the missing church.

"If it only had a spire," one said, "there'd be some chance." But as far as could be recollected, the building had a dumpy tower.

"Once caught, twice shy," said another; "let us find it this once, an' next time we'll have landmarks to dig it out by."

It was at sunrise that St. Piran, worn-out and heart-sick, let fall his spade and spoke from one of the tall mounds, where he had been digging for an hour.

"My children," he began, and the men uncovered their heads, "my children, we are going to be disgraced this day, and the best we can do is to pray that we may take it like men. Let us pray."

He knelt down on the great sand-hill, and the men and women around dropped on their knees also. And then St. Piran put up the prayer that has made his name famous all the world over.

3—The Prayer of St. Piran.

Hear us, O Lord, and be debonair: for ours is a particular case. We are not like the men of St. Neot or the men of St. Udy, who are forever importuning Thee upon the least occasion, praying at all hours and every day of the week. Thou knowest it is only with extreme cause that we bring ourselves to trouble Thee. Therefore regard our moderation in time past, and be instant to help us now. Amen.

There was silence for a full minute as he ceased; and then the kneeling parishioners lifted their eyes towards the top of the mound.

St. Piran was nowhere to be seen!

They stared into each other's faces. For a while not a sound was uttered. Then a woman began to sob—

"We've lost 'en! We've lost 'en!"

"Like Enoch, he's been taken!"

"Taken up in a chariot an' horses o' fire. Did any see 'en go?"

"An' what'll we do without 'en? Holy St. Piran, come back to us!"

"Hullo! hush a bit an' hearken!" cried Andrew Penhaligon, lifting a hand.

They were silent, and listening as he commanded, heard a muffled voice and a faint, calling as it were from the bowels of the earth.

"Fetch a ladder!" it said: "fetch a ladder! It's meself that's found ut, glory be to God! Holy queen av heaven! but me mouth is full av sand, an' it's burstin' I'll be if ye don't fetch a ladder quick!"

They brought a ladder and set it against the mound. Three of the men climbed up. At the top they found a big round hole, from the lip of which they scraped the sand away, discovering a patch of shingle roof, through which St. Piran—whose weight had increased of late—had broken and tumbled heels over head into his own church.

Three hours later there appeared on the eastern sky-line, against the yellow blaze of the morning, a large cavalcade that slowly pricked its way over the edge and descended the slopes of Newlyn Downs. It was the Visitation. In the midst rode St. Petroc, his crosier tucked under his arm, astride a white mule with scarlet ear-tassels and bells and a saddle of scarlet leather. He gazed across the sands to the sea, and turned to St. Neot, who towered at his side upon a flea-bitten grey.

"The parish seems to be deserted," said he: "not a man nor woman can I see, nor a trace of smoke above the chimneys."

St. Neot tightened his thin lips. In his secret heart he was mightily pleased.

"Eight in the morning," he answered, with a glance back at the sun. "They'll be all abed, I'll warrant you."

St. Petroc muttered a threat.

They entered the village street. Not a soul turned out at their coming. Every cottage door was fast closed, nor could any amount of knocking elicit an answer or entice a face to a window. In gathering wrath the visiting saints rode along the sea-shore to St. Piran's small hut.

Here the door stood open: but the hut was empty. A meagre breakfast of herbs was set out on the table, and a brand new scourge lay somewhat ostentatiously beside the platter. The visitors stood nonplussed, looked at each other, then eyed the landscape. Between barren sea and barren downs the beach stretched away, with not a human shape in sight. St. Petroc, choking with impotent wrath, appeared to study the hollow green breakers from between the long ears of his mule, but with quick sidelong glances right and left, ready to jump down the throat of the first saint that dared to smile.

After a minute or so St. Enodar suddenly turned his face inland, and held up a finger.

"Hark!" he shouted above the roar of the sea.

"What is it?"

"It sounds to me," said St. Petroc, after listening for some moments with his head on one side, "it sounds to me like a hymn."

"To be sure 'tis a hymn," said St. Enodar, "and the tune is 'Mullyon,' for a crown." And he pursed up his lips and followed the chant, beating time with his forefinger—

When, like a thief, the Midianite
Shall steal upon the camp,
O, let him find our armour bright,
And oil within our lamp!

"But where in the world does it come from?" asked St. Neot.

This could not be answered for the moment; but the saints turned their horses' heads from the sea, and moved slowly on the track of the sound, which at every step grew louder and more distinct.

It is at no appointed hours,
It is not by the dock,
That Satan, grisly wolf, devours
The unprotected flock

The visitors found themselves at the foot of an enormous sand-hill, from the top of which the chant was pouring as lava from a crater. They set their ears to the sandy wall. They walked round it, and listened again.

But ever prowls th' insidious foe,
And listens round the fold

This was too much. St. Petroc smote twice upon the sand-hill with his crozier, and shouted—

"Hi, there!"

The chant ceased. For at least a couple of minutes nothing

happened; and then St. Piran's bald head was thrust cautiously forward over the summit.

"Holy St. Petroc! Was it only you, after all? And St. Neot—and St. Udy O, glory be!"

"Why, who did you imagine we were?" St. Petroc asked, still in amazement.

"Why, throat-cutting Danes, to be sure, by the way you were comin' over the hills when we spied you, three hours back. An' the trouble we've had to cover up our blessed church out o' sight of thim marautherin' thieves! An' the intire parish gathered inside here an' singin' goodbye songs in expectation of imminent death! An' to think 'twas you holy men, all the while! But why didn't ye send word ye was comin', St. Petroc, darlint? For it's little but sand ye'll find in your mouths for breakfast, I'm thinkin'."

Lieutenant Lapenotiere

The night-porter at the Admiralty had been sleeping in his chair. He was red-eyed and wore his livery coat buttoned at random. He grumbled to himself as he opened the great door.

He carried a glass-screened candle, and held it somewhat above the level of his forehead—which was protuberant and heavily pock-marked. Under the light he peered out at the visitor, who stood tall and stiff, with uniform overcoat buttoned to the chin, between the Ionic pillars of the portico.

"Who's there?"

"Lieutenant Lapenotiere, of the *Pickle* schooner—with dispatches."

"Dispatches?" echoed the night-porter. Out beyond the screen of masonry that shut off the Board of Admiralty's forecourt from Whitehall, one of the tired post-horses started blowing through its nostrils on this foggy night.

"From Admiral Collingwood—Mediterranean Fleet off Cadiz—sixteen days," answered the visitor curtly. "Is everyone abed?"

"Admiral Collingwood? Why Admiral Collingwood?" The night-porter fell back a pace, opening the door a trifle wider. "Good God, sir! You don't say as how—"

"You can fetch down a Secretary or someone, I hope?" said Lieutenant Lapenotiere, quickly stepping past him into the long dim hall. "My dispatches are of the first importance. I have posted up from Falmouth without halt but for relays."

As the man closed the door, he heard his post-boy of the last relay slap one of the horses encouragingly before heading home to stable. The chaise wheels began to move on the cobbles.

"His Lordship himself will see you, sir. Of that I make no doubt," twittered the night-porter, fumbling with the bolt. "There was a terrible disturbance, back in July, when Captain Bettesworth arrived—not so late as this, to be sure, but towards midnight—and they waited till morning, to carry up the dispatches with his Lordship's chocolate. Thankful was I next day not to have been on duty at the time.... If you will follow me, sir—"

Lieutenant Lapenotiere had turned instinctively towards a door on the right. It admitted to the Waiting Room, and there were few officers in the service who did not know—and only too well—that Chamber of Hope Deferred.

"No, sir,.... this way, if you please," the night-porter corrected him, and opened a door on the left. "The Captains' Room," he announced, passing in and steering for the chimney-shelf, on which stood a pair of silver sconces each carrying three wax candles. These he took down, lit and replaced. "Ah, sir! Many's the time I've showed Lord Nelson himself into this room, in the days before Sir Horatio, and even after. And you were sayin'—"

"I said nothing."

The man moved to the door; but halted there and came back, as though in his own despite.

"I can't help it, sir.... Half a guinea he used to give me, regular. But the last time—and hard to believe 'twas little more than a month ago—he halts on his way out, and says he, searchin' awkward-like in his breeches' pocket with his left hand, 'Ned,' says he, 'my old friend'—aye, sir, his old friend he called me— 'Ned,' says he, pullin' out a fistful o' gold, 'my old friend,' says he, 'I'll compound with you for two guineas, this bein' the last time you may hold the door open for me, in or out. But you must pick 'em out,' says he, spreadin' his blessed fingers with the gold in 'em: 'for a man can't count money who's lost his right flapper.' Those were his words, sir. 'Old friend,' he called me, in that way of his."

Lieutenant Lapenotiere pointed to his left arm. Around the sleeve a black scarf was knotted.

"*Dead*, sir," the night-porter hushed his voice.

"Dead," echoed Lieutenant Lapenotiere, staring at the Turkey carpet, of which the six candles, gaining strength, barely illumined the pattern. "Dead, at the top of victory; a great victory. Go: fetch somebody down."

The night-porter shuffled off. Lieutenant Lapenotiere, erect and sombre, cast a look around the apartment, into which he had never before been admitted. The candles lit up a large painting—a queer bird's-eye view of Venice. Other pictures, dark and bituminous, decorated the panelled walls—portraits of dead admirals, a sea-piece or two, some charts. . . . This was all he discerned out in the dim light; and in fact he scanned the walls, the furniture of the room, inattentively. His stomach was fasting, his head light with rapid travel; above all, he had a sense of wonder that all this should be happening to *him*. For, albeit a distinguished officer, he was a modest man, and by habit considered himself of no great importance; albeit a brave man, too, he shrank at the thought of the message he carried—a message to explode and shake millions of men in a confusion of wild joy or grief.

For about the tenth time in those sixteen days it seemed to burst and escape in an actual detonation, splitting his head— there, as he waited in the strange room where never a curtain stirred. . . . It was a trick his brain played him, repeating, echoing the awful explosion of the French seventy-four *Achille*, which had blown up towards the close of the battle. When the ship was ablaze and sinking, his own crew had put off in boats to rescue the Frenchmen, at close risk of their own lives, for her loaded guns, as they grew red-hot, went off at random among rescuers and rescued. . . .

As had happened before when he felt this queer shock, his mind travelled back and he seemed to hear the series of discharges running up at short intervals to the great catastrophe. . . . To divert his thoughts, he turned to study the view of Venice above the chimney-piece. . . . and on a sudden faced about again.

He had a sensation that someone was in the room—someone standing close behind him.

But no. . . . For the briefest instant his eyes rested on an indistinct shadow—his own perhaps, cast by the candle-light? Yet why should it lie lengthwise there, shaped like a coffin, on the dark polished table that occupied the middle of the room?

The answer was that it did not. Before he could rub his eyes it had gone. Moreover, he had turned to recognise a living being. . . . and no living person was in the room, unless by chance (absurd supposition) one were hidden behind the dark red window curtains.

"Recognise" may seem a strange word to use; but here had lain the strangeness of the sensation—that the someone standing there was a friend, waiting to be greeted. It was with eagerness and a curious warmth of the heart that Lieutenant Lapenotiere had faced about—upon nothing.

He continued to stare in a puzzled way at the window curtains, when a voice by the door said:

"Good evening!—or perhaps, to be correct, good morning! You are Mr.—"

"Lapenotiere," answered the lieutenant, who had turned sharply. The voice—a gentleman's and pleasantly modulated—was not one he knew; nor did he recognise the speaker—a youngish, shrewd-looking man, dressed in civilian black, with knee-breeches. "Lapenotiere—of the *Pickle* schooner."

"Yes, yes—the porter bungled your name badly, but I guessed. Lord Barham will see you personally. He is, in fact, dressing with all haste at this moment. . . . I am his private secretary," explained the shrewd-looking gentleman in his quiet, business-like voice. "Will you come with me upstairs?"

Lieutenant Lapenotiere followed him. At the foot of the great staircase the secretary turned.

"I may take it, sir, that we are not lightly disturbing his Lordship—who is an old man."

"The news is of great moment, sir. Greater could scarcely be."

The secretary bent his head. As they went up the staircase Lieutenant Lapenotiere looked back and caught sight of the night-porter in the middle of the hall, planted there and gazing up, following their ascent.

On the first-floor landing they were met by a truly ridiculous spectacle. There emerged from a doorway on the left of the wide corridor an old gentleman clad in night-cap, night-shirt and bedroom slippers, buttoning his breeches and cursing vigorously; while close upon him followed a valet with dressing-gown on one arm, waistcoat and wig on the other, vainly striving to keep pace with his master's impatience.

"The braces, my lord—your Lordship has them forepart behind, if I may suggest—"

"Damn the braces!" swore the old gentleman. "Where is he? Hi, Tylney!" as he caught sight of the Secretary. "Where are we to go? My room, I suppose?"

"The fire is out there, my lord.... 'Tis past three in the morning. But after sending word to awake you, I hunted round and by good luck found a plenty of promising embers in the Board Room grate. On top of these I've piled what remained of my own fire, and Dobson has set a lamp there—"

"You've been devilish quick, Tylney. Dressed like a buck you are, too!"

"Your Lordship's wig," suggested the valet.

"Damn the wig!" Lord Barham snatched it and attempted to stick it on top of his night-cap, damned the night-cap, and, plucking it off, flung it to the man.

"I happened to be sitting up late, my lord, over the *Aeolus* papers," said Mr. Secretary Tylney.

"Ha?" Then, to the valet, "The dressing-gown there! Don't fumble! ...So this is Captain—"

"Lieutenant, sir: Lapenotiere, commanding the *Pickle* schooner."

The lieutenant saluted.

"From the Fleet, my lord—off Cadiz; or rather, off Cape Trafalgaro."

He drew the sealed dispatch from an inner breast-pocket and handed it to the First Lord.

"Here, step into the Board Room.... Where the devil are my spectacles?" he demanded of the valet, who had sprung forward to hold open the door.

Evidently the Board Room had been but a few hours ago the scene of a large dinner-party. Glasses, dessert-plates, dishes of fruit, decanters empty and half empty, cumbered the great mahogany table as dead and wounded, guns and tumbrils, might a battlefield. Chairs stood askew; crumpled napkins lay as they had been dropped or tossed, some on the floor, others across the table between the dishes.

"Looks cosy, eh?" commented the First Lord. "Maggs, set a screen around the fire, and look about for a decanter and some clean glasses."

He drew a chair close to the reviving fire, and glanced at the cover of the dispatch before breaking its seal.

"Nelson's handwriting?" he asked. It was plain that his old eyes, unaided by spectacles, saw the superscription only as a blur.

"No, my lord: Admiral Collingwood's," said Lieutenant Lapenotiere, inclining his head.

Old Lord Barham looked up sharply. His wig set awry, he made a ridiculous figure in his hastily donned garments. Yet he did not lack dignity.

"Why Collingwood?" he asked, his fingers breaking the seal. "God! you don't tell me—"

"Lord Nelson is dead, sir."

"Dead—dead? . . . . Here, Tylney—you read what it says. Dead? . . . No, damme, let the captain tell his tale. Briefly, sir."

"Briefly, sir—Lord Nelson had word of Admiral Villeneuve coming out of the Straits, and engaged the combined fleets off Cape Trafalgaro. They were in single line, roughly; and he bore down in two columns, and cut off their van under Dumanoir.

This was at dawn or thereabouts, and by five o'clock the enemy was destroyed."

"How many prizes?"

"I cannot say precisely, my lord. The word went, when I was signalled aboard the vice-admiral's flagship, that either fifteen or sixteen had struck. My own men were engaged, at the time, in rescuing the crew of a French seventy-four that had blown up; and I was too busy to count, had counting been possible. One or two of my officers maintain to me that our gains were higher. But the dispatch will tell, doubtless."

"Aye, to be sure. . . . Read, Tylney. Don't sit there clearing your throat, but read, man alive!" And yet it appeared that while the secretary was willing enough to read, the First Lord had no capacity, as yet, to listen. Into the very first sentence he broke with—

"No, wait a minute. 'Dead,' d'ye say. . . . My God! . . . lieutenant, pour yourself a glass of wine and tell us first how it happened."

Lieutenant Lapenotiere could not tell very clearly. He had twice been summoned to board the *Royal Sovereign*—he first time to receive the command to hold himself ready. It was then that, coming alongside the great ship, he had read in all the officers' faces an anxiety hard to reconcile with the evident tokens of victory around them. At once it had occurred to him that the admiral had fallen, and he put the question to one of the lieutenants—to be told that Lord Nelson had indeed been mortally wounded and could not live long; but that he must be alive yet, and conscious, since the *Victory* was still signalling orders to the fleet.

"I think, my lord," said he, "that Admiral Collingwood must have been doubtful, just then, what responsibility had fallen upon him, or how soon it might fall. He had sent for me to 'stand by' so to speak. He was good enough to tell me the news as it had reached him—"

Here Lieutenant Lapenotiere, obeying the order to fill his glass, let spill some of the wine on the table. The sight of the dark trickle on the mahogany touched some nerve of the brain: he saw it widen into a pool of blood, from which, as they picked up a shattered seaman and bore him below, a lazy stream crept across the deck of the flag-ship towards the scuppers. He moved his feet, as he had moved them then, to be out of the way of it: but recovered himself in another moment and went on—

"He told me, my lord, that the *Victory* after passing under the *Bucentaure's* stern, and so raking her that she was put out of action, or almost, fell alongside the *Redoutable*. There was a long swell running, with next to no wind, and the two ships could hardly have cleared had they tried. At any rate, they hooked, and it was then a question which could hammer the harder. The Frenchman had filled his tops with sharp-shooters, and from one of these— the mizen-top, I believe—a musket-ball struck down the admiral. He was walking at the time to and fro on a sort of gangway he had caused to be planked over his cabin sky-light, between the wheel and the ladder-way. . . . Admiral Collingwood believed it had happened about half-past one . . ."

"Sit down, man, and drink your wine," commanded the First Lord as the dispatch-bearer swayed with a sudden faintness.

"It is nothing, my lord—"

But it must have been a real swoon, or something very like it: for he recovered to find himself lying in an armchair. He heard the secretary's voice reading steadily on and on.... Also they must have given him wine, for he awoke to feel the warmth of it in his veins and coursing about his heart. But he was weak yet, and for the moment well content to lie still and listen.

Resting there and listening, he was aware of two sensations that alternated within him, chasing each other in and out of his consciousness. He felt all the while that he, John Richards Lapenotiere, a junior officer in His Majesty's service, was assisting in one of the most momentous events in his country's history; and alone in the room with these two men, he felt it as he had never begun to feel it amid the smoke and roar of the actual battle. He had seen the dead hero but half a dozen times in his life: he had never been honoured by a word from him: but like every other naval officer, he had come to look up to Nelson as to the splendid particular star among commanders. *There* was greatness: *there* was that which lifted men to such deeds as write man's name across the firmament! And, strange to say, Lieutenant Lapenotiere recognised something of it in this queer old man, in dressing-gown and ill-fitting wig, who took snuff and interrupted now with a curse and *anon* with a "bravo!" as the secretary read. He was absurd: but he was no common man, this Lord Barham. He had something of the ineffable aura of greatness.

But in the lieutenant's brain, across this serious, even awful sense of the moment and of its meaning, there played a curious secondary sense that the moment was not—that what was happening before his eyes had either happened before or was happening in some vacuum in which past, present, future and the ordinary divisions of time had lost their bearings. The great twenty-four-hour clock at the end of the Board Room, ticking on and on while the secretary read, wore an unfamiliar face. . . . Yes, time had gone wrong, somehow: and the events of the passage home to Falmouth, of the journey up to the doors of the Admiralty, though they ran on a chain, had no intervals to be measured by a clock, but followed one another like pictures on a wall. He saw the long, indigo-coloured swell thrusting the broken ships shoreward.

He felt the wind freshening as it southered and he left the fleet behind: he watched their many lanterns as they sank out of sight, then the glow of flares by the light of which dead-tired men were repairing damages, cutting away wreckage. His ship was wallowing heavily now, with the gale after her,—and now dawn was breaking clean and glorious on the swell off Lizard Point. A Mount's Bay lugger had spied them, and lying in wait, had sheered up close alongside, her crew bawling for news. He had not forbidden his men to call it back, and he could see the fellows' faces now, as it reached them from the speaking-trumpet: "Great victory—twenty taken or sunk—Admiral Nelson killed!"

They had guessed something, noting the *Pickle's* ensign at

half-mast: yet as they took in the purport of the last three words, these honest fishermen had turned and stared at one another; and without one answering word, the lugger had been headed straight back to the mainland.

So it had been at Falmouth. A ship entering port has a thousand eyes upon her, and the *Pickle's* errand could not be hidden. The news seemed in some mysterious way to have spread even before he stepped ashore there on the Market Strand. A small crowd had collected, and, as he passed through it, many doffed their hats. There was no cheering at all—no, not for this the most glorious victory of the war—outshining even the Nile or Howe's First of June.

He had set his face as he walked to the inn. But the news had flown before him, and fresh crowds gathered to watch him off. The post-boys knew. . . . and *they* told the post-boys at the next stage, and the next—Bodmin and Plymouth—not to mention the boatmen at Torpoint Ferry. But the countryside did not know: nor the labourers gathering in cider apples heaped under Devon apple-trees, nor, next day, the sportsmen banging off guns at the partridges around Salisbury. The slow, jolly life of England on either side of the high road turned leisurely as a wagon-wheel on its axle, while between hedgerows, past farm hamlets, church-towers and through the cobbled streets of market towns, he had sped and rattled with Collingwood's dispatch in his sealed case. The news had reached London with him. His last post-boys had carried it to their stables, and from stable to tavern. Tomorrow—today, rather—in an hour or two—all the bells of London would be ringing—or tolling! . . .

"He's as tired as a dog," said the voice of the secretary. "Seems almost a shame to waken him."

The lieutenant opened his eyes and jumped to his feet with an apology. Lord Barham had gone, and the Secretary hard by was speaking to the night-porter, who bent over the fire, raking it with a poker. The hands of the Queen Anne clock indicated a quarter to six.

"The First Lord would like to talk with you. . . . later in the day," said Mr. Tylney gravely, smiling a little these last words. He himself was white and haggard. "He suggested the early afternoon, say half-past two. That will give you time for a round sleep. . . . You might leave me the name of your hotel, in case he should wish to send for you before that hour."

"'The Swan with Two Necks,' Lad Lane, Cheapside," said Lieutenant Lapenotiere.

He knew little of London, and gave the name of the hostelry at which, many years ago, he had alighted from a West Country coach with his box and midshipman's kit. . . . A moment later he found himself wondering if it still existed as a house of entertainment. Well, he must go and seek it.

The secretary shook hands with him, smiling wanly.

"Few men, sir, have been privileged to carry such news as you have brought us tonight."

"And I went to sleep after delivering it," said Lieutenant Lapenotiere, smiling back.

The night-porter escorted him to the hall, and opened the great door for him. In the portico he bade the honest man good night, and stood for a moment, mapping out in his mind his way to "The Swan with Two Necks." He shivered slightly, after his nap, in the chill of the approaching dawn.

As the door closed behind him he was aware of a light shining, out beyond the screen of the fore-court, and again a horse blew through its nostrils on the raw air.

"Lord!" thought the lieutenant. "That fool of a post-boy cannot have mistaken me and waited all this time!"

He hurried out into Whitehall. Sure enough a chaise was drawn up there, and a post-boy stood by the near lamp, conning a scrap of paper by the light of it. No, it was a different chaise, and a different post-boy. He wore the buff and black, whereas the other had worn the blue and white. Yet he stepped forward confidently, and with something of a smile.

"Lieutenant Lapenotiere?" he asked, reaching back and holding up his paper to the lamp to make sure of the syllables.

"That is my name," said the amazed lieutenant.

"I was ordered here—five-forty-five—to drive you down to Merton."

"To Merton?" echoed Lieutenant Lapenotiere, his hand going to his pocket. The post-boy's smile, or so much as could be seen of it by the edge of the lamp, grew more knowing.

"I ask no questions, sir."

"But—but who ordered you?"

The post-boy did not observe, or disregarded, his bewilderment.

"A Briton's a Briton, sir, I hope? I ask no questions, knowing my place. . . . But if so be as you were to tell me there's been a great victory—" He paused on this.

"Well, my man, you're right so far, and no harm in telling you."

"Aye," chirruped the post-boy. "When the maid called me up with the order, and said as how *he* and no other had called with it—"

"He?"

The fellow nodded.

"She knew him at once, from his portraits. Who wouldn't? With his right sleeve pinned across so. . . . And, said I, 'Then there's been a real victory. Never would you see him back, unless. And I was right, sir!' he concluded triumphantly.

"Let me see that piece of paper."

"You'll let me have it back, sir?—for a memento," the post-boy pleaded. Lieutenant Lapenotiere took it from him—a plain half-sheet of note-paper roughly folded. On it was scribbled in pencil, back-hand wise, "Lt. Lapenotiere. Admiralty, Whitehall. At 6.30 a.m., not later. For Merton, Surrey."

He folded the paper very slowly, and handed it back to the post-boy.

"Very well, then. For Merton."

The house lay but a very little distance beyond Wimbledon. Its blinds were drawn as Lieutenant Lapenotiere alighted from the chaise and went up to the modest porch.

His hand was on the bell-pull. But some pressure checked

him as he was on the point of ringing. He determined to wait for a while and turned away towards the garden.

The dawn had just broken; two or three birds were singing. It did not surprise—at any rate, it did not frighten—Lieutenant Lapenotiere at all, when, turning into a short pleached alley, he looked along it and saw *him* advancing.

—Yes, *him*, with the pinned sleeve, the noble, seamed, eager face. They met as friends. . . . . In later years the lieutenant could never remember a word that passed, if any passed at all. He was inclined to think that they met and walked together in complete silence, for many minutes. Yet he ever maintained that they walked as two friends whose thoughts hold converse without need of words. He was not terrified at all. He ever insisted, on the contrary, that there, in the cold of the breaking day, his heart was light and warm as though flooded with first love—not troubled by it, as youth in first love is wont to be—but bathed in it; he, the ardent young officer, bathed in a glow of affection, ennobling, exalting him, making him free of a brotherhood he had never guessed.

He used also, in telling the story, to scandalise the clergyman of his parish by quoting the evangelists, and especially St. John's narrative of Mary Magdalen at the sepulchre.

For the door of the house opened at length; and a beautiful woman, scarred by knowledge of the world, came down the alley, slowly, unaware of him. Then (said he), as she approached, his hand went up to his pocket for the private letter he carried, and the shade at his side left him to face her in the daylight.

Mutual Exchange, Limited

Chapter 1

Millionaire though he was, Mr Markham (*nee* Markheim) never let a small opportunity slip. To be sure the enforced idleness of Atlantic crossing bored him and kept him restless; it affected him with *malaise* to think that for these five days, while the solitude of ocean swallowed him, men on either shore, with cables at their command, were using them to get rich on their own account—it might even be at his expense. The first day out from New York he had spent in his cabin, immersed in correspondence. Having dealt with this and exhausted it, on the second, third, and fourth days he found nothing to do. He never played cards; he eschewed all acquaintance with his fellow men except in the way of business; he had no vanity, and to be stared at on the promenade deck because of the fame of his wealth merely annoyed him. On the other hand, he had not the smallest excuse to lock himself up in his stuffy state-room. He enjoyed fresh air, and had never been seasick in his life.

It was just habit—the habit of never letting a chance go, or the detail of a chance—that on the fourth morning carried him the length of the liner, to engage in talk with the fresh-coloured young third officer busy on the high deck forward.

'A young man, exposed as you are, ought to insure himself,' said Mr Markham.

The third officer—by name Dick Rendal—knew something of the inquisitiveness and idle ways of passengers. This was his fifth trip in the *Carnatic*. He took no truck in passengers beyond showing them the patient politeness enjoined by the Company's rules. He knew nothing of Mr Markham, who dispensed with the services of a valet and dressed with a shabbiness only pardonable in the extremely rich. Mr Markham, 'the Insurance King,' had arrayed himself this morning in gray flannel, with a reach-me-down overcoat, cloth cap, and carpet slippers that betrayed his flat, Jewish instep. Dick Rendal sized him up for an insurance tout; but behaved precisely as he would have behaved on better information. He refrained from ordering the intruder aft; but eyed him less than amiably—being young, keen on his ship, and just now keen on his job.

'I saw you yesterday,' said Mr Markham. (It had blown more than half a gale, and late in the afternoon three heavy seas had come aboard. The third officer at this moment was employed with half a dozen seamen in repairing damages.) 'I was watching. As I judged, it was the nicest miss you weren't overboard. Over and above employers' liability you should insure. The Hands Across Mutual Exchange—that's your office.'

Mr Markham leaned back, and put a hand up to his inner breast-pocket—it is uncertain whether for his cigar-case, or for some leaflet relating to the Hands Across.

'Take care, sir!' said the third officer sharply. 'That stanchion—'

He called too late. The hand as it touched the breast-pocket, shot up and clawed at the air. With a voice that was less a cry than a startled grunt, Mr Markham pitched backwards off the fore-deck into the sea.

The third officer stared for just a fraction of a second; ran, seized a life-belt as the liner's length went shooting past; and hurled it—with pretty good aim, too—almost before a man of his working party had time to raise the cry of 'Man overboard!' Before the alarm reached the bridge, he had kicked off his shoes; and the last sound in his ears as he dived was the ping of the bell ringing down to the engine-room—a thin note, infinitely distant, speaking out of an immense silence.

Chapter 2

It was a beautifully clean dive; but in the flurry of the plunge the third officer forgot for an instant the right upward slant of the palms, and went a great way deeper than he had intended. By the time he rose to the surface the liner had slid by, and for a moment or two he saw nothing; for instinctively he came up facing aft, towards the spot where Mr Markham had fallen, and the long sea running after yesterday's gale threw up a ridge that seemed to take minutes—though in fact it took but a few seconds—to sink and heave up the trough beyond. By-and-by a life-belt swam up into sight; then another—at least a dozen had been flung; and beyond these at length, on the climbing crest of the swell two hundred yards away, the head and shoulders of Mr Markham.

By great good luck the first life-belt had fallen within a few feet of him, and Mr Markham had somehow managed to get within reach and clutch it—a highly creditable feat when it is considered that he was at best a poor swimmer, that the fall had knocked more than half the breath out of his body, that he had swallowed close on a pint of salt water, and that a heavy overcoat impeded his movements. But after this fair first effort Mr Markham, as his clothes weighed him down, began—as the phrase is—to make very bad weather of it. He made worse and worse weather of it as Dick Rendal covered the distance between them with a superlatively fine side-stroke, once or twice singing out to him to hold on, and keep a good heart. Mr Markham, whether he heard or no, held on with great courage, and even coolness—up to a point.

Then of a sudden his nerve deserted him. He loosed his hold of the life-belt, and struck out for his rescuer. Worse, as he sank in the effort and Dick gripped him, he closed and struggled. For half a minute Dick, shaking free of the embrace—and this only by striking him on the jaw and half stunning him as they rose on the crest of a swell—was able to grip him by the collar and drag him within reach of the life-belt. But here the demented man managed to wreathe his legs and arms in another and more terrible hold. The pair of them were now cursing horribly, cursing whenever a wave left choking them, and allowed them to cough and sputter for breath. They fought as two men whose lives had pent up an unmitigable hate for this moment. They fought, neither losing his hold, as their strength ebbed, and the weight of their clothes dragged them lower.

Dick Rendal's hand still clutched the cord of the life-belt, but both bodies were under water, fast locked, when the liner's boat at length reached the spot. They were hauled on board, as on a long line you haul a fish with a crab fastened upon him; and were laid in the stern-sheets, where their grip was with some difficulty loosened.

It may have happened in the struggle. Or again it may have happened when they were hoisted aboard and lay, for a minute or so, side by side on the deck. Both men were insensible; so far gone indeed that the doctor looked serious as he and his helpers began to induce artificial respiration.

The young third officer 'came round' after five minutes of this; but, strangely enough, in the end he was found to be suffering from a severer shock than Mr Markham, on whom the doctor operated for a full twenty minutes before a flutter of the eyelids rewarded him. They were carried away—the third officer, in a state of collapse, to his modest berth; Mr Markham to his white-and-gold deck-cabin. On his way thither Mr Markham protested cheerily that he saw no reason for all this fuss; he was as right now, or nearly as right, as the Bank.

CHAPTER 3

How's Rendal getting on?'

Captain Holditch, skipper of the *Carnatic*, put this question next morning to the doctor, and was somewhat surprised by the answer.

'Oh, Rendal's all right. That is to say, he will be all right. Just now he's suffering from shock. My advice—supposing, of course, you can spare him—is to pack him straightaway off to his people on a week's leave. In a week he'll be fit as a fiddle.'

The doctor paused and added, "Wish I could feel as easy about the millionaire.'

'Why, what's the matter with him? 'Struck me he pulled round wonderfully, once you'd brought him to. He talked as cheery as a grig.

'H'm—yes,' said the doctor; 'he has been talking like that ever since, only he hasn't been talking sense. Calls me names for keeping him in bed, and wants to get out and repair that stanchion. I told him it was mended. "Nothing on earth is the matter with me," he insisted, till I had to quiet him down with bromide. By the way, did you send off any account of the accident?'

'By wireless? No; I took rather particular pains to stop that—gets into the papers, only frightens the family and friends, who conclude things to be ten times worse than they are. Plenty of time at Southampton. Boat-express'll take him home ahead of the scare?'

'Lives in Park Lane, doesn't he?—that big corner house like a game-pie? . . . Ye-es, you were thoughtful, as usual. . . . Only someone might have been down to the docks to meet him. 'Wish I knew his doctor's address. Well, never mind—I'll fix him up so that he reaches Park Lane, anyway.'

'He ought to do something for Rendal,' mused Captain Holditch.

'He will, you bet, when his head is right—that's if a millionaire's head is ever right,' added the doctor, who held radical opinions on the distribution of wealth.

The captain ignored this. He never talked politics even when ashore.

'As plucky a rescue as ever I witnessed,' he answered the doctor. 'Yes, of course, I'll spare the lad. Slip a few clothes into his bag, and tell him he can get off by the first train. Oh, and by the way, you might ask him if he's all right for money; say he can draw on me if he wants any.'

The doctor took his message down to Dick Rendal; 'We're this moment passing Hurst Castle,' he announced cheerfully, 'and you may tumble out if you like. But first I'm to pack a few clothes for you; if you let me, I'll do it better than the steward. Shore-going clothes, my boy—where do you keep your cabin trunk? Eh? Suit-case, is it?—best leather, nickel locks—no, silver, as I'm a sinner! Hallo, my young friend!'—here the doctor looked up, mischief in his eye—'You never struck me as that sort of dude; and fathers and mothers don't fit their offspring out with silver locks to their suit-cases—or they've altered since my time. Well, you'll enjoy your leave all the better; and give her my congratulations. The Old Man says you may get off as soon as we're docked, and stay home till you've recovered. I dare say it won't be long before you feel better,' he wound up, with a glance at the suit-case.

'The Old Man? Yes—yes—Captain Holditch, of course,' muttered Dick from his berth.

The doctor looked at him narrowly for a moment; but, when he spoke again, kept by intention the same easy rattling tone.

'Decent of him, eh?—Yes, and by the way, he asked me to tell you that, if you shouldn't happen to be flush of money just now, that needn't hinder you five minutes. He'll be your banker, and make it right with the Board.'

Dick lay still for half a dozen seconds, as though the words took that time in reaching him. Then he let out a short laugh from somewhere high on his nose.

'My banker? Will he? Good Lord!'

'May be,' said the doctor, dryly; laying out a suit of mufti at the foot of the bed, 'the Old Man and I belong to the same date. I've heard that youngsters save money nowadays. But when I was your age that sort of offer would have hit the mark nine times out of ten.'

He delivered this as a parting shot. Dick, lying on his back and staring up at a knot in the woodwork over his bunk, received it placidly. Probably he did not hear. His brow was corrugated in a frown, as though he were working out a sum or puzzling over some problem. The doctor closed the door softly, and some minutes later paid a visit to Mr Markham, whom he found stretched on the couch of the white-and-gold deck-cabin, attired in a gray flannel sleeping-suit, and wrapped around the legs with a travelling rug of dubious hue.

'That's a good deal better,' he said cheerfully, after an examination, in which, while seeming to be occupied with pulses and temperature, he paid particular attention to the pupils of Mr Markham's eyes. 'We are nosing up the Solent fast—did you know it? Ten minutes ought to see us in Southampton Water; and I suppose you'll be wanting to catch the first train.'

'I wonder,' said Mr Markham vaguely, 'if the Old Man will mind.'

The doctor stared for a moment. 'I think we may risk it,' he said, after a pause; 'though I confess that, last night, I was doubtful. Of course, if you're going to be met, it's right enough.'

'Why should I be met?'

'Well, you see—I couldn't know, could I? Anyway, you ought to see your own doctor as soon as you get home. Perhaps, if you gave me his name, I might scribble a note to him, just to say what has happened. Even big-wigs, you know, don't resent being helped with a little information.'

Mr Markham stared. 'Lord!' said he, 'you're talking as if I kept a tame doctor! Why, man, I've never been sick nor sorry since I went to school.'

'That's not hard to believe. I've ausculted you—sound as a bell, you are: constitution strong as a horse's. Still, a shock is a shock. You've a family doctor, I expect—someone you ring up when your liver goes wrong, and you want to be advised to go to Marienbad or some such place—I'd feel easier if I could shift the responsibility on to him.'

Still Mr Markham stared. 'I've heard about enough of this shock to my system,' said he at length. 'But have it your own way. If you want me to recommend a doctor, my mother swears by an old boy in Craven Street, Strand. I don't know the number, but his name's Leadbetter, and he's death on croup.'

'Craven Street? That's a trifle off Park Lane, isn't it?—Still, Leadbetter, you say? I'll get hold of the directory, look up his address, and drop him a note or two on the case by this evening's post.

A couple of hours later Mr Markham and Dick Rendal almost rubbed shoulders in the crowd of passengers shaking hands with the ever polite Captain Holditch, and bidding the *Carnatic* goodbye with the usual parting compliments; but in the hurry and bustle no one noted that the pair exchanged neither word nor look of recognition. The skipper gave Dick an honest clap on the shoulder. 'Doctor's fixed you up, then? That's right. Make the best of your holiday, and I'll see that the Board does you justice,' and with that, turned away for more hand-shaking. One small thing he did remark. When it came to Mr Markham's turn, that gentleman, before extending a hand, lifted it to his forehead and gravely saluted. But great men—as Captain Holditch knew—have their eccentric ways.

Nor was it remarked, when the luggage came to be sorted out and put on board the boat express, that Dick's porter under his direction collected and wheeled off Mr Markham's; while Mr Markham picked up Dick's suit-case, walked away with it unchallenged to a third-class smoking compartment and deposited it on the rack. There were three other passengers in the compartment. 'Good Lord!' ejaculated one, as the millionaire stepped out to purchase an evening paper. 'Isn't that Markham? Well!—and travelling third!' 'Saving habit—second nature,' said another. 'That's the way to get rich, my boy.'

Meanwhile Dick, having paid for four places, and thereby secured a first-class solitude, visited the telegraph office, and shrank the few pounds in his pocket by sending a number of cablegrams.

On the journey up Mr Markham took some annoyance from the glances of his fellow-passengers. They were furtive, almost reverential, and this could only be set down to his exploit of yesterday. He thanked Heaven they forbore to talk of it.

Chapter 4

In the back-parlour of a bookseller's shop, between the Strand and the Embankment, three persons sat at tea; the proprietor of the shop, a gray little man with round spectacles and bushy eyebrows, his wife, and a pretty girl of twenty or twenty-one. The girl apparently was a visitor, for she wore her hat, and her jacket lay across the arm of an old horsehair sofa that stood against the wall in the lamp's half shadow; and yet the gray little bookseller and his little Dresden-china wife very evidently made no stranger of her. They talked, all three, as members of a family talk, when contented and affectionate; at haphazard, taking one another for granted, not raising their voices.

The table was laid for a fourth; and by-and-by they heard him coming through the shop—in a hurry too. The old lady, always sensitive to the sound of her boy's footsteps, looked up almost in alarm, but the girl half rose from her chair, her eyes eager.

'I know,' she said breathlessly. 'Jim has heard—'

'Chrissy here? That's right.' A young man broke into the room, and stood waving a newspaper. 'The *Carnatic's* arrived—here it is under "Stop Press"—I bought the paper as I came by Somerset House—"*Carnatic* arrived at Southampton 3.45 this afternoon. Her time from Sandy Hook, 5 days, 6 hours, 45 minutes."'

'Then she hasn't broken the record this time, though Dick was positive she would,' put in the old lady. During the last six months she had developed a craze for Atlantic records, and knew the performances of all the great liners by heart.

'You bad little mother!'—Jim wagged a forefinger at her. 'You don't deserve to hear another word.'

'Is there any more?'

'More? Just you listen to this—"Reports heroic rescue. Yesterday afternoon Mr Markham, the famous Insurance King, accidentally fell overboard from fore deck, and was gallantly rescued by a young officer named Kendal"—you bet that's a misprint for Rendal—error in the wire, perhaps—we'll get a later edition after tea—"who leapt into the sea and swam to the sinking millionaire, supporting him until assistance arrived. Mr Markham had by this afternoon recovered sufficiently to travel home by the Boat Express." There, see for yourselves!'

Jim spread the newspaper on the table.

'But don't they say anything about Dick?' quavered the mother, fumbling with her glasses, while Miss Chrissy stared at the print with shining eyes.

'Dick's not a millionaire, mother—though it seems he has been supporting one—for a few minutes anyway. Well, Chrissy, how does that make you feel?'

'You see, my dear,' said the little bookseller softly, addressing his wife, 'if any harm had come to the boy, they would have reported it for certain.'

They talked over the news while Jim ate his tea, and now and again interrupted with his mouth full; talked over it and speculated upon it in low, excited tones, which grew calmer by degrees. But still a warm flush showed on the cheeks of both the women, and the little bookseller found it necessary to take out his handkerchief at intervals and wipe his round spectacles.

He was wiping them perhaps for the twentieth time, and announcing that he must go and relieve his assistant in the shop, when the assistant's voice was heard uplifted close outside—as it seemed, in remonstrance with a customer.

'Hallo!' said the little bookseller, and was rising from his chair, when the door opened. A middle-aged, Jewish-looking man, wrapped to the chin in a shabby ulster and carrying a suit-case, stood on the threshold, and regarded the little party.

'Mother!' cried Mr Markham. 'Chrissy!'

He set down the suit-case and took two eager strides. Old Mrs. Rendal, the one immediately menaced, shrank back into Jim's arms as he started up with his throat working to bolt a mouthful of cake. Chrissy caught her breath.

'Who in thunder are you, sir?' demanded Jim.

'Get out of this, unless you want to be thrown out!'

'Chrissy!' again appealed Mr Markham, but in a fainter voice. He had come to a standstill, and his hand went slowly up to his forehead.

Chrissy pointed to the suitcase. 'It's—it's Dick's!' she gasped. Jim did not hear.

'Mr Wenham,' he said to the white-faced assistant in the doorway; 'will you step out, please, and fetch a policeman?'

'Excuse me.' Mr Markham took his hand slowly from his face, and spread it behind him, groping as he stepped backwards to the door. 'I—I am not well, I think'—he spoke precisely, as though each word as it came had to be held and gripped. 'The address'—here he turned on Chrissy with a vague, apologetic smile—'faces—clear in my head. Mistake—I really beg your pardon.'

'Get him some brandy, Jim,' said the little bookseller. 'The gentleman is ill, whoever he is.'

But Mr Markham turned without another word, and lurched past the assistant, who flattened himself against a bookshelf to give him room. Jim followed him through the shop; saw him cross the doorstep and turn away down the pavement to the left; stared in his wake until the darkness and the traffic swallowed him; and returned, softly whistling, to the little parlour.

'Drunk's the simplest explanation,' he announced.

'But how did he know my name?' demanded Chrissy. 'And the suitcase!'

'Eh?' He's left it—well, if this doesn't beat the band!—Here, Wenham nip after the man and tell him he left his luggage behind!' Jim stooped to lift the case by the handle.

'But it's Dick's!'

'Dick's?'

'It's the suitcase I gave him—my birthday present last April. See, there are his initials!'

Chapter 5

Dick Rendal, alighting at Waterloo, collected his luggage—or rather, Mr Markham's—methodically; saw it hoisted on a four-wheeler; and, handing the cabby two shillings, told him to deliver it at an address in Park Lane, where the butler would pay him his exact fare. This done, he sought the telegraph office and sent three more cablegrams, the concise wording of which he had carefully evolved on the way up from Southampton. These do not come into the story,—which may digress, however, so far as to tell that on receipt of one of them, the Vice-President of the Hands Across Central New York Office remarked to his secretary 'that the old warrior was losing no time. Leisure and ozone would appear to have bucked him up.' To which the secretary answered that it was lucky for civilisation if Mr Markham missed suspecting, or he'd infallibly make a corner in both.

Having despatched his orders, Dick Rendal felt in his pockets for a cigar-case; was annoyed and amused (in a sub-conscious sort of way) to find only a briar pipe and a pocketful of coarse-cut tobacco; filled and lit his pipe, and started to walk.

His way led him across Westminster Bridge, up through Whitehall, and brought him to the steps of that building which, among all the great London clubs, most exorbitantly resembles a palace. He mounted its perron with the springy confident step of youth; and that same spring and confidence of gait carried him past the usually vigilant porter. A marble staircase led him to the lordliest smoking-room in London. He frowned, perceiving that his favourite arm-chair was occupied by a somnolent Judge of the High Court, and catching up the *Revue des Deux Mondes*, settled himself in a window-bay commanding the great twilit square of the Horse Guards and the lamp-lit Mall.

He had entered the smoking-room lightly, almost jauntily; but—not a doubt of it—he was tired—so tired that he shuffled his body twice and thrice in the arm-chair before discovering the precise angle that gave superlative comfort....

'I beg your pardon, sir.'

Dick opened his eyes. A liveried footman stood over his chair, and was addressing him.

'Eh? Did I ring? Yes, you may bring me a glass of liqueur brandy. As quickly as possible, if you please; to tell the truth, George, I'm not feeling very well.'

The man started at hearing his name, but made no motion to obey the order.

'I beg your pardon, sir, but the secretary wishes to see you in his room.'

'The secretary? Mr Hood? Yes, certainly.' Dick rose. 'I—I am afraid you must give me your arm, please. A giddiness—the ship's motion, I suppose.'

The secretary was standing at his door in the great vestibule as Dick came down the staircase on the man's arm.

'I beg your pardon,' he said, 'but may I have your name? The porter does not recognise you, and I fear that I am equally at fault.'

'My name?'—with the same gesture that Mr Markham had used in the little back parlour, Dick passed a hand over his eyes. He laughed, and even to his own ears the laugh sounded vacant, foolish.

'Are you a member of the club, sir?'

'I—I thought I was.' The marble pillars of the atrium were swaying about him like painted cloths, the tesselated pavement heaving and rocking at his feet. 'Abominably stupid of me,' he muttered, 'unpardonable, you must think.'

The secretary looked at him narrowly, and decided that he was really ill; that there was nothing in his face to suggest the impostor.

'Come into my room for a moment,' he said, and sent the footman upstairs to make sure that no small property of the Club was missing. 'Here, drink down the brandy.... Feeling better? You are aware, no doubt, that I might call in the police and have you searched?'

For a moment Dick did not answer, but stood staring with rigid eyes. At length,—

'They—won't—find—what—I—want,' he said slowly, dropping out the words one by one. The secretary now felt certain that here was a genuine case of mental derangement. With such he had no desire to be troubled; and so, the footman bringing word that nothing had been stolen, he dismissed Dick to the street.

Chapter 6

The brandy steadying him, Dick went down the steps with

a fairly firm tread. But he went down into a world that for him was all darkness—darkness of chaos—carrying an entity that was not his, but belonged Heaven knew to whom.

The streets, the traffic, meant nothing to him. Their roar was within his head; and on his ears, nostrils, chest, lay a pressure as of mighty waters. Rapidly as he walked, he felt himself all the while to be lying fathoms deep in those waters, face downwards, with drooped head, held motionless there while something within him struggled impotently to rise to the surface. The weight that held him down, almost to bursting, was as the weight of tons.

The houses, the shop-fronts, the street-lamps, the throng of dark figures, passed him in unmeaning procession. Yet all the time his feet, by some instinct, were leading him towards the water; and by-and-by he found himself staring—still face downwards—into a black inverted heaven wherein the lights had become stars and swayed only a little.

He had, in fact, halted, and was leaning over the parapet of the Embankment, a few yards from Cleopatra's Needle; and as he passed the plinth some impression of it must have bitten itself on the retina; for coiled among the stars lay two motionless sphinxes green-eyed, with sheathed claws, watching lazily while the pressure bore him down to them, and down—and still down....

Upon this dome of night there broke the echo of a footfall. A thousand footsteps had passed him, and he had heard none of them. But this one, springing out of nowhere, sang and repeated itself and re-echoed across the dome, and from edge to edge. Dick's fingers drew themselves up like the claws of the sphinx. The footsteps drew nearer while he crouched: they were close to him. Dick leapt at them, with murder in his spring.

Where the two men grappled, the parapet of the Embankment opens on a flight of river-stairs. Mr Markham had uttered no cry; nor did a sound escape either man as, locked in that wrestle, they swayed over the brink.

They were hauled up, unconscious, still locked in each other's arms.

'Queer business,' said one of the rescuers as he helped to loosen their clasp, and lift the bodies on board the Royal Humane Society's float. Looks like murderous assault. But which of 'em done it by the looks, now?'

Five minutes later Dick's eyelids fluttered. For a moment he stared up at the dingy lamp swinging overhead; then his lips parted in a cry, faint, yet sharp—

'Take care, sir! That stanchion—'

But Mr Markham's first words were, 'Plucky! devilish plucky!—owe you my life, my lad.'

Grandfather, Hendry Watty
A Droll

'Tis the nicest miss in the world that I was born grandson of my own father's father, and not of another man altogether. Hendry Watty was the name of my grandfather that might have been; and he always maintained that to all intents and purposes he *was* my grandfather, and made me call him so—'twas such a narrow shave. I don't mind telling you about it. 'Tis a curious tale, too.

My grandfather, Hendry Watty, bet four gallons of eggy-hot that he would row out to the Shivering Grounds, all in the dead waste of the night, and haul a trammel there. To find the Shivering Grounds by night, you get the Gull Rock in a line with Tregamenna and pull out till you open the light on St. Anthony's Point; but everybody gives the place a wide berth because Archelaus Rowett's lugger foundered there, one time, with six hands on board; and they say that at night you can hear the drowned men hailing their names. But my grandfather was the boldest man in Port Loe, and said he didn't care. So one Christmas Eve by daylight he and his mates went out and tilled the trammel; and then they came back and spent the fore-part of the evening over the eggy-hot, down to Oliver's tiddly-wink, to keep my grandfather's spirits up and also to show that the bet was made in earnest.

'Twas past eleven o'clock when they left Oliver's and walked down to the cove to see my grandfather off. He has told me since that he didn't feel afraid at all, but very friendly in mind, especially towards William John Dunn, who was walking on his right hand. This puzzled him at the first, for as a rule he didn't think much of William John Dunn. But now he shook hands with him several times, and just as he was stepping into the boat he says, "You'll take care of Mary Polly, while I'm away." Mary Polly Polsue was my grandfather's sweetheart at that time. But why he should have spoken as if he was bound on a long voyage he never could tell; he used to set it down to fate.

"I will," said William John Dunn; and then they gave a cheer and pushed my grandfather off, and he lit his pipe and away he rowed all into the dead waste of the night. He rowed and rowed, all in the dead waste of the night; and he got the Gull Rock in a line with Tregamenna windows; and still he was rowing, when to his great surprise he heard a voice calling:

"*Hendry Watty! Hendry Watty!*"

I told you my grandfather was the boldest man in Port Loe. But he dropped his two paddles now, and made the five signs of Penitence. For who could it be calling him out here in the dead waste and middle of the night?

"*Hendry Watty! Hendry Watty! drop me a line.*"

My grandfather kept his fishing-lines in a little skivet under the stern-sheets. But not a trace of bait had he on board. If he had, he was too much a-tremble to bait a hook.

"*Hendry Watty! Hendry Watty! drop me a line, or I'll know why!*"

My poor grandfather by this had picked up his paddles again, and was rowing like mad to get quit of the neighbourhood, when something or somebody gave three knocks—*thump, thump, thump!*—on the bottom of the boat, just as you would knock on a door. The third thump fetched Hendry Watty upright on his legs. He had no more heart for disobeying, but having bitten his pipe-stem in half by this time—his teeth chattered so—he baited his hook with the broken bit and flung it overboard, letting the line run out in the stern-notch. Not halfway had it run before he felt a long pull on it, like the sucking of a dog-fish.

"*Hendry Watty! Hendry Watty! pull me in.*"

Hendry Watty pulled in hand over fist; and in came the lead sinker over the notch, and still the line was heavy; he pulled and he pulled, and next, all out of the dead waste of the night, came two white hands, like a washerwoman's, and gripped hold of the stern-board; and on the left of these two hands, on the little finger, was a silver ring, sunk very deep in the flesh. If this was bad, worse was the face that followed—a great white parboiled face, with the hair and whiskers all stuck with chips of wood and seaweed. And if this was bad for anybody, it was worse for my grandfather, who had known Archelaus Rowett before he was drowned out on the Shivering Grounds, six years before.

Archelaus Rowett climbed in over the stern, pulled the hook with the bit of pipe-stem out of his cheek, sat down in the stern-sheets, shook a small crayfish out of his whiskers, and said very coolly—

"If you should come across my wife—"

That was all my grandfather stayed to hear. At the sound of Archelaus's voice he fetched a yell, jumped clean over the side of the boat and swam for dear life. He swam and swam, till by the bit of the moon he saw the Gull Rock close ahead. There were lashin's of rats on the Gull Rock, as he knew: but he was a good deal surprised at the way they were behaving: for they sat in a row at the water's edge and fished, with their tails let down into the sea for fishing-lines: and their eyes were like garnets burning as they looked at my grandfather over their shoulders.

"Hendry Watty! Hendry Watty! You can't land here—you're disturbing the pollack."

"Bejimbers! I wouldn' do that for the world," says my grandfather: so off he pushes and swims for the mainland. This was a long job, and 'twas as much as he could do to reach Kibberick beach, where he fell on his face and hands among the stones, and there lay, taking breath.

The breath was hardly back in his body, before he heard footsteps, and along the beach came a woman, and passed close by to him. He lay very quiet, and as she came near he saw 'twas Sarah Rowett, that used to be Archelaus's wife, but had married another man since. She was knitting as she went by, and did not seem to notice my grandfather: but he heard her say to herself, "The hour is come, and the man is come."

He had scarcely begun to wonder over this, when he spied a ball of worsted yarn beside him that Sarah had dropped. 'Twas the ball she was knitting from, and a line of worsted stretched after her along the beach. Hendry Watty picked up the ball and followed the thread on tiptoe. In less than a minute he came near enough to watch what she was doing: and what she did was worth watching. First she gathered wreckwood and straw, and struck flint over touchwood and teened a fire. Then she unravelled her knitting: twisted her end of the yarn between finger and thumb—like a cobbler twisting a wax-end—and cast the end up towards the sky. It made Hendry Watty stare when the thread, instead of falling back to the ground, remained hanging, just as if 'twas fastened to something up above; but it made him stare more when Sarah Rowett began to climb up it, and away up till nothing could be seen of her but her ankles dangling out of the dead waste and middle of the night.

"*Hendry Watty! Hendry Watty!*"

It wasn't Sarah calling, but a voice far away out to sea.

"*Hendry Watty! Hendry Watty! send me a line.*"

My grandfather was wondering what to do, when Sarah speaks down very sharp to him, out of the dark:

"Hendry Watty! Where's the rocket apparatus? Can't you hear the poor fellow asking for a line?"

"I do," says my grandfather, who was beginning to lose his temper; "and do you think, ma'am, that I carry a Boxer's rocket in my trousers pocket?"

"I think you have a ball of worsted in your hand," says she. "Throw it as far as you can."

So my grandfather threw the ball out into the dead waste and middle of the night. He didn't see where it pitched, or how far it went.

"Right it is," says the woman aloft. "'Tis easy seen you're a hurler. But what shall us do for a cradle? Hendry Watty! Hendry

Watty!"

"Ma'am to *you*," says my grandfather.

"If you've the common feelings of a gentleman, I'll ask you kindly to turn your back; I'm going to take off my stocking."

So my grandfather stared the other way very politely; and when he was told he might look again, he saw she had tied the stocking to the line and was running it out like a cradle into the dead waste of the night.

"Hendry Watty! Hendry Watty! Look out below!"

Before he could answer, plump! a man's leg came tumbling past his ear and scattered the ashes right and left.

"Hendry Watty! Hendry Watty! Look out below!"

This time 'twas a great white arm and hand, with a silver ring sunk tight in the flesh of the little finger.

"Hendry Watty! Hendry Watty! Warm them limbs!"

My grandfather picked them up and was warming them before the fire, when down came tumbling a great round head and bounced twice and lay in the firelight, staring up at him. And whose head was it but Archelaus Rowett's, that he'd run away from once already, that night?

"Hendry Watty! Hendry Watty! Look out below!"

This time 'twas another leg, and my grandfather was just about to lay hands on it, when the woman called down:

"Hendry Watty! catch it quick! It's my own leg I've thrown down by mistake!"

The leg struck the ground and bounced high, and Hendry Watty made a leap after it....

And I reckon it's asleep he must have been: for what he caught was not Mrs. Rowett's leg, but the jib-boom of a deep-laden brigantine that was running him down in the dark. And as he sprang for it, his boat was crushed by the brigantine's forefoot and went down under his very boot-soles. At the same time he let out a yell, and two or three of the crew ran forward and hoisted him up to the bowsprit and in on deck, safe and sound.

But the brigantine happened to be outward-bound for the River Plate; so that, what with one thing and another, 'twas eleven good months before my grandfather landed again at Port Loe. And who should be the first man he sees standing above the cove but William John Dunn?

"I'm very glad to see you," says William John Dunn.

"Thank you kindly," answers my grandfather; "and how's Mary Polly?"

"Why, as for that," he says, "she took so much looking after, that I couldn't feel I was keeping her properly under my eye till I married her, last June month."

"You was always one to over-do things," said my grandfather.

"But if you was alive an' well, why didn' you drop us a line?"

Now when it came to talk about "dropping a line" my grandfather fairly lost his temper. So he struck William John Dunn on the nose a thing he had never been known to do before—and William John Dunn hit him back, and the neighbours had to separate them. And next day, William John Dunn took out a summons against him.

Well, the case was tried before the magistrates: and my grandfather told his story from the beginning, quite straightforward, just as I've told it to you. And the magistrates decided that, taking one thing with another, he'd had a great deal of provocation, and fined him five shillings. And there the matter ended. But now you know the reason why I'm William John Dunn's grandson instead of Hendry Watty's.

Not Here, O Apollo
A Christmas Story Heard at Midsummer

We sat and talked in the vicarage garden overlooking Mount's Bay. The long summer day lingered out its departure, although the full moon was up and already touching with a faint radiance the towers on St. Michael's Mount—'the guarded Mount'—that rested as though at anchor in the silver-grey offing. The land-breeze had died down with sunset; the Atlantic lay smooth as a lake below us, and melted, league upon league, without horizon into the grey of night. Between the vicar's fuchsia-bushes we looked down on it, we three—the vicar, the senior tutor and I.

I think the twilit hour exactly accorded with our mood, and it did not need the scent of the vicar's ten-week stocks, wafted across the garden, to touch a nerve of memory. For it was twenty years since we had last sat in this place and talked, and the summer night seemed to be laden with tranquil thoughts, with friendship and old regard. ...Twenty years ago I had been an undergraduate, and had made one of a reading-party under the senior tutor, who annually in the Long Vacation brought down two or three fourth-year men to bathe and boat and read Plato with him, for no pay but their friendship: and, generation after generation, we young men had been made welcome in this garden by the vicar, who happened to be an old member of our College and (as in time I came to see) delighted to renew his youth in ours. There had been daughters, too, in the old days. . . . But they had married, and the vicarage nest was empty long since.

The senior tutor, too, had given up work and retired upon his fellowship. But every summer found him back at his old haunts; and still every summer brought a reading-party to the Cove, in conduct now of a brisk junior fellow, who had read with me in our time and achieved a "first." In short, things at the cove were pretty much the same after twenty years, barring that a small colony of painters had descended upon it and made it their home. With them the undergraduates had naturally and quickly made friends, and the result was a cricket match—a grand Two-days' Cricket Match. They were all extremely serious about it, and the Oxford party—at their wits' end, no doubt, to make up a team against the artists—had bethought themselves of me, who dwelt at the other end of the duchy. They had written—they had even sent a two-page telegram—to me, who had not handled a bat for more years than I cared to count. It is delicious to be flattered by youth, especially for gifts you never possessed or possess no longer. I yielded and came. The season was midsummer, or a little after; the weather golden and glorious.

We had drawn stumps after the first day's play, and the evening was to be wound up with a sing-song in the great tent erected—a marvel to the "Covers," or native fishermen—on the cricket-field. But I no longer take kindly to such entertainments; and so, after a bathe and a quiet dinner at the inn, it came into my mind to take a stroll up the hill and along the cliffs, and pay an evening call on the old vicar, wondering if he would remember me.

I found him in his garden. The senior tutor was there too—"the grave man, nicknamed Adam"—and the vicar's wife, seated in a bee-hive straw chair, knitting. So we four talked happily for a while, until she left us on pretence that the dew was falling; and with that, as I have said, a wonderful silence possessed the garden fragrant with memories and the night-scent of flowers. . .

Then I let fall the word that led to the vicar's story. In old rambles, after long mornings spent with Plato, my eyes (by mirage, no doubt) had always found something Greek in the curves and colour of this coast; or rather, had felt the want of it. What that something was I could hardly have defined: but the feeling was always with me. It was as if at each bend of the shore I expected to find a temple with pillars, or a column crowning the next promontory; or, where the coast-track wound down to the little haven, to happen on a votive tablet erected to Poseidon or to "Helen's brothers, lucent stars"; nay, to meet with Odysseus' fisherman carrying an oar on his shoulder, or even, in an amphitheatre of the cliffs, to surprise Apollo himself and the Nine seated on a green plat whence a waterfall gushed down the coombe to the sandy beach.... This evening on my way along the cliffs—perhaps because I had spent a day bathing in sunshine in the company of white-flannelled youths—the old sensation had returned to haunt me. I spoke of it.

"'*Not here, O Apollo*—'" murmured the senior tutor.

"You quote against your own scepticism," said I. "The coast is right enough; it *is*"

Where Helicon breaks down
In cliff to the sea.

"It was made to invite the authentic gods—only the gods never found it out."

"Did they not?" asked the vicar quietly. The question took us a little aback, and after a pause his next words administered another small shock. "One never knows," he said, "when, or how near, the gods have passed. One may be listening to us in this garden, tonight....As for the Greeks—"

"Yes, yes, we were talking of the Greeks," the senior tutor (a convinced agnostic) put in hastily. "If we leave out Pytheas, no Greeks ever visited Cornwall. They are as mythical hereabouts as"— he hesitated, seeking a comparison—"as the Cornish wreckers; and *they* never existed outside of pious story-books."

Said the vicar, rising from his garden-chair, "I accept the omen. Wait a moment, you two." He left us and went across the dim lawn to the house, whence by and by he returned bearing a book under his arm, and in his hand a candle, which he set down unlit upon the wicker table among the coffee-cups.

"I am going," he said, "to tell you something which, a few years ago, I should have scrupled to tell. With all deference to your opinions, my dear Dick, I doubt if they quite allow you to understand the clergy's horror of chancing a heresy; indeed, I doubt if either of you quite guess what a bridle a man comes to wear who preaches a hundred sermons or so every year to a rural parish, knowing that nine-tenths of his discourse will assuredly be lost, while at any point in the whole of it he may be fatally misunderstood.... Yet as a man nears his end he feels an increasing desire to be honest, neither professing more than he knows, nor hiding any small article of knowledge as inexpedient to the Faith. The Faith, he begins to see, can take care of itself: for him, it is important to await his marching-orders with a clean breast. Eh, Dick?"

The senior tutor took his pipe from his mouth and nodded slowly.

"But what is your book?" he asked.

"My Parish Register. Its entries cover the years from 1660 to 1827. Luckily I had borrowed it from the vestry box, and it was safe on my shelf in the vicarage on the Christmas Eve of 1870, the night when the church took fire. That was in my second year as incumbent, and before ever you knew these parts."

"By six months," said the senior tutor. "I first visited the cove in July, 1871, and you were then beginning to clear the ruins. All the village talk still ran on the fire, with speculations on the cause of it."

"The cause," said the vicar, "will never be known. I may say that pretty confidently, having spent more time in guessing than will ever be spent by another man.... But since you never saw the old church as it stood, you never saw the heathen lovers in the south aisle."

"Who were they?"

"They were a group of statuary, and a very strange one; executed, as I first believed, in some kind of wax—but, pushing my researches (for the thing interested me) I found the material to be a white soapstone that crops out here and there in the crevices of our serpentine. Indeed, I know to a foot the spot from which the sculptor took it, close on two hundred years ago."

"It was of no great age, then?"

"No: and yet it bore all the marks of an immense age. For to begin with, it had stood five-and-twenty years in this very garden, exposed to all weathers, and the steatite (as they call it) is of all substances the most friable—is, in fact, the stuff used by tailors under the name of French chalk. Again, when, in 1719, my predecessor, old Vicar Hichens, removed it to the church and set it in the south aisle—or, at any rate, when he died and ceased to protect it—the young men of the parish took to using it for a hatstand, and also to carving their own and their sweethearts' names upon it during sermon-time. The figures of the sculpture were two; a youth and a maid, recumbent, and naked but for a web of drapery flung across their middles; and they lay on a roughly carved rock, over which the girl's locks as well as the drapery were made to hang limp, as though dripping with water.... One thing more I must tell you, risking derision; that to my ignorance the sculpture proclaimed its age less by these signs of weather and rough usage than by the simplicity of its design, its proportions, the chastity (there's no other word) of the two figures. They were classical, my dear Dick—what was left of them; Greek, and of the best period."

The senior tutor lit a fresh pipe, and by the flare of the match I saw his eyes twinkling.

"Praxiteles," he jerked out, between the puffs, "and in the age of Kneller! But proceed, my friend."

"And do you wait, my scoffer!" The vicar borrowed the box of matches, lit the candle—which held a steady flame in the still evening air—opened the book, and laid it on his knee while he adjusted his spectacles. "The story is here, entered on a separate leaf of the register and signed by Vicar Hichens' own hand. With your leave—for it is brief—I am going to read it through to you. The entry is headed:"

Concerning a group of Statuary now in the S. aisle of Lezardew Parish Church: set there by me in witness of God's Providence in operation, as of the corruption of man's heart, and for a warning to sinners to amend their ways.

In the year 1694, being the first of my vicariate, there lived in this Parish as hind to the farmer of Vellancoose a young man exceeding comely and tall of stature, of whom (when I came to ask) the people could tell me only that his name was Luke, and that as a child he had been cast ashore from a foreign ship; they said, a Portugal ship. [But the Portugals have swart complexions and are less than ordinary tall, whereas this youth was light-coloured and only brown by sunburn.] Nor could he tell me anything when I questioned him concerning his haveage; which I did upon report that he was courting my housemaiden Grace Pascoe, an honest good girl, whom I was loth to see waste herself upon an unworthy husband.

Upon inquiry I could not discover this Luke to be any way unworthy, saving that he was a nameless man and a foreigner and a backward church-goer. He told me with much simplicity that he could not remember to have had any parents; that Farmer Lowry had brought him up from the time he was shipwrecked and ever treated him kindly; and that, as for church-going, he had thought little about it, but would amend in this matter if it would give me pleasure. Which I thought a strange answer. When I went on to hint at his inclination for Grace Pascoe, he confused me by asking, with a look very straight and good-natured, if the girl had ever spoken to me on the matter; to which I was forced to answer that she had not. So he smiled, and I could not further press him.

Yet in my mind they would have made a good match; for the girl too was passing well-featured, and this Luke had notable gifts. He could read and write. The farmer spoke well of him, saying, "He has rewarded me many times over. Since his coming, thanks to the Lord, my farm prospers: and in particular he has a wonderful way with the beasts. Cattle or sheep, fowls, dogs, the wild things even, come to him almost without a call." He had also (the farmer told me) a wonderful knack of taking clay or mud and moulding it with his hands to the likeness of living creatures, of all sorts and sizes. In the kitchen by the great fire he would work at these images by hours together, to the marvel of everyone: but when the image was made, after a little while he always destroyed it; nor was it ever begged by anyone for a gift, there being a belief that, being fashioned by more than a man's skill, such things could only bring ill-luck to the possessors of them.

For months then I heard no more of Grace Pascoe's lover: nor (though he now came every Sunday to church) did I ever see looks pass between the vicarage pew (where she sat) and the Vellancoose pew (where he). But at the end of the year she came to me and told me she had given her word to a young farmer of Goldsithney, John Magor by name. In a worldly way this was a far better match for her than to take a nameless and landless man. Nor knew I anything against John Magor beyond some stray wildness natural to youth. He came of clean blood. He was handsome, almost as the other; tall, broad of chest, a prize-winner at wrestling-matches; and of an age when a good wife is usually a man's salvation.

I called their banns, and in due time married them. On the wedding-day, after the ceremony, I returned from church to find the young man Luke awaiting me by my house-door; who very civilly desired me to walk over to Vellancoose with him, which I did. There, taking me aside to an unused linhay, he showed me the sculpture, telling me (who could not conceal my admiration) that he had meant it for John and Grace Magor (as she now was) for a wedding-gift, but that the young woman had cried out against it as immodest and, besides, unlucky.

On the first count I could understand her rejecting such a gift; for the folk of these parts know nothing of statuary and count all nakedness immodest. Indeed, I wondered that the bridegroom had not taken Luke's freedom in ill part, and I said so: to which he answered, smiling, that no man ever quarrelled with him or could quarrel. "And now, sir," he went on, "my apprenticeship is up, and I am going on a long journey. Since you find my group pleasing I would beg you to accept it, or—if you had liefer—to keep it for me until I come again, as some day I shall."

"I do not wonder," said I, "at your wish to leave Lezardew Parish for the world where, as I augur, great fortune awaits you."

He smiled again at this and said that, touching his future, he had neither any hope nor any fear: and again he pressed me to accept the statuary. For a time I demurred, and in the end made it a condition that he altered the faces somewhat, concealing the likeness to John and Grace Magor: and to this he consented. "Yet," said he, "it will be the truer likeness when the time comes."

He was gone on the morrow by daybreak, and late that afternoon the farmer brought me the statuary in his haywagon. I had it set in the garden by the great filberd-tree, and there it has stood for near five-and-twenty years. (I ought to say that he had kept his promise of altering the faces, and thereby to my thinking had defaced their beauty: but beneath this defacement I still traced their first likeness.)

Now to speak of the originals. My way lying seldom by Goldsithney, I saw little of John and Grace Magor during the next few years, and nothing at all of them after they had left Goldsithney (their fortunes not prospering) and rented a smaller farm on the coast southward, below Rosudgeon: but what news came to me was ever of the same tenour. Their marriage had brought neither children nor other blessings. There were frequent quarrels, and the man had yielded to drinking; the woman, too, it was reported. She, that had been so trim a serving-maid, was become a slut with a foul tongue. They were cruelly poor with it all; for money does not always stick to unclean hands. I write all this to my reproach as well as to theirs, for albeit they dwelt in another parish it had been my Christian duty to seek them out. I did not, and I was greatly to blame.

To pass over many years and come to the 2nd of December last (1718). That night, about 11 o'clock, I sat in my library reading. It was blowing hard without, the wind W.N.W.; but I had forgotten the gale in my book, when a sound, as it were a distant outcry of many voices, fetched me to unbar the shutters and open the window to listen. The sound, whatever it was, had died away: I heard but the wind roaring and the surf on the beaches along the Bay: and I was closing the window again when, close at hand, a man's voice called to me to open the front door. I went out to the hall, where a lamp stood, and opened to him.

The light showed me the young man Luke, on whom I had not set eyes for these four-and-twenty years: nor, amazed and perturbed as I was, did it occur to me as marvellous that he had not aged a day. "There is a wreck," said he, "in the Porth below here; and you, sir, are concerned in it. Will you fetch a lantern and come with me?" He put this as a question, but in his tone was a command: and when I brought the lantern he took it from me and led the way. We struck across the Home Parc southward, thence across Gew Down and the Leazes, and I knew that he was making for the track which leads down to the sea by Prah Sands.

At the entry of the track he took off his coat and wrapped the lantern in it, though just there its light would have been most useful, or so I thought. But he led the way easily, and I followed with scarce a stumble. "We shall not need it," he said; "for see, there they are!" pointing to a small light that moved on the sands below us. "But who are they?" I asked. He strode down ahead of me, making swiftly for the light, and coming upon them in the noise of the gale we surprised a man and a woman, who at first cowered before us and then would have cast down their light and run. But my companion, unwrapping the lantern, held it high and so that the light shone on their faces. They were John Magor and his wife Grace.

Then I, remembering what cry of shipwrecked souls had reached to my library in the vicarage, and well guessing what work these wretches had been at, lifted my voice to accuse them. But the young man Luke stepped between us, and said he to them gently, "Come, and I will show what you seek." He went before us for maybe two hundred yards to the northern end of the beach, they behind him quaking, and I shepherding them in my righteous wrath. "Behold you," said he, and again lifted the lantern over a rock dark with seaweed (and yet the weed shone in the light)—"Behold you, what you have wrecked."

On their backs along the flat of the rock lay two naked bodies, of a youth and a maid, half-clasped one to another. He handed me the lantern for a better look, and in the rays of it the two wretches peered forward as if drawn against their will. I cannot well say if they or I first perceived the miracle; that these corpses, as they lay in the posture, so bore the very likeness of the two lovers on my sculptured slab. But I remember that, as John and Grace Magor screamed back and clung to me, and as by the commotion of them clutching at my knees the lantern fell and was extinguished, I heard the young man Luke say, "Yourselves, yourselves!"

I called to him to pick up the lantern; but he did not answer, and the two clinging wretches encumbered me. After a long while the clouds broke and the moon shone through them; and where he had stood there was no one. Also the slab of rock was dark, and the two drowned corpses had vanished with him. I pointed to it; but there was no tinder-box at hand to light the lantern again, and in the bitter weather until the dawn the two clung about me, confessing and rehearsing their sins.

I have great hopes that they are brought to a better way of life; and because (repent they never so much) no one is any longer likely to recognise in these penitents the originals upon whom it was moulded these many years ago, I am determined to move the statuary to a place in the S. aisle of our parish church, as a memorial, the moral whereof I have leave of John and Grace Magor to declare to all the parish. I choose to defer making it public, in tenderness, while they live: for all things point as yet to the permanent saving of their souls. But, as in the course of nature I shall predecease them, I set the record here in the Parish Register, as its best place.

  (Signed)   Malachi Hichens, B.D.
                 21st Jan., 1719.

"And is that all?" I asked.

"Yes and no," said the vicar, closing the book. "It is all that Mr. Hichens has left to help us: and you may or may not connect with it what I am going to relate of my own experience.... The old church, as you know, was destroyed by fire in the morning hours of Christmas Day, 1870. Throughout Christmas Eve and for a great part of the night it had been snowing, but the day broke brilliantly, on a sky without wind or cloud; and never have my eyes seen anything so terribly beautiful—ay, so sublime—as the sight which met them at the lych-gate.

"The old spire—which served as a sea-mark for the fishermen, and was kept regularly white-washed that it might be the more conspicuous—glittered in the morning sunshine from base to summit, as though matching its whiteness against that of the snow-laden elms: and in this frame of pure silver-work, burning without noise and with scarcely any smoke—this by reason of the excessive dryness of the woodwork—the church stood one glowing vault of fire. There was indeed so little smoke that at the first alarm, looking from my bedroom window, I had been incredulous; and still I wondered rather than believed, staring into this furnace wherein every pillar, nook, seat or text on the wall was distinctly visible, the south windows being burnt out and the great door thrown open and on fire.

"There was no entrance possible here, or indeed anywhere:

but, being half-distraught, I ran around to the small door of the north aisle. This, too, was on fire—or, rather, was already consumed; and you will say that I must have been wholly distraught when I tell you what I saw, looking in through the aperture through which it would have been death to pass. I saw *him*."

"You saw the young man Luke?" I asked, as he paused, inviting a word.

"He was standing by the stone figures within the porch.... And they crumbled—crumbled before my eyes in the awful heat. But he stood scatheless. He was young and comely; the hair of his head was not singed. He was as one of the three that walked in the midst of Nebuchadnezzar's furnace.... When the stone slab was crumbled to a handful of dust, he moved up the aisle and was gone.... That is all: but, as you accept your friend for a truthful man, explain, O sceptic!"

—And again there fell a silence in the garden.

Oceanus

1

My Dear Violet,—So you "gather from the tone of two or three recent letters that my spirit is creeping back to light and warmth again"? Well, after a fashion you are right. I shall never laugh again as I used to laugh before Harry's death. The taste has gone out of that carelessness, and I turn even from the remembrance of it. But I can be cheerful, with a cheerfulness which has found the centre of gravity. I am myself again, as people say. After months of agitation in what seemed to be chaos the lost atom has dropped back to its place in the scheme of things, and even aspires (poor mite!) to do its infinitesimal business intelligently. So might a mote in a sunbeam feel itself at one with God!

But when you assume that my recovery has been a gradual process, you are wrong. You will think me more than ever deranged; but I assure you that it has been brought about, not by long strivings, but suddenly—without preparation of mine—*and by the immediate hand of our dead brother.*

Yes; you shall have the whole tale. The first effect of the news of Harry's death in October last was simply to stun me. You may remember how once, years ago when we were children, we rode home together across the old racecourse after a long day's skating, our skates swinging at our saddle-bows; how Harry challenged us to a gallop; and how, midway, the roan mare slipped down neck over crop on the frozen turf and hurled me clean against the face of a stone dyke. I had been thrown from horseback more than once before, but somehow had always found the earth fairly elastic. So I had griefs before Harry died and took some rebound of hope from each: but that cast repeated in a worse degree the old shock—the springless brutal jar—of the stone dyke. With him the sun went out of my sky.

I understand that this torpor is quite common with men and women suddenly bereaved. I believe that a whole week passed before my brain recovered any really vital motion; and then such feeble thought as I could exert was wholly occupied with the desperate stupidity of the whole affair. If God were indeed shaping the world to any end, if any design of His underlay the activities of men, what insensate waste to quench such a heart and brain as Harry's!—to nip, as it seemed out of mere blundering wantonness, a bud which had begun to open so generously: to sacrifice that youth and strength, that comeliness, that enthusiasm, and all for nothing!

Had some campaign claimed him, had he been spent to gain a citadel or defend a flag, I had understood. But that he should be killed on a friendly mission; attacked in ignorance by those East Coast savages while bearing gifts to their king; deserted by the porters whose comfort (on their own confession) he had studied throughout the march; left to die, to be tortured, mutilated—and all for no possible good: these things I could not understand. At the end he might have escaped; but as he caught hold of his saddle by the band between the holsters, it parted: it was not leather, but faced paper, the job of some cheating contractor. I thought of this, too. And Harry had been through Chitral!

But though a man may hate, he cannot easily despise God for long. "He is great—but wasteful," said the American. We are the dust on His great hands, and fly as He claps them carelessly in the pauses of His work. Yet this theory would not do at all: for the unlucky particles are not dust, not refuse, but exquisite and exquisitely fashioned, designed to *live*, and to every small function of life adapted with the minutest care. There were nights indeed when, walking along the shore where we had walked together on the night before Harry left England and looking from the dark waters which divided me from his grave up to the nightly moon and to the stars around her, I could well believe God wasteful of little things.

Sirius flashing low, Orion's belt with the great nebula swinging like a pendant of diamonds; the ruby stars, Betelgueux and Aldebaran—my eyes went up beyond these to Perseus shepherding the Kids westward along the Milky way. From the right Andromeda flashed signals to him: and above sat Cassiopeia, her mother, resting her jewelled wrists on the arms of her throne. Low in the east Jupiter trailed his satellites in the old moon's path. As they all moved, silent, looking down on me out of the hollow spaces of the night, I could believe no splendid waste too costly for their perfection: and the Artificer who hung them there after millions of years of patient effort, if more intelligible than a God who produced them suddenly at will, certainly not less divine.

But walking the same shore by daylight I recognised that the shells, the mosses, the flowers I trampled on, were, each in its way, as perfect as those great stars: that on these—and on Harry—as surely as on the stars—God had spent, if not infinite pains, then at least so superlative a wisdom that to conceive of them as wastage was to deny the mind which called them forth.

There they were: and that He who had skill to create them could blunder in using them was simply incredible.

But this led to worse: for having to admit the infallible design, I now began to admire it as an exquisite scheme of evil, and to accuse God of employing supreme knowledge and skill to gratify a royal lust of cruelty. For a month and more this horrible theory justified itself in all innocent daily sights. Throughout my country walks I "saw blood." I heard the rabbit run squeaking before the weasel; I watched the butcher crow working steadily down the hedge. If I turned seaward I looked beneath the blue and saw the dog-fish gnawing on the whiting. If I walked in the garden I surprised the thrush dragging worms from the turf, the cat slinking on the nest, the spider squatting in ambush. Behind the rosy face of every well-nourished child I saw a lamb gazing up at the butcher's knife. My dear Violet, that was a hideous time!

And just then by chance a book fell into my hands—Lamartine's *Chute d'un Ange*. Do you know the Seventh and Tenth Visions of that poem, which describe the favourite amusements of the Men-gods? Before the Deluge, beyond the rude tents of the nomad shepherds, there rose city upon city of palaces built of jasper and porphyry, splendid and utterly corrupt; inhabited by men who called themselves gods and explored the subtleties of all sciences to minister to their vicious pleasures. At ease on soft couches, in hanging gardens set with fountains, these beings feasted with every refinement of cruelty. Kneeling slaves were their living tables; while for their food—

> *Tous les oiseaux de l'air, tous les poissons de l'onde,*
> *Tout ce qui vole ou nage ou rampe dans le monde,*
> *Mourant pour leur plaisir des plus cruels trepas*
> *De sanglantes savours composent leurs repas. . . .*

In these lines I believed that I discerned the very God of the universe, the God whom men worship—

> *Dans les infames jeux de leur divin loisir*
> *Le supplice de l'homme est leur premier plaisir.*
> *Pour que leur oeil feroce a l'envi s'en repaisse*
> *Des bourreaux devant eux en immolent sans cesse.*
> *Tantot ils font lutter, dans des combats affreux,*
> *L'homme contre la brute et les hommes entre eux,*
> *Aux longs ruisseaux de sang qui coulent de la veine,*
> *Aux palpitations des membres sur l'arene,*
> *Se levant a demi de leurs lits de repos*
> *Des frissons de plaisir fremissent sur leurs peaux.*
> *Le cri de la torture est leur douce harmonie,*
> *Et leur oeil dans son oeil boit sa lente agonie.*

I charged the Supreme Power with a cruelty deliberate, ruthless, serene. Nero the tyrant once commanded a representation in grim earnest of the Flight of Icarus; and the unhappy boy who took the part, at his first attempt to fly, fell headlong beside the emperor's couch and spattered him with blood and brains. For the emperor, says Suetonius, *perraro praesidere, ceterum accubans, parvis primum foraminibus, deinde toto podio adaperto, spectare consuerat*. So I believed that on the stage of this world men agonised for the delight of one cruel intelligence which watched from behind the curtain of a private box.

2

In this unhappy condition of mind, then, I was lying in my library chair here at Sevenhays, at two o'clock on the morning of January 4th. I had just finished another reading of the Tenth Vision and had tossed my book into the lap of an armchair opposite. Fire and lamp were burning brightly. The night outside was still and soundless, with a touch of frost.

I lay there, retracing in thought the circumstances of Harry's last parting from me, and repeating to myself a scrap here and there from the three letters he wrote on his way—the last of them, full of high spirits, received a full three weeks after the telegram which announced his death. There was a passage in this last letter describing a wonderful ride he had taken alone and by moonlight on the desert; a ride (he protested) which wanted nothing of perfect happiness but me, his friend, riding beside him to share his wonder. There was a sentence which I could not recall precisely, and I left my chair and was crossing the room towards the drawer in the writing-table where I kept his letters, when I heard a trampling of hoofs on the gravel outside, and then my Christian name called—with distinctness, but not at all loudly.

I went to the window, which was unshuttered; drew up the blind and flung up the sash. The moon, in its third quarter and about an hour short of its meridian, shone over the deodars upon the white gravel. And there, before the front door, sat Harry on his sorrel mare Vivandiere, holding my own Grey Sultan ready bridled and saddled. He was dressed in his old khaki riding suit, and his face, as he sat askew in his saddle and looked up towards my window, wore its habitual and happy smile.

Now, call this and what follows a dream, vision, hallucination, what you will; but understand, please, that from the first moment, so far as I considered the matter at all, I had never the least illusion that this was Harry in flesh and blood. I knew quite well all the while that Harry was dead and his body in his grave. But, soul or phantom—whatever relation to Harry this might bear—it had come to me, and the great joy of that was enough for the time. There let us leave the question. I closed the window, went upstairs to my dressing-room, drew on my riding-boots and overcoat, found cap, gloves, and riding-crop, and descended to the porch.

Harry, as I shall call him, was still waiting there on the off side of Grey Sultan, the farther side from the door. There could be no doubt, at any rate, that the grey was real horseflesh and blood, though he seemed unusually quiet after two days in stall. Harry freed him as I mounted, and we set off together at a walk, which we kept as far as the gate.

Outside we took the westward road, and our horses broke into a trot. As yet we had not exchanged a word; but now he asked a question or two about his people and his friends; kindly, yet most casually, as one might who returns after a week's holidaying. I answered as well as I could, with trivial news of their health. His mother had borne the winter better than usual—to be sure, there had been as yet no cold weather to speak of; but she and Ethel intended, I believed, to start for the south of France early in February. He inquired about you. His comments were such as a man makes on hearing just what he expects to hear, or knows beforehand. And for some time it seemed to be tacitly taken for granted between us that I should ask him no questions.

"As for me—" I began, after a while.

He checked the mare's pace a little. "I know," he said, looking straight ahead between her ears; then, after a pause, "it has been a bad time for you, You are in a bad way altogether. That is why I came."

"But it was for *you!*" I blurted out. "Harry, if only I had known why *you* were taken—and what it was to *you!*"

He turned his face to me with the old confident comforting smile.

"Don't you trouble about *that. That's* nothing to make a fuss about. Death?" he went on musing—our horses had fallen to a walk again—"It looks you in the face a moment: you put out your hands: you touch—and so it is gone. My dear boy, it isn't for us that you need worry."

"For whom, then?"

"Come," said he, and he shook Vivandiere into a canter.

3

I cannot remember precisely at what point in our ride the country had ceased to be familiar. But by-and-by we were climbing the lower slopes of a great down which bore no resemblance to the pastoral country around Sevenhays. We had left the beaten road for short turf—apparently of a copper-brown hue, but this may have been the effect of the moonlight. The ground rose steadily, but with an easy inclination, and we climbed with the wind at our backs; climbed, as it seemed, for an hour, or maybe two, at a footpace, keeping silence. The happiness of having Harry beside me took away all desire for speech.

This at least was my state of mind as we mounted the long lower slopes of the down. But in time the air, hitherto so exhilarating, began to oppress my lungs, and the tranquil happiness to give way to a vague discomfort and apprehension.

"What is this noise of water running?"

I reined up Grey Sultan as I put the question. At the same moment it occurred to me that this sound of water, distant and continuous, had been running in my ear for a long while.

Harry, too, came to a halt. With a sweep of the arm that embraced the dim landscape around and ahead, he quoted softly—

> *en detithei potamoio mega spenos Okeanoio antyga par pymaten sakeos pyka poietoio* . . . .

. . . and was silent again.

I recalled at once and distinctly the hot summer morning ten years back, when we had prepared that passage of the Eighteenth Book together in our study at Clifton; I at the table, Harry lolling in the cane-seated armchair with the Liddell and Scott open on his knees; outside, the sunny close and the fresh green of the lime-trees.

Now that I looked more attentively the bare down, on which we climbed like flies, did indeed resemble a vast round shield, about the rim of which this unseen water echoed. And the resemblance grew more startling when, a mile or so farther on our way, as the grey dawn overtook us, Harry pointed upwards and ahead to a small boss or excrescence now lifting itself above the long curve of the horizon.

At first I took it for a hummock or tumulus. Then, as the day whitened about us, I saw it to be a building—a tall, circular barrack not unlike the Colosseum. A question shaped itself on my lips, but something in Harry's manner forbade it. His gaze was bent steadily forward, and I kept my wonder to myself, and also the oppression of spirit which had now grown to something like physical torture.

When first the great barrack broke into sight we must have been at least two miles distant. I kept my eyes fastened on it as we approached, and little by little made out the details of its architecture. From base to summit—which appeared to be roofless—six courses of many hundred arches ran around the building, one above the other; and between each pair a course, as it seemed, of plain worked stone, though I afterwards found it to be sculptured in low relief. The arches were cut in deep relief and backed with undressed stone. The lowest course of all, however, was quite plain, having neither arches nor frieze; but at intervals corresponding to the eight major points of the compass—so far as I who saw but one side of it could judge—pairs of gigantic stone figures supported archways pierced in the wall; or sluices, rather, since from every archway but one a full stream of water issued and poured down the sides of the hill.

The one dry archway was that which faced us with open gate, and towards which Harry led the way; for oppression and terror now weighted my hand as with lead upon Grey Sultan's rein.

Harry, however, rode forward resolutely, dismounted almost in the very shadow of the great arch, and waited, smoothing his mare's neck. But for the invitation in his eyes, which were solemn, yet without a trace of fear, I had never dared that last hundred yards. For above the rush of waters I heard now a confused sound within the building—the thud and clanking of heavy machinery, and at intervals a human groan; and looking up I saw that the long friezes in *bas-relief* represented men and women tortured and torturing with all conceivable variety of method and circumstance—flayed, racked, burned, torn asunder, loaded with weights, pinched with hot irons, and so on without end.

And it added to the horror of these sculptures that while the limbs and even the dress of each figure were carved with elaborate care and nicety of detail, the faces of all—of those who applied the torture and of those who looked on, as well as of the sufferers themselves—were left absolutely blank. On the same plan the two Titans beside the great archway had no faces. The sculptor had traced the muscles of each belly in a constriction of anguish, and had suggested this anguish again in moulding the neck, even in disposing the hair of the head; but the neck supported, and the locks fell around, a space of smooth stone without a feature.

Harry allowed me no time to feed on these horrors. Signing to me to dismount and leave Grey Sultan at the entrance, he led me through the long archway or tunnel. At the end we paused again, he watching, while I drew difficult breath....

I saw a vast amphitheatre of granite, curving away on either hand and reaching up, tier on tier, till the tiers melted in the grey sky overhead. The lowest tier stood twenty feet above my head; yet curved with so lordly a perspective that on the far side of the arena, as I looked across, it seemed almost level with the ground; while the human figures about the great archway yonder were diminished to the size of ants about a hole... For there were human figures busy in the arena, though not a soul sat in any of the granite tiers above.

A million eyes had been less awful than those empty benches staring down in the cold dawn; bench after bench repeating the horror of the featureless carvings by the entrance-gate—repeating it in series without end, and unbroken, save at one point midway along the semicircle on my right, where the imperial seat stood out, crowned like a catafalque with plumes of purple horse-hair, and screened close with heavy purple hangings. I saw these curtains shake once or twice in the morning wind.

The floor of this amphitheatre I have spoken of as an arena; but as a matter of fact it was laid with riveted sheets of copper that recalled the dead men's shelves in the Paris *morgue*. The centre had been raised some few feet higher than the circumference, or possibly the whole floor took its shape from the rounded hill of which it was the apex; and from an open sluice immediately beneath the imperial throne a flood of water gushed with a force that carried it straight to this raised centre, over which it ran and rippled, and so drained back into the scuppers at the circumference. Before reaching the centre it broke and swirled around a row of what appeared to be tall iron boxes or cages, set directly in face of the throne. But for these ugly boxes the whole floor was empty. To and from these the little human figures were hurrying, and from these too proceeded the thuds and panting and the frequent groans that I had heard outside.

While I stood and gazed, Harry stepped forward into the arena. "This also?" I whispered.

He nodded, and led the way over the copper floor, where the water ran high as our ankles and again was drained off, until little dry spaces grew like maps upon the surface, and in ten seconds were flooded again. He led me straight to the cages, and I saw that while the roof and three sides of these were of sheet iron, the fourth side, which faced the throne, lay open. And I saw—in the first cage, a man scourged with rods; in the second, a body twisted on the rack; in the third, a woman with a starving babe, and a fellow that held food to them and withdrew it quickly (the torturers wore masks on their faces, and whenever blood flowed some threw handfuls of sawdust, and blood and sawdust together were carried off by the running water); in the fourth cage, a man tied, naked and helpless, whom a masked torturer pelted with discs of gold, heavy and keen-edged; in the fifth a brazier with irons heating, and a girl's body crouched in a corner—

"I will see no more!" I cried, and turned towards the great purple canopy. High over it the sun broke yellow on the climbing tiers of seats. "Harry! someone is watching behind those curtains! Is it—HE?"

Harry bent his head.

"But this is all that I believed! This is Nero, and ten times worse than Nero! Why did you bring me here?" I flung out my hand towards the purple throne, and finding myself close to a fellow who scattered sawdust with both hands, made a spring to tear his mask away. But Harry stretched out an arm.

"That will not help you," he said. "The man has no face."

"No face!"

"He once had a face, but it has perished. His was the face of these sufferers. Look at them."

I looked from cage to cage, and now saw that indeed all these sufferers—men and women—had but one face: the same wrung brow, the same wistful eyes, the same lips bitten in anguish. I knew the face. *We all know it.*

"His own Son! O devil rather than God!" I fell on my knees in the gushing water and covered my eyes.

"Stand up, listen and look!" said Harry's voice.

"What can I see? He hides behind that curtain."

"And the curtain?"

"It shakes continually."

"*That is with His sobs.* Listen! What of the water?"

"It runs from the throne and about the floor. It washes off the blood."

"That water is His tears. It flows hence down the hill, and washes all the shores of earth."

Then as I stood silent, conning the eddies at my feet, for the first time Harry took my hand.

"Learn this," he said. "There is no suffering in the world but ultimately comes to be endured by God."

Saying this, he drew me from the spot; gently, very gently led me away; but spoke again as we were about to pass into the shadow of the arch—

"Look once back: for a moment only."

I looked. The curtains of the imperial seat were still drawn close, but in a flash I saw the tiers beside it, and around, and away up to the sunlit crown of the amphitheatre, thronged with forms in white raiment. And all these forms leaned forward and bowed their faces on their arms and wept.

So we passed out beneath the archway. Grey Sultan stood outside, and as I mounted him the gate clashed behind. . . .

4

I turned as it clashed. And the gate was just the lodge-gate of Sevenhays. And Grey Sultan was trampling the gravel of our own drive. The morning sun slanted over the laurels on my right, and while I wondered, the stable clock struck eight.

The rest I leave to you; nor shall try to explain. I only know that, vision or no vision, my soul from that hour has gained a calm it never knew before. The sufferings of my fellows still afflict me; but always, if I stand still and listen, in my own room, or in a crowded street, or in a waste spot among the moors, I can hear those waters moving round the world—moving on their "priest-like task"—those lustral divine tears which are Oceanus.

Old Aeson

Judge between me and my guest, the stranger within my gates, the man whom in his extremity I clothed and fed.

I remember well the time of his coming, for it happened at the end of five days and nights during which the year passed from strength to age; in the interval between the swallow's departure and the redwing's coming; when the tortoise in my garden crept into his winter quarters, and the equinox was on us, with an east wind that parched the blood in the trees, so that their leaves for once knew no gradations of red and yellow, but turned at a stroke to brown, and crackled like tin-foil.

At five o'clock in the morning of the sixth day I looked out. The wind still whistled across the sky, but now without the obstruction of any cloud. Full in front of my window Sirius flashed with a whiteness that pierced the eye. A little to the right, the whole constellation of Orion was suspended clear over a wedge-like gap in the coast, wherein the sea could be guessed rather than seen. And, travelling yet further, the eye fell on two brilliant lights, the one set high above the other—the one steady and a fiery red, the other yellow and blazing intermittently—the one Aldebaran, the other revolving on the lighthouse top, fifteen miles away.

Half-way up the east, the moon, now in her last quarter and decrepit, climbed with the dawn close at her heels. And at this hour they brought in the stranger, asking if my pleasure were to give him clothing and hospitality.

Nobody knew whence he came—except that it was from the

wind and the night—seeing that he spoke in a strange tongue, moaning and making a sound like the twittering of birds in a chimney. But his journey must have been long and painful; for his legs bent under him, and he could not stand when they lifted him. So, finding it useless to question him for the time, I learnt from the servants all they had to tell—namely, that they had come upon him, but a few minutes before, lying on his face within my grounds, without staff or scrip, bareheaded, spent, and crying feebly for succour in his foreign tongue; and that in pity they had carried him in and brought him to me.

Now for the look of this man, he seemed a century old, being bald, extremely wrinkled, with wide hollows where the teeth should be, and the flesh hanging loose and flaccid on his cheek-bones; and what colour he had could have come only from exposure to that bitter night. But his eyes chiefly spoke of his extreme age. They were blue and deep, and filled with the wisdom of years; and when he turned them in my direction they appeared to look through me, beyond me, and back upon centuries of sorrow and the slow endurance of man, as if his immediate misfortune were but an inconsiderable item in a long list. They frightened me. Perhaps they conveyed a warning of that which I was to endure at their owner's hands. From compassion, I ordered the servants to take him to my wife, with word that I wished her to set food before him, and see that it passed his lips.

So much I did for this stranger. Now learn how he rewarded me.

He has taken my youth from me, and the most of my substance, and the love of my wife.

From the hour when he tasted food in my house, he sat there without hint of going. Whether from design, or because age and his sufferings had really palsied him, he came back tediously to life and warmth, nor for many days professed himself able to stand erect. Meanwhile he lived on the best of our hospitality. My wife tended him, and my servants ran at his bidding; for he managed early to make them understand scraps of his language, though slow in acquiring ours—I believe out of calculation, lest someone should inquire his business (which was a mystery) or hint at his departure. I myself often visited the room he had appropriated, and would sit for an hour watching those fathomless eyes while I tried to make head or tail of his discourse. When we were alone, my wife and I used to speculate at times on his probable profession. Was he a merchant?—an aged mariner?—a tinker, tailor, beggarman, thief? We could never decide, and he never disclosed.

Then the awakening came. I sat one day in the chair beside his, wondering as usual. I had felt heavy of late, with a soreness and languor in my bones, as if a dead weight hung continually on my shoulders, and another rested on my heart. A warmer colour in the Stranger's cheek caught my attention; and I bent forward, peering under the pendulous lids. His eyes were livelier and less profound. The melancholy was passing from them as breath fades off a pane of glass. *He was growing younger.* Starting up, I ran across the room, to the mirror.

There were two white hairs in my forelock; and, at the corner of either eye, half a dozen radiating lines. I was an old man.

Turning, I regarded the stranger. He sat phlegmatic as an Indian idol; and in my fancy I felt the young blood draining from my own heart, and saw it mantling in his cheeks. Minute by minute I watched the slow miracle—the old man beautified. As buds unfold, he put on a lovely youthfulness; and, drop by drop, left me winter.

I hurried from the room, and seeking my wife, laid the case before her. "This is a ghoul," I said, "that we harbour: he is sucking my best blood, and the household is clean bewitched." She laid aside the book in which she read, and laughed at me. Now my wife was well-looking, and her eyes were the light of my soul. Consider, then, how I felt as she laughed, taking the stranger's part against me. When I left her, it was with a new suspicion in my heart. "How shall it be," I thought, "if after stealing my youth, he go on to take the one thing that is better?"

In my room, day by day, I brooded upon this—hating my

own alteration, and fearing worse. With the Stranger there was no longer any disguise. His head blossomed in curls; white teeth filled the hollows of his mouth; the pits in his cheeks were heaped full with roses, glowing under a transparent skin. It was Aeson renewed and thankless; and he sat on, devouring my substance.

Now having probed my weakness, and being satisfied that I no longer dared to turn him out, he, who had half-imposed his native tongue upon us, constraining the household to a hideous jargon, the bastard growth of two languages, condescended to jerk us back rudely into our own speech once more, mastering it with a readiness that proved his former dissimulation, and using it henceforward as the sole vehicle of his wishes. On his past life he remained silent; but took occasion to confide in me that he proposed embracing a military career, as soon as he should tire of the shelter of my roof.

And I groaned in my chamber; for that which I feared had come to pass. He was making open love to my wife. And the eyes with which he looked at her, and the lips with which he coaxed her, had been mine; and I was an old man. Judge now between me and this guest.

One morning I went to my wife; for the burden was past bearing, and I must satisfy myself. I found her tending the plants on her window-ledge; and when she turned, I saw that years had not taken from her comeliness one jot. And I was old.

So I taxed her on the matter of this stranger, saying this and that, and how I had cause to believe he loved her.

"That is beyond doubt," she answered, and smiled.

"By my head, I believe his fancy is returned!" I blurted out.

And her smile grew radiant, as, looking me in the face, she answered, "By my soul, husband, it is."

Then I went from her, down into my garden, where the day grew hot and the flowers were beginning to droop. I stared upon them and could find no solution to the problem that worked in my heart. And then I glanced up, eastward, to the sun above the privet-hedge, and saw *him* coming across the flower beds, treading them down in wantonness. He came with a light step and a smile, and I waited for him, leaning heavily on my stick.

"Give me your watch!" he called out, as he drew near.

"Why should I give you my watch?" I asked, while something worked in my throat.

"Because I wish it; because it is gold; because you are too old, and won't want it much longer."

"Take it," I cried, pulling the watch out and thrusting it into his hand. "Take it—you who have taken all that is better! Strip me, spoil me—"

A soft laugh sounded above, and I turned. My wife was looking down on us from the window, and her eyes were both moist and glad.

"Pardon me," she said, "it is you who are spoiling the child."

Our Lady of Gwithian

Mary, mother, well thou be!
Mary, mother, think on me;
Sweete Lady, maiden clean,
Shield me from ill, shame, and teen;
Shield me, Lady, from villainy
And from all wicked company!
                    Speculum Christiani.

Here is a little story I found one day among the legends of the Cornish Saints, like a chip in porridge. If you love simplicity, I think it may amuse you.

Lovey Bussow was wife of Daniel Bussow, a tin-streamer of Gwithian Parish. He had brought her from Camborne, and her neighbours agreed that there was little amiss with the woman if you overlooked her being a bit weak in the head. They set her down as "not exactly." At the end of a year she brought her husband a fine boy. It happened that the child was born just about the time of year the tin-merchants visited St. Michael's Mount; and the father—who streamed in a small way, and had no beast of burden but his donkey, or "naggur"—had to load up panniers and drive his tin down to the shore-market with the rest, which for him meant an absence of three weeks, or a fortnight at the least.

So Daniel kissed his wife and took his leave; and the neighbours, who came to visit her as soon as he was out of the way, all told her the same story—that until the child was safely baptised it behoved her to be very careful and keep her door shut for fear of the Piskies. The Piskies, or fairy-folk (they said), were themselves the spirits of children that had died unchristened, and liked nothing better than the chance to steal away an unchristened child to join their nation of mischief.

Lovey listened to them, and it preyed on her mind. She reckoned that her best course was to fetch a holy man as quickly as possible to baptise the child and make the cross over him. So one afternoon, the mite being then a bare fortnight old, she left him asleep in his cradle and, wrapping a shawl over her head, hurried off to seek Meriden the Priest.

Meriden the Priest dwelt in a hut among the sandhills, a bowshot beyond St. Gwithian's Chapel on the seaward side, as you go out to Godrevy. He had spent the day in barking his nets, and was spreading them out to dry on the short turf of the towans; but on hearing Lovey's errand, he good-naturedly dropped his occupation and, staying only to fill a bottle with holy water, walked back with her to her home.

As they drew near, Lovey was somewhat perturbed to see that the door, which she had carefully closed, was standing wide open. She guessed, however, that a neighbour had called in her absence, and would be inside keeping watch over the child. As she reached the threshold, the dreadful truth broke upon her: the kitchen was empty, and so was the cradle!

It made her frantic for a while. Meriden the Priest offered what consolation he could, and suggested that one of her neighbours had called indeed, and finding the baby alone in the cottage, had taken it off to her own home to guard it. But this he felt to be a forlorn hope, and it proved a vain one. Neither search nor inquiry could trace the infant. Beyond a doubt the Piskies had carried him off.

When this was established so that even the hopefullest of the good-wives shook her head over it, Lovey grew calm of a sudden and (as it seemed) with the calm of despair. She grew obstinate too.

"My blessed cheeld!" she kept repeating. "The tender worm of 'en! But I'll have 'en back, if I've to go to the naughty place to fetch 'en. Why, what sort of a tale be I to pitch to my Dan'l, if he comes home and his firstborn gone?"

They shook their heads again over this. It would be a brave blow for the man, but (said one to another) he that marries a fool must look for thorns in his bed.

"What's done can't be undone," they told her. "You'd best let a two-three of us stay the night and coax 'ee from frettin'. It's bad for the system, and you so soon over childbirth."

Lovey opened her eyes wide on them.

"Lord's sake!" she said, "you don't reckon I'm goin' to sit down under this? What?—and him the beautifullest, straightest cheeld that ever was in Gwithian Parish! Go'st thy ways home, every wan. Piskies steal my cheeld an' Dan'l's, would they? I'll pisky 'em!"

She showed them forth—"put them to doors" as we say in the Duchy—everyone, the priest included. She would have none of their consolation.

"You mean it kindly, naybors, I don't say; but tiddn' what I happen to want. I wants my cheeld back; an' I'll *have'n* back, what's more!"

They went their ways, agreeing that the woman was doited. Lovey closed the door upon them, bolted it, and sat for hours staring at the empty cradle. Through the unglazed window she could see the stars; and when these told her that midnight was near, she put on her shawl again, drew the bolt, and fared forth over the towans. At first the stars guided her, and the slant of the night-wind on her face; but by and by, in a dip between the hills, she spied her mark and steered for it. This was the spark within St. Gwithian's Chapel, where day and night a tiny oil lamp, with a floating wick, burned before the image of Our Lady.

Meriden the Priest kept the lamp filled, the wick trimmed, year in and year out. But he, good man, after remembering Lovey in his prayers, was laid asleep and snoring within his hut, a bowshot away. The chapel-door opened softly to Lovey's hand, and she crept up to Mary's image, and abased herself before it.

"Dear Aun' Mary," she whispered, "the Piskies have taken my

cheeld! You d'knaw what that means to a poor female—you there, cuddlin' your liddle Jesus in the crook o' your arm. An' you d'knaw likewise what these Piskies be like; spiteful li'l toads, same as you or I might be if happen we'd died unchristened an' hadn' no share in heaven nor hell nor middle-earth. But that's no excuse. Aun' Mary, my dear, I want my cheeld back!" said she. That was all Lovey prayed. Without more ado she bobbed a curtsy, crept from the chapel, closed the door, and way-to-go back to her cottage.

When she reached it and struck a light in the kitchen she more than half expected to hear the child cry to her from his cradle. But, for all that Meriden the Priest had told her concerning the Virgin and her power, there the cradle stood empty.

"Well-a-well!" breathed Lovey. "The gentry are not to be hurried, I reckon. I'll fit and lie down for forty winks," she said; "though I do think, with her experience Mary might have remembered the poor mite would be famished afore this, not to mention that the milk in me is beginnin' to hurt cruel."

She did off some of her clothes and lay down, and even slept a little in spite of the pain in her breasts; but awoke a good two hours before dawn, to find no baby restored to her arms, nor even (when she looked) was it back in its cradle. "This'll never do," said Lovey. On went her shawl again, and once again she faced the night and hurried across the towans to St. Gwithian's Chapel. There in her niche stood Our Lady, quite as though nothing had happened, with the infant Christ in her arms and the tiny lamp burning at her feet.

"Aun' Mary, Aun' Mary," said Lovey, speaking up sharp, "this iddn' no sense 't all! A person would think time was no objic, the way you stick there starin', ain' my poor cheeld leary with hunger afore now—as you, bein' a mother, oft to knaw. Fit an' fetch 'en home to me quick. Aw, do'ee co', that's a dear soul!"

But Our Lady stood there and made no sign.

"I don't understand 'ee 't all," Lovey groaned. "'Tiddn' the way I'd behave in your place, and you d'knaw it."

Still Our Lady made no sign.

Lovey grew desperate.

"Aw, very well, then!" she cried. "Try what it feels like without your liddle Jesus!"

And reaching up a hand, she snatched at and lifted the Holy Child that fitted into a stone socket on Our Lady's arm. It came away in her grasp, and she fled, tucking it under her shawl.

All the way home Lovey looked for the earth to gape and swallow her, or a hand to reach down from heaven and grip her by the hair; and all the way she seemed to hear Our Lady's feet padding after her in the darkness. But she never stopped nor stayed until she reached home; and there, flinging in through the door and slamming to the bolt behind her, she made one spring for the bed, and slid down in it, cowering over the small stone image.

Rat-a-tat! tat!—someone knocked on the door so that the cottage shook.

"Knock away!" said Lovey. "Whoever thee be, thee 'rt not my cheeld."

Rat-a-tat! tat!

"My cheeld wouldn' be knockin': he's got neither strength nor sproil for it. An' you may fetch Michael and all his Angels, to tear me in pieces," said Lovey; "but till I hear my own cheeld creen to me, I'll keep what I have!"

Thereupon Lovey sat up, listening. For outside she heard a feeble wail.

She slipped out of bed. Holding the image tight in her right arm, she drew the bolt cautiously. On the threshold at her feet, lay her own babe, nestling in a bed of bracken.

She would have stooped at once and snatched him to her. But the stone Christling hampered her, lying so heavily in her arm. For a moment, fearing trickery, she had a mind to hurl it far out of doors into the night.... It would fall without much hurt into the soft sand of the towans. But on a second thought she held it forth gently in her two hands.

"I never meant to hurt 'en, Aun' Mary," she said. "But a firstborn's a firstborn, be we gentle or simple."

In the darkness a pair of invisible hands reached forward and took her hostage.

When it was known that the Piskies had repented and restored Lovey Bussow's child to her, the neighbours agreed that fools have most of the luck in this world; but came nevertheless to offer their congratulations. Meriden the Priest came also. He wanted to know how it had happened; for the Piskies do not easily surrender a child they have stolen.

Lovey—standing very demure, and smoothing her apron down along her thighs—confessed that she had laid her trouble before Our Lady.

"A miracle, then!" exclaimed his Reverence. "What height! What depth!"

"That's of it," agreed Lovey. "Aw, b'lieve me, your Reverence, we mothers understand wan another."

Phoebus on Halzaphron

God! of whom music
And song and blood are pure,
The day is never darkened
That had thee here obscure.

Early in 1897 a landslip on the tall cliffs of Halzaphron—which face upon Mount's Bay, Cornwall, and the Gulf Stream of the Atlantic—brought to light a curiosity. The slip occurred during the night of January 7th to 8th, breaking through the roof of a cavern at the base of the cliff and carrying many hundreds of tons of rock and earth down into deep water. For some weeks what remained of the cavern was obliterated, and in the rough weather then prevailing no one took the trouble to examine it; since it can only be approached by sea. The tides, however, set to work to sift and clear the detritus, and on Whit-Monday a party of pleasure-seekers from Penzance brought their boat to shore, landed, and discovered a stairway of worked stone leading up from the back of the cavern through solid rock.

The steps wound spirally upward, and were cut with great accuracy; but the drippings from the low roof of the stairway had worn every tread into a basin and filled it with water. Green slippery weeds coated the lowest stairs; those immediately above were stained purple and crimson by the growth of some minute fungus; but where darkness began, these colours passed through rose-pink into a delicate ivory-white—a hard crust of lime, crenulated like coral by the ceaseless trickle of water which deposited it.

At first the explorers supposed themselves on the track of a lost holy well. They had no candles, but by economising their stock of matches they followed up the mysterious and beautiful staircase until it came to a sudden end, blocked by the fallen mass of cliff. Still in ignorance whither it led or what purpose it had served, they turned back and descended to the sunshine again; when one of the party, scanning the cliff's face, observed a fragment—three steps only—jutting out like a cornice some sixty or seventy feet overhead.

This seemed to dispose of the holy well theory, and suggested that the stairway had reached to the summit, where perhaps an entrance might be found. The party returned to Penzance, and their report at once engaged the attention of the local Antiquarian Society; a small subscription list was opened, permission obtained from the owner of the property, and within a week a gang of labourers began to excavate on the cliff-top directly above the jutting cornice. The ground here showed a slight depression, and the soil proved unexpectedly deep and easy to work. On the second day, at a depth of seven feet, one of the men announced that he had come upon rock. But having spaded away the loose earth, they discovered that his pick had struck upon the edge of an extremely fine tessellated pavement, the remains apparently of a Roman villa.

Yet could this be a Roman villa? That the Romans drove their armies into Cornwall is certain enough; their coins, ornaments, and even pottery, are still found here and there; their camps can be traced. That they conquered and colonised it, however, during any of the four hundred years they occupied Britain has yet to be proved. In other parts of England the plough turns up memorials of that quiet home life with its graces which grew around these settlers and comforted their exile; and the commonest of these is the tessellated pavement with its emblems of the younger gods, the vintage, the warm south. But in the remote west, where the Celts held their savage own, no such traces have ever been found.

Could this at last be one? The pavement, cleared with care,

proved of a disappointing size, measuring 8 feet by 4 at the widest. The *tessellae* were exceptionally beautiful and fresh in color; and each separate design represented some scene in the story of Apollo. No Bacchus with his panther-skin and Maenads, no Triton and Nymphs, no loves of Mars and Venus, no Ganymede with the eagle, no Leda, no Orpheus, no Danaë, no Europa—but always and only Apollo! He was guiding his car; he was singing among the Nine; he was drawing his bow; he was flaying Marsyas; above all—the only repeated picture—he was guiding the oxen of Admetus, goad in hand, with the glory yet vivid about his hair. Could it (someone suggested) be the pavement of a temple? And, if so, how came a temple of the sun-god upon this unhomely coast?

The discovery gave rise to a small sensation and several ingenious theories, one enthusiastic philologer going so far as to derive the name Halzaphron from the Greek, interpreting it as "the salt of the west winds" or "Zephyrs," and to assert roundly that the temple (he assumed it to be a temple) dated far back beyond the Roman Invasion. This contention, though perhaps no more foolish than a dozen others, undoubtedly met with the most ridicule.

And yet in my wanderings along that coast I have come upon broken echoes, whispers, fragments of a tale, which now and again, as I tried to piece them together, wakened a suspicion that the derided philologer, with his false derivation, was yet "hot," as children say in the game of hide-and-seek.

For the stretch of sea overlooked by Halzaphron covers the lost land of Lyonnesse. Take a boat upon a clear, calm day, and, drifting, peer over the side through its shadow, and you will see the tops of tall forests waving below you. Walk the shore at low water and you may fill your pockets with beech-nuts, and sometimes—when a violent tide has displaced the sand—stumble on the trunks of large trees. Geologists dispute whether the Lyonnesse disappeared by sudden catastrophe or gradual subsidence, but they agree in condemning the fables of Florence and William of Worcester, that so late as November, 1099, the sea broke in and covered the whole tract between Cornwall and the Scillies, overwhelming on its way no less than a hundred and forty churches! They prove that, however it befell, we must date the inundation some centuries earlier. Now if my story be true—But let it be told:

★★★★★

In the year of the great tide Graul, son of Graul, was king in the Lyonnesse. He lived at peace in his city of Maenseyth, hard by the Sullêh, where the foreign traders brought their ships to anchor—sometimes from Tyre itself, oftener from the Tyrian colonies down the Spanish coast; and he ruled over a peaceful nation of tinners, herdsmen, and charcoal-burners. The charcoal came from the great forest to the eastward where Cara Clowz in Cowz, the gray rock in the wood, overlooked the Cornish frontier; his cattle pastured nearer, in the plains about the foot of the Wolves' Cairn; and his tinners camped and washed the ore in the valley-bottoms—for in those days they had no need to dig into the earth for metal, but found plenty by puddling in the river-beds.

So King Graul ruled happily over a happy people until the dark morning when a horseman came galloping to the palace of Maenseyth with a cry that the tide had broken through Crebawethan and was sweeping north and west upon the land, drowning all in its path. "Hark!" said he, "already you may hear the roar of it by Bryher!"

Yann, the king's body-servant, ran at once to the stables and brought three horses—one for Queen Niotte; one for her only child, the Princess Gwennolar; and for King Graul the red stallion, Rubh, swiftest and strongest in the royal stalls, one of the Five Wonders of Lyonnesse. More than six leagues lay between them and the Wolves' Cairn, which surely the waters could never cover; and toward it the three rode at a stretch gallop, King Graul only tightening his hand on the bridle as Rubh strained to outpace the others. As he rode he called warnings to the herdsmen and tinners who already had heard the far roar of waters and were fleeing to the hills. The cattle raced ahead of him, around him, beside him; he passed troop after troop; and among them, in fellowship, galloped foxes, badgers, hares, rabbits, weasels; even small field-mice were skurrying and entangling themselves in the long grasses, and toppling head over heels in their frenzy to escape.

But before they reached the Wolves' Cairn the three riders were alone again. Rubh alone carried his master lightly, and poised his head to sniff the wind. The other two leaned on their bridles and lagged after him, and even Rubh bore against the left-hand rein until it wearied the king's wrist. He wondered at this; but at the base of the cairn he wondered no longer, for the old gray wolf, for whose head Graul had offered a talent of silver, was loping down the hillside in full view, with her long family at her heels. She passed within a stone's throw of the king and gave him one quiet, disdainful look out of her green eyes as she headed her pack to the southward.

Then the king understood. He looked southward and saw the plain full of moving beasts. He looked northward, and two miles away the rolling downs were not, but in their place a bright line stretched taut as a string, and the string roared as if a great finger were twanging it.

Queen Niotte's horse had come to a standstill. Graul lifted and set her before him on Rubh's crupper, and called to Gwennolar to follow him. But Gwennolar's horse, too, was spent, and in a little while he drew rein and lifted her, too, and set her on the stallion's broad back behind him. Then forward he spurred again and southward after the wolves—with a pack fiercer than wolves shouting at Rubh's heels, nearer and yet nearer.

And Rubh galloped, yet not as before; for this Gwennolar was a witch—a child of sixteen, golden-tressed, innocent to look upon as a bird of the air. Her parents found no fault in her, for she was their only one. None but the Devil, whom she had bound to serve her for a year and a day, knew of her lovers—the dark young sailors from the ships of Tyre, who came ashore and never sailed again nor were seen—or beneath what beach their bodies lay in a row. To-day his date was up, and in this flood he was taking his wages.

Gwennolar wreathed her white arms around her father and clung to him, while her blown hair streamed like gold over his beard. And King Graul set his teeth and rode to save the pair whom he knew to be dearest and believed to be best. But if Niotte weighed like a feather, Gwennolar with her wickedness began to weigh like lead—and more heavily yet, until the stallion could scarcely heave his strong loins forward, as now the earth grew moist about his hoofs. For far ahead of the white surge-line the land was melting and losing its features; trickles of water threading the green pastures, channelling the ditches, widening out into pools among the hollows—traps and pitfalls to be skirted, increasing in number while the sun sank behind and still the great rock of Cara Clowz showed far away above the green forest.

Rubh's head was leaning and his lungs throbbed against the king's heels. Yet he held on. He had overtaken the wolves; and Graul, thinking no longer of deliverance, watched the pack streaming beside him but always falling back and a little back until even the great gray dam dropped behind. A minute later a scream rang close to his ear; the stallion leaped as if at a waterbrook, and as suddenly sank backward with a dozen wolves on his haunches.

"Father!" shrieked Gwennolar. "Father!" He felt her arms dragged from around his neck. With an arm over his wife Niotte he crouched, waiting for the fangs to pierce his neck. And while he waited, to his amazement the horse staggered up, shook himself, and was off with a bound, fleet as an arrow, fleeter than ever before, yet not fleeter than the pack now running again and fresh beside him. He looked back. Gwennolar rose to her knees on the turf where the wolves had pulled her down and left her unhurt; she stretched out both arms to him, and called once. The sun dipped behind her, and between her and the sun the tide—a long bright-edged knife—came sweeping and cut her down. Then it seemed as if the wolves had relinquished to the waters not their prey only but their own fierce instinct; for the waves paused at the body and played with it, nosing and tumbling it over and over, lifting it curiously, laying it down again on the green knoll, and then withdrawing in a circle while they took heart to rush upon it all together and toss it high, exultant and shouting. And during that pause the fugitives gained many priceless furlongs.

They reached the skirts of the great forest and dashed into its twilight, crouching low while Rubh tore his way between the gray beech-trunks and leaped the tangles of brier, but startled no life from bough or undergrowth. Beast and reptile had fled inland; and the birds hung and circled over the tree-tops without thought of roosting. Graul's right arm tightened about his wife's waist, but his left hand did no more than grasp the rein. He trusted to the stallion, and through twilight and darkness alike Rubh held his course.

When at length he slackened speed and came to a halt with a shudder, Graul looked up and saw the stars overhead and a glimmering scarp of granite, and knew it for the gray rock, Cara Clowz. By the base of it he lowered Niotte to the ground, dismounted, and began to climb, leading Rubh by the bridle and seeking for a pathway. Behind him the voices of crashing trees filled the windless night. He found a ledge at length, and there the three huddled together—Niotte between swooning and sleep, Graul seated beside her, and Rubh standing patient, waiting for the day. When the crashing ceased around them, the king could hear the soft flakes of sweat dripping from the stallion's belly, and saw the stars reflected now from the floor where his forest had stood. Day broke, and the Lyonnesse had vanished. Forest and pasture, city, mart and haven—away to the horizon a heaving sea covered all. Of his kingdom there remained only a thin strip of coast, marching beside the Cornish border, and this sentinel rock, standing as it stands today, then called Cara Clowz, and now St. Michael's Mount.

If you have visited it, you will know that the mount stands about half a mile from the mainland; an island except at low water, when you reach it by a stone causeway. Here, on the summit,

Graul and Niotte built themselves a house, asking no more of life than a roof to shelter them; for they had no child to build for, and their spirit was broken. The little remnant of their nation settled in Marazion on the mainland, or southward along the strip of coast, and set themselves to learn a new calling. As the sea cast up the bodies of their drowned cattle and the trunks of uprooted trees, they took hides and timber and fashioned boats and launched forth to win their food. They lowered nets and wicker pots through the heaving floor deep into the twilight, and, groping across their remembered fields, drew pollack and conger, shellfish and whiting from rocks where shepherds had sat to watch their sheep, or tinners gathered at noonday for talk and dinner.

At first it was as if a man returning at night to his house and, finding it unlit, should feel in the familiar cupboard for food and start back from touch of a monstrous body, cold and unknown. Time and use deadened the shock. They were not happy, for they remembered days of old; but they endured, they fought off hunger, they earned sleep; and their king, as he watched from Cara Clowz their dark sails moving out against the sunset, could give thanks that the last misery had been spared his people.

But there were dawns which discovered one or two missing from the tale of boats, home-comings with heavy news for freight, knots of women and children with blown wet hair awaiting it, white faces and the wails of widow and orphan. The days drew in and this began to happen often—so often that a tale grew with it and spread, until it had reached all ears but those of King Graul and Queen Motte.

One black noon in November a company of men crossed the sands at low-water and demanded to speak with the king.

"Speak, my children," said Graul. He knew that they loved him and might count on his sharing the last crust with them.

"We are come," said the spokesman, "not for ourselves, but for our wives and children. For us life is none too pleasant; but they need men's hands to find food for them, and at this rate there will soon be no men of our nation left."

"But how can I help you?" asked the king.

"That we know not; but it is your daughter Gwennolar who undoes us. She lies out yonder beneath the waters, and through the night she calls to men, luring them down to their death. I myself—all of us here—have heard her; and the younger men it maddens. With singing and witch fires she lures our boats to the reefs and takes toll of us, lulling even the elders to dream, cheating them with the firelight and voices of their homes."

Now the thoughts of Graul and Niotte were with their daughter continually. That she should have been lost and they saved, who cared so little for life and nothing for life without her—that was their abiding sorrow and wonder and self-reproach. Why had Graul not turned Rubh's head perforce and ridden back to die with her, since help her he could not? Many times a day he asked himself this; and though Niotte's lips had never spoken it, her eyes asked it too. At night he would hear her breath pause at his side, and knew she was thinking of their child out yonder in the cold waters.

"She calls to us also," he answered, and checked himself.

"So it is plain her spirit is alive yet, and she must be a witch," said the spokesman, readily.

The king rent his clothes. "My daughter is no witch!" he cried. "But I left her to die, and she suffers."

"Our lads follow her. She calls to them and they perish."

"It is not Gwennolar who calls, but some evil thing which counterfeits her. She was innocent as the day. Nevertheless your sons shall not perish, nor you accuse her. From this day your boats shall have a lantern on this rock to guide them, and I and my wife will tend it with our own hands."

Thenceforward at sunset with their own hands Graul and Niotte lit and hung out a lantern from the niche which stands to this day and is known as St. Michael's Chair; and trimmed it, and tended it the night through, taking turns to watch. Niotte, doited with years and sorrow, believed that it shone to signal her lost child home. Her hands trembled every night as Graul lit the wick, and she arched her palms above to shield it from the wind.

She was happier than her husband.

Gwennolar's spell defied the lantern and their tottering pains. Boats were lost, men perished as before. The people tried a new appeal. It was the women's turn to lay their grief at the king's door. They crossed the sands by ones and twos—-widows, childless mothers, maids betrothed and bereaved—and spread their dark skirts and sat before the gateway. Niotte brought them food with her own hands; they took it without thanks. All the day they sat silent, and Graul felt their silence to be heavier than curses—nay, that their eyes did indeed curse as they sat around and watched the lighting of the lantern, and Niotte, nodding innocently at her arched hands, told them, "See, I pray; cannot you pray too?"

But the king's prayer was spoken in the morning, when the flame and the stars grew pale together and the smoke of the extinguished lamp sickened his soul in the clean air. His gods were gone with the oaks under which he had worshipped; but he stood on a rock apart from the women and, lifting both hands, cried aloud: "If there be any gods above the tree-tops, or any in the far seas whither the old fame of King Graul has reached; if ever I did kindness to a stranger or wayfarer, and he, returning to his own altars, remembered to speak of Graul of Lyonnesse: may I, who ever sought to give help, receive help now! From my youth I have believed that around me, beyond sight as surely as within it, stretched goodness answering the goodness in my own heart; yea, though I should never travel and find it, I trusted it was there. O trust, betray me not! O kindness, how far soever dwelling, speak comfort and help! For I am afflicted because of my people."

Seven mornings he prayed thus on his rock: and on the seventh, his prayer ended, he stood watching while the sunrays, like dogs shepherding a flock, searched in the mists westward and gathered up the tale of boats one by one. While he counted them, the shoreward breeze twanged once like a harp, and he heard a fresh young voice singing from the base of the cliff at his feet—

*There lived a king in Argos,—
A merchantman in Tyre
Would sell the King his cargoes,
But took his heart's desire:
Sing Io, Io, Io!—*

Graul looked toward his wife. "That will be the boy Laian," said Motte; "he sits on the rock below and sings at his fishing."

"The song is a strange one," said Graul; "and never had Laian voice like that."

The singer mounted the cliff—

*The father of that merry may
A thousand towns he made to pay,
And lapp'd the world in fire!*

He stood before them—a handsome, smiling youth, with a crust of brine on his blue sea-cloak, and the light of the morning in his hair. "Salutation, O Graul!" said he, and looked so cordial and well-willing that the king turned to him from the dead lamp and the hooded women as one turns to daylight from an evil dream.

"Salutation, O Stranger!" he answered. "You come to a poor man, but are welcome—you and your shipmates."

"I travel alone," said the youth; "and my business—"

But the king put up his hand. "We ask no man his business until he has feasted."

"I feast not in a house of mourning; and my business is better spoken soon than late, seeing that I heal griefs."

"If that be so," answered Graul, "you come to those who are fain of you." And then and there he told of Gwennolar. "The blessing of blessings rest on him who can still my child's voice and deliver her from my people's curse!"

The Stranger listened, and threw back his head. "I said I could heal griefs. But I cannot cure fate; nor will a wise man ask it. Pain you must suffer, but I can soothe it; sorrow, but I can help you to forget; death, but I can brace you for it."

"Can death be welcomed," asked Graul, "save by those who

find life worse?"

"You shall see." He stepped to the mourning women, and took the eldest by the hand. At first he whispered to her—in a voice so low that Graul heard nothing, but saw her brow relax, and that she listened while the blood came slowly back to her cheeks.

"Of what are you telling her?" the king demanded.

"Hush!" said the stranger, "Go, fetch me a harp."

Graul brought a harp. It was mute and dusty, with a tangle of strings; but the stranger set it against his knee, and began to mend it deftly, talking the while in murmurs as a brook talks in a covert of cresses. By and by as he fitted a string he would touch and make it hum on a word—softly at first, and with long intervals—as though all its music lay dark and tangled in chaos, and he were exploring and picking out a note here and a note there to fit his song. There was trouble in his voice, and restlessness, and a low, eager striving, and a hope which grew as the notes came oftener, and lingered and thrilled on them. Then his fingers caught the strings together, and pulled the first chord: it came out of the depths with a great sob—a soul set free.

Other souls behind it rose to his fingers, and he plucked them forth, faster and faster—some wailing, some laughing fiercely, but each with the echo of a great pit, the clang of doors, and the mutter of an army pressing at its heels. And now the mourners leaned forward, and forgot all except to listen, for he was singing the Creation. He sang up the stars and set them in procession; he sang forth the sun from his chamber; he lifted the heads of the mountains and hitched on their mantles of green forest; he scattered the uplands with sheep, and the upper air with clouds; he called the west wind, and it came with a rustle of wings; he broke the rock into water and led it dancing down the cliffs, and spread it in marshes, and sent it spouting and hurrying in channels.

Flowers trooped to the lip of it, wild beasts slunk down to drink; armies of corn spread in rank along it, and men followed with sickles, chanting the hymn of Linus; and after them, with children at the breast, women stooped to glean or strode upright bearing baskets of food. Over their heads days and nights hurried in short flashes, and the seasons overtook them while they rested, and drowned them in showers of bloom, and overtopped their bodies with fresh corn: but the children caught up the sickles and ran on. To some—shining figures in the host—he gave names; and they shone because they moved in the separate light of divine eyes watching them, rays breaking the thickets or hovering down from heights where the gods sat at their ease.

But before this the men had brought their boats to shore, and hurried to the Mount, drawn by his harping. They pressed around him in a ring; and at first they were sad, since of what he sang they remembered the like in Lyonnesse—plough and sickle and flail, nesting birds and harvest, flakes of ore in the river-beds, dinner in the shade, and the plain beyond winking in the noon-day heat. They had come too late for the throes of his music, when the freed spirit trembled for a little on the threshold, fronting the dawn, but with the fire of the pit behind it and red on its trailing skirt. The song rolled forward now like a river, sweeping them past shores where they desired to linger.

But the stranger fastened his eyes on them, and sang them out to broad bars and sounding tumbling seas, where the wind piped, and the breeze came salt, and the spray slapped over the prow, hardening men to heroes. Then the days of their regret seemed to them good only for children, and the life they had loathed took a new face; their eyes opened upon it, and they saw it whole, and loved it for its largeness. "Beyond! beyond! beyond!"—they stared down on the fingers plucking the chords, but the voice of the harp sounded far up and along the horizon.

And with that quite suddenly it came back, and was speaking close at hand, as a friend telling them a simple tale; a tale which all could understand, though of a country unknown to them. Thus it ran:

> In Hellas, in the kingdom of Argos, there lived two brothers, Cleobis and Biton—young men, well to do, and of

great strength of body, so that each had won a crown in the public games. Now, once, when the Argives were keeping a festival of the goddess Hera, their mother had need to be driven to the temple in her chariot, but the oxen did not return from the field in time. The young men, therefore, seeing that the hour was late, put the yoke on their own necks, and drew the car in which their mother sat, and brought her to the temple, which was forty-five stades away. This they did in sight of the multitude assembled; and the men commended their strength, while the women called her blessed to be the mother of such sons. But she, overjoyed at the deed and its renown, entered the temple and, standing before the image of Hera, prayed the goddess to grant her two sons, Cleobis and Biton, the greatest boon which could fall to man. After she had prayed, and they had sacrificed and eaten of the feast, the young men sat down in the temple and fell asleep, and never awoke again, but so made an end with life. In this wise the blessing of Hera came to them; and the men of Argos caused statues to be made of them and set up at Delphi, for a memorial of their piety and its reward.

Thus quietly the great song ended, and Graul, looking around on his people, saw on their faces a cheerfulness they had not known since the day of the flood.

"Sir," said he, "yours is the half of my poor kingdom and yours the inheritance, if you will abide with us and sing us more of these songs."

"For that service," answered the stranger, "I am come; but not for the reward. Give me only a hide of land somewhere upon your cliffs, and there will I build a house and sing to all who have need of me."

So he did; and the fable goes on to say that never were known in the remnant of Lyonesse such seasons as followed, nor ever will be. The fish crowded to the nets, the cliffs waved with harvest. Heavy were the nets to haul and laborious was the reaping, but the people forgot their aches when the hour came to sit at the

Stranger's feet and listen, and drink the wine which he taught them to plant. For his part he toiled not at all, but descended at daybreak and nightfall to bathe in the sea, and returned with the brine on his curls and his youth renewed upon him. He never slept; and they, too, felt little need of sleep, but drank and sang the night away, refreshed by the sacred dews, watching for the moon to rise over the rounded cornfields, or for her feet to touch the sea and shed silver about the boats in the offing.

Out yonder Gwennolar sang and took her toll of life as before; but the people heeded less, and soon forgot even when their dearest perished. Other things than sorrow they began to unlearn. They had been a shamefaced race; the men shy and the women chaste. But the Stranger knew nothing of shame; nor was it possible to think harm where he, their leader, so plainly saw none. Naked he led them from the drinking-bout down the west stairway to the bathing-pool, and naked they plunged in and splashed around him and laughed as the cool shock scattered the night's languor and the wine-fumes. What mattered anything?—what they did, or what they suffered, or what news the homecoming boats might bring? They were blithe for the moment and lusty for the day's work, and with night again would come drink and song of the amorous gods; or if by chance the Singer should choose another note and tell of Procris or of Philomela, they could weep softly for others' woes and, so weeping, quite forget their own.

And the fable goes on to say that for three years by these means the stranger healed the griefs of the people of Lyonnesse, until one night when they sat around he told them the story of Ion; and if the stranger were indeed Phoebus Apollo himself, shameless was the telling. But while they listened, wrapped in the story, a cry broke on the night above the murmur of the beaches—a voice from the cliff below them, calling "Repent! Repent!"

They leaped to their feet at once, and hurried down the stairway. But the beach was empty; and though they hunted for an hour, they found no one. Yet the next night and every night after the same voice called "Repent! Repent!" They hurled down stones upon it and threatened it with vengeance; but it was not to be scared. And by and by the stranger missed a face from his circle, then another. At length came a night when he counted but half of his company.

He said no word of the missing ones; but early next morning, when the folk had set out to their labours in the fields, he took a staff and walked along the shore toward the Mount. A little beyond Parc-an-als, where a spring gushes from the face of the cliff, he came upon a man who stood under it catching the trickle in a stone basin, and halted a few paces off to watch him. The man's hair and beard were long and unkempt, his legs bare, and he wore a tattered tunic which reached below the knees and was caught about his waist with a thong girdle. For some minutes he did not perceive the singer; but turned at length, and the two eyed each other awhile.

Then the singer advanced smiling, while the other frowned.

"Thou hast followed me," he said.

"I have followed and found thee," the other answered.

"Thy name?"

"Leven," said the man. "I come out of Ireland."

"The Nazarite travels far; but this spot He overlooked on his travels, and the people had need. I brought them help; but they desert me now—for thee doubtless?"

The saint bent his head. The singer laughed.

"He is strong, but the old gods bear no malice. I go tonight to join their sleep, but I have loved this folk in a fashion. I pitied their woes and brought them solace: I taught them to forget—and in the forgetting maybe they have learned much that thou wilt have to unteach. Yet deal gently with them. They are children, and too often you holy men come with bands of iron. Shall we sit and talk awhile together, for their sakes?"

And the fable says that for a long day St. Leven sat on the sands of the Porth which now bears his name, and talked with the singer; and, that in consequence, to this day the descendants of the people of Lyonnesse praise God in cheerfuller hymns than the rest of the world uses—so much so that a company of minstrels visiting them not long ago were surprised in the midst of a drinking-chorus to find the audience tittering, and to learn afterward that they had chanted the most popular local burying-tunes!

Twilight had fallen before the stranger rose and took his farewell. On his way back he spied a company approaching along the dusky shore, and drew aside behind a rock while they passed toward the saint's dwelling. He found his own deserted. Of his old friends either none had come or none had waited; and away on a distant beach rose the faint chant of St. Patrick's Hymn of the Guardsman:

> *Christ the eye, the ear, the heart,*
> *Christ above, before, behind me;*
> *From the snare, the sword, the dart,*
> *On the Trinity I bind me—*
> *Christi est salus,*
> *Christi est salus,*
> *Salus tua, Domine, sit semper nobiscum!*

Psyche

Among these million Suns how shall the strayed Soul find her way back to earth?

The man was an engine-driver, thick-set and heavy, with a short beard grizzled at the edge, and eyes perpetually screwed up, because his life had run for the most part in the teeth of the wind. The lashes, too, had been scorched off. If you penetrated the mask of oil and coal-dust that was part of his working suit, you found a reddish-brown phlegmatic face, and guessed its age at fifty. He brought the last down train into Lewminster station every night at 9.45, took her on five minutes later, and passed through Lewminster again at noon, on his way back with the Galloper, as the porters called it.

He had reached that point of skill at which a man knows every pound of metal in a locomotive; seemed to feel just what was in his engine the moment he took hold of the levers and started up; and was expecting promotion. While waiting for it, he hit on the idea of studying a more delicate machine, and married a wife. She was the daughter of a woman at whose house he lodged, and her age was less than half of his own. It is to be supposed he loved her.

A year after their marriage she fell into low health, and her husband took her off to Lewminster for fresher air. She was lodging alone at Lewminster, and the man was passing Lewminster station on his engine, twice a day, at the time when this tale begins.

People—especially those who live in the West of England—

remember the great fire at the Lewminster Theatre; how, in the second Act of the *Colleen Bawn*, a tongue of light shot from the wings over the actors' heads; how, even while the actors turned and ran, a sheet of fire swept out on the auditorium with a roaring wind, and the house was full of shrieks and blind death; how men and women were turned to a white ash as they rose from their seats, so fiercely the flames outstripped the smoke. These things were reported in the papers, with narratives and ghastly details, and for a week all England talked of Lewminster.

This engine-driver, as the 9.45 train neared Lewminster, saw the red in the sky. And when he rushed into the station and drew up, he saw that the country porters who stood about were white as corpses.

"What fire is that?" he asked one.

"'Tis the theayter! There's a hundred burnt a'ready, and the rest treadin' each other's lives out while we stand talkin', to get 'pon the roof and pitch theirselves over!"

Now the engine-driver's wife was going to the play that night, and he knew it. She had met him at the station, and told him so, at midday.

But there was nobody to take the train on, if he stepped off the engine; for his fireman was a young hand, and had been learning his trade for less than three weeks.

So when the five minutes were up—or rather, ten, for the porters were bewildered that night—this man went on out of the station into the night. Just beyond the station the theatre was plain to see, above the hill on his left, and the flames were leaping from the roof; and he knew that his wife was there. But the train was never taken down more steadily, nor did a single passenger guess what manner of man was driving it.

At Drakeport, where his run ended, he stepped off the engine, walked from the railway-sheds to his mother-in-law's, where he still lodged, and went up-stairs to his bed without alarming a soul.

In the morning, at the usual hour, he was down at the station again, washed and cleanly dressed. His fireman had the Galloper's engine polished, fired up, and ready to start.

"Mornin'," he nodded, and looking into his driver's eyes, dropped the handful of dirty lint with which he had been polishing. After shuffling from foot to foot for a minute, he ended by climbing down on the far side of the engine.

"Oldster," he said, "'tis mutiny p'raps; but s'help me, if I ride a mile longside that new face o' your'n!"

"Maybe you're right," his superior answered wearily. "You'd best go up to the office, and get somebody sent down i' my place. And while you're there, you might get me a third-class for Lewminster."

So this man travelled up to Lewminster as passenger, and found his young wife's body among the two score stretched in a stable-yard behind the smoking theatre, waiting to be claimed. And the day after the funeral he left the railway company's service. He had saved a bit, enough to rent a small cottage two miles from the cemetery where his wife lay. Here he settled and tilled a small garden beside the high-road.

Nothing seemed to be wrong with the man until the late summer, when he stood before the Lewminster magistrates charged with a violent and curiously wanton assault.

It appeared that one dim evening, late in August, a mild gentleman, with Leghorn hat, spectacles, and a green gauze net, came sauntering by the garden where the ex-engine-driver was pulling a basketful of scarlet runners: that the prisoner had suddenly dropped his beans, dashed out into the road, and catching the mild gentleman by the throat had wrenched the butterfly net from his hand and belaboured him with the handle till it broke.

There was no defence, nor any attempt at explanation. The mild gentleman was a stranger to the neighbourhood. The magistrates marvelled, and gave his assailant two months.

At the end of that time the man came out of gaol and went quietly back to his cottage.

Early in the following April he conceived a wish to build a small greenhouse at the foot of his garden, by the road, and spoke to the local mason about it. One Saturday afternoon the mason came over to look at the ground and discuss plans. It was bright weather, and while the two men talked a white butterfly floated past them—the first of the year.

Immediately the mason broke off his sentence and began to chase the butterfly round the garden: for in the West country there is a superstition that if a body neglect to kill the first butterfly he may see for the season, he will have ill luck throughout the year. So he dashed across the beds, hat in hand.

"I'll hat 'en—I'll hat 'en! No, fay! I'll miss 'en, I b'lieve. Shan't be able to kill 'n if hor's wunce beyond th' gaate—stiddy, my son! Wo-op!"

Thus he yelled, waving his soft hat: and the next minute was lying stunned across a carrot-bed, with eight fingers gripping the back of his neck and two thumbs squeezing on his windpipe.

There was another assault case heard by the Lewminster bench; and this time the ex-engine-driver received four months. As before, he offered no defence: and again the magistrates were possessed with wonder.

Now the explanation is quite simple. This man's wits were sound, save on one point. He believed—why, God alone knows, who enabled him to drive that horrible journey without a tremor of the hand—that his wife's soul haunted him in the form of a white butterfly or moth. The superstition that spirits take this shape is not unknown in the West; and I suppose that as he steered his train out of the station, this fancy, by some odd freak of memory, leaped into his brain, and held it, hour after hour, while he and his engine flew forward and the burning theatre fell further and further behind. The truth was known a fortnight after his return from prison, which happened about the time of barley harvest.

A harvest-thanksgiving was held in the parish where he lived; and he went to it, being always a religious man. There were sheaves and baskets of vegetables in the chancel; fruit and flowers on the communion-table, with twenty-one tall candles burning above them; a processional hymn; and a long sermon. During the sermon, as the weather was hot and close, someone opened the door at the west end.

And when the preacher was just making up his mind to close the discourse, a large white moth fluttered in at the west door.

There was much light throughout the church; but the great blaze came, of course, from the twenty-one candles upon the altar. And towards this the moth slowly drifted, as if the candles sucked her nearer and nearer, up between the pillars of the nave, on a level with their capitals. Few of the congregation noticed her, for the sermon was a stirring one; only one or two children, perhaps, were interested—and the man I write of. He saw her pass over his head and float up into the chancel. He half-rose from his chair.

"My brothers," said the preacher, "if two sparrows, that are sold for a farthing, are not too little for the care of this infinite Providence—"

A scream rang out and drowned the sentence. It was followed by a torrent of vile words, shouted by a man who had seen, now for the second time, the form that clothed his wife's soul shrivelled in unthinking flames. All that was left of the white moth lay on the altar-cloth, among the fruit at the base of the tallest candlestick.

And because the man saw nothing but cruelty in the Providence of which the preacher spoke, he screamed and cursed, till they overpowered him and took him forth by the door. He was wholly mad from that hour.

Sindbad on Burrator

I heard this story in a farmhouse upon Dartmoor, and I give it in the words of the local doctor who told it. We were a reading-party of three undergraduates and a Christ Church don. The don had slipped on a boulder, two days before, while fishing the River Meavy, and sprained his ankle; hence Dr. Miles's visit. The two had made friends over the don's fly-book and the discovery that what the doctor did not know about Dartmoor trout was not worth knowing; hence an invitation to extend his visit over dinner. At dinner the talk diverged from sport to the ancient tin-works, stone circles, camps and *cromlechs* on the *tors* about us, and from there to touch speculatively on the darker side of the old religions: hence at length the doctor's story, which he told over the pipes and whisky, leaning his arms upon the table and gazing at it rather than at us, as though drawing his memories out of depths below its polished surface.

It must be thirty—yes, thirty—years ago (he said) since I met the man, on a bright November morning, when the Dartmoor hounds were drawing Burrator Wood. Burrator House in those days belonged to the Rajah Brooke—Brooke of Sarawak—who had bought it from Harry Terrell; or rather it had been bought for him by the Baroness Burdett Coutts and other admirers in England. Harry Terrell—a great sportsman in his day—had been loth enough to part with it, and when the bargain was first proposed, had named at random a price which was about double what he had given for the place. The *rajah* closed with the sum at once, asked him to make a list of everything in the house, and put a price on whatever he cared to sell. Terrell made a full list, putting what seemed to him fair prices on most of the furniture, and high ones—prohibitive he thought—on the sticks he had a fancy to keep. The *rajah* glanced over the paper in his grand manner, and says he, "I'll take it all."

"Stop! stop!" cried Terrell, "I bain't going to let you have the bed I was married in!"

"As you please; we'll strike out the bed, then," the *rajah* answered. That is how he took possession.

Burrator House, as I daresay you know, faces across the Meavy upon Burrator Wood; and the wood, thanks to Terrell, had always been a sure draw for a fox. I had tramped over from Tavistock on this particular morning,—for I was new to the country, a young man looking around me for a practice, and did not yet possess a horse,—and I sat on the slope above the house, at the foot of the *tor*, watching the scene on the opposite bank. The fixture, always a favourite one, and the *rajah's* hospitality—which was noble, like everything about him—had brought out a large and brightly-dressed field; and among them, in his black coat, moved Terrell on a horse twice as good as it looked. He had ridden over from his new home, and I daresay in the rush of old associations had forgotten for the while that the familiar place was no longer his.

The *rajah*, a statue of a man, sat on a tall grey at the covert's edge, directly below me; and from time to time I watched him through my field-glass. He had lately recovered from a stroke of paralysis, and was (I am told) the wreck of his old self; but the old fire lived in the ashes. He sat there, tall, lean, upright as a ramrod, with his eyes turned from the covert and gazing straight in front, over his horse's ears, on the rushing Meavy. He had forgotten the hounds; his care for his guests was at an end; and I wondered what thoughts, what memories of the East, possessed him. There is always a loneliness about a great man, don't you think? But I have never felt one to be so terribly—yes, terribly—alone as the *rajah* was that morning among his guests and the Devonshire *tors*.

"Every inch a king," said a voice at my elbow, and a little man settled himself down on the turf beside me. I set down my glasses with a start. He was a spare dry fellow of about fifty, dressed in what I took for the working suit of a mechanic. Certainly he did not belong to the moor. He wore no collar, but a dingy yellow handkerchief knotted about his throat, and both throat and face were seamed with wrinkles—so thickly seamed that at first glance you might take them for tattoo-marks; but I had time for a second, for without troubling to meet my eyes he nodded towards the *rajah*.

"I've cut a day's work and travelled out from Plymouth to get a sight of him; and I've a wife will pull my hair out when I get home and she finds I haven't been to the docks to-day; and I've had no breakfast but thirty grains of opium; but he's worth it."

"Thirty grains of opium!" I stared at him, incredulous. He did not turn, but, still with his eyes on the valley below us, stretched out a hand. It's fingers were gnarled, and hooked like a bird's claw, and on the little finger a ruby flashed in the morning sunlight—not a large ruby, but of the purest pigeon's-blood shade, and in any case a stone of price.

"You see this? My wife thinks it a sham one, but it's not. And some day, when I'm drunk or in low water, I shall part with it—but not yet. You've an eye for it, I see,"—and yet he was not looking towards me,—"but the *rajah*, yonder, and I are the only two within a hundred miles that can read what's in the heart of it."

He gazed for a second or two at the stone, lifted it to his ear as if listening, and lowering his hand to the turf, bent over it and gazed again. "Ay, *he* could understand and see into you, my beauty! *He* could hear the little drums tum-a-rumbling, and the ox-bells and bangles tinkling, and the shuffle of the elephants going by; *he* could read the lust in you, and the blood and the sun flickering and licking round the *kris* that spilt it—for it's the devil you have in you, my dear. But we know you—he and I—he and I. Ah! there you go," he muttered as the hounds broke into cry, and the riders swept round the edge of the copse towards the sound of a view-halloo. "There you go," he nodded after the *rajah*; "but ride as you will, the East is in you, great man—its gold in your blood, its dust in your eyelids, its own stink in your nostril; and, ride as you will, you can never escape it."

He clasped his knees and leaned back against the slope, following the grey horse and its rider with idolatrous gaze; and I noted that one of the clasped hands lacked the two middle fingers.

"You know him?" I asked. "You have seen him out there, at Sarawak?"

"I never saw him; but I heard of him." He smiled to himself. "It's not easy to pass certain gates in the East without hearing tell of the Rajah Brooke."

For a while he sat nursing his knee while I filled and lit a pipe. Then he turned abruptly, and over the flame of the match I saw his eyes, the pupils clouded around the iris and, as it were, withdrawn inward and away from the world. "Ever heard of Cagayan Sulu?" he asked.

"Never," said I. "Who or what is it?"

"It's an island," said he. "It lies a matter of eighty miles off the north-east corner of Borneo—facing Sandakan, as you might say."

"Who owns it?"

He seemed to be considering the question. "Well," he answered slowly, "if you asked the Spanish Government I suppose they'd tell you the King of Spain; but that's a lie. If you asked the natives—the Hadji Hamid, for instance—you'd be told it belonged to them; and that's half a lie. And if you asked the Father of Lies he might tell you the truth and call me for witness. I lost two fingers there—the only English flesh ever buried in those parts—so I've bought my knowledge."

"How did you come there?" I asked,—"if it's a fair question."

He chuckled without mirth. "As it happens, that's *not* a fair question. But I'll tell you this much, I came there with a brass band."

I began to think the man out of his mind.

"With the instruments, that is. I'd dropped the bandmaster on the way. Look here," he went on sharply, "the beginning is funny enough, but I'm telling you no lies. We'll suppose there was a ship, a British man-of-war—name not necessary just now."

"I think I understand," I nodded.

"Oh no, you don't," said he. "I'm not a deserter—at least not exactly—or I shouldn't be telling this to you. Well, we'll suppose this ship bound from Labuan to Hong-Kong with orders to keep along the north side of Borneo, to start with, and do a bit of exploring by the way. This would be in 'forty-nine, when the British Government had just taken over Labuan. *Very* good. Next we'll suppose the captain puts in at Kudat, in Marudu Bay, to pay a polite call on the *rajah* there or some understrapper of the *sultan's*, and takes his ship's band ashore by way of compliment, and that the band gets too drunk to play 'Annie Laurie.'" He chuckled again. "I never saw such a band as we were, down by the water's edge; and O'Hara, the bandmaster, took on and played the fool to such a tune, while we waited for the boat to take us aboard, that for the very love I bore him I had to knock him down and sit on him in a quiet corner.

"While I sat keeping guard on him I must have dropped asleep myself; for the next I remember was waking up to find the beach deserted and the boat gone. This put me in a sweat, of course; but after groping some while about the foreshore (which was as dark as the inside of your hat), I tripped over a rope and so found a native boat. O'Hara wouldn't wake, so I just lifted him on board like a sack, tossed in his cornet and my bombardon, tumbled in on top of them, and started to row for dear life towards the ship's light in the offing.

"But the *rajah*, or rather his servants, had filled us up with a kind of sticky drink that only begins to work when you think it about time to leave off. I must have pulled miles towards that ship, and every time I cast an eye over my shoulder her light was shining just as far away as ever. At last I remember feeling sure I was bewitched, and with that I must have tumbled off the thwart in a sound sleep.

"When I awoke I had both arms round the bombardon; there wasn't a sight of land, or of the ship, anywhere; and, if you please, the sun was near sinking! This time I managed to wake up O'Hara. We had splitting headaches, the pair of us; but we snatched up our instruments and started to blow on them like mad. Not a soul heard, though we blew till the sweat poured down us, and kept up the concert pretty well all through the night. You may think it funny, and I suppose we did amount to something like a joke—we two bandsmen booming away at the Popular Airs of Old England and the Huntsmen's Chorus under those everlasting stars. You wouldn't say so, if you had been the audience when O'Hara broke down and began to confess his sins.

"Luckily the sea kept smooth, and next morning I took the oars in earnest. We had no compass, and I was famished; but I stuck to it, steering by the sun and pulling in the direction where I supposed land to lie. O'Hara kept a look-out. We saw nothing, however, and down came the night again.

"Though the hunger had been gnawing and griping me for hours, yet—dog-tired as I was—I curled myself at the bottom of the boat and slept, and dreamed I was on board ship again and in my hammock. A sort of booming in my ears awoke me. Looking up I saw daylight around—clear morning light and blue sky—and right overhead, as it were, a great cliff standing against the blue. And there in the face of day O'Hara sat on the thwart, tugging like mad, now cricking his neck almost to stare up at the cliff, and now grinning down at me in silly triumph.

"With that I caught at the meaning of the sound in my ears. 'You infernal fool!' I shouted, staggering up and making to snatch the paddle from him. 'Get her nose round to it and back her!' For it was the noise of breaking water.

"But I was too late. Our boat, I must tell you, was a sort of Dutch pram, about twelve feet long and narrowing at the bows, which stood well out of water; handy enough for beaching, but not to be taken through breakers, by reason of its sitting low in the stern. O'Hara, as I yelled at him, pulled his starboard paddle and brought her (for these prams spin round easily) almost broadside on to a tall comber. As we slid up the side of it and hung there, I had a glimpse of a steep clean fissure straight through the wall of rock ahead; and in that instant O'Hara sprawled his arms and toppled overboard. The boat and I went by him with a rush. I saw a hand and wrist lifted above the foam, but when I looked back for them they were gone—gone as I shot over the bar and through the cleft into smooth water. I shouted and pulled back to the edge of the breakers; but he was gone, and I never saw him again.

"I suppose it was ten minutes before I took heart to look about me. I was floating on a lake of the bluest water I ever set eyes on, and as calm as a pond except by the entrance where the spent waves, after tumbling over the bar, spread themselves in long ripples, widening and widening until the edge of them melted and they were gone. The banks of the lake rose sheer from its edge, or so steeply that I saw no way of climbing them—walls you might call them, a good hundred feet high, and widening gradually towards the top, but in a circle as regular as ever you could draw with a pair of compasses. Any fool could see what had happened—that here was the crater of a dead volcano, one side of which had been broken into by the sea; but the beauty of it, sir, coming on top of my weakness, fairly made me cry. For the walls at the top were fringed with palms and jungle trees, and hung with creepers like curtains that trailed over the face of the cliff and down among the ferns by the shore. I leaned over the boat and stared into the water. It was clear, clear—you've no notion how clear; but no bottom could I see. It seemed to sink right through and into the sea on the other side of the world!

"Well, all this was mighty pretty, but it didn't tell me where to find a meal; so I baled out the boat and paddled along the eastern edge of the lake searching the cliffs for a path, and after an hour or so I hit on what looked to me like a foot-track, zigzagging up through the creepers and across the face of the rock. I determined to try it, made the boat fast to a clump of fern, slung

223

O'Hara's cornet on to my side-belt and began to climb.

"I saw no marks of footsteps; but the track was a path all right, though a teazer. A dozen times I had to crawl on hands and knees under the creepers—creepers with stems as thick as my two wrists—and once, about two-thirds of the way up, I was forced to push sideways through a crevice dripping with water, and so steep under foot that I slid twice and caked myself with mud. I very nearly gave out here; but it was do or die, and after ten minutes more of scratching, pushing, and scrambling, I reached the top and sat down to mop my face and recover.

"I daresay it was another ten minutes before I fetched breath enough and looked about me; and as I turned my head, there, close behind me, lay another crater with another lake smiling below, all blue and peaceful as the one I had left! I gazed from one to the other. This new crater had no opening on the sea; its sides were steeper, though not quite so tall; and either my eyes played me a trick or its water stood at a higher level. I stood there, comparing the two, when suddenly against the skyline, and not two hundred yards away, I caught sight of a man.

"He was walking towards me around the edge of the crater, and halting every now and then to stare down at my boat. He might be a friend, or he might be a foe; but anyway it was not for me, in my condition, to choose which, so I waited for him to come up. And first I saw that he carried a spear, and wore a pair of wide dirty-white trousers and a short coat embroidered with gold; and next that he was a true Malay, pretty well on in years, with a greyish beard falling over his chest. He had no shirt, but a scarlet sash wrapped about his waist and holding a *kris* and two long pistols handsomely inlaid with gold. In spite of his weapons he seemed a benevolent old boy.

"He pointed towards my boat and tried me with a few questions, first in his own language, then in Spanish, of which I knew very little beyond the sound. But I spread out my hands towards the sea, by way of explaining our voyage, and then pointed to my mouth. If he understood he seemed in no hurry. He tapped O'Hara's cornet gingerly with two fingers. I unstrung it and made shift to play 'Home, Sweet Home.' This delighted him; he nodded, rubbed his hands, and stepped a few paces from me, then turned and began fingering his spear in a way I did not like at all. 'It's a matter of taste, sir,' said I, or words to that effect, dropping the cornet like a hot potato; but he pointed towards it, and then over a ridge inland, and I gathered I must pick it up and follow him—which I did, and pretty quick.

"From the top of this ridge we faced across a small plain bounded on the north with a tier of hills, most of which seemed by their shape to be volcanoes, and out of action—for the sky lay quite blue and clear above them. The way down into this plain led through jungle; but the plain itself had been cleared of all but small clumps dotted here and there, which gave it, you might say, the look of an English park; and about half-way across, in a clear stretch of *lalang* grass, stood a village of white huts huddling round a larger and much taller house.

"The old man led me straight towards this, and, coming closer, I saw that the large house had a rough glacis about it and a round wall pierced with loopholes. A number of goats were feeding here and a few small cattle; also the ground about the village had been cleared and planted with fruit-trees,—mangoes, bananas, limes, and oranges,—but as yet I saw no inhabitants. The old Malay, who had kept ahead of me all the way, walking at a fair pace, here halted and once more signed to me to blow on the cornet. I obeyed, of course, this time with 'The British Grenadiers.' I declare to you it was like starting a swarm of bees.

"You wouldn't believe the troops that came pouring out of those few huts—the women in loose trousers pretty much like the men's, but with arms bare and loose *sarongs* flung over their right shoulders, the children with no more clothes than a pocket-handkerchief apiece. I can't tell you what first informed me of my guide's rank among them—whether the *salaams* they offered him, or the richness of his dress—he was the only one with gold lace and the only one who carried pistols—or the air with which he paraded me through the crowd, waving the people back to right and left, and clearing a way to a narrow door in the wall around the great house. A man armed with a long fowling-piece saluted him at the entry; and once inside he pointed from the house to his own breast, as much as to say, 'I am the chief, and this is mine.' I saluted him humbly.

"A verandah ran around the four sides of the house, with a trench between it and the fortified wall. A plank bridge led across the trench to the verandah steps, where my master—or, to call him by his right name, Hadji Hamid—halted again and clapped his hands. A couple of young Malay women, dressed like those I had passed in the street, ran out in answer, and were ordered to bring me food. While it was preparing I rested on a low chair, blinking at the sunlight on the fortified wall. It had been pierced, on the side of the house, for eleven guns, but six of the embrasures were empty, and of the five pieces standing no two were alike in size, age, or manufacture, and the best seemed to be a nine-pounder, strapped to its carriage with rope.

"Hadji Hamid saw what I was looking at, and chuckled to himself solemnly. All through the meal—which began with a mess of rice and chopped fowl and ended with bananas—he sat beside me, chewing betel, touching this thing and that, naming it in his language and making me repeat the words after him. He smiled at every mistake, but never lost his patience; indeed it was clear that my quickness delighted him, and I did my best, wondering all the while what he meant to do with me.

"Well, to be short, sir, he intended to keep me. I believe he would have done it for the sake of the cornet; but before I had finished eating, up stepped a sentry escorting a man with my bombardon under his arm. I had left it, as you know, in the boat, and had heard no order given; but the boat I never saw again, and here was my bombardon. Hadji Hamid took it in both hands, felt it all over, patted it, and ended by turning it over to me and calling in dumb show for a tune. I tell you, my performance was a success.

"At the first blast he leaned back suddenly in his chair; at the second he turned a kind of purple under his yellow skin; but at the third he caught hold of his stomach and began to roll in his seat and laugh. You never saw a man laugh like it. He made scarcely any sound; he was too near apoplexy to speak; but the tears ran down his face, and one minute his hand would be up waving feebly to me to stop, the next he'd be signalling to go on again. I wanted poor O'Hara; he used to give himself airs and swear at my playing, but among these people he and his cornet would have had to stand down.

"They gave me a bed that night in a corner of the verandah, and next morning my master came himself to wake me, and took me down to the village bathing-pool, just below the fortifications. It hurt my modesty to find the whole mob of inhabitants gathered there and waiting, and it didn't set me at ease, exactly, to notice that each man carried his spear. For one nasty moment I pictured a duck-hunt, with me playing duck. But there was no cause for alarm. At a signal from Hamid, who stripped and led the way, in we tumbled together—men, women, and children—the men first laying their spears on the bank beside their clothes. Six remained on shore to keep guard, and were relieved after five minutes by another six from the pool. There was a good deal of splashing and horse-play, but nothing you could call immodest, though my fair skin came in for an amount of attention I had to get used to.

"My breakfast was served to me alone, and soon after I was summoned to attend my master in one of the state rooms of the house. I found him on a shaded platform, seated opposite an old native as well-dressed and venerable-looking as himself, but stouter. The pair lolled on cushions at either end of the platform, smoking and smoothing their grey beards. I understood that the visitor was a personage and (somehow) that he had been sent for expressly to hear and be astonished by my performance.

"The two instruments were brought in upon cushions, and I began to play. The visitor—who had less sense of humour than Hamid—did not laugh at all. Instead, he took the mouthpiece of his *tchibouk* slowly from his lips and held it at a little distance, while his mouth and eyes opened wider and wider. Hamid eyed him keenly, with a kind of triumph under his lids; and the triumph grew as the old man's stare lit up with a jealousy there was no mistaking.

"This, too, passed as I wound up with a flourish and stood at attention, waiting for orders. The visitor put out his hand, but as I offered him the bombardon he waved it aside impatiently and pointed to the cornet. I passed it up to him; he patted and examined it for a while, laid it on his knee, and the two men began talking in low voices.

"I could see that compliments were passing; but you'll guess I wasn't prepared for what followed. Hamid stood up suddenly and whispered to one of his six guards stationed below the platform. The man went out, and returned in five minutes followed by a girl. Now that the island girls were beautiful I had already discovered that morning, and this one was no exception—a small thing about five feet, with glossy black hair and the tiniest feet and hands. She seemed to me to walk nervously, as if brought up for punishment; and a thought took me—and I shall be glad of it when I come to die—that if they meant to ill-use her I might do worse than assault that venerable pair with my bombardon and end my adventures with credit.

"My eyes were so taken up with the girl that for a full minute I paid no attention to my master. She had come to a halt under the platform, a couple of paces from me, with her eyes cast down upon the floor; and he on the platform was speaking. By and by he stopped, and glancing up I saw that he was motioning me to leave the room. Well, they had made no show as yet of ill-treating her; so I flung her one more look and obeyed, feeling pretty mean. I went out into the verandah, walked the length of it and turned—and there stood the girl right before me! Her little feet had followed me so softly that I had heard nothing; and now, as I stared at her, she crept close with a sort of sidelong motion, and knelt at my feet, at the same moment drawing her *sarong* over her head to hide it. Then the truth came upon me—I was married!

"Aoodya was her name. What else can I tell you about her,

to describe her? She was a child, and all life came as play to her, yet she understood love to the tips of her little madder-brown fingers. She was my teacher, too, and I sat at her feet day after day and learned while she drilled the island-language into me; learned by the hour while she untwisted her hair and rubbed it with grated cocoanut, and broke off her toilet to point to this thing and that and tell me its name, laughing at my mistakes or flipping bits of betel at me by way of reward. I had no wife at home to vex my conscience at all. All day we played about Hamid's verandah like two children, and Hamid watched us with a sort of twinkle in his eye, seemingly well content. It was plain he had taken a fancy to me, and I thought, as time passed, he grew friendlier.

"I blessed the old fellow, too. Had he not given me Aoodya? I puzzled my head over this favour, until Aoodya explained. 'You see,' she said, 'it was done to oblige the Hadji Hassan.' This was the old man who had listened to my performance on the bombardon. He lived in a stockaded house on the far side of the island, the chieftancy of which he and Hamid shared between them and without dispute.

"'How should it oblige Hassan?' I asked.

"'Because Hassan could not see or hear my lord and lover without longing to possess such a man for his very own. As who could?' And here she blew me a kiss.

"'Thank you, jewel of my heart,' said I; 'but yet I don't see. Was it me he wanted, or the *bombardon?*'

"'I fancy he thought of you together; but of course he did not ask for the big thing—that would have been greedy. He would be content with the little one, the what-you-call cornet; and—don't you see?'

"'No doubt it's stupid of me, my dear,' said I, 'but I'll be shot if I do.'

"She was sitting with a lapful of *pandanus* leaves, blue and green, weaving a mat of them while we talked, and had just picked out a beater from the tools scattered round her—a flat piece of board with a bevelled edge, and shaped away to a handle. 'Stupid!' she says to me, just like so, and at the same time raps me over the hand smartly. 'He thought—if peradventure there came to us a little one—'

"'*With* a what-you-call cornet?'—I clapped my hand to my mouth over a guffaw; and, with that, She—who had started laughing too—came to a stop, with her eyes fastened on the back of it. I saw them stiffen, and the pretty round pupils draw in and shrink to narrow slits like a cat's, and her arm went back slowly behind her, and her bosom leaned nearer and nearer. I thought she was going to spring at me, and as my silly laugh died out I turned my hand and held it palm outward, to fend her off. On the back of it was a drop of blood where the bevelled edge of the beater had by accident broken the skin.

"Somehow this movement of mine seemed to fetch her to bearings. Her hand came slowly forward again, hesitated, seemed to hover for a moment at her throat, then went swiftly down to her bosom between bodice and flesh, and came up again tugging after it what looked to me a piece of coarse thread. She tossed it into my lap as I still sat there cross-legged, and with that sprang up and raced away from me, down to the verandah. There was no chance of catching her, and I was (to tell the truth) a bit too much taken aback to try. I picked up the string. On it was threaded a silk purse no bigger than a shilling; and from this I shook into my palm a small stone like an opal. I turned it over once or twice, put it back in the purse, and stowed string, purse, and all in my breeches' pocket.

"I strolled down the verandah to our quarters in search of Aoodya, but the room was empty; and after that I'm afraid I smoked and sulked for the rest of the day, until nightfall. After playing the Hadji Hamid through his meal I went out to our favourite seat on the edge of the dry ditch, when she came to me out of nowhere across the withered grass of the compound.

"'Have you the charm, O beloved?' she whispered.

"'Oh, it's a charm, is it?' said I, partly sulky yet.

"'Yes, and you must never lose it—never part with it—never, above all, give it back to me. Promise me that, beloved; and I, who have wept much, am happy again.'

"So I promised, and she snuggled close to me, and all was as before. No more was said between us, and by next morning she seemed to have clean forgotten the affair. But I thought of it at times, and it puzzled me.

"Now, as I said, my master had taken a fancy to me quite apart from the bombardon, and a token of it was his constantly taking me out as companion on his walks. You may think it odd that he never troubled about my being an unbeliever—for of course he held by the Prophet, and so did all the islanders, Aoodya included. But in fact, though his people called themselves Mahommedans, each man treated his religion much as he chose, and Hamid talked to me as freely as if I had been his son.

"In this way I learned a deal of the island and its customs, and of the terms by which Hamid and Hassan between them shared its rule. But that any others laid claim to it I had no idea, until one day as we were walking on the coast, and not far from the crater where he had found me first, my master asked suddenly, 'Was I happy?'

"'Quite happy,' I answered.

"'You would not leave us if you could?' he went on, and began to laugh quiet-like, behind his beard. 'Oho! Love, love! I that am old have been merry in my day.' We walked for another mile, maybe, without speaking, and came to the edge of a valley. 'Look down yonder,' said he.

"Below us, and in the mouth of the valley, which grew broad and shallow as it neared the sea, I saw a hill topped by a round wall and compound. There might have been half a dozen houses within the compound, all thatched, and above them stood up a flag painted in red and yellow stripes, and so stiff in the breeze that with half an eye you could tell it was no bunting but a sheet of tin.

"Hullo!' said I. 'Spaniards?'

"'Puf!' Hamid grinned at the flag and spat. 'A Captain Marquinez inhabits there, with four Manila men and their wives. He is a sensible fellow, and does no harm, and if it pleases him to hoist that toy on a bamboo, he is welcome.'

"'They claim the island, then?'

"'What matters it if they claim? There was a letter once came to us from the Spanish Governor in Tolo. That man was a fool. He gave us warning that by order of the Government at Manila he would send a hundred men to build a fort inland and set up a garrison. Hassan and I took counsel together. 'He is a fool,' said Hassan; 'but we must answer him.' So we answered him thus. 'Send your men. Today they come; tomorrow they die—yet trouble not; *we* will bury them.'

"'Were they sent?' I asked.

"'They were not sent. He was a fool, yet within bounds. Nevertheless a time may come for us—not for Hassan and me, we shall die in our beds—but for our sons. Even for this we are prepared.' He would have said more, but checked himself. (I learned later on that the islanders kept one of the craters fortified for emergency, to make a last stand there; but they never allowed me to see the place.) 'We have gods of our own,' said Hamid slily, 'who will be helpful—the more so that we do not bother them over trifles. Also there are—other things; and the lake Sinquan, and another which you have not seen, are full of crocodiles.' He stamped his foot. 'My son, beneath this spot there has been fire, and still the men of Cagayan walk warily and go not without their spears. For you it is different; yet when you come upon aught that puzzles you, it were well to put no questions even to yourself.'

"'Not even about this?' I asked, and showed him the purse and stone which Aoodya had tossed to me.

"'You are in luck's way,' said he, 'whoever gave you that.' He pulled a small pouch from his breast, opened it, and showed me a stone exactly like mine. 'It is a cocoanut pearl. Keep it near to your hand, and forget not to touch it if you hear noises in the air or a man meet you with eyes like razors.'

"I wanted to ask him more, but he started to walk back hastily, and when I caught him up would talk of nothing but the sugar and sweet-potato crops, and the yield of cocoanut oil to be carried to Kudat at the next north-east monsoon. I noticed that the fruit-trees planted along the shore were old, and that scores of them had ceased bearing. 'They will last my day,' said he. 'Let my sons plant others if they so will.' He always spoke in this careless way of his children, and I believe he had many, for an islander keeps as many wives as he can afford; but they lived about the villages, and could not be told from the other inhabitants by any sign of rank or mark of favour he showed them.

"For a long while I believed that Aoodya must be a daughter of his. She always denied it, but owned that she had never known her mother and had lived in Hamid's house ever since she could remember. Anyhow, he took the greatest care of me, and never allowed me to join the expeditions which sailed twice a year from the island—to Palawan for paddy, and to the north of Borneo with oil and nuts and pandanus mats. He may have mistrusted me; but more likely he forbade it out of care for me and the music I played; for the *prahus* regularly came back with three or four of their number missing—either capsized on the voyage or blown away towards Tawi-Tawi, where the pirates accounted for them.

"Though I might not sail abroad he allowed me to join the tuburing parties off the shore. We would work along the reefs there in rafts of bamboo, towing with us two or three dug-outs filled with mashed *tubur*-roots. At the right spot the dug-outs would be upset, and after a while the fish came floating up on their sides, or belly uppermost, to be speared by us; for the root puddles the water like milk, and stupefies them somehow without hurting the flesh, which in an hour or so is fit to eat.

"We had been tuburing one afternoon, and put back with our baskets filled to a spit of the shore where we had left an old islander, Kotali by name, alone and tending a fire for our meal. Coming near we saw him stretched on the sand by his cooking-pots, and shouted to wake him, for his fire was low. Kotali did not stir. I was one of the first to jump ashore and run to him. He lay with his legs drawn up, his hands clenched, his eyes wide open and staring at us horribly. The man was as dead as a nail.

"I never saw people worse frightened. 'The Berbalangs!' said someone in a dreadful sort of whisper, and we started to run back to the raft for our lives—I with the rest, for the panic had taken hold of me, though I could see no sign of an enemy. I supposed these Berbalangs, named with such awe, to be pirates or marauders from Tawi-Tawi or some neighbouring island, and the first hint that reached me of anything worse was a wailing sound which grew as we ran, and overhauled us, until the air was filled with roaring, so that I swung round to defend myself, yet could see nothing. To my surprise a man who had been running beside me dropped on the sand, pulled a sigh of relief, and began to mop his face—and this in the very worst of the racket. 'They are gone by,' he shouted; 'the worse the noise the farther off they are. They have taken their fill to-day on poor old Kotali.'

"Suddenly the noise ceased altogether, and we picked up courage to return and bury the body. We had a basket of limes on the raft, and these were fetched and the juice squeezed over the grave; but no one seemed inclined to answer the questions I put about these Berbalangs. It seemed that unless they were close at hand there was ill-luck even in mentioning them, and I walked back to the village in a good deal of perplexity.

"I should tell you, sir, that by this time I was the father of a fine boy; and that Aoodya doted on him. When she was not feeding him or calling on me to admire his perfections, from the cleverness of his smile to the beautiful shape of his toes, he lay and slept, or kicked in a basket slung on a long bamboo fastened across the rafters, Aoodya would give the basket a pull, and this set it bobbing up and down on the spring of the bamboo for minutes at a time.

"Now when I reached home with my string of fish, I walked round to the back of the house to clean them before going in. This took me past the window of our room, and glancing inside—the window was unglazed, you understand—I saw Aoodya standing before the cradle and talking, quick and angry, with a man posted in the doorway opening on the verandah.

"I was not jealous. The thought never entered my head. But I dropped my fish and whipped round to the doorway in time to catch him as he turned to go, having heard my footstep belike.

"'Who the something-or-other are you?' I asked. 'And what's your business in my private house?'

"The man—a yellow-faced fellow, but young in figure—muttered something in a gibberish new to me, and made as if excusing himself. It gave me an ugly start to see that his eyes were yellow too, with long slits for pupils; but I saw too that he was afraid of me, and being in a towering rage myself, I out with my *kris*.

"'Now look here,' I said; 'I don't understand what you say, but maybe you understand this. Walk! And if I catch you here again, you'll need someone to sew you up.'

"I watched him as he went across the compound. The guard at the gate scarcely looked up, and if the thing hadn't been impossible, there, in the broad daylight, I could have fancied he saw no one. I turned to Aoodya and took her hands, for she was trembling from head to foot. At my touch she burst out sobbing, clung to my shoulder and begged me to protect her.

"'Why, of course I will,' said I, more cheerfully than I felt by a long sight. 'If I'd known you were frightened like this, I'd have slit his body to match his eyes. But who is he, at all?'

"'He—he said he was my brother!' she wailed, and clung to me again. 'I cannot—I cannot!'

"'I'll brother him!' cried I. 'But what is it he wants?'

"'I cannot—I cannot!' was all she would say; and now her sobs were so loud that the child woke up screaming and had to be soothed. And this seemed to do her good.

"Well, I got her to bed and asleep early that night; but before morning I had a worse fright than ever. Somehow in my dream I had a feeling come to me that the bed was empty, and sat up suddenly, half awake and scared. Aoodya had risen and was standing by the cradle, with one hand on its edge; in the other was the lamp—a clam-shell fastened in a split handle of bamboo, and holding a pith wick and a little oil. The flame wavered against her eyes as she held it up and peered into the baby's face—and her eyes were like as I had seen them once before, and devilish like the eyes I had seen in another face that afternoon.

"A man never knows what he can do till the call comes. There, betwixt sleep and waking, I knew that happiness had come to an end for us. Yet I slipped out of bed very softly, took the lamp from her as gentle as you please, set it on a stool and, turning, reached out for her two wrists and held them—for how long I can't tell you. She didn't try to fend me away, or struggle at all, and not a word did I utter, but stood holding her—the babe asleep beside us—and listened to her breathing until it grew easier, and she leaned to me, weak as water.

"Then I let go, and lifting the child's head from the pillow pulled Aoodya's charm, the cocoanut pearl, from my neck and hung it about his. 'That's for you, sonny,' said I, 'and if the Berbalangs come along you can pass them on to your father.' I faced round on Aoodya with a smile which no doubt was thin enough, though honestly meant to hearten her. 'It's all right, old girl. Come back to bed,' said I, and held her in my arms until I fell asleep in the dawn.

"But of course it was not all right; and after two days spent with this dismal secret between us, and Aoodya all the while play-acting at her old tricks of love for me and the babe—as if, God knows, I doubted they, and not the horror, were her real self—I could stand it no longer, but did what I ought to have done before; sought out my master and made a clean breast of it.

"I could see that it took the old man between wind and water. When I had done he sat for some time pulling his beard and eyeing me once or twice rather queerly, as I thought.

"'My friend,' said he at last, 'I suppose you will be suspecting me; yet I give you my word—and the Hadji Hamid is no liar—that if Aoodya is a Berbalang, or a daughter of Berbalangs, the same was unknown to me when I married you.'

"'I'll believe that,' I answered; 'the more by token that I never suspected you.'

"'She had no known father, which (as you know) is held a

disgrace among us; so much a disgrace that she grew up without suitors in spite of her looks and my favour. Therefore I seized my chance of giving her a husband, and in that I am not guiltless towards you; but of anything worse I was ignorant, and for proof I am going to help you if I can.' He frowned to himself, still tugging at his beard. 'Her mother was of good family, on this side of the island. Therefore she cannot be pure Berbalang, and most likely the Berbalangs have no more than a fetch upon her'—he used a word new to me, but 'fetch' I took to be the meaning of it. 'If so, we must go to them and persuade them to take it off. They owe me something; for though, as we value peace and quiet, Hassan and I leave them alone in their own dirty village and ask no tax nor homage, we could make things uncomfortable if we chose. Yes, yes,' said he, 'I think it can be done; but it will be dangerous. You are wearing your cocoanut pearl, of course?'

"I told him that I had given it up to the baby.

"He nodded. 'Yes, that was well done; but you must borrow it for the day. Run and fetch it at once; we have a long walk before us.'

"So I ran back, and without telling Aoodya, who was washing her linen behind the house, slipped the pearl off the child's neck and returned to Hamid. I found him, with two spears in his hand, waiting for me. He gave me one, and forth we set.

"The Berbalangs' village stands on a sort of table-land in the hills which rise all the way to Mount Tebulian, near the centre of the island. After the first two miles I found myself in strange country, and Hamid kept silence and signed to me to do the same. In this way we sweated up the slopes until, a little after noon, we reached a pass, and saw the roofs of the village over the edge of a broad step, as it were, half a mile above us. Here we sat down, and Hamid, drawing a couple of limes from his pocket, explained that I must on no account taste any food the Berbalangs set before us unless I first sprinkled it with lime juice. It might look like curried fish, but would, as likely as not, be human flesh disguised, the taste of which would destroy my soul and convert me into a Berbalang; a touch of the lime juice would turn such food back to its proper shape and show me what I was being asked to eat.

"We now moved forward again, very cautiously, and soon came to the village. The houses, perhaps a dozen in all, were scandalously dirty, otherwise pretty much like those in Hamid's own village. But not a living creature could be seen. Hamid, I could tell, was puzzled, and even a bit frightened. He put a good face on it, all the same, and began to walk from house to house, keeping his spear handy as he peered in at the doors. Still not a soul could we find, barring an old goat tethered and a few roaming fowls. The stink of the place sickened us, and I wanted to run, though we came across no actual horrors. In one room we found a pan of rice lately boiled and still smoking, and sprinkled it with lime juice. It remained good rice. Out into the street we went, and Hamid, growing bolder, raised a loud halloo. The noise of it sent the fowls scudding, and the hills around took it up and echoed it.

"He looked at me. 'They must be out on the hunt,' said he.

"'Good Lord!' I gasped. 'And the child at home—without the pearl!' I turned and plunged for it down the slope like a madman.

"What to do I had no idea; but I hadn't a doubt that the Berbalangs were after Aoodya or the child, or both, and I headed for home with the wind singing by my ears. At the foot of the pass I looked back. Hamid was following, skipping from one lava stone to another at a pace that did credit to his old legs. He waved a hand and called—as I thought, to encourage me; and away down I pounded.

"I must have reached the edge of the plain in twenty minutes (the climb had taken us more than two hours), and, once there, I squeezed my elbows into my sides and settled into stride. Luckily the season was dry, and a fire, three weeks before, had swept over the tall *lalang* grass, leaving a thin layer of ash, which made running easy. For all that, I was pretty near dead beat when I reached the compound and ran past the sentry. The man cried out at sight of me as I went by; but I thought he was just pattering out his challenge, being taken unawares; and knowing he would not let off his musket if he recognised me, I paid no attention.

"I had prepared myself (as I thought) for anything—to find Aoodya dead beside the child, or to find them both unharmed and flourishing as I had left them. But what happened was that I burst in and stared around an empty room. *That* knocked the wind out of my sails. I called twice, leaned my head against the door-post and panted; called again, and, getting no answer, walked stupidly back across the compound to the gate.

"The sentry there was pointing. I believe he was telling me, too, that Aoodya, with the child in her arms, had passed out some while before. But as he waved a hand towards the plain I saw a figure running there, and recognised Hamid. The old man was heading, not towards us, but for the seashore, and, plain as daylight, he was heading there with a purpose. I remembered now his cry to me from the head of the pass. So I pressed elbows to side again and lit out after him.

"He was making for a thick patch of jungle between us and the sea, and though I had run at least a mile out of the way I soon began to overhaul him. But long before I reached the clump he had found an opening in it and dived out of sight, and I overtook him only when the growth thinned suddenly by the edge of a crater, plunging down to a lake so exactly like Sinquan that I had to look about me and take my bearings before making sure that this was another, and one I had never yet seen.

"I caught him by the arm, and we peered down the slope together. At the foot of it, and by the edge of the lake, there ran a strip of white beach; and there, and almost directly below us, were gathered the Berbalangs.

"They were moving and pushing into place in a sort of circle around a small bundle which at first sight I took for a heap of clothes. At that distance they seemed harmless enough, and, barring the strangeness of the spot, might have been an ordinary party of islanders forming up for a dance. But when, all of a sudden, the ring came to a standstill, and a figure stepped out of it towards the bundle in the centre, my wits came back to me, and I flung up both arms, shouting 'Aoodya! Aoodya!'

"She must have made three paces in the time my voice took to reach her. She was close to the child. Then she halted and stood for a moment gazing up at me. I saw something bright drop from her. And with that she stooped, caught up the child, and was racing up the slope towards us.

"'Steady!' muttered Hamid, as a man broke from the circle, plucked up the knife from the sand and rushed after her. 'Steady!' he said again.

"Aoodya had a start of twenty yards or more, and in the first half-minute she actually managed to better it. Hamid, beside me, rubbed a bullet quickly on the rind of one of his lime-fruits and rammed it home. He took an eternal time about it; and below, now, the man was gaining. Unluckily their courses brought them into line, and twice the old man cursed softly and lowered his piece.

"Flesh and blood could not stand this. I let out a groan and sprang down the cliff. It was madness, and at the third step all foothold slipped from under me; but my clutch was tight on a fistful of creepers, and their tendrils were tough as a ship's rope. So down I went, now touching earth, now fending off from the rock with my feet, now missing hold and sprawling into a mass of leaves and roots, among which I clutched wildly and checked myself by the first thing handy—until, with the crack of Hamid's musket above, the vine, or whatever it was to which I clung for the moment, gave way as if shorn by the bullet, and I pitched a full twenty feet with a rush of loose earth and dust.

"I fell almost at the heels of Aoodya's enemy, upon a ledge along which he was swiftly running her down. Hamid's bullet had missed him, and before I could make the third in the chase he was forty yards ahead. I saw his bare shoulders parting the creepers—threading their way in and out like a bobbin, and jogging as the pace fell slower; for now we were all three in difficulties. Perhaps Aoodya had missed the track; at any rate the ledge we were now following grew shallower as it curved over the corner of the beach and ran sheer over the water of the lake. A jungle tree leaned out here, with a clear drop of a hundred feet. As I closed on my man, he swerved and began to clamber out along the trunk; and over his shoulder I saw Aoodya, with the babe in the crick of her arm, upon a bough which swayed and sank beneath her.

"I clutched at his ankle. He reached back with a hiss of his breath and jabbed his knife down on my left hand, cutting across the two middle fingers and pinning me through the small bones to the trunk. I tell you, sir, I scarcely felt it. My right went down to my waist and pulled out the *kris* there. He was the man I had caught within the verandah three days before; these were the same eyes shining, like a cat's, back into mine, and what I had promised him then I gave him now. But it was Hamid who killed him. For as my *kris* went into the flank of him, above the hip, Hamid's second shot cut down through his neck. His face at the moment rested sideways against the branch, and I suppose the bullet passed through to the bough and cost me Aoodya. For as the Berbalang fell, the bough seemed to rip away from where his cheek had rested, and Aoodya, with my child in her arms, swung back under my feet and dropped like a stone into the lake.

"I can't tell you, sir, how long I lay stretched out along that trunk, with the Berbalang's knife still pinned through my hand. I was staring down into the water. Aoodya and my child never rose again; but the Berbalang came to the surface at once and floated, bobbing for a while on the ripple, his head thrown back, his brown chest shining up at me, and the blood spreading on the water around it.

"It was Hamid who unpinned me and led me away. He had made shift to climb down, and while binding up my wounded hand pointed towards the beach. It was empty. The crowd of Berbalangs had disappeared.

"He found the track which Aoodya had missed, and as he led me up and out of the crater I heard him talking—talking. I suppose he was trying to comfort me—he was a good fellow; but at the top I turned on him, and 'Master,' I said, 'you have tried to do me much kindness, but today I have bought my quittance.' With that I left him standing and walked straight over the brow of the hill. I never looked behind me until I reached the Spaniards' compound, and called out at the gate to be let pass.

"Captain Marquinez was lying in a hammock in the cool of his verandah when the gate-keeper took me to him. He was, I think, the weariest man I ever happened on. 'So you want to leave the island?' said he when my tale was out. 'Yes, yes, I believe you; I've learnt to believe anything of those devils up yonder. But you must wait a fortnight, till the relief-boat arrives from Jola'—"

Here the story-teller broke off as a rider upon a grey horse came at a foot-pace round the slope of Burrator below us and passed on without seeing. It was the *rajah*, returning solitary from the hunt, and his eyes were still fastened ahead of him.

"Ah, great man! England is a weary hole for the likes of you and me. It's here they talk of the East, but we have loved it and hated it and known it, and remember. Our eyes have seen—our eyes have seen."

He stood up, pulled himself together with a kind of shiver, and suddenly shambled away across the slope, having said no goodbye, but leaving me there at gaze.

Step o' One Side
The Story is told by James Pascoe of Menadarva, in the Clay District of Cornwall

1

I was a small boy when Joseph Pooke laid a sort of spell on our parish; and as the beginnings of it happened in the bar-kitchen of 'Step o' One Side' (which is our local name for the Wesley Arms, by reason of its standing, respectable yet in some ways convenient, a short step off the main street), I can only report of them by hearsay; my chief witness being Sam Trudgian, a clay-worker and a moderately sober man all his days.

This Joseph Pooke, then, came on a Friday night in December and out of a tearing sou'westerly gale, to the astonishment of the company seated around on bench and settle and all the cosier for the squalls of rain bursting against the windows. For you must know that the little off-parlour beyond the bar-kitchen served, in those days on Friday nights, for a sort of counting-house, where the three Clay-lords (as we called them), who owned the great One-and-All Pit, paid out the men's wages; which done, they would light their long pipes and linger for a couple of hours over two goes apiece of brandy-hot and discuss the news of the day.

Old Zebedee and Cornelius Bunt, brothers and twins .it that, were the two seniors, both equally rich by repute; with William Pendrea, their sister's son—they being unmarried—for junior partner and manager. Lawyer Simmons of St. Austell regularly made up the fourth; and there they would sit content with the world, a door and a curtain only dividing them off from the big kitchen-bar where the men handselled their pay—thirty it might be and more, thinning down to a dozen as the staider ones sloped away home to their wives.

Well, there the place was full—Renatus Lowry, the landlord, stirring the great fire and taking orders; his wife behind the bar mixing '*Schenacrum*' (which is ale and rum with ingredients); and their daughter Annie, a slip of a girl all but husband-high, slicing lemons or running to and from the back-kitchen with the kettle. And in the midst of this busy-all the front door banged to, and close on the sound of it the foreigner walked in. I should explain perhaps that any with a face unknown or a stranger in any way from outside the parish is a 'foreigner' to us in Menadarva. But this man had the look of a far-travelled man as he stood a moment framed in the kitchen doorway, the lamplight glistering on the wet that poured off the rim of his sou'wester and down his yellow oilskin. Also when he pulled off his headpiece and the company caught sight that a pair of earrings glinted behind the draggle of his side locks, it took them aback to hear him speak good Cornish.

'Evenin', neighbours all!' says he, taking in the room with a smile and a bit of a laugh. 'A red light at times may be a warnin', but ashore and through red curtains it spells good entertainment—or should, eh, missus?' He turned to Mrs. Lowry.

'For them as can pay and behave themselves,' answered that cautious woman. Her husband just at that moment came from the inner room, a tray of empty glasses in hand. Belike the bang of the door had fetched him forth of a sudden.

'Hullo!' says he with a stare, handing the tray to the woman; and then: 'What's this?—a wreck ashore?'

'Timbers sound, I hope,' says the stranger, tapping a longish bundle wrapped in tarpaulin that he carried under his left arm. With no more ado he stepped across to the fire-place, unslung a haversack from his shoulder, set down the bundle, and slowly stripped himself of his oilskins—a well-set fellow, broad of shoulder, and cased in good sea-cloth. His boots, too, though mired, were stout and serviceable.

'You're kindly welcome anyways, my son,' said Renatus, perhaps noting this. 'A seaman, I reckon?'

'Miner. And my name's Pooke—Joseph Pooke—St. Joseph was in the tin trade once, as maybe you've heard tell. But you've made no bad cast at it, either: seem' that I've come here by way of The Horn.'

This made all stare, respectfully.

'Plymouth bound?'

'Not tonight, anyway. And I've not broke ship, if that's what you're hintin'.'

'For shame, Renatus!' put in the wife across the counter. 'Cattychisin' like this, and him just in from the weather.' The sight of the man's good clothes had reassured her, no doubt.

He stepped to the bar. 'Thank 'ee, ma'am. And as for your husband's name I can read it from the notice above the dresser: *Renatus Lowry, licensed to sell Beer, Spirituous Liquors And Tobacco*. Well, that's a suggestion. What about drinks all round, if the company will name their fancy?' He pulled out a fistful of silver and slid a couple of half-crowns across. 'That's a pretty piece, too, you keep here.'

'I'll trouble you to speak respectful of my daughter,' Mrs. Lowry fired up.

'Certainly, ma'am. But I was speakin' of your counter. A prettier piece of copper, nor a brighter kept as proud to image two handsome faces, hasn' delighted the eye this long while. I'm a miner, ma'am, as I said just now; and by haveage—my father and mother having broken up home under Cam Brea and gone out to the States with a cousin or two in the 'forty-nine when the mines closed, down-along. In Nevada I was born and reared. Underground mostly. . . . Drinks around, landlord, if you please! . . . And what might be *your* name, my dear?' he asks the girl. 'N. or M? as the book says.'

'Annie, sir,' answers she, bending low, and her hand shaking a bit as she pushed his drink towards him so that it spilt a drop.

'Careless, Annie!' says the mother.

'Annie?—Annie Lowry? Eh now—"Maxwellton braes are bonny." . . . No, ma'am, I'm not teasin' your daughter. 'Tis the name of an old song, and the world-widest on earth I reckon.'

'Is it out of Wesley?' she asked.

''Tis a tune two innocents have sung together often enough, each holding a corner of Wesley's hymn-book. And you shall hear it, with the company's leave.'

He went over to the corner, unwrapped a long box from the tarpaulin, drew from it fiddle and bow. Now I should tell you we have a great ear for music in Menadarva. So all waited agog while he resined and tuned, and it didn't need a scrape of his foot when ready, nor the flourish he gave to his bow, to call for silence.

First he played the air of the old song in single notes, very quiet and true: next he repeated it, holding the fiddle to his ear and plucking the strings: then it went under his chin again and fetched out the thing in great chords 'so as (I am quoting Sam) you didn't scarcely know the fiddle's inside from your own.' And with that he started off on variations faster and faster till the tune mazed itself in a kind of devil's jig. In the whirl of it (says Sam) you couldn't tell man from music, nor the music from the play of his wrists and the glint of his earrings; till sudden with a stamp of his foot he broke off, waited whilst you might count five and then, soft as before, plucked out the tune, note by note.

With that it was over. In the middle of the clapping Sam turned—he didn't know why—towards the girl Annie, and her face was white as a peeled hazel. Belike, though, he was the only one to mark this, the others slewing about at the moment towards the inner doorway, where stood the Clay-lords themselves, fetched forth by the music.

'Brayvo! Brayvo!' cackled the twins together. 'But who the devil is it?' asked Lawyer Simmons.

Pendrea, as manager, took charge. 'That's a rare gift of yours, my man,' says he. 'Travellin' in music, eh?'

'Travellin' *to* music,' the stranger corrected him. 'Joseph Pooke's my name, at your service; mining's my occupation—

metalliferous; and the jig I played just now is the tune I travel to, mostly. You may call it "Over the Hills and Far Away."'

Pendrea stood and eyed him a bit, finger on chin. He was a leading Methodist and took a great interest in his choir, so that all guessed what worked in his mind. 'Know anything about clay?'

'Adam was made of it, I've heard tell.'

'China-clay, I mean.'

'—and the sons of Adam hereabouts dig it for the making of things to be broken, like their father and other vessels of promise.'

'Well, if you 're minded for a job'—Pendrea flushed a trifle as he said it, being a masterful man and not caring to be answered thus before company—'come to my office tomorrow, at ten sharp.'

'Likely I may, when I've slept upon it'—with a side glance at the landlady.

'Annie, girl, fit and heat the warming-pan,' commanded she.

2

In this way Joseph Pooke came to us, to take charge, as you might say, of the parish. Next morning he signed on at the Great Goonburrow Pit, under the 'One and All,' and moved in his traps to Aunt Sandercock's, over her General Store; and—it being Saturday—took a longish walk over the moors. Sunday morning he attended church, and the Methodists reckoned they had lost him. But evening found him seated in chapel, just as attentive as to the parson's sermon; and singing, when the hymn came, in a clear light tenor.

Pendrea got hold of him afterwards. 'Glad to see you're one of the Connexion.'

'It's news to me,' answered Pooke. 'But there's a wheeze in that harmonium of yours that I could cure, if you gave me leave to try.'

Within a week, having fitted up a bench and conjured some tools out of goodness knows where, he had the instrument to pieces and refitted, bit by bit.

'You've made it speak like an angel,' said Miss Lasky, the choir leader, with a blush for her forwardness.

'Well,' said he, 'God Almighty *might* make an angel speak like a harmonium; but He's merciful. A harmonium's the devil at the best, if you'll excuse me. Your choir, now; a better set of natural voices you couldn't get together, not if you combed the Pacific slope; and yet all singing *tremolo* and because of *this*.' He banged his palm on the lid.

'But, but, Mr. Pooke—I *like* to hear them sing *tremolo!* It shows that their feelings are moved.'

She remembered his answer to this and told it to me years after. 'Music don't wobble, miss, any more than the stars singing their Maker's name.'

'Oh!' said Miss Lasky, puzzled. 'I didn't know you were religious—in that sense,' she went on, recovering herself and being (as I can guess now) not more averse than most spinsters of her age from discussing religion with a man.

He made no answer then; but later, being called in to train the choir, with no help but his fiddle he taught them how to hit their notes clean every time, till they chorused away like larks, unaccompanied, and the fame of it drew folks of a Sunday from miles around to hear.

Before this, though, he had a wood shed built at the back of Aunt Sandercock's, with a whole gamut of tools and gadgets. And by degrees *it* came about that if you wanted watch or clock put to rights, or your pump wouldn't work, or your chimney smoked, or you had a tooth to be pulled, or a child with the croup, or a swarm of bees to be hived, Pooke was your man.

With all this he never again played the fiddle in public, save to give the note at choir practices. 'This clay-heaving deadens the touch,' he explained one night to the company in 'Step o' One Side.' 'Metal and clay be two different things. Fire made 'em both; but in metal—gold, silver, tin, copper, call it what you will— fire's in the veins working, and you follow it like a lover—eh, Miss Annie? While, with clay, what is it but ashes, burnt out and dead.'

None the less he did his job at the works well enough, and specially in packing a truck. Only one day, happening to cross the pit with Pendrea, says he with a jerk of his thumb back towards where a two-three men were shovelling. ' There's a cornice of over-hang yonder. None too safe as I reckon.'

Now it may be that Pendrea had started to envy the man's popularity. At any rate he answered stiff and in the hearing of several: 'Your job's over there with the loading, I believe.'

'Sorry,' said Pooke polite. 'But my father was killed by a fall of rock; and the shock so told on my mother that my brother Noah was born a week later, before his time. Whereby, being his older by nine years, I had to look after him as he grew up. She being weak of health, her terror day and night was of earth or rock giving way and smothering him. Woman's foolishness, no doubt; but that 's how I grew up nervous about overhang.'

Two days later, as fate would have it, nine or ten tons of that very cornice came down and crushed a couple of workers. Reuben Oates and Jim Narcarrow by name. Pooke, as one of the foremost on the spot, to dig out the bodies, had to give evidence at the inquest, but not a word did he speak to cast any blame on Pendrca, and the other witnesses took their cue from him. So the verdict was 'Accidental death' and no more, though whisperings went around.

He never took advantage of the manager over this, unless you count a day when he walked into the office and asked for a week off.

'It's like this,' he answered Pendrea—'I was in that church of yours, on hands and knees, after hours, rubbing at a couple of brasses, when old Parson Vine came stumbling in, blind as a bat, and fairly pitched over me. Like leap-frog it was. And so, one thing leading to another, I told him that two of his organ-pipes were rotten as touch and proved it by poking a hole in 'em with my finger. And I want the hire of a lorry, too, if you'll oblige.'

'You're not joining our friends the Anglicans, I hope?'

'Nothing worse than helping brotherly love,' said Pooke. So

off he drove next day, and came back inside a week with four brand-new organ pipes, and in ten days had all the rest gilded to correspond.

But his last feat was with the Parish Band, which included church and chapel alike, but had been going to pieces ever since the death of old 'Waxy' Cann, their bandmaster. He spent three weeks going around collecting the old instruments and refitting them; and then turned to the piles of old music scores. 'B flat, B flat —the whole dam lot!'

"Tis the easiest key to play,' explained Archie Govett, leader and first cornet.

'Yes, and like kissing your sister.' With that he set to work again, transposing the better pieces back into their proper keys. Hours it must have cost him and reams of music sheets; but by August he had Menadarva Band fit to enter for the County Competition at Redruth, and that albeit he never put lip to the brass or the reeds himself. 'I was brought up on strings,' he'd say. 'If you want to know what brass can do, or a silver cornet, you should hear my brother Noah.'

It was during these practices that he started—and, once started, kept on going—with talk about this wonderful brother of his. 'He's a masterpiece, is Noah! Built for the brass, as you might say: six foot two, forty-eight round the chest at nineteen, and yet will fetch forth a note like a maid's whisper and not a slur in it.' Seemingly, too, this nonesuch had other accomplishments— 'could sing a high tenor, most pleasing, and shift a ton of broken rock against any two men of near his size,' and so on, and so on.

Well, the explanation came before we wanted; and with it the blow fell.

In mid-August the band, with Pooke as conductor, fared down to Redruth in a four-horse brake. They didn't carry off the Cup; but they brought home second prize, with a special for the 'Self-Chosen Item,' which was no less a teaser than the overture to *Semir ami de;* which again made excuse for a grand supper in 'Step o' One Side.' Having, of course, to speak to the toast of his health: 'You'll do better next time,' he said, 'and why? Because I'm leaving you, and by the five-forty tomorrow. . . . Passage booked back to the States on the *Dalmatic,* sailing Southampton, Tuesday. But 'tis no losers you'll be. You've heard me tell, often enough, of my brother Noah? Well, among his other merits he always does as I tell him. We've arranged to exchange jobs, and he'll be arriving, as we've planned, towards the end of March next. And so I thank you, friends all!' He lifted his glass and sat down of a sudden, the company left to stare as though they'd seen a ghost through the tobacco-smoke.

Next morning there was some talk of a testimonial, but no time for it. The band assembled in the afternoon and played him down to the station: and the last we saw of him was a hand waving from the carriage window at the bend of the curve.

3

It is here that, in a small way, I happen into the story, and with a confession. The train gone, and the crowd trooping back to the village to drink to the hero's health, it came into my unregenerate head (such temptations do assail a boy rising ten) that the coast lay clear for a raid on Mr. Rosveare's summer orchard of quarendens and ribstones on the hither side of the railway line.

It was latish, and the young moon already clear between the apple-branches, when I started to fetch a circuit for home, first across a net-work of sidings, and then in cover of a line of clay-trucks anchored and waiting delivery at Tray jetties. Here, to the right of my path, ran a stream that came down past the end of our garden, where was a plank for crossing.

But before I came to this a sound fetched me up short. Queer it was, and human, sobbing between the noises of the running water; and for the instant—there being no other cottage nigh—I could think of nothing but that *it* must be mother out in the garden and in some terrible distress. Heart in mouth I ran towards the plank, but was fetched up again in my stride.

Years ago, in the days before the railway reclaimed the marsh, and when barges plied high up our stream until the clay-washings choked it, someone had planted an old iron cannon for a bollard. Time had sunk it to half its height and plugged up the mouth with driftings of sand and clay-dust.... And there on it a girl was seated, rocking herself and sobbing.

'Twas the maid Annie Lowry. But what with the slip of the moon slanting down an angle of light through a break in the double line of trucks on the clay-dust spread everywhere white as snow, and here in a black shawl half covering her white frock, like a ghost she frighted me, and as like a ghost I must have come upon her, the clay muffling my tread.

'What are you doing here, boy?' she gasped out, jumping to her feet. 'Go away!'

Well, as for the question I reckoned it belonged to me, and I put it back on her. 'But if you're in trouble, Miss Annie,' I said, 'there's my mother handy, and you know her.'

She cut me short. 'I don't want your mother, Jim Pascoe'—she wiped her eyes bravely—'and I want nothing of you but to go away. There's nothing the matter with me, either.'

'If that's so,' I stammered, taken aback by the flat lie, 'won't you have an apple?'

Upon this she broke into a high laugh. But it ended quick, overtaken by a sort of guggle in her throat.

'You funny boy!... Yes, I'll take your apple.... And I'll give you something in change for it— and a promise.'

'What's that?' I asked.

She put down her head close and whispered. 'I'll give you a kiss, Jim, if you promise never—never on your oath—to tell any soul that you saw me here.'

Well, it happened to me so, at that age: and I vow that as she bent and kissed my cheek a glory of heaven broke all about me, and her breath was all flowers and fire. It was over in a moment, and she held out a hand for my apple.

'Word of honour you won't tell?'

'Not for wild horses, Miss Annie!'

Upon that she told me to run, and I ran.

4

'*Balearic timed Plymouth Saturday next Brother to wire arrival,*'—So Joseph Pooke was as good as his promise. The cablegram reached the Clay Company's office on the Wednesday before Easter, and the telegram from Plymouth on the Saturday morning (our post office receiving none on Good Friday). So again there was no time for organizing preparations to welcome the paragon. But Pendrea hurried around to engage the old lodgings at Aunt Sandercock's, enlisted some women to rig up a public tea in the Wesleyan School Room—*it* being a holiday, of course—and got together a small reception committee, including the vicar, to meet the 4.45 train. The stationmaster, too, was good enough to lay a score of fog-detonators up the line by way of welcome.

The banging of these may have shaken our man a bit. Anyhow, as the train drew in he had his head thrust out as if to inquire about the accident, and heaved forth upon the platform before Pendrea, hurrying up, had time to reach the compartment door.

So there Noah Pooke landed among us, with a kind of wondering smile on him: a monstrous fine fellow for all to see, strapping in height, with shoulders to match, in noways resembling his light-limbed brother, and least of all in his face, which was fair-complexioncd and pinkish, the lower part straggled over by a thin growth of beard, hay-coloured and curly. In his left fist he clenched the brass-handled case, which we guessed to contain the famous cornet; in his right a carpet-bag (or 'grip,' as he called it), which he had to set down for the hand-shaking. But to the case he stuck until, the school room reached, he looked around and stowed the thing carefully under his chair. Then with a vague sort of smile he cast a second look over the feast, and the first word he said was 'Fattening.'

One of the helpers pushed a plate of jam and cream splits under his nose. 'Come now, Mr. Noah, make a beginning!'—this with a blush for using his Christian name so forwardly.

'Thank 'ee, miss—a cup of tea and one slice of bread-and-butter. No sugar, if you please. Doctor's orders.'

He retrieved himself, however, at Easter Service in chapel next morning, with a cornet solo, O *for the Wings of a Dove*! clear as an angel speaking and persuading. There was no question but he must take over his brother's charge of the choir—and of the band, too, next session.

Also when, on Tuesday, he started work at the pits he soon showed that, though no match with his brother at packing, he could heave clay with the best or a trifle better.

But—no one could tell just why or how or when it began—for some reason or other the practices of band and choir fell away by degrees from the standard to which his brother had worked them—that is, unless you accept Sam Trudgian's explanation: 'When the billies slurred up so much as a note, Joseph would hammer the desk and cry "Dammit," no matter how holy the edifice; whereas with this chap 'tis "No, no," or "Shall we try again?" at the strongest.'

Aunt Sandercock, too, had an early word about him. You couldn't say she whispered it, either, that being foreign to the pitch of her voice. She kept Wyandots, and the freshness of their eggs was dear to her as her Bible. 'But every morning, sure as I lays—or sets, if you'll excuse me—his egg afore him, he looks at it, then up at me with "Are you sartin 'tis quite fresh, Mrs. Sandercock?" There's limits to innocence, if you ask me!'

Now I should tell you that from first sight of him I had worshipped the man for his strength and stature; and he clinched it on the day when he promoted me to tap the triangle in the band. Fine and proud my mother was when she buttoned the frogs of my uniform jacket, though she didn't know I'd had to fight two boys for *it*. The worse shock, therefore, *it* gave me when she fell to discussing him with Father over our Sunday dinner. At the mention of Noah Pooke I had pricked up my young ears.

Mother was saying '—and one of these days there'll be a scandal. Twice during sermon the minister faced around, lookin' where the noise came from.'

'Asleep,' suggested father, 'or wind, maybe. He suffers from it, as the parish knows.'

'He's soft as'—Mother shifted knife to fork hand and pushed finger half-way towards the figgy-duff she was carving—'as *that*. Put in with the bread and took out with the cakes.'

I flared up at this, though it misbecame my years. 'Mr. Pooke is the finest man in Menadarva,' I blurted out; 'and the handsomest, and the kindest.'

'When you've finished your plate,' said father after a slow stare, 'you just run along to garden and listen if the bees be threat'nin' a second swarm.'

Then, within a month, all of a sudden my hero's stock went up; it being gossiped about that he was courting the Lowry maid. They had been met in the dusk, walking out together. 'A promising match, too,' the parish agreed, while yet some added, ' Likely enough 'twill be the making of him,' Annie being reckoned a girl with a head on her shoulders.

But at the end of five weeks or so another rumour went round that the courtship had been broken off. And one evening in the bar-kitchen—Annie being away at the back somewhere, washing up—Bert Leggo, an impudent chap, tackled her mother for news of it. 'You'd better ask her,' answered Mrs. Lowry short and sharp. 'Some time when you've stopped winkin' and don't mind having an ear boxed.'

Anyway, it told upon Noah, who took to walking by nights, all alone, and going by day (as the word goes), looking a man that had lost sixpence and found a farthing. And the band went down to Redruth and came back without a prize.

But it was not until close on Christmas that the crash came.

5

The vicar had a niece, or grandniece, down for a visit; an upstanding lady, with a full, deep *contralto* voice and reputed to be making a fortune at the concerts in London. These artists, I'm told, can never rest on a holiday: and what must she do but get up a concert?—proceeds to be given to an Ambulance Class that had been formed after the accident at the pit and was already short of funds. This was an object for which church and chapel could work together, and they made a fine success of it up to a point. The band made up in noise what they'd unlearnt of Joseph Pooke's teaching. The vicar read out to us how the waters came down in all sorts of way at Lodore, and later quavered out ' O that we two were maying!' with the postmistress—of all the unlikeliest capers! After that came an item or too, and then, of course, our visitor bore away the bell with some Italian thing, all runs and shakes.

All encored this, as in duty bound, and she gave us *Caller Herrin* , with wonderful effect from her lower throat, as you might say. Next came Noah's turn; and, pulling himself together, as it were, he rendered *The Lost Chord* and *I Dreamt that I Dwelt* in his best style; so outstanding that when he ended the lady came up in her imperative way, shook him by the hand and almost kissed him. 'Wonderful!' she cried out, turning on the audience. 'This gentleman must really, yes really, try an *obbligato* to me with Miss—I forget your name for the moment—I'm so excited— oh, yes!—with Miss Hender at the piano, of course.' So Noah had to blush and bow.

Well, when the lady's next turn came and she sang *Bid me discourse,* he managed it to admiration, bending over Miss Hender's shoulder and fitting in, soft, on the right notes. And in the storm of applause Miss Hender found herself gently pushed off the music-stool and the lady seated in her place.

'You'll not need any score for this,' says the lady. 'It's the dear old *Annie Laurie,* key of G,' and she struck a couple of chords. Noah's cornet went up to his lips. He kept his smile but both his hands shook.

Maxwellton braes are bonny.

—And just then a voice—Bert Leggo's—spoke up from somewhere at the back: 'Damme! the man's blubbing.' It was true, too! Big tears were running down his cheeks as he puffed them for the next stave. There's no saying whether he heard Leggo or not. Anyway he lowered his cornet, looking about him as one dazed, tucked the thing—quick—under his arm, and fled off at the back of the platform.

6

That broke him. From that day he went about, eyes down, shunning his fellows, pitiful to see; the worst being that he kept his silly smile, full of pain as his eyes would be when he lifted them. Soon Aunt Sandercock let out that she dusted his tool-bench every morning and 'though he'll sit there half the night, wasting good oil at eleven three-farthings a gallon, there's every tool in its place untouched, same as I left it—and him the untidiest by habit that ever I lodged.' Soon, too, he took to lying a-bed and turning up late at the pit; until there came a Friday when Pendrea very reasonably lost his temper and sacked him on the spot.

Next morning I overtook and ran past him to catch up with a parcel of boys on the road to the moors—a waste of land that stretched for three miles and more at the back of the pits. It was unreclaimed for clay as yet; all peat, heather, and bog-plants, criss-crossed by small brown trickles of streams in which our game was to hunt for minnows, efts, dragon-flies, anything we could fetch home in pickle-jars.

He was carrying a fishing-rod, jointed up in a bag, and his cornet-case in his right hand. After passing him, something moved me to halt; and as he came up he must have read in my face what I couldn't put into words. For he bade me run after the rest, and then, still with that smile of his, 'Joseph is a fruitful bough,' said he; 'but Issachar a strong ass couching down between two burdens'—words that puzzled me at the time and puzzled me later when I found them in the Scriptures.

There were trout, small but plenty, lower down where the main stream made a long bend by the west; and when we parted he would be after these. But I never heard of his taking any, that day or after. What happened was that he wandered far off, away from sight, and there played tunes to himself on his key-bugle by the water. Times again, while hunting for minnows, we boys would hear the lonesome notes of it floating up, wailing across the moor. Sometimes it might be *Trafalgar's Bay* or *Come, cheer up, my Lads;* but always, and whatever the tune, it put you in mind of a creature lost and in pain.

And there the man died.

They found him stretched out by a small stream, his rod (unspliced) and his key-bugle on the bank beside him. Staring up and smiling he lay: death must have come upon him mercifully. The vicar pursed out the money to pay all expenses with a balance for the headstone: it appeared that of late he had been getting remittances from the States and paying them out quietly to the poor fellow.

But that doesn't quite end the story. One evening, towards Christmas, Joseph Pooke returned to Menadarva —it turned out, to visit the grave and settle up with the vicar. One or two put *it* about they had passed his ghost in the dusk. But it wasn't his ghost, nor his business alone with the vicar.

For that night the girl Annie ran off with him, to be married in London. . . . Yes, by licence and all in form: for two days later the proper certificate came to 'Step o' One Side,' with word she was off to the States with the best man in the world: and later Mr. Lowry showed around the photographs of two healthy children, twins.

'And a very ordinary pair,' was Sam Trudgian's comments. 'Heavy, like that unfortunate uncle of theirs, if you ask me. But 'tis curious how gifts will skip about in families.'

The Affair of Bleakirk-on-Sands

(*The events, which took place on November 23, 186-, are narrated by Reuben Cartwright, Esq., of Bleakirk Hall, Bleakirk-on-Sands, in the North Riding of Yorkshire.*)

A rough, unfrequented bridle-road rising and dipping towards the coast, with here and there a glimpse of sea beyond the sad-coloured moors: straight overhead, a red and wintry sun just struggling to assert itself: to right and left, a stretch of barren down still coated white with hoar-frost.

I had flung the reins upon my horse's neck, and was ambling homewards. Between me and Bleakirk lay seven good miles, and we had come far enough already on the chance of the sun's breaking through; but as the morning wore on, so our prospect of hunting that day faded further from us. It was now high noon, and I had left the hunt half an hour ago, turned my face towards the coast, and lit a cigar to beguile the way. When a man is twenty-seven he begins to miss the fun of shivering beside a frozen cover.

The road took a sudden plunge among the spurs of two converging hills. As I began to descend, the first gleam of sunshine burst from the dull heaven and played over the hoar-frost. I looked up, and saw, on the slope of the hill to the right, a horseman also descending.

At first glance I took him for a brother sportsman who, too, had abandoned hope of a fox. But the second assured me of my mistake. The stranger wore a black suit of antique, clerical cut, a shovel hat, and gaiters; his nag was the sorriest of ponies, with a shaggy coat of flaring yellow, and so low in the legs that the broad flaps of its rider's coat all but trailed on the ground. A queerer turnout I shall never see again, though I live to be a hundred.

He appeared not to notice me, but pricked leisurably down the slope, and I soon saw that, as our paths ran and at the pace we were going, we should meet at the foot of the descent: which we presently did.

"Ah, indeed!" said the stranger, reining in his pony as though now for the first time aware of me: "I wish you a very good day, sir. We are well met."

He pulled off his hat with a fantastic politeness. For me, my astonishment grew as I regarded him more closely. A mass of lanky, white hair drooped on either side of a face pale, pinched, and extraordinarily wrinkled; the clothes that wrapped his diminutive body were threadbare, greasy, and patched in all directions. Fifty years' wear could not have worsened them; and, indeed, from the whole aspect of the man, you might guess him a century old, were it not for the nimbleness of his gestures and his eyes, which were grey, alert, and keen as needles.

I acknowledged his salutation as he ranged up beside me.

"Will my company, sir, offend you? By your coat I suspect your trade: *venatorem sapit*—hey?"

His voice exactly fitted his eyes. Both were sharp and charged with expression; yet both carried also a hint that their owner had lived long in privacy. Somehow they lacked touch.

"I am riding homewards," I answered.

"Hey? Where is that?"

The familiarity lay rather in the words than the manner; and I did not resent it.

"At Bleakirk."

His eyes had wandered for a moment to the road ahead; but now he turned abruptly, and looked at me, as I thought, with some suspicion. He seemed about to speak, but restrained himself, fumbled in his waistcoat pocket, and producing a massive snuff-box, offered me a pinch. On my declining, he helped himself copiously; and then, letting the reins hang loose upon his arm, fell to tapping the box.

"To me this form of the herb *nicotiana* commends itself by its cheapness: the sense is tickled, the purse consenting—like the complaisant husband in Juvenal: you take me? I am well acquainted with Bleakirk-*super-sabulum*. By the way, how is Squire Cartwright of the Hall?"

"If," said I, "you mean my father, Angus Cartwright, he is dead these twelve years."

"Hey?" cried the old gentleman, and added after a moment, "Ah, to be sure, time flies—*quo dives Tullus et*—Angus, eh? And yet a hearty man, to all seeming. So you are his son." He took another pinch. "It is very sustaining," he said.

"The snuff?"

"You have construed me, sir. Since I set out, just thirteen hours since, it has been my sole *viaticum*." As he spoke he put his hand nervously to his forehead, and withdrew it.

"Then," thought I, "you must have started in the middle of the night," for it was now little past noon. But looking at his face, I saw clearly that it was drawn and pinched with fasting. Whereupon I remembered my flask and sandwich-box, and pulling them out, assured him, with some apology for the offer, that they were at his service. His joy was childish. Again he whipped off his hat, and clapping it to his heart, swore my conduct did honour to my dead father; "and with Angus Cartwright," said he, "kindness was intuitive. Being a habit, it outran reflection; and his whisky, sir, was undeniable. Come, I have a fancy. Let us dismount, and, in heroic fashion, spread our feast upon the turf; or, if the hoar-frost deter you, see, here are boulders, and a running brook to dilute our cups; and, by my life, a foot-bridge, to the rail of which we may tether our steeds."

Indeed, we had come to a hollow in the road, across which a tiny beck, now swollen with the rains, was chattering bravely. Falling in with my companion's humour, I dismounted, and, after his example, hitched my mare's rein over the rail. There was a raciness about the adventure that took my fancy. We chose two boulders from a heap of lesser stones close beside the beck, and divided the sandwiches, for though I protested I was not hungry, the old gentleman insisted on our sharing alike. And now, as the liquor warmed his heart and the sunshine smote upon his back, his eyes sparkled, and he launched on a flood of the gayest talk—yet always of a world that I felt was before my time.

Indeed, as he rattled on, the feeling that this must be some Rip Van Winkle restored from a thirty years' sleep grew stronger and stronger upon me. He spoke of Bleakirk, and displayed a knowledge of it sufficiently thorough—intimate even—yet of the old friends for whom he inquired many names were unknown to me, many familiar only through their epitaphs in the windy cemetery above the cliff. Of the rest, the pretty girls he named were now grandmothers, the young men long since bent and rheumatic; the youngest well over fifty. This, however, seemed to depress him little. His eyes would sadden for a moment, then laugh again. "Well, well," he said, "wrinkles, bald heads, and the deafness of the tomb—we have our day notwithstanding. Pluck the bloom of it—hey? a commonplace of the poets."

"But, sir," I put in as politely as I might, "you have not yet told me with whom I have the pleasure of lunching."

"Gently, young sir." He waved his hand towards the encircling moors. "We have feasted *more Homerico*, and in Homer, you remember the host allowed his guest fourteen days before asking that question. Permit me to delay the answer only till I have poured libation on the turf here. Ah! I perceive the whisky is exhausted: but water shall suffice. May I trouble you—my joints are stiff—to fill your drinking-cup from the brook at your feet?"

I took the cup from his hands and stooped over the water. As I did so, he leapt on me like a cat from behind. I felt a hideous blow on the nape of the neck: a jagged flame leapt up: the sunshine turned to blood—then to darkness. With hands spread out, I stumbled blindly forward and fell at full length into the beck.

When my senses returned, I became aware, first that I was lying, bound hand and foot and securely gagged, upon the turf;

secondly, that the horses were still tethered, and standing quietly at the foot-bridge; and, thirdly, that my companion had resumed his position on the boulder, and there sat watching my recovery.

Seeing my eyes open, he raised his hat and addressed me in tones of grave *punctilio*.

"Believe me, sir, I am earnest in my regret for this state of things. Nothing but the severest necessity could have persuaded me to knock the son of my late esteemed friend over the skull and gag his utterance with a stone—to pass over the fact that it fairly lays my sense of your hospitality under suspicion. Upon my word, sir, it places me in a cursedly equivocal position!"

He took a pinch of snuff, absorbed it slowly, and pursued.

"It was necessary, however. You will partly grasp the situation when I tell you that my name is Teague—the Reverend William Teague, Doctor of Divinity, and formerly incumbent of Bleakirk-on-Sands."

His words explained much, though not everything. The circumstances which led to the Reverend William's departure from Bleakirk had happened some two years before my birth: but they were startling enough to supply talk in that dull fishing village for many a long day. In my nursery I had heard the tale that my companion's name recalled: and if till now I had felt humiliation, henceforth I felt absolute fear, for I knew that I had to deal with a madman.

"I perceive by your eyes, sir," he went on, "that with a part of my story you are already familiar: the rest I am about to tell you. It will be within your knowledge that late on a Sunday night, just twenty-nine years ago, my wife left the Vicarage-house, Bleakirk, and never returned; that subsequent inquiry yielded no trace of her flight, beyond the fact that she went provided with a small hand-bag containing a change of clothing; that, as we had lived together for twenty years in the entirest harmony, no reason could then, or afterwards, be given for her astonishing conduct. Moreover, you will be aware that its effect upon me was tragical; that my lively emotions underneath the shock deepened into a settled gloom; that my faculties (notoriously eminent) in a short time became clouded, nay, eclipsed—necessitating my removal (I will not refine) to a madhouse. Hey, is it not so?"

I nodded assent as well as I could. He paused, with a pinch between finger and thumb, to nod back to me. Though his eyes were now blazing with madness, his demeanour was formally, even affectedly, polite.

"My wife never came back: naturally, sir—for she was dead."

He shifted a little on the boulders, slipped the snuff-box back into his waistcoat pocket, then crossing his legs and clasping his hands over one knee, bent forward and regarded me fixedly.

"I murdered her," he said slowly, and nodded.

A pause followed that seemed to last an hour. The stone which he had strapped in my mouth with his bandanna was giving me acute pain; it obstructed, too, what little breathing my emotion left me; and I dared not take my eyes off his. The strain on my nerves grew so tense that I felt myself fainting when his voice recalled me.

"I wonder now," he asked, as if it were a riddle—"I wonder if you can guess why the body was never found?"

Again there was an intolerable silence before he went on.

"Lydia was a dear creature: in many respects she made me an admirable wife. Her affection for me was canine—positively. But she was fat, sir; her face a jelly, her shoulders mountainous. Moreover, her voice!—it was my cruciation—monotonously, regularly, desperately voluble. If she talked of archangels, they became insignificant—and her themes, in ordinary, were of the pettiest. Her waist, sir, and my arm had once been commensurate: now not three of Homer's heroes could embrace her. Her voice could once touch my heart-strings into music; it brayed them now, between the millstones of the commonplace. Figure to yourself a man of my sensibility condemned to live on these terms!"

He paused, tightened his grasp on his knee, and pursued.

"You remember, sir, the story of the baker in Langius? He narrates that a certain woman conceived a violent desire to bite the naked shoulders of a baker who used to pass underneath her window with his wares. So imperative did this longing become, that at length the woman appealed to her husband, who (being a good-natured man, and unwilling to disoblige her) hired the baker, for a certain price, to come and be bitten. The man allowed her two bites, but denied a third, being unable to contain himself for pain.

"The author goes on to relate that, for want of this third bite, she bore one dead child, and two living. My own case," continued the Reverend William, "was somewhat similar. Lydia's unrelieved babble reacted upon her bulk, and awoke in me an absorbing, fascinating desire to strike her. I longed to see her quiver. I fought against the feeling, stifled it, trod it down: it awoke again. It filled my thoughts, my dreams; it gnawed me like a vulture. A hundred times while she sat complacently turning her inane periods, I had to hug my fist to my breast, lest it should leap out and strike her senseless. Do I weary you? Let me proceed:—

"That Sunday evening we sat, one on each side of the hearth, in the vicarage drawing-room. She was talking—talking; and I sat tapping my foot and whispering to myself, 'You are too fat, Lydia, you are too fat.' Her talk ran on the two sermons I had preached that day, the dresses of the congregation, the expense of living, the parish ailments—inexhaustible, trivial, relentless. Suddenly she looked up and our eyes met. Her voice trailed off and dropped like a bird wounded in full flight. She stood up and took a step towards me. 'Is anything the matter, William?' she asked solicitously. 'You are too fat, my dear,' I answered, laughing, and struck her full in the face with my fist.

"She did not quiver much—not half enough—but dropped like a half-full sack on to the carpet. I caught up a candle and examined her. Her neck was dislocated. She was quite dead."

The madman skipped up from his boulder, and looked at me with indescribable cunning.

"I am so glad, sir," he said, "that you did not bleed when I struck you; it was a great mercy. The sight of blood affects me—

ah!" he broke off with a subtle quiver and drew a long breath. "Do you know the sands by Woeful Ness—the Twin Brothers?" he asked.

I knew that dreary headland well. For half a mile beyond the grey church and vicarage of Bleakirk it extends, forming the northern arm of the small fishing-bay, and protecting it from the full set of the tides. Towards its end it breaks away sharply, and terminates in a dorsal ridge of slate-coloured rock that runs out for some two hundred feet between the sands we call the Twin Brothers. Of these, that to the south, and inside the bay, is motionless, and bears the name of the 'Dead-Boy;' but the 'Quick-Boy,' to the north, shifts continually. It is a quicksand, in short; and will swallow a man in three minutes.

"My mind," resumed my companion, "was soon made up. There is no murder, thought I, where there is no corpse. So I propped Lydia in the armchair, where she seemed as if napping, and went quietly upstairs. I packed a small hand-bag carefully with such clothes as she would need for a journey, descended with it, opened the front door, went out to be sure the servants had blown out their lights, returned, and hoisting my wife on my shoulder, with the bag in my left hand, softly closed the door and stepped out into the night. In the shed beside the garden-gate the gardener had left his wheelbarrow. I fetched it out, set Lydia on the top of it, and wheeled her off towards Woeful Ness. There was just the rim of a waning moon to light me, but I knew every inch of the way.

"For the greater part of it I had turf underfoot; but where this ended and the rock began, I had to leave the barrow behind. It was ticklish work, climbing down; for footing had to be found, and Lydia was a monstrous weight. Pah! how fat she was and clumsy—lolling this way and that! Besides, the bag hampered me. But I reached the foot at last, and after a short rest clambered out along the ridge as fast as I could. I was sick and tired of the business.

"Well, the rest was easy. Arrived at the furthest spit of rock, I tossed the bag from me far into the northern sand. Then I turned to Lydia, whom I had set down for the moment. In the moonlight her lips were parted as though she were still chattering; so I kissed her once, because I had loved her, and dropped her body over into the Quick-Boy Sand. In three minutes or so I had seen the last of her.

"I trundled home the barrow, mixed myself a glass of whisky, sat beside it for half an hour, and then aroused the servants. I was cunning, sir; and no one could trace my footprints on the turf and rock of Woeful Ness. The missing hand-bag, and the disarray I had been careful to make in the bedroom, provided them at once with a clue—but it did not lead them to the Quick-Boy. For two days they searched; at the end of that time it grew clear to them that grief was turning my brain. Your father, sir, was instant with his sympathy—at least ten times a day I had much ado to keep from laughing in his face. Finally two doctors visited me, and I was taken to a madhouse.

"I have remained within its walls twenty-nine years; but no—I have never been thoroughly at home there. Two days ago I discovered that the place was *boring* me. So I determined to escape; and this to a man of my resources presented few difficulties. I borrowed this pony from a stable not many yards from the madhouse wall; he belongs, I think, to a chimney-sweep, and I trust that, after serving my purpose, he may find a way back to his master."

I suppose at this point he must have detected the question in my eyes, for he cried sharply.

"You wish to know my purpose? It is simple." He passed a thin hand over his forehead. "I have been shut up, as I say, for twenty-nine years, and I now discover that the madhouse bores me. If they re-take me—and the hue and cry must be out long before this—I shall be dragged back. What, then, is my proposal? I ride to Bleakirk and out along the summit of Woeful Ness. There I dismount, turn my pony loose, and, descending along the ridge, step into the sand that swallowed Lydia. Simple, is it not? *Excessi, evasi, evanui.* I shall be there before sunset—which reminds me," he added, pulling out his watch, "that my time is nearly up. I regret to leave you in this plight, but you see how I am placed. I felt, when I saw you, a sudden desire to unbosom myself of a secret which, until the past half-hour, I have shared with no man.

"I see by your eyes again that if set at liberty you would interfere with my purpose. It is unfortunate that scarcely a soul ever rides this way—I know the road of old. But tomorrow is Sunday: I will scribble a line and fix it on the church-door at Bleakirk, so that the parish may at least know your predicament before twenty-four hours are out. I must now be going. The bandanna about your mouth I entreat you to accept as a memento. With renewed apologies, sir, I wish you good-day; and count it extremely fortunate that you did not bleed."

He nodded in the friendliest manner, turned on his heel, and walked quietly towards the bridge. As he untethered his pony, mounted, and ambled quietly off in the direction of the coast, I lay stupidly watching him. His black coat for some time lay, a diminishing blot, on the brown of the moors, stood for a brief moment on the sky-line, and vanished.

I must have lain above an hour in this absurd and painful position, wrestling with my bonds, and speculating on my chances of passing the night by the beck-side. My ankles were tied with my own handkerchief, my wrists with the thong of my own whip, and this especially cut me. It was knotted immovably; but by rolling over and rubbing my face into the turf, I contrived at length to slip the gag down below my chin. This done, I sat up and shouted lustily.

For a long time there was no reply but the whinnying of my mare, who seemed to guess something was wrong, and pulled at her tether until I thought she would break away. I think I called a score of times before I heard an answering "Whoo-oop!" far back on the road, and a scarlet coat, then another, and finally a dozen or more appeared on the crest of the hill. It was the hunt returning.

They saw me at once, and galloped up, speechless from sheer amazement. I believe my hands were loosened before a word was spoken. The situation was painfully ridiculous; but my story was partly out before they had time to laugh, and the rest of it was gasped to the accompaniment of pounding hoofs and cracking whips.

Never did the Netherkirk Hunt ride after fox as it rode after the Rev. William Teague that afternoon. We streamed over the moor, a thin red wave, like a rank of charging cavalry, the whip even forgetting his tired hounds that straggled aimlessly in our wake. On the hill above Bleakirk we saw that the tide was out, and our company divided without drawing rein, some four horsemen descending to the beach, to ride along the sands out under Woeful Ness, and across the Dead-Boy, hoping to gain the ridge before the madman and cut him off. The rest, whom I led by a few yards, breasted the height above and thundered past the grey churchyard wall. Inside it I caught a flying glimpse of the yellow pony quietly cropping among the tombs. We had our prey, then, enclosed in that peninsula as in a trap; but there was one outlet.

I remember looking down towards the village as we tore along, and seeing the fisher-folk run out at their doors and stand staring at the two bodies of horsemen thus rushing to the sea. The riders on the beach had a slight lead of us at first; but this they quickly lost as their horses began to be distressed in the heavy sand. I looked back for an instant. The others were close at my heels; and, behind again, the bewildered hounds followed, yelping mournfully. But neither man nor hound could see him whom they hunted, for the cliff's edge hid the quicksand in front.

Presently the turf ceased. Dismounting, I ran to the edge and plunged down the rocky face. I had descended about twenty feet, when I came to the spot where, by craning forward, I could catch sight of the spit of rock, and the Quick-Boy Sand to the right of it.

The sun—a blazing ball of red—was just now setting behind us, and its level rays fell full upon the man we were chasing. He stood on the very edge of the rocks, a black spot against the luminous yellow of sea and sand. He seemed to be meditating. His back was towards us, and he perceived neither his pursuers above nor the heads that at this moment appeared over the ridge behind him, and not fifteen yards away. The party on the beach had dismounted and were clambering up stealthily. Five seconds more and they could spring upon him.

But they underestimated a madman's instinct. As if for no reason, he gave a quick start, turned, and at the same instant was aware of both attacking parties. A last gleam of sunlight fell on the snuff-box in his left hand; his right thumb and fore-finger hung arrested, grasping the pinch. For fully half a minute nothing happened; hunters and hunted eyed each other and waited. Then carrying the snuff to his nose, and doffing his hat, with a satirical sweep of the hand and a low bow, he turned again and tripped off the ledge into the jaws of the Quick-Boy.

There was no help now. At his third step the sand had him by the ankles. For a moment he fought it, then, throwing up his arms, sank forward, slowly and as if bowing yet, upon his face. Second by second we stood and watched him disappear. Within five minutes the ripples of the Quick-Boy Sand met once more above him.

In the course of the next afternoon the Vicar of Bleakirk called at the Hall with a paper which he had found pinned to the church door. It was evidently a scrap torn from an old letter, and bore, scribbled in pencil by a clerkly hand, these words: "The young Squire Cartwright in straits by the foot-bridge, six miles toward Netherkirk. *Orate pro anima Guliemli Teague.*"

The Bend of the Road

1

Just outside the small country station of M—— in Cornwall, a viaduct carries the Great Western Railway line across a coombe, or narrow valley, through which a tributary trout-stream runs southward to meet the tides of the L—— River. From the carriage-window as you pass you look down the coombe for half a mile perhaps, and also down a road which, leading out from M—— Station a few yards below the viaduct, descends the left-hand slope at a sharp incline to the stream; but whether to cross it or run close beside it down the valley bottom you cannot tell, since, before they meet, an eastward curve of the coombe shuts off the view.

Both slopes are pleasantly wooded, and tall beeches, interset here and there with pines—a pretty contrast in the spring—spread their boughs over the road; which is cut cornice-wise, with a low parapet hedge to protect it along the outer side, where the ground falls steeply to the water-meadows, that wind like a narrow green riband edged by the stream with twinkling silver.

For the rest, there appears nothing remarkable in the valley: and certainly Mr. Molesworth, who crossed and recrossed it regularly on Tuesdays, Thursdays, and Saturdays, on his way to and from his banking business in Plymouth, would have been puzzled to explain why, three times out of four, as his train rattled over the viaduct, he laid down his newspaper, took the cigar from his mouth, and gazed down from the window of his first-class smoking carriage upon the green water-meadows and the curving road. The Great Western line for thirty miles or so on the far side of Plymouth runs through scenery singularly beautiful, and its many viaducts carry it over at least a dozen coombes more strikingly picturesque than this particular one which alone engaged his curiosity.

The secret, perhaps, lay with the road. Mr. Molesworth, who had never set foot on it, sometimes wondered whither it led and into what country it disappeared around the base of the slope to which at times his eyes travelled always wistfully. He had passed his forty-fifth year, and forgotten that he was an imaginative man. Nevertheless, and quite unconsciously, he let his imagination play for a few moments every morning—in the evening, jaded with business, he forgot as often as not to look—along this country road. Somehow it had come to wear a friendly smile, inviting him: and he on his part regarded it with quite a friendly interest. Once or twice, half-amused by the fancy, he had promised himself to take a holiday and explore it.

Years had gone by, and the promise remained unredeemed, nor appeared likely to be redeemed; yet at the back of his mind he was always aware of it. Daily, as the train slowed down and stopped at M— Station, he spared a look for the folks on the platform. They had come by the road; and others, alighting, were about to take the road.

They were few enough, as a rule: apple-cheeked farmers and country-wives with their baskets, bound for Plymouth market; on summer mornings, as likely as not, an angler or two, thick-booted, carrying rods and creels, their hats wreathed with March-browns or palmers on silvery lines of gut; in the autumn, now and then, a sportsman with his gun; on Monday mornings half a dozen navy lads returning from furlough, with stains of native earth on their shoes and the edges of their wide trousers.... The faces of all these people wore an innocent friendliness: to Mr. Molesworth, a childless man, they seemed a childlike race, and mysterious as children, carrying with them like an aura the preoccupations of the valley from which they emerged. He decided that the country below the road must be worth exploring; that spring or early summer must be the proper season, and angling his pretext. He had been an accomplished fly-fisher in his youth, and wondered how much of the art would return to his hand when, after many years, it balanced the rod again.

Together with his fly-fishing, Mr. Molesworth had forgotten most of the propensities of his youth. He had been born an only son of rich parents, who shrank from exposing him to the rigours and temptations of a public school. Consequently, when the time came for him to go up to Oxford, he had found no friends there and had made few, being sensitive, shy, entirely unskilled in games, and but moderately interested in learning. His vacations, which he spent at home, were as dull as he had always found them under a succession of well-meaning, middle-aged tutors—until, one August day, as he played a twelve-pound salmon, he glanced up at the farther bank and into a pair of brown eyes which were watching him with unconcealed interest.

The eyes belonged to a yeoman-farmer's daughter: and young Molesworth lost his fish, but returned next day, and again day after day, to try for him. At the end of three weeks or so, his parents—he was a poor hand at dissimulation—discovered what was happening, and interfered with promptness and resolution. He had not learnt the art of disobedience, and while he considered how to begin (having, indeed, taken his passion with a thoroughness that did him credit), Miss Margaret, sorely weeping, was packed off on a visit to her mother's relations near Exeter, where, three months later, she married a young farmer-cousin and emigrated to Canada.

In this way Mr. Molesworth's love-making and his fly-fishing had come to an end together. Like Gibbon, he had sighed as a lover, and (Miss Margaret's faithlessness assisting) obeyed as a son. Nevertheless, the sequel did not quite fulfil the hopes of his parents, who, having acted with decision in a situation which took them unawares, were willing enough to make amends by providing him with quite a large choice of suitable partners. To their dismay it appeared that he had done with all thoughts of matrimony: and I am not sure that, as the years went on, their dismay did not deepen into regret. To the end he made them an admirable son, but they went down to their graves and left him unmarried.

In all other respects he followed irreproachably the line of life they had marked out for him. He succeeded to the directorate of the bank in which the family had made its money, and to those unpaid offices of local distinction which his father had adorned. As a banker he was eminently 'sound'—that is to say, cautious, but not obstinately conservative; as a Justice of the Peace, scrupulous, fair, inclined to mercy, exact in the performance of all his duties. As High Sheriff he filled his term of office and discharged it adequately, but without ostentation. Respecting wealth, but not greatly caring for it—as why should he?—every year without effort he put aside a thousand or two. Men liked him, in spite of his shyness: his good manners hiding a certain fastidiousness of which he was aware without being at all proud of it. No one had ever treated him with familiarity. One or two at the most called him friend, and these probably enjoyed a deeper friendship than they knew. Everyone felt him to be, behind his reserve, a good fellow.

Regularly thrice a week he drove down in his phaeton to the small country station at the foot of his park, and caught the 10.27 up-train: regularly as the train started he lit the cigar which, carefully smoked, was regularly three-parts consumed by the time he crossed the M—— viaduct; and regularly, as he lit it, he was conscious of a faint feeling of resentment at the presence of Sir John Crang.

Nine mornings out of ten, Sir John Crang (who lived two stations down the line) would be his fellow-traveller; and, three times out of five, his only companion. Sir John was an ex-Civil Servant, knighted for what were known vaguely as 'services in Burmah,' and, now retired upon a derelict country seat in Cornwall, was making a bold push for local importance, and dividing his leisure between the cultivation of roses (in which he excelled) and the directorship of a large soap-factory near the

Plymouth docks. Mr. Molesworth did not like him, and might have accounted for his dislike by a variety of reasons. He himself, for example, grew roses in a small way as an amateur, and had been used to achieve successes at the local flower-shows until Sir John arrived and in one season beat him out of the field. This, as an essentially generous man, he might have forgiven; but not the loud dogmatic air of patronage with which, on venturing to congratulate his rival and discuss some question of culture, he had been bullied and set right, and generally treated as an ignorant junior. Moreover, he seemed to observe—but he may have been mistaken— that, whatever rose he selected for his buttonhole, Sir John would take note of it and trump next day with a finer bloom.

But these were trifles. Putting them aside, Mr. Molesworth felt that he could never like the man who—to be short—was less of a gentleman than a highly coloured and somewhat aggressive imitation of one. Most of all, perhaps, he abhorred Sir John's bulging glassy eyeballs, of a hard white by contrast with his coppery skin—surest sign of the cold sensualist. But in fact he took no pains to analyse his aversion, which extended even to the smell of Sir John's excellent but Burmese cigars. The two men nodded when they met, and usually exchanged a remark or two on the weather. Beyond this they rarely conversed, even upon politics, although both were Conservatives and voters in the same electoral division.

The day of which this story tells was a Saturday in the month of May 188—, a warm and cloudless morning, which seemed to mark the real beginning of summer after an unusually cold spring. The year, indeed, had reached that exact point when for a week or so the young leaves are as fragrant as flowers, and the rush of the train swept a thousand delicious scents in at the open windows. Mr. Molesworth had donned a white waistcoat in honour of the weather, and wore a bud of a Capucine rose in his buttonhole. Sir John had adorned himself with an enormous glowing Sénateur Vaisse. (Why not a Paul Neyron while he was about it? wondered Mr. Molesworth, as he surveyed the globular bloom.)

"Now in the breast a door flings wide—"

It may have been the weather that disposed Sir John to talk to-day. After commending it, and adding a word or two in general in praise of the West-country climate, he paused and watched Mr. Molesworth lighting his cigar.

"You're a man of regular habits?" he observed unexpectedly, with a shade of interrogation in his voice.

Mr. Molesworth frowned and tossed his match out of window.

"I believe in regular habits myself." Sir John, bent on affability, laid down his newspaper on his knee. "There's one danger about them, though: they're deadening. They save a man the bother of thinking, and persuade him he's doing right, when all the reason is that he's done the same thing a hundred times before. I came across that in a book once, and it seemed to me dashed sound sense. Now here's something I'd like to ask you—have you any theory at all about dreams?"

"Dreams?" echoed Mr. Molesworth, taken aback by the inconsequent question.

"There's a Society—isn't there?—that makes a study of 'em and collects evidence. Man wakes up, having dreamt that friend whom he knows to be abroad is standing by his bed; lights his candle or turns on the electric-light and looks at his watch; goes to sleep again, tells his family all about it at breakfast, and a week or two later learns that his friend died at such-and-such an hour, and the very minute his watch pointed to. That's the sort of thing."

"You mean the Psychical Society?"

"That's the name. Well, I'm a case for 'em. Anyway, I can knock the inside out of one of their theories, that dreams are a sort of memory-game, made up of scenes and scraps and such-like out of your waking consciousness—isn't that the lingo? Now, I've never had but one dream in my life; but I've dreamt it two or three score of times, and I dreamt it last night."

"Indeed?" Mr. Molesworth was getting mildly interested.

"And I'm not what you'd call a fanciful sort of person," went on Sir John, with obvious veracity. "Regular habits—rise early and to bed early; never a day's trouble with my digestion; off to sleep as soon as my head touches the pillow. You can't call my dream a nightmare, and yet it's unpleasant, somehow."

"But what is it?"

"Well,"—Sir John seemed to hesitate—"you might call it a scene. Yes, that's it—a scene. There's a piece of water and a church beside it—just an ordinary-looking little parish church, with a tower but no pinnacles. Outside the porch there's a tallish stone cross—you can just see it between the elms from the churchyard gate; and going through the gate you step over a sort of grid—half a dozen granite stones laid parallel, with spaces between."

"Then it must be a Cornish church. You never see that contrivance outside the Duchy: though it's worth copying. It keeps out sheep and cattle, while even a child can step across it easily."

"But, my dear sir, I never saw Cornwall—and certainly never saw or heard of this contrivance—until I came and settled here, eight years ago: whereas I've been dreaming this, off and on, ever since I was fifteen."

"And you never actually saw the rest of the scene? the church itself, for instance?"

"Neither stick nor stone of it: I'll take my oath. Mind you, it isn't *like* a church made up of different scraps of memory. It's just that particular church, and I know it by heart, down to a scaffold-hole, partly hidden with grass, close under the lowest string-course of the tower, facing the gate."

"And inside?"

"I don't know. I've never been inside. But stop a moment—you haven't heard the half of it yet! There's a road comes downhill to the shore, between the churchyard wall—there's a heap of greyish silvery-looking stuff, by the way, growing on the coping—something like lavender, with yellow blossoms—Where was I? Oh yes, and on the other side of the road there's a tall hedge with elms above it. It breaks off where the road takes a bend around and in front of the churchyard gate, with a yard or two of turf on the side towards the water, and from the turf a clean drop of three feet, or a little less, on to the foreshore. The foreshore is all grey stones, round and flat, the sort you'd choose to play what's called ducks-and-drakes. It goes curving along, and the road with it, until the beach ends with a spit of rock, and over the rock a kind of cottage (only bigger, but thatched and whitewashed just like a cottage) with a garden, and in the garden a laburnum in flower, leaning slantwise," —Sir John raised his open hand and bent his forefinger to indicate the angle—"and behind the cottage a reddish cliff with a few clumps of furze overhanging it, and the turf on it stretching up to a larch plantation …."

Sir John paused and rubbed his forehead meditatively.

"At least," he resumed, "I *think* it's a larch plantation; but the scene gets confused above a certain height. It's the foreshore, and the church and the cottage that I always see clearest. Yes, and I forgot to tell you—I'm a poor hand at description—that there's a splash of whitewash on the spit of rock, and an iron ring fixed there, for warping-in a vessel, maybe: and sometimes there's a boat, out on the water.…"

"You describe it vividly enough," said Mr. Molesworth as Sir John paused and, apparently on the point of resuming his story, checked himself, tossed his cigar out of the window, and chose a fresh one from his pocket-case. "Well, and what happens in your dream?"

Sir John struck a match, puffed his fresh cigar alight, deliberately examined the ignited end, and flung the match away. "Nothing happens. I told you it was just a scene, didn't I?"

"You said that somehow the dream was an unpleasant one."

"So I did. So it is. It makes me damnably uncomfortable every time I dream it; though for the life of me I can't tell you why."

"The picture as you draw it seems to me quite a pleasant one."

"So it is, again."

"And you say nothing happens?"

"Well—" Sir John took the cigar from his mouth and looked at it— "nothing ever happens in it, definitely: nothing at all. But always in the dream there's a smell of lemon verbena—it comes from the garden—and a curious hissing noise—and a sense of a black man's being somehow mixed up in it all...."

"A black man?"

"Black or brown... in the dream I don't think I've ever actually seen him. The hissing sound—it's like the hiss of a snake, only ten times louder—may have come into the dream of late years. As to that I won't swear. But I'm dead certain there was always a black man mixed up in it, or what I may call a sense of one: and that, as you will say, is the most curious part of the whole business."

Sir John flipped away the ash of his cigar and leant forward impressively.

"If I wasn't, as I say, dead sure of his having been in it from the first," he went on, "I could tell you the exact date when he took a hand in the game: because," he resumed after another pause, "I once actually saw what I'm telling you."

"But you told me," objected Mr. Molesworth, "that you had never actually seen it."

"I was wrong then. I saw it once, in a Burmese boy's hand at Maulmain. The old Eastern trick, you know: palmful of ink and the rest of it. There was nothing particular about the boy except an ugly scar on his cheek (caused, I believe, by his mother having put him down to sleep in the fireplace while the clay floor of it was nearly red-hot under the ashes). His master called himself his grandfather—a holy-looking man with a white beard down to his loins: and the pair of them used to come up every year from Mergui or some such part, at the Full Moon of Taboung, which happens at the end of March and is the big feast in Maulmain. The pair of them stood close by the great entrance of the Shway Dagone, where the three roads meet, and just below the long flights of steps leading up to the pagoda. The second day of the feast I was making for the entrance with a couple of naval officers I had picked up at the Club, and my man, Moung Gway, following as close as he could keep in the crowd. Just as we were going up the steps, the old impostor challenged me, and, partly to show my friends what the game was like—for they were new to the country—I stopped and found a coin for him. He poured the usual dollop of ink into the boy's hand, and, by George, sir, next minute I was staring at the very thing I'd seen a score of times in my dreams but never out of them. I tell you, there's more in that Eastern hanky-panky than meets the eye; beyond that I'll offer no opinion.

"Outside the magic I believe the whole business was a put-up job, to catch my attention and take me unawares. For when I stepped back, pretty well startled, and blinking from the strain of keeping my attention fixed on the boy's palm, a man jumped forward from the crowd and precious nearly knifed me. If it hadn't been for Moung Gway, who tripped him up and knocked him sideways, I should have been a dead man in two twos—for my friends were taken aback by the suddenness of it. But in less than a minute we had him down and the handcuffs on him; and the end was, he got five years' hard, which means hefting chain-shot from one end to another of the prison square and then hefting it back again.

"There was a rather neat little Burmese girl, you see—a sort of niece of Moung Gway's—who had taken a fancy to me; and this turned out to be a disappointed lover, just turned up from a voyage to Cagayan in a paddy-boat. I believed he had fixed it up with the venerable one to hold me with the magic until he got in his stroke. Venomous beggars, those Burmans, if you cross 'em in the wrong way! The fellow got his release a week before I left Maulmain for good, and the very next day Moung Gway was found, down by the quays, dead as a haddock, with a wound between the shoulder-blades as neat as if he'd been measured for it. Oh, I could tell you a story or two about those fellows!"

"It's easily explained, at any rate," Mr. Molesworth suggested, "why you see a dark-skinned man in your dream."

"But I tell you, my dear sir, he has been a part of the dream from the beginning... before I went to Wren's, and long before ever I thought of Burmah. He's as old as the church itself, and the foreshore and the cottage—the whole scene, in fact—though I can't say he's half as distinct. I can't tell you in the least, for instance, what his features are like. I've said that the upper part of the dream is vague to me; at the end of the foreshore, that is, where the cottage stands; the church tower I can see plainly enough to the very top. But over by the cottage— above the porch, as you may say—everything seems to swim in a mist: and it's up in that mist the fellow's head and shoulders appear and vanish. Sometimes I think he's looking out of the window at me, and draws back into the room as if he didn't want to be seen; and the mist itself gathers and floats away with the hissing sound I told you about...."

Sir John's voice paused abruptly. The train was drawing near the M—— viaduct, and Mr. Molesworth from force of habit had turned his eyes to the window, to gaze down the green valley. He withdrew them suddenly, and looked around at his companion.

"Ah, to be sure," he said vaguely; "I had forgotten the hissing sound."

It was curious, but as he spoke he himself became aware of a loud hissing sound filling his ears. The train lurched and jolted heavily.

"Hullo!" exclaimed Sir John, half rising in his seat, "something's wrong." He was staring past Mr. Molesworth and out of the window. "Nasty place for an accident, too," he added in a slow, strained voice.

The two men looked at each other for a moment. Sir John's face wore a tense expression—a kind of galvanised smile. Mr. Molesworth closed his eyes, instinctively concealing his sudden sickening terror of what an accident just there must mean: and for a second or so he actually had a sensation of dropping into space. He remembered having felt something like it in dreams three or four times in his life: and at the same instant he remembered a country superstition gravely imparted to him in childhood by his old nurse, that if you dreamt of falling and didn't wake up before reaching the bottom, you would surely die. The absurdity of it chased away his terror, and he opened his eyes and looked about him with a short laugh....

The train still jolted heavily, but had begun to slow down, and Mr. Molesworth drew a long breath as a glance told him that they were past the viaduct. Sir John had risen, and was leaning out of the farther window. Something had gone amiss, then. But what?

He put the question aloud. Sir John, his head and shoulders well outside the carriage-window, did not answer. Probably he did not hear.

As the train ran into M—— Station and came to a standstill, Mr. Molesworth caught a glimpse of the station-master, in his gold-braided cap, by the door of the booking-office. He wore a grave, almost a scared look. The three or four country-people on the sunny platform seemed to have their gaze drawn by the engine, and somebody ahead there was shouting. Sir John Crang, without a backward look, flung the door open and stepped out. Mr. Molesworth was preparing to follow—and by the cramped feeling in his fingers was aware at the same instant that he had been gripping the arm-rest almost desperately—when the guard of the train came running by and paused to thrust his head in at the open doorway to explain.

"Engine's broken her coupling-rod, sir—just before we came to the viaduct. Mercy for us she didn't leave the rails."

"Mercy indeed, as you say," Mr. Molesworth assented. "I suppose we shall be hung up here until they send a relief down?"

The guard—Mr. Molesworth knew him as 'George' by name, and by habit constantly polite—turned and waved his flag hurriedly, in acknowledgment of the shouting ahead, before answering—

"You may count on half an hour's delay, sir. Lucky it's no worse. You'll excuse me—they're calling for me down yonder."

He ran on, and Mr. Molesworth stepped out upon the platform, of which this end was already deserted, all the passengers having alighted and hurried forward to inspect the damaged engine. A few paces beyond the door he met the station-master racing back to despatch a telegram.

"It seems that we've had a narrow escape," said Mr. Molesworth.

The station-master touched his hat and plunged into his office. Mr. Molesworth, instead of joining the crowd around the engine, halted before a small pile of luggage on a bench outside the waiting-room and absent-mindedly scanned the labels.

Among the parcels lay a fishing-rod in a canvas case and a wicker creel, the pair of them labelled and bearing the name of an acquaintance of his— a certain Sir Warwick Moyle, baronet and county magistrate, beside whom he habitually sat at Quarter Sessions.

"I had no idea," Mr. Molesworth mused, "that Moyle was an angler. It would be a fair joke, anyway, to borrow his rod and fill up the time.— How long before the relief comes down?" he asked, intercepting the station-master as he came rushing out from his office and slammed the door behind him.

"Maybe an hour, sir, before we get you started again. I can't honestly promise you less than forty minutes."

"Very well, then: I'm going to borrow Sir Warwick's rod, there, and fill up the time," said Mr. Molesworth, pointing at it.

The station-master apparently did not hear; at any rate he passed on without remonstrance. Mr. Molesworth slung the creel over his shoulder, picked up the rod, and stepped out beyond the station gateway upon the road.

2

The road ran through a cutting, sunless, cooled by many small springs of water trickling down the rock-face, green with draperies of the hart's-tongue and common polypody ferns; and emerged again into warmth upon a curve of the hillside facing southward down the coombe, and almost close under the second span of the viaduct, where the tall trestles plunged down among the tree-tops like gigantic stilts, and the railway left earth and spun itself across the chasm like a line of gossamer, its crisscrossed timbers so delicately pencilled against the blue that the whole structure seemed to swing there in the morning breeze. Above it, in heights yet more giddy, the larks were chiming; and Mr. Molesworth's heart went up to those clear heights with a sudden lift.

In all the many times he had crossed the viaduct he had never once guessed—he could not have imagined—how beautiful it looked from below. He stood and gazed, and drew a long breath. Was it the escape from dreadful peril, with its blessed revulsion of feeling, that so quickened all his senses dulled by years of habit? He could not tell. He gave himself up to the strange and innocent excitement.

Why had he never till now—and now only by accident—obeyed the impulse to descend this road and explore? He was rich: he had not even the excuse of children to be provided for: the Bank might surely have waited for one day. He did not want much money. His tastes were simple—Was not the happiness at this moment thrilling him a proof that his tastes were simple as a child's? Lo, too, his eyes were looking on the world as freshly as a child's! Why had he so long denied them a holiday? Why do men chain themselves in prisons of their own making?

What had the station-master said? It might be an hour—certainly not less than forty minutes—before the train could be restarted. Mr. Molesworth looked at his watch. Forty minutes to explore the road: forty minutes' holiday! He laughed, pocketed the watch again, and took the road briskly, humming a song.

Suppose he missed his train? Why, then, the bank must do without him today, as it would have to do without him, one of these days, when he was dead. He thought of his fellow-directors' faces, and laughed again. He felt morally certain of missing that train. What kind of world would it be if money grew in birds' nests, or if leaves were currency and withered in autumn? Would it include truant-schools for bankers?...

He that is down needs fear no fall,
He that is low, no pride;

He that is humble ever shall
Have God to be his guide.

Fullness to such a burden is
That go on pilgrimage—

Mr. Molesworth did not actually sing these words. The tune he hummed was a wordless one, and, for that matter, not even much of a tune. But he afterwards declared very positively that he sang the sense of them, being challenged by the birds calling in contention louder and louder as the road dipped towards the stream, and by the music of lapsing water which now began to possess his ear. For some five or six furlongs the road descended under beech-boughs, between slopes carpeted with last year's leaves: but by and by the beeches gave place to an oak coppice with a matted undergrowth of the whortleberry; and where these in turn broke off, and a plantation of green young larches climbed the hill, the wild hyacinths ran down to the stream in sheet upon sheet of blue.

Mr. Molesworth rested his creel on the low hedge above one of these sheets of blue, and with the music of the stream in his ears began to unpack Sir Warwick Moyle's fishing-rod. For a moment he paused, bethinking himself, with another short laugh, that, without flies, neither rod nor line would catch him a fish. But decidedly fortune was kind to him today: for, opening the creel, he found Sir Warwick's fly-book within it, bulging with hooks and flies by the score—nay, by the hundred. He unbuckled the strap and was turning the leaves to make his choice, when his ear caught the sound of footsteps, and he lifted his eyes to see Sir John Crang coming down the road.

"Hullo!" hailed Sir John. "I saw you slip out of the station and took a fancy that I'd follow. Pretty little out-of-the-way spot, this. Eh? Why, where on earth did you pick up those angling traps?"

"I stole them," answered Mr. Molesworth deliberately, choosing a fly. He did not in the least desire Sir John's company, but somehow found himself too full of good-nature to resent it actively.

"Stole 'em?"

"Well, as a matter of fact, they belong to a friend of mine. They were lying ready to hand in the station, and I borrowed them without leave. He won't mind."

"You're a cool one, I must say." It may be that the recent agitation of his feelings had shaken Sir John's native vulgarity to the surface. Certainly he spoke now with a commonness of idiom and accent he was usually at pains to conceal. "You must have a fair nerve altogether, for all you're such a quiet-looking chap. Hadn't even the curiosity—had you?—to find out what had gone wrong; but just picked up a handy fishing-rod and strolled off to fill up the time till damages were repaired. Look here. Do you know, or don't you, that 'twasn't by more than a hair's-breadth we missed going over that viaduct?"

"I knew we must have had a narrow escape."

"And you can be tying the fly there on to that gut as steady as a doctor picking up an artery! Well, I envy you. Look at *that!*" Sir John held out a brown, hairy, shaking hand. "And I don't reckon myself a coward, either."

Mr. Molesworth knew that the man's record had established at any rate his reputation for courage. He had, in fact, been a famous hunter-out of Dacoity.

"I didn't know you went in for that sort of thing," pursued Sir John, watching Mr. Molesworth, who, with a penknife, was trimming the ends of gut. "Don't mind my watching your first cast or two, I hope? I won't talk. Anglers don't like being interrupted, I know."

"I shall be glad of your company: and please talk as much as you choose. To tell the truth, I haven't handled a rod for years, and I'm making this little experiment to see if I've quite lost the knack, rather than with any hope of catching fish."

It appeared, however, that he had not lost the knack, and after the first cast or two, in the pleasure of recovered skill, his senses abandoned themselves entirely to the sport. Sir John had lit a cigar and seated himself amid the bracken a short distance back from the brink, to watch: but whether he conversed or not Mr. Molesworth could not tell. He remembered afterwards that at the end of twenty minutes or so—probably when his cigar was finished—Sir John rose and announced his intention of strolling some way farther down the valley—"to soothe his nerves a bit," as he said, adding, "So long! I see you're going to miss that train, to a certainty."

Yes, it was certain enough that Mr. Molesworth would miss his train. He fished down the stream slowly, the song and dazzle of the water filling his ears, his vision; his whole being soothed and lulled less by the actual scene than by a hundred memories it awakened or set stirring. He was young again—a youth of twenty with romance in his heart. The plants and grasses he trod were the asphodels, sundew, water-mint his feet had crushed—crushed into fragrance—five-and-twenty years ago....

So deeply preoccupied was he that, coming to a bend where the coombe suddenly widened, and the stream without warning cast its green fringe of alders like a slough and slipped down a beach of flat pebbles to the head waters of a tidal creek, Mr. Molesworth rubbed his eyes with a start. Had the stream been a Naiad she could not have given him the go-by more coquettishly.

He rubbed his eyes, and then with a short gasp of wonder—almost of terror—involuntarily looked around for Sir John. Here before him was a shore, with a church beside it, and at the far end a whitewashed cottage— surely the very shore, church, cottage, of Sir John's dream! Yes, there was the stone cross before the porch; and here the grid-fashioned church stile; and yonder under the string-course the scaffold-hole with the grass growing out of it!

If Mr. Molesworth's hands had been steady when he tied on his May-fly, they trembled enough now as he hurriedly put up his tackle and disjointed his rod: and still, and again while he hastened across to the cottage above the rocky spit—the cottage with the larch plantation above and in the garden a laburnum aslant and in bloom—his eyes sought the beach for Sir John.

The cottage was a large one, as Sir John had described. It was, in fact, a waterside inn, with its name, The Saracen's Head, painted in black letters along its whitewashed front and under a swinging signboard. Looking up at the board Mr. Molesworth discerned, beneath its dark varnish, the shoulders, scimitar, and grinning face of a turbaned Saracen, and laughed aloud between incredulity and a sense of terror absurdly relieved. This, then, was Sir John's black man!

But almost at the same moment another face looked over the low hedge—the face of a young girl in a blue sun-bonnet: and Mr. Molesworth put out a hand to the gate to steady himself.

The girl—she had heard his laugh, perhaps—gazed down at him with a frank curiosity. Her eyes were honest, clear, untroubled: they were also extremely beautiful eyes: and they were more. As Mr. Molesworth to his last day was prepared to take oath, here were the very eyes, as here was the very face and here the very form, of the Margaret whom he had suffered for, and suffered to be lost to him, twenty-five years ago. It was Margaret, and she had not aged one day.

In Margaret's voice, too, seeing that he made no motion to enter, she spoke down to him across the hedge.

"Are you a friend, sir, of the gentleman that was here just now?"

"Sir John Crang?" Mr. Molesworth just managed to command his voice.

"I don't know his name, sir. But he left his cigar-case behind. I found it on the settle five minutes after he had gone, and ran out to search for him...."

Mr. Molesworth opened the gate and held out a hand for the case. Yes: he recognised it. It bore Sir John's monogram in silver.

"I will give it to him," he said. Without exactly knowing why, he followed her into the inn-kitchen. Yes, he would take a pint of her ale. "The home-brewed?" Yes, certainly, the home-brewed.

She brought it in a pewter tankard, exquisitely polished. The polish of it caught and cast back the sunlight in prismatic circles on the scoured deal table. The girl—Margaret—stood for a moment in the fuller sunlight by the window, lingering there to pick a dead leaf from a geranium on the ledge.

"Which way did Sir John go?"

"I *thought* he took the turning along the shore; but I didn't notice particularly which way he went. He said he had come down the valley, and I took it for granted he would be going on."

Mr. Molesworth drank his beer and stood up. "There are only two ways, then, out of this valley?"

"Thank you, sir—" As he paid her she dropped a small curtsey—"Yes, only two ways—up the valley or along the shore. The road up the valley leads to the railway station."

"By the way, there was an accident at the station this morning?"

"Indeed, sir?" Her beautiful eyes grew round. "Nothing serious, I hope?"

"It might have been a very nasty one indeed," said Mr. Molesworth, and paused. "I think I'll take a look along the shore before returning. I don't want to miss my friend, if I can help it."

"You can see right along it from the rock beyond the garden," said the girl, and Mr. Molesworth went out.

As he reached the spit of rock, the sunlight playing down the waters of the creek dazzled him for a moment. Rubbing his eyes, he saw, about two hundred yards along the foreshore, a boat grounded, and two figures beside it on the beach: and either his sight was playing him a trick or these two were struggling together.

He ran towards them. Almost as he started, in one of the figures he recognised Sir John. The other had him by the shoulders, and seemed to be dragging him by main force towards the boat. Mr. Molesworth shouted as he rushed up to the fray. The assailant turned—turned with a loud hissing sound—and, releasing Sir John, swung up a hand with something in it that flashed in the sun as he struck at the newcomer: and as Mr. Molesworth fell, he saw a fierce brown face and a cage of white, gleaming teeth bared in a savage grin....

He picked himself up, the blood running warm over his eyes, and, as he stood erect for a moment, down over his white waistcoat. But the dusky face of his antagonist had vanished, and, with it, the whole scene. In place of the foreshore with its flat grey stones, his eye travelled down a steep green slope. The hissing sound continued in his ears, louder than ever, but it came with violent jets of steam from a locomotive, grotesquely overturned some twenty yards below him. Fainting, he saw and sank across the body of Sir John Crang, which lay with face upturned among the June grasses, staring at the sky.

3

Statement by W. Pitt Ferguson, M.D., of Lockyer Street, Plymouth.

The foregoing narrative has been submitted to me by the writer, who was well acquainted with the late Mr. Molesworth. In my opinion it conveys a correct impression of that gentleman's temperament and character: and I can testify that in the details of his psychical adventures on the valley road leading to St. A——'s Church it adheres strictly to the account given me by Mr. Molesworth himself shortly after the accident on the M— viaduct, and repeated by him several times with insistence during the illness which terminated mortally some four months later. The manner in which the narrative is presented may be open to criticism: but of this, as one who has for some years eschewed the reading of fiction, I am not a fair judge. It adds, at any rate, nothing in the way of 'sensation' to the story as Mr. Molesworth told it: and of its improbability I should be the last to complain, who am to add, of my own positive observation, some evidence which will make it appear yet more startling, if not wholly incredible.

The accident was actually witnessed by two men, cattle-jobbers, who were driving down the valley road in a light cart or 'trap,' and were within two hundred yards of the viaduct when they saw the train crash through the parapet over the second span (counting from the west), and strike and plunge down the slope. In their evidence at the inquest, and again at the Board of Trade inquiry, these men agree that it took them from five to eight minutes only to alight, run down and across the valley (fording the stream on their way), and scramble up to the scene of the disaster: and they further agree that one of the first sad objects on which their eyes fell was the dead body of Sir John Crang with Mr. Molesworth, alive but sadly injured and bleeding, stretched across it. Apparently they had managed to crawl from the wreck of the carriage before Sir John succumbed, or Mr. Molesworth had managed to drag his companion out— whether dead or alive cannot be told—before himself fainting from loss of blood.

The toll of the disaster, as is generally known, amounted to twelve killed and seventeen more or less seriously injured. Help having been summoned from M—— Station, the injured—or as many of them as could be removed— were conveyed in an ambulance train to Plymouth. Among them was Mr. Molesworth, whose apparent injuries were a broken hip, a laceration of the thigh, and an ugly, jagged scalp-wound. Of all these he made, in time, a fair recovery: but what brought him under my care was the nervous shock from which his brain, even while his body healed, never made any promising attempt to rally. For some time after the surgeon had pronounced him cured he lingered on, a visibly dying man, and died in the end of utter nervous collapse.

Yet even within a few days of the end his brain kept an astonishing clearness: and to me, as well as to the friends who visited him in hospital and afterwards in his Plymouth lodgings—for he never returned home again, being unable to face another railway journey—he would maintain, and with astonishing vigour and lucidity of description, that he had actually in very truth travelled down the valley in company with Sir John Crang, and seen with his own eyes everything related in the foregoing paper. Now, as a record of what did undeniably pass through the brain of a cultivated man in some catastrophic moments, I found these recollections of his exceedingly interesting.

As no evidence is harder to collect, so almost none can be of higher importance, than that of man's sensations at the exact moment when he passes, naturally or violently, out of this present life into whatever may be beyond. Partly because Mr. Molesworth's story, which he persisted in, had this scientific value; partly in the hope of diverting his mind from the lethargy into which I perceived it to be sinking; I once begged him to write the whole story down. To this, however, he was unequal. His will betrayed him as soon as he took pen and paper.

The entire veracity of his recollection he none the less affirmed again and again, and with something like passion, although aware that his friends were but humouring him while they listened and made pretence to believe. The strong card—if I may so term it—in his evidence was undoubtedly Sir John Crang's cigar-case. It was found in Mr. Molesworth's breast-pocket when they undressed him at the hospital, and how it came there I confess I cannot explain. It may be that it had dropped on the grass from Sir John's pocket, and that Mr. Molesworth, under the hallucination which undoubtedly possessed him, picked it up, and pocketed it before the two cattle-drovers found him. It is an unlikely hypothesis, but I cannot suggest a likelier.

A fortnight before his death he sent for a lawyer and made his will, the sanity of which no one can challenge. At the end he directed that his body should be interred in the parish churchyard of St. A—, 'as close as may be to the cross by the church porch.' As a last challenge to scepticism this surely was defiant enough.

It was my duty to attend the funeral. The coffin, conveyed by train to M— Station, was there transferred to a hearse, and the procession followed the valley road. I forget at what point it began to be impressed upon me, who had never travelled the road before, that Mr. Molesworth's 'recollections' of it had been so exact that they compelled a choice between the impossibility of accepting his story and the impossibility of doubting the assurance of so entirely honourable a man that he had never travelled the road in his life. At first I tried to believe that his recollections of it—detailed as they were—might one by one have been suggested by the view from the viaduct. But, honestly, I was soon obliged to give this up: and when we arrived at the creek's head and the small churchyard beside it, I confessed myself confounded. Point by point, and at every point, the actual scene reproduced Mr. Molesworth's description.

I prefer to make no comment on my last discovery. After the funeral, being curious to satisfy myself in every particular, I walked across the track to the inn—The Saracen's Head—which again answered Mr. Molesworth's description to the last detail. The house was kept by a widow and her daughter: and the girl—an extremely good-looking young person—made me welcome. I concluded she must be the original of Mr. Molesworth's illusion—perhaps the strangest of all his illusions—and took occasion to ask her (I confess not without a touch of trepidation) if she remembered the day of the accident. She answered that she remembered it well. I asked if she remembered any visitor, or visitors, coming to the inn on that day. She answered, None: but that now I happened to speak of it, somebody must have come that day while she was absent on an errand to the Vicarage (which lies some way along the shore to the westward): for on returning she found a fishing-rod and creel on the settle of the inn-kitchen.

The creel had a luggage-label tied to it, and on the label was written 'Sir W. Moyle.' She had written to Sir Warwick about it more than a month ago, but had not heard from him in answer. [It turned out that Sir Warwick had left England, three days after the accident, on a yachting excursion to Norway.]

"And a cigar-case?" I asked. "You don't remember seeing a cigar-case?"

She shook her head, evidently puzzled. "I know nothing about a cigar-case," she said. "But you shall see the rod and fishing-basket."

She ran at once and fetched them. Now that rod and that creel (and the fly-book within it) have since been restored to Sir Warwick Moyle. He had left them in care of the station-master at M——, whence they had been missing since the day of the accident. It was suspected that they had been stolen, in the confusion that day prevailing at the little station, by some ganger on the relief-train.

The girl, I am convinced, was honest, and had no notion how they found their way to the kitchen of The Saracen's Head: nor—to be equally honest—have I.

The Haunted Dragoon

Beside the Plymouth road, as it plunges downhill past Ruan Lanihale church towards Ruan Cove, and ten paces beyond the lych-gate—where the graves lie level with the coping, and the horseman can decipher their inscriptions in passing, at the risk of a twisted neck—the base of the churchyard wall is pierced with a low archway, festooned with toad-flax and fringed with the hart's-tongue fern. Within the archway bubbles a well, the water of which was once used for all baptisms in the parish, for no child sprinkled with it could ever be hanged with hemp. But this belief is discredited now, and the well neglected: and the events which led to this are still a winter's tale in the neighbourhood. I set them down as they were told me, across the blue glow of a wreck-wood fire, by Sam Tregear, the parish bedman. Sam himself had borne an inconspicuous share in them; and because of them Sam's father had carried a white face to his grave.

My father and mother (said Sam) married late in life, for his trade was what mine is, and 'twasn't till her fortieth year that my mother could bring herself to kiss a gravedigger. That accounts, maybe, for my being born rickety and with other drawbacks that only made father the fonder. Weather permitting, he'd carry me off to churchyard, set me upon a flat stone, with his coat folded under, and talk to me while he delved. I can mind, now, the way he'd settle lower and lower, till his head played hidey-peep with me over the grave's edge, and at last he'd be clean swallowed up, but still discoursing or calling up how he'd come upon wonderful towns and kingdoms down underground, and how all the kings and queens there, in dyed garments, was offering him meat for his dinner every day of the week if he'd only stop and hobbynob with them—and all such gammut. He prettily doted on me—the poor old ancient!

But there came a day—a dry afternoon in the late wheat harvest—when we were up in the churchyard together, and though father had his tools beside him, not a tint did he work, but kept travishing back and forth, one time shading his eyes and gazing out to sea, and then looking far along the Plymouth road for minutes at a time. Out by Bradden Point there stood a little dandy-rigged craft, tacking lazily to and fro, with her mains'le all shiny-yellow in the sunset. Though I didn't know it then, she was the Preventive boat, and her business was to watch the Hauen: for there had been a brush between her and the *Unity* lugger, a fortnight back, and a Preventive man shot through the breast-bone, and my mother's brother Philip was hiding down in the town. I minded, later, how that the men across the vale, in Farmer Tresidder's wheat-field, paused every now and then, as they pitched the sheaves, to give a look up towards the churchyard, and the gleaners moved about in small knots, causeying and glancing over their shoulders at the cutter out in the bay; and how, when all the field was carried, they waited round the last load, no man offering to cry the *Neck*, as the fashion was, but lingering till sun was near down behind the slope and the long shadows stretching across the stubble.

"Sha'n't thee go underground today, father?" says I, at last.

He turned slowly round, and says he, "No, sonny. 'Reckon us'll climb skywards for a change.'"

And with that, he took my hand, and pushing abroad the belfry door began to climb the stairway. Up and up, round and round we went, in a sort of blind-man's-holiday full of little glints of light and whiff's of wind where the open windows came; and at last stepped out upon the leads of the tower and drew breath.

"There's two-an'-twenty parishes to be witnessed from where we're standin', sonny—if ye've got eyes," says my father.

Well, first I looked down towards the harvesters and laughed to see them so small: and then I fell to counting the church-towers dotted across the high-lands, and seeing if I could make out two-and-twenty. 'Twas the prettiest sight—all the country round looking as if 'twas dusted with gold, and the Plymouth road winding away over the hills like a long white tape. I had counted thirteen churches, when my father pointed his hand out along this road and called to me—

"Look'ee out yonder, honey, an' say what ye see!"

"I see dust," says I.

"Nothin' else? Sonny boy, use your eyes, for mine be dim."

"I see dust," says I again, "an' suthin' twinklin' in it, like a tin can—"

"Dragooners!" shouts my father; and then, running to the side of the tower facing the harvest-field, he put both hands to his mouth and called:

"*What have 'ee? What have 'ee?*"—very loud and long.

"*A neck—a neck!*" came back from the field, like as if all shouted at once—dear, the sweet sound! And then a gun was fired, and craning forward over the coping I saw a dozen men running across the stubble and out into the road towards the Hauen; and they called as they ran, "*A neck—a neck!*"

"Iss," says my father, "'tis a neck, sure 'nuff. Pray God they save en! Come, sonny—"

But we dallied up there till the horsemen were plain to see, and their scarlet coats and armour blazing in the dust as they came. And when they drew near within a mile, and our limbs ached with crouching—for fear they should spy us against the sky—father took me by the hand and pulled hot foot down the stairs. Before they rode by he had picked up his shovel and was shovelling out a grave for his life.

Forty valiant horsemen they were, riding two-and-two (by reason of the narrowness of the road) and a captain beside them—men broad and long, with hairy top-lips, and all clad in scarlet jackets and white breeches that showed bravely against their black war-horses and jet-black holsters, thick as they were wi' dust. Each man had a golden helmet, and a scabbard flapping by his side, and a piece of metal like a half-moon jingling from his horse's cheek-strap. 12 D was the numbering on every saddle, meaning the Twelfth Dragoons.

Tramp, tramp! they rode by, talking and joking, and taking no more heed of me—that sat upon the wall with my heels dangling above them—than if I'd been a sprig of stonecrop. But the captain, who carried a drawn sword and mopped his face with a handkerchief so that the dust ran across it in streaks, drew rein, and looked over my shoulder to where father was digging.

"Sergeant!" he calls back, turning with a hand upon his crupper; "didn't we see a figger like this a-top o' the tower, some way back?"

The sergeant pricked his horse forward and saluted. He was the tallest, straightest man in the troop, and the muscles on his arm filled out his sleeve with the three stripes upon it—a handsome red-faced fellow, with curly black hair.

Says he, "That we did, sir—a man with sloping shoulders and a boy with a goose neck." Saying this, he looked up at me with a grin.

"I'll bear it in mind," answered the officer, and the troop rode on in a cloud of dust, the sergeant looking back and smiling, as if 'twas a joke that he shared with us. Well, to be short, they rode down into the town as night fell. But 'twas too late, Uncle Philip having had fair warning and plenty of time to flee up towards the little secret hold under Mabel Down, where none but two families knew how to find him. All the town, though, knew he was safe, and lashins of women and children turned out to see the comely soldiers hunt in vain till ten o'clock at night.

The next thing was to billet the warriors. The captain of the troop, by this, was pesky cross-tempered, and flounced off to the "Jolly Pilchards" in a huff. "Sergeant," says he, "here's an inn, though a damned bad 'un, an' here I means to stop. Somewheres about there's a farm called Constantine, where I'm told the men can be accommodated. Find out the place, if you can, an' do your best: an' don't let me see yer face till tomorra," says he.

So Sergeant Basket—that was his name—gave the salute, and rode his troop up the street, where—for his manners were mighty winning, notwithstanding the dirty nature of his errand—he soon found plenty to direct him to Farmer Noy's, of Constantine; and up the coombe they rode into the darkness, a dozen or more going along with them to show the way, being won by their martial bearing as well as the sergeant's very friendly way of speech.

Farmer Noy was in bed—a pock-marked, lantern-jawed old gaffer of sixty-five; and the most remarkable point about him was the wife he had married two years before—a young slip of a girl but just husband-high. Money did it, I reckon; but if so, 'twas a bad bargain for her. He was noted for stinginess to such a degree that they said his wife wore a brass wedding-ring, weekdays, to save the genuine article from wearing out. She was a Ruan woman, too, and therefore ought to have known all about him. But woman's ways be past finding out.

Hearing the hoofs in his yard and the sergeant's *stram-a-ram* upon the door, down comes the old curmudgeon with a candle held high above his head.

"What the devil's here?" he calls out. Sergeant Basket looks over the old man's shoulder; and there, halfway up the stairs, stood Madam Noy in her night rail—a high-coloured ripe girl, languishing for love, her red lips parted and neck all lily-white against a loosened pile of dark-brown hair.

"Be cussed if I turn back!" said the sergeant to himself; and added out loud—

"Forty souldjers, in the king's name!"

"Forty devils!" says old Noy.

"They're devils to eat," answered the sergeant, in the most friendly manner; "an', begad, ye must feed an' bed 'em this night—or else I'll search your cellars. Ye are a loyal man—eh, farmer? An' your cellars are big, I'm told."

"Sarah," calls out the old man, following the sergeant's bold glance, "go back an' dress yersel' dacently this instant! These here honest souldjers—forty damned honest gormandisin' souldjers—be come in His Majesty's name, forty strong, to protect honest folks' rights in the intervals of eatin' 'em out o' house an' home. Sergeant, ye be very welcome i' the king's name. Cheese an' cider ye shall have, an' I pray the mixture may turn your forty stomachs."

In a dozen minutes he had fetched out his stable-boys and farm-hands, and, lantern in hand, was helping the sergeant to picket the horses and stow the men about on clean straw in the outhouses. They were turning back to the house, and the old man was turning over in his mind that the sergeant hadn't yet said a word about where he was to sleep, when by the door they found Madam Noy waiting, in her wedding gown, and with her hair freshly braided.

Now, the farmer was mortally afraid of the sergeant, knowing he had thirty ankers and more of contraband liquor in his cellars, and minding the sergeant's threat. None the less his jealousy got the upper hand.

"Woman," he cries out, "to thy bed!"

"I was waiting," said she, "to say the Cap'n's bed—"

"Sergeant's," says the dragoon, correcting her.

"—Was laid i' the spare room."

"Madam," replies Sergeant Basket, looking into her eyes and bowing, "a soldier with my responsibility sleeps but little. In the first place, I must see that my men sup."

"The maids be now cuttin' the bread an' cheese and drawin' the cider."

"Then, Madam, leave me but possession of the parlour, and let me have a chair to sleep in."

By this they were in the passage together, and her gaze devouring his regimentals. The old man stood a pace off, looking sourly. The sergeant fed his eyes upon her, and Satan got hold of him.

"Now if only," said he, "one of you could play cards!"

"But I must go to bed," she answered; "though I can play cribbage, if only you stay another night."

For she saw the glint in the farmer's eye; and so Sergeant

Basket slept bolt upright that night in an arm-chair by the parlour fender. Next day the dragooners searched the town again, and were billeted all about among the cottages. But the sergeant returned to Constantine, and before going to bed—this time in the spare room—played a game of cribbage with Madam Noy, the farmer smoking sulkily in his armchair.

"Two for his heels!" said the rosy woman suddenly, halfway through the game. "Sergeant, you're cheatin' yoursel' an' forgettin' to mark. Gi'e me the board; I'll mark for both."

She put out her hand upon the board, and Sergeant Basket's closed upon it. 'Tis true he had forgot to mark; and feeling the hot pulse in her wrist, and beholding the hunger in her eyes, 'tis to be supposed he'd have forgot his own soul.

He rode away next day with his troop: but my uncle Philip not being caught yet, and the government set on making an example of him, we hadn't seen the last of these dragoons. 'Twas a time of fear down in the town. At dead of night or at noonday they came on us—six times in all: and for two months the crew of the *Unity* couldn't call their souls their own, but lived from day to day in secret closets and wandered the country by night, hiding in hedges and straw-houses. All that time the revenue men watched the Hauen, night and day, like dogs before a rat-hole.

But one November morning 'twas whispered abroad that Uncle Philip had made his way to Falmouth, and slipped across to Guernsey. Time passed on, and the dragooners were seen no more, nor the handsome devil-may-care face of Sergeant Basket. Up at Constantine, where he had always contrived to billet himself, 'tis to be thought pretty Madam Noy pined to see him again, kicking his spurs in the porch and smiling out of his gay brown eyes; for her face fell away from its plump condition, and the hunger in her eyes grew and grew. But a more remarkable fact was that her old husband—who wouldn't have yearned after the dragoon, ye'd have thought—began to dwindle and fall away too. By the New Year he was a dying man, and carried his doom on his face. And on New Year's Day he straddled his mare for the last time, and rode over to Looe, to Doctor Gale's.

"Goody-losh!" cried the doctor, taken aback by his appearance— "What's come to ye, Noy?"

"Death!" says Noy. "Doctor, I hain't come for advice, for before this day week I'll be a clay-cold corpse. I come to ax a favour. When they summon ye, before lookin' at my body—that'll be past help—go you to the little left-top corner drawer o' my wife's bureau, an' there ye'll find a packet. You're my executor," says he, "and I leaves ye to deal wi' that packet as ye thinks fit."

With that, the farmer rode away home-along, and the very day week he went dead.

The doctor, when called over, minded what the old chap had said, and sending Madam Noy on some pretence to the kitchen, went over and unlocked the little drawer with a duplicate key, that the farmer had unhitched from his watch-chain and given him. There was no parcel of letters, as he looked to find, but only a small packet crumpled away in the corner. He pulled it out and gave a look, and a sniff, and another look: then shut the drawer, locked it, strode straight downstairs to his horse and galloped away.

In three hours' time, pretty Madam Noy was in the constables' hands upon the charge of murdering her husband by poison.

They tried her, next Spring Assize, at Bodmin, before the Lord Chief Justice. There wasn't evidence enough to put Sergeant Basket in the dock alongside of her—though 'twas freely guessed he knew more than anyone (saving the prisoner herself) about the arsenic that was found in the little drawer and inside the old man's body. He was subpoena'd from Plymouth, and cross-examined by a great hulking King's Counsel for three-quarters of an hour. But they got nothing out of him. All through the examination the prisoner looked at him and nodded her white face, every now and then, at his answers, as much as to say, "That's right—that's right: they shan't harm thee, my dear." And the love-light shone in her eyes for all the court to see. But the sergeant never let his look meet it. When he stepped down at last she gave a sob of joy, and fainted bang-off.

They roused her up, after this, to hear the verdict of *Guilty* and her doom spoken by the judge. "Pris'ner at the bar," said the Clerk of Arraigns, "have ye anything to say why this court should not pass sentence o' death?"

She held tight of the rail before her, and spoke out loud and clear—

"My Lord and gentlemen all, I be a guilty woman; an' I be ready to die at once for my sin. But if ye kill me now, ye kill the child in my body—an' he is innocent."

Well, 'twas found she spoke truth; and the hanging was put off till after the time of her delivery. She was led back to prison, and there, about the end of June, her child was born, and died before he was six hours old. But the mother recovered, and quietly abode the time of her hanging.

I can mind her execution very well; for father and mother had determined it would be an excellent thing for my rickets to take me into Bodmin that day, and get a touch of the dead woman's hand, which in those times was considered an unfailing remedy. So we borrowed the parson's manure-cart, and cleaned it thoroughly, and drove in together.

The place of the hangings, then, was a little door in the prison-wall, looking over the bank where the railway now goes, and a dismal piece of water called Jail-pool, where the townsfolk drowned most of the dogs and cats they'd no further use for. All the bank under the gallows was that thick with people you could almost walk upon their heads; and my ribs were squeezed by the crowd so that I couldn't breathe freely for a month after. Back across the pool, the fields along the side of the valley were lined with booths and sweet-stalls and standings—a perfect Whitsun-fair; and a din going up that cracked your ears.

But there was the stillness of death when the woman came forth, with the sheriff and the chaplain reading in his book, and the unnamed man behind—all from the little door. She wore a strait black gown, and a white kerchief about her neck—a lovely woman, young and white and tearless.

She ran her eye over the crowd and stepped forward a pace,

as if to speak; but lifted a finger and beckoned instead: and out of the people a man fought his way to the foot of the scaffold. 'Twas the dashing sergeant, that was here upon sick-leave. Sick he was, I believe. His face above his shining regimentals was grey as a slate; for he had committed perjury to save his skin, and on the face of the perjured no sun will ever shine.

"Have you got it?" the doomed woman said, many hearing the words.

He tried to reach, but the scaffold was too high, so he tossed up what was in his hand, and the woman caught it—a little screw of tissue-paper.

"I must see that, please!" said the sheriff, laying a hand upon her arm.

"'Tis but a weddin'-ring, sir"—and she slipped it over her finger. Then she kissed it once, under the beam, and, lookin' into the dragoon's eyes, spoke very slow—

"*Husband, our child shall go wi' you; an' when I want you he shall fetch you.*"

—and with that turned to the sheriff, saying:

"I be ready, sir."

The sheriff wouldn't give father and mother leave for me to touch the dead woman's hand; so they drove back that evening grumbling a good bit. 'Tis a sixteen-mile drive, and the ostler in at Bodmin had swindled the poor old horse out of his feed, I believe; for he crawled like a slug. But they were so taken up with discussing the day's doings, and what a mort of people had been present, and how the sheriff might have used milder language in refusing my father, that they forgot to use the whip. The moon was up before we got halfway home, and a star to be seen here and there; and still we never mended our pace.

'Twas in the middle of the lane leading down to Hendra Bottom, where for more than a mile two carts can't pass each other, that my father pricks up his ears and looks back.

"Hullo!" says he; "there's somebody gallopin' behind us."

Far back in the night we heard the noise of a horse's hoofs, pounding furiously on the road and drawing nearer and nearer.

"Save us!" cries father; "whoever 'tis, he's comin' down th' lane!" And in a minute's time the clatter was close on us and someone shouting behind.

"Hurry that crawlin' worm o' yourn—or draw aside in God's name, an' let me by!" the rider yelled.

"What's up?" asked my father, quartering as well as he could. "Why! Hullo! Farmer Hugo, be that you?"

"There's a mad devil o' a man behind, ridin' down all he comes across. A's blazin' drunk, I reckon—but 'tisn' *that*—'tis the horrible voice that goes wi' en—Hark! Lord protect us, he's turn'd into the lane!"

Sure enough, the clatter of a second horse was coming down upon us, out of the night—and with it the most ghastly sounds that ever creamed a man's flesh. Farmer Hugo pushed past us and sent a shower of mud in our faces as his horse leapt off again, and 'way-to-go down the hill. My father stood up and lashed our old grey with the reins, and down we went too, bumpity-bump for our lives, the poor beast being taken suddenly like one possessed. For the screaming behind was like nothing on earth but the wailing and sobbing of a little child—only tenfold louder. 'Twas just as you'd fancy a baby might wail if his little limbs was being twisted to death.

At the hill's foot, as you know, a stream crosses the lane—that widens out there a bit, and narrows again as it goes up t'other side of the valley. Knowing we must be overtaken further on—for the screams and clatter seemed at our very backs by this—father jumped out here into the stream and backed the cart well to one side; and not a second too soon.

The next moment, like a wind, this thing went by us in the moonlight—a man upon a black horse that splashed the stream all over us as he dashed through it and up the hill. 'Twas the scarlet dragoon with his ashen face; and behind him, holding to his cross-belt, rode a little shape that tugged and wailed and raved. As I stand here, sir, 'twas the shape of a naked babe!

Well, I won't go on to tell how my father dropped upon his knees in the water, or how my mother fainted off. The thing was gone, and from that moment for eight years nothing was seen or heard of Sergeant Basket. The fright killed my mother. Before next spring she fell into a decline, and early next fall the old man—for he was an old man now—had to delve her grave. After this he went feebly about his work, but held on, being wishful for me to step into his shoon, which I began to do as soon as I was fourteen, having outgrown the rickets by that time.

But one cool evening in September month, father was up digging in the yard alone: for 'twas a small child's grave, and in the loosest soil, and I was off on a day's work, thatching Farmer Tresidder's stacks. He was digging away slowly when he heard a rattle at the lych-gate, and looking over the edge of the grave, saw in the dusk a man hitching his horse there by the bridle.

'Twas a coal-black horse, and the man wore a scarlet coat all powdered with pilm; and as he opened the gate and came over the graves, father saw that 'twas the dashing dragoon. His face was still a slaty-grey, and clammy with sweat; and when he spoke, his voice was all of a whisper, with a shiver therein.

"Bedman," says he, "go to the hedge and look down the road, and tell me what you see."

My father went, with his knees shaking, and came back again.

"I see a woman," says he, "not fifty yards down the road. She is dressed in black, an' has a veil over her face; an' she's comin' this way."

"Bedman," answers the dragoon, "go to the gate an' look back along the Plymouth road, an' tell me what you see."

"I see," says my father, coming back with his teeth chattering, "I see, twenty yards back, a naked child comin'. He looks to be callin', but he makes no sound."

"Because his voice is wearied out," says the dragoon. And with that he faced about, and walked to the gate slowly.

"Bedman, come wi' me an' see the rest," he says, over his shoulder.

He opened the gate, unhitched the bridle and swung himself heavily up in the saddle.

Now from the gate the bank goes down pretty steep into the road, and at the foot of the bank my father saw two figures waiting. 'Twas the woman and the child, hand in hand; and their eyes burned up like coals: and the woman's veil was lifted, and her throat bare.

As the horse went down the bank towards these two, they reached out and took each a stirrup and climbed upon his back, the child before the dragoon and the woman behind. The man's face was set like a stone. Not a word did either speak, and in this fashion they rode down the hill towards Ruan sands. All that my father could mind, beyond, was that the woman's hands were passed round the man's neck, where the rope had passed round her own.

No more could he tell, being a stricken man from that hour. But Aunt Polgrain, the house-keeper up to Constantine, saw them, an hour later, go along the road below the town-place; and Jacobs, the smith, saw them pass his forge towards Bodmin about midnight. So the tale's true enough. But since that night no man has set eyes on horse or riders.

The Haunted Yacht
A Yarn

If anyone cares to buy the yawl *Siren*, he may have her for 200 pounds, or a trifle less than the worth of her ballast, as lead goes nowadays. For sufficient reasons—to be disclosed in the course of this narrative—I am unable to give her builder's name, and for reasons quite as sufficient I must admit the figures of her registered tonnage (29.56), cut on the beam of her forecastle, to be a fraud. I will be perfectly frank; there is a mystery about the yacht. But I gave 400 pounds for her in the early summer of 1890, and thought her dirt cheap. She was built under the old "Thames rule," that is, somewhere between 1875 and 1880, and was therefore long and narrow to begin with. She has been lengthened since.

Nevertheless, though nobody could call her a dry boat, she will behave herself in any ordinary sea, and come about quicker than most of her type. She is fast, has sound timbers and sheathing that fits her like a skin, and her mainmast and bowsprit are particularly fine spars of Oregon pine; her mizzen doesn't count for much. Let me mention the newest of patent capstans—I put this into her myself—cabins panelled in teak and pitch-pine and cushioned with red morocco, two suits of sails, besides a big spinnaker that does not belong to her present rig, a serviceable dinghy—well, you can see for yourselves without my saying more, that, even to break up, she is worth quite double the money.

In what follows I shall take leave here and there to alter a name or suppress it. With these exceptions you shall hear precisely how the *Siren* came into my hands.

Early in 1890 I determined, for the sake of my health, to take a longer holiday than usual, and spend the months of July, August, and September in a cruise about the Channel. My notion was to cross over to the French coast, sail down as far as Cherbourg, recross to Salcombe, and thence idle westward to Scilly, and finish up, perhaps, with a run over to Ireland. This, I say, was my notion: you could not call it a plan, for it left me free to anchor in any port I chose, and to stay there just as long as it amused me. One fixed intention I had, and one only—to avoid the big regattas. Money had to be considered, and I thought at first of hiring. I wanted something between twenty-five and forty tons, small enough to be worked by myself and a crew of three or at most three men and a boy, and large enough to keep us occupied while at sea.

Of course, I studied the advertisement columns, and for some time found nothing that seemed even likely to suit. But at last in *The Field*, and in the left-hand bottom corner—where it had been squeezed by the lists of the usual well-known agencies—I came on the following:—

> YAWL, 35 tons. For immediate SALE, that fast and comfortable cruiser *Siren*. Lately refitted and now in perfect condition throughout. Rigging, etc., as good as new. Cabin appointments of unusual richness and taste. 400 pounds. Apply, Messrs. Dewy and Moss, Agents and Surveyors, Portside Street, F——.

On reading this I took Lloyd's *Yacht Register* from its shelf, and hunted for further details. *Sirens* crowd pretty thickly in the Register; only a little less thickly than *Undines*. Including *Sirenes* and *Sirenas*, I found some fourteen—and not a yawl amongst them, nor anything of her tonnage. There were two more in Lloyd's *List of American Yachts*—one a centre-board schooner, the other a centre-board sloop; and, in a further list, I came upon a *Siren* that had changed her name to *Mirage*—a screw-schooner of one hundred and ninety tons, owned by no less a person than the Marquis of Ormonde. On the whole it seemed pretty clear that Lloyd knew not of the existence of this "fast and comfortable cruiser" of thirty-five tons.

However, if half the promises of the advertisement were genuine, the chance ought not to be lost for lack of further inquiry. So I sat down there and then and wrote a letter to the poetically-named Dewy and Moss, asking some questions in detail about the boat, and, in particular, where she was to be seen.

The answer came by return of post. The boat had been laid up since the autumn in a sheltered creek of the F— River, about three-quarters of a mile up from the harbour side, where Messrs. Dewy and Moss transacted business. The keys lay at their office, and she could be inspected at any time. Her sails, gear, and movable furniture were stored in a roomy loft at the back of Messrs, Dewy and Moss's own premises. Their client was a lady who wished to keep her name concealed—at any rate during the preliminaries; but they had full power to conduct the sale. The yacht was a bargain. The lady wished to be rid of it at once; but they might mention that she would not take a penny less than the quoted price of 400 pounds. They would be happy to deal with me in that or any other line of business; and they enclosed their card.

The card bore witness to the extraordinary versatility of Messrs. Dewy and Moss, if to nothing else. Here is the digest of it:—

> Auctioneers; Practical Valuers; House and Estate Agents; Business Brokers; Ship Brokers; Accountants and Commission Merchants; Servants' Registry Office; Fire, Life, Accident, and Plate Glass Insurance Effected; Fire Claims prepared and adjusted; Live Stock Insured; Agents for Gibson's Non-Slipping Cycles; Agents for Packington's Manures, the best and cheapest for all crops; Valuations for Probate; Emigration Agents; Private Arrangements negotiated with Creditors; Old Violins cleaned and repaired; Vice-Consulate for Norway and Sweden.

I cannot say this card produced quite the impression which its composers no doubt desired. It seemed to me that Messrs. Dewy and Moss had altogether too many strings to their bow.

And the railway journey to F—— was a long one. So I hesitated for two days; and on the late afternoon of the third found myself some three hundred miles from home, standing in a windy street full of the blown odours of shipping, and pulling at a bell which sounded with terrifying alacrity just on the other side of the door. A window was thrown up, right above me, and a head appeared (of Dewy, as it turned out), and invited me to come upstairs.

Mr. Dewy met me on the landing, introduced himself, and led me into his office, where a fat young woman sat awkwardly upon a wooden chair several inches too high for her. Hastily reviewing the many professional capacities in which Mr. Dewy could serve her, I decided that she must be a cook in search of a place. The agent gave me the only other chair in the room—it was clear that in their various feats of commercial dexterity the firm depended very little upon furniture—and balanced himself on the edge of his knee-hole table. He was a little, round man, and his feet dangled three inches from the floor. He looked honest enough, and spoke straightforwardly.

"You have come about the yacht, sir. You would wish to inspect her at once? This is most unfortunate! Your letter only reached us this afternoon. The fact is, my partner, Mr. Moss, has gone off for the day to N—— to attend a meeting of the Amateur Bee-keepers' Association—my partner is an enthusiast upon bee-culture."

The versatility of Moss began to grow bewildering. "—and will not be back until late tonight. As for me," he consulted his watch, "I am due in half an hour's time to conduct the rehearsal of a service of song at the Lady Huntingdon's Chapel, down the street, where I play the harmonium."

The diversity of Dewy dazed me.

"You are staying the night at F——?" he said.

"Why, yes. I sleep at the Ship Inn, but hoped to leave early tomorrow."

"Of course you could inspect the sails and gear at once; they are in the loft behind." He jerked a thumb over his shoulder.

"So I understand, but it would be better to see the boat first."

"Naturally, naturally. I hope you see how I am placed? You would not desire me, I feel sure, to disappoint the chapel members who will be waiting presently for their rehearsal. Stay . . . perhaps you would not greatly object to rowing up and inspecting the yacht by yourself? Here are the keys, and my boat is at your disposal; or, if you prefer it, a waterman—"

"Nothing would suit me better, if you don't mind my using the boat."

"It will be a favour, sir, your using her, I assure you. This way, if you please."

He jumped down from the table and led the way downstairs, and through some very rickety back premises to the quay door, where his boat lay moored to a frape. As I climbed down and cast off, Mr. Dewy pulled out his watch again.

"The evenings are lengthening, and you will have plenty of time. Half an hour to high water; you will have the tide with you each way. The keys will open everything on board. By the way, you can't miss her—black, with a tarnished gilt line, moored beside a large white schooner, just three-quarters of a mile up. You can tie up the boat to the frape on your return; tomorrow will do for the keys; at your service any time after nine a.m. Good evening, sir!"

Mr. Dewy turned and hurried back to his client, whose presence during our interview he had completely ignored.

The sun had dropped behind the tall hills that line the western shore of the beautiful F—— River; but a soft yellow light, too generously spread to dazzle, suffused the whole sky, and was reflected on the tide that stole up with scarcely a ripple. A sharp bend of the stream brought me in sight of the two yachts, not fifty yards away—their inverted reflections motionless as themselves; I rested on my oars and drifted up towards them, conning the black yawl carefully.

She struck me as too big for a 35-tonner, fore-shortened though she lay—a wall-sided narrow boat, but a very pretty specimen of her type. Her dismantled masts were painted white, and her upper boards had been removed, of course.

Hullo!

There was a man standing on her deck.

She lay with her nose pointing up the river and her stern towards me. The man stood by her wheel (for some idiotic reason, best known to himself, her builder had given her a wheel instead of a tiller), which was covered up with tarpaulin. He stood with a hand on this tarpaulin case, and looked back over his shoulder towards me—a tall fellow with a reddish beard and a clean-shaven upper lip. I was drifting close by this time—he looking curiously at me—and I must have been studying his features for half a minute before I hailed him.

"Yacht ahoy!" I called out. "Is that the *Siren?*"

Getting no answer, I pulled the boat close under the yacht's side, made her fast, and climbed on board by way of the channels.

"This is the *Siren*, eh?" I said, looking down her deck towards the wheel.

There was no man to be seen.

I stared around for a minute or so; ran to the opposite side and looked over; ran aft and leaned over her taffrail; ran forward and peered over her bows. Her counter was too short to conceal a man, and her stem had absolutely no overhang at all; yet no man was to be seen, nor boat nor sign of a man. I tried the companion: it was covered and padlocked. The sail-hatch and fore-hatch were also fastened and padlocked, and the skylights covered with tarpaulin and screwed firmly down. A mouse could not have found its way below, except perhaps by the stove-pipe or the pipe leading down to the chain-locker.

I was no believer in ghosts, but I had to hit on some theory there and then. My nerves had been out of order for a month or two, and the long railway journey must have played havoc with them. The whole thing was a hallucination. So I told myself while pulling the coverings off the skylights, but somehow got mighty little comfort out of it; and I will not deny that I fumbled a bit with the padlock on the main hatchway, or that I looked down a second time before setting foot on the companion ladder.

She was a sweet ship; and the air below, though stuffy, had no taste of bilge in it. I explored main cabin, sleeping cabins, forecastle. The movable furniture had been taken ashore, as I had been told; but the fixtures were in good order, the decorations in good taste. Not a panel had shrunk or warped, nor could I find any leakage. At the same time I could find no evidence that she had been visited lately by man or ghost. The only thing that seemed queer was the inscription "29.56" on the beam in the forecastle. It certainly struck me that the surveyor must have under-registered her, but for the moment I thought little about it.

Passing back through the main cabin I paused to examine one or two of the fittings—particularly a neat glass-fronted bookcase, with a small sideboard below it, containing three drawers and a cellaret. The bookcase was empty and clean swept; so also were the drawers. At the bottom of the cellaret I found a couple of flags stowed—a tattered yellow quarantine-signal tightly rolled into a bundle, and a red ensign neatly folded. As I lifted out the latter, there dropped from its folds and fell upon the cabin floor—a book.

I picked it up—a thin *quarto* bound in black morocco, and rather the worse for wear. On its top side it bore the following inscription in dingy gilt letters:—

JOB'S HOTEL, PENLEVEN,
VISITORS' BOOK.
J. JOB, *Proprietor.*

Standing there beneath the skylight I turned its pages over, wondering vaguely how the visitors' book of a small provincial hotel had found its way into that drawer. It contained the usual assortment of conventional praise and vulgar jocosity:—

> Mr. and the Hon. Mrs. Smith of Huddersfield, cannot speak too highly of Mrs. Job's ham and eggs.—September 15, 1881.

Arrived wet through after a 15-mile tramp along the coast; but thanks to Mr. and Mrs. Job were soon steaming over a comfortable fire.—John and Annie Watson, March, 1882.

Note appended by a humorist:

Then you sat on the hob, I suppose.

There was the politely patronising entry:

Being accustomed to Wolverhampton, I am greatly pleased with this coast.—F. B. W.

The poetical effusion:

Majestic spot! Say, doth the sun in heaven Behold aught to equal thee, wave-washed Penleven? etc.

Lighter verse:

*Here I came to take my ease,
Agreeably disappointed to find no fl—
Mrs. Job, your bread and butter
Is quite too utterly, utterly utter!
J. Harper, June 3rd, 1883.*

The contemplative man's ejaculation:

It is impossible, on viewing these Cyclopean cliffs, to repress the thought, How great is Nature, how little Man!

(A note: *So it is, old chap!* and a reproof in another hand: *Shut up! can't you see he's suffering?*)

The last entry was a brief one:

J. MacGuire, Liverpool. September 2nd, 1886.

Twilight forced me to close the book and put it back in its place. As I did so, I glanced up involuntarily towards the skylight, as if I half expected to find a pair of eyes staring down on me. Yet the book contained nothing but these mere trivialities. Whatever my apprehension, I was (as "J. Harper" would have said) "agreeably disappointed." I climbed on deck again, relocked the hatch, replaced the tarpaulins, jumped into the boat and rowed homewards. Though the tide favoured me, it was dark before I reached Mr. Dewy's quay-door. Having, with some difficulty, found the frape, I made the boat fast. I groped my way across his back premises and out into the gaslit street; and so to the Ship Inn, a fair dinner, and a sound night's sleep.

At ten o'clock next morning I called on Messrs. Dewy and Moss. Again Mr. Dewy received me, and again he apologised for the absence of his partner, who had caught an early train to attend a wrestling match at the far end of the county. Mr. Dewy showed me the sails, gear, cushions, etc., of the *Siren*—everything in surprising condition. I told him that I meant business, and added—

"I suppose you have all the yacht's papers?"

He stroked his chin, bent his head to one side, and asked, "Shall you require them?"

"Of course," I said; "the transfer must be regular. We must have her certificate of registry, at the very least."

"In that case I had better write and get them from my client."

"Is she not a resident here?"

"I don't know," he said, "that I ought to tell you. But I see no harm—you are evidently, sir, a *bona fide* purchaser. The lady's name is Carlingford—a widow—residing at present in Bristol."

"This is annoying," said I; "but if she lives anywhere near the Temple Mead Station, I might skip a train there and call on her. She herself desired no delay, and I desire it just as little. But the papers are necessary."

After some little demur, he gave me the address, and we parted. At the door I turned and asked, "By the way, who was the fellow on board the *Siren* last night as I rowed up to her?"

He gave me a stare of genuine surprise. "A man on board? Whoever he was, he had no business there. I make a point of looking after the yacht myself."

I hurried to the railway station. Soon after six that evening I knocked at Mrs. Carlingford's lodgings in an unattractive street of Bedminster, that unattractive suburb. A small maid opened the door, took my card, and showed me into a small sitting-room on the ground floor. I looked about me—a round table, a horsehair couch, a walnut sideboard with glass panels, a lithograph of John Wesley being rescued from the flames of his father's rectory, a coloured photograph—

As the door opened behind me and a woman entered, I jumped back almost into her arms. The coloured photograph, staring at me from the opposite wall above the mantelshelf, was a portrait—a portrait of the man I had seen on board the *Siren!*

"Who is that?" I demanded, wheeling round without ceremony.

But if I was startled, Mrs. Carlingford seemed ready to drop with fright. The little woman—she was a very small, shrinking creature, with a pallid face and large nervous eyes—put out a hand against the jamb of the door, and gasped out—

"Why do you ask? What do you want?"

"I beg your pardon," I said; "it was merely curiosity. I thought I had seen the face somewhere."

"He was my husband."

"He is dead, then?"

"Oh, why do you ask? Yes; he died abroad." She touched her widow's cap with a shaking finger, and then covered her face with her hands. "I was there—I saw it. Why do you ask?" she repeated.

"I beg your pardon sincerely," I said; "it was only that the portrait reminded me of somebody—But my business here is quite different. I am come about the yacht *Siren* which you have advertised for sale."

She seemed more than ever inclined to run. Her voice scarcely rose above a whisper.

"My agents at F— have full instructions about the sale."

"Yes, but they tell me you have the papers. I may say that I have seen the yacht and gear and am ready to pay the price you ask for immediate possession. I said as much to Mr. Dewy. But the papers, of course—"

"Are they necessary?"

"Certainly they are. At least the certificate of registry or, failing that, some reference to the port of registry, if the transfer is to be made. I should also like to see her warrant if she has one, and her sailmaker's certificate. Messrs. Dewy and Moss could draw up the inventory."

She still hesitated. At length she said, "I have the certificate; I will fetch it. The other papers, if she had any, have been lost or destroyed. She never had a warrant. I believe my husband belonged to no Yacht Club. I understand very little of these matters."

She left the room, and returned in five minutes or so with the open document in her hand.

"But," said I, looking over it, "this is a certificate of a vessel called the *Wasp*."

"Ah, I must explain that. I wished the boat to change her name with the new owner. Her old name—it has associations—painful ones—I should not like anyone else to know her as the *Wasp*."

"Well," I admitted, "I can understand that. But, see here, she is entered as having one mast and carrying a cutter rig."

"She was a cutter originally. My husband had her lengthened, in 1886, I think by five feet, and turned her into a yawl. It was abroad, at Malaga—"

"A curious port to choose."

"She was built, you see, as long ago as 1875. My husband used to say she was a broad boat for those days, and could be lengthened successfully and turned into quite a new-looking vessel. He gave her an entirely new sheathing, too, and all her spars are new. She was not insured, and, being in a foreign port, it was understood he would have her newly registered when he returned, which he fully intended. So no alterations were made in the certificate here, and, I believe, her old tonnage is still carved up somewhere inside her."

This was true enough. The figures on the certificate, 29.56, were those I had seen on the beam in the forecastle.

"My husband never lived to reach England, and when she

came back to F——, though she was visited, of course, by the Custom House officer and coastguard, nobody asked for her certificate, and so the alterations in her were never explained. She was laid up at once in the F—— River, and there she has remained."

Certain structural peculiarities in the main cabin—scarcely noted at the time, but now remembered—served to confirm Mrs. Carlingford's plainly told story. On my return to London that night I hunted up some back volumes of Hunt, and satisfied myself on the matter of the *Wasp* and her owner, William Carlingford. And, to be short, the transfer was made on a fresh survey, the cheque sent to Mrs. Carlingford, and the yawl *Siren* passed into my hands.

All being settled, I wrote to my old acquaintance, Mr. Dewy, asking him to fit the vessel out, and find me a steady skipper and crew—not without some apprehension of hearing by return of post that Dewy and Moss were ready and willing to sign articles with me to steer and sail the yacht in their spare moments. Perhaps the idea did not occur to them. At any rate they found me a crew, and a good one; and I spent a very comfortable three months, cruising along the south-western coast, across to Scilly, from Scilly to Cork and back to Southampton, where on September 29, 1891, I laid the yacht up for the winter.

Thrice since have I applied to Messrs. Dewy and Moss for a crew, and always with satisfactory results. But I must pass over 1892 and 1893 and come to the summer of 1894; or, to be precise, to Wednesday, the 11th of July. We had left Plymouth that morning for a run westward; but, the wind falling light towards noon, we found ourselves drifting, or doing little more, off the entrance of the small fishing haven of Penleven. Though I had never visited Penleven I knew, on the evidence of many picture-shows, that the place was well worth seeing. Besides, had I not the assurances of the Visitors' Book in my cabin? It occurred to me that I would anchor for an hour or two in the entrance of the haven, and eat my lunch ashore at Mr. Job's hotel. Mr. Job would doubtless be pleased to recover his long-lost volume, and I had no more wish than right to retain it.

Job's hotel was unpretending. Mrs. Job offered me ham and eggs and, as an alternative, a cut off a boiled silver-side of beef, if I did not mind waiting for ten minutes or so, when her husband would be back to dinner. I said that I would wait, and added that I should be pleased to make Mr. Job's acquaintance on his return, as I had a trifling message for him.

About ten minutes later, while studying a series of German lithographs in the coffee-room, I heard a heavy footstep in the passage and a knock at the door; and Mr. Job appeared, a giant of a man, with a giant's girth and red cheeks, which he sufflated as a preliminary of speech.

"Good day, Mr. Job," said I. "I won't keep you from your dinner, but the fact is, I am the unwilling guardian of a trifle belonging to you." And I showed him the Visitors' Book.

I thought the man would have had an apoplectic fit there on the spot. He rolled his eyes, dropped heavily upon a chair, and began to breathe hard and short.

"Where—where—?" he gasped, and began to struggle again for breath.

I said, "For some reason or other the sight of this book distresses you, and I think you had better not try to speak for a bit. I will tell you exactly how the book came into my possession, and afterwards you can let me have your side of the story, if you choose." And I told him just what I have told the reader.

At the conclusion, Mr. Job loosed his neckcloth and spoke—

"That book, sir, ought to be lyin' at the bottom of the sea. It was lost on the evening of September the 3rd, 1886, on board a yacht that went down with all hands. Now I'll tell you all about it. There was a gentleman called Blake staying over at Port William that summer—that's four miles up the coast, you know."

I nodded.

". . . staying with his wife and one son, a tall young fellow, aged about twenty-one, maybe. They came from Liverpool—and they had a yacht with them, that they kept in Port William harbour, anchored just below the bridge. She would be about thirty tons—a very pretty boat. They had only one hired hand for crew; used to work her themselves for the most part; the lady was extraordinary clever at the helm, or at the sheets either. Very quiet people they were. You might see them most days that summer, anchored out on the whiting grounds. What was she called? The *Queen of Sheba*—cutter-rigged-quite a new boat. It was said afterwards that the owner, Mr. Blake, designed her himself. She used often to drop anchor off Penleven. Know her? Why of course I'd know her; 'specially considerin' what happened.

"'What was that?' A very sad case; it made a lot of talk at the time. One day—it was the third of September, '86—Mr. and Mrs. Blake and the son, they anchored off the haven and came up here to tea. I supposed at the time they'd left their paid hand, Robertson, on board; but it turned out he was left home at Port William that day, barkin' a small mainsail that Mr. Blake had bought o' purpose for the fishin'. Well, Mrs. Blake she ordered tea, and while my missus was layin' the cloth young Mr. Blake he picks up that very book, sir, that was lyin' on the sideboard, and begins readin' it and laffin'.

"My wife, she goes out of the room for to cut the bread-and-butter, and when she comes back there was the two gentlemen by the window studyin' the book with their backs to the room, and Mrs. Blake lyin' back in the chair I'm now sittin' on, an' her face turned to the wall—so. The young Mr. Blake he turns round and says, 'This here's a very amusin' book, Mrs. Job. Would you mind my borrowing it for a day or two to copy out some of the poetry? I'll bring it back next time we put into Penleven.' Of course my wife says, 'No, she didn't mind.' Then the elder Mr. Blake he says, 'I see you had a visitor here yesterday—a Mr. MacGuire. Is he in the house?' My wife said, 'No; the gentleman had left his traps, but he'd started that morning to walk to Port William to spend the day.' Nothing more passed. They had their tea, and paid for it, and went off to their yacht. I saw that book in the young man's hand as he went down the passage.

"Well, sir, it was just duskin' in as they weighed and stood up towards Port William, the wind blowing pretty steady from the south'ard. At about ten minutes to seven o'clock it blew up in a sudden little squall—nothing to mention; the fishing-boats just noticed it, and that was all. But it was reckoned that squall capsized the *Queen of Sheba*. She never reached Port William, and no man ever clapped eyes on her after twenty minutes past six, when Dick Crego declares he saw her off the Blowth, half-way towards home, and going steady under all canvas. The affair caused a lot of stir, here and at Port William, and in the newspapers. Short-handed as they were, of course they'd no business to carry on as they did—'specially as my wife declares from her looks that Mrs. Blake was feelin' faint afore they started. She always seemed to me a weak, timmersome woman at the best; small and ailin' to look at."

"And Mr. Blake?"

"Oh, he was a strong-made gentleman: tall, with a big red beard."

"The son?"

"Took after his father, only he hadn't any beard; a fine up-standing pair."

"And no trace was ever found of them?"

"Not a stick nor a shred."

"But about this Visitors' Book? You'll swear they took it with them? See, there's not a stain of salt-water upon it."

"No, there isn't; but I'll swear young Mr. Blake had it in his hand as he went from my door."

I said, "Mr. Job, I've kept you already too long from your dinner. Go and eat, and ask them to send in something for me. Afterwards, I want you to come with me and take a look at my yacht, that is lying just outside the haven."

As we started from the shore Mr. Job, casting his eyes over the *Siren*, remarked, "That's a very pretty yawl of yours, sir." As we drew nearer, he began to eye her uneasily.

"She has been lengthened some five or six feet," I said; "she was a cutter to begin with."

"Lord help us!" then said Mr. Job, in a hoarse whisper. "She's the *Queen of Sheba*. I'd swear to her run anywhere—ay, or to that queer angle of her hawse-holes."

A close examination confirmed Mr. Job that my yacht was no other than the lost *Queen of Sheba*, lengthened and altered in rig. It persuaded me, too. I turned back to Plymouth, and, leaving the boat in Cattewater, drove to the Millbay Station and took a ticket for Bristol. Arriving there just twenty-four hours after my interview with Mr. Job, I made my way to Mrs. Carlingford's lodgings.

She had left them two years before; nothing was known of her whereabouts. The landlady could not even tell me whether she had moved from Bedminster: And so I had to let the matter rest.

But just fourteen days ago I received the following letter, dated from a workhouse in one of the Midland counties:—

> Dear Sir,—I am a dying woman, and shall probably be dead before this reaches you. The doctor says he cannot give me forty-eight hours. It is *angina pectoris*, and I suffer horribly at times. The yacht you purchased of me is not the *Wasp*, but the *Queen of Sheba*. My husband designed her. He was a man of some property near Limerick; and he and my son were involved in some of the Irish troubles between 1881 and 1884. It was said they had joined one of the brotherhoods, and betrayed their oaths. This I am sure was not true. But it is certain we had to run for fear of assassination.
>
> After a year in Liverpool we were forced to fly south to Port William, where we brought the yacht and lived for some time in quiet, under our own names. But we knew this could not last, and had taken measures to escape when need arose. My husband had chanced, while at Liverpool, upon an old yacht, dismantled and rotting in the Mersey—but of about the same size as his own and still, of course, upon the register. He bought her of her owner—a Mr. Carlingford, and a stranger—for a very few pounds, and with her—what he valued far more— her papers; but he never completed the transfer at the Custom House.
>
> His plan was, if pressed, to escape abroad, and pass his yacht off as the *Wasp*, and himself as Mr. Carlingford. All the while we lived at Port William the *Queen of Sheba* was kept amply provi-

sioned for a voyage of at least three weeks, when the necessity overtook us, quite suddenly— the name of a man, MacGuire, in the Visitors' Book of a small inn at Penleven. We left Penleven at dusk that evening, and held steadily up the coast until darkness. Then we turned the yacht's head, and ran straight across for Morlaix; but the weather continuing fine for a good fortnight (our first night at sea was the roughest in all this time), we changed our minds, cleared Ushant, and held right across for Vigo; thence, after re-victualling, we cruised slowly down the coast and through the Straits, finally reaching Malaga.

There we stayed and had the yacht lengthened. My husband had sold his small property before ever we came to Port William, and had managed to invest the whole under the name of Carlingford. There was no difficulty about letters of credit. At each port on the way we had shown the *Wasp's* papers, and used the name of Carlingford; and at Lisbon we read in an English newspaper about the supposed capsizing of the *Queen of Sheba.* Still, we had not only to persuade the officials at the various ports that our boat was the *Wasp.* We knew that our enemies were harder to delude, and our next step was to make her as unlike the *Wasp* or the *Queen of Sheba* as possible.

This we did by lengthening her and altering her rig. But it proved useless, as I had always feared it would. The day after we sailed from Malaga, a Spanish-speaking seaman, whom we had hired there as extra hand, came aft as if to speak to my husband (who stood at the wheel), and, halting a pace or two from him, lifted a revolver, called him by name, and shot him dead. Before he could turn, my son had knocked him senseless, and in another minute had tumbled him overboard. We buried my husband in the sea, next day.

We held on, we two alone, past Gibraltar— I steering and my son handling all the sails—and ran up for Cadiz. There we made deposition of our losses, inventing a story to account for them, and my son took the train for Paris, for we knew that our enemies had tracked the yacht, and there would be no escape for him if he clung to her. I waited for six days, and then engaged a crew and worked the yacht back to F—. I have never since set eyes on my son; but he is alive, and his hiding is known to myself and to one man only—a member of the brotherhood, who surprised the secret.

To keep that man silent I spent all my remaining money; to quiet him I had to sell the yacht; and now that money, too, is gone, and I am dying in a workhouse. God help my son now! I deceived you, and yet I think I did you no great wrong. The yacht I sold you was my own, and she was worth the money. The figures on the beam were cut there by my husband before we reached Vigo, to make the yacht correspond with the *Wasp's* certificate. If I have wronged you, I implore your pardon.—
   Yours truly,
              Catherine Blake.

Well, that is the end of the story. It does not, I am aware, quite account for the figure I saw standing by the *Siren's* wheel. As for the *Wasp*, she has long since rotted to pieces on the waters of the Mersey. But the question is, Have I a right to sell the *Siren?* I certainly have a right to keep her, for she is mine, sold to me in due form by her rightful owner, and honestly paid for. But then I don't want to keep her!

The Horror on the Stair

Particulars concerning the end of Mistress Catherine Johnstone, late of Givens, in Ayrshire; from a private relation made by the young woman Kirstie Maclachlan to the Reverend James Souttar, A.M., Minister of the Parish of Wyliebank, and by him put into writing.

I had been placed in my parish of Wyliebank about a twelvemonth before making acquaintance with Mr. Johnstone, the minister at Givens, twelve miles away. This would be in the year 1721, and from that until the date of his death (which happened in the autumn of 1725) I saw him in all not above a dozen times. To me he appeared a douce, quiet man, commonplace in the pulpit and not over-learned, strict in his own behaviour, methodical in his duties, averse from gossip of all kinds, having himself a great capacity for silence, whereby he seemed perhaps wiser than he was, but not (I think) more charitable. He had greatly advanced his fortunes by marriage.

This marriage made him remarkable, who else had passed as quite ordinary; but not for the money it brought him. Of his wife I knew no more than my neighbours. She was a daughter of Sir John Telfair, of Balgarnock, a gentleman of note in Renfrewshire; and the story ran concerning her that, at the age of sixteen, having a spite against one of the maidservants, she had pretended to be bewitched and persecuted by the devil, and upheld the imposture so cleverly, with rigors, convulsions, foaming at the mouth and spitting forth of straws, chips and cinders, pins and bent nails, that the Presbytery ordained a public fast against witchcraft, and by warrant of Privy Council a Commission visited Balgarnock to take evidence of her condition.

In the presence of these commissioners, of whom the Lord Blantyre was president, the young lady flatly accused one Janet Burns, her mother's still-room maid, of tormenting her with aid of the black art, and for witness showed her back and shoulders covered with wales, some blue and others freshly bleeding; and further, in the midst of their interrogatories cast herself into a trance, muttering and offering faint combat to divers unseen spirits, and all in so lifelike a manner that, notwithstanding they could discover no evident proof of guilt, these wise gentry were overawed and did commit the woman Janet Burns to take her trial for witchcraft at Paisley. There, poor soul, as she was escorted to the prison, the town rabble met her with sticks and stones and closed the case; for on her way a cobble cast by some unknown hand struck her upon the temple, and falling into the arms of the guard, she never spoke after, but breathed her last breath as they forced her through the mob to the prison gates.

This was the tale told to me; and long before I heard it the reprobation of the vulgar had swung back from Janet Burns and settled upon her accuser. Certain it was that swiftly upon the woman's murder—as I may well call it—Miss Catherine made a recovery, nor was thereafter troubled with fits, swoons or ailments calling for public notice. Indeed, she was shunned by all, and lived (as well as I could discover) in complete seclusion for twenty years, until the minister of Givens sought her out with an offer of marriage.

By this time she was near forty; a thin, hard-featured spinster, dwelling alone with her mother the Lady Balgarnock. Her two younger sisters had married early—the one to Captain Luce, of Dunragit in Wigtownshire, the other to a Mr. Forbes, of whom I know nothing save that his house was in Edinburgh: and as they had no great love for Miss Catherine, so they neither sought her company nor were invited to Balgarnock. Her father, Sir John, had deceased a few months before Mr. Johnstone presented himself.

He made a short courtship of it. The common tongues accused him (as was to be expected) of coming after her money; whereas she and her old mother lived a cat-and-dog life together, and she besides was of an age when women will often marry the first man that offers. But I now believe, and (unless I mistake) the history will show, that the excuse vulgarly made for her did not touch the real ground of her decision. At any rate, she married him and lived from 1718 to 1725 in the manse at Givens, where I made her acquaintance.

I had been warned what to expect. The parishioners of Givens seldom had sight of her, and set it down to pride and contempt of her husband's origin. (He had been a weaver's son from Falkirk, who either had won his way to the Marischal College of Aberdeen by strength of will and in defiance of natural dullness, or else had started with wits but blunted them in carving his way thither.) She rarely set foot beyond the manse garden, the most of her time being spent in a roomy garret under the slates, where she spun a fine yarn and worked it into thread of the kind which is yet known as "Balgarnock thread," and was invented by her or by her mother—for accounts differ as to this. I have beside me an advertisement clipped from one of the newspapers of twenty years ago, which says:

> The Lady Balgarnock and her eldest daughter having attained to great perfection in making whitening and twisting of SEWING THREED which is as cheap and white, and known by experience to be much stronger than the Dutch, to prevent people's being imposed upon by other Threed which may be sold under the name of Balgarnock Threed, the Papers in which the Lady Balgarnock at Balgarnock, or Mrs. Johnstone her eldest daughter, at Givens, do put up their Threed shall, for direction, have thereupon their Coat of Arms, '*Azure*, a ram's head caboshed *or*.' Those who want the said Threed, which is to be sold from fivepence to six shillings per ounce, may write to the Lady Balgarnock at Balgarnock, or Mrs. Johnstone at Givens, to the care of the Postmaster at Glasgow; and may call for the same in Edinburgh at John Seton, Merchant, his shop in the Parliament Close, where they will be served either in Wholesale or Retail, and will be served in the same manner at Glasgow, by

William Selkirk, Merchant, in Trongate.

In this art, then, the woman spent most of her days, preparing the thread with her own hands and bleaching her materials on a large slate raised upon brackets in the window of her garret. And, if one may confess for all, glad enough were Mr. Johnstone's guests when this wife of his rose from the table and departed upstairs. For a colder, more taciturn and discomfortable hostess could not be conceived. She would scarcely exchange a word through the meal—no, not with her husband, though he watched and seemed to forestall her wants with a tender officiousness. To see her seated there in black (which was her only wear), with her back to the window, her eyes on the board, and, as it seemed, the shadow of a long-past guilt brooding about her continually, gave me a feeling as of cold water dripping down the spine. And even the husband, though he pretended to observe nothing, must have known my relief when she withdrew and left us with the decanters.

Now I had tholed this penance, maybe, a dozen times, and could never win a speech from Mrs. Johnstone, nor a look, to show that she regarded me while present or remembered me after I had gone. So you may think I was surprised one day when the minister came riding over with word that his wife wanted a young girl for companion and to help her with the spinning, and had thought of me as likely to show judgment in recommending one. The girl must be sixteen, or thereabout, of decent behaviour and tractable, no gadder or lover of finery, healthy, able to read, an early riser, and, if possible, devout. For her parentage I need not trouble myself, if I knew of a girl suitable in these other respects.

It happened that I had of late been contriving some odd work about the manse for the girl Kirstie Maclachlan, not that the work needed doing, but to help her old mother; for we had no assessment for the poor, and the Session was often at its wits' end to provide relief, wherein as a man without family cares I could better assist than some of my neighbours. The girl's mother was a poor feckless creature who had left Wyliebank in her youth to take service in Glasgow, and there, beguiled at first by some villain, had gone from bad to worse through misguidance rather than wantonness, and at last crept home to her native parish to starve, if by starving she could save her child—then but an infant—from the city and its paths of destruction.

This, in part by her own courage, and in part by the help of the charitable, she had managed to do, and lived to see Kirstie grow to be a decent, religiously minded young woman. Nor did the lass want for good looks in a sober way, nor for wit when it came to reading books; but in speech she was shy beyond reason, and would turn red and stammer if a stranger but addressed her. I think she could never forget that her birth had been on the wrong side of the blanket, and, supposing folks to be pitying her for it, sought to avoid them and their kindness.

It was Kirstie, then, whom I ventured to commend to Mr. Johnstone for his lady's requirements; and after some talk between us the good man sent for her and was satisfied with her looks and the few answers which, in her stammering way, she managed to return to his questions. When he set off homeward it was on the understanding that she should follow him to Givens on foot, which she did the next day with her stock of spare clothes in a kerchief. Nor, although I twice visited Givens during her service there, did I ever see her at the manse, but twice only before she returned to us with the tale I am to set down—the first time at the burying of her mother here in Wyliebank, and the second at Givens, when I was called thither to inter her master who died very suddenly by the bursting of a blood-vessel in the brain.

After that she went to live with the widow in lodgings in Edinburgh; and from her, some fifteen months later, I received the news, in a letter most neatly indited, that Mrs. Johnstone had perished by her own hand, and a request to impart it to all in this parish whom it might concern. The main facts she told me then in writing, but the circumstances (being ever a sensible girl) she kept to transmit to me by word of mouth, rightly judging that the public enquiry had no business with them.

It seems, then, that Kirstie's first introduction to Mrs. Johnstone was none too cheerful; indeed, it came near to scaring her out of her senses. She arrived duly at Givens shortly before five of the afternoon (a warm day in June) and went straight to the manse, where the door was opened to her by Mr. Johnstone, who had seen her from the parlour window. He led the way back to the parlour, and, after a question or two upon her journey, took her up the main stairs to the landing. Here he halted and directed her up a narrow flight to her garret, which lay off to the right, at the very top.

The door stood ajar, and facing it was another door, wide open, through which a ray of the evening sun slanted across the stairhead. Kirstie, with her bundle in one hand and the other upon the hasp, turned to look down upon the minister, to make sure she was entering the right chamber. He stood at the foot of the stairs, and his eyes were following her (as she thought) with a very curious expression; but before he could nod she happened to throw a glance into the room opposite, and very nearly dropped her bundle.

Yet there was nothing to be scared at; merely the figure of an elderly woman in black bent over her spinning-wheel there in the dim light. It was Mrs. Johnstone, of course, seated at her work; but it came upon the girl with suddenness, like an apparition, and the fright, instead of passing, began to take hold of her as the uncanny woman neither spoke nor looked up. The room about her was bare, save for some hanks of yarn littered about the boards and a great pile of it drying on a tray by the window. The one ray of sunlight seemed to pass over this without searching the corners under the sloping roof, and fell at Kirstie's feet.

She has told me that she must have stood there for minutes with her heart working like a pump. When she looked down the stair again the minister was gone. She pulled her wits together, stepped quickly into her own room, and, having closed the door behind her, sat down on the bed to recover.

Being a lass of spirit, she quickly reasoned herself out of this foolishness, rose, washed, changed her stockings, put off her shawl for cap and apron, and—albeit in trepidation—presented herself once more at the door of Mrs. Johnstone's garret.

"Please you, mistress," she managed to say, "I am Kirstie Maclachlan, the new maid from Wyliebank."

Mrs. Johnstone looked up and fixed her with a pair of eyes that (she declared) searched her through and through; but all she said was, "The minister tells me you can read."

"Yes, mistress."

"What books have you brought?"

Kirstie, to be sure, had two books in her bundle—a Bible and John Bunyan's *Grace Abounding*, the both of them gifts from me. Mrs. Johnstone commanded her to fetch the second and start reading at once; "for," she explained, not unkindly, "it will suit you best, belike, to begin with something familiar; and if I find you read well and pleasantly, we will get a book from the manse library."

So the girl found a stool in the corner, and, seating herself near the window, began to read by the waning light. She had, indeed, an agreeable voice, and I had taken pains to teach her. She read on and on, gathering courage, yet uncertain if Mrs. Johnstone approved; who said no word, but continued her spinning until darkness settled down on the garret and blurred the print on the page.

At last she looked up, and, much to Kirstie's surprise, with a sigh. "That will do, girl, you read very nicely. Run down and find your supper, and after that the sooner you get to bed the better. We rise early in this house. Tomorrow I will put you in the way of your duties."

Downstairs Kirstie met the minister who had been taking a late stroll in the garden and now entered by the back-door. He halted under the lamp in the passage. "Well," he asked, "what did she say?"

"She bade me get my supper and be early in the morning," Kirstie answered simply.

For some reason this seemed to relieve him. He hung up his hat and stood pulling at his fingers until the joints cracked, which was a trick with him. "She needs to be soothed," he said. "If you read much with her, you must come to me to choose the books; yet she must think she has chosen them herself. We must manage that somehow. The great thing is to keep her mind soothed."

Kirstie did not understand. A few minutes later as she went up the stairs to her room the door opposite still remained open. All was dark within, but whether or not Mrs. Johnstone sat there in the darkness she could not tell.

The next morning she entered on her duties, which were light enough. Indeed, she soon suspected that her mistress had sought a companion rather than a servant, and at first had much to-do to find employment. Soon, however, Mrs. Johnstone took her into confidence, and began to impart the mysteries of whitening and twisting the famous Balgarnock thread; and so by degrees, without much talk on either side, there grew a strange affection betwixt them. Sure, Kirstie must have been the first of her sex to whom the strange woman showed any softness; and on her part the girl asserts that she was attracted from the first by a sort of pity, without well knowing for what her pity was demanded.

The minister went no farther with his confidences: he could see that Kirstie suited, and seemed resolved to let well alone. The wife never spoke of herself; and albeit, if Kirstie's reading happened to touch on the sources of Christian consolation, she showed some eagerness in discussing them, it was done without any personal or particular reference. Yet, even in those days, Kirstie grew to feel that terror was in some way the secret of her mistress's strangeness; that for the present the poor woman knew herself safe and protected from it, but also that there was ever a danger of that barrier falling—whatever it might be—and leaving her exposed to some enemy, from the thought of whom her soul shrank.

I do not know how Kirstie became convinced that, whoever or whatever the enemy might be, Mr. Johnstone was the phylactery. She herself could give no grounds for her conviction beyond his wife's anxiety for his health and well-being. I myself never observed it in a woman, and if I had, should have set it down to ordinary wifely concern. But Kirstie assures me, first, that it was not ordinary, and, secondly, that it was not at all wifely—that Mrs. Johnstone's care of her husband had less of the ministering unselfishness of a woman in love than of the eager concern of a gambler with his stake.

The girl (I need not say) did not put it thus, yet this in effect was her report. And she added that this anxiety was fitful to a degree: at times the minister could hardly take a walk without being fussed over and forced to change his socks on his return; at others, and for days together, his wife would resign the care of him to Providence, or at any rate to Fate, and trouble herself not at all about his goings-out or his comings-in, nor whether he wore a great-coat or not, nor if he returned wet to the skin and neglected to change his wear.

Well, the girl was right, as was proved on the afternoon when Mr. Johnstone, taking his customary walk upon the Kilmarnock road, fell and burst a blood-vessel, and was borne home to the manse on a gate. The two women were seated in the garret as usual when the crowd entered the garden; and with the first sound of the bearers' feet upon the path, which was of smooth pebbles compacted in lime, Mrs. Johnstone rose up, with a face of a sudden so grey and terrible that Kirstie dropped the book from her knee.

"It has come!" said the poor lady under her breath, and put out a hand as if feeling for some stick of furniture to lean against. "It has come!" she repeated aloud, but still hoarsely; and with that she turned to the lass with a most piteous look, and "Oh, Kirstie, girl," she cried, "you won't leave me? I have been kind to you—say you won't leave me!"

Before Kirstie well understood, her mistress's arms were about her and the gaunt woman clinging to her body and trembling like a child. "You will save me, Kirstie? You will live here and not forsake me? There is nobody now but you!" she kept crying over and over.

The girl held her firmly with a grasp above the elbows to steady her and allay the trembling, and, albeit dazed herself, uttered what soothing words came first to her tongue. "Why, mistress, who thinks of leaving you? Not I, to be sure. But let me get you to bed, and in an hour you will be better of this fancy, for fancy it must be."

"He is dead, I tell you," Mrs. Johnstone insisted, "and they are bringing him home. Hark to the door—that was never your master's knock—and the voices!"

She was still clinging about Kirstie when the cook came panting up the stairs and into the room with a white face; for it was true, and the minister had breathed his last between the garden gate and his house door.

★★★★★★

As I have said, I rode over from Wyliebank four days later to read the burial service. The widow was not to be seen, and of Kirstie, who ever hid herself from the sight of strangers, I caught but a glimpse. She did not follow the coffin, but remained upstairs (as I suppose) comforting her mistress. The other poor distracted servants, between tears and ignorance, made but a sorry business of entertaining the company, so that but half a dozen at most cared to return to the house, of whom I was not one.

The manse had to be vacated, and within a week or two I heard that Mrs. Johnstone had sold a great part of her furniture, dismissed all her household but Kirstie, and retired to a small cottage a little further up the street and scarcely a stone's-throw from the manse.

"She made," says Kirstie, "little show of mourning for her husband, nor for months afterwards did she return to the terror she had shown that day in the garret, yet I am sure that from the hour of his death she never knew peace of mind. She had fitted up a room in the cottage with her wheel and bleaching boards, and we spent all our time in reading or thread-making. At night my cot would be strewn in her bedroom, and we slept with a candle burning on the table between us; but once or twice I woke to see her laid on her side, or resting on her elbow, with her face towards me and her eyes fixed upon mine across the light. This used to frighten me, and she must have seen it, for always she would stammer that I need not be alarmed, and beg me to go to sleep again like a good child. I soon came to see that, whatever her own terror might be, she had the utmost dread of my catching it, and that her hope lay in keeping me cheerful. Since I had nothing on my mind at that time, and knew of no cause for fear, I used to sleep soundly enough; but I begin to think that my mistress slept scarcely at all. I cannot remember once waking without finding her awake and her eyes watching me as I say.

"She herself would not set foot outside the cottage for weeks together, and if by chance we did take a walk it would be towards sunset, when the fields were empty and the folk mostly gathered on the green at the far end of the village. There was a footpath led across these fields at the back of the cottage, and here at such an hour she would sometimes consent to take the air, leaning on my arm; but if any wayfarer happened to come along the path I used to draw her aside into the field, where we made believe to be gathering of wild flowers. She had a dislike of meeting strangers and a horror of being followed; the sound of footsteps on the path behind us would drive her near crazy."

I think 'twas this frequent pretence of theirs to be searching for wild flowers which brought the suspicion of witchcraft upon them among the population of Givens. The story of the woman's youth was remembered against her, if obscurely. Folks knew that she had once been afflicted or possessed by an evil spirit, and from this 'twas a short step to accuse her of gathering herbs at nightfall for the instruction of Kirstie in the black art. In the end the rumour drove them from Givens, and in this manner.

Though the widow so seldom showed herself abroad, in her care for Kirstie's cheerfulness she persuaded the girl to take a short walk every morning through the village. In truth Kirstie hated it. More and more as her mistress clung to her she grew to cling to her mistress; it seemed as if they two were in partnership against the world, and the part of protector which she played so watchfully and courageously for her years took its revenge upon her. For what makes a child so engaging as his trust in the fellow-creatures he meets and his willingness to expect the best of them? To Kirstie, yet but a little way past childhood, all men and women were possible enemies, to be suspected and shunned. She took her walk dutifully because Mrs. Johnstone commanded it, and because shops must be visited and groceries purchased; but it was penance to her, and she would walk a mile about to avoid a knot of gossips or to wile the time away until a shop emptied.

But one day in the long main street she was fairly caught by a mob of boys hunting and hooting after a negro man. They paid no heed to Kirstie, who shrank into a doorway as he passed down the causeway—a seaman, belike, trudging to Irvine or Saltcoats. He seemed by his gait to be more than half drunk, and by the way he shook his stick back at the boys and cursed them; but they would not be shaken off, and in the end he took refuge in the "Leaping Fish," where his tormentors gathered about the doorway and continued their booing until the landlord came forth and dispersed them.

By this time Kirstie had bolted from the doorway and run home. She said nothing of her adventure to Mrs. Johnstone; but in the dusk of the evening a riot began in the street a little way below the cottage. The black seaman had been drinking all day, and on leaving the "Leaping Fish," had fallen into a savage quarrel with a drover. Two or three decent fellows stopped the fight and pulled him off; but they had done better by following up their kindness and seeing him out of the village, for he was now planted with his back to a railing, brandishing his stick and furiously challenging the whole mob. So far as concerned him the mischief ended by his overbalancing to aim a vicious blow at an urchin, and crashing down upon the kerb, where he lay and groaned, while the blood flowed from an ugly cut across the eyebrow.

For a while the crowd stood about him in some dismay. A few were for carrying him back to the public-house; but at some evil prompting a voice cried out, "Take him to the widow Johnstone's! A witch should know how to deal with her sib, the black man." I believe so godless a jest would never have been played, had not the cottage stood handy and (as one may say) closer than their better thoughts. But certain it is that they hoisted the poor creature and bore him into Mrs. Johnstone's garden, and began to fling handfuls of gravel at the upper windows, where a light was burning.

At the noise of it against the pane Mrs. Johnstone, who was bending over the bedroom fire and heating milk for her supper, let the pan fall from her hand. For the moment Kirstie thought she would swoon. But helping her to a seat in the armchair, the brave lass bade her be comforted—it could be naught but some roystering drunkard—and herself went downstairs and unbarred the door. At the sight of her—so frail a girl—quietly confronting them with a demand to know their business, the crowd fell back a step or two, and in that space of time by God's providence arrived Peter Lawler, the constable, a very religious man, who gave the ringleaders some advice and warning they were not likely to forget. Being by this made heartily ashamed of themselves, they obeyed his order to pick up the man from the doorstep, where he lay at Kirstie's feet, and carry him back to the "Leaping Fish;" and so slunk out of the garden.

When all were gone Kirstie closed and bolted the door and returned upstairs to her mistress, whom she found sitting in her chair and listening intently.

"Who was it?" she demanded.

"Oh, nothing to trouble us, ma'am; but just a poor wandering blackamoor I met in the street today. The people, it seems, were bringing him here by mistake."

"A blackamoor!" cried Mrs. Johnstone, gasping. "A blackamoor!"

Now Kirstie was for running downstairs again to fetch some milk in place of what was spilt, but at the sound of the woman's voice she faced about.

"Pick together the silver, Kirstie, and fetch me my bonnet!"

At first Mrs. Johnstone began to totter about the room without aim, but presently fell to choosing this and that of her small possessions and tossing them into the seat of the armchair in a nervous hurry which seemed to gather with her strength. "Quick, lass! Did he see you?... ah, but that would not tell him. What like was he?" She pulled herself together and her voice quavered across the room. "Lass, lass, you will not forsake me? Do not speir now, but do all that I say. You promised—you did promise!" All this while she was working in a fever of haste, pulling even the quilt from the bed and anon tossing it aside as too burdensome. She was past all control. "Do not speir of me," she kept repeating.

"What, ma'am? Are we leaving?" Kirstie stammered once; but the strong will of the woman—mad though she might be—was upon her, and by-and-by the girl began packing in no less haste than her mistress. "But will you not tell me, ma'am?" she entreated between her labours.

"Not here! not here!" Mrs. Johnstone insisted. "Help me to get away from here!"

It was two in the morning when the women unlatched the door of the cottage and crept forth across the threshold—and across the stain of blood which lay thereon, only they could not see it. They took the footpath, each with a heavy bundle beneath her arm, and turning their backs on Givens walked resolutely forward for three miles to the cross-roads where the Glasgow coach would be due to pass in the dawn. Upon the green there beside the sign-post Kirstie believes that she slept while Mrs. Johnstone kept guard over the bundles; but she remembers little until she found herself, as if by magic, on the coach-top and dozing on a seat behind the driver.

From Glasgow, after a day's halt, they took another coach to Edinburgh, and there found lodgings in a pair of attics high aloft in one of the great houses, or lands, which lie off Parliament Square to the north. The building—a warren you might call it—had six stories fronting the square, the uppermost far overhanging, and Kirstie affirms that her window, pierced in the very eaves, stood higher than the roof of St. Giles' Church.

Hither in due course a carrier's cart conveyed Mrs. Johnstone's sticks of furniture, and here for fifteen months the two women lay as close as two needles in a bottle of hay. The house stood upon a ridge, and at the back of it a dozen double flights of stairs dived into courts and cellars far below the level of the front. It was by these—a journey in themselves— that Kirstie sometimes made exit and entrance when she had business at the shops, and she has counted up to me a list, which seemed without end, of the offices, workshops, and tenements she passed on her way, beginning with a wine store in the basement, mounting to *perruquiers'* and law-stationers' shops, and so up past bookbinders', felt-maker's, painters', die-sinkers', milliners' workrooms, to landings on which, as the roof was neared, the tenants herded closer and yet closer in meaner and yet meaner poverty.

The most of Kirstie's business was with Mr. John Seton, the agent, to whom she carried the thread spun by her mistress in the attic, and from whom she received the moneys and accounts of profits. Once or twice, at their first coming, Mrs. Johnstone had descended for a walk in the streets; but by this time the unhappy lady had it fixed in her mind that she was being watched and followed, and shook with apprehension at every corner. So pitiable indeed were the glances she flung behind her, and so frantic the precautions she used to shake off her supposed pursuers and return by circuitous ways, that Kirstie pressed her to no more such expeditions.

To the girl, still ignorant of the cause of this terror, her mistress was evidently mad. But mad or no, she grew daily weaker in health and her handiwork began to worsen in quality, until Kirstie was forced to use deceit and sell only her own thread to Mr. Seton, though she pretended to dispose of Mrs. Johnstone's, and accounted for the falling off in profit by a feigned tale of brisker competition among their Dutch rivals—an imposture in which the agent helped her, telling the same story in writing; for Mrs. Johnstone, whose eye for a bargain continued as sharp as ever, had actually begun to suspect the lass of robbing her.

About this time as Kirstie passed down the stairs she took notice that a new tradesman had set up business on the landing below. At first she wondered that a barber—for this was his trade—should task his customers to climb so many flights from the street; but it seemed that the fellow knew what he was about, for after the first week she never descended without meeting a customer or two mounting to his door or being followed down by one with his wig powdered and chin freshly scraped. The barber himself she never saw, though once, when the door stood ajar, she caught a glimpse of his white jacket and apron.

She believed that he entered into occupation at Michaelmas; at any rate, he had been plying his trade for close on two months, when on November 17th, 1739, and at a quarter to three in the afternoon, Kirstie went down to the Parliament Close to carry a packet of thread to Mr. Seton. The packet was smaller than usual, for Mrs. Johnstone had not been able to finish her weekly quantity; but this did not matter, since for a month past she had made none that was saleworthy.

Now this Mr. Seton was a pleasant man, in age almost threescore, and full of interest in Mrs. Johnstone, having done business for her and her mother, the Lady Balgarnock, pretty well all his life. And so it often happened that, while weighing the thread and making out his receipt for it, he would invite Kirstie to his office, in the rear of the shop, and discuss her mistress's health or some late news of the city, or advise her upon any small difficulty touching which she made bold to consult him—as, for instance, this pious deception in the matter of the thread.

But today in the midst of their discourse Kirstie felt a sudden uneasiness. Explain it she could not. Yet there came to her a sense, almost amounting to certainty, that Mrs. Johnstone was in trouble and had instant need of her. She had left her but a few minutes, and in ordinary health; there was no reason to be given for this apprehension. Nevertheless, as I say, she felt it as urgent as though her mistress's own voice were calling. Mr. Seton observed her change of colour, and broke off his chat to ask what was amiss. She knew that if she stayed to explain he would laugh at her for a silly fancy; and if it were more than a fancy, why then to explain would be a loss of precious time. Pleading, therefore, some forgotten duty, she left the good man hurriedly, and hastening out through the shop ran across Parliament Close and up the great staircase as fast as her legs could take her.

By the time she reached the fourth flight of stairs she began to feel ashamed of the impulse which brought her, and to argue with herself against it; but at the same time her ears were open and listening for any unusual sound in the rooms above. There was no such sound until she had mounted halfway up the sixth flight, when she heard a light footstep cross the landing, and, looking up, saw the barber's door very gently closing and shutting out a glimpse of his white jacket.

For the moment she thought little of this. The latch had scarcely clicked before she reached the landing outside, from which the last flight ran straight up to her mistress's door. It stood open, though she had closed it less than a quarter of an hour before. This was the first time she had found it open on her return.

She caught at the stair-rail. Through the door and over the line of the topmost stair she could just see the upper panes of the window at the back of Mrs. Johnstone's room. A heavy beam crossed the ceiling in front of the window, and from it, from a hook she had used that morning for twisting her yarn, depended a black bundle.

The bundle—it was big and shapeless—swayed ever so slightly between her and the yellow light sifted through the window. She tottered up, her knees shaking, and flung herself into the room with a scream.

While she fumbled, still screaming, at the bundle hanging from the beam, a step came swiftly up the stair, and the barber stood in the doorway. She recognised him by his white suit, and on the instant saw his face for the first time. He was a negro.

He laid a finger on his lips. Somehow the light showed them to her blood-red, although the rest of his features, barring the whites of his eyes, were all but indiscernible in the dusk. And somehow Kirstie felt a silence imposed on her by this gesture. He stepped across the boards swiftly and silently as a cat, found a stool, and set it under the beam. In the act of mounting it he signalled to Kirstie to run downstairs for help.

Silent as he, Kirstie slipped out at the door: on the threshold she glanced over her shoulder and saw him upon the stool fumbling with one hand at the yarn-rope, and with the other searching his apron pocket for a knife or razor. She ran down the garret stairs, down the next flight....

Here, on the landing, she paused. She had not screamed since the black man first appeared in the doorway. She was not screaming now; she felt that she could not even raise the faintest cry. But a suspicion fastened like a hand on the back of her neck and held her.

She hesitated for a short while, and began to climb the stairs again. From the landing she looked up into the room. The black man was still on the stool, his hand still on the rope. He had not cut the bundle down— was no longer even searching for a knife.

She had been deceived. The man, whoever he was, had dismissed her when every moment was precious, and was himself not even trying to help. Nay, it might be…

She fought down the horror of it and rushed up the stair to fight the thing, man or devil, and save her mistress. On her way she fumbled for the scissors in her pocket. As she broke into the garret the barber, leaving the bundle to swing from its rope, stepped off the stool and, darting to a corner of the room, seemed to stand at bay there. Kirstie sprang toward the stool and hacked at the rope. As the body dropped she faced around on the man's corner, meaning to kill or be killed.

But there was no man in the corner. Her eyes searched into its dusk, and met only the shadow of the sloping attic. He had gone without a sound. There had been no sound in the room but the thud of Mrs. Johnstone's body, and this thud seemed to Kirstie to be taken up and echoed by the blow of her own forehead upon the boards as she fell across the feet of her mistress.

The Lady of the Ship

Or so much as is told of her by Paschal Tonkin, steward and majordomo to the lamented John Milliton, of Pengersick Castle, in Cornwall: of her coming in the Portugal Ship, anno 1526; her marriage with the said Milliton and alleged sorceries; with particulars of the Barbary men wrecked in Mount's Bay and their entertainment in the town of Market Jew.

My purpose is to clear the memory of my late and dear master; and to this end I shall tell the truth and the truth only, so far as I know it, admitting his faults, which, since he has taken them before God, no man should now aggravate by guess-work. That he had traffic with secret arts is certain; but I believe with no purpose but to fight the Devil with his own armoury. He never was a robber as Mr. Thomas St. Aubyn and Mr. William Godolphin accused him; nor, as the vulgar pretended, a lustful and bloody man. What he did was done in effort to save a woman's soul; as Jude tells us, "*Of some have compassion, that are in doubt; and others save, having mercy with fear, pulling them out of the fire, hating even the garment spotted by the flesh*"—though this, alas! my dear master could not. And so with Jude I would end, praying for all of us and ascribing praise *to the only wise God, our Saviour, who is able to guard us from stumbling and set us faultless before His presence with exceeding joy.*

It was in January, 1526, after a tempest lasting three days, that the ship called the *Saint Andrew*, belonging to the King of Portugal, drove ashore in Gunwallo Cove, a little to the southward of Pengersick. She was bound from Flanders to Lisbon with a freight extraordinary rich—as I know after a fashion by my own eyesight, as well as from the inventory drawn up by Master Francis Porson, an Englishman, travelling on board of her as the King of Portugal's factor. I have a copy of it by me as I write, and here are some of Master Porson's items:—

8,000 cakes of copper, valued by him at £3,224.
18 blocks of silver,   "   "   "   " £2,250.
Silver vessels, plate, patens, ewers and pots, beside
    pearls, precious stones, and jewels of gold.
Also a chest of coined money, in amount £6,240.

There was also cloth of arras, tapestry, rich hangings, satins, velvets, silks, camlets, says, satins or Bruges, with great number of bales of Flemish and English cloth; 2,100 barber's basins; 3,200 laten candlesticks; a great chest of shalmers and other instruments of music; four sets of armour for the King of Portugal, much harness for his horses, and much beside—the whole amounting at the least computation to £16,000[1] in value. And this I can believe on confirmation of what I myself saw upon the beach.

But let me have done with Master Porson and his tale, which runs that the *Saint Andrew*, having struck at the mouth of the cove, there utterly perished; yet, by the grace and mercy of Almighty God, the greater part of the crew got safely to land, and by help of many poor folk dwelling in the neighbourhood saved all that was most valuable of the cargo. But shortly after (says he) there came on the scene three gentlemen, Thomas Saint Aubyn, William Godolphin, and John Milliton, with about sixty men armed in manner of war with bows and swords, and made an assault on the shipwrecked sailors and put them in great fear and jeopardy; and in the end took from them all they had saved from the wreck, amounting to 10,000 pounds worth of treasure—"which," says he, "they will not yield up, nor make restitution, though they have been called upon to do so."

So much then for the factor's account, which I doubt not he believed to be true enough; albeit on his own confession he had lain hurt and unconscious upon the beach at the time, and

---
1. Worth about £150,000 at time of first publication.

his tale rested therefore on what he could learn by hearsay after his recovery; when—the matter being so important—he was at trouble to journey all the way to London and lay his complaint before the Portuguese ambassador. Moreover he made so fair a case of it that the ambassador obtained of the English Court a commissioner, Sir Nicholas Fleming, to travel down and push enquiries on the spot—where Master Porson did not scruple to repeat his accusation, and to our faces (having indeed followed the commissioner down for that purpose).

I must say I thought him a very honest man—not to say a brave one, seeing what words he dared to use to Mr. Saint Aubyn in his own house at Clowance, calling him a mere robber. I was there when he said it and made me go hot and cold, knowing (if he did not) that for two pins Mr. Saint Aubyn might have had him drowned like a puppy. However, he chose to make nothing of an insult from a factor. "*Mercator tantum,*" replied he, snapping his fingers, and to my great joy; for any violence might have spoiled the story agreed on between us—that is, between Mr. Saint Aubyn, Mr. Godolphin, and me who acted as deputy for my master.

This story of ours, albeit less honest, had more colour of the truth than Master Porson's hearsay. It ran that Mr. Saint Aubyn, happening near Gunwallo, heard of the wreck and rode to it, where presently Mr. Godolphin and my master joined him and helped to save the men; that, in attempting to save the cargo also, a man of Mr. Saint Aubyn's—one Will Carnarthur—was drowned; that, in fact, very little was rescued; and, seeing the men destitute and without money to buy meat and drink, we bought the goods in lawful bargain with the master. As for the assault, we denied it, or that we took goods to the value of ten thousand pounds from the sailors. All that was certainly known to be saved amounted to about 20 pounds worth; and, in spite of many trials to recover more, which failed to pay the charges of labour, the bulk of the cargo remained in the ship and was broken up by the seas.

This was our tale, false in parts, yet a truer one than either of us, who uttered it, believed. The only person in the plot (so to say) who knew it to be true in substance was my master. I, his deputy, took this version from him to Clowance with a mind glad enough to be relieved by my duty from having any opinion on the matter. On the one hand, I had the evidence of my senses that the booty had been saved, and too much wit to doubt that any other man would conclude it to be in my master's possession. On the other, I had never known him lie or deceive, or engage me to further any deceit; his word was his bond, and by practice my word was his bond also.

Further, of this affair I had already begun to wonder if a man's plain senses could be trusted, as you will hear reason by-and-by. As for Mr. Saint Aubyn and Mr. Godolphin, they had no doubt at all that my master was lying, and that I had come wittingly to further his lie. They would have drawn on him (I make no doubt) had he brought the tale in person. From me, his intermediate, they took it as the best to suit with the known truth and present to the commissioner. All Cornishmen are cousins, you may say. It comes to this, rather: these gentlemen chose to accept my master's lie, and settle with him afterwards, rather than make a clean breast and be forced to wring their small shares out of the Exchequer. A neighbour can be persuaded, terrified, forced; but London is always a long way off, and London lawyers are the devil. I say freely that (knowing no more than they did, or I) these two gentlemen followed a reasonable policy.

But, after we had fitted Sir Nicholas with our common story, and as I was mounting my horse in Clowance courtyard, Mr. Saint Aubyn came close to my stirrup and said this by way of parting:

"You will understand, Mr. Tonkin, that today's tale is for to-day. But by God I will come and take my share—you may tell your master—and a trifle over! And the next time I overtake you I promise to put a bullet in the back of your scrag neck."

For answer to this—seeing that Master Porson stood at an easy distance with his eye on us—I saluted him gravely and rode out of the courtyard.

Now the manner of the wreck was this, and our concern with it. So nearly as I can learn, the *Saint Andrew* came ashore at two hours after noon: the date, the 20th of January, 1526, and the weather at the time coarse and foggy with a gale yet blowing from the south-west or a good west of south, but sensibly abating, and the tide wanting an hour before low water.

It happened that Mr. Saint Aubyn was riding, with twenty men at his back, homeward from Gweek, where he had spent three days on some private business, when he heard news of the wreck at a farmhouse on the road to Helleston: and so turning aside, he, whose dwelling lay farthest from it, came first to the cove. The news reached us at Pengersick a little after three o'clock; as I remember because my master was just then settled to dinner. But he rose at once and gave word to saddle in haste, at the same time bidding me make ready to ride with him, and fifteen others.

So we set forth and rode—the wind lulling, but the rain coming down steadily—and reached Gunwallo Cove with a little daylight to spare. On the beach there we found most of the foreigners landed, but seven of them laid out starkly, who had been drowned or brought ashore dead (for the yard had fallen on board, the day before, and no time left in the ship's extremity to bury them): and three as good as dead—among whom was Master Porson, with a great wound of the scalp; also everywhere great piles of freight, chests, bales, and casks—a few staved and taking damage from salt water and rain, but the most in apparent good condition.

The crew had worked very busily at the salving, and to the great credit of men who had come through suffering and peril of death. Mr. Saint Aubyn's band, too, had lent help, though by this time the flowing of the tide forced them to give over. But the master (as one might say) of their endeavours was neither the Portuguese captain nor Mr. Saint Aubyn, but a young damsel whom I must describe more particularly.

She was standing, as we rode down the beach, nigh to the water's edge; with a group of men about her, and Mr. Saint

Aubyn himself listening to her orders. I can see her now as she turned at our approaching and she and my master looked for the first time into each other's eyes, which afterwards were to look so often and fondly. In age she appeared eighteen or twenty; her shape a mere girl's, but her face somewhat older, being pinched and peaked by the cold, yet the loveliest I have ever seen or shall see. Her hair, which seemed of a copper red, darkened by rain, was blown about her shoulders, and her drenched blue gown, hitched at the waist with a snakeskin girdle, flapped about her as she turned to one or the other, using more play of hands than our home-bred ladies do.

Her feet were bare and rosy; ruddied doubtless, by the wind and brine, but I think partly also by the angry light of the sun-setting which broke the weather to seaward and turned the pools and the wetted sand to the colour of blood. A hound kept beside her, shivering and now and then lowering his muzzle to sniff the oreweed, as if the brine of it puzzled him: a beast in shape somewhat like our grey-hounds, but longer and taller, and coated like a wolf.

As I have tried to describe her she stood amid the men and the tangle of the beach; a shape majestical and yet (as we drew closer) slight and forlorn. The present cause of her gestures we made out to be a dark-skinned fellow whom two of Saint Aubyn's men held prisoner with his arms trussed behind him. On her other hand were gathered the rest of the Portuguese, very sullen and with dark looks whenever she turned from them to Saint Aubyn and from their language to the English. He, I could see, was perplexed, and stood fingering his beard: but his face brightened as he came a step to meet my master.

"Ha!" said he, "you can help us, Milliton. You speak the Portuguese, I believe?" (For my master was known to speak most of the languages of Europe, having caught them up in his youth when his father's madness forced him abroad. And I myself, who had accompanied him so far as Venice, could pick my way in the *lingua Franca*.) "This fellow"—pointing at the prisoner—"has just drawn a knife on the lady here; and indeed would have killed her, but for this hound of hers. My fellows have him tight and safe, as you see: but I was thinking by your leave to lodge him with you, yours being the nearest house for the safe keeping of such. But the plague is," says he, "there seems to be more in the business than I can fathom: for one half of these drenched villains take the man's part, while scarce one of them seems too well disposed towards the lady: although to my knowledge she has worked more than any ten of them in salving the cargo. And heaven help me if I can understand a word of their chatter!"

My master lifted his cap to her; and she lifted her eyes to him, but never a word did she utter, though but a moment since she had been using excellent English. Only she stood, slight and helpless and (I swear) most pitiful, as one saying, "Here is my judge. I am content."

My master turned to the prisoner and questioned him in the Portuguese. But the fellow (a man taller than the rest and passably straight-looking) would confess nothing but that his name was Gil Perez of Lagos, the boatswain of the wrecked ship. Questioned of the assault, he shook his head merely and shrugged his shoulders. His face was white: it seemed to me unaccountably, until glancing down I took note of a torn wound above his right knee on the inside, where the hound's teeth had fastened.

"But who is the captain of the ship?" my master demanded in Portuguese; and they thrust forward a small man who seemed not over-willing. Indeed his face had nothing to commend him, being sharp and yellow, with small eyes set too near against the nose.

"Your name?" my master demanded of him too.

"Affonzo Cabral," he answered, and plunged into a long tale of the loss of his ship and how it happened. Cut short in this and asked concerning the lady, he shrugged his shoulders and replied with an oath he knew nothing about her beyond this, that she had taken passage with him at Dunquerque for Lisbon, paying him beforehand and bearing him a letter from the Bishop of Cambrai, which conveyed to him that she was bound on some secret mission of politics to the Court of Lisbon.

As I thought, two or three of the men would have murmured something here, but for a look from her, who, turning to my master, said quietly in good English:

"That man is a villain. My name is Alicia of Bohemia, and my mission not to be told here in public. But he best knows why he took me for passenger, and how he has behaved towards me. Yourselves may see how I have saved his freight. And for the rest, sir"—here she bent her eyes on my master very frankly—"I have proved these men, and claim to be delivered from them."

At this my master knit his brows: and albeit he was a young man (scarce past thirty) and a handsome, the deep wedge-mark showed between them as I had often seen it show over the nose of the old man his father.

"I think," said he to Mr. Saint Aubyn, "this should be inquired into at greater leisure. With your leave my men shall take the prisoner to Pengersick and have him there in safe keeping. And if"—with a bow—"the Lady Alicia will accept my poor shelter it will be the handier for our examining of him. For the rest, cannot we be of service in rescuing yet more of the cargo?"

But this for the while was out of question: the *Saint Andrew* lying well out upon the strand, with never fewer than four or five ugly breakers between her and shore; and so balanced that every sea worked her to and fro. Moreover, her mizzen mast yet stood, as by a miracle, and the weight of it so strained at her seams that (thought I) there could be very little left of her by the next ebb.

By now, too, the night was closing down, and we must determine what to do with the cargo saved. Mr. Godolphin, who had arrived with his men during my master's colloquy, was ready with an offer of wains and pack-horses to convey the bulk of it to the outhouses at Godolphin. But this, when I interpreted it, the Portuguese captain would not hear. Nor was he more tractable to Mr. Saint Aubyn's offer to set a mixed guard of our three companies upon the stuff until daybreak. He plainly had his doubts of such protection: and I could not avoid some respect for his wisdom while showing it by argument to be mere perversity. To my master's persuasions and mine he shook his head: asking for the present to be allowed a little fuel and refreshment for his men, who would camp on the beach among their goods. And to this, in the end, we had to consent. Several times before agreeing—and perhaps more often than need was—my master consulted with the Lady Alicia. But she seemed indifferent what happened to the ship. Indeed, she might well have been overwearied.

At length, the Portugals having it their own way, we parted: Mr. Saint Aubyn riding off to lodge for the night with Mr. Godolphin, who took charge of the three wounded men; while we carried the Lady Alicia off to Pengersick (whither the prisoner Gil Perez had been marched on ahead), she riding pillion behind my Master, and the rest of us at a seemly distance.

On reaching home I had first to busy myself with orders for the victuals to be sent down to the foreigners at the cove, and afterwards in snatching my supper in the great hall, where already I saw my master and the strange lady making good cheer together at the high table. He had bidden the housekeeper fetch out some robes that had been his mother's, and in these antique fittings the lady looked not awkwardly (as you might suppose), but rather like some player in a masque. I know not how 'twas: but whereas (saving my respect) I had always been to my dear master as a brother, close to his heart and thoughts, her coming did at once remove him to a distance from me, so that I looked on the pair as if the dais were part of some other world than this, and they, pledging each other up there and murmuring in foreign tongues and playing with glances, as two creatures moving through a play or pisky tale without care or burden of living, and yet in the end to be pitied.

My fast broken, I bethought me of our prisoner; and catching up some meats and a flask of wine, hurried to the strong room where he lay. But I found him stretched on his pallet, and turning in a kind of fever: so returned and fetched a cooling draught in place of the victuals, and without questioning made him drink it. He thanked me amid some rambling, light-headed talk—the most of it too quickly poured out for me to catch; but by-and-by grew easier and drowsy. I left him to sleep, putting off questions for the morning.

But early on the morrow—between five and six o'clock—came Will Hendra, a cowkeeper, into our courtyard with a strange tale; one that disquieted if it did not altogether astonish me. The tale—as told before my master, whom I aroused to hear it—ran thus: that between midnight and one in the morning the Portugals in the cove had been set upon and beaten from the spoils by a number of men with pikes (no doubt belonging to Saint Aubyn or Godolphin, or both), and forced to flee to the cliffs. But (here came in the wonder) the assailants, having mastered the field, fell on the casks, chests, and packages, only to find them utterly empty or filled with weed and gravel! Of freight—so Will Hendra had it from one of Godolphin's own men, who were now searching the cliffs and caverns—not twelve-pennyworth remained on the beach. The Portugals must have hidden or made away with it all. He added that their captain had been found at the foot of the cliffs with his head battered in; but whether by a fall or a blow taken in the affray, there was no telling.

My master let saddle at once and rode away for the cove without breaking his fast. And I went about my customary duties until full daybreak, when I paid a visit to the strong room, to see how the prisoner had slept.

I found him sitting up in bed and nursing his leg, the wound of which appeared red and angry at the edges. I sent, therefore, for a fomentation, and while applying it thought no harm to tell him the report from the cove. To my astonishment it threw him into a transport, though whether of rage or horror I could not at first tell. But he jerked his leg from my grasp, and beating the straw with both fists he cried out—

"I knew it! I knew it would be so! She is a witch—a daughter of Satan, or his leman! It is her doing, I tell you. It is she who has killed that fool Affonzo. She is a witch!" He fell back on the straw, his strength spent, but still beat weakly with his fists, gasping "Witch—witch!"

"Hush!" said I. "You are light-headed with your hurt. Lie quiet and let me tend it."

"As for my hurt," he answered, "your tending it will do no good. The poison of that hound of hell is in me, and nothing for me but to say my prayers. But listen you"—here he sat up again and plucked me by the shoulder as I bent over his leg. "The freight is not gone, and good reason for why: it was never landed!"

"Hey?" said I, incredulous.

"It was never landed. The men toiled as she ordered—Lord, how they toiled! Without witch-craft they had never done the half of it. I tell you they handled moonshine—wove sand. The riches they brought ashore were emptiness; vain shows that already have turned to chips and straw and rubbish. Nay, sir"—for I drew back before these ravings—"listen for the love of God, before the poison gets hold of me! Soon it will be too late.... The evening before we sailed from Dunquerque, we were anchored out in the tide. It was my watch. I was leaning on the rail of the poop when I caught sight of her first. She was running for her life across the dunes—running for the waterside—she and her hound beside her. Away behind her, like ants dotted over the rises of the sand, were little figures running and pursuing.

"Down by the waterside one boat was waiting, with a man in it—or the Devil belike—leaning on his oars. She whistled; he pulled close in shore. She leapt into the boat with the dog at her heels, and was half-way across towards our ship before the first of those after her reached the water's edge. When she hailed us I ran and fetched Affonzo the master. The rest I charge to his folly. It was he who handed her up the ship's side. How the dog came on board I know not: only that I leaned over the bulwarks to have a look at him, but heard a pattering noise, and there he was on deck behind me and close beside his mistress. The boat and rower had vanished—under the ship's stern, as I supposed, but now I have my doubts. I saw no more of them, anyhow.

"By this time Affonzo was reading her letter. The crowd by

the water's edge had found a boat at length—how, I know not; but it was a very little one, holding but six men besides the one rower, and then over-laden. They pulled towards us and hailed just as the lady took the master's promise and went down to seek her cabin: and one of the men stood up, a tall gentleman with a chain about his neck. Affonzo went to the side to parley with him.

"The tall man with the chain cried out that he was mayor or provost—I forget which—and the woman must be given up as a proved witch who had laid the wickedest spells upon many citizens of Dunquerque. All this he had to shout; for Affonzo, who—either ignorantly or by choice—was already on Satan's side, would not suffer him to come aboard or even nigh the ship's ladder. Moreover, he drove below so many of our crew as had gathered to the side to listen, commanding me with curses to see to this.

"Yet I heard something of the mayor's accusation; which was that the woman had come to Dunquerque, travelling as a great lady with a retinue of servants and letters of commendation to the religious houses, on which and on many private persons of note she had bestowed relics of our Lord and the saints, pretending it was for a penance that she journeyed and gave the bounties: but that, at a certain hour, these relics had turned into toads, adders, and all manner of abominable offal, defiling the holy places and private shrines, in some instances the very church altars: that upon the outcry her retinue had vanished, and she herself taken to flight as we saw her running.

"At all this Affonzo scoffed, threatening to sink the boat if further troubled with their importunities. And, the provost using threats in return, he gave order to let weigh incontinently and clear with the tide, which by this was turned to ebb. And so, amid curses which we answered by display of our guns, we stood out from that port. Of the master's purpose I make no guess. Either he was bewitched, or the woman had taken him with her beauty, and he dreamed of finding favour with her.

"This only I know, that on the second morning, she standing on deck beside him, he offered some familiar approach; whereupon the dog flew at him, and I believe would have killed him, but was in time called off by her. Within an hour we met with the weather which after three days drove us ashore. Now whether Affonzo suspected her true nature or not—as I know he had taken a great fear of her—I never had time to discover. But I know her for a witch, and for a witch I tried to make away with her. For the rest, may God pardon me!"

All this the man uttered not as I have written it, but with many gasping interruptions; and afterwards lay back as one dead. Before I could make head or tail of my wonder, I heard cries and a clatter from the courtyard, and ran out to see what was amiss.

In the courtyard I found my master with a dozen men closing the bolts of the great gate against a company who rained blows and hammerings on the outside of it. My master had dismounted, and while he called his orders the blood ran down his face from a cut above the forehead. As for the smoking horses on which they had ridden in, these stood huddling, rubbing shoulders, and facing all ways like a knot of frightened colts.

All the bolts being shut, my master steps to the grille and speaking through it, "Saint Aubyn," says he, "between gentlemen there are fitter ways to dispute than brawling with servants. I am no thief or robber; as you may satisfy yourself by search and question, bringing, if you will, Mr. Godolphin and three men to help you under protection of my word. If you will not, then I am ready for you at any time of your choosing. But I warn you that, if any man offers further violence to my gate, I send Master Tonkin to melt the lead, of which I have good store. So make your choice."

He said it in English, and few of those who heard him could understand. And after a moment Saint Aubyn, who was a very courteous gentleman for all his hot temper, made answer in the same tongue.

"If I cannot take your word, Pengersick," said he, "be sure no searching will satisfy me. But that some of your men have made off with the goods, with or without your knowledge, I am convinced."

"If they have—" my master was beginning, when Godolphin's sneering laugh broke in on his words from the other side of the gate.

"'*If!*' '*If!*' There are too many *if's* in this parley for my stomach. Look ye, Pengersick, will you give up the goods or no?"

Upon this my master changed his tone. "As for Mr. Godolphin, I have this only to say: the goods are neither his nor mine; they are not in my keeping, nor do I believe them stolen by any of my men. For the words that have passed between us today, he knows me well enough to be sure I shall hold him to account, and that soon: and to that assurance commending him, I wish you both a very good day."

So having said, he strolled off towards the stables, leaving me to listen at the gate, where by-and-by, after some disputing, I had the pleasure to hear our besiegers draw off and trot away towards Godolphin. Happening to take a glance upwards at the house-front, I caught sight of the strange lady at the window of the guest-chamber, which faced towards the south-east. She was leaning forth and gazing after them: but, hearing my master's footsteps as he came from the stables, she withdrew her eyes from the road and nodded down at him gaily.

But as he went indoors to join her at breakfast I ran after, and catching him in the porch, besought him to have his wound seen to. "And after that," said I, "there is another wounded man who needs your attention. Unless you take his deposition quickly, I fear, sir, it may be too late."

His eyebrows went up at this, but contracted again upon the twinge of his wound. "I will attend to him first," said he shortly, and led the way to the strong room. "Hullo!" was his next word, as he came to the door—for in my perturbation and hurry I had forgotten to lock it.

"He is too weak to move," I stammered, as my poor excuse.

"Nevertheless it was not well done," he replied, pushing past me.

The prisoner lay on his pallet, gasping, with his eyes wide

open in a rigor. "Take her away!" he panted. "Take her away! She has been here!"

"Hey?" I cried: but my master turned on me sharply. To this day I know not how much of evil he suspected.

"I will summon you if I need you. For the present you will leave us here alone."

Nor can I tell what passed between them for the next half-an-hour. Only that when he came forth my master's face was white and set beneath its dry smear of blood. Passing me, who waited at the end of the corridor, he said, but without meeting my eyes:

"Go to him. The end is near."

I went to him. He lay pretty much as I had left him, in a kind of stupor; out of which, within the hour, he started suddenly and began to rave. Soon I had to send for a couple of our stablemen; and not too soon. For by this he was foaming at the mouth and gnashing, the man in him turned to beast and trying to bite, so that we were forced to strap him to his bed. I shall say no more of this, the most horrible sight of my life. The end came quietly, about six in the evening: and we buried the poor wretch that night in the orchard under the chapel wall.

All that day, as you may guess, I saw nothing of the strange lady. And on the morrow until dinner-time I had but a glimpse of her. This was in the forenoon. She stood, with her hound beside her, in an embrasure of the wall, looking over the sea: to the eye a figure so maidenly and innocent and (in a sense) forlorn that I recalled Gil Perez' tale as the merest frenzy, and wondered how I had come to listen to it with any belief. Her seaward gaze would be passing over the very spot where we had laid him: only a low wall hiding the freshly turned earth. My master had ridden off early: I could guess upon what errand.

He returned shortly after noon, unhurt and looking like a man satisfied with his morning's work. And at dinner, watching his demeanour narrowly, I was satisfied that either he had not heard the prisoner's tale or had rejected it utterly. For he took his seat in the gayest spirits, and laughed and talked with the stranger throughout the meal. And afterwards, having fetched an old lute which had been his mother's, he sat and watched her fit new strings to it, rallying her over her tangle. But when she had it tuned and, touching it softly, began the first of those murmuring heathenish songs to which I have since listened so often, pausing in my work, but never without a kind of terror at beauty so far above my comprehending—why, then my master laughed no more.

He had met Godolphin that morning and run him through the thigh. And that bitterest enemy of ours still wore a crutch a month later, when we faced Master Porson before the commissioner in Saint Aubyn's house at Clowance. At that conference (not to linger over the time between) the Commissioner showed himself pardonably suspicious of us all. He was a dry, foxy-faced man, who spoke little and at times seemed scarce to be listening; but rather turning over some deeper matters in his brain behind his grey-coloured eyes. But at length, Mr. Saint Aubyn having twice or thrice made mention of the Lady Alicia and her presence on the beach, this Sir Nicholas looked up at me sharply, and said he—"By all accounts this lady was a passenger shipped by the master at Dunquerque. It seems she was a foreign lady of birth, bearing letters commendatory to the Court of Lisbon."

"That was his story of it," Master Porson assented. "I was below and busy with the cargo at the time, and knew nothing of her presence on board until we had cleared the harbour."

"And at this moment she is a guest of Mr. Milliton's at Pengersick?" pursued Sir Nicholas, still with his eyes upon mine. I bowed, feeling mightily uneasy. "It is most necessary that I should take her evidence—and Mr. Milliton's. In all the statements received by me Mr. Milliton bears no small part: his house lies at no distance from Gunwallo Cove: and I have heard much of your Cornish courtesy. It appears to me singular, therefore, that although I have been these four days in his neighbourhood no invitation has reached me to visit his house and have audience with him: and it argues small courtesy that on coming here today in full expectation of seeing him, I should be fobbed off with a deputy."

"Though but a deputy," I protested, "I have my master's entire confidence."

"No doubt," said he drily. "But it would be more to the point if you had mine. It is imperative that I see Mr. Milliton of Pengersick and hear his evidence, as also this Lady Alicia's: and you may bear him my respects and say that I intend to call upon him tomorrow."

I bowed. It was all I could do: since the truth (for different reasons) could neither be told to him nor to the others. And the truth was that for two days my master and the strange lady had not been seen at Pengersick! They had vanished, and two horses with them: but when and how I neither knew nor dared push inquiries to discover. Only the porter could have told me had he chosen; but when I questioned him he looked cunning, shook his head, and as good as hinted that I would be wiser to question nobody, but go about my business as if I shared the secret.

And so I did, imitating the porter's manner even before Dame Tresize, the housekeeper. But it rankled that, even while instructing me—as he did on the eve of his departing—in the part I was to play at Clowance, my master had chosen to shut me out of this part of his confidence. And now on the road home from Clowance I carried an anxious heart as well as a sore. To tell the truth—that my master was away—I had not been able, knowing how prompt Saint Aubyn and Godolphin might be to take the advantage and pay us an unwelcome visit. "And indeed," thought I, "if my master hides one thing from me, why not another? The stuff may indeed be stored with us: though I will not believe it without proof." The commissioner would come, beyond a doubt. To discover my master's absence would quicken his suspicions: to deny him admittance would confirm them.

I reached home, yet could get no sleep for my quandary. But a little before the dawning, while I did on my clothes, there came a knocking at the gate followed by a clatter of hoofs in the courtyard; and hurrying down, with but pause to light my lantern, I found my master there and helping the strange lady to dismount, with the porter and two sleepy grooms standing by and holding torches. Beneath the belly of the lady's horse stood her hound, his tongue lolling and his coat a cake of mire. The night had been chilly and the nostrils of the hard-ridden beasts made a steam among the lights we held, while above us the upper frontage of the house stood out clear between the growing daylight and the waning moon poised above the courtlege-wall in the south-west.

"Hey! Is that Paschal?" My master turned as one stiff with riding. His face was ghastly pale, yet full of a sort of happiness: and I saw that his clothes were disordered and his boots mired to their tops. "Good luck!" cried he, handing the lady down. "We can have supper at once."

"Supper?" I repeated it after him.

"Or breakfast—which you choose. Have the lights lit in the hall, and a table spread. My lady will eat and drink before going to her room."

"'My lady'?" was my echo again.

"Just so—my lady, and my wife, and henceforward your mistress. Lead the way, if you please! Afterwards I will talk."

I did as I was ordered: lit the lights about the dais, spread the cloth with my own hands, fetched forth the cold meats and—for he would have no servants aroused—waited upon them in silence and poured the wine, all in a whirl of mind. My mistress (as I must now call her) showed no fatigue, though her skirts were soiled as if they had been dragged through a sea of mud. Her eyes sparkled and her bosom heaved as she watched my master, who ate greedily. But beyond the gallant words with which he pledged her welcome home to Pengersick nothing was said until, his hunger put away, he pushed back his chair and commanded me to tell what had happened at Clowance: which I did, pointing out the ticklish posture of affairs, and that for a certainty the commissioner might be looked for in within a few hours.

"Well," said my master, "I see no harm in his coming, nor any profit. The goods are not with us: never were with us: and there's the end of it."

But I was looking from him to my mistress, who with bent brows sat studying the table before her.

"Master Paschal," said she after a while, as one awaking from thought, "has done his business zealously and well. I will go to my room now and rest: but let me be aroused when this visitor comes, for I believe that I can deal with him." And she rose and walked away to the stair, with the hound at her heels.

A little later I saw my master to his room: and after that had some hours of leisure in which to fret my mind as well over what had happened as what was likely to. It was hard on noon when the commissioner arrived: and with him Master Porson. I led them at once to the hall and, setting wine before them, sent to learn when my master and mistress would be pleased to give audience. The lady came down almost at once, looking very rosy and fresh. She held a packet of papers, and having saluted the commissioner graciously, motioned me to seat myself at the table with paper and pen.

Sir Nicholas began with some question touching her business on board the *Saint Andrew*: and in answer she drew a paper from the top of her packet. It was spotted with sea-water, but (as I could see) yet legible. The commissioner studied it, showed it to Master Porson (who nodded), and handing it back politely, begged her for some particulars concerning the wreck.

Upon this she told the story clearly and simply. There had been a three days' tempest: the ship had gone ashore in such and such a manner: a great part of the cargo had undoubtedly been landed. It was on the beach when she had left it under conduct of Mr. Milliton, who had shown her great kindness. On whomsoever its disappearance might be charged, of her host's innocence she could speak.

My master appearing just now saluted the commissioner and gave his version very readily.

"You may search my cellars," he wound up, "and, if you please, interrogate my servants. My livery is known by everyone in this neighbourhood to be purple and tawny. The seamen can tell you if any of their assailants wore these colours."

"They assure me," said Sir Nicholas, "that the night was too dark for them to observe colours: and for that matter to disguise them would have been a natural precaution. There was a wounded man brought to your house—one Gil Perez, the boatswain."

"He is dead, as you doubtless know, of a bite received from this lady's hound as he was attacking her with a knife."

"But why, madam"—the factor turned to my mistress—"should this man have attacked you?"

She appeared to be expecting this question, and drew from her packet a second paper, which she unfolded quietly and spread on the table, yet kept her palm over the writing on it while she answered, "Those who engage upon missions of State must look to meet with attacks, but not to be asked to explain them. The mob at Dunquerque pursued me upon a ridiculous charge, yet was wisely incited by men who invented it, knowing the true purpose of my mission." She glanced from the commissioner to Master Porson. "Sir Nicholas Fleming—surely I have heard his name spoken, as of a good friend to the Holy Father and not too anxious for the emperor's marriage with Mary Tudor?" The commissioner started in his chair, while she turned serenely upon his companion. "And Master Porson," she continued, "as a faithful servant of His Majesty of Portugal will needs be glad to see a princess of Portugal take Mary Tudor's place. Eh?"—for they were eyeing each the other like two detected schoolboys—"It would seem, sirs, that though you came together, you were better friends than you guessed. Glance your eye, Master Porson, over this paper which I shall presently entrust to you for furtherance; and you will agree with Sir Nicholas that the prudent course for both of you is to forget, on leaving this house, that any such person as I was on board the *Saint Andrew.*"

The two peered into the parchment and drew back. "The emperor—" I heard the commissioner mutter with an intake of breath.

"And, as you perceive, in his own handwriting." She folded up the paper and, replacing it, addressed my master. "Your visitors, sir, deserve some refreshment for their pains and courtesy."

And that was the end of the conference. What that paper contained I know as little as I know by what infernal sorcery it was prepared. Master Porson folded it up tight in his hand, glancing dubiously at Sir Nicholas. My lady stood smiling upon them both for a moment, then dismissed me to the kitchens upon a pretended errand. They were gone when I returned, nor did I again set eyes upon the commissioner or the factor. It is true that the emperor did about this time break his pledge with our King Henry and marry a princess of Portugal; and some of high office in England were not sorry therefore. But of this enough.

As the days wore on and we heard no more of the wreck, my master and mistress settled down to that retirement from the world which is by custom allowed to the newly married, but which with them was to last to the end. A life of love it was; but—God help us!—no life of happiness; rather, in process of days, a life of torment. Can I tell you how it was? At first to see them together was like looking through a glass upon a picture; a picture gallant and beautiful yet removed behind a screen and not of this world. Suppose now that by little and little the glass began to be flawed, or the picture behind it to crumble (you could not tell which) until when it smiled it smiled wryly, until rocks toppled and figures fell askew, yet still kept up their pretence of play against the distorted woodland. Nay, it was worse than this: fifty times worse. For while the fair show tottered, my master and mistress clung to their love; and yet it was just their love which kept the foundations rocking.

They lived for each other. They neither visited nor received visits. Yet they were often, and by degrees oftener, apart; my master locked up with his books, my mistress roaming the walls with her hound or seated by her lattice high on the seaward side of the castle. Sometimes (but this was usually on moonlit nights or windless evenings when the sun sank clear to view over our broad bay) she would take up her lute and touch it to one of those outlandish love-chants with which she had first wiled my master's heart to her. As time went on, stories came to us that these chants, which fell so softly on the ears of us as we went about the rooms and gardens, had been heard by fishermen riding by their nets far in the offing—so far away (I have heard) as the Scillies; and there were tales of men who, as they listened, had seen the ghosts of drowned mariners rising and falling on the moon-rays, or floating with their white faces thrown back while they drank in the music; yea, even echoing the words of the song in whispers like the flutter of birds' wings.

When first the word crept about that she was a witch I cannot certainly say. But in time it did; and, what is more—though I will swear that no word of Gil Perez' confession ever passed my lips—the common folk soon held it for a certainty that the cargo saved from the *Saint Andrew* had been saved by her magic only; that the plate and rich stuffs seen by my own eyes were but cheating *simulacra*, and had turned into rubbish at midnight, scarce an hour before the assault on the Portuguese.

I have wondered since if 'twas this rumour and some belief in it which held Messrs. Saint Aubyn and Godolphin from offering any further attack on us. You might say that it was open to them, so believing, to have denounced her publicly. But in our country Holy Church had little hold—scarce more than the king's law itself in such matters; and within my memory it has always come easier to us to fear witch-craft than to denounce it. Also (and it concerns my tale) the three years which followed the stranding of the *Saint Andrew* were remarkable for a great number of wrecks upon our coast.

In that short time we of our parish and the men of St. Hilary upon our north were between us favoured with no fewer than fourteen; the most of them vessels of good burden. Of any hand in bringing them ashore I know our gentry to have been innocent. Still, there were pickings; and finding that my master held aloof from all share in such and (as far as could be) held his servants aloof, our neighbours, though not accepting this for quittance, forbore to press the affair of the *Saint Andrew* further than by spreading injurious tales and whispers.

The marvel was that we of Pengersick (who reaped nothing of this harvest) fell none the less under suspicion of decoying the vessels ashore. More than once in my dealings with the fishermen and tradesmen of Market Jew, I happened on hints of this; but nothing which could be taken hold of until one day a certain Peter Chynoweth of that town, coming drunk to Pengersick with a basket of fish, blurted out the tale. Said he, after I had beaten him down to a reasonable price, "'Twould be easy enough, one would think, to spare an honest man a groat of the fortune Pengersick makes on these dark nights."

"Thou lying thief!" said I. "What new slander is this?"

"Come, come," says he, looking roguish; "that won't do for me that have seen the false light on Cuddan Point more times than I can count; and so has every fisherman in the bay."

Well, I kicked him through the gate for it, and flung his basket after him; but the tale could not be so dismissed. "It may be," thought I, "someone of Pengersick has engaged upon this wickedness on his own account;" and for my master's credit I resolved to keep watch.

I took therefore the porter into my secret, who agreed to let me through the gate towards midnight without telling a soul. I took a sheepskin with me and a poignard for protection; and for a week, from midnight to dawn, I played sentinel on Cuddan Point, walking to and fro, or stretched under the lee of a rock whence I could not miss any light shown on the headland, if Peter Chynoweth's tale held any truth.

By the eighth trial I had pretty well made up my mind (and without astonishment) that Peter Chynoweth was a liar. But scarcely had I reached my post that night when, turning, I descried a radiance as of a lantern, following me at some fifty paces. On the instant I gripped my poignard and stepped behind a boulder. The light drew nearer, came, and passed me. To my bewilderment it was no lantern, but an open flame, running close along the turf and too low for anyone to be carrying it: nor was the motion that of a light which a man carries. Moreover, though it passed me within half-a-dozen yards and lit up the stone I stood behind, I saw nobody and heard no footstep, though the wind (which was south-westerly) blew from it to me. In this breeze the flame quivered, though not violently but as it were a ball of fire rolling with a flickering crest.

It went by, and I followed it at something above walking pace until upon the very verge of the head-land, where I had no will to risk my neck, it halted and began to be heaved up and down much like the poop-light of a vessel at sea. In this play it continued for an hour at least; then it came steadily back towards me by the way it had gone, and as it came I ran upon it with my dagger. But it slipped by me, travelling at speed towards the mainland; whither I pelted after it hot-foot, and so across the fields towards Pengersick. Strain as I might, I could not overtake it; yet contrived to keep it within view, and so well that I was bare a hundred yards behind when it came under the black shadow of the castle and without pause glided across the dry moat and so up the face of the wall to my lady's window, which there overhung. And into this window it passed before my very eyes and vanished.

I know not what emboldened me, but from the porter's lodge I went straight up to my master's chamber, where (though the hour must have been two in the morning or thereabouts) a light was yet burning. Also—but this had become ordinary—a smell of burning gums and herbs filled the passage leading to his door. He opened to my knock, and stood before me in his dressing-gown of sables—a tall figure of a man and youthful, though already beginning to stoop. Over his shoulder I perceived the room swimming with coils of smoke which floated in their wreaths from a brazier hard by the fireplace.

I think his first motion was to thrust me away; but I caught him by the hand, and with many protestations broke into my tale, giving him no time to forbid me. And presently he drew me inside, and shutting the door, stood upright by the table, facing me with his fingers on the rim as if they rested there for support.

"Paschal," said he, when at length I drew back, "this must not come to my lady's ears. She has been ailing of late."

"Ay, sir, and long since: of a disease past your curing."

"God help us! I hope not," said he; then broke out violently: "She is innocent, Paschal; innocent as a child!"

"Innocent!" cried I, in a voice which showed how little I believed.

"Paschal," he went on, "you are my servant, but my friend also, I hope. Nay, nay, I know. I swear to you, then, these things do but happen in her sleep. In her waking senses she is mine, as one day she shall be mine wholly. But at night, when her will is dissolved in sleep, the evil spirit wakes and goes questing after its master."

"Mahound?" I stammered, quaking.

"Be it Satan himself," said he, very low and resolute, "I will win her from him, though my own soul be the ransom."

"Dear my master," I began, and would have implored him on my knees; but he pointed to the door. "I will win her," he repeated. "What you have seen tonight happens more rarely now. Moreover, the summer is beginning—"

He paused: yet I had gathered his meaning. "There will be less peril for the ships for a while," said I.

Said he: "To *them* she intends no harm. It is for her master the light waves. Paschal, I am an unhappy man!" He flung a hand to his forehead, but recovering himself peered at me under the shadow of it. "If you could watch—often—as you have done tonight—you might protect others from seeing—"

The wisdom of this at least I saw, and gave him my promise readily. Upon this understanding (for no more could be had) I withdrew me.

The next day, therefore, I moved my bed to a turret-chamber on the angle of the south-eastern wall whence I could keep my lady's window in view. I was never a man to need much sleep: but if, through the year which followed, the apparition escaped once or twice without my cognisance, I dare take oath this was the extent of it. It appeared more rarely, as my master had promised: and in the end (I think) scarce above once a month. In form it never varied from the cresseted globe of flame I had first seen, and always it took the path across the fields towards Cuddan Point. No sound went with it, or announced its going or return: and while it was absent, my lady's chamber would be utterly dark and silent. My custom was not to follow it (which I had proved to be useless), but to let myself out and patrol the walls, satisfying myself that no watchers lurked about the castle. I understood now that Pengersick was reported throughout the neighbourhood to be haunted: and such a report is not the worst protection. These vague tales kept aloof the country people who, but for them, had almost certainly happened on the secret. And night after night while I watched, my master wrestled with the Evil One in his room.

The last time I saw the apparition was on the night of May 10th, 1529, more than three years after my lady's first coming to Pengersick. I was prepared for it: for she had been singing at her window a great part of the afternoon, and I had learnt to be warned by this mood. The night was a dark one, with flying clouds and a stiff breeze blowing up from the south-east. The flame left my lady's window at the usual hour—a few minutes after midnight—but returned some while before its due time. In ordinary it would be away for an hour and a half, or from that to two hours, but this night I had scarcely begun my rounds before I saw it returning across the fields. Nor was this the only surprise. For as I watched it up the wall and saw it gain my lady's window, I heard the hound within lift up its voice in a long, shuddering howl.

I lost no time, but made my way to my master's room. He, too, had heard the dog's howl, and was strangely perturbed. "It means something. It means something," he kept repeating. He had already run to his wife's chamber, but found her in a deep slumber and the hound (which always slept on the floor at her bed's foot) composing itself to sleep again, with jowl dropped on its fore-paws.

The next morning I had fixed to ride into the Market Jew to

fetch a packet of books which was waiting there for my master. But at the entrance of the town I found the people in great commotion, the cause of which turned out to be a group of Turk men gathered at the hither end of the causeway leading to the Mount. One told me they were Moslems (which indeed was apparent at first sight) and that their ship had run ashore that night, under the Mount; but with how much damage was doubtful. She lay within sight, in a pretty safe position, and not so badly fixed but I guessed the next tide would float her if her bottom were not broken.

The Moslems (nine in all) had rowed ashore in their boat and landed on the causeway; but with what purpose they had no chance to explain: for the inhabitants, catching sight of their knives and scimitars, could believe in nothing short of an intent to murder and plunder; and taking courage in numbers, had gathered (men and women) to the causeway-head to oppose them. To be sure these fears had some warrant in the foreigners' appearance: who with their turbans, tunics, dark faces and black naked legs made up a show which Market Jew had never known before nor (I dare say) will again.

Nor had the mildness of their address any effect but to raise a fresh commotion. For, their leader advancing with outstretched hands and making signals that he intended no mischief but rather sued for assistance, at once a cry went up, "The Plague!" "The Plague!" at which I believe the crowd would have scattered like sheep had not a few sturdy volunteers with pikes and boat-hooks forbidden his nearer approach.

Into this knot the conference had locked itself when I rode up and—the crowd making way for me—addressed the strangers in the *lingua Franca*, explaining that my Master of Pengersick was a magistrate and would be forward to help them either with hospitality or in lending aid to get their ship afloat; further that they need have no apprehension of the crowd, which had opposed them in fear, not in churlishness; yet it might be wise for the main body to stay and keep guard over the cargo while their spokesman went with me to Pengersick.

To this their leader at once consented; and we presently set forth together, he walking by my horse with an agile step and that graceful bearing which I had not seen since my days of travel: a bearded swarthy man, extraordinarily handsome in Moorish fashion and distinguished from his crew not only by authority as patron of the ship, but by a natural dignity. I judged him about forty. Me he treated with courtesy, yet with a reticence which seemed to say he reserved his speech for my master. Of the wreck he said nothing except that his ship had been by many degrees out of her bearings: and knowing that the Moorish disasters in Spain had thrown many of their chiefs into the trade of piracy I was contented to smoke such an adventurer in this man, and set him down for one better at fighting than at navigation.

With no more suspicion than this I reached Pengersick and, bestowing the stranger in the hall, went off to seek my master. For the change that came over my dear lord's face as he heard my errand I was in no way prepared. It was terrible.

"Paschal," he cried, sinking into a chair and spreading both hands helplessly on the table before him, "it is *he!* Her time is come, and mine!"

It was in vain that I reasoned, protesting (as I believed) that the stranger was but a chance pirate cast ashore by misadventure; and as vain that, his fears infecting me, I promised to go down and get rid of the fellow on some pretence.

"No," he insisted, "the hour is come. I must face it: and what is more, Paschal, I shall win. Another time I shall be no better prepared. Bring him to my room and then go and tell my lady that I wish to speak with her."

I did so. On ushering in the stranger I saw no more than the bow with which the two men faced each other: for at once my master signalled me to run on my further errand. Having delivered my message at my lady's door, I went down to the hall, and lingering there, saw her pass along the high gallery above the dais towards my lord's room, with the hound at her heels.

Thence I climbed the stair to my own room: locked the door and anon unlocked it, to be ready at sudden need. And there I paced hour after hour, without food, listening. From the courtyard came the noise of the grooms chattering and splashing: but from the left wing, where lay my master's rooms, no sound at all. Twice I stole out along the corridors and hung about the stair head: but could hear nothing, and crept back in fear to be caught eavesdropping.

It was about five in the afternoon (I think), all was still in the courtyard, when I heard the click of a latch and, running to the window, saw the porter closing his wicket gate. A minute later, on a rise beyond the wall, I spied the Moor. His back was towards the castle and he was walking rapidly towards Market Jew: and after him padded my lady's hound.

I hurried along the passages and knocked at my master's door. No one answered. I could not wait to knock again, but burst it open.

On the floor at my feet lay my master, and hard by the window my mistress with her hands crossed upon a crucifix. My master had no crucifix: but his face wore a smile—a happier one than it had worn for years.

The Laird's Luck

In a General Order issued from the Horse-Guards on New Year's Day, 1836, His Majesty, King William IV., was pleased to direct, through the Commander-in-Chief, Lord Hill, that "with the view of doing the fullest justice to Regiments, as well as to Individuals who had distinguished themselves in action against the enemy," an account of the services of every Regiment in the British Army should be published, under the supervision of the Adjutant General.

With fair promptitude this scheme was put in hand, under the editorship of Mr. Richard Cannon, Principal Clerk of the Adjutant General's Office. The duty of examining, sifting, and preparing the records of that distinguished Regiment which I shall here call the Moray Highlanders (concealing its real name for reasons which the narrative will make apparent) fell to a certain Major Reginald Sparkes; who in the course of his researches came upon a number of pages in manuscript sealed under one cover and docketed "Memoranda concerning Ensign D.M.J. Mackenzie. J.R., Jan. 3rd, 1816"—the initials being those of Lieut.-Colonel Sir James Ross, who had commanded the 2nd Battalion of the Morays through the campaign of Waterloo. The cover also bore, in the same handwriting, the word "Private," twice underlined.

Of the occurrences related in the enclosed papers—of the private ones, that is—it so happened that of the four eye-witnesses none survived at the date of Major Sparkes' discovery. They had, moreover, so carefully taken their secret with them that the Regiment preserved not a rumour of it. Major Sparkes' own commission was considerably more recent than the Waterloo year, and he at least had heard no whisper of the story. It lay outside the purpose of his inquiry, and he judiciously omitted it from his report. But the time is past when its publication might conceivably have been injurious; and with some alterations in the names—to carry out the disguise of the Regiment—it is here given.

The reader will understand that I use the IPSISSIMA VERBA *of Colonel Ross.*—Q)

1

I had the honour of commanding my regiment, the Moray Highlanders, on the 16th of June, 1815, when the late Ensign David Marie Joseph Mackenzie met his end in the bloody struggle of Quatre Bras (his first engagement). He fell beside the colours, and I gladly bear witness that he had not only borne himself with extreme gallantry, but maintained, under circumstances of severest trial, a coolness which might well have rewarded me for my help in procuring the lad's commission. And yet at the moment I could scarcely regret his death, for he went into action under a suspicion so dishonouring that, had it been proved, no amount of gallantry could have restored him to the respect of his fellows. So at least I believed, with three of his brother officers who shared the secret.

These were Major William Ross (my half-brother), Captain Malcolm Murray, and Mr. Ronald Braintree Urquhart, then our senior ensign. Of these, Mr. Urquhart fell two days later, at Waterloo, while steadying his men to face that heroic shock in which Pack's skeleton regiments were enveloped yet not overwhelmed by four brigades of the French infantry. From the others I received at the time a promise that the accusation against young Mackenzie should be wiped off the slate by his death, and the affair kept secret between us. Since then, however, there has come to me an explanation which—though hard indeed to credit—may, if true, exculpate the lad. I laid it before the others, and they agreed that if, in spite of precautions, the affair should ever come to light, the explanation ought also in justice to be forthcoming; and hence I am writing this memorandum.

It was in the late September of 1814 that I first made acquaintance with David Mackenzie. A wound received in the Battle of Salamanca—a shattered ankle—had sent me home invalided, and on my partial recovery I was appointed to command the 2nd Battalion of my regiment, then being formed at Inverness. To this duty I was equal; but my ankle still gave trouble (the splinters from time to time working through the flesh), and in the late summer of 1814 I obtained leave of absence with my step-brother, and spent some pleasant weeks in cruising and fishing about the Moray Firth. Finding that my leg bettered by this idleness, we hired a smaller boat and embarked on a longer excursion, which took us almost to the south-west end of Loch Ness.

Here, on September 18th, and pretty late in the afternoon, we were overtaken by a sudden squall, which carried away our mast (we found afterwards that it had rotted in the step), and put us for some minutes in no little danger; for my brother and I, being inexpert seamen, did not cut the tangle away, as we should have done, but made a bungling attempt to get the mast on board, with the rigging and drenched sail; and thereby managed to knock a hole in the side of the boat, which at once began to take in water. This compelled us to desist and fall to baling with might and main, leaving the raffle and jagged end of the mast to bump against us at the will of the waves.

In short, we were in a highly unpleasant predicament, when a coble or row-boat, carrying one small lug-sail, hove out of the dusk to our assistance. It was manned by a crew of three, of whom the master (though we had scarce light enough to distinguish features) hailed us in a voice which was patently a gentleman's. He rounded up, lowered sail, and ran his boat alongside; and while his two hands were cutting us free of our tangle, inquired very civilly if we were strangers. We answered that we were, and desired him to tell us of the nearest place alongshore where we might land and find a lodging for the night, as well as a carpenter to repair our damage.

"In any ordinary case," said he, "I should ask you to come aboard and home with me. But my house lies five miles up the lake; your boat is sinking, and the first thing is to beach her. It happens that you are but half a mile from Ardlaugh and a decent carpenter who can answer all requirements. I think, if I stand by you, the thing can be done; and afterwards we will talk of supper."

By diligent baling we were able, under his direction, to bring our boat to a shingly beach, over which a light shone warm in a cottage window. Our hail was quickly answered by a second light. A lantern issued from the building, and we heard the sound of footsteps.

"Is that you, Donald?" cried our rescuer (as I may be permitted to call him).

Before an answer could be returned, we saw that two men were approaching; of whom the one bearing the lantern was a grizzled old carlin with bent knees and a stoop of the shoulders. His companion carried himself with a lighter step. It was he who advanced to salute us, the old man holding the light obediently; and the rays revealed to us a slight, up-standing youth, poorly dressed, but handsome, and with a touch of pride in his bearing.

"Good evening, gentlemen." He lifted his bonnet politely, and turned to our rescuer. "Good evening, Mr. Gillespie," he said—I thought more coldly. "Can I be of any service to your friends?"

Mr. Gillespie's manner had changed suddenly at sight of the young man, whose salutation he acknowledged more coldly and even more curtly than it had been given. "I can scarcely claim them as my friends," he answered. "They are two gentlemen, strangers in these parts, who have met with an accident to their boat: one so serious that I brought them to the nearest landing, which happened to be Donald's." He shortly explained our mishap, while the young man took the lantern in hand and inspected the damage with Donald.

"There is nothing," he announced, "which cannot be set right in a couple of hours; but we must wait till morning. Meanwhile if, as I gather, you have no claim on these gentlemen, I shall beg them to be my guests for the night."

We glanced at Mr. Gillespie, whose manners seemed to have deserted him. He shrugged his shoulders. "Your house is the nearer," said he, "and the sooner they reach a warm fire the better for them after their drenching." And with that he lifted his cap to us, turned abruptly, and pushed off his own boat, scarcely regarding our thanks.

A somewhat awkward pause followed as we stood on the beach, listening to the creak of the thole-pins in the departing boat. After a minute our new acquaintance turned to us with a slightly constrained laugh.

"Mr. Gillespie omitted some of the formalities," said he. "My name is Mackenzie—David Mackenzie; and I live at Ardlaugh Castle, scarcely half a mile up the glen behind us. I warn you that its hospitality is rude, but to what it affords you are heartily welcome."

He spoke with a high, precise courtliness which contrasted oddly with his boyish face (I guessed his age at nineteen or twenty), and still more oddly with his clothes, which were threadbare and patched in many places, yet with a deftness which told of a woman's care. We introduced ourselves by name, and thanked him, with some expressions of regret at inconveniencing (as I put it, at hazard) the family at the Castle.

"Oh!" he interrupted, "I am sole master there. I have no parents living, no family, and," he added, with a slight sullenness which I afterwards recognised as habitual, "I may almost say, no friends: though to be sure, you are lucky enough to have one fellow-guest to-night—the minister of the parish, a Mr. Saul, and a very worthy man."

He broke off to give Donald some instructions about the boat, watched us while we found our plaids and soaked valises, and then took the lantern from the old man's hand. "I ought to have explained," said he, "that we have neither cart here nor carriage: indeed, there is no carriage-road. But Donald has a pony."

He led the way a few steps up the beach, and then halted, perceiving my lameness for the first time. "Donald, fetch out the pony. Can you ride bareback?" he asked: "I fear there's no saddle but an old piece of sacking." In spite of my protestations the pony was led forth; a starved little beast, on whose over-sharp ridge I must have cut a sufficiently ludicrous figure when hoisted into place with the valises slung behind me.

The procession set out, and I soon began to feel thankful for my seat, though I took no ease in it. For the road climbed steeply from the cottage, and at once began to twist up the bottom of a ravine so narrow that we lost all help of the young moon. The path, indeed, resembled the bed of a torrent, shrunk now to a trickle of water, the voice of which ran in my ears while our host led the way, springing from boulder to boulder, avoiding pools, and pausing now and then to hold his lantern over some slippery place. The pony followed with admirable caution, and my brother trudged in the rear and took his cue from us. After five minutes of this the ground grew easier and at the same time steeper, and I guessed that we were slanting up the hillside and away from the torrent at an acute angle. The many twists and angles, and the utter darkness (for we were now moving between trees) had completely baffled my reckoning when—at the end of twenty minutes, perhaps—Mr. Mackenzie halted and allowed me to come up with him.

I was about to ask the reason of this halt when a ray of his lantern fell on a wall of masonry; and with a start almost laughable I knew we had arrived. To come to an entirely strange house at night is an experience which holds some taste of mystery even for the oldest campaigner; but I have never in my life received such a shock as this building gave me—naked, unlit, presented to me out of a darkness in which I had imagined a steep mountain scaur dotted with dwarfed trees—a sudden abomination of desolation standing, like the prophet's, where it ought not. No light showed on the side where we stood—the side over the ravine; only one pointed turret stood out against the faint moonlight glow in the upper sky: but feeling our way around the gaunt side of the building, we came to a back court-yard and two windows lit. Our host whistled, and helped me to dismount.

In an angle of the court a creaking door opened. A woman's voice cried, "That will be be you, Ardlaugh, and none too early! The minister—"

She broke off, catching sight of us. Our host stepped hastily to the door and began a whispered conversation. We could hear that she was protesting, and began to feel awkward enough. But whatever her objections were, her master cut them short.

"Come in, sirs," he invited us: "I warned you that the fare would be hard, but I repeat that you are welcome."

To our surprise and, I must own, our amusement, the woman caught up his words with new protestations, uttered this time at the top of her voice.

"The fare hard? Well, it might not please folks accustomed to city feasts; but Ardlaugh was not yet without a joint of venison in the larder and a bottle of wine, maybe two, maybe three, for any guest its master chose to make welcome. It was 'an ill bird that 'filed his own nest'"—with more to this effect, which our host tried in vain to interrupt.

"Then I will lead you to your rooms," he said, turning to us as soon as she paused to draw breath.

"Indeed, Ardlaugh, you will do nothing of the kind." She ran into the kitchen, and returned holding high a lighted torch—a grey-haired woman with traces of past comeliness, overlaid now by an air of worry, almost of fear. But her manner showed only a defiant pride as she led us up the uncarpeted stairs, past old portraits sagging and rotting in their frames, through bleak corridors, where the windows were patched and the plastered walls discoloured by fungus. Once only she halted. "It will be a long way to your apartments. A grand house!" She had faced round on us, and her eyes seemed to ask a question of ours. "I have known it filled," she added—"filled with guests, and the drink and fiddles never stopping for a week. You will see it better tomorrow. A grand house!"

I will confess that, as I limped after this barbaric woman and her torch, I felt some reasonable apprehensions of the bedchamber towards which they were escorting me. But here came another surprise. The room was of moderate size, poorly furnished, indeed, but comfortable and something more. It bore traces of many petty attentions, even—in its white dimity curtains and valances—of an attempt at daintiness. The sight of it brought quite a pleasant shock after the dirt and disarray of the corridor. Nor was the room assigned to my brother one whit less habitable. But if surprised by all this, I was fairly astounded to find in each room a pair of candles lit—and quite recently lit—beside the looking-glass, and an ewer of hot water standing, with a clean towel upon it, in each wash-hand basin. No sooner had the woman departed than I visited my brother and begged him (while he unstrapped his valise) to explain this apparent miracle. He could only guess with me that the woman had been warned of our arrival by the noise of footsteps in the courtyard, and had dispatched a servant by some back stairs to make ready for us.

Our valises were, fortunately, waterproof. We quickly exchanged our damp clothes for dry ones, and groped our way together along the corridors, helped by the moon, which shone through their uncurtained windows, to the main staircase. Here we came on a scent of roasting meat—appetising to us after our day in the open air—and at the foot found our host waiting for us. He had donned his Highland dress of ceremony—velvet jacket, phillabeg and kilt, with the tartan of his clan—and looked (I must own) extremely well in it, though the garments had long since lost their original gloss. An apology for our rough touring suits led to some few questions and replies about the regimental tartan of the Morays, in the history of which he was passably well informed.

Thus chatting, we entered the great hall of Ardlaugh Castle—a tall, but narrow and ill-proportioned apartment, having an open timber roof, a stone-paved floor, and walls sparsely decorated with antlers and round targes—where a very small man stood warming his back at an immense fireplace. This was the Reverend Samuel Saul, whose acquaintance we had scarce time to make before a cracked gong summoned us to dinner in the adjoining room.

The young Laird of Ardlaugh took his seat in a roughly carved chair of state at the head of the table; but before doing so treated me to another surprise by muttering a Latin grace and crossing himself. Up to now I had taken it for granted he was a member of the Scottish Kirk. I glanced at the minister in some mystification; but he, good man, appeared to have fallen into a brown study, with his eyes fastened upon a dish of apples which adorned the centre of our promiscuously furnished board.

Of the furniture of our meal I can only say that poverty and decent appearance kept up a brave fight throughout. The table-cloth was ragged, but spotlessly clean; the silver-ware scanty and worn with high polishing. The plates and glasses displayed a noble range of patterns, but were for the most part chipped or cracked. Each knife had been worn to a point, and a few of them joggled in their handles. In a lull of the talk I caught myself idly counting the darns in my table-napkin.

They were—if I remember—fourteen, and all exquisitely stitched. The dinner, on the other hand, would have tempted men far less hungry than we—grilled steaks of salmon, a roast haunch of venison, grouse, a milk-pudding, and, for dessert, the dish of apples already mentioned; the meats washed down with one wine only, but that wine was claret, and beautifully sound. I should mention that we were served by a grey-haired retainer, almost stone deaf, and as hopelessly cracked as the gong with which he had beaten us to dinner. In the long waits between the courses we heard him quarrelling outside with the woman who had admitted us; and gradually—I know not how—the conviction grew on me that they were man and wife, and the only servants of our host's establishment. To cover the noise of one of their altercations I began to congratulate the Laird on the quality of his venison, and put some idle question about his care for his deer.

"I have no deer-forest," he answered. "Elspeth is my only housekeeper."

I had some reply on my lips, when my attention was distracted by a sudden movement by the Rev. Samuel Saul. This honest man had, as we shook hands in the great hall, broken into a flood of small talk. On our way to the dining-room he took me, so to speak, by the button-hole, and within the minute so drenched me with gossip about Ardlaugh, its climate, its scenery, its crops, and the dimensions of the parish, that I feared a whole evening of boredom lay before us. But from the moment we seated ourselves at table he dropped to an absolute silence. There are men, living much alone, who by habit talk little during their meals; and the minister might be reserving himself. But I had almost forgotten his presence when I heard a sharp exclamation, and, looking across, saw him take from his lips his wine-glass of claret and set it down with a shaking hand. The laird, too, had heard, and bent a darkly questioning glance on him. At once the little man—whose face had turned to a sickly white—began to stammer and excuse himself.

"It was nothing—a spasm. He would be better of it in a moment. No, he would take no wine: a glass of water would set him right—he was more used to drinking water," he explained, with a small, nervous laugh.

Perceiving that our solicitude embarrassed him, we resumed our talk, which now turned upon the last peninsular campaign and certain engagements in which the Morays had borne part; upon the stability of the French Monarchy, and the career (as we believed, at an end) of Napoleon. On all these topics the Laird showed himself well informed, and while preferring the part of listener (as became his youth) from time to time put in a question which convinced me of his intelligence, especially in military affairs.

The minister, though silent as before, had regained his colour; and we were somewhat astonished when, the cloth being drawn and the company left to its wine and one dish of dessert, he rose and announced that he must be going. He was decidedly better, but (so he excused himself) would feel easier at home in his own manse; and so, declining our host's offer of a bed, he shook hands and bade us goodnight. The laird accompanied him to the door, and in his absence I fell to peeling an apple, while my brother drummed with his fingers on the table and eyed the faded hangings. I suppose that ten minutes elapsed before we heard the young man's footsteps returning through the flagged hall and a woman's voice uplifted.

"But had the minister any complaint, whatever—to ride off without a word? She could answer for the collops—"

"Whist, woman! Have done with your clashin', ye doited old fool!" He slammed the door upon her, stepped to the table, and with a sullen frown poured himself a glass of wine. His brow cleared as he drank it. "I beg your pardon, gentlemen; but this indisposition of Mr. Saul has annoyed me. He lives at the far end of the parish—a good seven miles away—and I had invited him expressly to talk of parish affairs."

"I believe," said I, "you and he are not of the same religion?"

"Eh?" He seemed to be wondering how I had guessed. "No, I was bred a Catholic. In our branch we have always held to the Old Religion. But that doesn't prevent my wishing to stand well with my neighbours and do my duty towards them. What disheartens me is, they won't see it." He pushed the wine aside, and for a while, leaning his elbows on the table and resting his chin on his knuckles, stared gloomily before him. Then, with sudden boyish indignation, he burst out: "It's an infernal shame; that's it—an infernal shame! I haven't been home here a twelvemonth, and the people avoid me like a plague. What have I done? My father wasn't popular—in fact, they hated him. But so did I. And he hated me, God knows: misused my mother, and wouldn't endure me in his presence.

"All my miserable youth I've been mewed up in a school in England—a private seminary. Ugh? what a den it was, too! My mother died calling for me—I was not allowed to come: I hadn't seen her for three years. And now, when the old tyrant is dead, and I come home meaning—so help me!—to straighten things out and make friends—come home, to the poverty you pretend not to notice, though it stares you in the face from every wall—come home, only asking to make the best of of it, live on good terms with my fellows, and be happy for the first time in my life—damn them, they won't fling me a kind look! What have I *done?*—that's what I want to know.

"The queer thing is, they behaved more decently at first. There's that Gillespie, who brought you ashore: he came over the first week, offered me shooting, was altogether as pleasant as could be. I quite took to the fellow. Now, when we meet, he looks the other way! If he has anything against me, he might at least explain: it's all I ask. What have I done?"

Throughout this outburst I sat slicing my apple and taking now and then a glance at the speaker. It was all so hotly and honestly boyish! He only wanted justice. I know something of youngsters, and recognised the cry. Justice! It's the one thing every boy claims confidently as his right, and probably the last thing on earth he will ever get. And this boy looked so handsome, too, sitting in his father's chair, petulant, restive under a weight too heavy (as anyone could see) for his age. I couldn't help liking him.

My brother told me afterwards that I pounced like any recruiting-sergeant. This I do not believe. But what, after a long pause, I said was this: "If you are innocent or unconscious of offending, you can only wait for your neighbours to explain themselves. Meanwhile, why not leave them? Why not travel, for instance?"

"Travel!" he echoed, as much as to say, "You ought to know, without my telling, that I cannot afford it."

"Travel," I repeated; "see the world, rub against men of your age. You might by the way do some fighting."

He opened his eyes wide. I saw the sudden idea take hold of him, and again I liked what I saw.

"If I thought—" He broke off. "You don't mean—" he began, and broke off again.

"I mean the Morays," I said. "There may be difficulties; but at this moment I cannot see any real ones."

By this time he was gripping the arms of his chair. "If I thought—"he harked back, and for the third time broke off. "What a fool I am! It's the last thing they ever put in a boy's head at that infernal school. If you will believe it, they wanted to make a priest of me!"

He sprang up, pushing back his chair. We carried our wine into the great hall, and sat there talking the question over before the fire. Before we parted for the night I had engaged to use all my interest to get him a commission in the Morays; and I left him pacing the hall, his mind in a whirl, but his heart (as was plain to see) exulting in his new prospects.

And certainly, when I came to inspect the castle by the next morning's light, I could understand his longing to leave it. A gloomier, more pretentious, or worse-devised structure I never set eyes on. The Mackenzie who erected it may well have been (as the saying is) his own architect, and had either come to the end of his purse or left his heirs to decide against planting gardens, laying out approaches or even maintaining the pile in decent repair. In place of a drive a grassy cart-track, scored deep with old ruts, led through a gateless entrance into a courtyard where the slates had dropped from the roof and lay strewn like autumn leaves. On this road I encountered the young laird returning from an early tramp with his gun; and he stood still and pointed to the castle with a grimace.

"A white elephant," said I.

"Call it rather the corpse of one," he answered. "Cannot you imagine some *genie* of the Oriental Tales dragging the beast across Europe and dumping it down here in a sudden fit of disgust? As a matter of fact my grandfather built it, and cursed us with poverty thereby. It soured my father's life. I believe the only soul honestly proud of it is Elspeth."

"And I suppose," said I, "you will leave her in charge of it when you join the Morays?"

"Ah!" he broke in, with a voice which betrayed his relief: "you are in earnest about that? Yes Elspeth will look after the castle, as she does already. I am just a child in her hand. When a man has one only servant it's well to have her devoted." Seeing my look of surprise, he added, "I don't count old Duncan, her husband; for he's half-witted, and only serves to break the plates. Does it surprise you to learn that, barring him, Elspeth is my only retainer?"

"H'm," said I, considerably puzzled—I must explain why.

★★★★★

I am by training an extraordinarily light sleeper; yet nothing had disturbed me during the night until at dawn my brother knocked at the door and entered, ready dressed.

"Hullo!" he exclaimed, "are you responsible for this?" and he pointed to a chair at the foot of the bed where lay, folded in a neat pile, not only the clothes I had tossed down carelessly overnight, but the suit in which I had arrived. He picked up this latter, felt it, and handed it to me. It was dry, and had been carefully brushed.

"Our friend keeps a good valet," said I; "but the queer thing is that, in a strange room, I didn't wake. I see he has brought hot water too."

"Look here," my brother asked: "did you lock your door?"

"Why, of course not—the more by token that it hasn't a key."

"Well," said he, "mine has, and I'll swear I used it; but the same thing has happened to me!"

This, I tried to persuade him, was impossible; and for the while he seemed convinced. "It *must* be," he owned; "but if I didn't lock that door I'll never swear to a thing again in all my life."

*****

The young laird's remark set me thinking of this, and I answered after a pause, "In one of the pair, then, you possess a remarkably clever valet."

It so happened that, while I said it, my eyes rested, without the least intention, on the sleeve of his shooting-coat; and the words were scarcely out before he flushed hotly and made a motion as if to hide a neatly mended rent in its cuff. In another moment he would have retorted, and was indeed drawing himself up in anger, when I prevented him by adding—

"I mean that I am indebted to him or to her this morning for a neatly brushed suit; and I suppose to your freeness in plying me with wine last night that it arrived in my room without waking me. But for that I could almost set it down to the supernatural."

I said this in all simplicity, and was quite unprepared for its effect upon him, or for his extraordinary reply. He turned as white in the face as, a moment before, he had been red. "Good God!" he said eagerly, "you haven't missed anything, have you?"

"Certainly not," I assured him. "My dear sir—"

"I know, I know. But you see," he stammered, "I am new to these servants. I know them to be faithful, and that's all. Forgive me; I feared from your tone one of them—Duncan perhaps—"

He did not finish his sentence, but broke into a hurried walk and led me towards the house. A minute later, as we approached it, he began to discourse half-humorously on its more glaring features, and had apparently forgotten his perturbation.

I too attached small importance to it, and recall it now merely through unwillingness to omit any circumstance which may throw light on a story sufficiently dark to me. After breakfast our host walked down with us to the loch-side, where we found old Donald putting the last touches on his job. With thanks for our entertainment we shook hands and pushed off: and my last word at parting was a promise to remember his ambition and write any news of my success.

2

I anticipated no difficulty, and encountered none. The *Gazette* of January, 1815, announced that David Marie Joseph Mackenzie, gentleman, had been appointed to an ensigncy in the —th Regiment of Infantry (Moray Highlanders); and I timed my letter of congratulation to reach him with the news. Within a week he had joined us at Inverness, and was made welcome.

I may say at once that during his brief period of service I could find no possible fault with his bearing as a soldier. From the first he took seriously to the calling of arms, and not only showed himself punctual on parade and in all the small duties of barracks, but displayed, in his reserved way, a zealous resolve to master whatever by book or conversation could be learned of the higher business of war. My junior officers—though when the test came, as it soon did, they acquitted themselves most creditably—showed, as a whole, just then no great promise. For the most part they were young lairds, like Mr. Mackenzie, or cadets of good Highland families; but, unlike him, they had been allowed to run wild, and chafed under harness. One or two of them had the true Highland addiction to card-playing; and though I set a pretty stern face against this curse—as I dare to call it—its effects were to be traced in late hours, more than one case of shirking "rounds," and a general slovenliness at morning parade.

In such company Mr. Mackenzie showed to advantage, and I soon began to value him as a likely officer. Nor, in my dissatisfaction with them, did it give me any uneasiness—as it gave me no surprise—to find that his brother-officers took less kindly to him. He kept a certain reticence of manner, which either came of a natural shyness or had been ingrained in him at the Roman Catholic seminary. He was poor, too; but poverty did not prevent his joining in all the regimental amusements, figuring modestly but sufficiently on the subscription lists, and even taking a hand at cards for moderate stakes. Yet he made no headway, and his popularity diminished instead of growing. All this I noted, but without discovering any definite reason. Of his professional promise, on the other hand, there could be no question; and the men liked and respected him.

Our senior ensign at this date was a Mr. Urquhart, the eldest son of a West Highland laird, and heir to a considerable estate. He had been in barracks when Mr. Mackenzie joined; but a week later his father's sudden illness called for his presence at home, and I granted him a leave of absence, which was afterwards extended. I regretted this, not only for the sad occasion, but because it deprived the battalion for a time of one of its steadiest officers, and Mr. Mackenzie in particular of the chance to form a very useful friendship. For the two young men had (I thought) several qualities which might well attract them each to the other, and a common gravity of mind in contrast with their companions' prevalent and somewhat tiresome frivolity. Of the two I judged Mr. Urquhart (the elder by a year) to have the more stable character. He was a good-looking, dark-complexioned young Highlander, with a serious expression which, without being gloomy, did not escape a touch of melancholy. I should judge this melancholy of Mr. Urquhart's constitutional, and the boyish sullenness which lingered on Mr. Mackenzie's equally handsome face to have been imposed rather by circumstances.

Mr. Urquhart rejoined us on the 24th of February. Two days later, as all the world knows, Napoleon made his escape from Elba; and the next week or two made it certain not only that the allies must fight, but that the British contingent must be drawn largely, if not in the main, from the second battalions then drilling up and down the country. The 29th of March brought us our marching orders; and I will own that, while feeling no uneasiness about the great issue, I distrusted the share my raw youngsters were to take in it.

On the 12th of April we were landed at Ostend, and at once marched up to Brussels, where we remained until the middle of June, having been assigned to the 5th (Picton's) Division of the Reserve. For some reason the Highland regiments had been massed into the Reserve, and were billeted about the capital, our own quarters lying between the 92nd (Gordons) and General Kruse's Nassauers, whose lodgings stretched out along the Louvain road; and although I could have wished some harder and more responsible service to get the Morays into training, I felt what advantage they derived from rubbing shoulders with the fine fellows of the 42nd, 79th, and 92nd, all First Battalions toughened by Peninsular work.

The gaieties of life in Brussels during these two months have been described often enough; but among the military they were chiefly confined to those officers whose means allowed them to keep the pace set by rich civilians, and the Morays played the part of amused spectators. Yet the work and the few gaieties which fell to our share, while adding to our experiences, broke up to some degree the old domestic habits of the battalion. Excepting on duty I saw less of Mr. Mackenzie and thought less about him; he might be left now to be shaped by active service. But I was glad to find him often in company with Mr. Urquhart.

I come now to the memorable night of June 15th, concerning which and the end it brought upon the festivities of Brussels so much has been written. All the world has heard of the Duchess of Richmond's ball, and seems to conspire in decking it out with pretty romantic fables. To contradict the most of these were waste of time; but I may point out (1) that the ball was over and, I believe, all the company dispersed, before the actual alarm awoke the capital; and (2) that all responsible officers gathered there shared the knowledge that such an alarm was impending, might arrive at any moment, and would almost certainly arrive within a few hours.

News of the French advance across the frontier and attack on General Zieten's outposts had reached Wellington at three o'clock that afternoon. It should have been brought five hours earlier; but he gave his orders at once, and quietly, and already our troops were massing for defence upon Nivelles. We of the Reserve had secret orders to hold ourselves prepared. Obedient to a hint from their commander-in-chief, the generals of division and brigade who attended the duchess' ball withdrew themselves early on various pleas. Her Grace had honoured me with an invitation, probably because I represented a Highland regiment; and Highlanders (especially the Gordons, her brother's regiment) were much to the fore that night with reels, flings, and strathspeys. The many withdrawals warned me that something was in the wind, and after remaining just so long as seemed respectful, I took leave of my hostess and walked homewards across the city as the clocks were striking eleven.

We of the Morays had our headquarters in a fairly large building—the Hôtel de Liège—in time of peace a resort of *commis-voyageurs* of the better class. It boasted a roomy hall, out of which opened two coffee-rooms, converted by us into guard- and mess-room. A large drawing-room on the first floor overlooking the street served me for sleeping as well as working quarters, and to reach it I must pass the *entresol*, where a small apartment had been set aside for occasional uses. We made it, for instance, our ante-room, and assembled there before mess; a few would retire there for smoking or card-playing; during the day it served as a waiting-room for messengers or any one whose business could not be for the moment attended to.

I had paused at the entrance to put some small question to the sentry, when I heard the crash of a chair in this room, and two voices broke out in fierce altercation. An instant after, the mess-room door opened, and Captain Murray, without observing me, ran past me and up the stairs. As he reached the *entresol*, a voice—my brother's—called down from an upper landing, and demanded, "What's wrong there?"

"I don't know, Major," Captain Murray answered, and at the same moment flung the door open. I was quick on his heels, and he wheeled round in some surprise at my voice, and to see me interposed between him and my brother, who had come running downstairs, and now stood behind my shoulder in the entrance.

"Shut the door," I commanded quickly. "Shut the door, and send away anyone you may hear outside. Now, gentlemen, explain yourselves, please."

Mr. Urquhart and Mr. Mackenzie faced each other across a small table, from which the cloth had been dragged and lay on the floor with a scattered pack of cards. The elder lad held a couple of cards in his hand; he was white in the face.

"He cheated!" He swung round upon me in a kind of indignant fury, and tapped the cards with his forefinger.

I looked from him to the accused. Mackenzie's face was dark, almost purple, rather with rage (as it struck me) than with shame.

"It's a lie." He let out the words slowly, as if holding rein on his passion. "Twice he's said so, and twice I've called him a liar." He drew back for an instant, and then lost control of himself. "If that's not enough—." He leapt forward, and almost before Captain Murray could interpose had hurled himself upon Urquhart.

The table between them went down with a crash, and Urquhart went staggering back from a blow which just missed his face and took him on the collar-bone before Murray threw both arms around the assailant.

"Mr. Mackenzie," said I, "you will consider yourself under arrest. Mr. Urquhart, you will hold yourself ready to give me a full explanation. Whichever of you may be in the right, this is a disgraceful business, and dishonouring to your regiment and the cloth you wear: so disgraceful, that I hesitate to call up the guard and expose it to more eyes than ours. If Mr. Mackenzie"—I turned to him again—"can behave himself like a gentleman, and accept the fact of his arrest without further trouble, the scandal can at least be postponed until I discover how much it is necessary to face. For the moment, sir, you are in charge of Captain Murray. Do you understand?"

He bent his head sullenly. "He shall fight me, whatever happens," he muttered.

I found it wise to pay no heed to this. "It will be best," I said to Murray, "to remain here with Mr. Mackenzie until I am ready for him. Mr. Urquhart may retire to his quarters, if he will—I advise it, indeed—but I shall require his attendance in a few minutes. You understand," I added significantly, "that for the present this affair remains strictly between ourselves." I knew well enough that, for all the king's regulations, a meeting would inevitably follow sooner or later, and will own I looked upon it as the proper outcome, between gentlemen, of such a quarrel. But it was not for me, their colonel, to betray this knowledge or my feelings, and by imposing secrecy I put off for the time all the business of a formal challenge with seconds. So I left them, and requesting my brother to follow me, mounted to my own room. The door was no sooner shut than I turned on him.

"Surely," I said, "this is a bad mistake of Urquhart's? It's an incredible charge. From all I've seen of him, the lad would never be guilty …" I paused, expecting his assent. To my surprise he did not give it, but stood fingering his chin and looking serious.

"I don't know," he answered unwillingly. "There are stories against him."

"What stories?"

"Nothing definite." My brother hesitated. "It doesn't seem fair to him to repeat mere whispers. But the others don't like him."

"Hence the whispers, perhaps. They have not reached me."

"They would not. He is known to be a favourite of yours. But they don't care to play with him." My brother stopped, met my look, and answered it with a shrug of the shoulders, adding, "He wins pretty constantly."

"Any definite charge before tonight's?"

"No: at least, I think not. But Urquhart may have been put up to watch."

"Fetch him up, please," said I promptly; and seating myself at the writing-table I lit candles (for the lamp was dim), made ready the writing materials and prepared to take notes of the evidence.

Mr. Urquhart presently entered, and I wheeled round in my chair to confront him. He was still exceedingly pale—paler, I thought, than I had left him. He seemed decidedly ill at ease, though not on his own account. His answer to my first question made me fairly leap in my chair.

"I wish," he said, "to qualify my accusation of Mr. Mackenzie. That he cheated I have the evidence of my own eyes; but I am not sure how far he knew he was cheating."

"Good heavens, sir!" I cried. "Do you know you have accused that young man of a villainy which must damn him for life? And now you tell me—" I broke off in sheer indignation.

"I know," he answered quietly. "The noise fetched you in upon us on the instant, and the mischief was done."

"Indeed, sir," I could not avoid sneering, "to most of us it would seem that the mischief was done when you accused a brother-officer of fraud to his face."

He seemed to reflect. "Yes, sir," he assented slowly; "it is done. I saw him cheat: that I must persist in; but I cannot say how far he was conscious of it. And since I cannot, I must take the consequences."

"Will you kindly inform us how it is possible for a player to cheat and not know that he is cheating?"

He bent his eyes on the carpet as if seeking an answer. It was long in coming. "No," he said at last, in a slow, dragging tone, "I cannot."

"Then you will at least tell us exactly what Mr. Mackenzie did."

Again there was a long pause. He looked at me straight, but with hopelessness in his eyes. "I fear you would not believe me. It would not be worthwhile. If you can grant it, sir, I would ask time to decide."

"Mr. Urquhart," said I sternly, "are you aware you have brought against Mr. Mackenzie a charge under which no man of honour can live easily for a moment? You ask me without a word of evidence in substantiation to keep him in torture while I give you time. It is monstrous, and I beg to remind you that, unless your charge is proved, you can—and will—be broken for making it."

"I know it, sir," he answered firmly enough; "and because I knew it, I asked—perhaps selfishly—for time. If you refuse, I will at least ask permission to see a priest before telling a story which I can scarcely expect you to believe." Mr. Urquhart too was a Roman Catholic.

But my temper for the moment was gone. "I see little chance," said I, "of keeping this scandal secret, and regret it the less if the consequences are to fall on a rash accuser. But just now I will have no meddling priest share the secret. For the present, one word more. Had you heard before this evening of any hints against Mr. Mackenzie's play?"

He answered reluctantly, "Yes."

"And you set yourself to lay a trap for him?"

"No, sir; I did not. Unconsciously I may have been set on the watch: no, that is wrong—I *did* watch. But I swear it was in every hope and expectation of clearing him. He was my friend. Even when I saw, I had at first no intention to expose him until—"

"That is enough, sir," I broke in, and turned to my brother. "I have no option but to put Mr. Urquhart too under arrest. Kindly convey him back to his room, and send Captain Murray to me. He may leave Mr. Mackenzie in the *entresol*."

My brother led Urquhart out, and in a minute Captain Murray tapped at my door. He was an honest Scot, not too sharp-witted, but straight as a die. I am to show him this description, and he will cheerfully agree with it.

"This is a hideous business, Murray," said I as he entered. "There's something wrong with Urquhart's story. Indeed, between ourselves it has the fatal weakness that he won't tell it."

Murray took a minute to digest this, then he answered, "I don't know anything about Urquhart's story, sir. But there's something wrong about Urquhart." Here he hesitated.

"Speak out, man," said I: "in confidence. That's understood."

"Well, sir," said he, "Urquhart won't fight."

"Ah! so that question came up, did it?" I asked, looking at him sharply.

He was not abashed, but answered, with a twinkle in his eye, "I believe, sir, you gave me no orders to stop their talking, and in a case like this—between youngsters—some question of a meeting would naturally come up. You see, I know both the lads. Urquhart I really like; but he didn't show up well, I must own—to be fair to the other, who is in the worse fix."

"I am not so sure of that," I commented; "but go on."

He seemed surprised. "Indeed, Colonel? Well," he resumed, "I being the sort of fellow they could talk before, a meeting was discussed. The question was how to arrange it without seconds—that is, without breaking your orders and dragging in outsiders. For Mackenzie wanted blood at once, and for awhile Urquhart seemed just as eager. All of a sudden, when…." here he broke off suddenly, not wishing to commit himself.

"Tell me only what you think necessary," said I.

He thanked me. "That is what I wanted," he said. "Well, all of a sudden, when we had found out a way and Urquhart was discussing it, he pulled himself up in the middle of a sentence, and with his eyes fixed on the other—a most curious look it was—he waited while you could count ten, and, 'No,' says he, 'I'll not fight you at once'—for we had been arranging something of the sort—'not tonight, anyway, nor tomorrow,' he says. 'I'll fight you; but I won't have your blood on my head *in that way*.' Those were his words. I have no notion what he meant; but he kept repeating them, and would not explain, though Mackenzie tried him hard and was for shooting across the table. He was repeating them when the major interrupted us and called him up."

"He has behaved ill from the first," said I. "To me the whole affair begins to look like an abominable plot against Mackenzie. Certainly I cannot entertain a suspicion of his guilt upon a bare assertion which Urquhart declines to back with a tittle of evidence."

"The devil he does!" mused Captain Murray. "That looks bad for him. And yet, sir, I'd sooner trust Urquhart than Mackenzie, and if the case lies against Urquhart—"

"It will assuredly break him," I put in, "unless he can prove the charge, or that he was honestly mistaken."

"Then, sir," said the captain, "I'll have to show you this. It's ugly, but it's only justice."

He pulled a sovereign from his pocket and pushed it on the writing-table under my nose.

"What does this mean?"

"It is a marked one," said he.

"So I perceive." I had picked up the coin and was examining it.

"I found it just now," he continued, "in the room below. The upsetting of the table had scattered Mackenzie's stakes about the floor."

"You seem to have a pretty notion of evidence," I observed sharply. "I don't know what accusation this coin may carry; but why need it be Mackenzie's? He might have won it from Urquhart."

"I thought of that," was the answer. "But no money had

changed hands. I enquired. The quarrel arose over the second deal, and as a matter of fact Urquhart had laid no money on the table, but made a pencil-note of a few shillings he lost by the first hand. You may remember, sir, how the table stood when you entered."

I reflected. "Yes, my recollection bears you out. Do I gather that you have confronted Mackenzie with this?"

"No. I found it and slipped it quietly into my pocket. I thought we had trouble enough on hand for the moment."

"Who marked this coin?"

"Young Fraser, sir, in my presence. He has been losing small sums, he declares, by pilfering. We suspected one of the orderlies."

"In this connection you had no suspicion of Mr. Mackenzie?"

"None, sr." He considered for a moment, and added: "There was a curious thing happened three weeks ago over my watch. It found its way one night to Mr. Mackenzie's quarters. He brought it to me in the morning; said it was lying, when he awoke, on the table beside his bed. He seemed utterly puzzled. He had been to one or two already to discover the owner. We joked him about it, the more by token that his own watch had broken down the day before and was away at the mender's. The whole thing was queer, and has not been explained. Of course in that instance he was innocent: everything proves it. It just occurred to me as worth mentioning, because in both instances the lad may have been the victim of a trick."

"I am glad you did so," I said; "though just now it does not throw any light that I can see." I rose and paced the room. "Mr. Mackenzie had better be confronted with this, too, and hear your evidence. It's best he should know the worst against him; and if he be guilty it may move him to confession."

"Certainly, sir," Captain Murray assented. "Shall I fetch him?"

"No, remain where you are," I said; "I will go for him myself."

I understood that Mr. Urquhart had retired to his own quarters or to my brother's, and that Mr. Mackenzie had been left in the *entresol* alone. But as I descended the stairs quietly I heard within that room a voice which at first persuaded me he had company, and next that, left to himself, he had broken down and given way to the most childish wailing. The voice was so unlike his, or any grown man's, that it arrested me on the lowermost stair against my will. It resembled rather the sobbing of an infant mingled with short strangled cries of contrition and despair.

"What shall I do? What shall I do? I didn't mean it—I meant to do good! What shall I do?"

So much I heard (as I say) against my will, before my astonishment gave room to a sense of shame at playing, even for a moment, the eavesdropper upon the lad I was to judge. I stepped quickly to the door, and with a warning rattle (to give him time to recover himself) turned the handle and entered.

He was alone, lying back in an easy chair—not writhing there in anguish of mind, as I had fully expected, but sunk rather in a state of dull and hopeless apathy. To reconcile his attitude with the sounds I had just heard was merely impossible; and it bewildered me worse than any in the long chain of bewildering incidents. For five seconds or so he appeared not to see me; but when he grew aware his look changed suddenly to one of utter terror, and his eyes, shifting from me, shot a glance about the room as if he expected some new accusation to dart at him from the corners. His indignation and passionate defiance were gone: his eyes seemed to ask me, "How much do you know?" before he dropped them and stood before me, sullenly submissive.

"I want you upstairs," said I: "not to hear your defence on this charge, for Mr. Urquhart has not yet specified it. But there is another matter."

"Another?" he echoed dully, and, I observed, without surprise.

I led the way back to the room where Captain Murray waited. "Can you tell me anything about this?" I asked, pointing to the sovereign on the writing-table.

He shook his head, clearly puzzled, but anticipating mischief.

"The coin is marked, you see. I have reason to know that it was marked by its owner in order to detect a thief. Captain Murray found it just now among your stakes."

Somehow—for I liked the lad—I had not the heart to watch his face as I delivered this. I kept my eyes upon the coin, and waited, expecting an explosion—a furious denial, or at least a cry that he was the victim of a conspiracy. None came. I heard him breathing hard. After a long and very dreadful pause some words broke from him, so lowly uttered that my ears only just caught them.

"This too? O my God!"

I seated myself, the lad before me, and Captain Murray erect and rigid at the end of the table. "Listen, my lad," said I. "This wears an ugly look, but that a stolen coin has been found in your possession does not prove that you've stolen it."

"I did not. Sir, I swear to you on my honour, and before Heaven, that I did not."

"Very well," said I: "Captain Murray asserts that he found this among the moneys you had been staking at cards. Do you question that assertion?"

He answered almost without pondering. "No, sir. Captain Murray is a gentleman, and incapable of falsehood. If he says so, it was so."

"Very well again. Now, can you explain how this coin came into your possession?"

At this he seemed to hesitate; but answered at length, "No, I cannot explain."

"Have you any idea? Or can you form any guess?"

Again there was a long pause before the answer came in low and strained tones: "I can guess."

"What is your guess?"

He lifted a hand and dropped it hopelessly. "You would not believe," he said.

I will own a suspicion flashed across my mind on hearing

these words—the very excuse given a while ago by Mr. Urquhart—that the whole affair was a hoax and the two young men were in conspiracy to fool me. I dismissed it at once: the sight of Mr. Mackenzie's face, was convincing. But my temper was gone.

"Believe you?" I exclaimed. "You seem to think the one thing I can swallow as creditable, even probable, is that an officer in the Morays has been pilfering and cheating at cards. Oddly enough, it's the last thing I'm going to believe without proof, and the last charge I shall pass without clearing it up to my satisfaction. Captain Murray, will you go and bring me Mr. Urquhart and the major?"

As Captain Murray closed the door I rose, and with my hands behind me took a turn across the room to the fireplace, then back to the writing-table.

"Mr. Mackenzie," I said, "before we go any further I wish you to believe that I am your friend as well as your colonel. I did something to start you upon your career, and I take a warm interest in it. To believe you guilty of these charges will give me the keenest grief. However unlikely your defence may sound—and you seem to fear it—I will give it the best consideration I can. If you are innocent, you shall not find me prejudiced because many are against you and you are alone. Now, this coin—" I turned to the table.

The coin was gone.

I stared at the place where it had lain; then at the young man. He had not moved. My back had been turned for less than two seconds, and I could have sworn he had not budged from the square of carpet on which he had first taken his stand, and on which his feet were still planted. On the other hand, I was equally positive the incriminating coin had lain on the table at the moment I turned my back.

"It is gone!" cried I.

"Gone?" he echoed, staring at the spot to which my finger pointed. In the silence our glances were still crossing when my brother tapped at the door and brought in Mr. Urquhart, Captain Murray following.

Dismissing for a moment this latest mystery, I addressed Mr. Urquhart. "I have sent for you, sir, to request in the first place that here in Mr. Mackenzie's presence and in colder blood you will either withdraw or repeat and at least attempt to substantiate the charge you brought against him."

"I adhere to it, sir, that there was cheating. To withdraw would be to utter a lie. Does he deny it?"

I glanced at Mr. Mackenzie. "I deny that I cheated," said he sullenly.

"Further," pursued Mr. Urquhart, "I repeat what I told you, sir. He *may*, while profiting by it have been unaware of the cheat. At the moment I thought it impossible; but I am willing to believe—"

"*You* are willing!" I broke in. "And pray, sir, what about me, his colonel, and the rest of his brother officers? Have you the coolness to suggest—"

But the full question was never put, and in this world it will never be answered. A bugle call, distant but clear, cut my sentence in half. It came from the direction of the Place d'Armes. A second bugle echoed, it from the height of the Montagne du Parc, and within a minute its note was taken up and answered across the darkness from quarter after quarter.

We looked at one another in silence. "Business," said my brother at length, curtly and quietly.

Already the rooms above us were astir. I heard windows thrown open, voices calling questions, feet running.

"Yes," said I, "it is business at length, and for the while this inquiry must end. Captain Murray, look to your company. You, Major, see that the lads tumble out quick to the alarm-post. One moment!"—and Captain Murray halted with his hand on the door—"It is understood that for the present no word of tonight's affair passes our lips." I turned to Mr. Mackenzie and answered the question I read in the lad's eyes. "Yes, sir; for the present I take off your arrest. Get your sword. It shall be your good fortune to answer the enemy before answering me."

To my amazement Mr. Urquhart interposed. He was, if possible, paler and more deeply agitated than before. "Sir, I entreat you not to allow Mr. Mackenzie to go. I have reasons—I was mistaken just now—"

"Mistaken, sir?"

"Not in what I saw. I refused to fight him—under a mistake. I thought—"

But I cut his stammering short. "As for you," I said, "the most charitable construction I can put on your behaviour is to believe you mad. For the present you, too, are free to go and do your duty. Now leave me. Business presses, and I am sick and angry at the sight of you."

It was just two in the morning when I reached the alarm-post. Brussels by this time was full of the rolling of drums and screaming of pipes; and the regiment formed up in darkness rendered tenfold more confusing by a mob of citizens, some wildly excited, others paralysed by terror, and all intractable. We had, moreover, no small trouble to disengage from our ranks the wives and families who had most unwisely followed many officers abroad, and now clung to their dear ones bidding them farewell. To end this most distressing scene I had in some instances to use a roughness which it still afflicts me to remember. Yet in actual time it was soon overhand dawn scarcely breaking when the Morays with the other regiments of Pack's brigade filed out of the park and fell into stride on the road which leads southward to Charleroi.

In this record it would be immaterial to describe either our march or the since-famous engagement which terminated it. Very early we began to hear the sound of heavy guns far ahead and to make guesses at their distance; but it was close upon two in the afternoon before we reached the high ground above Quatre Bras, and saw the battle spread below us like a picture. The Prince of Orange had been fighting his ground stubbornly since seven in the morning. Ney's superior artillery and far superior cavalry had forced him back, it is true; but he still covered the cross-roads which were the key of his defence, and his position remained sound, though it was fast becoming critical. Just as we arrived, the French, who had already mastered the farm of Piermont, on the left of the Charleroi road, began to push their skirmishers into a thicket below it and commanding the road running east to Namur. Indeed, for a short space they had this road at their mercy, and the chance within grasp of doubling up our left by means of it.

This happened, I say, just as we arrived; and Wellington, who had reached Quatre Bras a short while ahead of us (having fetched a circuit from Brussels through Ligny, where he paused to inspect Field-Marshal Blücher's dispositions for battle), at once saw the danger, and detached one of our regiments, the 95th Rifles, to drive back the *tirailleurs* from the thicket; which, albeit scarcely breathed after their march, they did with a will, and so regained the Allies' hold upon the Namur road. The rest of us meanwhile defiled down this same road, formed line in front of it, and under a brisk cannonade from the French heights waited for the next move.

It was not long in coming. Ney, finding that our artillery made poor play against his, prepared to launch a column against us. Warned by a cloud of skirmishers, our light companies leapt forward, chose their shelter, and began a very pretty exchange of musketry. But this was preliminary work only, and soon the head of a large French column appeared on the slope to our right, driving the Brunswickers slowly before it. It descended a little way, and suddenly broke into three or four columns of attack. The mischief no sooner threatened than Picton came galloping along our line and roaring that our division would advance and engage with all speed. For a raw regiment like the Morays this was no light test; but, supported by a veteran regiment on either hand, they bore it admirably.

Dropping the Gordons to protect the road in case of mishap, the two brigades swung forward in the prettiest style, their skirmishers running in and forming on either flank as they advanced. Then for a while the work was hot; but, as will always happen when column is boldly met by line, the French quickly had enough of our enveloping fire, and wavered. A short charge with the bayonet finished it, and drove them in confusion up the slope: nor had I an easy task to resume a hold on my youngsters and restrain them from pursuing too far. The brush had been sharp, but I had the satisfaction of knowing that the Morays had behaved well. They also knew it, and fell to jesting in high good-humour as General Pack withdrew the brigade from the ground of its exploit and posted us in line with the 42nd and 44th regiments on the left of the main road to Charleroi.

To the right of the Charleroi road, and some way in advance of our position, the Brunswickers were holding ground as best they could under a hot and accurate artillery fire. Except for this, the battle had come to a lull, when a second mass of the enemy began to move down the slopes: a battalion in line heading two columns of infantry direct upon the Brunswickers, while squadron after squadron of lancers crowded down along the road into which by weight of numbers they must be driven. The Duke of Brunswick, perceiving his peril, headed a charge of his lancers upon the advancing infantry, but without the least effect. His horsemen broke. He rode back and called on his infantry to retire in good order. They also broke, and in the attempt to rally them he fell mortally wounded.

The line taken by these flying Brunswickers would have brought them diagonally across the Charleroi road into our arms, had not the French lancers seized this moment to charge straight down it in a body. They encountered, and the indiscriminate mass was hurled on to us, choking and overflowing the causeway. In a minute we were swamped—the two Highland regiments and the 44th bending against a sheer weight of French horsemen.

So suddenly came the shock that the 42nd had no time to form square, until two companies were cut off and well-nigh destroyed; *then* that noble regiment formed around the horsemen who could boast of having broken it, and left not one to bear back the tale. The 44th behaved more cleverly, but not more intrepidly: it did not attempt to form square, but faced its rear rank round and gave the Frenchmen a volley; before they could checks their impetus the front rank poured in a second; and the light company, which had held its fire, delivered a third, breaking the crowd in two, and driving the hinder-part back in disorder and up the Charleroi road. But already the fore-part had fallen upon the Morays, fortunately the last of the three regiments to receive the shock. Though most fortunate, they had least experience, and were consequently slow in answering my shout.

A wedge of lancers broke through us as we formed around the two standards, and I saw Mr. Urquhart with the king's colours hurled back in the rush. The pole fell with him, after swaying within a yard of a French lancer, who thrust out an arm to grasp it. And with that I saw Mackenzie divide the rush and stand—it may have been for five seconds—erect, with his foot upon the standard. Then three lancers pierced him, and he fell. But the lateral pressure of their own troopers broke the wedge which the French had pushed into us. Their leading squadrons were pressed down the road and afterwards accounted for by the Gordons. Of the seven-and-twenty assailants around whom the Morays now closed, not one survived.

Towards nightfall, as Ney weakened and the Allies were reinforced, our troops pushed forward and recaptured every important position taken by the French that morning. The Morays, with the rest of Picton's division, bivouacked for the night in and around the farmstead of Gemiancourt.

So obstinately had the field been contested that darkness fell before the wounded could be collected with any thoroughness; and the comfort of the men around many a camp-fire was disturbed by groans (often quite near at hand) of some poor comrade or enemy lying helpless and undiscovered, or exerting his shattered limbs to crawl towards the blaze. And these interruptions at length became so distressing to the Morays, that two or three officers sought me and demanded leave to form a fatigue party of volunteers and explore the hedges and thickets with lanterns. Among them was Mr. Urquhart: and having readily given leave and accompanied them some little way on their search, I was bidding them goodnight and good-speed when I found him standing at my elbow.

"May I have a word with you, Colonel?" he asked.

His voice was low and serious. Of course I knew what subject filled his thoughts. "Is it worth while, sir?" I answered. "I have lost to-day a brave lad for whom I had a great affection. For him the account is closed; but not for those who liked him and are still concerned in his good name. If you have anything further against him, or if you have any confession to make, I warn you that this is a bad moment to choose."

"I have only to ask," said he, "that you will grant me the first convenient hour for explaining; and to remind you that when I besought you not to send him into action to-day, I had no time to give you reasons."

"This is extraordinary talk, sir. I am not used to command the Morays under advice from my subalterns. And in this instance I had reasons for not even listening to you." He was silent. "Moreover," I continued, "you may as well know, though I am under no obligation to tell you, that I do most certainly not regret having given that permission to one who justified it by a signal service to his king and country."

"But would you have sent him *knowing* that he must die? Colonel," he went on rapidly, before I could interrupt, "I beseech you to listen. I knew he had only a few hours to live. I saw his wraith last night. It stood behind his shoulder in the room when in Captain Murray's presence he challenged me to fight him. You are a Highlander, sir: you may be sceptical about the second sight; but at least you must have heard many claim it. I swear positively that I saw Mr. Mackenzie's wraith last night, and for that reason, and no other, tried to defer the meeting. To fight him, knowing he must die, seemed to me as bad as murder. Afterwards, when the alarm sounded and you took off his arrest, I knew that his fate must overtake him—that my refusal had done no good. I tried to interfere again, and you would not hear. Naturally you would not hear; and very likely, if you had, his fate would have found him in some other way. That is what I try to believe. I hope it is not selfish, sir; but the doubt tortures me."

"Mr. Urquhart," I asked, "is this the only occasion on which you have possessed the second sight, or had reason to think so?"

"No, sir."

"Was it the first or only time last night you believed you were granted it?"

"It was the *second* time last night," he said steadily.

We had been walking back to my bivouac fire, and in the light of it I turned and said: "I will hear your story at the first opportunity. I will not promise to believe, but I will hear and weigh it. Go now and join the others in their search."

He saluted, and strode away into the darkness. The opportunity I promised him never came. At eleven o'clock next morning we began our withdrawal, and within twenty-four hours the Battle of Waterloo had begun. In one of the most heroic feats of that day—the famous resistance of Pack's brigade—Mr. Urquhart was among the first to fall.

3

Thus it happened that an affair which so nearly touched the honour of the Morays, and which had been agitating me at the very moment when the bugle sounded in the Place d'Armes, became a secret shared by three only. The regiment joined in the occupation of Paris, and did not return to Scotland until the middle of December.

I had ceased to mourn for Mr. Mackenzie, but neither to regret him nor to speculate on the mystery which closed his career, and which, now that death had sealed Mr. Urquhart's lips, I could no longer hope to penetrate, when, on the day of my return to Inverness, I was reminded of him by finding, among the letters and papers awaiting me, a visiting-card neatly indited with the name of the Reverend Samuel Saul. On inquiry I learnt that the minister had paid at least three visits to Inverness during the past fortnight, and had, on each occasion, shown much anxiety to learn when the battalion might be expected.

He had also left word that he wished to see me on a matter of much importance.

Sure enough, at ten o'clock next morning the little man presented himself. He was clearly bursting to disclose his business, and our salutations were scarce over when he ran to the door and called to someone in the passage outside.

"Elspeth! Step inside, woman. The housekeeper, sir, to the late Mr. Mackenzie of Ardlaugh," he explained, as he held the door to admit her.

She was dressed in ragged mourning, and wore a grotesque and fearful bonnet. As she saluted me respectfully I saw that her eyes indeed were dry and even hard, but her features set in an expression of quiet and hopeless misery. She did not speak, but left explanation to the minister.

"You will guess, sir," began Mr. Saul, "that we have called to learn more of the poor lad." And he paused.

"He died most gallantly," said I: "died in the act of saving the colours. No soldier could have wished for a better end."

"To be sure, to be sure. So it was reported to us. He died, as one might say, without a stain on his character?" said Mr. Saul, with a sort of question in his tone.

"He died," I answered, "in a way which could only do credit to his name."

A somewhat constrained silence followed. The woman broke it. "You are not telling us all," she said, in a slow, harsh voice.

It took me aback. "I am telling all that needs to be known," I assured her.

"No doubt, sir, no doubt," Mr. Saul interjected. "Hold your tongue, woman. I am going to tell Colonel Ross a tale which may or may not bear upon anything he knows. If not, he will interrupt me before I go far; but if he says nothing I shall take it I have his leave to continue. Now, sir, on the 16th day of June last, and at six in the morning—that would be the day of Quatre Bras—"

He paused for me to nod assent, and continued. "At six in the morning or a little earlier, this woman, Elspeth Mackenzie, came to me at the Manse in great perturbation. She had walked all the way from Ardlaugh. It had come to her (she said) that the young Laird abroad was in great trouble since the previous evening. I asked, 'What trouble? Was it danger of life, for instance?'—asking it not seriously, but rather to compose her; for at first I set down her fears to an old woman's whimsies. Not that I would call Elspeth old precisely—"

Here he broke off and glanced at her; but, perceiving she paid little attention, went on again at a gallop. "She answered that it was worse—that the young Laird stood very near disgrace, and (the worst of all was) at a distance she could not help him. Now, sir, for reasons I shall hereafter tell you, Mr. Mackenzie's being in disgrace would have little surprised me; but that she should know of it, he being in Belgium, was incredible. So I pressed her, and she being distraught and (I verily believe) in something like anguish, came out with a most extraordinary story: to wit, that the Laird of Ardlaugh had in his service, unbeknown to him (but, as she protested, well known to her), a familiar spirit—or, as we should say commonly, a 'brownie'—which in general served him most faithfully but at times erratically, having no conscience nor any Christian principle to direct him. I cautioned her, but she persisted, in a kind of wild terror, and added that at times the spirit would, in all good faith, do things which no Christian allowed to be permissible, and further, that she had profited by such actions. I asked her, 'Was thieving one of them?' She answered that it was, and indeed the chief.

"Now, this was an admission which gave me some eagerness to hear more. For to my knowledge there were charges lying against young Mr. Mackenzie—though not pronounced—which pointed to a thief in his employment and presumably in his confidence. You will remember, sir, that when I had the honour of meeting you at Mr. Mackenzie's table, I took my leave with much abruptness. You remarked upon it, no doubt. But you will no longer think it strange when I tell you that there—under my nose—were a dozen apples of a sort which grows nowhere within twenty miles of Ardlaugh but in my own Manse garden. The tree was a new one, obtained from Herefordshire, and planted three seasons before as an experiment. I had watched it, therefore, particularly; and on that very morning had counted the fruit, and been dismayed to find twelve apples missing.

"Further, I am a pretty good judge of wine (though I taste it rarely), and could there and then have taken my oath that the claret our host set before us was the very wine I had tasted at the table of his neighbour Mr. Gillespie. As for the venison—I had already heard whispers that deer and all game were not safe within a mile or two of Ardlaugh. These were injurious tales, sir, which I had no mind to believe; for, bating his religion, I saw everything in Mr. Mackenzie which disposed me to like him. But I knew (as neighbours must) of the shortness of his purse; and the multiplied evidence (particularly my own Goodrich pippins staring me in the face) overwhelmed me for a moment.

"So then, I listened to this woman's tale with more patience—or, let me say, more curiosity—than you, sir, might have given it. She persisted, I say, that her master was in trouble; and that the trouble had something to do with a game of cards, but that Mr. Mackenzie had been innocent of deceit, and the real culprit was this spirit I tell of—"

Here the woman herself broke in upon Mr. Saul. "He had nae conscience—he had nae conscience. He was just a poor luck-child, born by mischance and put away without baptism. He had nae conscience. How should he?"

I looked from her to Mr. Saul in perplexity.

"Whist!" said he; "we'll talk of that anon."

"We will not," said she. "We will talk of it now. He was my own child, sir, by the young Laird's own father. That was before he was married upon the wife he took later—"

Here Mr. Saul nudged me, and whispered: "The old Laird—had her married to that daunderin' old half-wit Duncan, to cover things up. This part of the tale is true enough, to my knowledge."

"My bairn was overlaid, sir," the woman went on; "not by purpose, I will swear before you and God. They buried his poor body without baptism; but not his poor soul. Only when the young laird came, and my own bairn clave to him as Mackenzie to Mackenzie, and wrought and hunted and mended for him—it was not to be thought that the poor innocent, without knowledge of God's ways—"

She ran on incoherently, while my thoughts harked back to the voice I had heard wailing behind the door of the *entresol* at Brussels; to the young Laird's face, his furious indignation, followed by hopeless apathy, as of one who in the interval had learnt what he could never explain; to the marked coin so mysteriously spirited from sight; to Mr. Urquhart's words before he left me on the night of Quatre Bras.

"But he was sorry," the woman ran on; "he was sorry—sorry. He came wailing to me that night; yes, and sobbing. He meant no wrong; it was just that he loved his own father's son, and knew no better. There was no priest living within thirty miles; so I dressed, and ran to the minister here. He gave me no rest until I started."

I addressed Mr. Saul. "Is there reason to suppose that, besides this woman and (let us say) her accomplice, anyone shared the secret of these pilferings?"

"Ardlaugh never knew," put in the woman quickly. "He may have guessed we were helping him; but the lad knew nothing, and may the saints in heaven love him as they ought! He trusted me with his purse, and slight it was to maintain him. But until too late, he never knew—no, never, sir!"

I thought again of that voice behind the door of the *entresol*.

"Elspeth Mackenzie," I said, "I and two other living men alone know of what your master was accused. It cannot affect him; but these two shall hear your exculpation of him. And I will write the whole story down, so that the world, if it ever hears the charge, may also hear your testimony, which of the two (though both are strange) I believe to be not the less credible."

The Legend of Sir Dinar

A puff of north-east wind shot over the hill, detached a late December leaf from the sycamore on its summit, and swooped like a wave upon the roofs and chimney-stacks below. It caught the smoke midway in the chimneys, drove it back with showers of soot and wood-ash, and set the townsmen sneezing who lingered by their hearths to read the morning newspaper. Its strength broken, it fell prone upon the main street, scattering its fine dust into fan-shaped figures, then died away in eddies towards the south. Among these eddies the sycamore leaf danced and twirled, now running along the ground upon its edge, now whisked up to the level of the first-storey windows. A nurse, holding up a three-year-old child behind the pane, pointed after the leaf—

"Look—there goes Sir Dinar!"

Sir Dinar was the youngest son and the comeliest of King Geraint, who had left Arthur's Court for his own western castle of Dingerein in Roseland, where Portscatho now stands, and was buried, when his time came, over the Nare, in his golden boat with his silver oars beside him. To fill his siege at the Round Table he sent, in the lad's sixteenth year, this Dinar, who in two years was made knight by King Arthur, and in the third was turned into an old man before he had achieved a single deed of note.

For on the fifth day after he was made knight, and upon the Feast of Pentecost, there began the great quest of the Sancgrael, which took Sir Lancelot from the Court, Sir Perceval, Sir Bors,

Sir Gawaine, Sir Galahad, and all the flower of the famous brotherhood. And because, after their going, it was all sad cheer at Camelot, and heavy, empty days, Sir Dinar took two of his best friends aside, both young knights, Sir Galhaltin and Sir Ozanna le Coeur Hardi, and spoke to them of riding from the Court by stealth. "For," he said, "we have many days before us, and no villainy upon our consciences, and besides are eager. Who knows, then, but we may achieve this adventure of the Sancgrael?" These listened and imparted it to another, Sir Sentrail: and the four rode forth secretly one morning before the dawn, and set their faces towards the north-east wind.

The day of their departure was that next after Christmas, the same being the Feast of Saint Stephen the Martyr. And as they rode through a thick wood, it came into Sir Dinar's mind that upon this day it was right to kill any bird that flew, in remembrance that when Saint Stephen had all but escaped from the soldiers who guarded him, a small bird had sung in their ears and awakened them. By this, the sky was growing white with the morning, but nothing yet clear to the sight: and while they pressed forward under the naked boughs, their horses' hoofs crackling the frosted undergrowth, Sir Dinar was aware of a bird's wing ruffling ahead, and let fly a bolt without warning his companions; who had forgotten what morning it was, and drew rein for a moment.

But pressing forward again, they came upon a gerfalcon lying, with long lunes tangled about his feet and through his breast the hole that Sir Dinar's bolt had made. While they stooped over this bird the sun rose and shone between the tree-trunks, and lifting their heads they saw a green glade before them, and in the midst of the glade three pavilions set, each of red sendal, that shone in the morning. In the first pavilion slept seven knights, and in the second a score of damsels, but by the door of the third stood a lady, fair and tall, in a robe of samite, who, as they drew near to accost her, inquired of them—

"Which of you has slain my gerfalcon?"

And when Sir Dinar confessed and began to make his excuse,

"Silly knight!" said she, "who couldst not guess that my falcon, too, was abroad to avenge the blessed Stephen. Or dost think that it was a hawk, of all birds, that sang a melody in the ears of his guards?"

With that she laughed, as if pacified, and asked of their affairs; and being told that they rode in search of the Sancgrael, she laughed again, saying—

"Silly knights all, that seek it before you be bearded! For three of you must faint and die on the quest, and you, sir," turning to Sir Dinar, "must many times long to die, yet never reach nearer by a foot."

"Let it be as God will," answered Sir Dinar. "But hast thou any tidings, to guide us?"

"I have heard," said she, "that it was seen latest in the land of Gore, beyond Trent Water." And with her white finger she pointed down a narrow glade that led to the north-west. So they thanked her and pricked on, none guessing that she herself was King Urience' wife, of Gore, and none other than Queen Morgan le Fay, the famous enchantress, who for loss of her gerfalcon was lightly sending Sir Dinar to his ruin.

So all that day they rode, two and two, in the strait alley that she had pointed out; and by her enchantments she made the winter trees to move with them, serried close on either hand, so that, though the four knights wist nothing of it, they advanced not a furlong for all their haste. But towards nightfall there appeared close ahead a blaze of windows lit and then a tall castle with dim towers soaring up and shaking to the din of minstrelsy. And finding a great company about the doors, they lit down from their horses and stepped into the great hall, Sir Dinar leading them. For a while their eyes were dazed, seeing that sconces flared along the walls and the place was full of knights and damsels brightly clad, and the floor shone. But while they were yet blinking, a band of maidens came and unbuckled their arms and cast a shining cloak upon each; which was hardly done when a lady came towards them out of the throng, and though she was truly the Queen Morgan le Fay, they knew her not at all, for by her necromancy she had altered her countenance.

"Come, dance," said she, "for in an instant the musicians will begin."

The other three knights tarried awhile, being weary with riding; but Sir Dinar stepped forward and caught the hand of a damsel, and she, as she gave it, looked in his eyes and laughed. She was dressed all in scarlet, with scarlet shoes, and her hair lay on her shoulders like waves of burnished gold. As Sir Dinar set his arm about her, with a crash the merry music began; and floating out with him into the dance, her scarlet shoes twinkling and her tossed hair shaking spices under his nostrils, she leaned back a little on his arm and laughed again.

Sir Galhaltin was leaning by the doorway, and he heard her laugh and saw her feet twinkle like blood-red moths, and he called to Sir Dinar. But Sir Dinar heard only the brassy music, nor did any of the dancers turn their heads, though Sir Galhaltin called a second time and more loudly. Then Sir Sentrail and Sir Ozanna also began to call, fearing they knew not what for their comrade. But the guests still drifted by as they were clouds, and Sir Dinar, with the red blood showing beneath the down on his cheeks, smiled always and whirled with the woman upon his arm.

By and by he began to pant, and would have rested: but she denied him.

"For a moment only," he said, "because I have ridden far today."

But "No" she said, and hung a little more heavily upon his arm, and still the music went on. And now, gating upon her, he was frightened; for it seemed she was growing older under his eyes, with deep lines sinking into her face, and the flesh of her neck and bosom shrivelling up, so that the skin hung loose and gathered in wrinkles. And now he heard the voices of his companions calling about the door, and would have cast off the sorceress and run to them. But when he tried, his arm was welded around her waist, nor could he stay his feet.

The three knights now, seeing the sweat upon his white face

and the looks he cast towards them, would have broken in and freed him: but they, too, were by enchantment held there in the doorway. So, with their eyes starting, they must needs stay there and watch; and while they stood the boards became as molten brass under Sir Dinar's feet, and the hag slowly withered in his embrace; and still the music played, and the other dancers cast him never a look as he whirled round and round again. But at length, with never a stay in the music, his partner's feet trailed heavily, and, bending forward, she shook her white locks clear of her gaunt eyes, and laughed a third time, bringing her lips close to his. And the poison of death was in her lips as she set them upon his mouth. With that kiss there was a crash. The lights went out, and the music died away in a wail: and the three knights by the door were caught away suddenly and stunned by a great wind.

Awaking, they found themselves lying in the glade where they had come upon the three red pavilions. Their horses were cropping at the turf, beside them, and Sir Dinar's horse stood in sight, a little way off. But Sir Dinar was already deep in the forest, twirling and spinning among the rotten leaves, and on his arm hung a corrupting corpse. For a whole day they sought him and found him not (for he heard nothing of their shouts), and towards evening mounted and rode forward after the Sancgrael; on which quest they died, all three, each in his turn.

But Sir Dinar remained, and twirled and skipped till the body he held was a skeleton; and still he twirled, till it dropped away piecemeal; and yet again, till it was but a stain of dust on his ragged sleeve. Before this his hair was white and his face wizened with age.

But on a day a knight in white armour came riding through the forest, leaning somewhat heavily on his saddle-bow: and was aware of an old decrepit man that ran towards him, jigging and capering as if for gladness, yet caught him by the stirrup and looked up with rheumy tears in his eyes.

"In God's name, who art thou?" asked the knight. He, too, was past his youth; but his face shone with a marvellous glory.

"I am young Sir Dinar, that was made a knight of the Round Table but five days before Pentecost. And I know thee. Thou art Sir Galahad, who shouldst win the Sancgrael: therefore by Christ's power rid me of this enchantment."

"I have not won it yet," Sir Galahad answered, sighing. "Yet, poor comrade, I may do something for thee, though I cannot stay thy dancing."

So he stretched out his hand and touched Sir Dinar: and by his touch Sir Dinar became a withered leaf of the wood. And when mothers and nurses see him dancing before the wind, they tell this story of him to their children.

The Magic Shadow

Once upon a time there was born a man-child with a magic shadow.

His case was so rare that a number of doctors have been disputing over it ever since and picking his parents' histories and genealogies to bits, to find the cause. Their inquiries do not help us much. The father drove a cab; the mother was a charwoman and came of a consumptive family. But these facts will not quite account for a magic shadow. The birth took place on the night of a new moon, down a narrow alley into which neither moon nor sun ever penetrated beyond the third-storey windows—and that is why the parents were so long in discovering their child's miraculous gift. The hospital-student who attended merely remarked that the babe was small and sickly, and advised the mother to drink sound port-wine while nursing him,—which she could not afford.

Nevertheless, the boy struggled somehow through five years of life, and was put into smallclothes. Two weeks after this promotion his mother started off to scrub out a big house in the fashionable quarter, and took him with her: for the house possessed a wide garden, laid with turf and lined with espaliers, sunflowers, and hollyhocks, and as the month was August, and the family away in Scotland, there seemed no harm in letting the child run about in this paradise while she worked. A flight of steps descended from the drawing-room to the garden, and as she knelt on her mat in the cool room it was easy to keep an eye on him. Now and then she gazed out into the sunshine and called; and the boy stopped running about and nodded back, or shouted the report of some fresh discovery.

By-and-by a sulphur butterfly excited him so that he must run up the broad stone steps with the news. The woman laughed, looking at his flushed face, then down at his shoe-strings, which were untied: and then she jumped up, crying out sharply—"Stand still, child—stand still a moment!"

She might well stare. Her boy stood and smiled in the sun, and his shadow lay on the whitened steps. Only the silhouette was not that of a little breeched boy at all, but of a little girl in petticoats; and it wore long curls, whereas the charwoman's son was close-cropped.

The woman stepped out on the terrace to look closer. She twirled her son round and walked him down into the garden, and backwards and forwards, and stood him in all manner of positions and attitudes, and rubbed her eyes. But there was no mistake: the shadow was that of a little girl.

She hurried over her charing, and took the boy home for his father to see before sunset. As the matter seemed important, and she did not wish people in the street to notice anything strange, they rode back in an omnibus. They might have spared their haste, however, as the cab-driver did not reach home till supper-time, and then it was found that in the light of a candle, even when stuck inside a carriage-lamp, their son cast just an ordinary shadow. But next morning at sunrise they woke him up and carried him to the house-top, where the sunlight slanted between the chimney-stacks: and the shadow was that of a little girl.

The father scratched his head. "There's money in this, wife. We'll keep the thing close; and in a year or two he'll be fit to go round in a show and earn money to support our declining years."

With that the poor little one's misfortunes began. For they shut him in his room, nor allowed him to play with the other children in the alley—there was no knowing what harm might come to his precious shadow. On dark nights his father walked him out along the streets; and the boy saw many curious things under the gas-lamps, but never the little girl who inhabited his shadow. So that by degrees he forgot all about her. And his father kept silence.

Yet all the while she grew side by side with him, keeping pace with his years. And on his fifteenth birthday, when his parents took him out into the country and, in the sunshine there, revealed his secret, she was indeed a companion to be proud of—neat of figure, trim of ankle, with masses of waving hair; but whether blonde or brunette could not be told; and, alas! she had no eyes to look into.

"My son," said they, "the world lies before you. Only do not forget your parents, who conferred on you this remarkable shadow."

The youth promised, and went off to a showman. The showman gladly hired him; for, of course, a magic shadow was a rarity, though not so well paying as the Strong Man or the Fat Woman, for these were worth seeing every day, whereas for weeks at a time, in dull weather or foggy, our hero had no shadow at all. But he earned enough to keep himself and help the parents at home; and was considered a success.

One day, after five years of this, he sought the Strong Man, and sighed. For they had become close friends.

"I am in love," he confessed.

"With your shadow?"

"No."

"Not with the Fat Woman!" the Strong Man exclaimed, with a start of jealousy.

"No. I have seen her that I mean these three days in the Square, on her way to music lesson. She has dark brown eyes and wears yellow ribbons. I love her."

"You don't say so! She has never come to our performance, I hope."

"It has been foggy ever since we came to this town."

"Ah, to be sure. Then there's a chance: for, you see, she would never look at you if she knew of—of that other. Take my advice—go into society, always at night, when there is no danger;

get introduced; dance with her; sing serenades under her window; then marry her. Afterwards—well, that's your affair."

So the youth went into society and met the girl he loved, and danced with her so vivaciously and sang serenades with such feeling beneath her window, that at last she felt he was all in all to her. Then the youth asked to be allowed to see her father, who was a retired colonel; and professed himself a man of substance. He said nothing of the shadow: but it is true he had saved a certain amount. "Then to all intents and purposes you are a gentleman," said the retired colonel; and the wedding-day was fixed.

They were married in dull weather, and spent a delightful honeymoon. But when spring came and brighter days, the young wife began to feel lonely; for her husband locked himself, all the day long, in his study—to work, as he said. He seemed to be always at work; and whenever he consented to a holiday, it was sure to fall on the bleakest and dismallest day in the week.

"You are never so gay now as you were last Autumn. I am jealous of that work of yours. At least," she pleaded, "let me sit with you and share your affection with it."

But he laughed and denied her: and next day she peered in through the keyhole of his study.

That same evening she ran away from him: having seen the shadow of another woman by his side.

Then the poor man—for he had loved his wife—cursed the day of his birth and led an evil life. This lasted for ten years, and his wife died in her father's house, unforgiving.

On the day of her funeral, the man said to his shadow—"I see it all. We were made for each other, so let us marry. You have wrecked my life and now must save it. Only it is rather hard to marry a wife whom one can only see by sunlight and moonlight."

So they were married; and spent all their life in the open air, looking on the naked world and learning its secrets. And his shadow bore him children, in stony ways and on the bare mountain-side. And for every child that was born the man felt the pangs of it.

And at last he died and was judged: and being interrogated concerning his good deeds, began—

"We two—"—and looked around for his shadow. A great light shone all about; but she was nowhere to be seen. In fact, she had passed before him, and his children remained on earth, where men already were heaping them with flowers and calling them divine.

Then the man folded his arms and lifted his chin.

"I beg your pardon," he said, "I am simply a sinner."

There are in this world certain men who create. The children of such are poems, and the half of their soul is female. For it is written that without woman no new thing shall come into the world.

The Miracle of the White Wolf

1.—The Tale of Snorri Gamlason

In the early summer of 1358, with the breaking up of the ice, there came to Brattahlid, in Greenland, a merchant-ship from Norway, with provisions for the Christian settlements on the coast. The master's name was Snorri Gamlason, and it happened that as he sailed into Eric's Fiord and warped alongside the quay, word was brought to him that the Bishop of Garda had arrived that day in Brattahlid, to hold a confirmation. Whereupon this Snorri went ashore at once, and, getting audience of the bishop, gave him a little book, with an account of how he had come by it.

The book was written in Danish, and Snorri could not understand a word of it, being indeed unable to read or to write; but he told this tale:—

His ship, about three weeks before, had run into a calm, which lasted for three days and two nights, and with a northerly drift she fell away, little by little, towards a range of icebergs which stretched across and ahead of them in a solid chain. But about noon of the third day the colour of the sky warned him of a worse peril, and soon there came up from the westward a bank of fog, with snow in it, and a wind that increased until they began to hear the ice grinding and breaking up—as it seemed—all around them. Snorri steered at first for the southward, where had been open water; but by and by found that even here were drifting bergs. He therefore put his helm down and felt his way through the weather by short boards, and so, with the most of his men stationed forward to keep a look-out, fenced, as it were, with the danger, steering and tacking, until by God's grace the fog lifted, and the wind blew gently once more.

And now in the clear sunshine he saw that the storm had been more violent than any had supposed; since the wall of ice, which before had been solid, was now burst and riven in many places, and in particular to the eastward, where a broad path of water lay before them almost like a canal, but winding here and there. Towards this Snorri steered, and entered it with a fair breeze.

They had come, he said, but to the second bend of this waterway, when a seaman, who had climbed the mast on the chance of spying an outlet, called out in surprise that there was a ship ahead of them, but two miles off, and running down the channel before the wind, even as they. At first he found no credit for this tale, and even when those on deck spied her mast and yard overtopping a gap between two bergs, they could only set it down for a mirage or cheat of eyesight in the clear weather.

But by and by, said Snorri, they could not doubt they were in chase of a ship, and, further, that they were fast overtaking her. For she steered with no method, and shook with every slant of wind, and anon went off before it like a helpless thing, until in the end she was fetched up by the jutting foot of a berg, and there shook her sail, flapping with such noise that Snorri's men heard it, though yet a mile away.

They bore down upon her, and now took note that this sail of hers was ragged and frozen, so that it flapped like a jointed board, and that her rigging hung in all ways and untended, but stiff with rime; and drawing yet nearer, they saw an ice-line about her hull, so deep that her timbers seemed bitten through, and a great pile of frozen snow upon her poop, banked even above her tiller; but no helmsman, and no living soul upon her.

Then Snorri let lower his boat, and was rowed towards her; and, coming alongside, gave a hail, which was unanswered. But from the frozen pile by the tiller there stuck out a man's arm, ghastly to see. Snorri climbed on board by the waist, where her sides were low and a well reached aft from the mast to the poop. There was a cabin beneath the poop, and another and larger room under the deck forward, between the step of the mast and the bows. Into each of these he broke with axes and bars, and in the one found nothing but some cooking-pots and bedding; but in the other—that is, the after-cabin—the door, as he burst it in, almost fell against a young man seated by a bed.

So life-like was he that Snorri called aloud in the doorway, but anon, peering into the gloomy place, perceived the body to be frozen upright and stiff, and that on the bed lay another body, of a lady slight and young, and very fair. She, too, was dead and frozen; yet her cheeks, albeit white as the pillow against which they rested, had not lost their roundness. Snorri took note also of her dress and of the coverlet reaching from the bed's foot to her waist, that they were of silk for the most part, and richly embroidered, and her shift and the bed-sheets about her of fine linen. The man's dress was poor and coarse by comparison; yet he carried a sword, and was plainly of gentle nurture. The sword Snorri drew from its sheath and brought away; also he took a small box of jewels; but little else could he find on the ship, and no food of any kind.

His design was to leave the ship as he found it, carrying away only these tokens that his story, when he arrived at Brattahlid, might be received with faith; and to direct where the ship might be sought for. But as he quitted the cabin some of his men shouted from the deck, where they had discovered yet another body frozen in a drift. This was an old man seated with crossed legs and leaning against the mast, having an ink-horn slung about his neck, and almost hidden by his grey beard, and on his knee a book, which he held with a thumb frozen between two pages.

This was the book which Snorri had brought to Brattahlid, and which the Bishop of Garda read aloud to him that same afternoon, translating as he went; the ink being fresh, the writing clerkly, and scarcely a page damaged by the weather. It bore no title; but the bishop, who afterwards caused his secretary to take a copy of the tale, gave it a very long one, beginning:

God's mercy shown in a Miracle upon certain castaways from Jutland, at the Feast of the Nativity of His Blessed Son, our Lord, in the year *MCCCLVII.*, whereby He made dead trees to put forth in leaf, and comforted desperate men with summer in the midst of the Frozen Sea ... with much beside.

But all this appears in the tale, which I will head only with the name of the writer.

2.—Peter Kurt's Manuscript [1]

Now that our troubles are over, and I sit by the mast of our late unhappy ship, not knowing if I am on earth or in paradise, but full-fed and warm in all my limbs, yea pierced and glowing with the love of Almighty God, I am resolved to take pen and use my unfrozen ink in telling out of what misery His hand hath led us to this present Eden.

I who write this am Peter Kurt, and I was the steward of my master Ebbe while he dwelt in his own castle of Nebbegaard. Poor he was then, and poor, I suppose, he is still in all but love and the favour of God; but in those days the love was but an old servant's (to wit, my own), and the favour of God not evident, but the poverty, on the other hand, bitterly apparent in all our housekeeping. We lived alone, with a handful of servants—sometimes as few as three—in the castle which stands between the sandhills and the woods, as you sail into Veile Fiord.

All these woods, as far away as to Rosenvold, had been the good knight his father's, but were lost to us before Ebbe's birth, and leased on pledge to the Knight Borre, of Egeskov, of whom I am to tell; and with them went all the crew of verderers, huntsmen, grooms, prickers, and ostringers that had kept Nebbegaard cheerful the year round. His mother had died at my master's birth, and the knight himself but two years after, so that the lad

---

[1] The courtship of Ebbe, the poor esquire of Nebbegaard, and the maiden Mette is a traditional tale of West Jutland. A version of it was Englished by Thorpe from Carit Etlar's *Eventyr og Folkesagen fra Jylland*: but this, while it tells of Ebbe's adventures at the "Bride-show," and afterwards at the hunting-party, contains no account of the lovers' escape and voyage, or of the miracle which brought them comfort at the last. Indeed, Master Kurt contradicts the common tale in many ways, but above all in his ending, wherein (although he narrates a miracle) I find him worthy of belief.

grew up in his poverty with no heritage but a few barren acres of sand, a tumbling house, and his father's sword, and small prospect of winning the broad lands out of Borre's clutches.

Nevertheless, under my tutoring he grew into a tall lad and a bold, a good swordsman, skilful at the tilt and in handling a boat; but not talkative or free in his address of strangers. The most of his days he spent in fishing, or in the making and mending of gear; and his evenings, after our lesson in sword-play, in the reading of books (of which Nebbegaard had good store), and specially of the Icelanders, skalds and sagamen; also at times in the study of Latin with me, who had been bred to the priesthood, but left it for love of his father, my foster-brother, and now had no ambition of my own but to serve this lad and make him as good a man.

But there were days when he would have naught to do with fishing or with books; dark days when I forbore and left him to mope by the dunes, or in the great garden which had been his mother's, but was now a wilderness untended. And it was then that he first met with the lady Mette.

For as he walked there one morning, a little before noon, a swift shadow passed overhead between him and the sun, and almost before he could glance upward a body came dropping out of the sky and fell with a thud among the rose-bushes by the eastern wall. It was a heron, and after it swooped the bird which had murdered it; a white ger-falcon of the kind which breeds in Greenland, but a trained bird, as he knew by the sound of the bells on her legs as she plunged through the bushes. Ebbe ran at once to the corner where the birds struggled; but as he picked up the pelt he happened to glance towards the western wall, and in the gateway there stood a maiden with her hand on the bridle of a white palfrey. Her dog came running towards Ebbe as he stood. He beat it off, and carrying the pelt across to its mistress, waited a moment silently, cap in hand, while she called the great falcon back to its lure and leashed it to her wrist, which seemed all too slight for the weight.

Then, as Ebbe held out the dead heron, she shook her head

and laughed. "I am not sure, sir, that I have any right to it. We flushed it yonder between the wood and the sandhills, and, though I did not stay to consider, I think it must belong to the owner of the shore-land."

"It is true," said Ebbe, "that I own the shore-land, and the forest, too, if law could enforce right. But for the bird you are welcome to it, and to as many more as you care to kill."

Upon this she knit her brows. "The forest? But I thought that the forest was my father's? My name," said she, "is Mette, and my father is the Knight Borre, of Egeskov."

"I am Ebbe of Nebbegaard, and," said he, perceiving the mirth in her eyes, "you have heard the rhyme upon me—*Ebbe from Nebbe, with all his men good, Has neither food nor firing-wood.*"

"I had not meant to be discourteous," said she contritely; "but tell me more of these forest-lands."

"Nay," answered Ebbe, "hither comes riding your father with his men. Ask him for the story, and when he has told it you may know why I cannot make him or his daughter welcome at Nebbegaard."

To this she made no reply, but with her hand on the palfrey's bridle went slowly back to meet her father, who reined up at a little distance and waited, offering Ebbe no salutation. Then a groom helped her to the saddle, and the company rode away towards Egeskov, leaving the lad with the dead bird in his hand.

For weeks after this meeting he moped more than usual. He had known before that Sir Borre would leave no son, and that the lands of Nebbegaard, if ever to be won back, must be wrested from a woman—and this had ever troubled him. It troubled me the less because I hoped there might be another way than force; and even if it should come to that, Sir Borre's past treachery had killed in me all kindness towards his house, male or female.

He and my old master and five other knights of the eastern coast had been heavily oppressed by the Lord of Trelde, Lars Trolle, who owned many ships, and, though no better than a pirate, claimed a right of levying tribute along the shore that faces Funen, upon pretence of protecting it. After enduring many raids and paying toll under threat for years, these seven knights banded together to rid themselves of this robber; but word of their meetings being carried to Trolle, he came secretly one night to Nebbegaard with three ships' crews, broke down the doors, and finding the seven assembled in debate, made them prisoners and held them at ransom. My master, a poor man, could only purchase release by the help of his comrade, Borre, who found the ransom, but took in exchange the lands of Nebbegaard, to hold them until repaid out of their revenues; but of these he could never after be brought to give an account. We on our side had lost the power to enforce it, and behind his own strength he could now threaten us with Lars Trolle's, to whom he had been reconciled.

Therefore I felt no tenderness for Sir Borre's house, if by any means our estates could be recovered. But after this meeting with Sir Borre's daughter, I could see that my young lord went heavily troubled; and I began to think of other means than force.

It may have been six months later that word fame to us of great stir and bustle at Egeskov. Sir Borre, being aged, and anxious to see his daughter married before he died, had proclaimed a bride-show. Now the custom is, and the rule, that any suitor (so he be of gentle birth) may offer himself in these contests; nor will the parents begin to bargain until he has approved himself,—a wise plan, since it lessens the disputing, which else might be endless. So when this news reached us I looked at my master, and he, perceiving what I would say, answered it.

"If Holgar will carry me," said he, "we will ride to Egeskov."

This Holgar was a stout roan horse, foaled at Nebbegaard, but now well advanced in years, and the last of that red stock for which our stables had been famous.

"He will carry you thither," said I; "and by God's grace, bring you home with a bride behind you."

Upon this my master hung his head. "Peter," he said, "do not think I attempt this because it is the easier way."

"It comes easier than fighting with a woman," I answered.

"But you will find it hard enow when the old man begins to haggle."

I did not know then that the lad's heart was honestly given to this maid; but so it was, and had been from the moment when she stood before him in the gateway.

So to Egeskov we rode, and there found no less than forty suitors assembled, and some with a hundred servants in retinue. Sir Borre received us with no care to hide his scorn, though the hour had not come for putting it into words; and truly my master's arms were old-fashioned, and with the dents they had honourably taken when they cased his father, made a poor battered show, for all my scouring.

Nevertheless, I had no fear when his turn came to ride the ring. Three rides had each wooer under the lady Mette's eyes, and three rings Ebbe carried off and laid on the cushion before her. She stooped and passed about his neck the gold chain which she held for the prize; but I think they exchanged no looks. Only one other rider brought two rings, and this was a son of Lars Trolle, Olaf by name, a tall young knight, and well-favoured, but disdainful; whom I knew Sir Borre must favour if he could.

I could not see that the maiden favoured him above the rest, yet I kept a close eye upon this youth, and must own that in the jousting which followed he carried himself well. For this the most of the wooers had fresh horses, and I drew a long breath when, at the close of the third course, my master, with two others, remained in the lists. For it had been announced to us that the last courses should be ridden on the morrow. But now Sir Borre behaved very treacherously, for perceiving (as I am sure) that the horse Holgar was overwearied and panting, he gave word that the sport should not be stayed.

More by grace of Heaven it was than by force of riding that Ebbe unhorsed his next man, a knight's son from Smalling; but in the last course, which he rode against Olaf of Trolle, who had stood a bye, his good honest beast came to the tilt-cloth with knees trembling, and at a touch rolled over, though between the two lances (I will swear) there was nothing to choose. I was quick to pick up my dear lad; but he would have none of my comfort, and limped away from the lists as one who had borne himself shamefully. Yea, and my own heart was hot as I led Holgar back to stable, without waiting to see the prize claimed by one who, though a fair fighter, had not won it without foul aid.

Having stalled Holgar I had much ado to find his master again, and endless work to persuade him to quit his sulks and join the other suitors in the hall that night, when each presented his bride-gift. Even when I had won him over, he refused to take the coffer I placed in his hands, though it held his mother's jewels, few but precious. But entering with the last, as became his humble rank of esquire, he laid nothing at the lady's feet save his sword and the chain that she herself had given him.

"You bring little, Squire Ebbe," said the Knight Borre, from his seat beside his daughter.

"I bring what is most precious in the world to me," said Ebbe.

"Your lance is broken, I believe?" said the old knight scornfully.

"My lance is not broken," he answered; "else you should have it to match your word." And rising, without a look at Mette, whose eyes were downcast, he strode back to the door.

I had now given up hope, for the maid showed no sign of kindness, and the old man and the youth were like two dogs—the very sight of the one set the other growling. Yet—since to leave in a huff would have been discourteous—I prevailed on my master to bide over the morrow, and even to mount Holgar and ride forth to the hunt which was to close the bride-show. He mounted, indeed, but kept apart and well behind Mette and her brisk group of wooers. For, apart from his lack of inclination, his horse was not yet recovered; and by and by, as the prickers started a deer, the hunt swept ahead of him and left him riding alone.

He had a mind to turn aside and ride straight back to Nebbegaard, whither he had sent me on to announce him (and dismally enough I obeyed), when at the end of a green glade he spied Mette returning alone on her white palfrey.

"For I am tired of this hunting," she told him, as she came near. "And you? Does it weary you also, that you lag so far behind?"

"It would never weary me," he answered; "but I have a weary horse."

"Then let us exchange," said she. "Though mine is but a palfrey, it would carry you better. Your roan betrayed you yesterday, and it is better to borrow than to miss excelling."

"My house," answered Ebbe, still sulkily, "has had enough borrowing of Egeskov; and my horse may be valueless, but he is one of the few things dear to me, and I must keep him."

"Truly then," said she, "your words were nought, last night, when you professed to offer me the gifts most precious to you in the world."

And before he could reply to this, she had pricked on and was lost in the woodland.

Ebbe sat for a while as she left him, considering, at the crossing of two glades. Then he twitched Holgar's rein and turned back towards Nebbegaard. But at the edge of the wood, spying a shepherd seated below in the plain by his flock, he rode down to the man, and called to him and said—

"Go this evening to Egeskov and greet the lady Mette, and say to her that Ebbe of Nebbegaard could not barter his good horse, the last of his father's stable. But that she may know he was honest in offering her the thing most precious to him, tell her further what thou hast seen."

So saying, he alighted off Holgar, and, smoothing his neck, whispered a word in his ear. And the old horse turned his muzzle and rubbed it against his master's left palm, whose right gripped a dagger and drove it straight for the heart. This was the end of the roan stock of Nebbegaard.

My master Ebbe reached home that night with the mire thick on his boots. Having fed him, I went to the stables, and finding no Holgar made sure that he had killed the poor beast in wrath for his discomforture at the tilt. The true reason he gave me many days after. I misjudged him, judging him by his father's temper.

On the morrow of the bride-show the suitors took their leave of Egeskov, under promise to return again at the month's end and hear how the lady Mette had chosen. So they went their ways, none doubting that the fortunate one would be Olaf of Trelde; and, for me, I blamed myself that we had ever gone to Egeskov.

But on the third morning after the bride-show I changed this advice very suddenly; for going at six of the morning to unlock our postern gate, as my custom was, I found a tall black stallion tethered there and left without a keeper. His harness was of red leather, and each broad crimson rein bore certain words embroidered: on the one "*A Straight Quarrel is Soonest Mended*" on the other, "*Who Will Dare Learns Swiftness.*"

Little time I lost in calling my master to admire, and having read what was written, he looked in my eyes and said, "I go back to Egeskov."

"That is well done," said I; "may the Almighty God prosper it!"

"But," said he doubtfully, "if I determine on a strange thing, will you help me, Peter? I may need a dozen men; men without wives to miss them."

"I can yet find a dozen such along the fiord," I answered.

"And we go on a long journey, perhaps never to return to Nebbegaard."

"Dear master," said I, "what matter where my old bones lie after they have done serving you?" He kissed me and rode away to Egeskov.

"I thought that the Squire of Nebbe had done with us," Sir Borre began to sneer, when Ebbe found audience. "But the bride-show is over, my man, and I give not my answer for a month yet."

"Your word is long to pledge, and longer to redeem," said Ebbe. "I know that, were I to wait a twelvemonth, you would not of free will give me Mette."

"Ah, you know that, do you? Well, then, you are right, Master Lackland, and the greater your impudence in hoping to wile from me through my daughter what you could not take by force."

Ebbe replied, "I was prepared to find it difficult, but let that pass. As touching my lack of land, I have Nebbegaard left; a poor estate and barren, yet I think you would be glad of it, to add to the lands of which you robbed us."

"Well," said Borre, "I would give a certain price for it, but not my daughter, nor anything near so precious to me."

"Give me one long ship," said Ebbe; "the swiftest of your seven which ride in the strait between Egeskov and Stryb. You shall take Nebbegaard for her, since I am weary of living at home and care little to live at all without Mette."

Borre's eyes shone with greed. "I commend you," said he; "for a stout lad there is nothing like risking his life to win a fortune. Give me the deeds belonging to Nebbegaard, and you shall have my ship *Gold Mary*."

"By your leave," said Ebbe, "I have spent some time in watching your ships upon the fiord; and the ship in my mind was the *White Wolf*."

Sir Borre laughed to find himself outwitted, for the *White Wolf* could outsail all his fleet. But in any case he had the better of the bargain and could afford to show some good-humour. Moreover, though he knew not that Mette had any tenderness for this youth, his spirits rose at the prospect of getting him out of the way.

So the bargain was struck, and as Nebbe rode homewards to his castle for the last time, he met the shepherd who had taken his former message. The man was waiting for him, and (as you guess) by Mette's orders.

"Tell the lady Mette," said Ebbe, "that I have sold Nebbegaard for the *White Wolf*, and that two nights from now my men will be aboard of her; also that I sup with her father that evening before the boat takes me off from the Bent Ness."

So it was that two nights later Ebbe supped at Egeskov, and was kept drinking by the old knight for an hour maybe after the lady Mette had risen and left the hall for her own room.

And at the end, after the last speeding-cup, needs must Sir Borre (who had grown friendly beyond all belief) see him to the gate and stand there bare-headed among his torch-bearers while my master mounted the black stallion that was to bear him to Bent Ness, three miles away, where I waited with the boat.

But as Ebbe shook his rein, and moved out of the torchlight, came the damsel Mette stealing out of the shadow upon the far side of the horse. He reached down a hand, and she took it, and sprang up behind him.

"For this bout, Sir Borre, I came with a fresh horse!" called my master blithely; and so, striking spur, galloped off into the dark.

Little chance had Sir Borre to overtake them. The stallion was swift, our boat waiting in the lee of the Ness, the wind southerly and fresh, the *White Wolf* ready for sea, with sail hoisted and but one small anchor to get on board or cut away if need were. But there was no need. Before the men of Egeskov reached the Ness and found there the black stallion roaming, its riders were sailing out of the Strait with a merry breeze. So began our voyage.

My master was minded to sail for Norway and take service under the king. But first, coming to the island of Laeso, he must put ashore and seek a priest, by whom he and the lady Mette were safely made man and wife. Two days he spent at the island, and then, with fresh store of provisions, we headed northward again.

It was past Skagen that our troubles began, with a furious wind from the north-east against which there was no contending, so that we ran from it and were driven for two days and a night into the wide sea. Even when it lessened, the wind held in the east; and we, who could handle the ship, but knew little of reckoning, crept northward again in the hope to sight the coast of Norway. For two days we held on at this, lying close by the wind, and in good spirits, although our progress was not much;

but on the third blew another gale—this time from the south-east—and for a week gale followed gale, and we went in deadly peril, yet never losing hope. The worst was the darkness, for the year was now drawing towards Yule, and as we pressed farther north we lost almost all sight of the sun.

At length, with the darkness and the bitter cold and our stores running low, we resolved to let the wind take us with what swiftness it might to whatsoever land it listed; and so ran westward, with darkness closing upon us, and famine and a great despair.

But the lady Mette did not lose heart, and the worst of all (our failing cupboard) we kept from her, so that she never lacked for plenty. Truly her cheerfulness paid us back, and her love for my master, the like of which I had not seen in this world; no, nor dreamed of. Hand in hand this pair would sit, watching the ice which was our prison and the great North Lights, she close against Ebbe's side for warmth, and (I believe) as happy us a bird; he trembling for the end. The worst was to see her at table, pressing food to his mouth and wondering at his little hunger; while his whole body cried out for the meat, only it could not be spared.

Though she must know soon, none of us had the heart to tell her; and not out of pity alone, but because with her must die out the last spark by which we warmed ourselves.

But there came a morning—I write it as of a time long ago, and yet it was but yesterday, praise be unto God!—there came a morning when I awoke and found that two of our men had died in the plight, of frost and famine. They must be hidden before my mistress discovered aught; and so before her hour of waking we weighted and dropped the bodies overside into deep water; for the ice had not yet wholly closed about us. Now as I stooped, I suppose that my legs gave way beneath me. At any rate, I fell; and in falling struck my head against the bulwarks, and opened my eyes in that unending dusk to find the lady Mette stooping over me.

Then somehow I was aware that she had called for wine to

force down my throat, and had been told that there was no wine; and also that with this answer had come to her the knowledge, full and sudden, of our case. Better had we done to trust her than to hide it all this while, for she turned to Ebbe, who stood at her shoulder, and "Is not this the feast of Yule?" she asked. My master bent his head, but without answering.

"Ah!" she cried to him. "Now I know what I have longed to know, that your love is less than mine, for you can love yet be doubtful of miracles; while to me, now that I have loved, no miracle can be aught but small." She bowed herself over me. "Art dying, old friend? Look up and learn that God, being Love, deserts not lovers."

Then she stooped and gathered, as I thought, a handful of snow from the deck; but lo! when she pressed it to my lips, and I tasted, it was heavenly manna.

And looking up past her face I saw the ribbons of the North Lights fade in a great and wide sunlight, bathing the deck and my frozen limbs. Nor did they feel it only, but on the wind came the noise of bergs rending, springs breaking, birds singing, many and curious. And with that, as I am a sinful man, I gazed up into green leaves; for either we had sailed into Paradise or the timbers of the *White Wolf* were swelling with sap and pushing forth bough upon bough. Yea, and there were roses at the mast's foot, and my fingers, as I stretched them, dabbled in mosses. While I lay there, breathing softly, as one who dreams and fears to awake, I heard her voice talking among the noises of birds and brooks, and by the scent it seemed to be in a garden; but whether it spake to me or to Ebbe I knew not, nor cared.

> The Lord is my Shepherd, and guides me, wherefore I lack nothing. He maketh me to lie down in green pastures: He leadeth me by comfortable streams: He reviveth my soul. Yea, though I walk through the valley of the shadow of death, I will fear no harm: Thy rod and Thy staff they comfort me."

But, a little after, I knew that the voice spake to my master, for it said: "Let us go forth into the field, O beloved: let us lodge in the villages: let us get up betimes to the vineyard and see if the vine have budded, if its blossom be open, the pomegranates in flower. Even there will I give thee my love." Then looking again I saw that the two had gone from me and left me alone.

But, blessed be God, they took not away the vision, and now I know certainly that it is no cheat. For here sit I, dipping my pen into the unfrozen ink, and, when a word will not come, looking up into the broad branches and listening to the birds till I forget my story. It is long since they left me; but I am full fed, and the ship floats pleasantly. After so much misery I am as one rocked on the bosom of God; and the pine resin has a pleasant smell.

The Mystery of Joseph Laquedem

A Jew, unfortunately slain on the sands of Sheba Cove, in the parish of Ruan Lanihale, August 15, 1810: or so much of it as is hereby related by the Rev. Endymion Trist, B.D., then vicar of that parish, in a letter to a friend.

My dear J——,—You are right, to be sure, in supposing that I know more than my neighbours in Ruan Lanihale concerning the unfortunate young man, Joseph Laquedem, and more than I care to divulge; in particular concerning his tragical relations with the girl Julia Constantine, or July, as she was commonly called. The vulgar knowledge amounts to little more than this— that Laquedem, a young Hebrew of extraordinary commercial gifts, first came to our parish in 1807 and settled here as managing secretary of a privateering company at Porthlooe; that by his aptitude and daring in this and the illicit trade he amassed a respectable fortune, and at length opened a private bank at Porthlooe and issued his own notes; that on August 15, 1810, a forced "run" which, against his custom, he was personally supervising, miscarried, and he met his death by a carbine-shot on the sands of Sheba Cove; and, lastly, that his body was taken up and conveyed away by the girl Julia Constantine, under the fire of the preventive men.

The story has even in our time received what I may call some fireside embellishments; but these are the facts, and the parish knows little beyond them. I (as you conjecture) know a great deal more; and yet there is a sense in which I know nothing more. You and I, my old friend, have come to an age when men do not care to juggle with the mysteries of another world, but knowing that the time is near when all accounts must be rendered, desire to take stock honestly of what they believe and what they do not. And here lies my difficulty. On the one hand I would not make public an experience which, however honestly set down, might mislead others, and especially the young, into rash and mischievous speculations. On the other, I doubt if it be right to keep total silence and withhold from devout and initiated minds any glimpse of truth, or possible truth, vouchsafed to me. As the Greek said, "*Plenty are the thyrsus-bearers, but few the illuminate*"; and among these few I may surely count my old friend.

It was in January 1807—the year of the abominable business of Tilsit—that my churchwarden, the late Mr. Ephraim Pollard, and I, in cleaning the south wall of Lanihale Church for a fresh coat of whitewash, discovered the frescoes and charcoal drawings, as well as the brass plaque of which I sent you a tracing; and I think not above a fortnight later that, on your suggestion, I set to work to decipher and copy out the old churchwardens' accounts. On the Monday after Easter, at about nine o'clock P.M., I was seated in the vicarage parlour, busily transcribing, with a couple of candles before me, when my housekeeper Frances came in with a visiting-card, and the news that a stranger desired to speak with me. I took the card and read "Mr. Joseph Laquedem."

"Show the gentleman in," said I.

Now the fact is, I had just then a few guineas in my chest, and you know what a price gold fetched in 1807. I dare say that for twelve months together the most of my parishioners never set eyes on a piece, and any that came along quickly found its way to the Jews. People said that government was buying up gold, through the Jews, to send to the armies. I know not the degree of truth in this, but I had some five and twenty guineas to dispose of, and had been put into correspondence with a Mr. Isaac Laquedem, a Jew residing by Plymouth Dock, whom I understood to be offering 25s. 6d. per guinea, or a trifle above the price then current.

I was fingering the card when the door opened again and admitted a young man in a caped overcoat and tall boots bemired high above the ankles. He halted on the threshold and bowed.

"Mr.—?"

"Joseph Laquedem," said he in a pleasant voice.

"I guess your errand," said I, "though it was a Mr. Isaac Laquedem whom I expected.—Your father, perhaps?"

He bowed again, and I left the room to fetch my bag of guineas. "You have had a dirty ride," I began on my return.

"I have walked," he answered, lifting a muddy boot. "I beg you to pardon these."

"What, from Torpoint Ferry? And in this weather? My faith, sir, you must be a famous pedestrian!"

He made no reply to this, but bent over the guineas, fingering them, holding them up to the candlelight, testing their edges with his thumbnail, and finally poising them one by one on the tip of his forefinger.

"I have a pair of scales," suggested I.

"Thank you, I too have a pair in my pocket. But I do not need them. The guineas are good weight, all but this one, which is possibly a couple of grains short."

"Surely you cannot rely on your hand to tell you that?"

His eyebrows went up as he felt in his pocket and produced a small velvet-lined case containing a pair of scales. He was a decidedly handsome young man, with dark intelligent eyes and a slightly scornful—or shall I say ironical?—smile. I took particular note of the steadiness of his hand as he adjusted the scales and weighed my guinea.

"To be precise," he announced, "1.898, or practically one and nine-tenths short."

"I should have thought," said I, fairly astounded, "a lifetime too little for acquiring such delicacy of sense!"

He seemed to ponder. "I dare say you are right, sir," he answered, and was silent again until the business of payment was concluded. While folding the receipt he added, "I am a connoisseur of coins, sir, and not of their weight alone."

"Antique, as well as modern?"

"Certainly."

"In that case," said I, "you may be able to tell me something about this": and going to my bureau I took out the brass plaque which Mr. Pollard had detached from the planks of the church wall. "To be sure, it scarcely comes within the province of numismatics."

He took the plaque. His brows contracted, and presently he laid it on the table, drew my chair towards him in an absent-minded fashion, and, sitting down, rested his brow on his open palms. I can recall the attitude plainly, and his bent head, and the rain still glistening in the waves of his black hair.

"Where did you find this?" he asked, but without looking up.

I told him. "The engraving upon it is singular. I thought that possibly—"

"Oh, that," said he, "is simplicity itself. An eagle displayed, with two heads, the legs resting on two gates, a crescent between, an imperial crown surmounting—these are the arms of the Greek Empire, the two gates are Rome and Constantinople. The question is, how it came where you found it? It was covered with plaster, you say, and the plaster whitewashed? Did you discover anything near it?"

Upon this I told him of the frescoes and charcoal drawings, and roughly described them.

His fingers began to drum upon the table.

"Have you any documents which might tell us when the wall was first plastered?"

"The parish accounts go back to 1594—here they are: the Registers to 1663 only. I keep them in the vestry. I can find no mention of plastering, but the entries of expenditure on white-washing occur periodically, the first under the year 1633." I turned the old pages and pointed to the entry "*Ite paide to George mason for a dayes work about the churche after the Jew had been, and white wassche is vjd.*"

"A Jew? But a Jew had no business in England in those days. I wonder how and why he came." My visitor took the old volume and ran his finger down the leaf, then up, then turned back a page. "Perhaps this may explain it," said he. "*Ite deliued Mr. Beuill to make puision for the companie of a fforeste barke yt came ashoare iiis ivd.*" He broke off, with a finger on the entry, and rose. "Pray forgive me, sir; I had taken your chair."

"Don't mention it," said I. "Indeed I was about to suggest that you draw it to the fire while Frances brings in some supper."

To be short, although he protested he must push on to the inn at Porthlooe, I persuaded him to stay the night; not so much, I confess, from desire of his company, as in the hope that if I took him to see the frescoes next morning he might help me to elucidate their history.

I remember now that during supper and afterwards my guest allowed me more than my share of the conversation. He made an admirable listener, quick, courteous, adaptable, yet with something in reserve (you may call it a facile tolerance, if you will) which ended by irritating me. Young men should be eager, fervid, *sublimis cupidusque*, as I was before my beard grew stiff. But this young man had the air of a spectator at a play, composing himself to be amused. There was too much wisdom in him and too little emotion. We did not, of course, touch upon any religious question—indeed, of his own opinions on any subject he disclosed extraordinarily little: and yet as I reached my bedroom that night I told myself that here, behind a mask of good manners, was one of those perniciously modern young men who have run through all beliefs by the age of twenty, and settled down to a polite but weary atheism.

I fancy that under the shadow of this suspicion my own manner may have been cold to him next morning. Almost immediately after breakfast we set out for the church. The day was sunny and warm; the atmosphere brilliant after the night's rain. The hedges exhaled a scent of spring. And, as we entered the churchyard, I saw the girl Julia Constantine seated in her favourite angle between the porch and the south wall, threading a chain of daisies.

"What an amazingly handsome girl!" my guest exclaimed.

"Why, yes," said I, "she has her good looks, poor soul!"

"Why 'poor soul'?"

"She is an imbecile, or nearly so," said I, fitting the key in the lock.

We entered the church. And here let me say that, although I furnished you at the time of their discovery with a description of the frescoes and the ruder drawings which overlay them, you can scarcely imagine the grotesque and astonishing *coup d'oeil* presented by the two series. To begin with the frescoes, or original series. One, as you know, represented the Crucifixion. The head of the Saviour bore a large crown of gilded thorns, and from the wound in His left side flowed a continuous stream of red gouts of blood, extraordinarily intense in colour (and intensity of colour is no common quality in fresco-painting). At the foot of the cross stood a Roman soldier, with two female figures in dark-coloured drapery a little to the right, and in the background a man clad in a loose dark upper coat, which reached a little below the knees.

The same man reappeared in the second picture, alone, but carrying a tall staff or hunting spear, and advancing up a road, at the top of which stood a circular building with an arched doorway and, within the doorway, the head of a lion. The jaws of this beast were open and depicted with the same intense red as the Saviour's blood.

Close beside this, but further to the east, was a large ship, under sail, which from her slanting position appeared to be mounting over a long swell of sea. This vessel had four masts; the two foremost furnished with yards and square sails, the others with lateen-shaped sails, after the Greek fashion; her sides were decorated with six gaily painted bands or streaks, each separately charged with devices—a golden saltire on a green ground, a white crescent on a blue, and so on; and each masthead bore a crown with a flag or streamer fluttering beneath.

Of the frescoes these alone were perfect, but fragments of

others were scattered over the wall, and in particular I must mention a group of detached human limbs lying near the ship—a group rendered conspicuous by an isolated right hand and arm drawn on a larger scale than the rest. A gilded circlet adorned the arm, which was flexed at the elbow, the hand horizontally placed, the forefinger extended towards the west in the direction of the picture of the Crucifixion, and the thumb shut within the palm beneath the other three fingers.

So much for the frescoes. A thin coat of plaster had been laid over them to receive the second series, which consisted of the most disgusting and fantastic images, traced in black. One of these drawings represented Satan himself—an erect figure, with hairy paws clasped in a supplicating posture, thick black horns, and eyes which (for additional horror) the artist had painted red and edged with a circle of white. At his feet crawled the hindmost limb of a peculiarly loathsome monster with claws stuck in the soil. Close by a nun was figured, sitting in a pensive attitude, her cheek resting on the back of her hand, her elbow supported by a hideous dwarf, and at some distance a small house, or prison, with barred windows and a small doorway crossed with heavy bolts.

As I said, this upper series had been but partially scraped away, and as my guest and I stood at a little distance, I leave you to imagine, if you can, the incongruous tableau; the Prince of Darkness almost touching the mourners beside the cross; the sorrowful nun and grinning dwarf side by side with a ship in full sail, which again seemed to be forcing her way into a square and forbidding prison, etc.

Mr. Laquedem conned all this for some while in silence, holding his chin with finger and thumb.

"And it was here you discovered the plaque?" he asked at length.

I pointed to the exact spot.

"H'm!" he mused, "and that ship must be Greek or Levantine by its rig. Compare the crowns on her masts, too, with that on the plaque . . ." He stepped to the wall and peered into the frescoes. "Now this hand and arm—"

"They belong to me," said a voice immediately behind me, and turning, I saw that the poor girl had followed us into the church.

The young Jew had turned also. "What do you mean by that?" he asked sharply.

"She means nothing," I began, and made as if to tap my forehead significantly.

"Yes, I do mean something," she persisted. "They belong to me. I remember—"

"What do you remember?"

Her expression, which for a moment had been thoughtful, wavered and changed into a vague foolish smile. "I can't tell . . . something . . . it was sand, I think . . ."

"Who is she?" asked Mr. Laquedem.

"Her name is Julia Constantine. Her parents are dead; an aunt looks after her—a sister of her mother's."

He turned and appeared to be studying the frescoes. "Julia Constantine—an odd name," he muttered. "Do you know anything of her parentage?"

"Nothing except that her father was a labourer at Sheba, the manor-farm. The family has belonged to this parish for generations. I believe July is the last of them."

He faced round upon her again. "*Sand*, did you say? That's a strange thing to remember. How does *sand* come into your mind? Think, now."

She cast down her eyes; her fingers plucked at the daisy-chain. After a while she shook her head. "I can't think," she answered, glancing up timidly and pitifully.

"Surely we are wasting time," I suggested. To tell the truth I disapproved of his worrying the poor girl.

He took the daisy-chain from her, looking at me the while with something between a "by-your-leave" and a challenge. A smile played about the corners of his mouth.

"Let us waste a little more." He held up the chain before her and began to sway it gently to and fro. "Look at it, please, and stretch out your arm; look steadily. Now your name is Julia Constantine, and you say that the arm on the wall belongs to you. Why?"

"Because ... if you please, sir, because of the mark."

"What mark?"

"The mark on my arm."

This answer seemed to discompose as well as to surprise him. He snatched at her wrist and rolled back her sleeve, somewhat roughly, as I thought. "Look here, sir!" he exclaimed, pointing to a thin red line encircling the flesh of the girl's upper arm, and from that to the arm and armlet in the fresco.

"She has been copying it," said I, "with a string or ribbon, which no doubt she tied too tightly."

"You are mistaken, sir; this is a birthmark. You have had it always?" he asked the girl.

She nodded. Her eyes were fixed on his face with the gaze of one at the same time startled and confiding; and for the moment he too seemed to be startled. But his smile came back as he picked up the daisy-chain and began once more to sway it to and fro before her.

"And when that arm belonged to you, there was sand around you—eh! Tell us, how did the sand come there?"

She was silent, staring at the pendulum-swing of the chain. "Tell us," he repeated in a low coaxing tone.

And in a tone just as low she began, "There was sand ... red sand ... it was below me ... and something above ... something like a great tent." She faltered, paused and went on, "There were thousands of people...." She stopped.

"Yes, yes—there were thousands of people on the sand—"

"No, they were not on the sand. There were only two on the sand ... the rest were around ... under the tent ... my arm was out ... just like this...."

The young man put a hand to his forehead. "Good Lord!" I heard him say, "the amphitheatre!"

"Come, sir," I interrupted, "I think we have had enough of this jugglery."

But the girl's voice went on steadily as if repeating a lesson:—

"And then you came—"

"*I!*" His voice rang sharply, and I saw a horror dawn in his eyes, and grow. "*I!*"

"And then you came," she repeated, and broke off, her mind suddenly at fault. Automatically he began to sway the daisy-chain afresh. "We were on board a ship . . . a funny ship . . . with a great high stern. . . ."

"Is this the same story?" he asked, lowering his voice almost to a whisper; and I could hear his breath going and coming.

"I don't know . . . one minute I see clear, and then it all gets mixed up again . . . we were up there, stretched on deck, near the tiller . . . another ship was chasing us . . . the men began to row, with long sweeps. . . ."

"But the sand," he insisted, "is the sand there?"

"The sand? . . . Yes, I see the sand again . . . we are standing upon it . . . we and the crew . . . the sea is close behind us . . . some men have hold of me . . . they are trying to pull me away from you. . . . Ah!—"

And I declare to you that with a sob the poor girl dropped on her knees, there in the aisle, and clasped the young man about the ankles, bowing her forehead upon the insteps of his high boots. As for him, I cannot hope to describe his face to you. There was something more in it than wonder—something more than dismay, even—at the success of his unhallowed experiment. It was as though, having prepared himself light-heartedly to witness a play, he was seized and terrified to find himself the principal actor. I never saw ghastlier fear on human cheeks.

"For God's sake, sir," I cried, stamping my foot, "relax your cursed spells! Relax them and leave us! This is a house of prayer."

He put a hand under the girl's chin, and, raising her face, made a pass or two, still with the daisy-chain in his hand. She looked about her, shivered and stood erect. "Where am I?" she asked. "Did I fall? What are you doing with my chain?" She had relapsed into her habitual childishness of look and speech.

I hurried them from the church, resolutely locked the door, and marched up the path without deigning a glance at the young man. But I had not gone fifty yards when he came running after.

"I entreat you, sir, to pardon me. I should have stopped the experiment before. But I was startled—thrown off my balance. I am telling you the truth, sir!"

"Very likely," said I. "The like has happened to other rash meddlers before you."

"I declare to you I had no thought—" he began. But I interrupted him:

"'No thought,' indeed! I bring you here to resolve me, if you can, a curious puzzle in archaeology, and you fall to playing devil's pranks upon a half-witted child. 'No thought!'—I believe you, sir."

"And yet," he muttered, "it is an amazing business: the sand—the *velarium*—the outstretched arm and hand—*pollice compresso*—the exact gesture of the gladiatorial shows—"

"Are you telling me, pray, of gladiatorial shows under the Eastern Empire?" I demanded scornfully.

"Certainly not: and that," he mused, "only makes it the more amazing."

"Now, look here," said I, halting in the middle of the road, "I'll hear no more of it. Here is my gate, and there lies the highroad, on to Porthlooe or back to Plymouth, as you please. I wish you good morning, sir; and if it be any consolation to you, you have spoiled my digestion for a week."

I am bound to say the young man took his dismissal with grace. He halted then and there and raised his hat; stood for a moment pondering; and, turning on his heel, walked quickly off towards Porthlooe.

It must have been a week before I learnt casually that he had obtained employment there as secretary to a small company owning the *Lord Nelson* and the *Hand-in-hand* privateers. His success, as you know, was rapid; and naturally in a gossiping parish I heard about it—a little here, a little there—in all a great deal. He had bought the *Providence* schooner; he had acted as freighter for Minards' men in their last run with the *Morning Star*; he had slipped over to Cork and brought home a Porthlooe prize illegally detained there; he was in London, fighting a salvage case in the Admiralty Court; . . . Within twelve months he was accountant of every trading company in Porthlooe, and agent for receiving the moneys due to the Guernsey merchants. In 1809, as you know, he opened his bank and issued notes of his own. And a year later he acquired two of the best farms in the parish, Tresawl and Killifreeth, and held the fee simple of the harbour and quays.

During the first two years of his prosperity I saw little of the man. We passed each other from time to time in the street of Porthlooe, and he accosted me with a politeness to which, though distrusting him, I felt bound to respond. But he never offered conversation, and our next interview was wholly of my seeking.

One evening towards the close of his second year at Porthlooe, and about the date of his purchase of the *Providence* schooner, I happened to be walking homewards from a visit to a sick parishioner, when at Cove Bottom, by the miller's footbridge, I passed two figures—a man and a woman standing there and conversing in the dusk. I could not help recognising them; and halfway up the hill I came to a sudden resolution and turned back.

"Mr. Laquedem," said I, approaching them, "I put it to you, as a man of education and decent feeling, is this quite honourable?"

"I believe, sir," he answered courteously enough, "I can convince you that it is. But clearly this is neither the time nor the place."

"You must excuse me," I went on, "but I have known Julia since she was a child."

To this he made an extraordinary answer. "No longer?" he asked; and added, with a change of tone, "Had you not forbidden me the vicarage, sir, I might have something to say to you."

"If it concern the girl's spiritual welfare—or yours—I shall be happy to hear it."

"In that case," said he, "I will do myself the pleasure of calling upon you—shall we say tomorrow evening?"

He was as good as his word. At nine o'clock next evening—about the hour of his former visit—Frances ushered him into my parlour. The similarity of circumstance may have suggested to me to draw the comparison; at any rate I observed then for the first time that rapid ageing of his features which afterwards became a matter of common remark. The face was no longer that of the young man who had entered my parlour two years before; already some streaks of grey showed in his black locks, and he seemed even to move wearily.

"I fear you are unwell," said I, offering a chair.

"I have reason to believe," he answered, "that I am dying." And then, as I uttered some expression of dismay and concern, he cut me short. "Oh, there will be no hurry about it! I mean, perhaps, no more than that all men carry about with them the seeds of their mortality—so why not I? But I came to talk of Julia Constantine, not of myself."

"You may guess, Mr. Laquedem, that as her vicar, and having known her and her affliction all her life, I take something of a fatherly interest in the girl."

"And having known her so long, do you not begin to observe some change in her, of late?"

"Why, to be sure," said I, "she seems brighter."

He nodded. "*I* have done that; or rather, love has done it."

"Be careful, sir!" I cried. "Be careful of what you are going to tell me! If you have intended or wrought any harm to that girl, I tell you solemnly—"

But he held up a hand. "Ah, sir, be charitable! I tell you solemnly our love is not of that kind. We who have loved, and lost, and sought each other, and loved again through centuries, have outlearned that rougher passion. When she was a princess of Rome and I a Christian Jew led forth to the lions—"

I stood up, grasping the back of my chair and staring. At last

I knew. This young man was stark mad.

He read my conviction at once. "I think, sir," he went on, changing his tone, "the learned antiquary to whom, as you told me, you were sending your tracing of the plaque, has by this time replied with some information about it."

Relieved at this change of subject, I answered quietly (while considering how best to get him out of the house), "My friend tells me that a similar design is found in Landulph Church, on the tomb of Theodore Paleologus, who died in 1636."

"Precisely; of Theodore Paleologus, descendant of the Constantines."

I began to grasp his insane meaning. "The race, so far as we know, is extinct," said I.

"The race of the Constantines," said he slowly and composedly, "is never extinct; and while it lasts, the soul of Julia Constantine will come to birth again and know the soul of the Jew, until—"

I waited.

"—Until their love lifts the curse, and the Jew can die."

"This is mere madness," said I, my tongue blurting it out at length.

"I expected you to say no less. Now look you, sir—in a few minutes I leave you, I walk home and spend an hour or two before bedtime in adding figures, balancing accounts; tomorrow I rise and go about my daily business cheerfully, methodically, always successfully. I am the long-headed man, making money because I know how to make it, respected by all, with no trace of madness in me. You, if you meet me tomorrow, shall recognise none. Just now you are forced to believe me mad. Believe it then; but listen while I tell you this:—When Rome was, I was; when Constantinople was, I was. I was that Jew rescued from the lions. It was I who sailed from the Bosphorus in that ship, with Julia beside me; I from whom the Moorish pirates tore her, on the beach beside Tetuan; I who, centuries after, drew those obscene figures on the wall of your church—the devil, the nun, and the barred convent—when Julia, another Julia but the same soul, was denied to me and forced into a nunnery. For the frescoes, too, tell *my* history. *I* was that figure in the dark habit, standing a little back from the cross. Tell me, sir, did you never hear of Joseph Kartophilus, Pilate's porter?"

I saw that I must humour him. "I have heard his legend," said I;[1] "and have understood that in time he became a Christian."

He smiled wearily. "He has travelled through many creeds; but he has never travelled beyond Love. And if that love can be purified of all passion such as you suspect, he has not travelled beyond forgiveness. Many times I have known her who shall save me in the end; and now in the end I have found her and shall be able, at length, to die; have found her, and with her all my dead loves, in the body of a girl whom you call half-witted—and shall be able, at length, to die."

And with this he bent over the table, and, resting his face on his arms, sobbed aloud. I let him sob there for a while, and then touched his shoulder gently.

He raised his head. "Ah," said he, in a voice which answered the gentleness of my touch, "you remind me!" And with that he deliberately slipped his coat off his left arm and, rolling up the shirt sleeve, bared the arm almost to the shoulder. "I want you close," he added with half a smile; for I have to confess that during the process I had backed a couple of paces towards the door. He took up a candle, and held it while I bent and examined the thin red line which ran like a circlet around the flesh of the upper arm just below the apex of the deltoid muscle. When I looked up I met his eyes challenging mine across the flame.

"Mr. Laquedem," I said, "my conviction is that you are possessed and are being misled by a grievous hallucination. At the same time I am not fool enough to deny that the union of flesh and spirit, so passing mysterious in everyday life (when we pause to think of it), may easily hold mysteries deeper yet. The Church Catholic, whose servant I am, has never to my knowledge de-

---

1. The legend is that as Christ left the judgment hall on His way to Calvary, Kartophilus smote Him, saying, "Man, go quicker!" and was answered, "I indeed go quickly; but thou shalt tarry till I come again."

nied this; yet has providentially made a rule of St. Paul's advice to the Colossians against intruding into those things which she hath not seen. In the matter of this extraordinary belief of yours I can give you no such comfort as one honest man should offer to another: for I do not share it. But in the more practical matter of your conduct towards July Constantine, it may help you to know that I have accepted your word and propose henceforward to trust you as a gentleman."

"I thank you, sir," he said, as he slipped on his coat. "May I have your hand on that?"

"With pleasure," I answered, and, having shaken hands, conducted him to the door.

From that day the affection between Joseph Laquedem and July Constantine, and their frequent companionship, were open and avowed. Scandal there was, to be sure; but as it blazed up like straw, so it died down. Even the women feared to sharpen their tongues openly on Laquedem, who by this time held the purse of the district, and to offend whom might mean an empty skivet on Saturday night. July, to be sure, was more tempting game; and one day her lover found her in the centre of a knot of women fringed by a dozen children with open mouths and ears.

He stepped forward. "Ladies," said he, "the difficulty which vexes you cannot, I feel sure, be altogether good for your small sons and daughters. Let me put an end to it." He bent forward and reverently took July's hand. "My dear, it appears that the depth of my respect for you will not be credited by these ladies unless I offer you marriage. And as I am proud of it, so forgive me if I put it beyond their doubt. Will you marry me?" July, blushing scarlet, covered her face with her hands, but shook her head. There was no mistaking the gesture: all the women saw it. "Condole with me, ladies!" said Laquedem, lifting his hat and including them in an ironical bow; and placing July's arm in his, escorted her away.

I need not follow the history of their intimacy, of which I saw, indeed, no more than my neighbours. On two points all accounts of it agree: the rapid ageing of the man during this period and the improvement in the poor girl's intellect. Some profess to have remarked an equally vehement heightening of her beauty; but, as my recollection serves me, she had always been a handsome maid; and I set down the transfiguration—if such it was—entirely to the dawn and growth of her reason. To this I can add a curious scrap of evidence. I was walking along the cliff track, one afternoon, between Porthlooe and Lanihale church-town, when, a few yards ahead, I heard a man's voice declaiming in monotone some sentences which I could not catch; and rounding the corner, came upon Laquedem and July. She was seated on a rock; and he, on a patch of turf at her feet, held open a small volume which he laid face downwards as he rose to greet me. I glanced at the back of the book and saw it was a volume of Euripides. I made no comment, however, on this small discovery; and whether he had indeed taught the girl some Greek, or whether she merely listened for the sake of hearing his voice, I am unable to say.

Let me come then to the last scene, of which I was one among many spectators.

On the morning of August 15th, 1810, and just about daybreak, I was awakened by the sound of horses' hoofs coming down the road beyond the vicarage gate. My ear told me at once that they were many riders and moving at a trot; and a minute later the jingle of metal gave me an inkling of the truth. I hurried to the window and pulled up the blind. Day was breaking on a grey drizzle of fog which drove up from seaward, and through this drizzle I caught sight of the last five or six scarlet plumes of a troop of dragoons jogging down the hill past my bank of laurels.

Now our parish had stood for some weeks in apprehension of a visit from these gentry. The riding-officer, Mr. Luke, had threatened us with them more than once. I knew, moreover, that a run of goods was contemplated: and without questions of mine—it did not become a parish priest in those days to know too much—it had reached my ears that Laquedem was himself in Roscoff bargaining for the freight. But we had all learnt confidence in him by this time—his increasing bodily weakness never seemed to affect his cleverness and resource—and no doubt occurred to me that he would contrive to checkmate this new move of the riding-officer's. Nevertheless, and partly I dare say out of curiosity, to have a good look at the soldiers, I slipped on my clothes and hurried downstairs and across the garden.

My hand was on the gate when I heard footsteps, and July Constantine came running down the hill, her red cloak flapping and her hair powdered with mist.

"Hullo!" said I, "nothing wrong, I hope?" She turned a white, distraught face to me in the dawn.

"Yes, yes! All is wrong! I saw the soldiers coming—I heard them a mile away, and sent up the rocket from the church-tower. But the lugger stood in—they *must* have seen!—she stood in, and is right under Sheba Point now—and *he*—"

I whistled. "This is serious. Let us run out towards the point; we—you, I mean—may be in time to warn them yet."

So we set off running together. The morning breeze had a cold edge on it, but already the sun had begun to wrestle with the bank of sea-fog. While we hurried along the cliffs the shoreward fringe of it was ripped and rolled back like a tent-cloth, and through the rent I saw a broad patch of the cove below; the sands (for the tide was at low ebb) shining like silver; the dragoons with their greatcoats thrown back from their scarlet breasts and their accoutrements flashing against the level rays. Seaward, the lugger loomed through the weather; but there was a crowd of men and black boats—half a score of them—by the water's edge, and it was clear to me at once that a forced run had been at least attempted.

I had pulled up, panting, on the verge of the cliff, when July caught me by the arm.

"*The sand!*"

She pointed; and well I remember the gesture—the very gesture of the hand in the fresco—the forefinger extended, the thumb shut within the palm. "*The sand* . . . he told me . . ."

Her eyes were wide and fixed. She spoke, not excitedly at all, but rather as one musing, much as she had answered Laquedem on the morning when he waved the daisy-chain before her.

I heard an order shouted, high up the beach, and the dragoons came charging down across the sand. There was a scuffle close by the water's edge; then, as the soldiers broke through the mob of free-traders and wheeled their horses round, fetlock deep in the tide, I saw a figure break from the crowd and run, but presently check himself and walk composedly towards the cliff up which climbed the footpath leading to Porthlooe. And above the hubbub of oaths and shouting, I heard a voice crying distinctly, "Run, man! Tis after thee they are! *Man, go faster!*"

Even then, had he gained the cliff-track, he might have escaped; for up there no horseman could follow. But as a trooper came galloping in pursuit, he turned deliberately. There was no defiance in his attitude; of that I am sure. What followed must have been mere blundering ferocity. I saw a jet of smoke, heard the sharp crack of a firearm, and Joseph Laquedem flung up his arms and pitched forward at full length on the sand.

The report woke the girl as with the stab of a knife. Her cry—it pierces through my dreams at times—rang back with the echoes from the rocks, and before they ceased she was half-way down the cliffside, springing as surely as a goat, and, where she found no foothold, clutching the grass, the rooted samphires and sea pinks, and sliding. While my head swam with the sight of it, she was running across the sands, was kneeling beside the body, had risen, and was staggering under the weight of it down to the water's edge.

"Stop her!" shouted Luke, the riding-officer. "We must have the man! Dead or alive, we must have'n!"

She gained the nearest boat, the free-traders forming up around her, and hustling the dragoons. It was old Solomon Tweedy's boat, and he, prudent man, had taken advantage of the skirmish to ease her off, so that a push would set her afloat. He asserts that as July came up to him she never uttered a word, but the look on her face said "Push me off," and though he was at that moment meditating his own escape, he obeyed and pushed the boat off "like a mazed man." I may add that he spent three months in Bodmin Gaol for it.

She dropped with her burden against the stern sheets, but leapt up instantly and had the oars between the thole-pins almost as the boat floated. She pulled a dozen strokes, and hoisted the main-sail, pulled a hundred or so, sprang forward and ran up the jib. All this while the preventive men were straining to get off two boats in pursuit; but, as you may guess, the free-traders did nothing to help and a great deal to impede. And first the crews tumbled in too hurriedly, and had to climb out again (looking very foolish) and push afresh, and then one of the boats had mysteriously lost her plug and sank in half a fathom of water. July had gained a full hundred yards' offing before the pursuit began in earnest, and this meant a good deal. Once clear of the point the small cutter could defy their rowing and reach away to the eastward with the wind just behind her beam. The riding-officer saw this, and ordered his men to fire. They assert, and we must believe, that their object was merely to disable the boat by cutting up her canvas.

Their first desultory volley did no damage. I stood there, high on the cliff, and watched the boat, making a spy-glass of my hands. She had fetched in close under the point, and gone about on the port tack—the next would clear—when the first shot struck her, cutting a hole through her jib, and I expected the wind to rip the sail up immediately; yet it stood. The breeze being dead on-shore, the little boat heeled towards us, her mainsail hiding the steerswoman.

It was a minute later, perhaps, that I began to suspect that July was hit, for she allowed the jib to shake and seemed to be running right up into the wind. The stern swung round and I strained my eyes to catch a glimpse of her. At that moment a third volley rattled out, a bullet shore through the peak halliards, and the mainsail came down with a run. It was all over.

The preventive men cheered and pulled with a will. I saw them run alongside, clamber into the cutter, and lift the fallen sail.

And that was all. There was no one on board, alive or dead. Whilst the canvas hid her, in the swift two minutes between the boat's putting about and her running up into the wind, July Constantine must have lifted her lover's body overboard and followed it to the bottom of the sea, There is no other explanation; and of the bond that knit these two together there is, when I ask myself candidly, no explanation at all, unless I give more credence than I have any wish to give to the wild tale which Joseph Laquedem told me. I have told you the facts, my friend, and leave them to your judgment.

The Paradise of Choice

It was not as in certain toy houses that foretell the weather by means of a man-doll and a woman-doll—the man going in as the woman comes out, and *vice versa*. In this case both man and woman stepped out, the man half a minute behind; so that the woman was almost at the street-corner while he hesitated just outside the door, blinking up at the sky, and then dropping his gaze along the pavement.

The sky was flattened by a fog that shut down on the roofs and chimneys like a tent-cloth, white and opaque. Now and then a yellowish wave rolled across it from eastward, and the cloth would be shaken. When this happened, the street was always filled with gloom, and the receding figure of the woman lost in it for a while.

The man thrust a hand into his trousers pocket, pulled out a penny, and after considering for a couple of seconds, spun it carelessly. It fell in his palm, tail up; and he regarded it as a sailor might a compass. The trident in Britannia's hand pointed westward, down the street.

"West it is," he decided with a shrug, implying that all the four quarters were equally to his mind. He was pocketing the coin, when footsteps approached, and he lifted his head. It was the woman returning. She halted close to him with an undecided manner, and the pair eyed each other.

We may know them as Adam and Eve, for both were beginning a world that contained neither friends nor kin. Both had very white hands and very short hair. The man was tall and meagre, with a receding forehead and a sandy complexion that should have been freckled, but was not. He had a trick of half-closing his eyes when he looked at anything, not screwing them up as seamen do, but appearing rather to drop a film over them like the inner eyelid of a bird. The woman's eyes resembled a hare's, being brown and big, and set far back, so that she seemed at times to be looking right behind her. She wore a faded look, from her dust-coloured hair to her boots, which wanted blacking.

"It all seems so wide," she began; "so wide—"

"I'm going west," said the man, and started at a slow walk. Eve followed, a pace behind his heels, treading almost in his tracks. He went on, taking no notice of her.

"How long were you in there?" she asked, after a while.

"Ten year'." Adam spoke without looking back. "'Cumulated jobs, you know."

"I was only two. Blankets it was with me. They recommended me to mercy."

"You got it," Adam commented, with his eyes fastened ahead.

The fog followed them as they turned into a street full of traffic. Its frayed edge rose and sank, was parted and joined again—now descending to the first-storey windows and blotting out the cabmen and passengers on omnibus tops, now rolling up and over the parapets of the houses and the sky-signs. It was noticeable that in the crowd that hustled along the pavement Adam moved like a puppy not yet waywise, but with lifted face, while Eve followed with her head bent, seeing nothing but his heels. She observed that his boots were hardly worn at all.

Three or four times, as they went along, Adam would eye a shop window and turn in at the door, while Eve waited. He returned from different excursions with a twopenny loaf, a red sausage, a pipe, box of lights and screw of tobacco, and a noggin or so of gin in an old soda-water bottle. Once they turned aside into a public, and had a drink of gin together. Adam paid.

Thus for two hours they plodded westward, and the fog and

crowd were with them all the way—strangers jostling them by the shoulder on the greasy pavement, hansoms splashing the brown mud over them—the same din for miles. Many shops were lighting up, and from these a yellow flare streamed into the fog; or a white when it came from the electric light; or separate beams of orange, green, and violet, when the shop was a druggist's.

Then they came to the railings of Hyde Park, and trudged down the hill alongside them to Kensington Gardens. It was yet early in the afternoon. Adam pulled up.

"Come and look," he said. "It's autumn in there," and he went in at the Victoria gate, with Eve at his heels.

"Mister, how old might you be?" she asked, encouraged by the sound of his voice.

"Thirty."

"And you've passed ten years in—in there." She jerked her head back and shivered a little.

He had stooped to pick up a leaf. It was a yellow leaf from a chestnut that reached into the fog above them. He picked it slowly to pieces, drawing full draughts of air into his lungs. "Fifteen," he jerked out, "one time and another. 'Cumulated, you know." Pausing, he added, in a matter-of-fact voice, "What I've took would come to less'n a pound's worth, altogether."

The gardens were deserted, and the pair roamed towards the centre, gazing curiously at so much of sodden vegetation as the fog allowed them to see. Their eyes were not jaded; to them a blade of grass was not a little thing.

They were down on the south side, amid the heterogeneous plants there collected, examining each leaf, spelling the Latin labels and comparing them, when the hour came for closing. In the dense atmosphere the park-keeper missed them. The gates were shut; and the fog settled down thicker with the darkness.

Then the man and the woman were aware, and grew afraid. They saw only a limitless plain of grey about them, and heard a murmur as of the sea rolling around it.

"This gaol is too big," whispered Eve, and they took hands.

The man trembled. Together they moved into the fog, seeking an outlet.

At the end of an hour or so they stumbled on a seat, and sat down for awhile to share the bread and sausage, and drink the gin. Eve was tired out and would have slept, but the man shook her by the shoulder.

"For God's sake don't leave me to face this alone. Can you sing?"

She began "*When other lips* . . ." in a whisper which gradually developed into a reedy *soprano*. She had forgotten half the words, but Adam lit a pipe and listened appreciatively.

"Tell you what," he said at the close; "you'll be able to pick up a little on the road with your singing. We'll tramp west to-morrow, and pass ourselves off for man and wife. Likely we'll get some farm work, down in the country. Let's get out of this."

They joined hands and started off again, unable to see a foot before them in the blackness. So it happened next morning that the park-keeper, coming at his usual hour to unlock the gates, found a man and a woman inside with their white faces pressed against the railings, through which they glared like caged beasts. He set them free, and they ran out, for his paradise was too big.

Now, facing west, they tramped for two days on the Bath road, leaving the fog behind them, and drew near Reading. It was a clear night as they approached it, and the sky studded with stars that twinkled frostily. Eleven o'clock sounded from a tower ahead. On the outskirts of the town they were passing an ugly modern villa with a large garden before it, when an old gentleman came briskly up the road and turned in at the gate.

Adam swung round on his heel and followed him up the path, begging. Eve hung by the gate.

"No," said the old gentleman, fitting his latchkey into the door, "I have no work to offer. Eh?—Is that your wife by the gate? Hungry?"

Adam whispered a lie in his ear.

"Poor woman, and to be on the road, in such a state, at this hour! Well, you shall share my supper before you search for a lodging. Come inside," he called out to Eve, "and be careful of the step. It's a high one."

He led them in, past the ground-floor rooms and up a flight of stairs. After pausing on the landing and waiting a long time for Eve to take breath, he began to ascend another flight.

"Are we going to have supper on the leads?" Adam wondered.

They followed the old gentleman up to the attics and into a kind of tower, where was a small room with two tables spread, the one with a supper, the other with papers, charts, and mathematical instruments.

"Here," said their guide, "is bread, a cold chicken, and a bottle of whisky. I beg you to excuse me while you eat. The fact is, I dabble in astronomy. My telescope is on the roof above, and to-night every moment is precious."

There was a ladder fixed in the room, leading to a trap-door in the ceiling. Up this ladder the old gentleman trotted, and in half a minute had disappeared, shutting the trap behind him.

It was half an hour or more before Adam climbed after him, with Eve, as usual, at his heels.

"My dear madam!" cried the astronomer, "and in your state!"

"I told you a lie," Adam said. "I've come to beg your pardon. May we look at the stars before we go?"

In two minutes the old gentleman was pointing out the constellations—the Great Bear hanging low in the north-east, pointing to the Pole star, and across it to Cassiopeia's bright zigzag high in the heavens; the barren square of Pegasus, with its long tail stretching to the Milky Way, and the points that cluster round Perseus; Arcturus, white Vega and yellow Capella; the Twins, and beyond them the Little Dog twinkling through a coppice of naked trees to eastward; yet further round the Pleiads climbing, with red Aldebaran after them; below them Orion's belt, and last of all, Sirius flashing like a diamond, white and red, and resting on the horizon where the dark pasture lands met the sky.

Then, growing flushed with his subject, he began to descant on these stars, their distances and velocities; how that each was a sun, careering in measureless space, each trailing a company of worlds that spun and hurtled round it; that the Dog-star's light shone into their eyes across a hundred trillion miles; that the star itself swept along a thousand miles in a minute. He hurled figures at them, heaping millions on millions. "See here"—and, turning the telescope on its pivot, he sighted it carefully. "Look at that small star in the Great Bear: that's Groombridge Eighteen-thirty. *He's* two hundred billions of miles away. *He* travels two hundred miles a second, does Groombridge Eighteen-thirty. In one minute Groombridge Eighteen-thirty could go from here to Hong-Kong."

"Then damn Groombridge Eighteen-thirty!"

It was uttered in the bated tone that night enforces: but it came with a groan. The old gentleman faced round in amazement.

"He means, sir," explained the woman, who had grown to understand Adam passing well, "my man means that it's all too big for us. We've strayed out of prison, sir, and shall feel safer back again, looking at all this behind bars."

She reached out a hand to Adam: and this time it was he that followed, as one blinded and afraid. In three months they were back again at the gates of the paradise they had wandered from. There stood a warder before it, clad in blue: but he carried no flaming sword, and the door opened and let them in.

The Penance of John Emmet

I have thought fit in this story to alter all the names involved and disguise the actual scene of it: and have done this so carefully that, although the story has a key, the reader who should search for it would not only waste his time but miss even the poor satisfaction of having guessed an idle riddle. He whom I call Parson West is now dead. He was an entirely conscientious man; which means that he would rather do wrong himself than persuade or advise another man—above all, a young man—to do it. I am sure therefore that in burying the body of John Emmet as he did, and enlisting my help, he did what he thought right, though the action was undoubtedly an illegal one.

Still, the question is one for casuists; and remembering how modest a value my old friend set on his own wisdom, I dare say that by keeping his real name out of the narrative I am obeying what would have been his wish. His small breach of the law he was (I know) prepared to answer for cheerfully, should the facts come to light. He has now gone where their discovery affects him not at all.

Parson West, then, when I made his acquaintance in 188-, had for thirty years been vicar of the coast-parish of Lansulyan. He had come to it almost fresh from Oxford, a young scholar with a head full of Greek, having accepted the living from his old college as a step towards preferment. He was never to be offered another. Lansulyan parish is a wide one in acreage, and the stipend exiguous even for a bachelor. From the first the parson eked out his income by preparing small annotated editions of the classics for the use of schools and by taking occasional pupils, of whom in 188- I was the latest. He could not teach me scholarship, which is a habit of mind; but he could, and in the end did, teach me how to win a scholarship, which is a sum of money paid annually. I have therefore a practical reason for thinking of him with gratitude: and I believe he liked me, while despising my Latinity and discommending my precociousness with tobacco.

His pupils could never complain of distraction. The church-town—a single street of cottages winding round a knoll of elms which hide the vicarage and all but the spire of St. Julian's Church—stands high and a mile back from the coast, and looks straight upon the Menawhidden reef, a fringe of toothed rocks lying parallel with the shore and half a mile distant from it. This reef forms a breakwater for a small inlet where the coombe which runs below Lansulyan meets the sea. Follow the road downhill from the church-town and along the coombe, and you come to a white-washed fishing haven, with a life-boat house and short sea-wall. The Porth is its only name.

On the whole, if one has to live in Lansulyan parish the Porth is gayer than the church-town, where from the vicarage windows you look through the trees southward upon ships moving up or down channel in the blue distance and the white water girdling Menawhidden; northward upon downs where herds of ponies wander at will between the treeless farms, and a dun-coloured British earthwork tops the high sky-line. Dwellers among these uplands, wringing their livelihood from the obstinate soil by labour which never slackens, year in and year out, from Monday morning to Saturday night, are properly despised by the inhabitants of the Porth, who sit half their time mending nets, cultivating the social graces, and waiting for the harvest which they have not sown to come floating past their doors. By consequence, if a farmer wishes to learn the spiciest gossip about his nearest neighbour, he must travel down to the Porth for it.

And this makes it the more marvellous that what I am about to tell, happening as it did at the very gates of the Porth, should have escaped the sharpest eyes in the place.

The vicar's custom was to read with me for a couple of hours in the morning and again for an hour and a half before dinner. We had followed this routine rigidly and punctually for three months or so when, one evening in June, he returned from the Porth a good ten minutes late, very hot and dusty, and even so took a turn or two up and down the room with his hands clasped behind his coat-tails before settling down to correct my *iambics*.

"John Emmet is dead," he announced, pausing before the window with his back towards me and gazing out upon the ill-kept lawn.

"Wasn't he the coxswain of the life-boat?" I asked.

"Ah, to be sure, you never saw him, did you? He took to his bed before you came . . . a long illness. Well, well, it's all over!" Parson West sighed. "He saved, or helped to save, a hundred and fifteen lives, first and last. A hundred and fifteen lives!"

"I've heard something of the sort down at the Porth. A hundred and fifty, I think they said. They seemed very proud of him down there."

"Why?" The vicar faced round on me, and added after a moment abruptly— "He didn't belong to them: he was not even born in this parish."

"Where then?"

He disregarded the question. "Besides, the number was a hundred and fifteen: that's just the pity."

I did not understand: but he had seated himself at table and was running through my *iambics*. In the third verse he underlined a false quantity with blue pencil and looked up for an explanation. While I confessed the fault, his gaze wandered away from me and fell upon his fingers drumming upon the table's edge. A slant of red sunshine touched the signet-ring on his little finger, which he moved up and down watching the play of light on the rim of the collet. He was not listening. By-and-by he glanced up, "I beg your pardon—" stammered he, and leaving the rest of my verses uncorrected, pointed with his pencil to the concluding one. "That's not Greek," he said.

"It's in Sophocles," I contended: and turning up the word in "Liddell and Scott," I pushed the big lexicon under his nose.

For a moment he paid no heed to the action; did not seem to grasp the meaning of it. Then for the first and last time in my acquaintance with him he broke into a passion of temper.

"What do you mean, Sir? It's offensive, I tell you: a downright offensive, ungentlemanly thing to do! Yes, Sir, ungentlemanly!" He crumpled up my verses and tossed them into the waste-paper basket. "We had better get on with our Tacitus." And "Offensive!" I heard him muttering once more, as he picked up the book and found his place. I began to construe. His outburst had disconcerted me, and no doubt I performed discreditably: but glancing up in some apprehension after a piece of guess-work which even to me carried no conviction, I saw that again he was not attending. After this, by boldly skipping each difficulty as it arose I managed to cover a good deal of ground with admirable fluency.

We dined together in silence that evening, and after dinner strolled out to the big filbert-tree under which, for a few weeks in the year, Parson West had his dessert laid and sipped his thin port—an old common-room fashion to which he clung. To the end of his days he had the white cloth removed before dessert, and the fruits and the one decanter set out upon polished mahogany.

I glanced at him while helping myself to strawberries and cream. He sat nervously folding and refolding the napkin on his knee. By-and-by he spoke, but without looking at me.

"I lost my temper this afternoon, and I beg your pardon, my boy."

I began to stammer my contrition for having offended him: but he cut me short with a wave of the hand. "The fact is," he explained, "I was worried by something quite different."

"By John Emmet's death," I suggested. He nodded, and looked at me queerly while he poured out a glass of Tarragona.

"He was my gardener years ago, before he set up market-gardening on his own account."

"That's queer too," said I.

"What's queer?" He asked it sharply.

"Why, to find a gardener cox'n of a life-boat."

"He followed the sea in early life. But I'll tell you what *is* queer, and that's his last wish. His particular desire was that I, and I alone, should screw down the coffin. He had Trudgeon the carpenter up to measure him, and begged this of me in Trudgeon's presence and the doctor's. What's more, I consented."

"That's jolly unpleasant," was my comment, for lack of a better.

The vicar sat silent for a while, staring across the lawn, while I watched a spider which had let itself down from a branch overhead and was casting anchor on the decanter's rim. With his next question he seemed to have changed the subject.

"Where do you keep your boat now?"

"Renatus Warne has been putting in a new strake and painting her. I shall have her down on the beach tomorrow."

"Ah, so that's it? I cast my eye over the beach this afternoon and couldn't see her. You haven't been trying for the conger lately."

"We'll have a try tomorrow evening if you'll come, Sir. I wish you would."

The vicar, though he seldom found time for the sport, was a famous fisherman. He shook his head; and then, leaning an arm on the table, gazed at me with sudden seriousness.

"Look here: could you make it convenient to go fishing for conger this next night or two—*and to go alone?*"

I saw that he had something more to say, and waited.

"The fact is," he went on after a glance towards the house, "I have a ticklish job to carry through—the queerest in all my experience; and unfortunately I want help as well as secrecy. After some perplexity I've resolved to ask you: because, upon my word, you're the only person I can ask. That doesn't sound flattering—eh? But it isn't your fitness I doubt, or your nerve. I've hesitated because it isn't fair to drag you into an affair which, I must warn you, runs counter to the law in a small way."

I let out a low whistle. "A smuggling job?" I suggested.

"Good Heavens, boy! What do you take me for?"

"I beg your pardon, then. But when you talk of a row-boat—at night—a job that wants secrecy—breaking the law—"

"I'll have to tell you the whole tale, I see: and it's only fair."

"Not a bit," said I stoutly. "Tell me what you want done and I'll do it. Afterwards tell me your reasons, if you care to. Indeed, Sir, I'd rather have it that way, if you don't mind. I was abominably disrespectful this afternoon—"

"No more about *that*."

"But I *was*: and with your leave, Sir, that's the form of apology I'll choose."

And I stood up with my hands in my pockets.

"Nonsense, nonsense," said the vicar, eyeing me with a twinkle. But I nodded back in the most determined manner.

"Your instructions, sir—that is, unless you prefer to get another helper."

"But I cannot," pleaded he. "That's the mischief."

"Very well, then. Your instructions, please." And thus I had my way.

This happened on a Tuesday. The next evening I walked down to the Porth and launched my boat. A row of idlers watched me from the long bench under the life-boat house, and a small knot on the beach inspected my fishing-gear and lent a hand to push off. "Ben't goin' alone, be 'e?" asked Renatus Warne. "Yes," said I. "The conger'll have 'ee then, sure enough." One or two offered chaffingly to come out and search for me if I shouldn't return before midnight; and a volley of facetious warnings followed me out upon the calm sea.

The beach was deserted, however, when I returned. I had hooked three fine conger; and having hauled up the boat and cleaned her, I made my way back to the vicarage, well pleased, getting to bed as the clock struck two in the morning.

This was Thursday; and in the evening, between seven and eight o'clock, I launched the boat again under the eyes of the population and started fishing on the inner grounds, well in sight of the Porth. Dusk fell, and with it the young moon dropped behind the western headland. Far out beyond Menawhidden the riding-lights of a few drifters sparkled in the darkness: but I had little to fear from them.

The moon had no sooner disappeared than I shifted my ground, and pulling slowly down in the shore's shadow (I had greased the leathers of my oars for silence), ran the boat in by the point under Gunner's Meadow, beached her cunningly between two rocks, and pulled a tarpaulin over to hide her white-painted interior. My only danger now lay in blundering against the coastguard: but by dodging from one big boulder to another and listening all the while for footsteps, I gained the withy bed at the foot of the meadow. The night was almost pitch-black, and no one could possibly detect the boat unless he searched for it.

I followed the little stream up the valley bottom, through an orchard, and struck away from it across another meadow and over the rounded shoulder of the hill to my right. This brought me in rear of a kitchen-garden and a lonely cob-walled cottage, the front of which faced down a dozen precipitous steps upon the road leading from Lansulyan to the Porth. The cottage had but one window in the back, in the upper floor; and just beneath it jutted out a lean-to shed, on the wooden side of which I rapped thrice with my knuckles.

"Hist!" The vicar leaned out from the dark window above. "Right: it's all ready. We must stow it in the outhouse. Trudgeon is down in the road below, waiting for me to finish."

No more was said. The vicar withdrew: after a minute I heard the planking creak: then something white glimmered in the opening of the window—something like a long bundle of linen, extruded inch by inch, then lowered on to the penthouse roof and let slide slowly down towards me.

"Got it?"

"Right." I steadied it a moment by its feet, then let it slide into my arms, and lowered it on to the gravelled path. It was the body of John Emmet, in his winding-sheet.

"Carry it into the shed," whispered the vicar. "I must show Trudgeon the coffin and hand him the keys. When I've got rid of him I'll come round."

Somehow, the second time of handling it was far worse than the first. The chill of the corpse seemed to strike through its linen wrappers. But I lifted it inside, shut the door upon it, and stood wiping my forehead, while the vicar closed the window cautiously, drew the blind, and pressed-to the clasp.

A minute later I heard him calling from the front, "Mr. Trudgeon—Mr. Trudgeon"; and Trudgeon's hob-nailed boots ascending the steps. Silence followed for many minutes: then a slant of candlelight faded off the fuchsia-bush round the corner, and the two men stumbled down the staircase—stood muttering on the doorstep while a key grated in the lock—stumbled down the steps and stood muttering in the sunken roadway. At length they said "Goodnight" and parted. I listened while the sound of their footsteps died away: Trudgeon's down the hill towards the Porth, the vicar's up towards the church-town.

After this I had some painful minutes. As they dragged by, an abominable curiosity took hold of me, an itch to open the door of the shed, strike a match, and have a look at the dead face I had never seen. Then came into my mind a passage in the *Republic* which I had read a fortnight before—how that one Leontius, the son of Aglaion, coming up one day from the Piraeus under the north wall of the city, observed some corpses lying on the ground at the place of execution; and how he fought between his desire to look and his abhorrence until at length, the fascination mastering him, he forced his eyes open with his fingers and ran up exclaiming, "Look, wretches, look! Feed your fill on the fair sight!" . . . My seat was an inverted flower-pot, and clinging to it I began to count. If the vicar did not arrive before I reached five hundred, why, then . . .

"*Hist!*" He had fetched his compass round by the back of the garden, treading so softly that the signal sounded almost in my ear and fetched me off my flower-pot in a nervous quake.

He wore a heavy pea-jacket, and, as a smell of hot varnish announced, carried a dark lantern beneath it. He had strapped this to his waist-belt to leave both hands free.

We lifted the body out and carried it across the meadow, the vicar taking the shoulders and I the heels. And now came the real hazard of the night. If the coastguard or any belated wanderer should blunder upon us, we stood convicted of kidnapping a corpse, and (as the vicar afterwards allowed) there was simply no explanation to be given. When we gained the orchard and pushed through the broken fence, every twig that crackled fetched my heart into my mouth: and I drew my first breath of something like ease when at length, in the withy bed at the foot of Gunner's Meadow, we laid our burden down behind the ruin of an old cob-wall and took a short rest before essaying the beach.

But that breath was hardly drawn before I laid a warning hand on the vicar's sleeve. Someone was coming down the cliff-track: the coastguard, no doubt. He halted on the wooden footbridge, struck a match and lit his pipe. From our covert not ten yards away I saw the glow on his face as he shielded the match in the hollow of both his hands. It was the coastguard—a fellow called Simms. His match lit, I expected him to resume his walk. But no: he loitered there. For what reason, on earth? Luckily his back was towards us now: but to me, as I cowered in the plashy mud and prayed against sneezing, it seemed that the damnatory smell of the vicar's lantern must carry for half a mile at least.

And now I heard another footstep, coming from the westward, and a loose stone kicked over the cliff. Another coastguard! The pair hailed each other, and stood on the footbridge talking together for a good three minutes.

Then to our infinite relief they parted with a "So long!" and each made slowly off by the way he had come. It was just a meeting of the patrols after all.

Another ten minutes must have gone by before we dared to lift the body again: and after a nervous while in crossing the beach we found the boat left high and dry by the ebb, and had an interminable job to get her down to the water without noise. I climbed in and took the oars: the vicar lifted a sizeable stone on board and followed.

"The Carracks," he whispered. "That's the spot he named to me."

So I pulled out towards the Carracks, which are three points of rock lying just within the main barrier of Menawhidden, where it breaks up towards its western end into a maze of islets. While I pulled, the vicar knelt on the bottom-boards and made fast the stone to John Emmet's feet.

Well, I need not tell the rest of our adventure at length. We reached the Carracks, and there the vicar pulled out a short surplice from the immense inner pocket of his pea-jacket, donned it, and read the burial service in due form by the light of his dark lantern: and by the light of it, as I arranged John Emmet's shroud, I had my first and last glimpse of his face—a thin face, old and hollow, with grey side-whiskers: a face extraordinarily pallid: in other circumstances perhaps not noticeable unless it were for a look of extreme weariness which had lasted even into the rest of death.

"We therefore commit his body to the deep, to be turned into corruption, looking for the resurrection of the body (when the sea shall give up her dead), and the life of the world to come. . . ."

Together we balanced it on the gunwale, and with the help of the stern-board tilted it over. It dropped, into fifteen fathoms of water.

There was another funeral next day in Lansulyan churchyard—where so many have come to be buried who never in life heard the name of Lansulyan: the harvest of Menawhidden, commemorated on weather-beaten stones and, within the church, on many tablets which I used to con on Sundays during the vicar's discourses. The life-boat men had mustered in force, and altogether there was a large attendance at the graveside. At one point a fit of coughing interrupted the vicar in his recital of the service. I was the one auditor, however, who understood the meaning of it.

That evening we took our dessert again under the great elm. Somehow I felt certain he would choose this hour for his explanation: and in due course it came.

"I'm a truth-speaking man by habit," he began after a long gaze upwards at the rooks now settling to roost and making a mighty pother of it. "But I'm afraid there's no getting round the fact that this afternoon I acted a lie. And yet, on the whole, my conscience is easy."

He sipped his wine, and went on meditatively—

"Morals have their court of equity as well as the law of the land: and with us"—the vicar was an old-fashioned Churchman—"that court is the private conscience. In this affair you insisted on putting your conscience into my hands. Well, I took the responsibility, and charge myself with any wrong you have committed, letting your confidence stand to your credit, as well as the service you have done for me—and another. Do you know the grey marble tablet on the south wall of the church—the *Nerbuddha* monument?"

I nodded.

"'*Sacred to the memory of Lieutenant-Colonel Victor Stanhope, C.B., and 105 Officers and Men of Her Majesty's 2-th Regiment of Foot, lost in the wreck of the Nerbuddha, East Indiaman, on Menawhidden, January 15th, 1857....*' Then follows a list of the officers. Underneath, if you remember, is a separate slab to the officers and crew of the *Nerbuddha*, who behaved admirably, all the senior officers keeping order to the last and going down with the ship."

I nodded again, for I knew the inscriptions pretty well by heart.

"The wreck happened in the first winter of my incumbency here. Then, as now, I had one pupil living with me, an excellent fellow. Dick Hobart was his name, his age seventeen or thereabouts, and my business to put some polish on a neglected education before he entered the army. His elder brother had been a college friend of mine, and indeed our families had been acquainted for years.

"Dick slept in the room you now occupy. He had a habit, which I never cured, of sitting up late over a pipe and a yellow-backed novel: and so he happened to be dressed that night when he saw the first signal of distress go up from Menawhidden. He came to my room at once and called me up: and while I tumbled out and began to dress, he ran down to Porth to give the alarm.

"The first signal, however, had been seen by the folks down there, and he found the whole place in a hubbub. Our first life-boat had arrived less than three months before; but the crew got her off briskly, and were pulling away lustily for the reef when it occurred to a few of those left behind that the sea running was not too formidable for a couple of seine-boats lying high on the beach: and within five minutes these were hauled down and manned with scratch crews—Dick Hobart among them.

"Three days of east wind had knocked up a heavy swell: but the wind was blowing a moderate gale only—nothing to account for a big ship (as she was already reported to be) finding herself on Menawhidden. Three signals only had been shown, and these in quick succession. We learned afterwards that she went down within twelve minutes of striking. She had dashed straight on the Carracks, with the wind well behind her beam, topmasts housed for the night, but, barring that, canvassed like a well-found ship sure of her sea-room. And the Carracks had torn the bottom out of her.

"The difficulty with the life-boat and two seine-boats was to find the position of the wreck, the night being pitch dark and dirty, and the calls and outcries of the poor creatures being swept down the wind to the westward. Our fellows pulled like Trojans, however, hailing and ahoying as they went; and about half-way down the line of Menawhidden they came on the first of the *Nerbuddha's* boats, laden with women and children, in charge of the fourth officer and half-a-dozen seamen. From her they learned the vessel's name and whereabouts, and having directed her on her way to the Porth, hurried forward again. They passed another boat similarly laden, and presently heard the distracting cries of swimmers, and drove straight into the wreckage and the struggling crowd of bodies. The life-boat rescued twenty-seven, and picked up four more on a second journey: the first seine-boat accounted for a dozen: the second (in which Hobart pulled an oar) was less fortunate, saving five only—and yet, as I shall tell you, my young friend had (and, for that matter, still has) abundant reason to be thankful for his voyage in her; for on that night he plucked from the sea the greatest treasure of his life.

"She—for it was a small girl of seven, and he took her from the arms of a seaman who died soon after being lifted into the boat-turned out to be the colonel's daughter. She had stood by her mother's side above the gangway while the women passed down the side into the boats: for that noble English lady had insisted that as it was the colonel's duty to follow his men, so it was for the colonel's wife to wait until every other woman and every child had filed past. The *Nerbuddha* had gone down under her as she stood there beside her husband, steadied by his hand on her shoulder. Both bodies were afterwards recovered.

"Altogether fifty-two were buried in this parish: other bodies were washed ashore or picked up from time to time, some at great distances up and down the Channel. In the end the list of those unaccounted for came to forty, or by other accounts thirty-six. That was my first experience of what Menawhidden could do. I have had many since: but to this day our little church—yes, even when we decorate it for harvest-festival and pile the sheaves within the Communion rails—remains for me the dark little building where the bodies lay in rows waiting to be identified, and where I and half-a-dozen volunteers took turns in keeping watch day and night while the windows shook and the damp oozed down the walls.

"The cause of the wreck was never made clear. The helmsman had gone, and the captain (his body was among the missing), and the first, second, and third officers. But two seamen who had been successively relieved at the wheel in the early hours of the night agreed on the course set by the captain. It was a course which must finally bring them straight on Menawhidden. Yet there was no evidence to show that the captain changed it. The men knew nothing of Channel navigation, and had simply obeyed orders. She had struck during the first mate's watch. The fourth officer (survivor) had also been on deck. He gave evidence that his superior, Mr. Rands, had said nothing about the course. For his own part he had supposed the ship to be a good fifteen miles from the coast. They had sighted no shorelights to warn them: but the weather was hazy. Five minutes before the catastrophe Mr. Rands had remarked that the wind was increasing, but had deferred shortening sail.

"The ship was an old one, but newly rigged throughout. Her compasses had been adjusted and the ship swung at Greenhithe, just before the voyage. Mr. Murchison, the captain, was a trusted commander of the H.E.I.C.: he came originally from Liverpool, and had worked his way up in the company's service: a positive man and something of a disciplinarian, almost a martinet—not a man who would bear crossing easily. He was in his cabin, but came on deck at once, ready dressed; and had, with Colonel Stanhope's assistance, kept admirable order, getting out the three boats as promptly as possible. A fourth had actually been launched, and was being manned when the vessel plunged and stove her in as she went down.

"That is as much as needs be told about the *Nerbuddha*. Let me get on to the happier part of the story, that which concerns Dick Hobart and the small girl whom by Heaven's mercy he helped to save. Her name was Felicia—Felicia Rose Derwent Stanhope in full. Her uncle and guardian, Sir John Derwent, came down and fetched her home, with the bodies of her father and mother. I have told you that Dick was just then waiting for his commission, which, by the way, his family could poorly afford to purchase. Well, in recognition of his 'gallantry' (as the old gentleman was good enough to term it) Sir John, who possessed a good deal of influence, had him gazetted within six weeks, and to the 2-th Regiment—'for which,' so ran the gracious letter bringing the news, 'you have performed the first of what I hope will be a long list of distinguished services.'

"Pretty, was it not? Yes, but there's prettier to come. Felicia, who was an only child and quite an heiress in a small way, kept up from the first a steady correspondence with her 'preserver': childish letters, to begin with, but Dick kept them all. In Bombay, in Abyssinia, for a few weeks in England (when he saw her for the first time since the wreck), then back in India again, he has told me since that the world held but one woman for him, and that was the little girl growing up to womanhood in her Bedfordshire home.

"Well it all happened as you are guessing. Dick, who had inherited a little money by this time, and was expecting his majority, returned to England in '72 on a long furlough. Needless to say he paid a visit to Cressingham, where Felicia lived under the wing of a widowed aunt: equally needless to say what happened there. The engagement was a short one—six weeks: and Dick flattered me immensely with an invitation to come up and perform the ceremony."

The vicar paused, refilled his glass, and leaning back gazed up at the now silent nests. "All this," thought I, "may be mighty interesting in its way, but what—"

"But what, you'll be asking, has all this to do with John Emmet? I'm coming to that. On the evening of my arrival at Cressingham, Dick, who was lodging at the village inn where I too had a room, took me over to pay my respects to the ladies. We had taken our leave and were passing down the pretty avenue of limes to the entrance gates, when he paused and hailed a man stooping over a fountain in the Italian garden on our left, and apparently clearing it of dead leaves.

"'Hi! John Emmet!'

"The man straightened his back, faced round, and came towards us, touching his hat.

"'This is the gentleman, John, who has come expressly to tie the knot next Wednesday. You must know,' said Dick, turning to me, 'that Miss Felicia and John Emmet are sworn friends, and he owes me a mighty grudge for taking her away. He's been gardener here for fifteen—sixteen—how many years is it, John?'

"'Then,' said I, 'I suppose you were here before the wreck of the *Nerbuddha*, and knew Miss Felicia's parents?'

"The man gave a start, and his hat, which he had pulled off, and with the brim of which he was fumbling, slipped from his fingers and rolled on the turf.

"'Oh, yes, I forgot!' put in Dick. 'I ought to have told you that Mr. West here is the Rector of Lansulyan, and was at the time of the wreck.'

"'Indeed, Sir!' John Emmet had recovered his hat, and confronted me with a face for which I spared a glance before bending my eyes on the daisies at my feet. 'I—I took service here some months after that event.'

"'Come, *Padre*'—these were the next words I heard—'if you wish to prod up all the daisies on Felicia's property, arise early tomorrow and begin. But if we're to dine at the Hall tonight it's time to be getting back to the inn and changing our clothes.'

"I looked up, and my eyes fell on the retreating back of John Emmet, already half-way towards the Italian garden."

"'Queer fellow, that—what's his name?—John Emmet,' said I late that night on our return to the inn, as Dick and I mixed our whiskey and prepared for a smoke before his sitting-room fire.

"'Tile loose, I fancy,' answered Dick, pausing with a lighted match in his hand. 'I've an idea that he owes me a grudge for coming here and carrying off Felicia.'

"'What gives you that notion?'

"'Well, you see he has always been a favourite of hers. She tells me that the hours she managed to steal and spend in the garden, chatting with John Emmet while he worked, were the happiest in her childhood. He seems to have been a kind of out-of-door protector to her, and I'll bet she twisted him round her small thumb.'

"'That's little enough to go upon,' was my comment. 'It struck me, on the contrary, that the man eyed you with some affection, not to say pride.'

"'Well, it's a small thing, but I can't help remembering how he took the news of Felicia's—of our engagement. You see, it happened at a fancy-dress dance.'

"'What happened?'

"'Don't be dense, *Padre*. Why, *it*—the engagement. The dance was given by some people who live two miles from here—people called Bargrave. Felicia and I drove over. She wore an old court dress of her grandmother's or great-grand-mother's: I'm no hand at costumes, and can only tell you that she looked particularly jolly in it. I went in uniform—mess uniform, that is. It's one of the minor advantages of the service that on these occasions a man hasn't to put on a cavalier's wig and look like a goat out for a holiday. Well, as I was saying, at this particular dance *it* happened. It was daybreak when we started to drive home; a perfect midsummer morning, sun shining, dew on the hedges, and the birds singing fit to split themselves.

"'Felicia and I had a lot to say to each other, naturally; and it occurred to us to stop the carriage at the gates and send it on while we walked up to the house together. We took the path leading through the Italian garden, and there—pretty well in the same place where you saw him this afternoon—we came on John Emmet, already out and at work: or rather he was leaning on a hoe and staring after the carriage as it moved up the avenue behind the limes. We came on him from behind, and, I suppose, suddenly. Anyhow, we scared him. I never saw such a face in my life as he turned on us! It went all white in an instant, and then slowly whiter. No doubt our dress was unusual: but I'm not accustomed to be taken for a ghost—'

"'Was it *you* who frightened him?'

"'Yes, I think so. He kept his eyes on me, anyway: and at first, when Felicia asked him to congratulate her, he didn't seem to hear. After a bit, however, he picked up his speech and muttered something about fate, and wishing her joy—I forget what. Felicia confessed afterwards that his face had fairly frightened her.'

"'Look here,' I asked; 'it may seem an irrelevant question, but has the 2-th made any changes in its uniform lately?—any important changes, I mean.'

"'No: the War Office has been obliging enough to leave us alone in that respect: out of sight out of mind, I suppose. In point of fact we've kept the same rig—officers and men—for something like a quarter of a century.' He paused. 'I see what you're driving at. The man, you think, may be an old deserter!'

"'Not so fast, please. Now here's another question. You remember the night after the wreck of the *Nerbuddha*: the night you took a turn in Lansulyan Church, watching the bodies? You came to me in the morning with a story which I chose to laugh at—'

"'About the face at the window, you mean?' Dick gave a mock shudder. 'I suppose my nerves were shaken. I've been through some queer things since: but upon my soul I'd as soon face the worst of them again as take another spell with a line of corpses in that church of yours.'

"'But—the face?'

"'Well, at the time I'd have sworn I saw it: peering in through the last window westward in the south aisle—the one above the font. I ran out, you remember, and found nobody: then I fetched a lantern and flashed it about the churchyard.'

"'There were gravestones in plenty a man could hide behind. Should you remember the face?'

"Dick considered for a while. 'No: it didn't strike me as a face so much as a pair of eyes; I remember the eyes only. They were looking straight into mine.'

"'Well, now. I've always guessed there was something queer about that *Nerbuddha* business: though till now I've never told a soul my chief reason for believing so. After you left me that night, and while I was dressing, it occurred to me from the last of the three signals—the only one I saw—that the wreck must be somewhere near the Carracks, and that Farmer Tregaskis had a seine-boat drawn up by the old pallace[1] at Gunner's Meadow, just opposite the Carracks.'"

"'It struck me that if it were possible to knock up Tregaskis and his boys and the farmhand who slept on the premises, and

---
1. Pilchard store.

get this boat launched through the surf, we should reach the wreck almost as soon as the lifeboat. So I took a lantern and ran across the fields to the farm. Lights were burning there in two or three windows, and Mrs. Tregaskis, who answered my knock, told me that her husband and the boys had already started off— she believed for Gunner's Meadow, to launch their boat. There had been talk of doing so, anyhow, before they set out. Accordingly, off I pelted hot-foot for the meadow, but on reaching the slope above it could see no lanterns either about the pallace or on the beach. It turned out afterwards that the Tregaskis family had indeed visited the beach, ten minutes ahead of me, but judging it beyond their powers to launch the boat short-handed through the surf, were by this time on their way towards the Porth. I thought this likely enough at the time, but resolved to run down and make sure.

"'Hitherto I had carried my lantern unlit: but on reaching the coombe bottom I halted for a moment under the lee of the pallace-wall to strike a match. In that moment, in a sudden lull of the breakers, it seemed to me that I heard a footstep on the loose stones of the beach; and having lit my candle hastily I ran round the wall and gave a loud hail. It was not answered: the sound had ceased: but hurrying down the beach with my lantern held high, I presently saw a man between me and the water's edge. I believe now that he was trying to get away unobserved: but finding this hopeless he stood still with his hands in his pockets, and allowed me to come up. He was bare-headed, and dressed only in shirt and trousers and boots. Somehow, though I did not recognise him, I never doubted for a moment that the man belonged either to my own or the next parish. I was a newcomer in those days, you remember.

"'"Hulloa!" said I, "where do you come from?"'

"'He stared at me stupidly and jerked his thumb over his shoulder towards the west. I inferred that he came from one of the shore-farms in that direction. He looked like a middle-aged farmer—a grizzled man with a serious, responsible face. "But you're wet through," I said, for his clothes were drenched.

"'For answer he pointed towards the surf, and lifting my lantern again, I detected a small cask floating a little beyond the breakers. Now before coming to Lansulyan I had heard some ugly tales of the wrecking done in these parts, and at the sight of this I fairly lost my temper. 'It seems to me,' said I, "a man of your age should be ashamed of himself, lurking here for miserable booty when there are lives to save! In God's name, if you have a spark of manhood in you, follow me to the Porth!" I swung off in a rage, and up the beach: after a moment I heard him slowly following. On the cliff track I swallowed down my wrath and waited for him to come up, meaning to expostulate more gently. He did not come up. I hailed twice, but he had vanished into the night.

"'Now this looked ugly. And on reflection, when I reached the Porth and heard men wondering how on earth a fine ship found herself on Menawhidden in such weather, it looked uglier yet. The fellow—now I came to think it over—had certainly shrunk from detection. Then, thirty hours later, came your story of the face, and upset me further. I kept my suspicions to myself, however. The matter was too grave for random talking: but I resolved to keep eyes and ears open, and if this horrible practice of wrecking did really exist, to expose it without mercy.

"'Well I have lived some years since in Lansulyan: and I am absolutely sure now that no such horrors exist, if they ever existed.'

"'But the man?' was Dick's query.

"'That's what I'm coming to. You may be sure I looked out for him: for, unlike you, I remembered the face I saw. Yet until today I have never seen it since.'

"'Until today?'

"'Yes. The man I saw on the beach was Miss Felicia's gardener, John Emmet. He has shaved his beard; but I'll swear to him.'

"All that Dick could do was to pull the pipe from his mouth and give a long whistle. 'But what do you make of it?' he asked with a frown.

"'As yet, nothing. Where does the man live?'

"'In a small cottage at the end of the village, just outside the gate of the kitchen-garden.'

"'Married?'

"'No: a large family lives next door and he pays the eldest girl to do some odd jobs of housework.'

"'Then tomorrow,' said I, 'I'll pay him a call.'

"'Seen your man?' asked Dick next evening, as we walked up towards the house, where again we were due for dinner.

"'I have just come from him: and what's more I have a proposition to make to Miss Felicia, if you and she can spare me an hour this evening.'

"The upshot of our talk was that, a week later, as I drove home from the station after my long railway journey, John Emmet sat by my side. He had taken service with me as gardener, and for nine years he served me well. You'll hardly believe it"—here the vicar's gaze travelled over the unkempt flower-beds—"but under John Emmet's hand this garden of mine was a picture. The fellow would have half a day's work done before the rest of the parish was out of bed. I never knew a human creature who needed less sleep—that's not the way to put it, though—the man *couldn't* sleep: he had lost the power (so he said) ever since the night the *Nerbuddha* struck.

"So it was that every afternoon found the day's work ended in my garden, and John Emmet, in my sixteen-foot boat, exploring the currents and soundings about Menawhidden. And almost every day I went with him. He had become a learner—for the third time in his life; and the quickest learner (in spite of his years) I have ever known, for his mind was bent on that single purpose. I should tell you that the Trinity House had discovered Menawhidden at last and placed the bell-buoy there—which is and always has been entirely useless: also that the Lifeboat Institution had listened to some suggestions of mine and were re-organising the service down at the Porth.

"And it was now my hope that John Emmet might become coxswain of the boat as soon as he had local knowledge to back up the seamanship and aptitude for command in which I knew him to excel every man in the Porth. There were jealousies, of course: but he wrangled with no man, and in the end I had my way pretty easily. Within four years of his coming John Emmet knew more of Menawhidden than any man in the parish; possibly more than all the parish put together. And today the parish is proud of him and his record.

"But they do not know—and you are to be one of the four persons in the world who know—that *John Emmet was no other than John Murchison, the captain who lost the 'Nerbuddha'*! He had come ashore in the darkness some five minutes before I had surprised him on the beach: had come ashore clinging to the keg which I saw floating just beyond the breakers. Then and there, stunned and confounded by the consequences of his carelessness, he had played the coward for the first and last time in his life. He had run away—and Heaven knows if in his shoes I should not have done the same. For two nights and a day a hideous fascination tied him to the spot. It was his face Dick had seen at the window. The man had been hiding all day in the trench by the north wall of the churchyard; as Dick ran out with a lantern he slipped behind a gravestone, and when Dick gave up the search, he broke cover and fled inland.

"He changed his name: let this be his excuse, he had neither wife nor child. The man knew something of gardening: he had a couple of pounds and some odd shillings in his pocket—enough to take him to one of the big midland towns—Wolverhampton, I think—where he found work as a jobbing gardener. But something of the fascination which had held him lurking about Lansulyan, drove him to Cressingham, which—he learned from the newspaper accounts of the wreck—was Colonel Stanhope's country seat. Or perhaps he had some vague idea that Heaven would grant him a chance to make amends. You understand now how the little Felicia became his idol.

"At Lansulyan he had but two desires. The first was to live until he had saved as many lives as his carelessness had lost in the *Nerbuddha*. For it was nothing worse, but mere forgetfulness to change the course: one of those dreadful lapses of memory which baffle all Board of Trade inquiry. You may light, and buoy, and beacon every danger along the coast, and still you leave that small kink in the skipper's brain which will cast away a ship for all your care. The second of his desires you have helped me to fulfil. He wished in death to be John Murchison again, and lie where his ship lies: lie with his grand error atoned for. John Emmet needs no gravestone: for John Emmet lived but to earn John Murchison's right to a half-forgotten tablet describing him as a brave man. And I believe that Heaven, which does not count by tally, has granted his wish."

The Roll-Call of the Reef

"Yes, sir," said my host, the quarryman, reaching down the relics from their hook in the wall over the chimneypiece; "they've hung here all my time, and most of my father's. The women won't touch 'em; they're afraid of the story. So here they'll dangle, and gather dust and smoke, till another tenant comes and tosses 'em out o' doors for rubbish. Whew! 'tis coarse weather, surely."

He went to the door, opened it, and stood studying the gale that beat upon his cottage-front, straight from the Manacle Reef. The rain drove past him into the kitchen, aslant like threads of gold silk in the shine of the wreck-wood fire. Meanwhile, by the same firelight, I examined the relics on my knee. The metal of each was tarnished out of knowledge. But the trumpet was evidently an old cavalry trumpet, and the threads of its party-coloured sling, though fretted and dusty, still hung together. Around the side-drum, beneath its cracked brown varnish. I could hardly trace a royal coat-of-arms and a legend running, "Per *Mare Per Terrain*"—the motto of the marines. Its parchment, though black and scented with wood-smoke, was limp and mildewed; and I began to tighten up the straps—under which the drumsticks had been loosely thrust—with the idle purpose of trying if some music might be got out of the old drum yet.

But as I turned it on my knee, I found the drum attached to the trumpet-sling by a curious barrel-shaped padlock, and paused to examine this. The body of the lock was composed of half a dozen brass rings, set accurately edge to edge; and, rubbing the brass with my thumb, I saw that each of the six had a series of letters engraved around it.

I knew the trick of it, I thought. Here was one of those word padlocks, once so common; only to be opened by getting the rings to spell a certain word, which the dealer confides to you.

My host shut and barred the door, and came back to the hearth.

"'Twas just such a wind—east by south—that brought in what you've got between your hands. Back in the year 'nine, it was; my father has told me the tale a score o' times. You're twisting round the rings, I see. But you'll never guess the word. Parson Kendall, he made the word, and he locked down a couple o' ghosts in their graves with it; and when his time came he went to his own grave and took the word with him."

"Whose ghosts, Matthew?"

"You want the story, I see, sir. My father could tell it better than I can. He was a young man in the year 'nine, unmarried at the time, and living in this very cottage, just as I be. That's how he came to get mixed up with the tale."

He took a chair, lighted a short pipe, and went on, with his eyes fixed on the dancing violet flames:

"Yes, he'd ha' been about thirty year old in January, eighteen 'nine. The storm got up in the night o' the twenty-first o' that month. My father was dressed and out long before daylight; he never was one to bide in bed, let be that the gale by this time was pretty near lifting the thatch over his head. Besides which, he'd fenced a small 'taty-patch that winter, down by Lowland Point, and he wanted to see if it stood the night's work. He took the path across Gunner's Meadow—where they buried most of the bodies afterward. The wind was right in his teeth at the time, and once on the way (he's told me this often) a great strip of oarweed came flying through the darkness and fetched him a slap on the cheek like a cold hand.

"But he made shift pretty well till he got to Lowland, and then had to drop upon hands and knees and crawl, digging his fingers every now and then into the shingle to hold on, for he declared to me that the stones, some of them as big as a man's head, kept rolling and driving past till it seemed the whole foreshore was moving westward under him. The fence was gone, of course; not a stick left to show where it stood; so that, when first he came to the place, he thought he must have missed his bearings. My father, sir, was a very religious man; and if he reckoned the end of the world was at hand—there in the great wind and night, among the moving stones—you may believe he was certain of it when he heard a gun fired, and, with the same, saw a flame shoot up out of the darkness to windward, making a sudden fierce light in all the place about.

"All he could find to think or say was, 'The Second Coming! The Second Coming! The Bridegroom cometh, and the wicked He will toss like a ball into a large country;' and being already upon his knees, he just bowed his head and 'bided, saying this over and over.

"But by'm by, between two squalls, he made bold to lift his head and look, and then by the light—a bluish colour 'twas—he saw all the coast clear away to Manacle Point, and off the Manacles in the thick of the weather, a sloop-of-war with topgallants housed, driving stern foremost toward the reef. It was she, of course, that was burning the flare. My father could see the white streak and the ports of her quite plain as she rose to it, a little outside the breakers, and he guessed easy enough that her captain had just managed to wear ship and was trying to force her nose to the sea with the help of her small bower anchor and the scrap or two of canvas that hadn't yet been blown out of her. But while he looked, she fell off, giving her broadside to it foot by foot, and drifting back on the breakers around Cam Du and the Varses. The rocks lie so thick thereabout that 'twas a toss up which she struck first; at any rate, my father could'nt tell at the time, for just then the flare died down and went out.

"Well, sir, he turned then in the dark and started back for Coverack to cry the dismal tidings—though well knowing ship and crew to be past any hope, and as he turned the wind lifted him and tossed him forward 'like a ball,' as he'd been saying, and homeward along the foreshore. As you know, 'tis ugly work, even by daylight, picking your way among the stones there, and my father was prettily knocked about at first in the dark. But by this 'twas nearer seven than six o'clock, and the day spreading. By the time he reached North Corner, a man could see to read print; hows'ever, he looked neither out to sea nor toward Coverack, but headed straight for the first cottage—the same that stands above North Corner today. A man named Billy Ede lived there then, and when my father burst into the kitchen bawling, 'Wreck! wreck!' he saw Billy Ede's wife, Ann, standing there in her clogs with a shawl over her head, and her clothes wringing wet.

"'Save the chap!' says Billy Ede's wife, Ann.

"'What d'ee mean by crying stale fish at that rate?'

"'But 'tis a wreck, I tell 'ee.'

"'I've a-zeed 'n, too; and so has everyone with an eye in his head.'

"And with that she pointed straight over my father's shoulder, and he turned; and there, close under Dolor Point, at the end of Coverack town, he saw another wreck washing, and the point black with people, like emmets, running to and fro in the morning light. While he stood staring at her, he heard a trumpet sounded on board, the notes coming in little jerks, like a bird rising against the wind; but faintly, of course, because of the distance and the gale blowing—though this had dropped a little.

"'She's a transport,' said Billy Ede's wife, Ann, 'and full of horse-soldiers, fine long men. When she struck they must ha' pitched the horses over first to lighten the ship, for a score of dead horses had washed in afore I left, half an hour back. An' three or four soldiers, too—fine long corpses in white breeches and jackets of blue and gold. I held the lantern to one. Such a straight young man!'

"My father asked her about the trumpeting.

"'That's the queerest bit of all. She was burnin' a light when me an' my man joined the crowd down there. All her masts had gone; whether they carried away, or were cut away to ease her,

I don't rightly know. Her keelson was broke under her and her bottom sagged and stove, and she had just settled down like a sitting hen—just the leastest list to starboard; but a man could stand there easy. They had rigged up ropes across her, from bulwark to bulwark, an' besides these the men were mustered, holding on like grim death whenever the sea made a clean breach over them, an' standing up like heroes as soon as it passed. The captain an' the officers were clinging to the rail of the quarterdeck, all in their golden uniforms, waiting for the end as if 'twas King George they expected.

"'There was no way to help, for she lay right beyond cast of line, though our folk tried it fifty times. And beside them clung a trumpeter, a whacking big man, an' between the heavy seas he would lift his trumpet with one hand, and blow a call; and every time he blew the men gave a cheer. There (she say)—hark 'ee now—there he goes agen! But you won't hear no cheering any more, for few are left to cheer, and their voices weak. Bitter cold the wind is, and I reckon it numbs their grip o' the ropes, for they were dropping off fast with every sea when my man sent me home to get his breakfast. Another wreck, you say? Well, there's no hope for the tender dears, if 'tis the Manacles. You'd better run down and help yonder; though 'tis little help any man can give. Not one came in alive while I was there. The tide's flowing, an' she won't hold together another hour, they say.'

"Well, sure enough, the end was coming fast when my father got down to the point. Six men had been cast up alive, or just breathing—a seaman and five troopers. The seaman was the only one that had breath to speak; and while they were carrying him into the town, the word went round that the ship's name was the *Despatch*, transport, homeward-bound from Corunna, with a detachment of the Seventh Hussars, that had been fighting out there with Sir John Moore. The seas had rolled her further over by this time, and given her decks a pretty sharp slope; but a dozen men still held on, seven by the ropes near the ship's waist, a couple near the break of the poop, and three on the quarterdeck. Of these three my father made out one to be the skipper; close by him clung an officer in full regimentals—his name, they heard after, was Captain Duncanfield; and last came the tall trumpeter; and if you'll believe me, the fellow was making shift there, at the very last, to blow 'God Save the King.' What's more, he got to 'Send us victorious,' before an extra big sea came bursting across and washed them off the deck—every man but one of the pair beneath the poop—and he dropped his hold before the next wave; being stunned, I reckon.

"The others went out of sight at once, but the trumpeter—being, as I said, a powerful man as well as a tough swimmer—rose like a duck, rode out a couple of breakers, and came in on the crest of the third. The folks looked to see him broke like an egg at their very feet; but when the smother cleared, there he was, lying face downward on a ledge below them; and one of the men that happened to have a rope round him—I forgot the fellow's name, if I ever heard it—jumped down and grabbed him by the ankle as he began to slip back. Before the next big sea, the pair were hauled high enough to be out of harm, and another heave brought them up to grass. Quick work, but master trumpeter wasn't quite dead; nothing worse than a cracked head and three staved ribs. In twenty minutes or so they had him in bed, with the doctor to tend him.

"Now was the time—nothing being left alive upon the transport—for my father to tell of the sloop he'd seen driving upon the Manacles. And when he got a hearing, though the most were set upon salvage, and believed a wreck in the hand, so to say, to be worth half a dozen they couldn't see, a good few volunteered to start off with him and have a look. They crossed Lowland Point; no ship to be seen on the Manacles nor anywhere upon the sea. One or two was for calling my father a liar. 'Wait till we come to Dean Point,' said he. Sure enough, on the far side of Dean Pont they found the sloop's mainmast washing about with half a dozen men lashed to it, men in red jackets, every mother's son drowned and staring; and a little further on, just under the Dean, three or four bodies cast up on the shore, one of them a small drummer-boy, side-drum and all; and nearby part of a ship's gig, with 'H.M.S. *Primrose*' cut on the stern-board.

"From this point on the shore was littered thick with wreckage and dead bodies—the most of them marines in uniform—and in Godrevy Cove, in particular, a heap of furniture from the captain's cabin, and among it a water-tight box, not much damaged, and full of papers, by which, when it came to be examined, next day, the wreck was easily made out to be the *Primrose*, of eighteen guns, outward bound from Portsmouth, with a fleet of transports for the Spanish war—thirty sail, I've heard, but I've never heard what became of them. Being handled by merchant skippers, no doubt they rode out the gale, and reached the Tagus safe and sound. Not but what the captain of the *Primrose*—Mein was his name—did quite right to try and club-haul his vessel when he found himself under the land; only he never ought to have got there, if he took proper soundings. But it's easy talking.

"The *Primrose*, sir, was a handsome vessel—for her size one of the handsomest in the king's service'—and newly fitted out at Plymouth Dock. So the boys had brave pickings from her in the way of brass-work, ship's instruments, and the like, let alone some barrels of stores not much spoiled. They loaded themselves with as much as they could carry, and started for home, meaning to make a second journey before the preventive men got wind of their doings, and came to spoil the fun. 'Hullo!' says my father, and dropped his gear, 'I do believe there's a leg moving?' and running fore, he stooped over the small drummer-boy that I told you about. The poor little chap was lying there, with his face a mass of bruises, and his eyes closed; but he had shifted one leg an inch or two, and was still breathing.

"So my father pulled out a knife, and cut him free from his drum—that was lashed on to him with a double turn of Manila rope—and took him up and carried him along here to this very room that we're sitting in. He lost a good deal by this; for when he went back to fetch the bundle he'd dropped, the preventive men had got hold of it, and were thick as thieves along the foreshore; so that 'twas only by paying one or two to look the other way that he picked up anything worth carrying off: which you'll allow to be hard, seeing that he was the first man to give news of the wreck.

"Well, the inquiry was held, of course, and my father gave evidence, and for the rest they had to trust to the sloop's papers, for not a soul was saved besides the drummer-boy, and he was raving in a fever, brought on by the cold and the fright. And the seaman and the five troopers gave evidence about the loss of the *Despatch*. The tall trumpeter, too, whose ribs were healing, came forward and kissed the book; but somehow his head had been hurt in coming ashore, and he talked foolish-like, and 'twas easy seen he would never be a proper man again. The others were taken up to Plymouth, and so went their ways; but the trumpeter stayed on in Coverack; and King George, finding he was fit for nothing, sent him down a trifle of a pension after a while-enough to keep him in board and lodging, with a bit of tobacco over.

"Now the first time that this man—William Tallifer he called himself—met with the drummer-boy, was about a fortnight after the little chap had bettered enough to be allowed a short walk out of doors, which he took, if you please, in full regimentals. There never was a soldier so proud of his dress. His own suit had shrunk a brave bit with the salt water; but into ordinary frock an' corduroys he declared he would not get, not if he had to go naked the rest of his life; so my father—being a good-natured man, and handy with the needle—turned to and repaired damages with a piece or two of scarlet cloth cut from the jacket of one of the drowned Marines. Well, the poor little chap chanced to be standing, in this rig out, down by the gate of Gunner's Meadow, where they had buried two score and over of his comrades. The morning was a fine one, early in March month; and along came the cracked trumpeter, likewise taking a stroll.

"'Hullo!' says he; 'good mornin'! And what might you be doin' here?'

"'I was a-wishin',' says the boy, 'I had a pair o' drumsticks. Our lads were buried yonder without so much as a drum tapped or a musket fired; and that's not Christian burial for British soldiers.'

"'Phut!' says the trumpeter, and spat on the ground; 'a parcel of Marines!'

"The boy eyed him a second or so, and answered up: 'If I'd a tav of turf handy, I'd bung it at your mouth, you greasy cavalryman, and learn you to speak respectful of your betters. The Marines are the handiest body o' men in the service.'

"The trumpeter looked down on him from the height of six-foot two, and asked: 'Did they die well?'

"'They died very well. There was a lot of running to and fro at first, and some of the men began to cry, and a few to strip off their clothes. But when the ship fell off for the last time, Captain Mein turned and said something to Major Griffiths, the commanding officer on board, and the major called out to me to beat to quarters. It might have been for a wedding, he sang it out so cheerful. We'd had word already that 'twas to be parade order; and the men fell in as trim and decent as if they were going to church. One or two even tried to shave at the last moment. The major wore his medals.

"'One of the seamen, seeing I had work to keep the drum steady—the sling being a bit loose for me, and the wind what you remember—lashed it tight with a piece of rope; and that saved my life afterward, a drum being as good as a cork until it's stove, I kept beating away until every man was on decks and then the major formed them up and told them to die like British soldiers, and the chaplain was in the middle of a prayer when she struck. In ten minutes she was gone. That was how they died, cavalryman.'

"'And that was very well done, drummer of the Marines. What's your name?'

"'John Christian.'

"'Mine's William George Tallifer, trumpeter, of the Seventh Light Dragoons—the Queen's Own. I played "God Save the King" while our men were drowning. Captain Duncanfield told me to sound a call or two, to put them in heart; but that matter of "God Save the King" was a notion of my own. I won't say anything to hurt the feelings of a Marine, even if he's not much over five-foot tall; but the Queen's Own Hussars is a tearin' fine regiment. As between horse and foot, 'tis a question o' which gets a chance. All the way from Sahagun to Corunna 'twas we that took and gave the knocks—at Mayorga and Rueda, and Bennyventy.'—The reason, sir, I can speak the names so pat, is that my father learnt 'em by heart afterward from the trumpeter, who was always talking about Mayorga and Rueda and Bennyventy.'—We made the rear-guard, under General Paget; and drove the French every time; and all the infantry did was to sit about in wine-shops till we whipped 'em out, an' steal an' straggle an' play the tomfool in general.

"' And when it came to a stand-up fight at Corunna, .'twas we that had to stay seasick aboard the transports, an' watch the infantry in the thick o' the caper. Very well they behaved, too—specially the Fourth Regiment, an' the Forty-Second Highlanders, an' the Dirty Half-Hundred. Oh, ay; they're decent regiments, all three. But the Queen's Own Hussars is a tearin' fine regiment. So you played on your drum when the ship was goin' down? Drummer John Christian, I'll have to get you a new pair of sticks.'

"The very next day the trumpeter marched into Helston, and got a carpenter there to turn him a pair of box-wood drumsticks for the boy. And this was the beginning of one of the most curious friendships you ever heard tell of. Nothing delighted the pair more than to borrow a boat off my father and pull out to the rocks where the *Primrose* and the *Despatch* had struck and sunk; and on still days 'twas pretty to hear them out there off the Manacles, the drummer playing his tattoo—for they always took their music with them—and the trumpeter practising calls, and making his trumpet speak like an angel. But if the weather turned roughish, they'd be walking together and talking; leastwise the youngster listened while the other discoursed about Sir John's campaign in Spain and Portugal, telling how each little skirmish befell; and of Sir John himself, and General Baird, and General Paget, and Colonel Vivian, his own commanding officer, and what kind of men they were; and of the last bloody stand-up at Corunna, and so forth, as if neither could have enough.

"But all this had to come to an end in the late summer, for the boy, John Christian, being now well and strong again, must go up to Plymouth to report himself. 'Twas his own wish (for I believe King George had forgotten all about him), but his friend wouldn't hold him back. As for the trumpeter, my father had made an arrangement to take him on as lodger, as soon as the boy left; and on the morning fixed for the start, he was up at the door here by five o'clock, with his trumpet slung by his side, and all the rest of his belongings in a small valise. A Monday morning it was, and after breakfast he had fixed to walk with the boy some way on the road toward Helston, where the coach started. My father left them at breakfast together, and went out to meat the pig, and do a few odd morning jobs of that sort. When he came back, the boy was still at table, and the trumpeter sat with the rings in his hands, hitched, together just as they be at this moment.

"'Look at this,' he says to my father, showing him the lock. 'I picked it up off a starving brass-worker in Lisbon, and it is not one of your common locks that one word of six letters will open at any time. There's janius in this lock; for you've only to make the rings spell any six-letter word you please and snap down the lock upon that, and never a soul can open it—not the maker, even—until somebody comes along that knows the word you snapped it on. Now Johnny here's goin', and he leaves his drum behind him; for, though he can make pretty music on it, the parchment sags in wet weather, by reason of the sea-water getting at it; an' if he carries it to Plymouth, they'll only condemn it and give him another.

"'And, as for me, I shan't have the heart to put lip to the trumpet any more when Johnny's gone. So we've chosen a word together, and locked 'em together upon that; and, by your leave, I'll hang 'em here together on the hook over your fireplace. Maybe Johnny'll come back; maybe not. Maybe, if he comes, I'll be dead an' gone, and he'll take 'em apart an' try their music for old sake's sake. But if he never comes, nobody can separate 'em; for nobody besides knows the word. And if you marry and have sons, you can tell 'em that here are tied together the souls of Johnny Christian, drummer of the Marines, and William George Tallifer, once trumpeter of the Queen's Own Hussars. Amen.'

"With that he hung the two instruments 'pon the hook there; and the boy stood up and thanked my father and shook hands; and the pair went out of the door, toward Helston.

"Somewhere on the road they took leave of one another; but nobody saw the parting, nor heard what was said between them. About three in the afternoon the trumpeter came walking back over the hill; and by the time my father came home from the fishing, the cottage was tidied up, and the tea ready, and the whole place shining like a new pin. From that time for five years he lodged here with my father, looking after the house and tilling the garden. And all the while he was steadily failing; the hurt in his head spreading, in a manner, to his limbs. My father watched the feebleness growing on him, but said nothing. And from first to last neither spake a word about the drummer, John Christian; nor did any letter reach them, nor word of his doings.

"The rest of the tale you're free to believe, sir, or not, as you please. It stands upon my father's words, and he always declared he was ready to kiss the Book upon it, before judge and jury. He said, too, that he never had the wit to make up such a yarn; and he defied any one to explain about the lock, in particular, by any other tale. But you shall judge for yourself.

"My father said that about three o'clock in the morning, April fourteenth, of the year 'fourteen, he and William Tallifer were sitting here, just as you and I, sir, are sitting now. My father had put on his clothes a few minutes before, and was mending his spiller by the light of the horn lantern, meaning to set off before daylight to haul the trammel. The trumpeter hadn't been to bed at all. Toward the last he mostly spent his nights (and his days, too) dozing in the elbow-chair where you sit at this minute. He was dozing then (my father said) with his chin dropped forward on his chest, when a knock sounded upon the door, and the door opened, and in walked an upright young man in scarlet regimentals.

"He had grown a brave bit, and his face the colour of wood-ashes; but it was the drummer, John Christian. Only his uniform was different from the one he used to wear, and the figures '38' shone in brass upon his collar.

"The drummer walked past my father as if he never saw him, and stood by the elbow-chair and said:

"'Trumpeter, trumpeter, are you one with me?'

"And the trumpeter just lifted the lids of his eyes, and answered: 'How should I not be one with you, drummer Johnny—Johnny boy? If you come, I count; if you march, I mark time; until the discharge comes.'

"'The discharge has come tonight,' said the drummer; and the word is Corunna no longer.' And stepping to the chimney-place, he unhooked the drum and trumpet, and began to twist the brass rings of the lock, spelling the word aloud, so—'C-O-R-U-N-A.' When he had fixed the last letter, the padlock opened in his hand.

"'Did you know, trumpeter, that, when I came to Plymouth, they put me into a line regiment?'

"'The 38th is a good regiment,' answered the old hussar, still in his dull voice; 'I went back with them from Sahagun to Corunna. At Corunna they stood in General Fraser's division, on the right. They behaved well.

"'But I'd fain see the Marines again,' says the drummer, handing him the trumpet; 'and you, you shall call once more for the Queen's Own. Matthew,' he says, suddenly, turning on my father—and when he turned, my father saw for the first time that his scarlet jacket had a round hole by the breast-bone, and that the blood was welling there—'Matthew, we shall want your boat.'

"Then my father rose on his legs like a man in a dream, while they two slung on, the one his drum, and t'other his trumpet. He took the lantern and went quaking before them down to the shore, and they breathed heavily behind him; and they stepped into his boat, and my father pushed off.

"'Row you first for Dolor Point,' says the drummer. So my father rowed them past the white houses of Coverack to Dolor Point, and there, at a word, lay on his oars. And the trumpeter, William Tallifer, put his trumpet to his mouth and sounded the reveille. The music of it was like rivers running.

"'They will follow,' said the drummer. Matthew, pull you now for the Manacles.

"So my father pulled for the Manacles, and came to an easy close outside Carn Du. And the drummer took his sticks and beat a tattoo, there by the edge of the reef; and the music of it was like a rolling chariot.

"'That will do,' says he, breaking off; 'they will follow. Pull now for the shore under Gunner's Meadow.'

"Then my father pulled for the shore and ran his boat in under Gunner's Meadow. And they stepped out, all three, and walked up to the meadow. By the gate the drummer halted, and began his tattoo again, looking out toward the darkness over the sea.

"And while the drum beat, and my father held his breath, there came up out of the sea and the darkness a troop of many men, horse and foot, and formed up among the graves; and others rose out of the graves and formed up—drowned Marines with bleached faces, and pale Hussars, riding their horses, all lean and shadowy. There was no clatter of hoofs or accoutrements, my father said, but a soft sound all the while like the beating of a bird's wing; and a black shadow lay like a pool about the feet of all. The drummer stood upon a little knoll just inside the gate, and beside him the tall trumpeter, with hand on hip, watching them gather; and behind them both my father, clinging to the gate. When no more came, the drummer stopped playing, and said, 'Call the roll.'

"Then the trumpeter stepped toward the end man of the rank and called, 'Troop Sergeant-Major Thomas Irons,' and the man answered in a thin voice, 'Here.'

"'Troop Sergeant-Major Thomas Irons, how is it with you?'

"The man answered, 'How should it be with me? When I was young, I betrayed a girl; and when I was grown, I betrayed a friend, and for these I must pay. But I died as a man ought. God save the King!'

"The trumpeter called to the next man, 'Trooper Henry Buckingham,' and the next man answered, 'Here.'

"'Trooper Henry Buckingham, how is it With you?'

"'How should it be with me? I was a drunkard, and I stole, and in Lugo, in a Wine-shop, I killed a man. But I died as a man should. God save the King!'

"So the trumpeter went down the line; and when he had finished, the drummer took it up, hailing the dead Marines in their order. Each man answered to his name, and each man ended with 'God save the King!' When all were hailed, the drummer stepped back to his mound, and called:

"'It is well. You are content, and we are content to join you. Wait, now, a little while.'

"With this he turned and ordered my father to pick up the lantern, and lead the way back. As my father picked it up, he heard the ranks of the dead men cheer and call, 'God save the King!' all together, and saw them waver and fade back into the dark, like a breath fading off a pane.

"But when they came back here to the kitchen, and my father set the lantern down, it seemed they'd both forgot about him. For the drummer turned in the lantern-light—and my father could see the blood still welling out of the hole in his breast—and took the trumpet-sling from around the other's neck, and locked drum and trumpet together again, choosing the letters on the lock very carefully. While he did this, he said.

"'The word is no more Corunna, but Bayonne. As you left out an "n" in Corunna, so must I leave out an "n" in Bayonne.' And before snapping the padlock, he spelt out the word slowly—'B-A-Y-O-N-E.' After that, he used no more speech; but turned and hung the two instruments back on the hook; and then took the trumpeter by the arm; and the pair walked out into the darkness, glancing neither to right nor left.

"My father was on the point of following, when he heard a sort of sigh behind him; and there, sitting in the elbow-chair, was the very trumpeter he had just seen walk out by the door! If my father's heart jumped before, you may believe it jumped quicker now. But after a bit, he went up to the man asleep in the chair and put a hand upon him. It was the trumpeter in flesh and blood that he touched; but though the flesh was warm, the trumpeter was dead.

"Well, sir, they buried him three days after; and at first my father was minded to say nothing about his dream (as he thought it). But the day after the funeral, he met Parson Kendall coming from Helston market; and the parson called out: 'Have 'ee heard the news the coach brought down this mornin'?' 'What news?' says my father. 'Why, that peace is agreed upon.' 'None too soon,' says my father. 'Not soon enough for our poor lads at Bayonne,' the parson answered. 'Bayonne!' cries my father, with a jump. 'Why, yes;' and the parson told him all about a great sally the French had made on the night of April 13th. 'Do you happen to know if the 38th Regiment was engaged?' my father asked. 'Come, now,' said Parson Kendall, 'I didn't know you was so well up in the campaign. But, as it happens, I do know that the 38th was engaged, for 'twas they that held a cottage and stopped the French advance.'

"Still my father held his tongue; and when, a week later, he walked in Helston and bought a 'Mercury' off the Sherborne rider, and got the landlord of the 'Angel' to spell out the list of killed and wounded, sure enough, there among the killed was Drummer John Christian, of the 38th Foot.

"After this there was nothing for a religious man but to make a clean breast. So my father went up to Parson Kendall, and told the whole story. The parson listened, and put a question or two, and then asked:

"'Have you tried to open the lock since that night?'

"'I haven't dared to touch it,' says my father.

"'Then come along and try.' When the parson came to the

cottage here, he took the things off the hook and tried the lock. 'Did he say "Bayonne?" The word has seven letters.'

"'Not if you spell it with one "n" as he did,' says my father.

"The parson spelt it out—'B-A-Y-O-N-E' 'Whew!' says he, for the lock had fallen open in his hand.

"He stood considering it a moment, and then he says: 'I tell you what. I shouldn't blab this all round the parish, if I was you. You won't get no credit for truth-telling, and a miracle's wasted on a set of fools. But if you like, I'll shut down the lock again upon a holy word that no one but me shall know, and neither drummer nor trumpeter, dead or alive, shall frighten the secret out of me.'

"'I wish to heaven you would, parson,' said my father.

"The parson chose the holy word there and then, and shut the lock back upon it, and hung the drum and trumpet back in their place. He is gone long since, taking the word with him. And till the lock is broken by force nobody will ever separate those two."

The Room of Mirrors

A late hansom came swinging round the corner into Lennox Gardens, cutting it so fine that the near wheel ground against the kerb and jolted the driver in his little seat. The jingle of bells might have warned me; but the horse's hoofs came noiselessly on the half-frozen snow, which lay just deep enough to hide where the pavement ended and the road began; and, moreover, I was listening to the violins behind the first-floor windows of the house opposite. They were playing the "*Wiener Blut.*"

As it was, I had time enough and no more to skip back and get my toes out of the way. The cabby cursed me. I cursed him back so promptly and effectively that he had to turn in his seat for another shot. The windows of the house opposite let fall their light across his red and astonished face. I laughed, and gave him another volley. My head was hot, though my feet and hands were cold; and I felt equal to cursing down any cabman within the four-mile radius. That second volley finished him. He turned to his reins again and was borne away defeated; the red eyes of his lamps peering back at me like an angry ferret's.

Up in the lighted room shadows of men and women crossed the blinds, and still the "*Wiener Blut*" went forward.

The devil was in that waltz. He had hold of the violins and was weaving the air with scents and visions—visions of Ascot and Henley; green lawns, gay sunshades, midsummer heat, cool rivers flowing, muslins rippled by light breezes; running horses and silken jackets; white tables heaped with roses and set with silver and crystal, jewelled fingers moving in the soft candle-light, bare necks bending, diamonds, odours, bubbles in the wine; blue water and white foam beneath the leaning shadow of sails; hot air flickering over stretches of moorland; blue again—Mediterranean blue—long facades, the din of bands and King Carnival parading beneath showers of blossom:—and all this noise and warmth and scent and dazzle flung out into the frozen street for a beggar's portion. I had gone under.

The door of the house opposite had been free to me once— and not six months ago; freer to me perhaps than to any other. Did I long to pass behind it again? I thrust both hands into my pockets for warmth, and my right hand knocked against something hard. Yes . . . just once. . . .

Suddenly the door opened. A man stood on the threshold for a moment while the butler behind him arranged the collar of his fur overcoat. The high light in the portico flung the shadows of both down the crimson carpet laid on the entrance-steps. Snow had fallen and covered the edges of the carpet, which divided it like a cascade of blood pouring from the hall into the street. And still overhead the "*Wiener Blut*" went forward.

The man paused in the bright portico, his patent-leather boots twinkling under the lamp's rays on that comfortable carpet. I waited, expecting him to whistle for a hansom. But he turned, gave an order to the butler, and stepping briskly down into the street, made off eastwards. The door closed behind him. He was the man I most hated in the world. If I had longed to cross the threshold a while back it was to seek him, and for no other reason.

I started to follow him, my hands still in my pockets. The snow muffled our footfalls completely, for as yet the slight northeast wind had frozen but the thinnest crust of it. He was walking briskly, as men do in such weather, but with no appearance of hurry. At the corner of Sloane Street he halted under a lamp, pulled out his watch, consulted it, and lit a cigarette; then set off again up the street towards Knightsbridge.

This halt of his had let me up within twenty paces of him. He never turned his head; but went on presenting me his back, a target not to be missed. Why not do it now? Better now and here than in a crowded thoroughfare. My right hand gripped the revolver more tightly. No, there was plenty of time: and I was curious to know what had brought Gervase out at this hour: why he had left his guests, or his wife's guests, to take care of themselves: why he chose to be trudging afoot through this infernally unpleasant snow.

The roadway in Sloane Street was churned into a brown mass like chocolate, but the last 'bus had rolled home and left it to freeze in peace. Half-way up the street I saw Gervase meet and pass a policeman, and altered my own pace to a lagging walk. Even so, the fellow eyed me suspiciously as I went by—or so I thought: and guessing that he kept a watch on me, I dropped still further behind my man. But the lamps were bright at the end of the street, and I saw him turn to the right by the great drapery shop at the corner.

Once past this corner I was able to put on a spurt. He crossed the roadway by the Albert Gate, and by the time he reached the park railings the old distance separated us once more. Half-way up the slope he came to a halt, by the stone drinking-trough: and flattening myself against the railings, I saw him try the thin ice in the trough with his finger-tips, but in a hesitating way, as if his thoughts ran on something else and he scarcely knew what he did or why he did it. It must have been half a minute before he recovered himself with a shrug of his shoulders, and plunging both hands deep in his pockets, resumed his pace.

As we passed Hyde Park Corner I glanced up at the clock there: the time was between a quarter and ten minutes to one. At the entrance of Down Street he turned aside again, and began to lead me a zigzag dance through the quiet thoroughfare: and I followed, still to the tune of the "*Wiener Blut.*"

But now, at the corner of Charles Street, I blundered against another policeman, who flashed his lantern in my face, stared after Gervase, and asked me what my game was. I demanded innocently enough to be shown the nearest way to Oxford Street, and the fellow, after pausing a moment to chew his suspicions, walked with me slowly to the south-west corner of Berkeley Square, and pointed northwards.

"That's your road," he growled, "straight on. And don't you forget it!"

He stood and watched me on my way. Nor did I dare to turn aside until well clear of the square. At the crossing of Davies and Grosvenor Streets, however, I supposed myself safe, and halted for a moment.

From the shadow of a porch at my elbow a thin voice accosted me.

"Kind gentleman—"

"Heh?" I spun round on her sharply: for it was a woman, stretching out one skinny hand and gathering her rags together with the other.

"Kind gentleman, spare a copper. I've known better days—I have indeed."

"Well," said I, "as it happens, I'm in the same case. And they couldn't be much worse, could they?"

She drew a shuddering breath back through her teeth, but still held out her hand. I felt for my last coin, and her fingers closed on it so sharply that their long nails scraped the back of mine.

"Kind gentleman—"

"Ay, they are kind, are they not?"

She stared at me, and in a nerveless tone let one horrible oath escape her.

"There'll be one less before morning," said I, "if that's any consolation to you. Goodnight!" Setting off at a shuffling run, I doubled back along Grosvenor Street and Bond Street to the point where I hoped to pick up the trail again. And just there, at the issue of Bruton Street, two constables stood ready for me.

"I thought as much," said the one who set me on my way. "Hi, you! Wait a moment, please;" then to the other, "Best turn his pockets out, Jim."

"If you dare to try—" I began, with my hand in my pocket: the next moment I found myself sprawling face downward on the sharp crust of snow.

"Hullo, constables!" said a voice. "What's the row?" It was Gervase. He had turned leisurely back from the slope of Conduit Street, and came strolling down the road with his hands in his pockets.

"This fellow, Sir—we have reason to think he was followin' you."

"Quite right," Gervase answered cheerfully, "of course he was."

"Oh, if you knew it, Sir—"

"Certainly I knew it. In fact, he was following at my invitation."

"What for did he tell me a lie, then?" grumbled the constable, chapfallen.

I had picked myself up by this time and was wiping my face. "Look here," I put in, "I asked you the way to Oxford Street, that and nothing else." And I went on to summarise my opinion of him.

"Oh! it's you can swear a bit," he growled. "I heard you just now."

"Yes," Gervase interposed suavely, drawing the glove from his right hand and letting flash a diamond finger-ring in the lamp-light. "He *is* a bit of a beast, policeman, and it's not for the pleasure of it that I want his company."

A sovereign passed from hand to hand. The other constable had discreetly drawn off a pace or two.

"All the same, it's a rum go."

"Yes, isn't it?" Gervase assented in his heartiest tone. "Here is my card, in case you're not satisfied."

"If *you're* satisfied, Sir—"

"Quite so. Goodnight!" Gervase thrust both hands into his pockets again and strode off. I followed him, with a heart hotter than ever—followed him like a whipped cur, as they say. Yes, that was just it. He who had already robbed me of everything else had now kicked even the pedestal from under me as a figure of tragedy. Five minutes ago I had been the implacable avenger tracking my unconscious victim across the city. Heaven knows how small an excuse it was for self-respect; but one who has lost character may yet chance to catch a dignity from circumstances; and to tell the truth, for all my desperate earnestness I had allowed my vanity to take some artistic satisfaction in the sinister chase. It had struck me—shall I say?—as an effective ending, nor had I failed to note that the snow lent it a romantic touch.

And behold, the unconscious victim knew all about it, and had politely interfered when a couple of unromantic "Bobbies" threatened the performance by tumbling the stalking avenger into the gutter! They had knocked my tragedy into harlequinade as easily as you might bash in a hat; and my enemy had refined the cruelty of it by coming to the rescue and ironically restarting the poor play on lines of comedy. I saw too late that I ought to have refused his help, to have assaulted the constable and been hauled to the police-station. Not an impressive wind-up, to be sure; but less humiliating than this! Even so, Gervase might have trumped the poor card by following with a gracious offer to bail me out!

As it was, I had put the whip into his hand, and must follow him like a cur. The distance he kept assured me that the similitude had not escaped him. He strode on without deigning a single glance behind, still in cold derision presenting me his broad back and silently challenging me to shoot. And I followed, hating him worse than ever, swearing that the last five minutes should not be forgotten, but charged for royally when the reckoning came to be paid.

I followed thus up Conduit Street, up Regent Street, and across the Circus. The frost had deepened and the mud in the roadway crackled under our feet. At the Circus I began to guess, and when Gervase struck off into Great Portland Street, and thence by half-a-dozen turnings northward by east, I knew to what house he was leading me.

At the entrance of the side street in which it stood he halted and motioned me to come close.

"I forget," he said with a jerk of his thumb, "if you still have the entry. These people are not particular, to be sure."

"I have not," I answered, and felt my cheeks burning. He could not see this, nor could I see the lift of his eyebrows as he answered—

"Ah? I hadn't heard of it. . . . You'd better step round by the mews, then. You know the window, the one which opens into the passage leading to Pollox Street. Wait there. It may be ten minutes before I can open."

I nodded. The house was a corner one, between the street and a by-lane tenanted mostly by cabmen; and at the back of it ran the mews where they stabled their horses. Half-way down this mews a narrow alley cut across it at right angles: a passage un-frequented by traffic, known only to the stablemen, and in the daytime used only by their children, who played hop-scotch on the flagged pavement, where no one interrupted them. You wondered at its survival—from end to end it must have measured a good fifty yards—in a district where every square foot of ground fetched money; until you learned that the house had belonged, in the 'twenties, to a nobleman who left a name for eccentric profligacy, and who, as owner of the land, could afford to indulge his humours. The estate since his death was in no position to afford money for alterations, and the present tenants of the house found the passage convenient enough.

My footsteps disturbed no one in the sleeping mews; and doubling back noiselessly through the passage, I took up my station beside the one low window which opened upon it from the blank back premises of the house. Even with the glimmer of snow to help me, I had to grope for the window-sill to make sure of my bearings. The minutes crawled by, and the only sound came from a stall where one of the horses had kicked through his thin straw bedding and was shuffling an uneasy hoof upon the cobbles. Then just as I too had begun to shuffle my frozen feet, I heard a scratching sound, the unbolting of a shutter, and Gervase drew up the sash softly.

"Nip inside!" he whispered. "No more noise than you can help. I have sent off the night porter. He tells me the bank is still going in the front of the house—half-a-dozen playing, perhaps."

I hoisted myself over the sill, and dropped inside. The wall of this annexe—which had no upper floor, and invited you to mistake it for a harmless studio—was merely a sheath, so to speak. Within, a corridor divided it from the true wall of the room: and this room had no window or top-light, though a handsome one in the roof—a dummy—beguiled the eyes of its neighbours.

There was but one room: an apartment of really fine proportions, never used by the tenants of the house, and known but to a few curious ones among its frequenters.

The story went that the late owner, Earl C——, had reason to believe himself persistently cheated at cards by his best friends, and in particular by a duke of the Blood Royal, who could hardly be accused to his face. The earl's sense of honour forbade him to accuse any meaner man while the big culprit went unrebuked. Therefore he continued to lose magnificently while he devised a new room for play: the room in which I now followed Gervase.

I had stood in it once before and admired the courtly and costly thoroughness of the earl's rebuke. I had imagined him conducting his expectant guests to the door, ushering them in with a wave of the hand, and taking his seat tranquilly amid the dead, embarrassed silence: had imagined him facing the royal duke and asking, "Shall we cut?" with a voice of the politest inflection.

For the room was a sheet of mirrors. Mirrors panelled the walls, the doors, the very backs of the shutters. The tables had mirrors for tops: the whole ceiling was one vast mirror. From it depended three great candelabra of cut-glass, set with reflectors here, there, and everywhere.

I had heard that even the floor was originally of polished brass. If so, later owners must have ripped up the plates and sold them: for now a few cheap Oriental rugs carpeted the unpolished boards. The place was abominably dusty: the striped yellow curtains had lost half their rings and drooped askew from their soiled vallances. Across one of the wall-panels ran an ugly scar. A smell of rat pervaded the air. The present occupiers had no use for a room so obviously unsuitable to games of chance, as they understood chance: and I doubt if a servant entered it once a month. Gervase had ordered candles and a fire: but the chimney was out of practice, and the smoke wreathed itself slowly about us as we stood surrounded by the ghostly company of our reflected selves.

"We shall not be disturbed," said Gervase. "I told the man I was expecting a friend, that our business was private, and that until he called I wished to be alone. I did not explain by what entrance I expected him. The people in the front cannot hear us. Have a cigar?" He pushed the open case towards me. Then, as I drew back, "You've no need to be scrupulous," he added, "seeing that they were bought with your money."

"If that's so, I will," said I; and having chosen one, struck a match. Glancing round, I saw a hundred small flames spurt up, and a hundred men hold them to a hundred glowing cigar-tips.

"After you with the match." Gervase took it from me with a steady hand. He, too, glanced about him while he puffed. "Ugh!" He blew a long cloud, and shivered within his furred overcoat. "What a gang!"

"It takes all sorts to make a world," said I fatuously, for lack of anything better.

"Don't be an infernal idiot!" he answered, flicking the dust off one of the gilt chairs, and afterwards cleaning a space for his elbow on the looking-glass table. "It takes only two sorts to make the world we've lived in, and that's you and I." He gazed slowly round the walls. "You and I, and a few fellows like us—not to mention the women, who don't count."

"Well," said I, "as far as the world goes—if you must discuss it—I always found it a good enough place."

"Because you started as an unconsidering fool: and because, afterwards, when we came to grips, you were the under-dog, and I gave you no time. My word—how I have hustled you!"

I yawned. "All right: I can wait. Only if you suppose I came here to listen to your moral reflections—"

He pulled the cigar from between his teeth and looked at me along it.

"I know perfectly well why you came here," he said slowly, and paused. "Hadn't we better have it out—with the cards on the table?" He drew a small revolver from his pocket and laid it with a light clink on the table before him. I hesitated for a moment, then followed his example, and the silent men around us did the same.

A smile curled his thin lips as he observed this multiplied gesture. "Yes," he said, as if to himself, "that is what it all comes to."

"And now," said I, "since you know my purpose here, perhaps you will tell me yours."

"That is just what I am trying to explain. Only you are so impatient, and it—well, it's a trifle complicated." He puffed for a moment in silence. "Roughly, it might be enough to say that I saw you standing outside my house a while ago; that I needed a talk with you alone, in some private place; that I guessed, if you saw me, you would follow with no more invitation; and that, so reasoning, I led you here, where no one is likely to interrupt us."

"Well," I admitted, "all that seems plain sailing."

"Quite so; but it's at this point the thing grows complicated." He rose, and walking to the fireplace, turned his back on me and spread his palms to the blaze. "Well," he asked, after a moment, gazing into the mirror before him, "why don't you shoot?"

I thrust my hands into my trouser-pockets and leaned back staring—I daresay sulkily enough—at the two revolvers within grasp. "I've got my code," I muttered.

"The code of—these mirrors. You won't do the thing because it's not the thing to do; because these fellows"—he waved a hand and the ghosts waved back at him—"don't do such things, and you haven't the nerve to sin off your own bat. Come"— he strolled back to his seat and leaned towards me across the table—"it's not much to boast of, but at this eleventh hour we must snatch what poor credit we can. You are, I suppose, a more decent fellow for not having fired: and I—By the way, you did feel the temptation?"

I nodded. "You may put your money on that. I never see you without wanting to kill you. What's more, I'm going to do it."

"And I," he said, "knew the temptation and risked it. No: let's be honest about it. There was no risk: because, my good Sir, I know you to a hair."

"There was," I growled.

"Pardon me, there was none. I came here having a word to say to you, and these mirrors have taught me how to say it. Take a look at them—the world we are leaving—that's it: and a cursed second-hand, second-class one at that."

He paced slowly round on it, slewing his body in the chair.

"I say a second-class one," he resumed, "because, my dear Reggie, when all's said and done, we are second-class, the pair of us, and pretty bad second-class. I met you first at Harrow. Our fathers had money: they wished us to be gentlemen without well understanding what it meant: and with unlimited pocket-money and his wits about him any boy can make himself a power in a big school. That is what we did: towards the end we even set the fashion for a certain set; and a rank bad fashion it was. But, in truth, we had no business there: on every point of breeding we were outsiders. I suspect it was a glimmering consciousness of this that made us hate each other from the first. We understood one another too well. Oh, there's no mistake about it! Whatever we've missed in life, you and I have hated."

He paused, eyeing me queerly. I kept my hands in my pockets. "Go on," I said.

"From Harrow we went to college—the same business over again. We drifted, of course, into the same set; for already we had become necessary to each other. We set the pace of that set—were its apparent leaders. But in truth we were alone—you and I—as utterly alone as two shipwrecked men on a raft. The others were shadows to us: we followed their code because we had to be gentlemen, but we did not understand it in the least. For, after all, the roots of that code lay in the breeding and tradition of honour, with which we had no concern. To each other you and I were intelligible and real; but as concerned that code and the men who followed it by right of birth and nature, we were looking-glass men imitating—imitating—imitating."

"We set the pace," said I. "You've allowed that."

"To be sure we did. We even modified the code a bit—to its hurt; though as conscious outsiders we could dare very little. For instance, the talk of our associates about women—and no doubt their thoughts, too—grew sensibly baser. The sanctity of gambling debts, on the other hand, we did nothing to impair: because we had money. I recall your virtuous indignation at the amount of paper floated by poor W—— towards the end of the great baccarat term. Poor devil! He paid up—or his father did—and took his name off the books. He's in Ceylon now, I believe. At length you have earned a partial right to sympathise: or would have if only you had paid up."

"Take care, Gervase."

"My good Sir, don't miss my point. Wasn't I just as indignant with W——? If I'd been warned off Newmarket Heath, if I'd been shown the door of the hell we're sitting in, shouldn't I feel just as you are feeling? Try to understand!"

"You forget Elaine, I think."

"No: I do not forget Elaine. We left College: I to add money to money in my father's office; you to display your accomplishments in spending what your father had earned. That was the extent of the difference. To both of us, money and the indulgence it buys meant everything in life. All I can boast of is the longer sight. The office-hours were a nuisance, I admit: but I was clever enough to keep my hold on the old set; and then, after office-hours, I met you constantly, and studied and hated you—studied you because I hated you. Elaine came between us. You fell in love with her. That I, too, should fall in love with her was no coincidence, but the severest of logic. Given such a woman and two such men, no other course of fate is conceivable. She made it necessary for me to put hate into practice. If she had not offered herself, why, then it would have been somebody else:

that's all. Good Lord!" he rapped the table, and his voice rose for the first time above its level tone of exposition, "you don't suppose all my study—all my years of education—were to be wasted!"

He checked himself, eyed me again, and resumed in his old voice—

"You wanted money by this time. I was a solicitor—your old college friend—and you came to me. I knew you would come, as surely as I knew you would not fire that pistol just now. For years I had trained myself to look into your mind and anticipate its working. Don't I tell you that from the first you were the only real creature this world held for me? You were my only book, and I had to learn you: at first without fixed purpose, then deliberately. And when the time came I put into practice what I knew: just that and no more. My dear Reggie, you never had a chance."

"Elaine?" I muttered again.

"Elaine was the girl for you—or for me: just that again and no more."

"By George!" said I, letting out a laugh. "If I thought that!"

"What?"

"Why, that after ruining me, you have missed being happy!"

He sighed impatiently, and his eyes, though he kept them fastened on mine, seemed to be tiring. "I thought," he said, "I could time your intelligence over any fence. But tonight there's something wrong. Either I'm out of practice or your brain has been going to the deuce. What, man! You're shying at every bank! Is it drink, hey? Or hunger?"

"It might be a little of both," I answered. "But stay a moment and let me get things straight. I stood between you and Elaine—no, give me time—between you and your aims, whatever they were. Very well. You trod over me; or, rather, you pulled me up by the roots and pitched me into outer darkness to rot. And now it seems that, after all, you are not content. In the devil's name, why?"

"Why? Oh, cannot you see? . . . Take a look at these mirrors again—our world, I tell you. See—you and I—you and I—always you and I! Man, I pitched you into darkness as you say, and then I woke and knew the truth—that you were necessary to me."

"Hey?"

"*I can't do without you!*" It broke from him in a cry. "So help me God, Reggie, it is the truth!"

I stared in his face for half a minute maybe, and broke out laughing. "Jeshurun waxed fat and—turned sentimental! A nice copy-book job you make of it, too!"

"*Oh, send my brother back to me— I cannot play alone!*"

"Perhaps you'd like me to buy a broom and hire the crossing in Lennox Gardens? Then you'd be able to contemplate me all day long, and nourish your fine fat soul with delicate eating. Pah! You make me sick."

"It's the truth," said he quietly.

"It may be. To me it looks a sight more like *foie gras*. Can't do without me, can't you? Well, I can jolly well do without you, and I'm going to."

"I warn you," he said: "I have done you an injury or two in my time, but by George if I stand up and let you shoot me—well, I hate you badly enough, but I won't let you do it without fair warning."

"I'll risk it anyway," said I.

"Very well." He stood up, and folded his arms. "Shoot, then, and be hanged!"

I put out my hand to the revolver, hesitated, and withdrew it.

"That's not the way," I said. "I've got my code, as I told you before."

"Does the code forbid suicide?" he asked.

"That's a different thing."

"Not at all. The man who commits suicide kills an unarmed man."

"But the unarmed man happens to be himself."

"Suppose that in this instance your distinction won't work?

Look here," he went on, as I pushed back my chair impatiently, "I have one truth more for you. I swear I believe that what we have hated, we two, is not each other, but ourselves or our own likeness. I swear I believe we two have so shared natures in hate that no power can untwist and separate them to render each his own. But I swear also I believe that if you lift that revolver to kill, you will take aim, not at me, but by instinct at a worse enemy—yourself, vital in my heart."

"You have some pretty theories tonight," I sneered. "Perhaps you'll go on to tell me which of us two has been Elaine's husband, feeding daintily in Lennox Gardens, clothed in purple and fine linen, while the other—"

He interrupted me by picking up his revolver and striding to the fireplace again.

"So be it, since you will have it so. Kill me," he added, with a queer look, "and perhaps you may go back to Lennox Gardens and enjoy all these things in my place."

I took my station. Both revolvers were levelled now. I took sight along mine at his detested face. It was white but curiously eager—hopeful even. I lowered my arm, scanning his face still; and still scanning it, set my weapon down on the table.

"I believe you are mad," said I slowly. "But one thing I see—that, mad or not, you're in earnest. For some reason you want me to kill you; therefore that shall wait. For some reason it is torture to you to live and do without me: well, I'll try you with that. It will do me good to hurt you a bit." I slipped the revolver into my pocket and tapped it. "Though I don't understand them, I won't quarrel with your sentiments so long as you suffer from them. When that fails, I'll find another opportunity for this. Goodnight." I stepped to the door. "Reggie!"

I shut the door on his cry: crossed the corridor, and climbing out through the window, let myself drop into the lane.

As my feet touched the snow a revolver-shot rang out in the room behind me.

I caught at the frozen sill to steady myself: and crouching there, listened. Surely the report must have alarmed the house!

I waited for the sound of footsteps: waited for three minutes—perhaps longer. None came. To be sure, the room stood well apart from the house: but it was incredible that the report should have awakened no one! My own ears still rang with it.

Still no footsteps came. The horse in the stable close by was still shuffling his hoof on the cobbles. No other sound . . .

Very stealthily I hoisted myself up on the sill again, listened, dropped inside, and tip-toed my way to the door. The candles were still burning in the Room of Mirrors. And by the light of them, as I entered, Gervase stepped to meet me.

"Ah, it's you," I stammered. "I heard—that is, I thought—"

And with that I saw—recognised with a catch of the breath—that the figure I spoke to was not Gervase, but my own reflected image, stepping forward with pale face and ghastly from a mirror. Yet a moment before I could have sworn it was Gervase.

Gervase lay stretched on the hearthrug with his hand towards the fire. I caught up a candle, and bent over him. His features were not to be recognised.

As I straightened myself up, with the candle in my hand, for an instant those features, obliterated in the flesh, gazed at me in a ring, a hundred times repeated behind a hundred candles. And again, at a second glance, I saw that the face was not Gervase's but my own.

I set down the candle and made off, closing the door behind me. The horror of it held me by the hair, but I flung it off and pelted down the lane and through the mews. Once in the street I breathed again, pulled myself together, and set off at a rapid walk, southwards, but not clearly knowing whither.

As a matter of fact, I took the line by which I had come: with the single difference that I made straight into Berkeley Square through Bruton Street. I had, I say, no clear purpose in following this line rather than another. I had none for taking Lennox Gardens on the way to my squalid lodgings in Chelsea. I had a purpose, no doubt; but will swear it only grew definite as I came in sight of the lamp still burning beneath Gervase's portico.

There was a figure, too, under the lamp—the butler—bending there and rolling up the strip of red carpet. As he pulled its edges from the frozen snow I came on him suddenly.

"Oh, it's you, Sir!" He stood erect, and with the air of a man infinitely relieved.

"Gervase!"

The door opened wide and there stood Elaine in her ball-gown, a-glitter with diamonds.

"Gervase, dear, where have you been? We have been terribly anxious—"

She said it, looking straight down on me—on me—who stood in my tattered clothes in the full glare of the lamp. And then I heard the butler catch his breath, and suddenly her voice trailed off in wonder and pitiful disappointment.

"It's not Gervase! It's Reg—Mr. Travers. I beg your pardon. I thought—"

But I passed up the steps and stood before her: and said, as she drew back—

"There has been an accident. Gervase has shot himself." I turned to the butler. "You had better run to the police station. Stay: take this revolver. It won't count anything as evidence: but I ask you to examine it and make sure all the chambers are loaded."

A thud in the hall interrupted me. I ran in and knelt beside Elaine, and as I stooped to lift her—as my hand touched her hair—this was the jealous question on my lips—

"What has *she* to do with it. It is *I* who cannot do without him—who must miss him always!"

The Seventh Man

In a one-roomed hut, high within the Arctic Circle, and only a little south of the eightieth parallel, six men were sitting—much as they had sat, evening after evening, for months. They had a clock, and by it they divided the hours into day and night. As a matter of fact, it was always night. But the clock said half-past eight, and they called the time evening.

The hut was built of logs, with an inner skin of rough match-boarding, daubed with pitch. It measured seventeen feet by fourteen; but opposite the door four bunks—two above and two below—took a yard off the length, and this made the interior exactly square. Each of these bunks had two doors, with brass latches on the inner side; so that the owner, if he chose, could shut himself up and go to sleep in a sort of cupboard. But as a rule, he closed one of them only—that by his feet. The other swung back, with its brass latch showing. The men kept these latches in a high state of polish.

Across the angle of the wall, to the left of the door, and behind it when it opened, three hammocks were slung, one above another. No one slept in the uppermost.

But the feature of the hut was its fireplace; and this was merely a square hearth-stone, raised slightly above the floor, in the middle of the room. Upon it, and upon a growing mountain of soft grey ash, the fire burned always. It had no chimney, and so the men lost none of its warmth. The smoke ascended steadily and spread itself under the blackened beams and roof-boards in dense blue layers. But about eighteen inches beneath the spring of the roof there ran a line of small trap-doors with sliding panels, to admit the cold air, and below these the room was almost clear of smoke. A newcomer's eyes might have smarted, but these men stitched their clothes and read in comfort. To keep the up-draught steady they had plugged every chink and crevice in the match-boarding below the trap-doors with moss, and payed the seams with pitch. The fire they fed from a stack of drift and wreck wood piled to the right of the door, and fuel for the fetching strewed the frozen beach outside—whole trees notched into lengths by lumberers' axes and washed thither from they knew not what continent. But the wreck-wood came from their own ship, the *J. R. MacNeill*, which had brought them from Dundee.

They were Alexander Williamson, of Dundee, better known as The Gaffer; David Faed, also of Dundee; George Lashman, of Cardiff; Long Ede, of Hayle, in Cornwall; Charles Silchester, otherwise The Snipe, of Ratcliff Highway or thereabouts; and Daniel Cooney, shipped at Tromso six weeks before the wreck, an Irish-American by birth and of no known address.

The Gaffer reclined in his bunk, reading by the light of a smoky and evil-smelling lamp. He had been mate of the *J. R. MacNeill*, and was now captain as well as patriarch of the party. He possessed three books—the Bible, Milton's *Paradise Lost*, and an odd volume of *The Turkish Spy*. Just now he was reading *The Turkish Spy*. The lamplight glinted on the rim of his spectacles and on the silvery hairs in his beard, the slack of which he had tucked under the edge of his blanket. His lips moved as he read, and now and then he broke off to glance mildly at Faed and the Snipe, who were busy beside the fire with a greasy pack of cards; or to listen to the peevish grumbling of Lashman in the bunk below him.

Lashman had taken to his bed six weeks before with scurvy, and complained incessantly; and though they hardly knew it, these complaints were wearing his comrades' nerves to fiddle-strings—doing the mischief that cold and bitter hard work and the cruel loneliness had hitherto failed to do. Long Ede lay stretched by the fire in a bundle of skins, reading in his only book, the Bible, open now at the Song of Solomon. Cooney had finished patching a pair of trousers, and rolled himself in his hammock, whence he stared at the roof and the moonlight streaming up there through the little trap-doors and chivying the layers of smoke. Whenever Lashman broke out into fresh quaverings of self-pity, Cooney's hands opened and shut again, till the nails dug hard into the palm. He groaned at length, exasperated beyond endurance.

"Oh, stow it, George! Hang it all, man! . . ."

He checked himself, sharp and short: repentant, and rebuked by the silence of the others. They were good seamen all, and tender dealing with a sick shipmate was part of their code.

Lashman's voice, more querulous than ever, cut into the silence like a knife—

"That's it. You've thought it for weeks, and now you say it. I've knowed it all along. I'm just an encumbrance, and the sooner you're shut of me the better, says you. You needn't to fret. I'll be soon out of it; out of it—out there, alongside of Bill—"

"Easy there, matey." The Snipe glanced over his shoulder and laid his cards face downward. "Here, let me give the bed a shake up. It'll ease yer."

"It'll make me quiet, you mean. Plucky deal you care about easin' me, any of yer!"

"Get out with yer nonsense! Dan didn' mean it." The Snipe slipped an arm under the invalid's head and rearranged the pillow of skins and gunny-bags.

"He didn't, didn't he? Let him say it then . . ."

The Gaffer read on, his lips moving silently. Heaven knows how he had acquired this strayed and stained and filthy little *demi-octavo* with the arms of Saumarez on its book-plate—"*The Sixth Volume of Letters writ by a Turkish Spy, who liv'd Five-and-Forty Years Undiscovered at Paris: Giving an Impartial Account to the Divan at Constantinople of the most remarkable Transactions of Europe, And discovering several Intrigues and Secrets of the Christian Courts (especially of that of France),*" etc., etc. "Written originally in *Ara-*

bick. Translated into *Italian*, and from thence into *English* by the Translator of the First Volume. The Eleventh Edition. London: Printed for G. Strahan, S. Ballard"—and a score of booksellers—"*MDCCXLI.*" Heavens knows why he read it; since he understood about one-half, and admired less than one-tenth. The Oriental reflections struck him as mainly blasphemous. But the Gaffer's religious belief marked down nine-tenths of mankind for perdition: which perhaps made him tolerant. At any rate, he read on gravely between the puffs of his short clay—

> On the 19th of this moon, the king and the whole court were present at a ballet, representing the grandeur of the French monarchy. About the middle of the entertainment, there was an antique dance performed by twelve masqueraders, in the suppos'd form of daemons. But before they had advanced far in their dance, they found an interloper amongst 'em, who by encreasing the number to thirteen, put them quite out of their measure: for they practise every step and motion beforehand, till they are perfect. Being abashed therefore at the unavoidable blunders the thirteenth antique made them commit, they stood still like fools, gazing at one another: None daring to unmask, or speak a word; for that would have put all the spectators into a disorder and confusion. Cardinal Mazarini (who was the chief contriver of these entertainments, to divert the king from more serious thoughts) stood close by the young monarch, with the scheme of the ballet in his hand.
>
> Knowing therefore that this dance was to consist but of twelve antiques, and taking notice that there were actually thirteen, he at first imputed it to some mistake. But, afterwards, when he perceived the confusion of the dancers, he made a more narrow enquiry into the cause of this disorder. To be brief, they convinced the cardinal that it could be no error of theirs, by a kind of demonstration, in that they had but twelve antique dresses of that sort, which were made on purpose for this particular ballet. That which made it seem the greater mystery was, that when they came behind the scenes to uncase, and examine the matter, they found but twelve antiques, whereas on the stage there were thirteen ...

"Let him say it. Let him say he didn't mean it, the rotten

Irishman!"

Cooney flung a leg wearily over the side of his hammock, jerked himself out, and shuffled across to the sick man's berth.

"Av coorse I didn' mane it. It just took me, ye see, lyin' up yondher and huggin' me thoughts in this—wilderness. I swear to ye, George: and ye'll just wet your throat to show there's no bad blood, and that ye belave me." He took up a pannikin from the floor beside the bunk, pulled a hot iron from the fire, and stirred the frozen drink. The invalid turned his shoulder pettishly. "I didn't mane it," Cooney repeated. He set down the pannikin, and shuffled wearily back to his hammock.

The Gaffer blew a long cloud and stared at the fire; at the smoke mounting and the grey ash dropping; at David Faed dealing the cards and licking his thumb between each. Long Ede shifted from one cramped elbow to another and pushed his Bible nearer the blaze, murmuring, "Take us the foxes, the little foxes, that spoil our vines."

"Full hand," the Snipe announced.

"Ay." David Faed rolled the quid in his cheek. The cards were so thumbed and tattered that by the backs of them each player guessed pretty shrewdly what the other held. Yet they went on playing night after night; the Snipe shrilly blessing or cursing his luck, the Scotsman phlegmatic as a bolster.

"Play away, man. What ails ye?" he asked.

The Snipe had dropped both hands to his thighs and sat up, stiff and listening.

"Whist! Outside the door. . . ."

All listened. "I hear nothing," said David, after ten seconds.

"Hush, man—listen! There, again . . ."

They heard now. Cooney slipped down from his hammock, stole to the door and listened, crouching, with his ear close to the jamb. The sound resembled breathing—or so he thought for a moment. Then it seemed rather as if some creature were softly feeling about the door—fumbling its coating of ice and frozen snow.

Cooney listened. They all listened. Usually, as soon as they stirred from the scorching circle of the fire, their breath came from them in clouds. It trickled from them now in thin wisps of vapour. They could almost hear the soft grey ash dropping on the hearth.

A log spluttered. Then the invalid's voice clattered in—

"It's the bears—the bears! They've come after Bill, and next it'll be my turn. I warned you—I told you he wasn't deep enough. O Lord, have mercy . . . mercy . . . !" He pattered off into a prayer, his voice and teeth chattering.

"Hush!" commanded the Gaffer gently; and Lashman choked on a sob.

"It ain't bears," Cooney reported, still with his ear to the door. "Leastways . . . we've had bears before. The foxes, maybe . . . let me listen."

Long Ede murmured: "Take us the foxes, the little foxes . . ."

"I believe you're right," the Gaffer announced cheerfully. "A bear would sniff louder—though there's no telling. The snow was falling an hour back, and I dessay 'tis pretty thick outside. If 'tis a bear, we don't want him fooling on the roof, and I misdoubt the drift by the north corner is pretty tall by this time. Is he there still?"

"I felt something then . . . through the chink, here . . . like a warm breath. It's gone now. Come here, Snipe, and listen."

"'Breath,' eh? Did it *smell* like bear?"

"I don't know . . . I didn't smell nothing, to notice. Here, put your head down, close."

The Snipe bent his head. And at that moment the door shook gently. All stared; and saw the latch move up, up . . . and falteringly descend on the staple. They heard the click of it.

The door was secured within by two stout bars. Against these there had been no pressure. The men waited in a silence that ached. But the latch was not lifted again.

The Snipe, kneeling, looked up at Cooney. Cooney shivered and looked at David Faed. Long Ede, with his back to the fire, softly shook his feet free of the rugs. His eyes searched for the Gaffer's face. But the old man had drawn back into the gloom of his bunk, and the lamplight shone only on a grey fringe of beard. He saw Long Ede's look, though, and answered it quietly as ever.

"Take a brace of guns aloft, and fetch us a look round. Wait, if there's a chance of a shot. The trap works. I tried it this afternoon with the small chisel."

Long Ede lit his pipe tied down the ear-pieces of his cap, lifted a light ladder off its staples, and set it against a roof-beam: then, with the guns under his arm, quietly mounted. His head and shoulders wavered and grew vague to sight in the smoke-wreaths. "Heard anything more?" he asked. "Nothing since," answered the Snipe. With his shoulder Long Ede pushed up the trap. They saw his head framed in a panel of moonlight, with one frosty star above it. He was wriggling through. "Pitch him up a sleeping-bag, somebody," the Gaffer ordered, and Cooney ran with one. "Thank 'ee, mate," said Long Ede, and closed the trap.

They heard his feet stealthily crunching the frozen stuff across the roof. He was working towards the eaves over-lapping the door. Their breath tightened. They waited for the explosion of his gun. None came. The crunching began again: it was heard down by the very edge of the eaves. It mounted to the blunt ridge overhead; then it ceased.

"He will not have seen aught," David Faed muttered.

"Listen, you. Listen by the door again." They talked in whispers. Nothing; there was nothing to be heard. They crept back to the fire, and stood there warming themselves, keeping their eyes on the latch. It did not move. After a while Cooney slipped off to his hammock; Faed to his bunk, alongside Lashman's. The Gaffer had picked up his book again. The Snipe laid a couple of logs on the blaze, and remained beside it, cowering, with his arms stretched out as if to embrace it. His shapeless shadow wavered up and down on the bunks behind him; and, across the fire, he still stared at the latch.

Suddenly the sick man's voice quavered out—

"It's not him they want—it's Bill! They're after Bill, out there!

That was Bill trying to get in. . . . Why didn't yer open? It was Bill, I tell yer!"

At the first word the Snipe had wheeled right-about-face, and stood now, pointing, and shaking like a man with ague.

"Matey . . . for the love of God . . ."

"I won't hush. There's something wrong here tonight. I can't sleep. It's Bill, I tell yer. See his poor hammock up there shaking. . . ."

Cooney tumbled out with an oath and a thud. "Hush it, you white-livered swine! Hush it, or by—" His hand went behind him to his knife-sheath.

"Dan Cooney"—the Gaffer closed his book and leaned out—"go back to your bed."

"I won't, Sir. Not unless—"

"Go back."

"Flesh and blood—"

"Go back." And for the third time that night Cooney went back.

The Gaffer leaned a little farther over the ledge, and addressed the sick man.

"George, I went to Bill's grave not six hours agone. The snow on it wasn't even disturbed. Neither beast nor man, but only God, can break up the hard earth he lies under. I tell you that, and you may lay to it. Now go to sleep."

Long Ede crouched on the frozen ridge of the hut, with his feet in the sleeping-bag, his knees drawn up, and the two guns laid across them. The creature, whatever its name, that had tried the door, was nowhere to be seen; but he decided to wait a few minutes on the chance of a shot; that is, until the cold should drive him below. For the moment the clear tingling air was doing him good. The truth was Long Ede had begun to be afraid of himself, and the way his mind had been running for the last forty-eight hours upon green fields and visions of spring. As he put it to himself, something inside his head was melting. Biblical texts chattered within him like running brooks, and as they fleeted he could almost smell the blown meadow-scent. "Take us the foxes, the little foxes . . . for our vines have tender grapes . . . A fountain of gardens, a well of living waters, and streams from Lebanon . . . Awake, O north wind, and come, thou south . . . blow upon my garden, that the spices thereof may flow out . . ." He was light-headed, and he knew it. He must hold out. They were all going mad; were, in fact, three parts crazed already, all except the Gaffer. And the Gaffer relied on him as his right-hand man. One glimpse of the returning sun—one glimpse only—might save them yet.

He gazed out over the frozen hills, and northward across the ice-pack. A few streaks of pale violet—the ghost of the Aurora—fronted the moon. He could see for miles. Bear or fox, no living creature was in sight. But who could tell what might be hiding behind any one of a thousand hummocks? He listened. He heard the slow grinding of the ice-pack off the beach: only that. "Take us the foxes, the little foxes. . ."

This would never do. He must climb down and walk briskly, or return to the hut. Maybe there was a bear, after all, behind one of the hummocks, and a shot, or the chance of one, would scatter his head clear of these tom-fooling notions. He would have a search round.

What was that, moving . . . on a hummock, not five hundred yards away? He leaned forward to gaze.

Nothing now: but he had seen something. He lowered himself to the eaves by the north corner, and from the eaves to the drift piled there.

The drift was frozen solid, but for a treacherous crust of fresh snow. His foot slipped upon this, and down he slid of a heap.

Luckily he had been careful to sling the guns tightly at his back. He picked himself up, and unstrapping one, took a step into the bright moonlight to examine the nipples; took two steps: and stood stock-still.

There, before him, on the frozen coat of snow, was a footprint. No: two, three, four—many footprints: prints of a naked human foot: right foot, left foot, both naked, and blood in each print—a little smear.

It had come, then. He was mad for certain. He saw them: he put his fingers in them; touched the frozen blood. The snow before the door was trodden thick with them—some going, some returning.

"The latch . . . lifted . . ." Suddenly he recalled the figure he had seen moving upon the hummock, and with a groan he set his face northward and gave chase. Oh, he was mad for certain! He ran like a madman—floundering, slipping, plunging in his clumsy moccasins. "Take us the foxes, the little foxes . . . My beloved put in his hand by the hole of the door, and my bowels were moved for him . . . I charge you, O daughters of Jerusalem . . . I charge you . . . I charge you . . ."

He ran thus for three hundred yards maybe, and then stopped as suddenly as he had started.

His mates—they must not see these footprints, or they would go mad too: mad as he. No, he must cover them up, all within sight of the hut. And tomorrow he would come alone, and cover those farther afield. Slowly he retraced his steps. The footprints—those which pointed towards the hut and those which pointed away from it—lay close together; and he knelt before each, breaking fresh snow over the hollows and carefully hiding the blood. And now a great happiness filled his heart; interrupted once or twice as he worked by a feeling that someone was following and watching him. Once he turned northwards and gazed, making a telescope of his hands. He saw nothing, and fell again to his long task.

Within the hut the sick man cried softly to himself. Faed, the Snipe, and Cooney slept uneasily, and muttered in their dreams. The Gaffer lay awake, thinking. After Bill, George Lashman; and after George? . . . Who next? And who would be the last—the unburied one? The men were weakening fast; their wits and courage coming down at the end with a rush. Faed and Long Ede were the only two to be depended on for a day. The Gaffer liked Long Ede, who was a religious man. Indeed he had a growing suspicion that Long Ede, in spite of some amiable laxities of belief, was numbered among the Elect: or might be, if interceded for. The Gaffer began to intercede for him silently; but experience had taught him that such "wrestlings," to be effective, must be noisy, and he dropped off to sleep with a sense of failure . . .

The Snipe stretched himself, yawned, and awoke. It was seven in the morning: time to prepare a cup of tea. He tossed an armful of logs on the fire, and the noise awoke the Gaffer, who at once inquired for Long Ede. He had not returned. "Go you up to the roof. The lad must be frozen." The Snipe climbed the ladder, pushed open the trap, and came back, reporting that Long Ede was nowhere to be seen. The old man slipped a jumper over his suits of clothing—already three deep—reached for a gun, and moved to the door. "Take a cup of something warm to fortify," the Snipe advised. "The kettle won't be five minutes boiling." But the Gaffer pushed up the heavy bolts and dragged the door open.

"What in the! . . . Here, bear a hand, lads!"

Long Ede lay prone before the threshold, his out-stretched hands almost touching it, his moccasins already covered out of sight by the powdery snow which ran and trickled incessantly—trickled between his long, dishevelled locks, and over the back of his gloves, and ran in a thin stream past the Gaffer's feet.

They carried him in and laid him on a heap of skins by the fire. They forced rum between his clenched teeth and beat his hands and feet, and kneaded and rubbed him. A sigh fluttered on his lips: something between a sigh and a smile, half seen, half heard. His eyes opened, and his comrades saw that it was really a smile.

"Wot cheer, mate?" It was the Snipe who asked.

"I—I seen . . ." The voice broke off, but he was smiling still.

What had he seen? Not the sun, surely! By the Gaffer's reckoning the sun would not be due for a week or two yet: how many weeks he could not say precisely, and sometimes he was glad enough that he did not know.

They forced him to drink a couple of spoonfuls of rum, and wrapped him up warmly. Each man contributed some of his own bedding. Then the Gaffer called to morning prayers, and the three sound men dropped on their knees with him. Now, whether by reason of their joy at Long Ede's recovery, or because the old man was in splendid voice, they felt their hearts uplifted that morning with a cheerfulness they had not known for months. Long Ede lay and listened dreamily while the passion of the Gaffer's thanksgiving shook the hut. His gaze wandered over their bowed forms—"The Gaffer, David Faed, Dan Cooney, the Snipe, and—and George Lashman in his bunk, of course—and me." But, then, *who was the seventh?* He began to count. "There's myself—Lashman, in his bunk—David Faed, the Gaffer, the Snipe, Dan Cooney ... One, two, three, four—well, but that made *seven*. Then who was the seventh? Was it George who had crawled out of bed and was kneeling there? Decidedly there were five kneeling. No: there was George, plain enough, in his berth, and not able to move. Then who was the stranger? Wrong again: there was no stranger. He knew all these men—they were his mates. Was it—Bill? No, Bill was dead and buried: none of these was Bill, or like Bill. Try again—One, two, three, four, five—and us two sick men, seven. The Gaffer, David Faed, Dan Cooney—have I counted Dan twice? No, that's Dan, yonder to the right, and only one of him. Five men kneeling, and two on their backs: that makes seven every time. Dear God—suppose—"

The Gaffer ceased, and in the act of rising from his knees, caught sight of Long Ede's face. While the others fetched their breakfast-cans, he stepped over, and bent and whispered—

"Tell me. Ye've seen what?"

"Seen?" Long Ede echoed.

"Ay, seen what? Speak low—was it the sun?"

"The s—" But this time the echo died on his lips, and his face grew full of awe uncomprehending. It frightened the Gaffer.

"Ye'll be the better of a snatch of sleep," said he; and was turning to go, when Long Ede stirred a hand under the edge of his rugs.

"Seven ... count ..." he whispered.

"Lord have mercy upon us!" the Gaffer muttered to his beard as he moved away. "Long Ede; gone crazed!"

And yet, though an hour or two ago this had been the worst that could befall, the Gaffer felt unusually cheerful. As for the others, they were like different men, all that day and through the three days that followed. Even Lashman ceased to complain, and, unless their eyes played them a trick, had taken a turn for the better. "I declare, if I don't feel like pitching to sing!" the Snipe announced on the second evening, as much to his own wonder as to theirs. "Then why in thunder don't you strike up?" answered Dan Cooney, and fetched his concertina. The Snipe struck up, then and there—"Villikins and his Dinah"! What is more, the Gaffer looked up from his *Paradise Lost,* and joined in the chorus.

By the end of the second day, Long Ede was up and active again. He went about with a dazed look in his eyes. He was counting, counting to himself, always counting. The Gaffer watched him furtively.

Since his recovery, though his lips moved frequently, Long Ede had scarcely uttered a word. But towards noon on the fourth day he said an extraordinary thing.

"There's that sleeping-bag I took with me the other night. I wonder if 'tis on the roof still. It will be froze pretty stiff by this. You might nip up and see, Snipe, and"—he paused—"if you find it, stow it up yonder on Bill's hammock."

The Gaffer opened his mouth, but shut it again without speaking. The Snipe went up the ladder.

A minute passed; and then they heard a cry from the roof—a cry that fetched them all trembling, choking, weeping, cheering, to the foot of the ladder.

"Boys! boys!—the Sun!"

Months later—it was June, and even George Lashman had recovered his strength—the Snipe came running with news of the whaling fleet. And on the beach, as they watched the vessels come to anchor, Long Ede told the Gaffer his story. "It was a hall—a hallu—what d'ye call it, I reckon. I was crazed, eh?"

The Gaffer's eyes wandered from a brambling hopping about the lichen-covered boulders, and away to the sea-fowl wheeling above the ships: and then came into his mind a tale he had read once in *The Turkish Spy*. "I wouldn't say just that," he answered slowly.

"Anyway," said Long Ede, "I believe the Lord sent a miracle to us to save us all."

"I wouldn't say just that, either," the Gaffer objected. "I doubt it was meant just for you and me, and the rest were presairved, as you might say incidentally."

The Small People
To a Lady who had asked for a Fairy Tale.

You thought it natural, my dear lady, to lay this command on me at the dance last night. We had parted, two months ago, in London, and we met, unexpectedly and to music, in this corner of the land where (they say) the piskies still keep. And certainly, when I led you out upon the balcony (that you might not see the new moon through glass and lose a lucky month), it was not hard to picture the Small People at their play on the turf and among the dim flower-beds below us. But, as a matter of fact, they are dead, these Small People. They were the long-lived but not immortal spirits of the folk who inhabited Cornwall many thousands of years back—far beyond Christ's birth. They were "poor innocents," not good enough for heaven yet too good for the eternal fires; and when they first came, were of ordinary stature. But after Christ's birth they began to grow smaller and smaller, and at length turned into emmets and vanished from the earth.

The last I heard of them was a sad and serious little history, very different from the old legends. Part of it I was told by a hospital surgeon, of all people in the world. Part I learnt by looking at your beautiful gown last night, as you leant on the balcony-rail. You remember how heavy the dew was, and that I fetched a shawl for your shoulders. You did not wrap it so tightly round but that four marguerites in gold embroidery showed on the front of your bodice; and these come into the tale, the remainder of which I was taught this morning before breakfast, down among the cairns by the sea where the Small People's Gardens still remain—sheltered spots of green, with here and there some ferns and cliff-pinks left. For me they are libraries where sometimes I read for a whole summer's day; and with the help of the hospital surgeon, I bring you from them a story about your ball-gown which is perfectly true.

Twenty years ago—before the fairies had dwindled into ants, and when wayfarers were still used to turn their coats inside out, after nightfall, for fear of being "pisky-led"—there lived, down at the village, a girl who knew all the secrets of the Small People's Gardens. Where you and I discover sea-pinks only, and hear only the wash of the waves, she would go on midsummer nights and find flowers of every colour spread, and hundreds of little lights moving among them, and fountains and waterfalls and swarms of small ladies and gentlemen, dressed in green and gold, walking and sporting among them, or reposing on the turf and telling stories to the most ravishing soft music. This was as much as she would relate; but it is certain that the piskies were friends of hers. For, in spite of her nightly wanderings, her housework was always well and cleanly done before other girls were dressed—the morning milk fresh in the dairy, the step sanded, the fire lit and the scalding-pans warming over it. And as for her needlework, it was a wonder.

Some said she was a changeling; others that she had found the four-leaved clover or the fairy ointment, and rubbed her eyes with it. But it was her own secret; for whenever the people tried to follow her to the "Gardens," *whir! whir! whir!* buzzed in their ears, as if a flight of bees were passing, and every limb would feel as if stuck full of pins and pinched with tweezers, and they were rolled over and over, their tongues tied as if with cords, and at last, as soon as they could manage, they would pick themselves up, and hobble home for their lives.

Well, the history—which, I must remind you, is a true one—goes on to say that in time the girl grew ambitious, or fell in love (I cannot remember which), and went to London. In any case it must have been a strong call that took her: for there are no fairies in London. I regret that my researches do not allow me to tell you how the Small People at home took her departure; but we will suppose that it grieved them deeply. Nor can I say precisely how the girl fared for many years. I think her fortune contained both joy and sorrow for a while; and I suspect that many passages of her life would be sadly out of place in this story, even if they could be hunted out. Indeed, fairy-tales have to omit so much nowadays, and therefore seem so antiquated, that one marvels how they could ever have been in fashion.

But you may take it as sure that in the end this girl met with more sorrow than joy; for when next she comes into sight it is in London streets and she is in rags. Moreover, though she wears a flush on her cheeks, above the wrinkles it does not come of health or high spirits, but perhaps from the fact that in the twenty years' interval she has seen millions of men and women, but not one single fairy.

In those latter days I met her many times. She passed under your windows shortly before dawn on the night that you gave your dance, early in the season. You saw her, I think?—a woman who staggered a little, and had some words with the policeman at the corner: but, after all, a staggering woman in London is no such memorable sight. All day long she was seeking work, work, work; and after dark she sought forgetfulness. She found the one, in small quantities, and out of it she managed to buy the other, now and then, over the counter. But she had long given up looking for the fairies. The lights along the embankment had ceased to remind her of those in the Small People's Gardens; nor did the noise bursting from music-hall doors as she passed, recall the old sounds; and as for the scents, there were plenty in London, but none resembling that of the garden which you might smell a mile out at sea.

I told you that her needlework had been a marvel when she lived down at the village. Curiously enough, this was the one gift of the fairies that stayed by her, and it remained as wonderful as ever. Her most frequent employer was a flat-footed Jew with a large, fleshy face; and because she had a name for honesty, she was not seldom entrusted with costly pieces of stuff, and allowed to carry them home to turn into ball-dresses under the roof through the gaps of which, as she stitched, she could see the night pass from purple to black, and from black to the lilac of daybreak. There, with a hundred pounds' worth of silk and lace on her knee, she would sit and work a dozen hours to earn as many pence. With fingers weary and—But you know Hood's song, and no doubt have taken it to heart a dozen times.

It came to this, however, that one evening, when she had not eaten for forty hours, her employer gave her a piece of embroidery to work against time. The fact is, my dear lady, that you are very particular about having your commissions executed to the hour, and your dressmakers are anxious to oblige, knowing that you never squabble over the price. To be sure, you have never heard of the flat-footed Jew man—how should you? And we may believe that your dressmakers knew just as little of the poor woman who had used to be the friend of the Small People. But the truth remains that, in the press of your many pleasures, you were pardonably twenty-four hours late in ordering the gown in which you were to appear an angel.

Ah, madam! will it comfort you to hear that *you* were the one to reconcile the Small People with that poor sister of yours who had left them, twenty years before, and wanted them so sorely? The hospital doctor gave her complaint a long name, and I gather that it has a place by itself in books of pathology. But the woman's tale was that, after she had been stitching through the long night, the dawn came through the roof and found her with four marguerites still left to be embroidered in gold on the pieces of satin that lay in her lap. She threaded her needle afresh, rubbed her weary eyes, and began—when, lo! a miracle.

Instead of one hand, there were four at work—four hands, four needles, four lines of thread. *The four marguerites were all being embroidered at the same time!* The piskies had forgiven, had remembered her at last, after these many years, and were coming to her help, as of old. Ah, madam, the tears of thankfulness that ran from her hot eyes and fell upon those golden marguerites of yours!

Of course her eyes were disordered. There was only one flower, really. There was only one embroidered in the morning, when they found her sobbing, with your bodice still in her lap, and took her to the hospital; and that is why the dressmakers failed to keep faith with you for once, and made you so angry.

Dear lady, the piskies are not easily summoned, in these days.

The Talking Ships

He was a happy boy, for he lived beside a harbour, and just below the last bend where the river swept out of steep woodlands into view of the sea. A half-ruined castle, with a battery of antiquated guns, still made-believe to protect the entrance to the harbour, and looked across it upon a ridge of rocks surmounted by a wooden cross, which the Trinity pilots kept in repair. Between the cross and the fort, for as long as he could remember, a procession of ships had come sailing in to anchor by the great red buoy immediately beneath his nursery window. They belonged to all nations, and hailed from all imaginable ports; and from the day his nurse had first stood him upon a chair to watch them, these had been the great interest of his life.

He soon came to know them all—French brigs and *chasse-marees*, Russian fore-and-afters, Dutch billyboys, *galliots* from the East coast, and Thames hay-barges with vanes and wind-boards. He could tell you why the Italians were deep in the keel, why the Danes were manned by youngsters, and why these youngsters deserted, although their skippers looked, and indeed were, such good-natured fellows; what food the French crews hunted in the seaweed under the cliff, and when the Baltic traders would be driven southward by the ice. Once acquainted with a vessel, he would recognise her at any distance, though by what signs he could no more tell than we why we recognise a friend.

On his seventh birthday he was given a sailing boat, on condition that he learned to read; but, although he kept by the bargain honestly, at the end of a month he handled her better than he was likely to handle his book in a year. He had a companion and instructor, of course—a pensioner who had left the navy to become in turn fisherman, yachtsman, able seaman on board a dozen sailing vessels, and now yachtsman again. His name was Billy, and he taught the boy many mysteries, from the tying of knots to the reading of weather-signs; how to beach a boat, how to take a conger off the hook, how to gaff a cuttle and avoid its ink.... In return the boy gave him his heart, and even something like worship.

One fine day, as they tacked to and fro a mile and more from the harbour's mouth, whiffing for mackerel, the boy looked up from his seat by the tiller. "I say, Billy, did you speak?"

Billy, seated on the thwart and leaning with both arms on the weather gunwale, turned his head lazily. "Not a word this half-hour," he answered.

"Well now, I thought not; but somebody, or something—spoke just now." The boy blushed, for Billy was looking at him quizzically. "It's not the first time I've heard it, either," he went on; "sometimes it sounds right astern, and sometimes close beside me."

"What does it say?" asked Billy, re-lighting his pipe.

"I don't know that it *says* anything, and yet it seems to speak out quite clearly. Five or six times I've heard it, and usually on smooth days like this, when the wind's steady."

Billy nodded. "That's right, sonny; I've heard it scores of times. And they say.... But, there, I don't believe a word of it."

"What do they say?"

"They say that 'tis the voice of drowned men down below, and that they hail their names whenever a boat passes."

The boy stared at the water. He knew it for a floor through which he let down his trammels and crab-pots into wonderland—a twilight with forests and meadows of its own, in which all the marvels of all the fairy-books were possible; but the terror of it had never clouded his delight.

"Nonsense, Billy; the voice I hear is always quite cheerful and friendly—not a bit like a dead man's."

"I tell what I'm told," answered Billy, and the subject dropped.

But the boy did not cease thinking about the voice; and sometime after he came, as it seemed, upon a clue. His father had set him to read Shakespeare; and, taking down the first of twelve volumes from the shelf, he began upon the first play, *The Tempest*. He was prepared to yawn, but the first scene flung open a door to him, and he stepped into a new world, a childish Ferdinand roaming an Isle of Voices. He resigned Miranda to the grown-up prince, for whom (as he saw at a glance, being wise in the ways of story-books) she was eminently fitted. It was in Ariel, perched with harp upon the shrouds of the king's ship, that he recognised the unseen familiar of his own voyaging. "O spirit, be my friend—speak to me often!" As children will, he gave Prospero's island a local habitation in the tangled cliff-garden, tethered Caliban in the tool-shed, and watched the white surf far withdrawn, or listened to its murmur between the lordly boles of the red-currant bushes. For the first time he became aware of some limitations in Billy.

He had long been aware of some serious limitations in his nurse: she could not, for instance, sail a boat, and her only knot was a "granny." He never dreamed of despising her, being an affectionate boy; but more and more he went his own way without consulting her. Yet it was she who—unconsciously and quite as if it were nothing out of the way—handed him the clue.

A flagstaff stood in the garden on a grassy platform, halfway down the cliff-side, and the boy at his earnest wish had been given charge of it. On weekdays, as a rule he hoisted two flags—an ensign on the gaff, and a single code-flag at the masthead; but on Sundays he usually ran up three or four, and with the help of the code-book spelt out some message to the harbour. Sometimes, too, if an old friend happened to take up her moorings at the red buoy below, he would have her code-letters hoisted to welcome her, or would greet and speed her with such signals as K.T.N., "Glad to see you," and B.R.D., or B.Q.R., meaning "Goodbye," "A pleasant passage."

Skippers fell into the habit of dipping their flags to him as they were towed out to sea, and a few amused themselves while at anchor by pulling out their bags of bunting and signalling humorous conversations, though their topmasts reached so near to the boy's platform that they might with less labour have talked through a speaking-trumpet.

One morning before Christmas six vessels lay below at the buoy, moored stem to stem in two tiers of three; and, after hoisting his signal (C.P.B.H. for "Christmas Eve"), he ran indoors with the news that all six were answering with bushes of holly at their topmast heads, while one—a Danish *barquentine*—had rove stronger halliards and carried a tall fir-tree at the main, its branches reaching many feet above her truck.

"Christmas is Christmas," said his nurse. "When I was young, at such times there wouldn't be a ship in the harbour without its talking-bush."

"What is a talking-bush?" the boy asked.

"And you pretend to be a sailor! Well, well—not to know what happens on Christmas night when the clocks strike twelve!"

The boy's eyes grew round. "Do—the—ships—talk?"

"Why, of course they do! For my part, I wonder what Billy teaches you."

Late that evening, when the household supposed him to be in bed, the boy crept down through the moonlit garden to the dinghy which Billy had left on its frape under the cliff. But for their riding-lights, the vessels at the buoy lay asleep. The crews of the foreigners had turned in; the *Nubian*, of Runcorn, had no soul on board but a night-watchman, now soundly dozing in the forecastle; and the *Touch-me-not* was deserted. The *Touch-me-not* belonged to the port, and her skipper, Captain Tangye, looked after her in harbour when he had paid off all hands. Usually he slept on board; but tonight, after trimming his lamp, he had rowed ashore to spend Christmas with his family—for which, since he owned a majority of the shares, no one was likely to blame him. He had even left the accommodation-ladder hanging over her side, to be handy for boarding her in the morning.

All this the boy had noted; and accordingly, having pushed across in the dinghy, he climbed the *Touch-me-not's* ladder and dropped upon deck with a bundle of rugs and his father's great-coat under his arm.

He looked about him and listened. There was no sound at all but the lap of tide between the ships, and the voice of a preacher travelling over the water from a shed far down the harbour, where the Salvation Army was holding a midnight service. Captain Tangye had snugged down his ship for the night: ropes were coiled, deckhouses padlocked, the spokes of the wheel covered against dew and frost. The boy found the slack of a stout hawser coiled beneath the taffrail—a circular fort into which he crept with his rugs, and nestled down warmly; and then for half an hour lay listening. But only the preacher's voice broke the silence of the harbour. On—on it went, rising and falling. . . .

Away in the little town the church clock chimed the quarter. "It must have missed striking the hour," thought the boy, and he peered over the edge of his shelter. The preacher's voice had ceased; but another was speaking, and close beside him.

"You'd be surprised," it said, "how simple one's pleasures grow with age. This is the twelfth Christmas I've spent at home, and I assure you I quite look forward to it: that's a confession, eh?—from one who has sailed under Nelson and smelt powder in his time." The boy knew that he must be listening to the *Touch-me-not*, whose keelson came from an old line-of-battle ship. "To be sure," the voice went on graciously, "a great deal depends on one's company."

"Talking of powder," said the *Nubian*, creaking gently on her stern-moorings, "reminds me of a terrible adventure. My very first voyage was to the mouth of a river on the West Coast of Africa, where two native tribes were at war. Somehow, my owner—a scoundrelly fellow in the Midlands—had wind of the quarrel, and that the tribe nearest the coast needed gunpowder. We sailed from Cardiff with fifteen hundred barrels duly labelled, and the natives came out to meet us at the river-mouth and rafted them ashore; but the barrels, if you will believe me, held nothing but sifted coal-dust. Off we went before the trick was discovered, and with six thousand pounds' worth of ivory in my hold. But the worst villainy was to come; for my owner, pretending that he had opened up a profitable trade, and having his ivory to show for it, sold me to a London firm, who loaded me with real gunpowder and sent me out, six months later, to the same river, but with a new skipper and a different crew. The natives knew me at once, and came swarming out in canoes as soon as we dropped anchor.

"The captain, who of course suspected nothing, allowed them to crowd on board; and I declare that within five minutes they had clubbed him and every man of the crew and tossed their bodies to the sharks. Then they cut my hawsers and towed me over the river-bar; and, having landed a good half of my barrels, they built and lit a fire around them in derision. I can hear the explosion still; my poor upper-works have been crazy ever since. It destroyed almost all the fighters of the tribe, who had formed a ring to dance around the fire. The rest fled inland, and I never saw them again, but lay abandoned for months as they had anchored me, between the ruined huts and a sandy spit alive with mosquitoes—until somehow a British tramp-steamer heard of me at one of the trading stations up the coast.

"She brought down a crew to man and work me home. But my owner could not pay the salvage; so the parties who owned the steamer—a Runcorn firm—paid him fifty pounds and kept me for their services. A surveyor examined me, and reported that I should never be fit for much: the explosion had shaken me to pieces. I might do for the coasting trade—that was all; and in that I've remained."

"Owners are rogues, for the most part," commented the Danish *barquentine*, rubbing against the *Touch-me-nots* fender as if to nudge her. "There's the *Maria Stella Maris* yonder can tell us a tale of the food they store us with. She went through a mutiny once, I've heard."

"I'd rather not talk of it," put in the Italian hastily, and a shudder ran through her timbers. "It's a dreadful recollection, and I have that by my mizzen-mast which all the holystone in the world can never scour."

"But I've had a mutiny, too!" said the Dutch *galliot*, with a voice of great importance; and this time the boy felt sure that the vessels nudged one another.

"It happened," the *galliot* went on, "between my skipper and his *vrauw*, who was to all purpose our mate, and as good a mate as ever I sailed with. But she would not believe the world was round. The skipper took a Dutch cheese and tried to explain things: he moved the cheese round, as it might be, from west to east, and argued and argued, until at last, being a persevering man, he did really persuade her, but it took a whole voyage, and by the time he succeeded we were near home again, and in the North Sea Canal.

"The moment she was convinced, what must the woman do but go ashore to an aunt of hers who lived at Zaandam, and refuse to return on board, though her man went on his bended knees to her! 'I will not,' she said; 'and *that's* flat, at any rate.' The poor man had to start afresh, undo every one of his arguments, and prove the earth flat again, before she would trust herself to travel. It cost us a week, but for my part I didn't grudge it. Your cliffs and deep-water harbours don't appeal to me. Give me a canal with windmills and summer-houses where you can look in on the families drinking tea as you sail by; give me, above all, a canal on Sundays, when the folks walk along the towing-path in their best clothes, and you feel as if you were going to church with them."

"Give me rather," said the Norwegian *barque* from Christiansund, "a fiord with forests running straight up to the snow mountains, and water so deep that no ship's anchor can reach it."

"I have seen most waters," the Dane announced calmly and proudly. "As you see, I am very particular about my paint, for a ship ought to keep up her beauty and look as young as she can. But I have an ice-mark around my breast which is usually taken for a proof of experience, and as a philosopher I say that all waters are tolerable enough if one carries the talisman."

"But can a ship be beautiful?" and "What is the talisman?" asked the Italian and the *Nubian* together.

"One at a time, please. My dear," she addressed the Italian, "the point is, that men, whom we serve, think us beautiful indeed. It seems strange to us, who carry the thought of the forests we have left; and on warm days, when the sap awakes in us and tries to climb again, forgetting its weakness, we miss the green boughs and the moss at our feet and the birds overhead. But I have studied my reflection often enough in calm weather, and begin to see what men have in mind when they admire us."

"And the talisman?" asked the *Nubian* again.

"The talisman? There is no one cure for useless regret, but each must choose his own. With me it is the thought of the child after whom I was christened. The day they launched me was her first birthday, and she a small thing held in the crook of her mother's arm: when the bottle swung against my stem the wine spurted, and some drops of it fell on her face. The mother did not see me take the water—she was too busy wiping the drops away. But it was a successful launch, and I have brought the family luck, while she has brought them happiness.

"Because of it, and because our names are alike, her parents think of us together; and sometimes, when one begins to talk of *Thekla*, the other will not know for a moment which of us is meant. They drink my health, too, on her birthday, which is the fourteenth of May; and you know King Solomon's verse for the fourteenth—'She is like the merchants' ships, she bringeth her food from afar.' This is what I have done while she was growing; for King Solomon wrote it for a wife, of course. But now I shall yield up my trust, for when I return she is to be married. She shall bind that verse upon her with a coral necklace I carry for my gift, and it shall dance on her white throat when her husband leads her out to open the wedding-ball."

"Since you are so fond of children," said the *Touch-me-not*, "tell me, what shall we do for the one I have on my deck? He is the small boy who signalled Christmas to us from the garden above; and he dreams of nothing but the sea, though his parents wish him to stick to his books and go to college."

The Dane did not answer for a moment. She was considering. "Wherever he goes," she said at length, "and whatever he does, he will find that to serve much is to renounce much. Let us show him that what is renounced may yet come back in beautiful thoughts."

And it seemed to the boy that, as she ceased, a star dropped out of the sky and poised itself above the fir-tree on her main-topmast; and that the bare mast beneath it put forth branches, while upon every branch, as it spread, a globe of fire dropped from the star, until a gigantic Christmas-tree soared from the deck away up to heaven. In the blaze of it the boy saw the miracle run from ship to ship—the timber bursting into leaf with the song of birds and the scent of tropical plants. Across the avenue of teak which had been the *Nubian's* bulwarks he saw the Dutchman's galley, now a summer-house set in parterres of tulips.

Beyond it the sails of the *Maria Stella Maris*, shaken from the yards, were piling themselves into snowy mountains, their foot-ropes and braces trailing down and breaking into leaves and clusters of the vine. He heard the murmur of streams flowing, the hum of bees, the whetting of the scythes—even the stir of insects' wings among the grasses. From truck to keelson the ships were wavering, dissolving part from part into remote but unforgotten hiding-places whence the mastering adventurer had torn them to bind and yoke them in service. Divine the service, but immortal also the longing to return! "But there the glorious Lord will be unto us a place of broad rivers and streams; wherein shall go no galley with oars, neither shall gallant ship pass thereby."

The boy heard the words; but before he understood them a hand was on his shoulder, and another voice speaking above him.

"God bless us! it's you, is it? Here's a nice tale to tell your father, I must say!" He opened his eyes, and above Captain Tangye's shoulder the branches faded, the lights died out, and the masts stood stripped and bare for service against the cold dawn.

The Two Householders
Extract from the Memoirs of Gabriel Foot, Highwayman.

I will say this—speaking as accurately as a man may, so long afterwards—that when first I spied the house it put no desire in me but just to give thanks.

For conceive my case. It was near mid-night, and ever since dusk I had been tramping the naked moors, in the teeth of as vicious a nor'-wester as ever drenched a man to the skin, and then blew the cold home to his marrow. My clothes were sodden; my coat-tails flapped with a noise like pistol-shots; my boots squeaked as I went. Overhead, the October moon was in her last quarter, and might have been a slice of finger-nail for all the light she afforded. Two-thirds of the time the wrack blotted her out altogether; and I, with my stick clipped tight under my armpit, eyes puckered up, and head bent aslant, had to keep my wits alive to distinguish the road from the black heath to right and left. For three hours I had met neither man nor man's dwelling, and (for all I knew) was desperately lost. Indeed, at the cross-roads, two miles back, there had been nothing for me but to choose the way that kept the wind on my face, and it gnawed me like a dog.

Mainly to allay the stinging of my eyes, I pulled up at last, turned right-about-face, leant back against the blast with a hand on my hat, and surveyed the blackness behind. It was at this instant that, far away to the left, a point of light caught my notice, faint but steady; and at once I felt sure it burnt in the window of a house. "The house," thought I, "is a good mile off, beside the other road, and the light must have been an inch over my hat-brim for the last half-hour." This reflection—that on so wide a moor I had come near missing the information I wanted (and perhaps a supper) by one inch—sent a strong thrill down my back.

I cut straight across the heather towards the light, risking quags and pitfalls. Nay, so heartening was the chance to hear a fellow creature's voice, that I broke into a run, skipping over the stunted gorse that cropped up here and there, and dreading every moment to see the light quenched. "Suppose it burns in an upper window, and the family is going to bed, as would be likely at this hour—" The apprehension kept my eyes fixed on the bright spot, to the frequent scandal of my legs, that within five minutes were stuck full of gorse prickles.

But the light did not go out, and soon a flicker of moonlight gave me a glimpse of the house's outline. It proved to be a deal more imposing than I looked for—the outline, in fact, of a tall, square barrack, with a cluster of chimneys at either end, like ears, and a high wall, topped by the roofs of some outbuildings, concealing the lower windows. There was no gate in this wall, and presently I guessed the reason. I was approaching the place from behind, and the light came from a back window on the first floor.

The faintness of the light also was explained by this time. It shone behind a drab-coloured blind, and in shape resembled the stem of a wine-glass, broadening out at the foot; an effect produced by the half-drawn curtains within. I came to a halt, waiting for the next ray of moonlight. At the same moment a rush of wind swept over the chimney-stacks, and on the wind there seemed to ride a human sigh.

On this last point I may err. The gust had passed some seconds before I caught myself detecting this peculiar note, and trying to disengage it from the natural chords of the storm. From the next gust it was absent; and then, to my dismay, the light faded from the window.

I was half-minded to call out when it appeared again, this

time in two windows—those next on the right to that where it had shone before. Almost at once it increased in brilliance, as if the person who carried it from the smaller room to the larger were lighting more candles; and now the illumination was strong enough to make fine gold threads of the rain that fell within its radiance, and fling two shafts of warm yellow over the coping of the back wall. During the minute or more that I stood watching, no shadow fell on either blind.

Between me and the wall ran a ditch, into which the ground at my feet broke sharply away. Setting my back to the storm again, I followed the lip of this ditch around the wall's angle. Here it shallowed, and here, too, was shelter; but not wishing to mistake a bed of nettles or any such pitfall for solid earth, I kept pretty wide as I went on. The house was dark on this side, and the wall, as before, had no opening. Close beside the next angle there grew a mass of thick gorse bushes, and pushing through these I found myself suddenly on a sound high-road, with the wind tearing at me as furiously as ever.

But here was the front; and I now perceived that the surrounding wall advanced some way before the house, so as to form a narrow courtlage. So much of it, too, as faced the road had been whitewashed, which made it an easy matter to find the gate. But as I laid hand on its latch I had a surprise.

A line of paving-stones led from the gate to a heavy porch; and along the wet surface of these there fell a streak of light from the front door, which stood ajar.

That a door should remain six inches open on such a night was astonishing enough, until I entered the court and found it as still as a room, owing to the high wall. But looking up and assuring myself that all the rest of the facade was black as ink, I wondered at the carelessness of the inmates.

It was here that my professional instinct received the first jog. Abating the sound of my feet on the paving-stones, I went up to the door and pushed it softly. It opened without noise.

I stepped into a fair-sized hall of modern build, paved with red tiles and lit with a small hanging-lamp. To right and left were doors leading to the ground-floor rooms. Along the wall by my shoulder ran a line of pegs, on which hung half-a-dozen hats and great-coats, every one of clerical shape; and full in front of me a broad staircase ran up, with a staring Brussels carpet, the colours and pattern of which I can recall as well as I can today's breakfast. Under this staircase was set a stand full of walking-sticks, and a table littered with gloves, brushes, a hand-bell, a riding-crop, one or two dog-whistles, and a bedroom candle, with tinder-box beside it. This, with one notable exception, was all the furniture.

The exception—which turned me cold—was the form of a yellow mastiff dog, curled on a mat beneath the table. The arch of his back was towards me, and one forepaw lay over his nose in a natural posture of sleep. I leant back on the wainscotting with my eyes tightly fixed on him, and my thoughts sneaking back, with something of regret, to the storm I had come through.

But a man's habits are not easily denied. At the end of three minutes the dog had not moved, and I was down on the door-mat unlacing my soaked boots. Slipping them off, and taking them in my left hand, I stood up, and tried a step towards the stairs, with eyes alert for any movement of the mastiff; but he never stirred. I was glad enough, however, on reaching the stairs, to find them newly built, and the carpet thick. Up I went, with a glance at every step for the table which now hid the brute's form from me, and never a creak did I wake out of that staircase till I was almost at the first landing, when my toe caught a loose stair-rod, and rattled it in a way that stopped my heart for a moment, and then set it going in double-quick time.

I stood still with a hand on the rail. My eyes were now on a level with the floor of the landing, out of which branched two passages—one turning sharply to my right, the other straight in front, so that I was gazing down the length of it. Almost at the end, a parallelogram of light fell across it from an open door.

A man who has once felt it knows there is only one kind of silence that can fitly be called "dead." This is only to be found in a great house at midnight. I declare that for a few seconds after I rattled the stair-rod you might have cut the silence with a knife. If the house held a clock, it ticked inaudibly.

Upon this silence, at the end of a minute, broke a light sound—the *tink-tink* of a decanter on the rim of a wine-glass. It came from the room where the light was.

Now perhaps it was that the very thought of liquor put warmth into my cold bones. It is certain that all of a sudden I straightened my back, took the remaining stairs at two strides, and walked down the passage as bold as brass, without caring a jot for the noise I made.

In the doorway I halted. The room was long, lined for the most part with books bound in what they call "divinity calf," and littered with papers like a barrister's table on assize day. A leathern elbow-chair faced the fireplace, where a few coals burned sulkily, and beside it, on the corner of a writing table, were set an unlit candle and a pile of manuscripts. At the opposite end of the room a curtained door led (as I guessed) to the chamber that I had first seen illuminated. All this I took in with the tail of my eye, while staring straight in front, where, in the middle of a great square of carpet, between me and the windows, stood a table with a red cloth upon it. On this cloth were a couple of wax candles lit, in silver stands, a tray, and a decanter three-parts full of brandy. And between me and the table stood a man.

He stood sideways, leaning a little back, as if to keep his shadow off the threshold, and looked at me over his left shoulder—a bald, grave man, slightly under the common height, with a long clerical coat of preposterous fit hanging loosely from his shoulders, a white cravat, black breeches, and black stockings. His feet were loosely thrust into carpet slippers. I judged his age at fifty, or thereabouts; but his face rested in the shadow, and I could only note a pair of eyes, very small and alert, twinkling above a large expanse of cheek.

He was lifting a wine-glass from the table at the moment when I appeared, and it trembled now in his right hand. I heard a spilt drop or two fall on the carpet. This was all the evidence he showed of discomposure.

Setting the glass back, he felt in his breast-pocket for a handkerchief, failed to find one, and rubbed his hands together to get the liquor off his fingers.

"You startled me," he said, in a matter-of-fact tone, turning his eyes upon me, as he lifted his glass again, and emptied it. "How did you find your way in?"

"By the front door," said I, wondering at his unconcern.

He nodded his head slowly.

"Ah! yes; I forgot to lock it. You came to steal, I suppose?"

"I came because I'd lost my way. I've been travelling this God-forsaken moor since dusk—"

"With your boots in your hand," he put in quietly.

"I took them off out of respect to the yellow dog you keep."

"He lies in a very natural attitude—eh?"

"You don't tell me he was *stuffed?*"

The old man's eyes beamed a contemptuous pity.

"You are indifferent sharp, my dear sir, for a housebreaker. Come in. Set down those convicting boots, and don't drip pools of water in the doorway. If I must entertain a burglar, I prefer him tidy."

He walked to the fire, picked up a poker, and knocked the coals into a blaze. This done, he turned round on me with the poker still in his hand. The serenest gravity sat on his large, pale features.

"Why have I done this?" he asked.

"I suppose to get possession of the poker."

"Quite right. May I inquire your next move?"

"Why?" said I, feeling in my tail-pocket, "I carry a pistol."

"Which I suppose to be damp?"

"By no means. I carry it, as you see, in an oil-cloth case."

He stooped, and laid the poker carefully in the fender.

"That is a stronger card than I possess. I might urge that by pulling the trigger you would certainly alarm the house and the neighbourhood, and put a halter round your neck. But it strikes me as safer to assume you capable of using a pistol with effect at three paces. With what might happen subsequently I will not pretend to be concerned. The fate of your neck"—he waved a hand,—"well, I have known you for just five minutes, and feel but a moderate interest in your neck. As for the inmates of this house, it will refresh you to hear that there are none. I have lived here two years with a butler and female cook, both of whom I dismissed yesterday at a minute's notice, for conduct which I will not shock your ears by explicitly naming. Suffice it to say, I carried them off yesterday to my parish church, two miles away, married them and dismissed them in the vestry without characters. I wish you had known that butler—but excuse me; with the information I have supplied, you ought to find no difficulty in fixing the price you will take to clear out of my house instanter."

"Sir," I answered, "I have held a pistol at one or two heads in my time, but never at one stuffed with nobler indiscretion. Your chivalry does not, indeed, disarm me, but prompts me to desire more of your acquaintance. I have found a gentleman, and must sup with him before I make terms."

This address seemed to please him. He shuffled across the room to a sideboard, and produced a plate of biscuits, another of dried figs, a glass, and two decanters.

"Sherry and Madeira," he said. "There is also a cold pie in the larder, if you care for it."

"A biscuit will serve," I replied. "To tell the truth, I'm more for the bucket than the manger, as the grooms say: and the brandy you were tasting just now is more to my mind than wine."

"There is no water handy."

"I have soaked in enough tonight to last me with this bottle."

I pulled over a chair, laid my pistol on the table, and held out the glass for him to fill. Having done so, he helped himself to a glass and a chair, and sat down facing me.

"I was speaking, just now, of my late butler," he began, with a sip at his brandy. "Does it strike you that, when confronted with moral delinquency, I am apt to let my indignation get the better of me?"

"Not at all," I answered heartily, refilling my glass.

It appeared that another reply would have pleased him better.

"H'm. I was hoping that, perhaps, I had visited his offence too strongly. As a clergyman, you see, I was bound to be severe; but upon my word, sir, since Parkinson left I have felt like a man who has lost a limb."

He drummed with his fingers on the cloth for a few moments, and went on—

"One has a natural disposition to forgive butlers—Pharaoh, for instance, felt it. There hovers around butlers an atmosphere in which common ethics lose their pertinence. But mine was a rare bird—a black swan among butlers! He was more than a butler: he was a quick and brightly gifted man. Of the accuracy of his taste, and the unusual scope of his endeavour, you will be able to form some opinion when I assure you he modelled himself upon *me*."

I bowed, over my brandy.

"I am a scholar: yet I employed him to read aloud to me, and derived pleasure from his intonation. I talk with refinement: yet he learned to answer me in language as precise as my own. My cast-off garments fitted him not more irreproachably than did my amenities of manner. Divest him of his tray, and you would find his mode of entering a room hardly distinguishable from my own—the same urbanity, the same alertness of carriage, the same superfine deference towards the weaker sex. All—all my idiosyncrasies I saw reflected in him; and can you doubt that I was gratified? He was my *alter ego*—which, by the way, makes it harder for me to pardon his behaviour with the cook."

"Look here," I broke in; "you want a new butler?"

"Oh, you really grasp that fact, do you?" he retorted.

"Why, then," said I, "let me cease to be your burglar and let me continue here as your butler."

He leant back, spreading out the fingers of each hand on the table's edge.

"Believe me," I went on, "you might do worse. I have been

in my time a demy of Magdalen College, Oxford, and retain some Greek and Latin. I'll undertake to read the Fathers with an accent that shall not offend you. My taste in wine is none the worse for having been formed in other men's cellars. Moreover, you shall engage the ugliest cook in Christendom, so long as I'm your butler. I've taken a liking to you—that's flat—and I apply for the post."

"I give forty pounds a year," said he.

"And I'm cheap at that price."

He filled up his glass, looking up at me while he did so with the air of one digesting a problem. From first to last his face was grave as a judge's.

"We are too impulsive, I think," was his answer, after a minute's silence; "and your speech smacks of the amateur. You say, 'Let me cease to be your burglar and let me be your butler.' The aspiration is respectable; but a man might as well say, 'Let me cease to write sermons, let me paint pictures.' And truly, sir, you impress me as no expert even in your present trade."

"On the other hand," I argued, "consider the moderation of my demands; that alone should convince you of my desire to turn over a new leaf. I ask for a month's trial; if at the end of that time I don't suit, you shall say so, and I'll march from your door with nothing in my pocket but my month's wages. Be hanged, sir! but when I reflect on the amount you'll have to pay to get me to face tonight's storm again, you seem to be getting off dirt cheap!" cried I, slapping my palm on the table.

"Ah, if you had only known Parkinson!" he exclaimed.

Now the third glass of clean spirit has always a deplorable effect on me. It turns me from bright to black, from levity to extreme sulkiness. I have done more wickedness over this third tumbler than in all the other states of comparative inebriety within my experience. So now I glowered at my companion and cursed.

"Look here, I don't want to hear any more of Parkinson, and I've a pretty clear notion of the game you're playing. You want to make me drink, and you're ready to sit prattling there plying me till I drop under the table."

"Do me the favour to remember that you came, and are staying, on your own motion. As for the brandy, I would remind you that I suggested a milder drink. Try some Madeira."

He handed me the decanter, as he spoke, and I poured out a glass.

"Madeira!" said I, taking a gulp, "Ugh! it's the commonest Marsala!"

I had no sooner said the words than he rose up, and stretched a hand gravely across to me.

"I hope you will shake it," he said; "though, as a man who after three glasses of neat spirit can distinguish between Madeira and Marsala, you have every right to refuse me. Two minutes ago you offered to become my butler, and I demurred. I now beg you to repeat that offer. Say the word, and I employ you gladly; you shall even have the second decanter (which contains genuine Madeira) to take to bed with you."

We shook hands on our bargain, and catching up a candlestick, he led the way from the room.

Picking up my boots, I followed him along the passage and down the silent staircase. In the hall he paused to stand on tiptoe, and turn up the lamp, which was burning low. As he did so, I found time to fling a glance at my old enemy, the mastiff. He lay as I had first seen him—a stuffed dog, if ever there was one. "Decidedly," thought I, "my wits are to seek tonight;" and with the same, a sudden suspicion made me turn to my conductor, who had advanced to the left-hand door, and was waiting for me, with a hand on the knob.

"One moment!" I said: "This is all very pretty, but how am I to know you're not sending me to bed while you fetch in all the countryside to lay me by the heels?"

"I'm afraid," was his answer, "you must be content with my word, as a gentleman, that never, tonight or hereafter, will I breathe a syllable about the circumstances of your visit. However, if you choose, we will return upstairs."

"No; I'll trust you," said I; and he opened the door.

It led into a broad passage paved with slate, upon which three or four rooms opened. He paused by the second and ushered me into a sleeping-chamber, which, though narrow, was comfortable enough—a vast improvement, at any rate, on the mumpers' lodgings I had been used to for many months past.

"You can undress here," he said. "The sheets are aired, and if you'll wait a moment, I'll fetch a nightshirt—one of my own."

"Sir, you heap coals of fire on me."

"Believe me that for ninety-nine of your qualities I do not care a tinker's curse; but for your palate you are to be taken care of."

He shuffled away, but came back in a couple of minutes with the nightshirt.

"Goodnight," he called to me, flinging it in at the door; and without giving me time to return the wish, went his way upstairs.

Now it might be supposed I was only too glad to toss off my clothes and climb into the bed I had so unexpectedly acquired a right to. But, as a matter of fact, I did nothing of the kind. Instead, I drew on my boots and sat on the bed's edge, blinking at my candle till it died down in its socket, and afterwards at the purple square of window as it slowly changed to grey with the coming of dawn. I was cold to the heart, and my teeth chattered with an ague. Certainly I never suspected my host's word; but was even occupied in framing good resolutions and shaping out a reputable future, when I heard the front door gently pulled to, and a man's footsteps moving quietly to the gate.

The treachery knocked me in a heap for the moment. Then, leaping up and flinging my door wide, I stumbled through the uncertain light of the passage into the front hall. There was a fan-shaped light over the door, and the place was very still and grey. A quick thought, or, rather, a sudden, prophetic guess at the truth, made me turn to the figure of the mastiff curled under the hall table.

I laid my hand on the scruff of his neck. He was quite limp, and my fingers sank into the flesh on either side of the vertebrae.

Digging them deeper, I dragged him out into the middle of the hall and pulled the front door open to see the better.

His throat was gashed from ear to ear.

How many seconds passed after I dropped the senseless lump on the floor, and before I made another movement, it would puzzle me to say. Twice I stirred a foot as if to run out at the door. Then, changing my mind, I stepped over the mastiff, and ran up the staircase.

The passage at the top was now dark; but groping down it, I found the study door open, as before, and passed in. A sick light stole through the blinds—enough for me to distinguish the glasses and decanters on the table, and find my way to the curtain that hung before the inner room.

I pushed the curtain aside, paused for a moment, and listened to the violent beat of my heart; then felt for the door-handle and turned it.

All I could see at first was that the chamber was small; next, that the light patch in a line with the window was the white coverlet of a bed; and next that somebody, or something, lay on the bed.

I listened again. There was no sound in the room; no heart beating but my own. I reached out a hand to pull up the blind, and drew it back again. I dared not.

The daylight grew minute by minute on the dull oblong of the blind, and minute by minute that horrible thing on the bed took something of distinctness.

The strain beat me at last. I fetched a loud yell to give myself courage, and, reaching for the cord, pulled up the blind as fast as it would go.

The face on the pillow was that of an old man—a face waxen and peaceful, with quiet lines about the mouth and eyes, and long lines of grey hair falling back from the temples. The body was turned a little on one side, and one hand lay outside the bedclothes in a very natural manner. But there were two big dark stains on the pillow and coverlet.

Then I knew I was face to face with the real householder,

and it flashed on me that I had been indiscreet in taking service as his butler, and that I knew the face his ex-butler wore.

And, being by this time awake to the responsibilities of the post, I quitted it three steps at a time, not once looking behind me. Outside the house the storm had died down, and white daylight was gleaming over the sodden moors. But my bones were cold, and I ran faster and faster.

Widdershins
A Droll

Once upon a time there was a small farmer living in Wendron parish, not far from the church-town. Thaniel Teague was his name. This Teague happened to walk into Helston on a Furry-day, when the mayor and townspeople dance through the streets to the Furry-tune. In the evening there was a grand ball given at the Angel Hotel, and the landlord very kindly allowed Teague—who had stopped too late as it was—to look in through the door and watch the gentry dance the lancers.

Teague thought he had never seen anything so heavenly. What with one hindrance and another 'twas past midnight before he reached home, and then nothing would do for him but he must have his wife and six children out upon the floor in their night-clothes, practising the Grand Chain while he sang—

Out of my stony griefs
Bethel I'll raise!

The seventh child, the babby, they set down in the middle of the floor, like a nine-pin. And the worst of it was, the poor mite twisted his eyes so, trying to follow his mammy round and round, that he grew up with a cast from that hour.

'Tis of this child—Joby he was called—that I am going to tell you. Barring the cast, he grew up a very straight lad, and in due time began to think upon marrying. His father's house faced south, and as it came easier to him to look north-west than any other direction, he chose a wife from Gwinear parish. His elder brothers had gone off to sea for their living, and his sister had married a mine-captain: so when the old people died, Joby took over the farm and worked it, and did very well.

Joby's wife was very fond of him, though of course she didn't like that cast in his looks: and in many ways 'twas inconvenient too. If the poor man ever put hand on plough to draw a straight furrow, round to the north 'twould work as sure as a compass-needle. She consulted the doctors about it, and they did no good. Then she thought about consulting a conjurer; but being a timorous woman as well as not over-wise, she put it off for a while.

Now, there was a little fellow living over to Penryn in those times, Tommy Warne by name, that gave out he knew how to conjure. Folks believed in him more than he did himself: for, to tell truth, he was a lazy shammick, who liked most ways of getting a living better than hard work. Still, he was generally made pretty welcome at the farmhouses round, for he could turn a hand to anything and always kept the maids laughing in the kitchen. One morning he dropped in on Farmer Joby and asked for a job to earn his dinner; and Joby gave him some straw to spin for thatching. By dinner-time Tom had spun two bundles of such very large size that the farmer rubbed his chin when he looked at them.

"Why," says he, "I always thought you a liar—I did indeed. But now I believe you can conjure, sure enough."

As for Mrs. Joby, she was so much pleased that, though she felt certain the devil must have had a hand in it, she gave Tom an extra helping of pudding for dinner.

Sometime after this, Farmer Joby missed a pair of pack-saddles. Search and ask as he might, he couldn't find out who had stolen them, or what had become of them.

"Tommy Warne's a clever fellow," he said at last. "I must see if he can tell me anything." So he walked over to Penryn on purpose.

Tommy was in his doorway smoking when Farmer Joby came down the street. "So you'm after they pack-saddles," said he.

"Why, how ever did you know?"

"That's my business. Will it do if you find 'em after harvest?"

"To be sure 'twill. I only want to know where they be."

"Very well, then; after harvest they'll be found."

Home the farmer went. Sure enough, after harvest, he went to unwind Tommy's two big bundles of straw-rope for thatching the mow, and in the middle of each was one of his missing pack-saddles.

"Well, now," said Joby's wife, "that fellow must have a real gift of conjurin'! I wonder, my dear, you don't go and consult him about that there cross-eye of yours."

"I will, then," said Joby; and he walked over to Penryn again the very next market-day.

"'Cure your eyes,' is it?" said Tommy Warne. "Why, to be sure I can. Why didn't you ax me afore? I thought you *liked* squintin'."

"I don't, then; I hate it."

"Very well; you shall see straight this very night if you do what I tell you. Go home and tell your wife to make your bed on the roof of the four-poster; and she must make it widdershins, turnin' bed-tie and all against the sun, and puttin' the pillow where the feet come as a rule. That's all."

"Fancy my never thinkin' of anything so simple as that!" said Joby. He went home and told his wife. She made his bed on the roof of the four-poster, and widdershins, as he ordered; and they slept that night, the wife as usual, and Joby up close to the rafters.

But scarcely had Joby closed an eye before there came a rousing knock at the door, and in walked Joby's eldest brother, the sea-captain, that he hadn't seen for years.

"Get up, Joby, and come along with me if you want that eye of yours mended."

"Thank you, Sam, it's curin' very easy and nice, and I hope you won't disturb me."

"If 'tis Tommy Warne's cure you're trying, why then I'm part of it; so you'd best get up quickly."

"Aw, that's another matter, though you might have said so at first. I'd no notion you and Tommy was hand-'n-glove."

Joby rose up and followed his brother out of doors. He had nothing on but his night-shirt, but his brother seemed in a hurry, and he didn't like to object.

They set their faces to the road and they walked and walked, neither saying a word, till they came to Penryn. There was a fair going on in the town; swing-boats and shooting-galleries and lillybanger standings, and naphtha lamps flaming, and in the middle of all, a great whirly-go-round, with striped horses and boats, and a steam-organ playing "Yankee Doodle." As soon as they started Joby saw that the whole thing was going around widdershins; and his brother stood up under the naphtha-lamp and pulled out a sextant and began to take observations.

"What's the latitude?" asked Joby. He felt that he ought to say something to his brother, after being parted all these years.

"Decimal nothing to speak of," answered Sam.

"Then we ought to be nearing the Line," said Joby. He hadn't noticed the change, but now he saw that the boat they sat in was floating on the sea, and that Sam had stuck his walking-stick out over the stern and was steering.

"What's the longitude?" asked Joby.

"That doesn't concern us."

"'Tis west o' Grinnidge, I suppose?" Joby knew very little about navigation, and wanted to make the most of it.

"West o' Penryn," said Sam, very sharp and short. "'Twasn' Grinnidge Fair we started from."

But presently he sings out "Here we are!" and Joby saw a white line, like a popping-crease, painted across the blue sea ahead of them. First he thought 'twas paint, and then he thought 'twas catgut, for when the keel of their boat scraped over it, it sang like a bird.

"That was the Equator," said Sam. "Now let's see if your eyes be any better."

But when Joby tried them, what was his disappointment to find the cast as bad as ever?—only now they were slewing right the other way, towards the South Pole.

"I never thought well of this cure from the first," declared Sam. "For my part, I'm sick and tired of the whole business!" And with that he bounced up from the thwart and hailed a passing shark and walked down its throat in a huff, leaving Joby all alone on the wide sea.

"There's nice brotherly behaviour for you!" said Joby to himself. "Lucky he left his walking-stick behind. The best thing I can do is to steer along close to the Equator, and then I know where I am."

So he steered along close to the Line, and by and by he saw something shining in the distance. When he came nearer, 'twas a great gilt fowl stuck there with its beak to the Line and its wings sprawled out. And when he came close, 'twas no other than the cock belonging to the tower of his own parish church of Wendron!

"Well!" said Joby, "one has to travel to find out how small the world is. And what might you be doin' here, naybour?"

"Is that you, Joby Teague? Then I'll thank you to do me a good turn. I came here in a witch-ship last night, and the crew put this spell upon me because I wouldn't pay my footing to cross the Line. A nice lot, to try and steal the gilt off a church weather-cock! 'Tis ridiculous," said he, "but I can't get loose for the life o' me!"

"Why, that's as easy as ABC," said Joby. "You'll find it in any book of parlour amusements. You take a fowl, put its beak to the floor, and draw a chalk line away from it, right and left—"

Joby wetted his thumb, smudged out a bit of the Equator on each side of the cock's nose, and the bird stood up and shook himself.

"And now is there anything I can do for you, Joby Teague?"

"To be sure there is. I'm getting completely tired of this boat: and if you can give me a lift, I'll take it as a favour."

"No favour at all. Where shall we go visit?—the Antipodes?"

"No, thank you," said Toby. "I've heard tell they get up an' do their business when we honest folks be in our beds: and that kind o' person I never could trust. Squint or no squint, Wendron's Wendron, and that's where I'm comfortable."

"Well, it's no use loitering here, or we may get into trouble for what we've done to the Equator. Climb on my back," said the bird, "and home we go!"

It seemed no more than a flap of the wings, and Joby found himself on his friend's back on one of the pinnacles of Wendron Church and looking down on his own farm.

"Thankin' you kindly, soce, and now I think I'll be goin'," said he.

"Not till I've cured your eyesight, Joby," said the polite bird.

Joby by this time was wishing his eyesight to botheration; but before he could say a word, a breeze came about the pinnacles, and he was spinning around on the cock's back—spinning around widdershins— clutching the bird's neck and holding his breath.

"And now," the cock said, as they came to a standstill again, "I think you can see a hole in a ladder as well as any man."

Just then the bells in the tower below them began to ring merrily.

Said Joby, "What's that for, I wonder?"

"It looks to me," said the cock, "as if your wife was gettin' married again."

Sure enough, while the bells rang, Joby saw the door of his own house open, and his own wife come stepping towards the church, leaning on a man's arm. And who should that man be but Tommy Warne?

"And to think I've lived fifteen years with that woman, and never lifted my hand to her!"

Said the bird, "The wedding is fixed for eleven o'clock, and 'tis on the stroke now. If I was you, Joby, I'd climb down and put back the church clock."

"And so I would, if I knew how to get to it."

"You've but to slide down my leg to the parapet: and from the parapet you can jump right on to the string-course under the clock."

Joby slid down the bird's leg, and jumped on to the ledge. He had never before noticed a clock in Wendron Church tower; but there one was, staring him in the face.

"Now," cried his friend, "catch hold of the minute-hand and turn!" Joby did so—"Widdershins!" screamed the bird: "faster! faster!" Joby whizzed back the minute-hand with all his might.

"Aie, ul—ul—oo! Lemme go! 'Tis my arm you're pullin' off!" 'Twas his own wife's voice in his own four-poster. Joby had slid down the bedpost and caught hold of her arm, and was workin' it round like mad from right to left.

"I ax your pardon, my dear. I was thinkin' you was another man's bride."

"Indeed, I must say you wasn't behavin' like it," said she.

But when she got up and lit a candle, she was pleased enough. For Joby's eyes were as straight as yours or mine. And straight they have been ever since.

Daphnis

Has olim exuvias mihi perfidus ille reliquit,
Pignora cara sui: quae nunc ego limine in ipso,
Terra, tibi mando; debent haec pignora Daphnin—
Ducite ab urbe domum, mea, carmina, ducite Daphnin.

I knew the superstition lingered along the country-side: and I was sworn to find it. But the labourers and their wives smoothed all intelligence out of their faces as soon as I began to hint at it. Such is the way of them. They were my good friends, but had no mind to help me in this. Nobody who has not lived long with them can divine the number of small incommunicable mysteries and racial secrets chambered in their inner hearts and guarded by their hospitable faces. These alone the Celt withholds from the Saxon, and when he dies they are buried with him.

A chance word or two of my old nurse, by chance caught in some cranny of a child's memory and recovered after many days, told me that the charm was still practised by the woman-folk, or had been practised not long before her death. So I began to hunt for it, and, almost as soon, to believe the search hopeless. The new generation of girls, with their smart frocks, in fashion not more than six months behind London, their Board School notions, and their consuming ambition to "look like a lady"— were these likely to cherish a local custom as rude and primitive as the long-stone circles on the tors above? But they were Cornish; and of that race it is unwise to judge rashly. For years I had never a clue: and then, by Sheba Farm, in a forsaken angle of the coast, surprised the secret.

Sheba Farm stands high above Ruan sands, over which its windows flame at sunset. And I sat in the farm kitchen drinking cider and eating potato-cake, while the farmer's wife, Mrs. Bolverson, obligingly attended to my coat, which had just been soaked by a thunder-shower. It was August, and already the sun beat out again, fierce and strong. The bright drops that gemmed the tamarisk-bushes above the wall of the town-place were already fading under its heat; and I heard the voices of the harvesters up the lane, as they returned to the oat-field whence the storm had routed them. A bright parallelogram stretched from the window across the white kitchen-table, and reached the dim hollow of the open fire-place. Mrs. Bolverson drew the towel-horse, on which my coat was stretched, between it and the wood fire, which (as she held) the sunshine would put out.

"It's uncommonly kind of you, Mrs. Bolverson," said I, as she turned one sleeve of the coat towards the heat. "To be sure, if the women in these parts would speak out, some of them have done more than that for the men with an old coat."

She dropped the sleeve, faced round, and eyed me.

"What do you know of that?" she asked slowly, and as if her chest tightened over the words. She was a woman of fifty and more, of fine figure but a worn face. Her chief surviving beauty was a pile of light golden hair, still lustrous as a girl's. But her blue eyes—though now they narrowed on me suspiciously—must have looked out magnificently in their day.

"I fancy," said I, meeting them frankly enough, "that what you know and I don't on that matter would make a good deal."

She laughed harshly, almost savagely.

"You'd better ask Sarah Gedye, across the coombe. She buried a man's clothes one time, and—it might be worth your while to ask her what came o't."

If you can imagine a glint of moonlight running up the blade of a rapier, you may know the chill flame of spite and despite that flickered in her eyes then as she spoke.

"I take my oath," I muttered to myself, "I'll act on the invitation."

The woman stood straight upright, with her hands clasped behind her, before the deal table. She gazed, under lowered brows, straight out of window; and following that gaze, I saw across the coombe a mean mud hut, with a wall around it, that looked on Sheba Farm with the obtrusive humility of a poor relation.

"Does she—does Sarah Gedye—live down yonder?"

"What is that to you?" she enquired fiercely, and then was silent for a moment, and added, with another short laugh—

"I reckon I'd like the question put to her: but I doubt you've got the pluck."

"You shall see," said I; and taking my coat off the towel-horse, I slipped it on.

She did not turn, did not even move her head, when I thanked her for the shelter and walked out of the house.

I could feel those steel-blue eyes working like gimlets into my back as I strode down the hill and passed the wooden plank that lay across the stream at its foot. A climb of less than a minute brought me to the green gate in the wall of Sarah Gedye's garden patch; and here I took a look backwards and upwards at Sheba. The sun lay warm on its white walls, and the whole building shone against the burnt hillside. It was too far away for me to spy Mrs. Bolverson's blue print gown within the kitchen window, but I knew that she stood there yet.

The sound of a footstep made me turn. A woman was coming round the corner of the cottage, with a bundle of mint in her hand.

She looked at me, shook off a bee that had blundered against her apron, and looked at me again—a brown woman, lean and strongly made, with jet-black eyes set deep and glistening in an ugly face.

"You want to know your way?" she asked.

"No. I came to see you, if your name is Sarah Gedye."

"Sarah Ann Gedye is my name. What 'st want?"

I took a sudden resolution to tell the exact truth.

"Mrs. Gedye, the fact is I am curious about an old charm that was practised in these parts, as I know, till recently. The charm is this—When a woman guesses her lover to be faithless to her, she buries a suit of his old clothes to fetch him back to her. Mrs. Bolverson, up at Sheba yonder—"

The old woman had opened her mouth (as I know now) to curse me. But as Mrs. Bolverson's name escaped me, she turned her back, and walked straight to her door and into the kitchen. Her manner told me that I was expected to follow.

But I was not prepared for the face she turned on me in the shadow of the kitchen. It was grey as wood-ash, and the black eyes shrank into it like hot specks of fire.

"She—*she* set you on to ask me that?" She caught me by the coat and hissed out: "Come back from the door—don't let her see." Then she lifted up her fist, with the mint tightly clutched in it, and shook it at the warm patch of Sheba buildings across the valley.

"May God burn her bones, as He has smitten her body barren!"

"What do you know of this?" she cried, turning upon me again.

"I know nothing. That I have offered you some insult is clear: but—"

"Nay, you don't know—you don't know. No man would be such a hound. You don't know; but, by the Lord, you shall hear, here where you'm standin', an' shall jedge betwix' me an' that pale 'ooman up yonder. Stand there an' list to me.

"He was my lover more'n five-an'-thirty years agone. Who? That 'ooman's wedded man, Seth Bolverson. We warn't married"—this with a short laugh. "Wife or less than wife, he found me to his mind. She—she that egged you on to come an' flout me—was a pale-haired girl o' seventeen or so i' those times—a church-goin' mincin' strip of a girl—the sort you menfolk bow the knee to for saints. Her father owned Sheba Farm, an' she look'd across on my man, an' had envy on 'en, an' set her eyes to draw 'en. Oh, a saint she was! An' he, the poor shammick, went. 'Twas a good girl, you understand, that wished for to marry an' reform 'en. She had money, too. I? I'd ha' poured out my blood for 'en: that's all I cud do. So he went.

"As the place shines this day, it shone then. Like a moth it drew 'en. Late o' summer evenin's its windeys shone when down below here 'twas chill i' the hill's shadow. An' late at night the candles burned up there as he courted her. Purity and cosiness, you understand, an' down here—he forgot about down here. Before he'd missed to speak to me for a month, I'd hear 'en whistlin' up the hill, so merry as a grig. Well, he married her.

"They was married three months, an' 'twas harvest time come round, an' I in his vield a-gleanin'. For I was suffered near to that extent, seem' that the cottage here had been my fathers', an' was mine, an' out o't they culdn' turn me. One o' the hands, as they was pitchin', passes me an empty keg, an' says, 'Run you to the farm-place an' get it filled.' So with it I went to th' kitchen, and while I waited outside I sees his coat an' wesket 'pon a peg i' the passage. Well I knew the coat; an' a madness takin' me for all my loss, I unhitched it an' flung it behind the door, an', the keg bein' filled, picked it up agen and ran down home-along.

"No thought had I but to win Seth back. 'Twas the charm you spoke about: an' that same midnight I delved a hole by the dreshold an' buried the coat, whisperin', '*Man, come back, come back to me!*' as Aun' Lesnewth had a-taught me, times afore.

"But she, the pale woman, had a-seen me, dro' a chink o' the parlour-door, as I tuk the coat down. An' she knowed what I tuk it for. I've a-read it, times and again, in her wifely eyes; an' today you yoursel' are witness that she knowed. If Seth knowed—"

She clenched and unclenched her fist, and went on rapidly.

"Early next mornin', and a'most afore I was dressed, two constables came in by the gate, an' she behind 'em treadin' delicately, an' *he* at her back, wi' his chin dropped. They charged me wi' stealin' that coat—wi' stealin' it—that coat that I'd a-darned an' patched years afore ever *she* cuddled against its sleeve!"

"What happened?" I asked, as her voice sank and halted.

"What happened? She looked me i' the eyes scornfully; an' her own were full o' knowledge. An' wi' her eyes she coaxed and dared me to abase mysel' an' speak the truth an' win off jail. An' I, that had stole nowt, looked back at her an' said, 'It's true. I stole the coat. Now cart me off to jail; but handle me gently for the sake o' my child unborn.' When I spoke these last two words an' saw her face draw up wi' the bitterness o' their taste, I held out my wrists and clapped the handcuffs together like cymbals and laughed wi' a glad heart."

She caught my hand suddenly, and drawing me to the porch, pointed high above Sheba, to the yellow upland where the harvesters moved.

"Do 'ee see 'en there?—that tall young man by the hedge—there where the slope dips? That's my son, Seth's son, the straightest man among all. Neither spot has he, nor wart, nor blemish 'pon his body; and when she pays 'en his wages, Saturday evenin's, he says 'Thank 'ee, ma'am,' wi' a voice that's the very daps o' his father's. An' she's childless. Ah, childless woman! Childless woman! Go back an' carry word to her o' the prayer I've spoken upon her childlessness."

And "Childless woman!" "Childless woman!" she called twice again, shaking her fist at the windows of Sheba Farmhouse, that blazed back angrily against the westering sun.

ALSO FROM LEONAUR
AVAILABLE IN SOFTCOVER OR HARDCOVER WITH DUST JACKET

MR MUKERJI'S GHOSTS by S. Mukerji—Supernatural tales from the British Raj period by India's Ghost story collector.

KIPLINGS GHOSTS by Rudyard Kipling—Twelve stories of Ghosts, Hauntings, Curses, Werewolves & Magic.

THE COLLECTED SUPERNATURAL AND WEIRD FICTION OF WASHINGTON IRVING: VOLUME 1 by Washington Irving—Including one novel 'A History of New York', and nine short stories of the Strange and Unusual.

THE COLLECTED SUPERNATURAL AND WEIRD FICTION OF WASHINGTON IRVING: VOLUME 2 by Washington Irving—Including three novelettes 'The Legend of the Sleepy Hollow', 'Dolph Heyliger', 'The Adventure of the Black Fisherman' and thirty-two short stories of the Strange and Unusual.

THE COLLECTED SUPERNATURAL AND WEIRD FICTION OF JOHN KENDRICK BANGS: VOLUME 1 by John Kendrick Bangs—Including one novel 'Toppleton's Client or A Spirit in Exile', and ten short stories of the Strange and Unusual.

THE COLLECTED SUPERNATURAL AND WEIRD FICTION OF JOHN KENDRICK BANGS: VOLUME 2 by John Kendrick Bangs—Including four novellas 'A House-Boat on the Styx', 'The Pursuit of the House-Boat', 'The Enchanted Typewriter' and 'Mr. Munchausen' of the Strange and Unusual.

THE COLLECTED SUPERNATURAL AND WEIRD FICTION OF JOHN KENDRICK BANGS: VOLUME 3 by John Kendrick Bangs—Including twor novellas 'Olympian Nights', 'Roger Camerden: A Strange Story', and ten short stories of the Strange and Unusual.

THE COLLECTED SUPERNATURAL AND WEIRD FICTION OF MARY SHELLEY: VOLUME 1 by Mary Shelley—Including one novel 'Frankenstein or the Modern Prometheus', and fourteen short stories of the Strange and Unusual.

THE COLLECTED SUPERNATURAL AND WEIRD FICTION OF MARY SHELLEY: VOLUME 2 by Mary Shelley—Including one novel 'The Last Man', and three short stories of the Strange and Unusual.

THE COLLECTED SUPERNATURAL AND WEIRD FICTION OF AMELIA B. EDWARDS by Amelia B. Edwards—Contains two novelettes 'Monsieur Maurice', and 'The Discovery of the Treasure Isles', one ballad 'A Legend of Boisguilbert' and seventeen short stories to cill the blood.

AVAILABLE ONLINE AT **www.leonaur.com**
AND FROM ALL GOOD BOOK STORES